San Diego

Four Sun-Kissed Romances

CATHY MARIE HAKE
JOYCE LIVINGSTON

BARBOUR
PUBLISHING

Love Is Patient © 2003 by Cathy Marie Hake
Love Is Kind © 2003 by Joyce Livingston
Love Worth Finding © 2005 by Cathy Marie Hake
Love Worth Keeping © 2005 by Joyce Livingston

ISBN 1-59789-365-X

Cover image by Stephen Simpson/Getty Images

Scripture quotations are taken from the New American Standard Bible, © 1960, 1962, 1963, 1968, 1971, 1972, 1973, 1975, 1977, 1995 by The Lockman Foundation. Used by permission.

This book is a work of fiction. Names, characters, places, and incidents are either products of the author's imagination or used fictitiously. Any similarity to actual people, organizations, and/or events is purely coincidental.

Published by Barbour Publishing, Inc., P.O. Box 719, Uhrichsville, Ohio 44683, www.barbourbooks.com

Our mission is to publish and distribute inspirational products offering exceptional value and biblical encouragement to the masses.

Member of the
Evangelical Christian
Publishers Association

Printed in the United States of America.
5 4 3 2 1

Love Is Patient

by Cathy Marie Hake

Chapter 1

Granite Cliffs, California

Big, brown, puppy-dog eyes—Vanessa Zobel had always been a sucker for them. It was why she'd opened Whiskers, Wings, and Wags. Right now, she had not one, but two sets of large, soulful brown eyes trained on her. "May I help you?"

"Nobody can help me," the little boy across the counter said in a despondent tone.

Vanessa looked to the adult for an explanation. The tall, sable-haired man stared back at her for a moment, then glanced down at his shuffling son.

"We need to return this." The man set a quart-sized Zip-Tite plastic bag on the counter. It tilted toward the edge, so he caught and scooted the bag closer to the register. Blissfully untroubled by the changing current, the goldfish inside continued to swim tiny laps.

The little boy stuck out a grubby finger and rubbed the edge of the clear plastic bag. "I done wrong."

His confession didn't reveal much information, but he'd admitted responsibility for whatever the problem was. Vanessa hummed. "Is that so?"

"I really, really wanted Goldie. I knew he'd stay little and he'd be quiet."

The man rested his callused hand on the boy's shoulder. "Jeff—"

"I know, Dad. I done wrong." The little boy hung his head.

Kids sometimes shoplifted. Vanessa had experience dealing with customers in that realm, but she knew Jeff couldn't have stolen the fish. She looked at the father in puzzlement.

"I understand you give coupons to the school for free goldfish. Jeff forged my signature on the parental permission line."

"Ohh." The picture became clear. She looked from the child to the fish and back again at Jeff. His lower lip protruded in a quivering, almost-ready-to-cry pout. "Oh, my."

"Dad says I gotta—" His little chin rose as he sucked in a gulp of air. "Gotta give Goldie back to you."

Vanessa shot the broad-shouldered father a quick glance. The left side of his mouth kicked up into a rakish smile, and his eyes stayed steady as could be. He stood behind his son and kept a hand on his shoulder.

To Vanessa, it looked like a show of support during a difficult time. Still, the father's other palm flattened and scooted the bag farther away. Taking her cue from him, she walked around the counter and knelt in front of the little guy. Since she didn't know if he would be afraid of her dog, she rested a hand on Amber's golden coat in a silent show of reassurance. "Jeff, I think you're a mighty lucky young man."

"You mean I getta keep Goldie?" Hope flared in his big eyes.

"No, I'm afraid not." Vanessa took his little hand in hers as she shook her head. "I think you're blessed to have a daddy who loves you so much, he wants to teach you to be an honorable man."

"Is honor'ble like being honest?"

"That's part of it. It means being honest and fair and that folks know they can trust you to do the right thing."

Jeff twisted the toe of his well-worn sneaker on the linoleum floor. The sound of the rubber squeaking mixed with tweets, yips, and a parrot squawk. He jammed his hands into his pockets and muttered, "My dad's honor'ble."

"I try to be, son. It's not always easy."

Tears filled Jeff's eyes. "I wanna keep Goldie. Goldie likes me. What if he isn't happy here?"

"I'm sure the lady has lots of goldfish to keep Goldie company."

"Yes, I do. Goldie will need to get used to the water, though."

Though lines of bafflement creased his brow, a devastatingly handsome smile tilted the father's mouth. "Goldie's already a very good swimmer."

"I'll need to let him get used to the water temperature. It might be a bit of a shock to him otherwise, so we'll just slip him—bag and all—into the tank until the temperature equalizes. Then we'll let Goldie out so he can make friends with all of the other fish."

"We will? Do I get to help?"

Oops. Me and my big mouth. She wrinkled her nose and looked up at the father again. "It'll take about fifteen minutes."

Jeff tugged on his father's paint-splattered sweatshirt. "Dad, you said we were going to bring Goldie back if it took all day!"

Vanessa tried to smother her smile. She doubted the father meant he was willing to stick around for a fish reacclimation.

The father chuckled and rumpled Jeff's hair. "We can spare fifteen minutes."

Vanessa took the bag from the counter. "The fish tanks are right back here."

"Can I carry Goldie?" A quick look back into the dad's eyes let Vanessa know it was okay. "Sure." She handed the squishy package down to Jeff's little hands, then shoved up the right sleeve of his lightweight sweatshirt. "We'll even have you put his bag into the tank."

Jeff carried his tiny contraband through the store. Vanessa thought they made quite a procession—the boy and his fish, his father, then she and Amber bringing up the rear. Amber quietly sat at heel while the father clasped his big hands around his son's waist and lifted him. Jeff solemnly lowered the bag into the goldfish tank. Big tears filled his eyes.

"I know it's hard for you, son, but this is the way it has to be." The father set him back down.

"I knew it was bad to tell a lie. Writing a lie is wrong, too, huh?"

"Yes, it is."

Several of the fish in the tank darted by the plastic bag. A few nudged it. "It looks to me like Goldie's got a lot of fish who want to be his friend," Vanessa said. "You can watch them for awhile if you'd like. I need to do a little work around here, but I'll come back to help you let Goldie out of the bag."

Vanessa walked past several more tanks teeming with fish, around the corner display of hamsters, gerbils, and mice, then shoved a protruding bag of dog food into place on a shelf before she reached the back room.

"All done," Valene declared as she pulled a load of towels from the clothes dryer.

Vanessa smiled at her identical twin. "Hang on a second." She unfastened Val's clip, quickly finger-combed the shoulder-length, honey blond tresses back into order, and popped them back into a tidy ponytail that matched her own.

Val's blue eyes twinkled. "If you tell me I look pretty, I'm going to accuse you of being vain."

"Your soul is beautiful," Vanessa shot back. "I didn't say a word about the package God put it in."

"Oh, so He gave Mom and Dad a two-for-the-price-of-one deal on us?"

"Spoken like a business major." Vanessa laughed at their silly banter as she plucked a green jacket from amidst the towels and fastened it over Amber's back. "Speaking of deals, what would you think of us putting together a puppy package?"

"Not a bad idea—especially since you filled every last cage and pen last night."

"What can I say?" Vanessa spread her hands wide. "I love dogs. I need to get back out there." She smoothed the golden retriever's jacket, gave the animal an affectionate stroke, and started to push a cart out the door. "Let's go." She murmured the command, and Amber sedately walked alongside her.

"Whatcha doin'?" Jeff asked from over by the hamsters.

"I'm going to give all of the animals some fresh drinking water."

"Can I help?"

"You need to ask your daddy."

Jeff's father turned around from admiring a parrot. "I'll let him help. . . ." Glints of gold sparkled in his brown eyes. "If I can too."

Jeff scampered over. "Your dog's wearing clothes now!"

"Yes, she is. She's a special dog. Her name is Amber."

Jeff pursed his lips and squinted at the writing on the green jacket. He pointed at it. "That doesn't say Amber."

His father squatted down beside him. "Why don't you read it, sport?"

"J-joo-eye-dee." His little features twisted. "Jooeydie? What is that?"

"Sound it out again. Use the other sound for G, and keep the first vowel silent."

Jeff's face puckered. "Teacher says, 'When two vowels go walking, the first one does the talking.' "

"That's usually true, but this word is a rule breaker."

"G-eye-duh. Guide!" Jeff beamed as he ran his forefinger along the white lettering. "Guide pup-py in train-ing!"

"What a smart boy!" Vanessa smiled at how the father beamed from her praise every bit as much as the son.

"Jeff's six. I'm Nathan Adams." Laugh lines around his mouth deepened. "I'm sure he'll be glad to tell you how old I am, what we ate for lunch, and that I occasionally drive too fast."

"Vanessa Zobel," she provided with a quick laugh. "Twenty-four, a taco, and no speeding tickets. . .yet."

"Did Amber eat a taco, too?"

"No." She played with Amber's soft ears. "Amber isn't supposed to be a pet. She's going to be a working dog. We want to teach her to do her jobs without getting treats. It makes her happy for me to pat her and tell her she's a good girl."

Nathan hooked his thumbs in the front pockets of his tattered jeans. "So you'll train her and give her away?"

The gentle quality of his voice made Vanessa's heart melt. Most people focused on what a wonderful thing it was for the blind to receive such a dog. She did, too— or she wouldn't be training the dogs. Still, few ever understood the ache involved in relinquishing a puppy.

"This is my fourth guide puppy." She petted Amber and added, "She's a good dog. I'll miss her, but I know she'll be a wonderful companion helper for someone who needs her."

"Does she sleep here at night with all of the other animals?" Jeff continued to trace the letters on the jacket.

"No, Amber goes everywhere with me. It's my job to make sure she learns how to behave nicely wherever we are. In a few months, she'll go to San Francisco to a special doggy school where they'll teach her how to help a blind person."

"Someone's going to be lucky," Nathan said slowly as he looked into her eyes. "It looks like you've trained Amber magnificently."

"Does she wear that thing on her face 'cuz she's a working dog?"

"Yes." Vanessa glanced down at the green halterlike device. "It's a training tool called a gentle leader. That part around her muzzle is loose, so she can still open her mouth."

"Can she still eat?"

"Yes, she could, but I've trained her only to eat at special times from a bowl. She won't eat food she finds on the ground or that people offer her. See how the other part of it goes under her chin here and makes a collar? If I give the leash just a tiny pull, it steers her."

Nathan gave her an astonished look. "Power steering for puppies. Wow."

"How come all of the other dogs and cats are noisy, but Amber is quiet?"

"They're just babies. They need someone to love and train them." The door chimed. Vanessa craned her neck and spied one of her regular customers trundling into the shop. "Excuse me. I need to help Mrs. Rosetti."

She sold the usual pound of lamb-and-rice biscuits her regular bought each week, then came back to the father and son. "Would you like to help me give the animals fresh water to drink?"

In no time at all Nathan, Jeff, and Vanessa had refilled all the water bottles and dishes for the reptiles, rodents, birds, and kittens. Jeff's enthusiasm for the task far outstripped his ability, and his shirt showed it. Still, his father ignored the wet clothing and patiently helped his son. At each cage, habitat, or pen, Jeff decided he'd love to have that particular pet the most.

"Looks like you have a bona fide animal lover on your hands," she said to Nathan.

"He's decided anything worth having is worth collecting. We already have a rock collection, at least two hundred baseball cards, three oatmeal canisters of seashells, and enough Matchbox cars to jam our own freeway. If I let him have one pet, I'm sure our whole house would turn into one big menagerie."

As Vanessa raised a brow, she asked the teasing question, "And the problem with that would be. . . ?"

"I'm not about to debate that issue with you." Nathan shook his head and gave her a rueful grin. "Your bias is clear."

"True. I think pets are great." Vanessa parked the cart in the corner and spread her hands wide. "I can't think of anything better than being around animals!"

"Why are you stopping?" Nathan asked her.

"We can go release Goldie now."

Jeff stood on tiptoe and peeped over the edge of a pen holding a pair of cocker spaniels. "I wanna see the puppies. They're so little!"

"I'll tell you what: We'll use up the rest of the water in the pitcher. Then, we can let the goldfish free. Afterward, I'll take care of the rest of the dogs."

Nathan snagged one of a pair of cocker spaniels that bounded out of their pen when Vanessa opened the sliding door. She hastily grabbed the other and laughed as it licked her cheek. "You're gonna run me ragged, aren't you, Frack?"

"Frack?" Father and son asked in unison.

"Frack." She held up her wiggling puppy. "You snagged Frick—for which I'm eternally grateful."

"I wanna hold a puppy, too."

"I don't mind your holding a puppy, but perhaps we could find one that's a little less active." Vanessa playfully tousled Frack's ears, then set him back in his pen.

The shop's bell chimed again, announcing another customer.

"If you don't mind, I can help Jeff release the goldfish while you take care of those folks," Nathan offered.

"Fine. Thanks."

Lord, she prayed as she walked off, *see that guy? Gorgeous brown eyes, fabulous sense of honor and ethics, even a dollop of humor. You can find me one of those whenever You're ready.*

Two little girls stood with their mother at the door. "We've come to look at kittens."

"I hope all of the good ones aren't taken!" one girl said.

"I hope not, too." Vanessa smiled at them. *But I'm not talking about kittens.*

Chapter 2

Nathan watched the perky woman and her retriever head for the front of the shop. Her blond ponytail bounced as she walked. It had been a long time since he reacted to such a natural beauty. The moment they made eye contact, his brain went into a free fall, and he'd probably made a total fool of himself gawking at her. She hadn't laughed at how he fumbled and almost dropped that dumb goldfish—a fact for which he was grateful.

Most of all, he appreciated how she'd taken her cues from him and supported how he wanted to discipline Jeff. She hadn't made a big, hairy deal out of the matter, but the way she stood firm about putting Goldie back in the tank reinforced his parental decision. Still, the compassionate way she allowed Jeff to make sure Goldie had new friends would undoubtedly keep him from doing a total meltdown when they left.

"Dad, do you think Goldie will be okay?"

"The lady here is nice, sport. I think she'll do a great job keeping Goldie happy."

"Prob'ly." Jeff sighed. "I guess we can let him out of his bag now."

Jeff took his sweet time telling Goldie a half dozen "important" things. He then spoke to the rest of the tank's occupants, earnestly telling them all about their wonderful companion as if he'd owned the silly creature for months instead of overnight. Lower lip quivering, Jeff finally freed the fish.

Nathan watched tears fill his son's eyes. He quietly took the soggy bag from Jeff's hands and wished again he hadn't needed to do this. As kids went, Jeff was great, but Nathan wanted him to grow up to have integrity. Rewarding his dishonesty by letting him keep the fish would be a mistake.

"I can't tell which one is Goldie." Jeff trembled. "Can you?"

Oh, it would be so easy to lie.

"No, son, but I figure that's a good thing. It means Goldie fits right in and everybody is already playing with him."

"How are you doing, big guy?" Vanessa asked softly as she rounded the corner. Nathan watched as she knelt, opened her arms, and Jeff ran to her. She hugged him. "It's not easy to say good-bye, is it?"

Jeff shook his head and burrowed closer to her.

"I'll bet you'd rather grow up to be a good man like your daddy than to keep one little old goldfish."

"Yeah," he agreed, his voice muted against her shoulder. "I done wrong, but Dad said this would make it right."

"The next time you have to choose how to act, I'll bet you do a better job," Nathan said as he slipped his hands around Jeff's waist and lifted him high.

"We can't go yet, Dad. She promised I could hold a puppy."

"I need to get more water. Why don't you two go look at the dogs and decide which one Jeff wants to hold?"

Whiskers, Wings, and Wags certainly boasted a bumper crop of animals. Nathan and Jeff sauntered along the puppy wall. Every breed from Afghans to wiener dogs snuffled, yipped, and wagged from the bright clean pens and cages. A pair of puffball-sized huskies tussled over a toy, and a little Shar-Pei that looked like a rumpled tan sock napped in a corner.

"Does she got any spotty dogs like on the movie?"

"Does she have any spotty Dalmatians?" He tried to correct Jeff's grammar when they were alone. If other folks were around, Nathan preferred to ignore the usual childish mistakes. But Evie had loved fine literature, and she would have wanted their son to be well-spoken.

"Yeah, Dad. Dalmatians. I forgot that name."

Nathan scanned the pens. "Hmm. No, I don't see any."

"I don't carry them," Vanessa said as she approached. Amber walked at her side, yet a frisky black Lab strained every last inch of the leash Vanessa held in her other hand. "Dalmatians are charming to look at, but they tend to be very high-strung, so the pound ends up with lots of them. I'd rather let somebody rescue one than support someone to breed more litters."

Nathan listened to every word she said, but he was even more aware of Jeff's reaction. His son reached up, clutched his hand with a near-death grip and quivered with sheer excitement.

"Is that one for me?"

"Sure," Vanessa said. "Maybe we could let you go into a meeting enclosure so he'll stay corralled."

Jeff rocketed into the three-foot tall enclosure, and the Lab galloped right after him. Vanessa laughingly controlled him until Nathan closed the gate. It wobbled, and he inspected it. "You've got a loose screw."

"Plenty of folks have told me I have a screw loose. No one ever told me I have a loose screw."

Jeff enthusiastically petted the Lab. "My dad's in the 'struction business. He knows all 'bout screws an' lumber and stuff."

"You've got a handy dad."

"Uh-huh. Honor'ble too. I wanna grow up to be like him someday."

"Good for you. Those are fine qualities."

The minute Vanessa unhooked the leash, the Lab and Jeff tumbled into a tangle of legs and noise.

"Looks like they're getting along okay," she said after a minute. "I'll let them goof off while I give the rest of these babies a drink."

"Let me help," Nathan offered.

She held up her hand. "I'd rather you stay with Jeff. The puppy is already settling down, but I don't like to leave kids alone with unfamiliar dogs."

"Makes sense. Tell you what. Find a Phillips screwdriver, and I'll fix the hinge for you." Nathan grinned at how the Lab licked the hip of Jeff's jeans. "Do you have food in your pocket?"

"Beef jerky," Jeff confessed. "I wanted a snack while you got your hair cut. He's really smart to find it so fast, isn't he, Dad?"

"Yes, he is."

"Can he have some jerky?"

"No," Vanessa called over. "I have a jar of puppy biscuits on the ledge there. You may give him one of those."

The minute the puppy heard the rattle from the jar, he skidded over and sat on Nathan's foot. *Cute little thing. Hardly longer than my shoe.* "Hungry, boy?"

A yip served as an answer.

Vanessa went up front to help a few more customers. When she came back, she leaned over the wall and chuckled. Nathan didn't feel self-conscious in the least to have Jeff and the puppy both in his lap. As a matter of fact, he was enjoying every minute of it. He'd be hard-pressed to say which one of them wiggled more.

"I try to give each of the puppies a temporary name. The owners are free to change it, but it lets me love them a bit more while they're here. Do you guys have any suggestions for him?"

"Blackie?"

Nathan ruffled Jeff's hair. "That's not a bad suggestion, sport, but lots of dogs get named that. Why not think of things that are black?"

"Wheels. Tires. Licorice."

"Licorice!" Vanessa clapped. "I like that!"

"Lick for a nickname," Nathan added as the puppy laved his son's face.

Truthfully, Jeff and Lick were getting along famously, which surprised Nathan. Jeff had never shown much interest in animals, but he seemed to be enjoying this little jaunt to the pet store. *I didn't even realize he wanted that dumb fish, either. Maybe I should take him to the zoo. . . .*

"I'll make a little name tag for Lick's pen. He just came in last night."

"You've got a bumper crop of puppies." Nathan tilted his head toward the far wall.

"Spring." She smiled. "The early litters are here, and I just took in several new puppies last night. I'd rather sell puppies and kittens for Easter than bunnies."

"I like dogs better than bunnies," Jeff declared. He stroked Licorice and giggled as the puppy licked him avidly in response.

Nathan focused more attention on Vanessa than his son, since Jeff seemed content to play with the puppy. "What's wrong with rabbits?"

"Nothing." She shrugged. "Some folks do beautifully with them, but others don't realize the cute little bunny won't stay tiny and that he likes to eat plants."

"Dad, look. He's so neat!"

Nathan glanced down. "Yeah, he is." He looked back at Vanessa. "Sounds like you're more interested in making good matches than in making a buck."

She flushed with obvious pleasure. "I try."

"Can I give him another biscuit?"

"Sure," Nathan answered absently. The jar rattled. "I'll bet the dog treat manufacturers make a bundle off of you, Vanessa."

A wisp of hair came loose from her ponytail as she shook her head. She tucked the sunny strand back into the clip. "I like to use affection instead of treats."

"Dad, he's got lots and lots of little teeth."

"Yeah, he does." He couldn't recall the last time he'd been around anyone so cheerful. "Working here really suits you."

"It's a blessing to have a job I love."

"You found a screwdriver?"

"Yes—if you really don't mind. . . "

"Not at all."

Nathan shifted into a more comfortable position and continued to carry on some small talk with Vanessa as he fixed the hinge. Jeff broke in with little observations and nonsense, but since he and Licorice kept each other entertained, Nathan continued to focus on Vanessa. Jeff got more insistent, and Nathan put both hands on his son's shoulders to transmit that he needed to settle down and hush a bit.

"I'm gonna get it, aren't I?"

At the same time Jeff spoke, Vanessa asked, "Are you guys about done in there?"

"Yes."

"Wow, Dad. Thanks!"

"Huh?" Nathan gave his son a quick look. His little face radiated with joy.

"I'll take really good care of him. I promise!"

"What?" Nathan cast a baffled glance at Vanessa. She gave him a troubled look.

"He asked if he could have the puppy," she whispered, "and you said yes."

14

Chapter 3

*O*h, *great. The one time I don't give my kid undivided attention, I tell him he can have a dog? I didn't mean that he would get the dog; I meant if he kept interrupting he was going to be in trouble!* Nathan took a deep breath and turned back to crush Jeff's hopes.

"Jeff," Vanessa said as she entered the pen. She knelt and made direct eye contact with him. "This is all my fault. Your daddy was answering my question. He wasn't telling you that you could have the puppy."

Jeff wrapped his arms around the puppy's neck, hugged it close, and shook his head. His voice went adamant. "My dad is honor'ble. He said I could have my dog."

"Your daddy is an honorable man, but this was just a misunderstanding. A mistake," Vanessa tried again.

Nathan took a deep breath. "It's a fine puppy."

"See? My dad doesn't lie!"

Vanessa let out a soundless sigh.

"Why don't you let us talk about this for a few minutes?" Nathan asked her.

She stood, clasped her hands at her waist, and tilted her head toward the puppy. "The three of you, or the two of you?"

"Three," Jeff answered promptly. From the way he held onto the little Lab, she suspected a six-point earthquake wouldn't shake them apart.

Vanessa didn't say another word. After she let herself out of the enclosure, Nathan noticed she walked away without that cute bounce she'd had earlier.

Several minutes later, she returned. She seemed subdued. Instead of wearing that dazzling smile, she avoided making eye contact.

"Hey," he called softly, "we're going to take him. A boy needs a dog."

"Labs make good pets," she said as her face brightened a bit, but it still missed that sparkle he'd noticed earlier. "They do well with children."

"I guess I'd better buy some kibble." Nathan let himself out of the enclosure. "Jeff, you and Lick play for a few more minutes."

"Okay, Dad."

Ten minutes later, Nathan dumped the contents of a red plastic shopping basket onto the counter and shook his head. Two chew toys, a bottle of puppy shampoo, a leash, collar, food and water bowls, all accused him of being a pushover.

The large sheepskin bed and the ten-pound bag of puppy kibble leaning against the counter proved he'd done a royal job of painting himself into a very expensive commitment.

Me and my big mouth. I try to teach my son to show integrity and end up buying half of a pet store!

Vanessa caught a jingly ball that started to roll off the counter. From the minute she'd whispered that he'd accidentally agreed to get the dog, she'd changed. She couldn't seem to meet his eyes.

From their conversation, Nathan knew making a good match was important to her. He strove to find a way to reassure her. "Do you have a good vet you recommend?"

"We have a terrific vet who comes here one Saturday a month to give vaccinations—Dr. Bainbridge. If you buy the puppy shot package, it saves you all of the office visit charges."

"Good idea."

She leaned down and pulled out a few leaflets from beneath the counter. As she tucked them into a bag, she said, "I'm giving you the information on that package, as well as one of the vet's business cards."

"Thanks. I appreciate it."

She continued to avoid looking at him. "I'm also giving you a pet ID tag order form. Fill it out, and we'll order the tags. They're complimentary."

He reached over and captured her hand as she reached for one of the toys. "You don't need to throw in anything. Seriously, this was my choice."

"Hey, Dad!"

"Just a minute, sport."

Vanessa flashed him a strained smile and pulled away from his touch. "We've been putting together a new puppy package. The first bag of food, a toy, and the tags are included at no charge."

The nape of his neck started to prickle. Nathan wheeled around and stared at Vanessa as she quietly walked up to him and asked, "Are you sure you want to do this? I'll come up with some way to explain it to Jeff."

"There are two of you. Twins." He cast a quick look over his shoulder, then concentrated back on Vanessa. Even though her eyes radiated concern, that little spark was still there—both in her eyes and somewhere deep inside of him. He'd missed that with the other gal.

"We're identical. I'm sorry if you were confused. I didn't realize Valene had come out and started helping you."

He glanced down at Amber. "I should have guessed something was wrong. I didn't see your companion."

"Daa–aad. Look out. There are two—" Jeff galloped around the corner and skidded to a stop. Licorice didn't halt. He charged ahead.

"Whoa!" Vanessa dove for the little puppy.

Nathan got to him first. Licorice sniffed his neck and let out a happy sounding yap. Vanessa knelt right next to them. Nathan dipped his chin to keep the puppy from licking the ticklish spot beneath his left ear. "I don't want to hear another word about not taking this little fellow home. It's obvious he's chosen us."

✞

"Vanessa!" Nathan called as he hastened toward the young woman locking the pet shop door.

She cast a quick glance over her shoulder and grinned. "Hi. How are things going?"

"Not good. We need to talk." Nathan raked his fingers through his hair in a single, impatient swipe. "I'm going insane."

"And you think I have the directions to get there?" She finished locking the shop. "Why does everyone think I'm the crazy sister? No, wait. Don't answer that."

He eyed her white-and-orange baseball uniform with dismay. "Cleats?"

"They're a lot more comfortable than heels. My church team is playing across the street tonight."

A sick feeling churned in his stomach. "And you play."

Her smile gleamed. "Believe me, if I didn't, nobody would ever wrangle me into wearing this uniform. I look more like the Great Pumpkin than the shortstop."

He tilted his head to the side. "Shortstop, huh? No kidding. I would have pegged a bouncy gal like you to be the team mascot."

"That was back in high school. Valene was the class valedictorian; I was the class clown and mascot. I shouldn't complain about this uniform. Nothing could ever be as uncomfortable as the shark suit I wore."

"You wore an outfit made of sharkskin?"

"Worse," she moaned. "I wore a great big, gray-and-white plush—"

"Plush? A shark?"

"Oh, yes. Fins and all. You're looking at one of Granite Cliffs's great whites—retired, of course."

"Since you've retired, you'll have enough time to help me." Nathan felt a small spurt of satisfaction that he'd segued this smoothly. "We're um. . .having some trouble."

"We are?" She pointed across the street to the ball diamond in a silent invitation to walk along with her.

Nathan automatically stood to her left so he'd be on the outside. "Yeah, well—"

She didn't follow along. "I'm sorry, Nathan, but Amber walks at heel. You need to be on my right."

"Oh. Okay." He shifted.

"Let's go," she said, and they fell into step.

"See? That's what I need. Jeff and Lick are romping everywhere and tearing up the house and yard. I need obedience and control tips. Amber heard you and fell right into step with us."

"One down, one to go." She winked and added, "I think you do fine with Jeff. The puppy might take a bit of time."

"If you saw my place, you wouldn't say so. My son's decided wherever he goes, Lick should be there with him. Last night, he waited until my back was turned and decided Lick belonged in the tub with him."

"Oh, no!"

Nathan rubbed his forehead at the memory of the wet puppy, the soggy bathroom, and the water trail down the hallway. That was just a part of the trials he faced with this new acquisition. "Yes. The dog won't eat his kibble. Instead, he's chewed the leg of a dining chair and gnawed on a pillow from the sofa."

They stopped at the corner and prepared to cross the busy intersection. Amber halted and sat without any cue at all. A cat streaked by, but the dog didn't react.

"I can't believe that. I've chased after our puppy twice because he can't leave cats alone. You've got to help me."

"I guess I sort of got you into this." Vanessa started to cross the street.

"Are you going to get me out of it?" He matched her stride and added on in desperation, "I'm more than willing to pay the going rate."

"Licorice is too young yet for training, but we can reserve a spot for him in one of the classes I'll have in a little over a month."

"My sanity could be measured in milliseconds, not months."

"Uh-oh. That sounds serious."

He rubbed his aching temple with his fingertips. "The only pets I ever had were cats. Cats take care of themselves."

"Ah, yes. Cats train their owners; dogs are trained by their owners."

"You nailed it on the head. So tell me: What's available right now to get us through the nightmare stage?"

"You mean something like private puppy lessons?"

He shot her a grateful smile. "I thought you'd never offer!"

Her eyes widened and a hectic flush filled her cheeks. "I didn't!" He continued to stare at her, and she scrunched her nose. "Let me guess. You bought the Lab because you misspoke and honored your word, so you're standing there thinking I ought to do the same thing."

"I'm flexible with hours."

Vanessa leaned her back into the fence. One of her knees crooked outward and her heel fit into the chain link. "We have to have an understanding. I'm not good at minding what I say. Valene—she's one of those 'think first, then talk' kind of people. Me? I'm impulsive. She got the brain, and I got the mouth." She laughed self-consciously. "If I'm willing to work with you, you have to promise not to use my words against me. I'll be sunk if you do!"

"Fair enough. When can we start?"

She shrugged. "Tomorrow at seven?"

"In the morning?"

Vanessa groaned. "Oh, don't tell me you're one of those morning people!"

"No." He watched someone dump several bats and balls out of a canvas sack. "I'd be a night owl if Jeff weren't such an early riser. He got that from my wife."

"If she's a stay-home mom, I could work with her from ten to eleven."

Pain speared through him. "Evie died five years ago."

"I'm so sorry, Nathan."

He nodded his head in acknowledgment of her sympathy.

"Nate? Nate Adams!" Kip Gaterie jogged over and shook his hand. "Did Van talk you into joining the team? We could use a slugger like you!"

"You know each other?" Vanessa gave him an assessing look. "And you play ball?"

"Hang on a second here. I'm trying to get you to train a dog so I won't have to chase after him. Running after a ball isn't any more appealing."

"We were on a community ball team together almost five years ago." Kip looked at him steadily. "You can always change your mind. We'd be glad to have you, and we've got a bunch of rug rats about Jeff's age who could keep him company on the playground."

"Thanks, but I'll have to pass."

"That's a shame." Kip scuffed his foot in the red dirt. "Van, the park messed up on our reservation and only slotted us for an hour and a half. We're playing sudden death tonight, so we need to get out there."

"Okay."

As she turned to go, Nathan grabbed her arm. "Hey, if you're only going to play for a little while, I can go home and get Jeff and Lick. Could you work with us after the game?"

"You're really desperate, aren't you?"

"In a word, yes!"

She glanced at her bright yellow Tweety Bird watch. "Be here at seven thirty. I can't work miracles, but I'll try to give you a few starting tips."

"I gave up hoping for miracles years ago." He fished in his pocket for his keys, embarrassed by his sharp tone. "Have a good game. We'll be back later."

Chapter 4

Vanessa wondered at the depth of the bitterness in Nathan's words, but it was neither the time nor the place to ask him what had caused that shift in him. Instead, she shoved on her mitt and jogged out onto the ball diamond.

After a cursory warm-up, the game began. Valene sat in the bleachers. She liked individual sports like tennis and badminton, but when it came to team sports, she preferred to be a spectator. By contrast, Vanessa loved all sports. Back in junior high she'd begged and wheedled to have her twin join several teams with her, but their youth pastor once gave a lesson on accepting loved ones instead of trying to change them. His words hit home—Vanessa had spent the whole ride to Seaside Chapel trying to cajole Val into trying out for the junior high volleyball team. She'd spent the drive home apologizing. Now it all seemed to work out beautifully. Val always brought the team banner and would watch Amber while Van dashed around the bases.

Kip sat down on the bench next to Van in the dugout. He nudged her shoulder playfully. "What's with you and Nathan Adams?"

Vanessa gave him a startled look. "Nothing. I just sold him a puppy, and it needs a bit of training. Why?"

He shrugged. "He's a good guy."

She gave him a piercing look. "But?"

"Nate took his wife's death hard. They used to attend Mercy Springs. He stopped attending, and I kinda hoped maybe he was starting back into fellowship."

"I don't know a thing about where he stands with the Lord. The only thing I know is, I'm in the doghouse 'cuz he bought a rambunctious puppy from me." She squinted as a ball sailed through the air. Hopping to her feet, she screamed, "Run! Run, Todd!"

The team cheered as Todd sped across home plate. Kip headed out of the dugout and hefted a bat. He looked back at Vanessa and wagged the end of the bat in her direction. "You never know what God will use to bring a sheep back into the fold. Keep your heart and eyes open."

※

"There she is!" Jeff galloped toward the chain-link fence. Lick romped alongside him.

Nathan didn't need his son to point out where Vanessa was. He heard her first. She ran full tilt for third base, screaming like a heat-seeking missile the whole way. Her golden ponytail streamed behind her, and the left half of what had once been white-and-orange-striped baseball leggings now sported a calf-to-waist dusting of red that tattled on what must've been a world-class slide. She took a cue from the third-base coach and stopped. Energy high, she bobbed up and down on the base.

Nathan grinned as he continued to watch her. She cheered from third base, "You can do it, Della! Slug it!"

"I don't have your muscles, girlfriend!"

Cupping her hands around her mouth, Vanessa yelled back, "Then use your brains. Anyone has more of those than I do!"

Everyone on the diamond chuckled, but Nathan watched as the outfielders drew closer to the infield. The ball whizzed over the plate.

"Strike one!" The second pitch went wide. The third zoomed over the plate again. Della stood there the whole time and didn't swing at all.

"Della," Vanessa hollered, "I said to use your brains, not your looks."

Della lifted the bat off her shoulder and took an awkward stance. "I'm not getting filthy dirty like you do."

"Don't worry about that. I already collected all of the loose dirt. You ought to be fine."

"Do you girls mind if we play ball?" the opposing pitcher asked in a humored tone.

"If you insist." Della nodded. "I'm as ready as I'm gonna get."

Nathan's jaw dropped as he heard the bat crack and the ball sailed far out into center field. Vanessa and the runner on second base both ran home. Vanessa skipped back and forth along the foul line. "You did it, Della! You did it!"

"Pretty clever strategy," Nathan said through the fence to Kip. "Lulled the other team into complacency."

Kip shook his head. "Nope. We can't believe it, either. Della's never even connected. Van took her to the batting cages this week."

"What in the world is Della doing on a team if she can't hit?"

"It's not about winning—it's about having a good time." Kip stared at him. "Though I wasn't kidding that we could sure use you on our team."

Vanessa bounced over. "Jeff! Lick! Hiya, guys!"

Licorice jumped up onto the fence with a happy yip.

"Off." Vanessa's voice took on a firm quality. She added, "Give the command and jerk back on the leash."

"Off!" Nathan pulled the leash from Jeff and tugged it. To his surprise, Licorice got all four paws on the grass and gave him a baffled look.

"Good dog, good dog," Vanessa crooned. She glanced at her watch. "You're a little early. Val and Amber are over on the bleachers. You can join them, or I can meet you by the playground as soon as the game is done."

"No playground," Jeff said morosely. "Dad said I can't 'cuz I already took my bath."

"Maybe next time," Vanessa said.

Nathan watched his son brighten up again. Vanessa had a knack for saying the right thing. Licorice started to drag on the leash. "I guess we're off to the stands."

He greeted Valene and took a seat next to her. He leaned forward and read the scoreboard. "The Altar Egos?"

"Vanessa named the team when it got started. She came up with over a dozen possible names, but that one won the vote."

"Is she always this irrepressible?"

Valene choked back a laugh. "I don't think I've ever heard anyone label her that way, but you're right."

The teams swapped positions. Vanessa played shortstop.

"Altar Egos...," Nathan repeated as he spotted the big plastic banner someone had tied to the chain-link dugout. The bold black words on the orange-and-white-striped background intrigued Nathan: "BUT MAY IT NEVER BE THAT I WOULD BOAST, EXCEPT IN THE CROSS OF OUR LORD JESUS CHRIST." GALATIANS 6:14.

Kip said it was a game for fun—not for competition—but the banner's declaration backed up what might easily have been a politically correct comment.

Nathan watched as the Altar Egos' players teased each other as much as they congratulated the other team on good plays. Vanessa called, "Nice try!" to one of her teammates when he dropped a pop fly. He picked up the ball, fired it at her, and she snagged it in her glove. "Ned and his nuclear arm!"

She intrigued Nathan. If anyone had room to boast, surely it was Vanessa. A powerhouse hit and a talent for snagging line drives made her impressive to watch. Then again, so did her svelte figure. She'd been almost comical—a one-woman cheering squad for her friends. When the clock ran out and her team lost by one run, her grin didn't fade a bit.

As she came over to the bleachers, Jeff hopped up. "Guess what?" He didn't even pause to allow her to guess. "I got new spelling words on Monday, and you'll never in a million years guess what one of the words was. *Guide*—just like on Amber's jacket."

"Betcha you ace that test," Vanessa said. "Val, we're going to work a little with Licorice to see if we can find a few ways to calm him a bit. You can stay if you'd like, or you can take my car home. Amber and I could use the walk."

"I'd rather go work on my résumé. I saw a few positions in the career section that looked promising." Val squinted at the distance. "I have enough light to walk home. You keep the car."

"Not a chance," Nathan interrupted. "Jeff and I will give Vanessa a ride. We're messing up your schedule. It's the least we can do."

"Really, I can walk," Valene insisted. "I walk or jog four miles every day."

Nathan saw the worried look she shot Vanessa.

"We won't stay very long, Valene. Jeff has school tomorrow, and I need to have him in bed by eight thirty. After chasing him and Lick around this evening, I'll probably crash all of five minutes later."

"See? Pumpkin time isn't midnight; it's eight." Vanessa handed the keys to her sister. "Now promise me you'll juice up your résumé. It was too modest and bland."

"I'll see what I can do."

"What kind of job are you looking for?"

Valene shrugged. "I have my business degree. I kind of thought maybe a hospital business office."

"The minute you interview, you'll have every single hospital in Southern California after you," Vanessa declared. She stooped and said to Jeff, "My sister is a total brain. She's terrific at spelling words and math."

"Did you ever switch places for tests?" Jeff asked in a stage whisper.

Nathan wondered the same thing, but he wasn't sure he wanted to hear the answer—and he certainly didn't want Jeff to.

Vanessa wrinkled her nose. "It wouldn't have been right for us to swap places at school. We each got the grades we deserved. We did trade places at summer camp once so I could play baseball more and Valene got to swim."

"Van slid into second base and ruined my new jeans that day," Valene recalled.

"You look alike, but you're really different," Jeff decided.

Vanessa winked at Nathan. "That's one smart kid you have there. If your dog is half as clever, training him will be a piece of cake."

They spent about half an hour working with Licorice. Jeff started out like gangbusters, wanting to do everything. Licorice decided to yank free and make a mad dash across the park.

"Oh, no," Nathan groaned. He started to run after the puppy. It was the last thing he wanted to do.

"Nathan, clap and shout his name, but run the opposite way. He'll come chase you."

Less than a minute later, Licorice wiggled in Nathan's arms. "I can't believe it. That's all it takes? I've practically run a marathon twice today, catching this hairy little beast!"

Jeff plopped down on the grass and started to laugh. "Daddy needs to be trained more than the dog!"

Vanessa bit her lip and turned away, but from the way her shoulders shook, he knew she was thoroughly entertained. He bumped her hip with his and said in mock outrage, "Now look what you've done!"

"Saved you shoe leather?" she shot back.

"Who are you kidding?" He held up Licorice. "Knowing my luck, this little energetic four-legged headache is going to end up chewing on my shoes, anyway."

"Dad?"

Something in Jeff's tone made Nathan freeze. "What?"

Jeff ducked his head and lifted both shoulders. He said to his lap in a small voice, "He already did."

Nathan groaned. He turned back to Vanessa. "Shoes, a pillow, and a chair leg. Tell me the list of casualties ends there."

"You're in it for the long haul. It's not a three-strikes-and-he's-out proposition."

"You're the puppy pro." He couldn't help responding to her gentle humor and common sense. "Now what do I do?"

"Give him the chew toys. I don't have anything scheduled tomorrow evening. Bring him by the shop after closing, and we'll come up with some strategies."

"Okay. You're on. I can hold out that long."

⁂

The door to Whiskers, Wings, and Wags flew open. "Vanessa!" Jeff's shout almost covered the chimes. A split second later, Vanessa heard Nathan's low scold, "You're not a Scud missile, son. Use your indoor voice and your manners."

" 'Kay, Dad. Where is she?"

"I'm down here," Vanessa called. She lifted a hand and waved over the counter.

"Hey, Van," Nathan said, "about ready to go?"

Embarrassed to the core of her being, she looked up at Nathan and shook her head.

"No?"

"I'm. . .um. . .stuck."

Chapter 5

S tuck?" Nathan repeated, leaning farther over the counter to get a better look.

"Stuck? Vanessa's stuck?" Jeff repeated. He raced around the counter.

"Oh, brother." Vanessa rested her head against Amber's side. "Ever hear the old saying, 'Be careful what you pray for?' "

"What did you pray for, and why are you stuck?" Nathan moved Jeff off to the side and hunkered down.

"I dropped a receipt. It slipped down here behind the drawers. When I reached up to get it, my ring caught, and my hand is jammed."

Nathan thoughtfully pinched his lower lip between his forefinger and thumb. He raised his brows at Jeff. "Son, it looks like we have a genuine damsel in distress here."

"Are we gonna rescue her?"

"Sometimes, sport, a man's gotta do what a man's gotta do."

"Wait!"

"Did we scare you free, like Dad scares the hiccups outta me?"

"Don't I just wish." She looked up at Nathan. "Would you please flip over the CLOSED sign and lock the door?"

"Jeff, you heard her. You can do those things, can't you?"

" 'Course I can!" His tennis shoes squeaked on the linoleum as he ran back around the counter. The dead bolt made a solid clunk, and cardboard scraped across the glass as the sign flipped over.

Nathan didn't wait for his son to finish those simple tasks. He maneuvered onto the floor next to her and slid his hand up close to hers. With each inhalation he took, his chest pressed against her back. Every breath he let out ruffled her hair and made her shiver. He frowned and wrapped his other arm around her. "You're cold. How long have you been trapped down here?"

"Half of forever," she evaded.

"Oh. So she can't tell time, either," Jeff said from behind them.

"Son, we need to squirt some soap up onto Vanessa's hand. Go into the back room and see what you can find."

"Dog shampoo," she suggested. "It's the yellowish orange stuff by the big tub."

Nathan's fingers nudged the side of her hand. "Too bad we can't open the drawer, but it would knock you senseless."

"Thank you."

"Huh?" He twisted his head a bit and gave her a puzzled look.

"After finding me like this, I figured you were going to think I didn't have any sense at all."

"Just because Valene was valedictorian doesn't mean you're not bright. How about if you stop comparing yourself and always thinking you come out on the short end of the deal?"

If he'd barked the words at her or teased, it would have been easier. Since his voice went so soft and earnest, she gulped.

He tugged a bit on her wrist and muttered, "You're really jammed in there."

The whole situation struck her as so ludicrous, she started to giggle. "You know me—I took that old cliché to heart: 'Anything worth doing is worth doing right.'"

Nathan's arm tightened around her. "So you're saying this was worth doing?"

How am I supposed to answer that?

The patter of Jeff's shoes saved her from having to formulate an answer. "Here's the shampoo!" He climbed over their legs and sat next to Amber. While Nathan withdrew his hand and gooped it up with the unscented liquid, Jeff scratched his knee. "What did you pray for, Van?"

She jerked on her hand once again to no avail and confessed, "Patience."

"Here goes nothing." Nathan curled back around her and slid his hand up by her wrist. "My fingers are fatter than yours. If I shove my hand any higher, we'll both get stuck. Can you wiggle your hand to the side a little?"

"Which side?"

"That way." He nudged her a bit. "Good. I'll see if I can rub some of this slimy stuff on the metal bar here and on the edge of your hand. Afterward, if you jostle your hand over here, maybe we can work just enough of the soap under the ring to make your finger slip free."

"I don't even know if it'll come off." She fidgeted, hoping to spread the shampoo around. "Grandma gave one to each of us on our thirteenth birthday."

"You've never taken it off?"

"Nope."

"Wow," Jeff said. He gave her an incredulous look. "Dad said all rings have to come off sooner or later. He keeps his in his sock drawer."

Nathan went completely still. Vanessa closed her eyes for a moment, sensing the pain that rolled off him. He'd said very little about his wife, but what he had said made it clear he'd loved her dearly. It must have been heartrending to finally remove his wedding band.

He drew in a deep, steadying breath. In a tight voice, he ordered, "Now try to work your hand free."

A few, very long minutes later, she felt a little give. "Almost—it slipped a little bit."

"Good." Nathan clenched her elbow. "On the count of three. One, two, three!"

He yanked, she pulled, and her hand came free.

"Oh, thank you, thank you, thank you."

"So you got what you prayed for," Jeff said as he hugged Amber.

Nathan opened the drawer, pried the ring free, and shoved it back at Vanessa. He stared at his son and rasped, "Prayers are like dreams and wishes. Not all of them come true. Don't ever forget that."

✟

At least once a week, Nathan arranged for Vanessa to work with him, Jeff, and Licorice. Every weekend, he brought Jeff to Whiskers, Wings, and Wags to buy a bag of kibble.

"I can order this in larger bags. It comes in twenty and forty pounds," Vanessa offered.

"Not a chance." Nathan plunked a ten-dollar bill onto the counter. "Don't even start down that path. You could charm a snake into buying a pedicure, but I'm impervious to this particular sales pitch."

"A pedicured snake?"

He ignored her entertained echo. "Our place is small. I don't want to have to go out to the garage or backyard to grab a scoop of chow for the little beast."

"Isn't that funny? For some odd reason, I figured a man in the construction business would have a big old house."

"Old, yes; big, no. Evie and I bought an 1865 saltbox back in Massachusetts on our honeymoon." For the first time, the memory flitted though his mind without tearing a jagged hole in his heart.

"A saltbox? How charming!"

"You wouldn't have said that if you'd have seen it. The poor thing was slated for destruction. Evie went wild over it and said all the rickety old house needed was elbow grease and love, so we had the place all numbered, dismantled, and shipped out here. I put it back together on a big lot." Under his breath, he recalled, "We always figured we could add on."

"Dad's building me a fort. A giant one with a swing set underneath."

"Neato! Are you helping?"

Nathan grinned. "He's sanding the shutters and is going to paint them."

"If you need an extra pair of hands, I'm willing to help." She lifted her arms and fluttered her fingers in the air. "A pair of nice guys rescued me, so I can offer to be useful."

"Dad's putting a zebra in the backyard. He said he'd need lotsa help with that."

"A zebra?" Vanessa gawked at Nathan. "You really weren't kidding when you said if you got one animal, you'd end up with a menagerie!"

Nathan chuckled. "Jeff's got the wrong idea. It's a gazebo, not a zebra."

"No zebra?" His son gave him a dismayed look.

"No zebra. No cats, rats, birds, or lizards, either." He glanced about the pet shop and hoped he hadn't missed out on anything readily visible, because sure as the sun rose, if he missed something, Jeff would take that as a promise that he could have one. In the off chance he had overlooked a creature, Nathan shook his finger at his son—as much to keep his attention focused on him as anything else. "Don't press your luck. We have an agreement, and you're behind on your end of the deal."

Jeff blurted out a laugh and slapped his hand over his mouth.

"Just what is so funny?" Vanessa folded her arms on the counter and leaned forward.

"Dad made a joke about our agreement about Lick." Jeff whispered very blatant clues at a decibel only a first grader would consider secretive. "Behind. End."

Vanessa made a goofy face. "Well, buster, you'd better clean up your act. I'm not coming over to help on a fort or a gazebo if I have to tiptoe through the tulips."

"We don't got no flowers."

"Have," Nathan corrected. "We don't have any flowers." *Evie loved flowers, and I still can't stand to tend them.* He shoved away the thought and cleared his throat. "I don't have time to mess with detailed gardening. If something needs more than routine watering and an occasional trimming, you can bet it's not in my yard."

"Juggling a thriving business, a kid, and an energetic puppy would be enough for anyone." Vanessa's lips pursed, and the impish gleam in her eyes warned Nathan he'd better prepare himself for whatever she'd say next.

"The best thing for you would be some free time. You know—recreation."

"Is that so?" he asked sardonically.

"Absolutely. Something fun. Let you get out a bit. Be with good people. Enjoy fresh air."

"Are you—" Jeff bobbed and weaved from one side of his father's long, lean legs to the other "—sending Dad to summer camp?"

"Nope." Nathan ruffled his son's hair. "I think Van's trying to rope me into playing baseball."

"Where's her rope?"

"With the zebra?" Vanessa ventured in a playful tone.

"Sport, I need a minute with Vanessa. Why don't you go see if you can spot Goldie in the fish tank?" He waited until Jeff was out of earshot, then braced both hands on the counter. It took everything in him to keep from thundering, but he refused to lose control. "Forget it. Just forget this plan of yours to lure me back into church. I know the whole deal—sucker someone into an activity they like, then chip away the defenses until they start attending services. Well, it's not going to work, Vanessa. Not on me."

"Okay. I promise I won't ever invite you to worship. It doesn't mean you can't just have a good time with great people."

"You just don't get it, so I'm going to be blunt. My wife died. She was a devout believer. We prayed for a miracle, but she died an inch at a time of kidney failure. A good Christian man would have accepted it, but I didn't. I still haven't. Call me jaded or bitter or a backslider—I know all of the churchy terms for it. There's one thing I refuse to be, and that's a hypocrite. I'm not about to wear a mask and pretend everything is hunky-dory."

"Who said you have to?"

He slammed his fist on the counter. "I went to church the Sunday after the funeral. I needed God. I needed comfort. Instead, I ended up having to put up with half of the congregation weeping all over me. How was I supposed to console them when all I could do was look at my son and know God had taken away his mother?"

"I'm sorry you hurt." She slid her hand over his fist.

"What? No shock that I'd dare to be mad at God?"

Vanessa simply squeezed his clenched fist. "There's nothing wrong with being angry. God is bigger than your rage, and He's patient."

Her response caught him off guard. Embarrassed by his outburst, Nathan mumbled, "I'm not about to darken the door of a church."

"There aren't any stained-glass windows or sermons on a ball diamond." She waggled her brows. "And I'll help with your gazebo."

"You drive a hard bargain. Do you drive nails half as well?"

"Just you wait and see."

Chapter 6

Vanessa sat on the edge of the deck they'd just made for the gazebo and winced as Nathan yanked a splinter from his hand. "Want some help with that?"

"Naw. It's no big deal. I get 'em all the time."

"When you said you were building a gazebo, I didn't imagine anything quite this grand."

The leather of his tool belt made a slight stretching sound, and some of the tools clinked together as he laid back and supported himself on his elbows. He gave her a taunting grin. "In over your head?"

"I'm holding my own." She gave him a saucy smile. "Except for when it comes to tools. Your cordless power stuff is really nifty."

"Occupational benefit."

"Oh, come on. Who are you kidding? Even if you weren't in the construction business, you'd still have the biggest and best power tools made because they're big boys' toys."

"I collect toys; you collect things with fur, fins, or feathers. From where I sit, it seems like you shouldn't be throwing rocks, since you're living in a glass house."

"From where you sit?" Her ponytail swished impudently as she gawked around at the gazebo. "I might have glass walls to my so-called house, but this little house of yours has none at all!"

"Just you wait and see." He stood and pulled her to her feet. "This baby's going to be done in no time at all."

She picked up a drill, slipped her forefinger through the trigger loop, and made it whine. "Thanks to these toys."

"And thanks to you. It's a lot easier getting things done with an extra pair of hands."

"I'm having fun." She turned to go back to work. "We ought to be able to get the main beams up and the benches made today."

"I'm amazed. I thought Amber would go nuts over the whine of the drill. She just curls up out of the way, and the noise doesn't even faze her."

"It's all part of training her to ignore things. I've taken her to construction sites, parades, and high school basketball and football games. She's learned that noise, vibration, and movement aren't as important as being a good girl." Vanessa stroked Amber approvingly. "It's all a part of learning good puppy manners, and you are a perfect lady, aren't you?"

"Incredible. Why doesn't she stretch out?"

"That's part of her training too. We teach the dogs to 'be small.' She's going to have to fit under seats on a bus, ride in a plane and train, and be in auditoriums. If she stretches out, someone will step on her, or she'll become an obstacle."

"How'd you learn all of this?"

"There's a manual, and I go to puppy-raiser meetings twice a month."

"Meetings? What do you do?"

"One meeting is usually a combination business and obedience-training meeting. The second one is normally an outing. We take the puppies somewhere so they can be exposed to a challenging environment or situation and learn how to respond appropriately. It's a great group of people and dogs."

She reached over for another length of wood he'd already cut to size. "If you have any wood left over, you could make a doghouse for Lick."

"Why bother? He's sleeping in Jeff's room."

"I know we're in California, but it does rain every once in a while."

Nathan waved his hand to indicate the gazebo. "And this isn't enough shelter?"

"That all depends."

"On what?

She gave him a look of owl-eyed innocence. "If you like eau de wet puppy."

"Okay. I'm convinced. A doghouse is my next project."

"Then we'd better get back to work and finish this up."

A few hours later, they took another breather.

"This yard is huge." Vanessa scanned. "I'll bet you have a cool lawn mower."

"It all depends on what you think is cool. I hired the kid next door to mow and edge. He wanted to earn money for football."

"He's probably rich enough to own the team by now. What is this—an acre?"

"Three-quarters of an acre. I tried to keep the gazebo to scale. It would have looked pretty ridiculous to have one of those little scaled-down jobs back here."

"Yeah, well, Jeff's fort is so big, I'm expecting the U.S. Navy to billet a few officers in it."

Nathan bent his head over his palm and plucked out another splinter as he mumbled, "Jeff wanted the extra level and the rope netting. It wasn't that much more work."

"Did you really camp out up there last Friday?"

"Yup. Lanterns, sleeping bags, and mosquitoes." He turned toward the house and yelled, "Jeff, where's that lemonade?"

The door opened. Jeff stuck his head out and shouted, "I can't reach the glasses."

"Aren't there clean ones in the dishwasher?"

"Huh-unh. We forgot to run it. I can tell 'cuz there's still pasgetti on the plates."

"I'll go help him." Vanessa sprang to her feet. Amber accompanied her across the lawn and into the house. The minute she got inside, Vanessa sucked in a deep breath. She'd never been inside Nathan's house.

Clearly, a busy man, a little boy, and an undisciplined puppy lived here. School papers cluttered the refrigerator door and the coffee table. Both the telephone and the stove bore spaghetti sauce splatters, and a small bulletin board listed two baby-sitters, several fast-food places, and a few scrawled memos. Two pairs of muddy shoes—one small, the other huge—sat on the hearth, and a track of muddy paw prints zigzagged down the hall.

"The glasses are up there." Jeff pointed to a cupboard on the right side of the sink.

Vanessa opened it and spied a set of earthenware dishes adorned with pinkish flowers around the edges. It seemed so absurdly feminine in a father-and-son home, but that fact tugged at her heart. Clearly, Nathan still held his wife's memory dear, and he clung to the little things that still kept her alive in his heart. She must've been someone very special.

Bypassing the glass tumblers in favor of three mismatched plastic cups, Vanessa said, "These look like good ones to take to the backyard."

"I'll pour the lemonade."

"Okay." She fought the urge to take over. Nathan encouraged Jeff to be independent, and it wouldn't hurt anything if they had to wipe up a spill. She took the time to scan the house a bit more.

A woman's touch was still very evident. Wallpaper of dainty sprays of antique roses covered the far side of the kitchen, echoed by linoleum flooring that held a pattern of tiles with little rose-colored flowers. A five-foot-long pine board hung from the ceiling. Several decorator-quality baskets dangled from pegs on it.

"Forgive the mess," a deep voice said from behind her.

Vanessa jumped at the sound. "It's a wonderful place."

"Consuelo will be back on Monday. She's spending a week visiting her sister. She manages to keep Jeff out of trouble when he gets home from school and keeps the place from being a total pit. Three days on our own, and we've just about demolished the downstairs. Jeff and I were going to pick up a bit before you got here, but—"

"We got busy watching cartoons," Jeff interrupted.

Vanessa watched red creep up Nathan's neck. "Don't be embarrassed. I did the same thing. I was supposed to be sorting through the pots and pans, but I ate my cereal in front of the TV and got stuck on good old *Rocky and Bullwinkle* reruns."

Nathan swiped two of the glasses from the counter and handed her one. "*Rocky and Bullwinkle*, huh?"

"My favorite."

"So even as a kid, you had a thing for animals."

"Guilty as charged." She took a sip. "Great lemonade, Jeff."

"Thanks. Can the dogs drink some, too?"

"No," Nathan and Vanessa said in unison.

"Why not?"

Nathan looked at Vanessa. "You're the expert."

"People food isn't always healthy for dogs. Every once in a while, if your dad lets you, you can give Lick some of your leftovers."

"Oh, great," Jeff sighed. "Dad always finishes everything. We don't got no leftovers."

"We don't have any leftovers," Nathan corrected.

"That's what I said. Poor Licorice is gonna starve!"

Vanessa walked out of the kitchen and into the backyard before she burst into laughter.

A short while later, Nathan pounded one last nail into a board and asked, "Why are you sorting pots and pans?"

"Valene bought a condo. We're trying to decide who owns what."

"You mean the Dynamic Duo is splitting up?"

"Hard to imagine, isn't it? Actually, I think it's a great move—pardon the pun. Val landed a job in the business office at the hospital. The condo is close, so she won't have to worry about a long commute."

"It's not all that far—about twenty minutes or so?"

"Close enough to still meet and go to church and do things together."

"Outgoing as you are, you'll stay busy." He stuffed the hammer into his tool belt without even looking. "Aren't you worried Val will feel a bit lost?"

"I think it'll be a good change for her—she'll need a little nudging, but she'll make friends. If anything, I'm going to be lost without her. She's so organized and capable."

"Capable? Look at you, Van. You own and run a store. You have an active social life. You're great at sports, volunteer in the community, and are better with a hammer and saw than half of the men I hire. Don't sell yourself short."

She looked into his coffee-brown eyes and saw the sincerity there. His praise meant more to her than it probably ought to. Uncomfortable with the sudden closeness she felt, she wiped her palms on the sides of her jeans. "If I do something stupid like forgetting to pay the electricity bill so I lose my power, I'm going to sneak over and sleep in Jeff's fort."

Concern creased Nathan's forehead. "You're used to splitting rent. Are you going to be in trouble?"

"No, Val wouldn't ever leave me in the lurch. The shop's doing well. I can afford to live alone. Amber's good company, too, aren't you, girl?"

Amber wagged her tail.

Nathan looked across the yard at Jeff and Lick as they tumbled in the grass. "Any chance you'll train him to sit quietly?"

"Are you asking about Jeff or Licorice?"

"Hey! For that, I'm not going to volunteer to help Val move."

Chapter 7

J ust how much stuff have the two of you squirreled away in this place?" Nathan took in the pile of boxes and blinked in disbelief.

"This place has a lot of storage space," Valene murmured as she glanced about the apartment.

"She's only taking her stuff." Vanessa capped the black marker with a flourish after she finished writing "Kitchen—dishes. Breakable!" on a box.

"Not really. Vanessa's giving me a bunch of things that probably are rightfully hers."

"It's really an excuse for me to go buy new dishes. I want to get something different."

The shuffle of booted feet at the doorway made them all turn. "Kip! You came." Vanessa waved him in. "I nearly fought Val to the death so I could keep the coffeemaker. There's a fresh pot in the kitchen, if either of you men need to get juiced up with caffeine before we start."

"What? No doughnuts?" Kip crossed the room and slapped Nathan on the shoulder in greeting. "These two women are going to work us half to death, then let starvation complete the job."

"I suppose this is my cue to say something like, 'I made Grandma's cinnamon coffee cake,' but I probably ought to confess that Valene is taking the couch."

Nathan stared at the big, pale blue, fluffy-cushioned couch and rubbed his forehead. "How about if I go for the coffee, cake, and no couch?"

Kip flopped down on the couch. "You've obviously never tasted Vanessa's cooking! Me? I'll take the coffee and move the couch. I've tasted something she made once. Believe me, once was more than enough. It wasn't fit for human consumption."

"Hey!" Vanessa tossed the marker at him and headed into the kitchen. "Just because you don't know dog food when you see it. . ."

"Dog food?" Nathan looked from Kip to Valene for an explanation.

A shy smile lit Valene's face. "Van made special biscuits for Mrs. Culpepper's poodle. She's got heart problems and needs low sodium treats."

"It was Valentine's Day," Kip groused. "How was I supposed to know they weren't heart-shaped cookies? She had them on a plate!"

Van came back into the room. She balanced four mismatched holiday paper plates that held plastic forks and big, fragrant chunks of pastry.

Nathan happily swiped one, handed it to Valene, and took one for himself as Kip scrambled off the couch and dove for another. "Wow. I thought you were kidding when you said something about your granny's recipe."

"It's not cinnamon; it's her lemon cream cheese loaf," Vanessa said.

Nathan took a bite. It melted in his mouth. He quickly licked a pastry crumb off his lip. "For this, I'll even help move the couch."

"Careful." Kip gave a wary look around at the boxes. "They're bribing us. There's got to be a catch somewhere." His eyes narrowed. "Val, is your new condo an upstairs one?"

"Not a chance. By the time I get home from a four-mile run, I don't want to have to jog up the stairs."

Kip chuckled. "And I thought you were going to tell us Vanessa is afraid of heights."

Nathan gulped down the last bite of pastry and shook his head. "Vanessa is fearless."

She bumped into a stack of boxes and quoted, "I can do all things through Him who strengthens me."

"Then why did you want us to come help you move all of this junk?"

✝

The move only took the morning hours. Valene had everything organized and ready to go, and the men managed to wedge everything into the truck she'd rented. After a single trip, they'd hauled everything out and taken it into Val's new place. The twins' parents were out of town, but they called from their hotel and arranged for a local deli to furnish lunch. A four-foot submarine sandwich with all of the trimmings was delivered just as Nathan wheeled in a dolly with the last stack of boxes on it.

As they ate, Kip tossed a can of soda to Nathan and said, "We still have a spot for you on the team."

"I'm not going to church."

Vanessa startled at the vehemence of his tone.

Kip shrugged. "I didn't invite you to church. 'Course, you're welcome if you wanna come, but I'm talking about home plate, not the offering plate."

Aware he'd startled Vanessa and Valene, Nathan felt a niggling of guilt. He pushed it aside. There was nothing wrong with a man standing firm on an issue. Then again, there was nothing wrong with a guy playing ball, either. "Okay, here's the deal: I'll play. But don't expect me to warm a pew."

"We're in business."

"Business!" Vanessa glanced at her watch. "I have to mind the shop for a couple of hours. Jamie could only stay 'til two today. I'll be back at about six to help you unpack the boxes, Val." She hugged her sister, dashed for the door, and sang over her shoulder, "Thanks for lugging all of my sissy's stuff, guys!"

Vanessa sailed back through her sister's door at a few minutes after six.

"Next time I get a great idea and decide to move," Valene sighed as she plopped down on the couch, "shoot me."

Clinging to a large roasting pan with oven mitts, Vanessa stepped around a stack of towels and looked around the living room. "You've unpacked almost half of the boxes! We'll finish up later. For now. . ."

Valene gave her a weary smile. "Supper. Whatever it is, I'll eat it."

"Here you are." Vanessa set the roasting pan on the bare coffee table.

"Put the mitts under that! I don't want the wood ruined!"

Vanessa ignored her twin and lifted the lid with a flourish. "Ta da!"

"What in the world?" Val leaned forward and stared at the pan. Nestled inside was a cell phone with a colorful rectangle of paper taped to the bottom. She lifted the phone, and Vanessa started to laugh as Valene tore off the coupon and read aloud, "Free pizza?"

"But of course. Home delivery. And observe, Mam'selle. . ." She pulled out a red-and-white-checkered plastic tablecloth, spread it on the coffee table, and topped it with matching paper plates and napkins she'd stuffed into the roasting pan. "All you have to do is call. I already arranged for them to bring a large pizza with the works, soda, and salad. It'll take them twenty minutes to have it all here."

"What? No dessert?"

Vanessa gave her a wounded look. "Have you ever known me to skimp on the essentials?" She pulled a small gold box of chocolate truffles from the roasting pan and set it in the center of the table with all due consideration.

"Perfect. How about if we eat those while we wait for the pizza?"

"Be still, my beating heart!" Vanessa patted her chest theatrically. "Is that my always-sensible twin sister suggesting something that decadent?"

"I am being sensible. If I turn my back, you'll eat the hazelnut." She leaned forward, lifted the foil box's lid, and plucked out her favorite. After she called for the pizza, she crossed one leg beneath her on the sofa and made direct eye contact. "I want to talk to you for a minute about being sensible."

"Uh-oh. You just pasted on your serious look."

"I am serious. Van, Nathan is a troubled man. He's really resistant to anything having to do with God."

"I know." She stared at her sister and sighed. "What kind of Christian would I be to reject him instead of coming alongside him? He's mad at God. Really mad. I've been there too. Remember when Grandma died? I hurt so badly, I didn't pray all summer."

"Yeah, but from what Kip said, Nathan's been bitter for years now."

"Nathan hasn't made any secret of it. God is patient, Val. I figure we can either push Nathan away, or we can draw him back to the Lord. It's not something that will be fixed overnight. Baby steps—it's a matter of baby steps. You heard him—he'll join the team."

"Don't fall for him, Van. It'll break your heart."

Chapter 8

Nathan peeked in on Jeff. His son was sprawled across the bed sideways, the pillow lay on the floor, and the puppy was curled up at the head of the bed where the pillow belonged. Letting out a sigh, Nathan crossed the hardwood floor. His footsteps made a solid sound, but he doubted a full-volume Sousa march would rouse Jeff. Licorice's head lifted, and his tail made a rapid *whump, whump, whump* against the oak headboard.

"You don't belong up here." Nathan planned to scoop the puppy off the bed, place him on the floor, and have him trot out to the back door for one last pit stop. Once he reached for the dog, his plans altered.

Licorice's tongue darted out and lapped at Nathan's wrist. The speed of his tail wagging a drumbeat against the headboard doubled. Nathan picked him up, cradled him in his arms, and left the room. As he walked down the hall and reached the squeaky third step on the stairs, the puppy squirmed and snuffled until his little wet nose nudged at the base of Nathan's throat.

Nathan stopped on the stairs and looked down. "I'm Granite Cliffs' biggest pushover, you know. You're the living proof of that. If you weren't so cute, it would be downright embarrassing that I put up with you."

The small metal tags on Lick's collar jingled.

"Yeah. I know." Nathan carried him down the rest of the stairs, through the living room, and out the kitchen door. He put down the pooch and sat out in the gazebo. It was too early to turn in, and he had too many thoughts running though his mind to bother trying to follow the plot of any television show.

He took up a piece of sandpaper and started to rub out a small ding on the right edge of the western bench in the gazebo. After a few passes, his action halted. He didn't want to make that nick disappear.

Vanessa had been hammering a trellis on the side of the gazebo, and her hammer slipped. She'd been upset about the blemish in the bench, but it was such a minor imperfection, Nathan knew he could sand it smooth. For now, he'd still leave that nick there—it was like a reminder of the golden afternoon when they'd constructed this.

Vanessa. He'd felt a spurt of emotion when Kip showed up at her apartment this morning to help with the move. Were they dating? The thought turned his stomach. He had no right to be jealous or possessive. None whatsoever. He and

Vanessa were. . . *What are we?*

He couldn't exactly answer that nagging question. When Kip said he hadn't had any of Vanessa's cooking other than the dog biscuits, that had made Nathan breathe a little easier. As they'd all worked together to carry things out to the moving truck and haul them into Valene's new place, Nathan noticed Kip kept mixing up the sisters.

They both wore blue jeans and old, faded red Whiskers, Wings, and Wags T-shirts. Other than that, Kip must have been hit in the head with one too many wild pitches if he thought Van and Val were interchangeable. Val was a pretty young woman; Van was ravishingly beautiful. She just plain sparkled. Her moves carried an exuberance and grace that captivated Nathan.

They didn't even smell alike. Val wore something from one of those fancy bottles she'd carried into her new place in a basket; Vanessa would have given Carmen Miranda stiff competition in the fruit bowl category. Her hair smelled of strawberry shampoo, she chewed watermelon bubble gum, and when she sat beside him in the truck, she'd slicked peach gloss on her lips.

If all else failed, Kip could have just glanced down and seen that Amber shadowed Vanessa everywhere she went. *Well, maybe that isn't entirely true,* Nathan admitted to himself. *Amber stays with Valene when Vanessa is on the ball diamond.*

Licorice woofed softly. He'd grown appreciably in the past month. He'd barely been able to make it up a step that first day. Now, he undulated like a playful dolphin as he bounded up the four risers into the gazebo. Nathan groaned.

"Lick, is that mud on your nose and paws?"

Licorice skidded to a halt, leaving telltale streaks in his wake.

"What did you dig up this time?"

The puppy sank down, buried his muzzle in his paws, and made a pitiful, guilty whimper.

"Looks like I'm going to have to consult with Vanessa about what to do with a naughty little digger." Nathan leaned down and petted Lick's sleek black coat. In truth, he wasn't overly upset. It provided another good excuse to be with Vanessa again.

✝

"Do you have time for a puppy consultation?"

Vanessa clamped the receiver between her ear and her shoulder as she considered Nathan's question. She had her hands full, but she didn't want to miss what he had to say. "Uh-oh. What's Lick up to now?"

"Outsmarting me."

She didn't try to muffle her laughter. "Again?"

Silence on his end of the line might have meant he was offended, but when he spoke, his voice sounded more like he was chuckling than chiding. "You could be a little more sympathetic."

"Actually, I'm thinking how fortunate you are. Obviously Lick is a highly intelligent dog, so once he's trained, he's going to be a dreamboat."

"Right about now, I'd settle for a leaky canoe."

"Well, he's a puppy, so I can guarantee he's still leaky."

"You did warn me that you'd been class clown," Nathan muttered wryly.

"Let me put Nero down so I can hold the phone." She set aside the receiver, placed the black Lab puppy she'd just groomed into an enclosure, and came back. "Thanks for waiting."

"Let me get this straight," Nathan said with a tinge of amusement. "You're fiddling with Nero while my Rome is burning."

"That's about the size of it. He and Lick are from the same litter. The family who took him didn't check with their landlord, and they've been told they'll be evicted if they keep him."

"And I thought I had problems."

"It's really no problem at all. Valene is a little lonely. She's used to me and a dog, so I've decided to give Nero to her."

"She doesn't have a yard."

"No, she doesn't. For just about anyone else, I'd encourage them to have a smaller dog if it's going to be a house pet. Val loves to walk and jog. If anything, Nero will get plenty of exercise and provide an extra measure of safety for Val. Anyway, enough about Nero and Val. What do you need?"

"Help. I'm desperate. I tell you what: Jeff and I will bring Lick to baseball practice tonight. We'll snag some Picnicin' Chicken on the way. If we get to your shop right as it closes, we can eat in the park, and you can give me some pointers on what to do with the puppy."

"Sounds great. Feed Lick before you come—otherwise, he's going to want people food."

"Okay. Gotcha. Good tactic. See you later."

☩

Van and Amber were standing outside the pet shop when Nathan drove up. He drew alongside the curb and parked.

"There they are!" Jeff scrambled out of his seat belt and twisted to unlatch Lick from his puppy seat belt. The windows were rolled down, and he shouted, "We brought chicken and hot cherry flipovers for dessert!"

"Turnovers, sport." Nathan identified with Jeff's eager scramble to get out of the car. Clearly, if he and Vanessa did decide to pursue a relationship, he wouldn't have to worry whether Jeff liked her. Nathan got out of the car, grabbed the rustling plastic bag holding their supper, and snatched his mitt from the dashboard.

"All set?" Vanessa stooped and paid generous attention to Lick.

"You betcha." Jeff gawked around. "Dad said you gots another dog just like mine. Where is he?"

"I do have another puppy that's Licorice's brother. I left him in the shop, and I want to keep him a big surprise. I'm giving him to Valene after the game tonight. Can you keep it a secret?"

"Yep!" Jeff hopped in place.

Nathan tilted his head and slanted his eyes toward the clouds as he shrugged, hoping Vanessa would understand his meaning. Six-year-old boys weren't exactly reliable when it came to keeping confidences.

Vanessa's eyes twinkled with understanding. She rose and lifted an electric blue athletic bag.

"I'll take that." Nathan reached for it.

"Then put your glove inside. No use carrying a bunch of loose gear." She unzipped it and opened the flaps.

Nathan made a show of leaning forward and peering inside the bag. "You don't have a python in there that'll eat my all-time favorite mitt, do you?"

She let out a theatrical sigh. "I knew I forgot something!"

"Good thing. You'd be in big trouble if anything happened to my glove. I worked at a Christmas-tree lot my sophomore year of high school so I could earn enough money for it."

"Ah, yes." She gave him a pert smile. "The old sweeter-'cuz-I-earned-it item. Val and I shared our biggie, but I suppose that wouldn't come as any surprise."

"As different as you are from one another, it is. So tell me—what did the two of you want so badly?"

"A sound system for our bedroom. When we moved to our apartment, it was the only thing in the living room."

He dropped his mitt inside. As she zipped up the bag, he mused, "It didn't occur to me until now, but you don't have any snakes in the shop."

"Snakes are icky," Jeff declared.

"Val and my mom agree with you. The day I signed the papers for this shop, they made a point of telling me not to count on their help if I kept a single snake on the premises."

As he lifted the bag of gear, Nathan asked, "It's not much of a sacrifice, is it? You already offer a wide array of animals."

"I couldn't possibly handle snakes. They don't have wings or whiskers, and they don't wag. Are we ready to go?"

"Ready!" Jeff and Nathan declared in unison.

Jeff trotted ahead with Lick sort of trying to stay at heel. The two of them tangled about every third step, but that rated as a definite improvement.

Nathan stood to Van's right so Amber could walk at heel. With the supper bag in one hand and the athletic bag over the opposite shoulder, he didn't have a free hand. For a fleeting moment, he considered switching the picnic to his right hand so his left hand would be free to hold hers, but he dismissed that concept as soon as it flashed though his mind. He wasn't ready to jump into anything deep yet, and she seemed comfortable with matters as they stood. Most of him accepted that fact, but he still felt a twinge. He hadn't realized how lonely he'd become until he'd met Vanessa.

Laughter bubbled out of her as she watched Jeff and Lick. That sound acted like a breeze, scattering his gloomy clouds of thoughts. Nathan started to do something he hadn't done in years.

Chapter 9

As they strolled down the street, Nathan started to whistle. It felt right, just puckering up and letting loose a stream of notes. It wasn't until they were waiting at the light that he realized what tune he'd chosen.

Vanessa said the title just as his own awareness dawned. " 'How Much Is That Doggy in the Window?' "

He gave her a sheepish look. "I guess I'd better be careful not to give away the secret, either."

Jeff took his hand before they crossed the street. "I 'membered to look both ways."

"Good going."

"Dad, did you tell on Lick?"

He squeezed Jeff's hand. "Vanessa needs to know what Licorice is doing so she can help us make him a better puppy. She's not going to stop liking him just because he did something bad."

"Like the way you still love me, even when I done wrong?"

"Do wrong. And yes, just like I will always love you, no matter what you do. Still, that's not an excuse for you to do bad things. When you love someone, you try your hardest to do things that please them."

"Then everybody is happy. Right, Dad?"

"Right."

They reached the other side of the street, and Jeff shook free of his grasp. "We'll run over to the big tree. Can we sit under the tree for our picnic?"

Nathan shot Vanessa a quick look. "Wouldn't you rather sit at one of the picnic tables?"

"How about if we sit at a table under a tree? I don't mind sitting on the ground, but Lick is going to help himself to the food if it's down at his level. It's not fair to tempt him. He's too young to know better."

After they were seated and had started eating, Vanessa peeked under the table and asked Licorice, "So are they going to tell me what you did this time?"

"He dug a hole—a great big hole." Jeff drew a sizable circle in the air with his drumstick.

"Hmm."

"I read a few suggestions online," Nathan confessed. "I tried two of them. Both were abysmal failures."

"What did you do?"

"I blew up a balloon, put it in the hole, and covered it with dirt. Supposedly the loud pop was supposed to be a deterrent. The only thing it did was send him running to another spot, where he promptly started digging a new hole."

"Persistent little monster, isn't he?"

Nathan thought her voice held a blend of sympathy for him and a tad of amusement. He broke eye contact and scooped in a few hefty bites of coleslaw.

"So what else have you tried?"

"A squirt gun!" Jeff guffawed.

Nathan gave Vanessa his if-you-can't-beat-'em-join-'em grin. "We discovered Lick loves water. Silly animal came charging toward me and tried to drink from the Super Squirtmaster."

"So I gotta Squirtmaster to play with now." Jeff's delight couldn't be more clear.

"So much for my foray into effective canine discipline."

"Labs are water dogs." Vanessa took a quick sip of soda and set the can back onto the sun-bleached wooden tabletop. "The nice thing is, he'll love going to the beach with you."

"If he digs there," Nathan grumbled, "maybe he'll fall all the way through to China."

"Dad! You wouldn't let that happen, would you?"

"No, he was just teasing, Jeff. There are some things you can do to stop the digging. If you play with him more and tire him out, he won't have the energy to dig. There are a few products out on the market that keep a dog from digging, and you can spray them on the ground in key places where the digging will destroy special plants."

"Okay. I know the shop is already closed, but can I go ahead and pick up some of that tonight?"

"Sure." She slanted him a questioning look. "Have you been gardening?"

"Yeah. How'd you guess?"

"He planted flowers." Jeff's little body swayed back and forth in cadence with how he swung his legs. "But Lick dug most all of 'em up."

Vanessa's brows arched in surprise. "I thought you said you weren't much on flowers."

"A certain person who helped me build the gazebo pointed out the backyard would look a lot better if I planted some."

Her brows wiggled as she did a truly pathetic Groucho Marx imitation. "I'll bet that person was right."

"Who knows? The little black beast made mulch of them."

Vanessa rested her forearms on the picnic table and leaned forward. Her voice softened. "Nathan, Lick saw you digging in the dirt. He thought it was okay. Until he gets older, you'd do well not to set an example you don't want him to follow."

"Oh, brother! Do I feel stupid!"

"Now I'll make you feel downright smart: Go get some chicken wire. Put about an inch of dirt over it, and just comb flower seeds into the soil. He won't be able to dig, and you'll only spend a fraction of what you would for pony packs of flowers."

"For that, you deserve a cherry turnover."

✞

That Friday, after the game, Vanessa gathered her gear and collected Amber from Val. "Wanna go out for some ice cream?"

"Double fudge?"

"Double dips," Vanessa promised.

Deep laughter from behind made them turn around. Nathan rested his hands on his hips. "Double scoops of double fudge for twins. Don't tell me you don't see the humor in that."

"Dad, can we get ice cream, too?"

Vanessa saw the question in Nathan's eyes. "Sure, you guys can come along. We'll sit outside the shop so Nero and Lick can come along."

Jeff knelt between the two Lab puppies. Both turned as if on cue and licked him. "What about Amber? Won't she come?"

"Amber is allowed to go into most places like church and restaurants and stores because she's a service animal."

"Sis?"

Vanessa turned to Val. "Huh?"

"I hope you don't mind, but I changed his name. Nero was a madman, and I wanted something a little more. . .noble."

"I don't care one bit. What did you decide on?"

"Hero."

"Oh, that was clever. I'll bet he responded to it right away."

Valene beamed. "He did. He's so bright. I want him to start in with the next session of puppy obedience. When does it start?"

"Next Saturday."

Nathan knelt and scratched both Lick and Hero behind the ears. "Did you boys hear that? You're going to be classmates."

"Can they have ice cream, too, to cel'brate? You taked me out for ice cream when I started school."

"I don't know." Nathan looked up at Vanessa. "You didn't let us feed the dogs at our picnic."

"Amber eats twice a day. I give her treats, but not while I'm eating or socializing, because I don't want her to turn into a beggar."

Val hitched the strap of her purse higher on her shoulder. "We probably ought to use the same system we did back when you had Thane."

Vanessa nodded and explained to Nathan and Jeff, "I had my first guide puppy in my senior year of high school. We still had our family dog, a poodle named Fluffy. Fluffy wanted treats like she used to get—she was pretty spoiled. We taught the dogs that Fluffy got a treat when Thane got to go on an outing."

"Then I guess going on the trip is enough. Lick won't get a lick of ice cream."

Jeff giggled. "That was funny, Dad."

"Ice cream?" Kip sauntered up. "Are you going out for ice cream? I'm inviting myself along."

As they sat on the little wrought-iron patio set outside of the ice cream parlor, she watched Nathan wipe a dab of Very Berry from Jeff's face. He looked up at Vanessa just as she realized a little chocolate had dripped on her chin. He beat Kip to the stack of napkins in the center of the table and handed one to her. "So you got your first dog in high school. Why?"

"I love animals, and it seemed like a neat thing to do. Since we'd be in college in a year, it wasn't right for me to get a dog of my own and leave it behind with my folks."

"That makes sense, but then I'm running into a logic problem. You told me this is your fourth guide puppy, so you had to have a dog or two while you were in college."

"I listed puppy training on my college application under community service. The college admissions officer noticed it and mentioned that he'd give me clearance to have a puppy in classes as long as we didn't have any major accidents or disruptions."

"Did you?"

"Mom does a lot of volunteer work, and Dad was able to take the dogs to work with him at the phone company some days. Between Val and me juggling class schedules and our folks filling in, we breezed through college with the pups. Our first dog, Thane, was the biggest challenge. He was a riot."

Val choked back a giggle. "He about caused a riot on more than one occasion. The poor thing pitched a full-scale fit the first time he spied you in your shark suit. She came into the auditorium for a school assembly, and I think Thane thought the shark had eaten her."

"If Val hadn't let go of the leash, it wouldn't have been such a disaster. It took all but one member of the football team to catch Thane." Vanessa ignored her sister's don't-you-dare look and added, "The quarterback was a little preoccupied, flirting with my sister."

"Which is why she'd let go of the leash?" Nathan ventured as he gave Val a knowing grin. "Can't fault a man for having good taste."

"Sure can't," Kip agreed in a hearty tone.

"Thanks, guys—but you'll notice, my sister had the full attention of the rest of the team."

"Yeah," Vanessa snorted. "And who wouldn't, dressed up like a huge stuffed shark with a growling puppy clamped onto the fin?"

"What did you do?" Jeff wondered as several rivulets of ice cream ran down the cone, onto his hand.

"Yeah, Van," Kip nudged her arm. "What did you do?"

"A very funny dance," Val answered. "You started this, Van, so I'm telling the rest of the story. The dog wouldn't let go of the shark, and the shark kept running in a circle and wouldn't let go of the dog. There's a great picture of it in our yearbook as one of the football players took a dive toward them. The caption is BAIT AND TACKLE."

"Oh, well," Vanessa laughed. "What do I say? She's brainy, and I'm zany. I think I keep her guardian angel and mine busy enough for both of us."

"My mom is with the angels." Jeff's comment immediately changed the focus of the conversation.

"Then she's in a very happy place."

Vanessa heard her sister's sweet words as she watched Nathan wrap his arm around Jeff's shoulders. "That's right, son." His action bespoke support and love, yet he didn't let anyone give him that same comfort.

If he were a puppy or a kitten, she would have known a score of ways to coax him to draw close and let her give comfort. Originally he'd seemed bitter; now he had become matter-of-fact, like someone who woodenly recited a rote prayer but the meaning behind the words didn't register. Nathan built walls and constructed defenses she couldn't begin to get beyond. Until he was ready, no one would be able to reach him. All she could do was pray the Lord would work in his heart. . . and trust that when the time was right, God would have someone there to show His comfort and consolation to Nathan.

Chapter 10

Nathan sat in the shady courtyard with five other puppy owners. Had anyone asked, he would have said Vanessa looked like a luscious slice of lemon meringue pie, dressed in her crisp yellow walking shorts and a gauzy white blouse. He watched Vanessa demonstrate the simple commands she'd be working on with the "puppy kindergarten" members. Amber obediently followed each order.

"Just how long before Marzipan does all of those tricks?" one woman asked.

The burly man next to Nathan tried to untangle his beagle's leash from around his own legs and muttered, "Right about now, I'd settle for this mutt learning to sit. I'm going to fall and break my neck if Soupy keeps running circles around me."

After the session was over, folks wandered into Whiskers, Wings, and Wags to make some purchases. Jamie, the clerk who had been minding the store, slipped out for her lunch break. Nathan saw several other customers browsing, too.

"What if I hang out with Hero and Licorice for awhile in one of the enclosures so Val can help you out?"

One desperate glance at the line at the register, and Van gave him a grateful smile. "Bless you!"

Nathan watched the puppies frolic and listened to Vanessa's cheerful voice as she helped her customers. Her zest for life appealed to him. She was every bit as sunny and bouncy as her hair.

For the past five years, he'd had a deep shadow of grief over his life. Evie begged him not to run from life, to feel free to fall in love again. "God has someone special in store for you and Jeff. I have an assurance about that."

He'd shaken his head. He didn't want any other woman. Since Evie died, not a day went by that he hadn't looked around the home they'd lovingly restored and missed her. . .until he met Vanessa. Oh, there had been plenty of beautiful women who made it abundantly clear they'd be happy to be the new Mrs. Adams. Not one of them deserved a second look or thought.

How could it be? In one short month, Vanessa crashed right through all of his defenses. One month? One day. That very first day he'd been here, he'd changed. Nathan could hardly imagine it, but now he was sitting on the floor, two little black Labs playing with his shoelaces, and feeling perfectly content to hear Vanessa talk to old Mrs. Rosetti about the lamb-and-rice dog biscuits.

A father couldn't exactly dive into dating and courtship. Nathan resolved to take things slowly. He had Jeff to think of. Then again, he needed to kick things up a few notches. The thought that Vanessa and Kip might be an item had had him in knots. Now that he knew this wasn't the case, he wanted to be smart enough to start reeling her in. He wasn't about to sit back and let another man steal his sunshine.

"Who are your pals?"

Nathan didn't have to look up to identify the speaker. "Val, if you can't recognize your own four-legged kid, your sister's going to disown you."

She laughed. "It wouldn't be the first time she's been tempted."

He clipped a leash back onto Hero's collar, lifted him over the hip-high wall, and placed him in Val's arms. "Jeff's hoping you'll bring Hero to the park next Thursday for our baseball practice. He thinks the brothers need to play together."

"Smart kid you have there." Vanessa refilled the treat jar by the enclosure. "Puppies need to socialize so they learn to get along well."

Val agreed to the plan and left, but Nathan found he wasn't eager to go. He sauntered to the front of the shop and watched as Vanessa deftly straightened up a display of squeaky toys. He liked that about her—she managed to keep things tidy without making a big fuss or to-do about it.

"Do you think I'll ever manage to train Lick to be as obedient as Amber is?"

"I think you have an excellent start." She gave him a hundred-watt smile. "You have to remember I've worked with Amber for ten months. She was only eight weeks old when I got her, so we've had plenty of time to develop rapport. Several months from now, you and Lick will be a great team."

"Yeah, but probably not like you and Amber. You're with her twenty-four/seven."

"That bonding and intense teamwork do pay off. I won't pretend otherwise, but the world is full of well-behaved dogs that haven't been with their owners any more than you're with Lick."

"I hope you're right. I watched Val, and she seems to have Hero well in control—much better than I do Lick, and I've had him longer."

Vanessa's eyes twinkled. "She was moaning about how much better you are with Lick."

"No kidding?"

"It's the absolute truth. Everyone wants a cute little fluff ball, but they forget that the little guys have to learn the rules of the home, just like a child would. The first month with a puppy is always challenging. As of this week, you've passed that mark. You've had him for five weeks. Things ought to start improving a lot."

Her words carried the assurance he sought, but he wanted to keep visiting. Nathan shifted his weight and wondered, "Are you as hungry as I am?"

"I'm starving. Why?"

"Two reasons. First, because I thought we could go snag a burger. The second is, I think it's going to be a persistent issue after these Saturday classes."

"Why would that be?"

"Because every last dog in the class is named after food!"

Vanessa tickled a kitten through a cage and mused aloud, "Oh? I didn't even notice. There was Marzipan. And Pepper."

"I've got Licorice, and that guy next to me had Soupy. The English pug is Cheerio."

"But Val's dog is Hero. It doesn't—"

"Hero sandwich," Nathan reminded her.

Vanessa's laughter pealed through the air. "Know what? I limit the class to six. I had another request that I slotted for the next series: 'Brownie.'"

"So what do you say? Jamie ought to be coming back from her lunch break soon. She can hold down the fort while we fill up after our brainwashing ordeal."

"What about Lick?"

Oops. Blew it on that account. Nathan tapped the toe of his athletic shoe on the linoleum floor, then grinned. "How about if he takes a nap in the grooming room?"

"Poor baby. Is he tuckered out after his first day of puppy kindergarten?"

"Yes, but his daddy is trying to get on the teacher's good side by offering to take her out for lunch."

"I always thought you were supposed to take the teacher an apple."

"Oh, that's for teachers who have children for their pupils. Dogs are a different story entirely."

"Do tell." She shot him an entertained look.

"Kids take apples to the teacher; puppy owners take the teacher to apple pie."

"I thought I liked my job. I was wrong—I love it!"

Ah, Vanessa, he thought, *if only a slice of apple pie could change how I felt about my life and job. There was a time when I had that same enthusiasm you have, but it's been gone for years now.*

✝

Vanessa fumbled for the telephone. It shrilled again, and she groaned as her fingers curled around the receiver and lifted it. "Hullo?"

"Vanessa?"

"Nathan?" She squinted at the neon orange numbers on her alarm clock—*4:17? This has to be a nightmare. It's not really happening.*

"Listen, I'm sorry to bother you—"

She shook herself. "Is it Jeff? Is something wrong?" In an instant, she was blazingly awake.

"No, but yes. Here's the deal: I just got an emergency call. The night watchman from the apartment complex I've started over on Beach and Tenth says it looks like the second story is buckling."

"Oh, no!"

"Jeff's class is going—"

"Whale watching today," she remembered aloud. Jeff had chattered about the trip every chance he got. He'd been looking forward to it for three weeks. "As I recall, you were supposed to go along."

"I'd ask Consuelo to go, but she gets seasick. I know Mondays are your day off, and I hate to ask. . ."

"Oh, I love whale watching! I'd be happy to go."

"Even with a class of six-year-olds?"

"The more, the merrier. I need to take Amber out on a boat, anyway."

"You're a lifesaver. I'll bundle up Jeff and be there in about twenty minutes."

"Don't bother. I'll come there."

Vanessa hung up the phone, hopped off the mattress, and flung the covers up in a hasty pretense of making the bed. Knowing the sea breeze would be stiff, she wore a T-shirt beneath a fleecy sweatshirt. Jeans, thick socks, and a battered pair of tennis shoes finished the outfit, then she dashed into the bathroom to grab her toothbrush.

Vanessa stopped dead in her tracks and burst out laughing. She'd fallen asleep, reading in bed, so she hadn't taken off what little makeup she normally wore. Mascara formed smoky rings around her eyes, a crease from her pillowcase looked like an earthquake fault line down her left cheek, and static electricity made every last strand of hair stick straight out in a bizarre impression of an atomic dandelion.

"Maybe I am having a nightmare, after all." She quickly scrubbed away the raccoon rings with a damp washcloth and brushed her teeth. Practically snatching herself bald due to the hairbrush getting caught in numerous tangles, Vanessa grumbled, "I'm going to have to talk to that man. He'll just have to understand he needs to arrange to have emergencies at a decent hour."

Amber woofed from beside her.

"Hey, don't stand up for the man. We girls are supposed to stick together." Vanessa grabbed a handful of essentials, zipped back into her bedroom, and recalled lending Val her big leather purse. Without it, she knew she had to make do.

Fifteen minutes later, she stood on the doorstep to Nathan's old saltbox in the predawn chill. She shivered and tapped quietly on the door. It opened almost instantly.

"Van, I can't thank you enough. I—what in the world?" He stared at the bulging pillowcase in her hands and gave her a baffled look.

Vanessa cruised past him and refused to look him in the eye. "I'm not trick-or-treating. If you dare say anything, you're dead meat. I already told you I'm not a morning person."

"I didn't say a word."

She tried to act calm, cool, and collected as she pulled her windbreaker from the pillowcase. She should have put it on for the drive over, but she hadn't been functioning well enough to reason out that minor detail. Next, she withdrew Amber's leash and bright green jacket. A digital camera, a hairbrush, a tube of lip balm, a scrunchy for her hair, a visor, and a pair of sunglasses tumbled onto the coffee table as she upended the pillowcase.

Pretending to ignore Nathan's chuckle, she tossed the pillow onto the end of the couch, punched it a few times, toed out of her shoes, and flopped down. As she closed her eyes, she yawned.

Amber's paws pattered on the hardwood floor as she turned around in her customary triple circles before she plopped down directly next to the sofa. In contrast, Nathan's work boots sounded like a whole platoon of infantrymen as he approached. He detoured somewhere—but she refused to peek. All she wanted were twenty more winks. . .no, make that forty. A door latch popped open, then shut, and the infantry marched closer. "Here," Nathan growled softly. He covered Vanessa with a big, heavy blanket.

She didn't know where he'd gotten it from, and she didn't really care. As she snuggled a bit deeper into the cushions and blanket, she mumbled, "Better dig up an alarm clock for me."

"You won't need one. Jeff gets up at six-thirty on the dot."

"I'm not going to open my eyes, because if you're smiling at that revolting news, I'll have to crawl off the couch and leave."

"Thanks again, Van."

"G'night. G'bye."

The lock on the door clicked, and she dropped into a deep sleep filled with wild, disjointed dreams centering on talking puppies.

"I can't find my dad. Can you help me?"

"He's in the yard," she told the terrier.

"Thanks." The little pup trotted away. A door banged, and cold air washed over her as the little dog hollered, "Dad. Daaad! Where are you?"

Vanessa bolted from the couch. "Jeff!"

Chapter 11

Vanessa stumbled over Amber and skidded through the kitchen. The clock on the stove read 6:33. She sped through the doorway in her stocking feet and ran out onto the wet lawn. "Jeff!"

Where was he? She nearly got whiplash, scanning the property. Red-and-blue plaid pajamas made him easy to spot once she turned toward the far end of the backyard. Both of his feet—bare feet—were on the rope ladder to his fort.

"I can't find Dad. I thought I'd climb up here. I can see better if—"

"Honey, your dad's not out here. He had a problem at work."

"But you told me he was in the yard." Jeff hung there and gave her a bewildered look.

"I must've been talking in my sleep. Come on back in the house."

Jeff jumped onto the grass and headed back toward the door. He turned and watched Amber and Lick both take care of business and pointed at them with shameless glee. "See what good puppies we have?"

"Terrific ones." She took a step. "Eww yuck! Your lawn is soaking wet!"

"Unh-huh. Dad made the timer on the sprinklers to go on early so the grass is dry for me to play on all day." Jeff trotted past her, into the house, with both dogs in his wake.

She squished after him. Once inside, she peeled off her socks and scowled at them. "What time does school start?"

"Eight."

"Great. I can toss these in the dryer." She mentally clicked off the minutes before they'd have to leave and felt a burst of relief that there was plenty of time for her to regain dry socks. At least there was one good thing about Jeff being an early riser—it gave a bit of space for solving odd predicaments that came up.

"Dad's gotta get home 'fore then, though. We're going on a field trip, and we've gotta be at the school early."

"Just how early?" She decided to break the news about being the substitute, then mop up all of the wet foot and paw tracks on the linoleum.

"I dunno. It's on the paper." He banged his palm on the refrigerator door. The sheet of directions beneath his hand had a sketch of a whale in the upper right-hand corner.

"Thank You, Lord!" Vanessa snatched the page away from a pizza delivery magnet. She looked down at Jeff. "Know how I told you your dad had a great big problem at work? Well, since he figured he wouldn't get back in time, Amber and I are going to go with you instead."

"A dog can go to school?" Jeff's eyes got wider. "A dog wants to watch whales?"

"Isn't that cool?"

"Wow! Can I take Licorice too?"

"No, sport. Amber's allowed to come along because when she grows up, she'll be a working dog. Give me a second here so I can get the scoop on what we're doing today."

" 'Kay."

Vanessa read the paper. The teacher had chosen a picture that depicted the kind of whale they'd most likely see—a point in her favor, and one she promptly lost when Vanessa spotted the second-to-the-last line, "Be sure to be here early! We're leaving at seven-thirty!"

Vanessa flipped the paper onto the kitchen counter and glanced at the clock again. "We're on a tight schedule, sport. We have to be at school in less than an hour. You'd better hurry up and get dressed."

Jeff rocketed up the stairs and reappeared five minutes later in an orange tank top and blue-and-purple-striped shorts. "I'm ready!"

"Only if you want to turn into a snowman. You'll freeze your toes off in that outfit. C'mon. Let's go find you something a bit warmer." Vanessa took his hand and climbed the stairs. She felt a little funny, wandering around the private part of Nathan's house.

What had to be the master bedroom was directly across from the landing. Early morning sunlight slanted through a beautiful, oval stained-glass window and splashed puddles of amber, rose, and blue over the rumpled, eggshell-colored sheets of a sleigh bed. In his rush, Nathan had dropped several coins that lay in a haphazard path from the antique oak dresser to the door.

It took but a second to take in that view, and Vanessa wanted to hurry on past it. Three doors gaped ahead. "Where's your bedroom?"

"Over here." Jeff tugged her past a bathroom where the towels hung askew, into what still looked like a nursery. The wallpaper featured pastel zoo animals, yellow gingham curtains dressed the window, and a baby blue, three-drawer dresser stood against the far wall. All three drawers were ajar.

"Boy, you really were in a hurry," Vanessa said as she took in the garments spilling from each drawer. "How about if you find a pair of jeans, and I'll come up with a shirt?"

" 'Kay."

Vanessa straightened out the drawers as swiftly as she could while trying to be unobtrusive. She pretended to consider different shirts before settling on an undershirt and a bright yellow sweatshirt that would make him easy to spot in a crowd. She made his bed and set the clothes on it with a pat. "You change while I see about some breakfast."

"It's Monday," he said as though that fact had special significance.

"What does that have to do with breakfast?"

"Waffles and orange juice! We always have them on Monday." He even nodded as if to assert it was the routine every decent home ought to follow.

Once Vanessa reached the kitchen, she glanced at all of the cupboards and cabinets. Where does Nathan keep the waffle iron? She could wait a few minutes 'til Jeff came down to answer that question. In the meantime, since there wasn't a carton of orange juice in the refrigerator, she opened the freezer. There, in the door, just next to the can of orange juice, sat a box of toaster waffles.

"Quick and easy." She grabbed both items and spun around toward the counter. It struck her as odd that Nathan bought juice that had to be prepared and waffles that were premade, but then again, he probably grabbed them during a dash through the frozen-food section.

Jeff plunked down the stairs, and they sat at the table and ate while the puppies chomped on kibble. Jeff banged the heels of his tennis shoes on the rungs of his chair. "What did you make for lunch?"

Lunch! Oh, great. How could I forget about that? She gave him an I've-got-this-covered look. "We're a team. We're making lunch together."

He dawdled over a second waffle as she wiped down the toaster and put it away. Mouth full, he pointed at a cabinet. "We gots granola bars and fruit rollies up there."

It didn't take long to slap together a decent lunch. They brushed their teeth, and then Vanessa groaned, "I forgot to put my socks in the dryer!"

"You can wear some of mine."

"Thanks, but my feet are a bit bigger than yours."

He opened the dryer and fished out a crew sock with two black stripes at the top and another with no color striping but gray patches at the toe and heel. "Here. You can wear Dad's. We aren't gonna be late, are we? Teacher said if we're late, the bus will leave without us."

Vanessa yanked on the mismatched socks, ignored the fact that the heels poked out at ankle level, and shoved her feet into her tennis shoes. "You put Lick in the backyard. I'll grab my stuff, and we'll be outta here."

"Are you sure Dad won't come with us? The three of us always have fun together."

"Yeah, we do manage to have fun together, but if your dad woke me up early for anything other than an emergency, I'd dump him right off the boat."

She gathered all of the gear, snapped the leash and jacket on Amber, and they raced out the door. Jeff's school was a brisk half-mile walk, and they chattered the whole way there. The minute they reached the edge of the school grounds, Vanessa spied a tall, dark, handsome man leaning against a cinder-block wall. "Nathan!"

✢

Nathan strove to look casual, but it wasn't easy. Luckily, Jeff gave him a moment of diversion.

"Dad! You're here! You'd better be careful. 'Nessa said she'd dump you over the side of the boat if you showed up."

Vanessa's pink cheeks tattled that she hadn't counted on that little quip getting repeated. Nathan chuckled at her. "Gotta watch what you say around Jeff. He's got a knack for remembering the smallest things and repeating them at the most inopportune moment."

"So I noticed." She shrugged. "I deserved that. I ought to think before I speak, but that's a real weak point for me. I take it the apartment emergency isn't a massive crisis after all?"

"Yes and no. The watchman thought the second floor was buckling. It isn't. We designed it so the upstairs of the deluxe apartments will have either sunken baths or a raised platform for the bed and a lower conversation or play area."

"I see."

Nathan thought of how tired she'd been when she'd dragged herself to his front door earlier that morning. He quickly added, "But while I was there, I looked at the ceiling beams for the main entrance and noticed they're already warped a little. They'll continue to twist until they torque the supports and weaken the vaulted ceilings. I had to track down the manufacturer back East and read him the riot act. He's sending replacements on the train today. It's going to set us behind schedule a full three days. If I hadn't caught that, it would have been a real embarrassment."

"Doing quality work matters to you."

"Yes, it does." He raised his brows. "Am I forgiven, or are you planning to go through with that plot to dump me overboard and feed me to the whales?"

"There's nothing to forgive. Jeff and I had a fun morning. He's a great helper."

"Yeah, I fed the puppies and got Van some of your socks." Jeff giggled. "Hers got wet."

Nathan gave Vanessa a stricken look. "Lick didn't. . .um—"

"No! Oh, no, he didn't. I tromped out in the backyard on your just-watered lawn."

"Ah. Gotcha. One of the hazards of having a puppy."

"Nope. She didn't come out to get the puppies; she came out to get me!"

"Sport, what were you doing out in the backyard?"

"Vanessa said you were out there." Jeff tugged on Nathan's belt and stood up on tiptoe. In a stage whisper, he added, "Dad, she talks in her sleep!"

With a mock look of exasperation, Vanessa propped her hands on her hips and tapped her toe on the sidewalk. "And you, Jeffrey Adams, talk waaay too much while you're awake!"

"Yep!" Jeff giggled at her theatrics. With a gleeful look, he added, "Dad, guess what? Your socks are too big on her. Waaay too big."

"No kidding. Your dad's feet are huge." She pinched her jeans just above the knees and hiked them up several inches. "Have you ever seen anything so ridiculous?"

Nathan tilted back his head and roared.

"Listen, mister, it's not that funny!"

"Oh, yes, it is." He couldn't stop chuckling. "Let me guess. Jeff got those out of the dryer."

"How did you know?" Vanessa and Jeff both asked him.

Nathan copied Vanessa's action. He hiked up his own jeans and displayed a plain sock and a striped one. "I was in such a hurry to get out of the house this morning, I grabbed whatever was handy. I'm wearing the matching set!"

The look on Vanessa's face was priceless. She blinked, her face split into a huge grin, and giggles spilled out of her. When she finally calmed down, she announced, "It looks like you have everything well in hand. They don't need me as an extra chaperon, so I'm taking your funny socks and going home."

Nathan dared to reach over and grab her hand. "Actually, we do need you. When I got here, Miss Sanderly was having a conniption fit. It seems one of the mothers who offered to accompany us woke up with a toothache."

"You'll come, Vanessa, won't you? Pleeeze?" Jeff jigged at her side.

"Of course she will. She wouldn't miss this trip for anything." Nathan didn't want to give her an opportunity to back out. He knew he ought to feel guilty about roping her into this; the truth of it was, he didn't feel anything other than pure anticipation.

Chapter 12

"Val, you wouldn't have believed it," Vanessa told her sister as they met at church for the midweek service. "One of the other kids on the field trip didn't have a jacket. Nathan grabbed one out of the jump seat of his truck and gave it to the little boy."

"That's good. Remember the time we went whale watching and nearly froze?"

"Yes, but I thought we were done, and it turned out that was just the beginning."

"Oh?"

"They could live out of that truck for a week. No exaggeration—they have so much stuff all organized in the cab, NASA ought to ask for packing tips. Nathan started rummaging for food so he'd have a lunch to take."

"Well, we have energy bars and water in our cars."

Vanessa shook her head. "But we don't have cheese-and-crackers snack packs. A juice box."

"Sis, Jeff's a little kid. Nathan's got to keep munchies for him."

"If it stopped there, I wouldn't think a thing of it. Then he started pulling stuff out in earnest. Beef jerky. Dried apricots. A little can of peanuts. Granola bars. Those individual cups of applesauce and plastic spoons!"

Valene's eyes grew huge. "The man even had spoons?"

Muting her voice since they were entering the sanctuary, Vanessa said, "Yes. Spoons. And paper towels. Nathan packed a better lunch than I did!"

To her credit, Val muffled her laughter. As they slid into the pew, she wondered aloud, "Had he just gone grocery shopping or something?"

"No." Vanessa plunked her purse down and muttered, "He keeps earthquake supplies in his truck and car." She gave her sister a daffy look. "To top it all off, we cruised all day and didn't see a single whale."

"That's too bad."

"Jeff was so disappointed."

The music started, so their conversation ended abruptly. Vanessa stared at the back of the pew in front of her and let out a silent sigh. She'd struggled to get Jeff ready, lunches made, and the two of them to school on time; Nathan did it every single school day, and he managed it quite well. He operated on a smooth, near-perfect level, and she could be the poster girl for Insecurities Anonymous—well, she would be if they had anything more than a friendship. *But we don't. We're just pals.* That realization flooded her with an odd sense of relief. *Yeah. It's good Nathan is so good at handling things on his own. Sure it is. It works out well for him and Jeff.*

She continued to think of them until Kip slid into the pew and somehow managed to bump Val over so he sat between them. Once the service got underway, Pastor MacIntosh made announcements. After he mentioned one particular upcoming activity, Vanessa and Valene both leaned forward to make eye contact and exchanged a meaningful look.

✝

"He'd have such a good time."

Nathan stared out of the dugout, not wanting to look at Vanessa's pleading face. Kip sent a ball sailing into center field and made it to second base while folks cheered. Nathan hoped Van would get involved in the game and drop the subject.

"I'm working, but you can go with him, Nathan. If you're already busy, plenty of the parents are going, and they'd keep close watch on Jeff."

He didn't respond.

The shortstop caught a fly, and Kip got tagged out on third. Nathan bolted off the bench, eager to get out on the field, away from the conversation.

Vanessa halted him. "I'm sorry, Nathan. I didn't mean to pressure you. I promised I wouldn't invite you to church—I didn't stop to think you'd consider a primary department outing would fall under that heading. I just knew Jeff would enjoy going to the tide pools, and well—" She let out a gusty sigh. "I understand. It's with the church's primary department. I can see now it was a mistake for me to say anything."

Tears glossed her eyes. Nathan drew in a quick breath. Part of him caved in; the other part rebelled. She wasn't just a do-gooder, trying to involve his son in church—she really cared about Jeff. *But I'm not getting sucked into all of this church stuff.*

"I really blew it, didn't I?"

"Vanessa, let's just drop it for now and play ball."

"All right." She paused and added, "I'll drop it." As he began to walk off, he heard her mutter, "For now."

In the last inning, Nathan channeled all of his churning emotions into his swing. His grand slam bought the Altar Egos' triumph. As he ran the bases and touched home plate, the team and crowd went wild. Only he knew deep inside, the last thing he felt was victorious.

✝

Saturday, after the puppy kindergarten class, Nathan curled his hand around

Vanessa's arm. Shock jolted through her at the intensity of his gaze.

"Can you give me a minute?"

"Um, yeah. Sure. What is it, Nathan?"

"Saturday mornings aren't working out well for me." He let go of her. "The next few weeks will be impossible. Can you work with Jeff and me on training Lick on a catch-as-catch-can basis?"

A sick feeling churned in her stomach. She'd pressured him about the tide-pool trip for Jeff, and this seemed like a polite version of "So long, see ya later."

Lord, I'm so sorry. I need to learn to be patient. I acted in haste, and I've pushed him away from You.

Nathan tugged on Lick's leash to pull him back from sniffing at a patch of grass. Nathan kept his gaze trained downward. "Jeff really wants to go to the tide pools next Saturday. I can't be in two places at once."

"He'll love it! Be sure to take your camera and get pictures."

Nathan looked up, and the sparkle in his eye warmed her heart. He wasn't trying to bail out or to mollify her—she could see that he really wanted to go.

"It's been so long since I dug out the camera. Evie always took snapshots. I just haven't had the heart. When you took your camera whale watching, I got an attack of the guilts."

When he mentioned his wife, the sparkle in his eyes dimmed, and it made Vanessa want to comfort him. She sensed he'd not welcome anything overt, so instead, she went for simple reassurance. "Not that I got any great photos, anyway. We didn't see a single whale."

Nathan shrugged. "Since he didn't get to see any whales, I thought you were right—he ought to get a chance to see sea creatures somehow."

Vanessa nodded. If she said something right now, she'd probably make an utter fool of herself, either hugging him or blubbering for joy.

"It's not just next Saturday. If it were a matter of missing a single class, we'd probably be able to catch on and catch up. It's more complicated than that. The following Saturday, I'll be out of town, and the week after, I have an appointment with a client. Lick's just too knot-headed for me to believe we can miss three sessions in a row and train him to be obedient."

"I'm sure we can work out a few private training sessions."

"Great. If we can get him to behave, I'll be a happy camper. I don't expect him to ever be a model citizen like Amber."

"When we're through with him, he will be. It just takes patience. With patience, you can do just about anything."

⸸

Late that evening, Vanessa pulled a diskette out of her computer. *Lord, I just wanna say something here. I know I told Nathan all it took was patience to get things done. I did qualify it with a 'just about.' Well, I've been trying to make the accounts balance, and they won't. I can't. This doesn't just take patience—it's going to take a miracle!*

She grimaced at the memory of her sage words, then turned that grimace toward the shoebox full of receipts. Practice—she practiced plenty of things, but patience wasn't one of them. That commodity just hit an all-time low.

In sheer desperation, she filled a bag with gourmet doggy treats and hit the road. She tromped into Val's condo and cried, "I'm throwing myself on your mercy. I even brought bribes for Hero."

"It's the end of the month." Val arched a brow. "Let me guess: You can't get the books to balance."

"Bingo."

"Hero will be happy to have the treats. I, on the other hand, refuse to be bribed."

"Val, come on. I'm dying here."

"So am I. Here's the deal: You give Hero the rest of his puppy shots. I can't stand to do it myself, and Dr. Bainbridge's office is only open during the hours I work."

"I'm more than willing to do that. You've got a deal." Vanessa poured herself a cup of tea. "Then again, I would have been willing to do it for you anyway."

Val laughed. "I know. Just like I would have straightened out your record keeping for you anyway."

While Val clicked around on the computer and resolved all the quirks and misfiled information on Vanessa's ledger, Van dug through the cabinets and found a vase.

"What're you up to now?"

"Don't pay any attention to me. Just crunch the numbers." Vanessa pulled a variety of silk flowers from her athletic bag and put together an arrangement for Val's living room.

"All done," Val said.

"Me too. Take a look."

Val walked into the living room, and her face lit up. "That's perfect! I don't know how you do that kind of stuff. Arts and crafts are my waterloo."

"Yeah, well, you got the smarts; I got the crafts. Believe me, if I had to pick, I would have taken the brains."

"You do have brains," Val protested. She then grimaced. "But I'm worried you're not using them. We need to have a talk."

"Now what did I do?" Van turned sideways on the couch and watched as her twin searched for the right words. *Uh-oh. Whatever this is, it's a biggie. . . .*

Val paced across the floor and turned back. "I think you need to draw a definite line with Nathan."

"Draw a line?"

"He's not a believer. Well, he is, but he's not living his faith. He's bitter toward the Lord, and that's not the kind of man you ought to be dating."

Vanessa snorted. "Dating? You've gotta be kidding me. We have his son and two dogs everywhere we go. It's nothing romantic at all."

"Just because it starts off innocently doesn't mean it'll stay that way." Valene sat down and curled her hand around Vanessa's wrist. "You'd be wise to spend less time with him and more time with a man who is practicing a strong daily walk with Christ."

"We're not dating, Val, and Nathan will eventually restore his relationship with the Lord. Christ didn't turn His back on those who strayed. He said as a shepherd He'd search for every lost lamb. If all I ever do is hang out with Christians who have no doubts or questions, who's going to reach out to those who are out of relationship or hurting? That wouldn't be living my faith."

"You have a point, but I'm trying to make you see the difference between being casual friends and losing your heart. Nathan is handsome, well-to-do, and kind."

"I have several guy friends who are handsome or well-off, and they're all good-hearted. They're just friends."

"But how many of them would have called you at four in the morning to pinch-hit for their kid's field trip? Why did Nathan call you?"

"Let's see. For starters, my other friends don't have kids. As for Nathan, it was a Monday. Most people work on Mondays, but it's my day off. Nathan knows I love the ocean. Jeff and I are buddies. Besides—it's good for Amber to go on all different modes of transportation, and she hadn't been on a boat yet."

Val gave her an I'm-not-buying-your-story look.

"Get this: One of the kids came up to us and asked Jeff, 'Is she your dad's girlfriend?' and I said, 'Nope. Amber is my dog, not his.' See? I made it clear I'm not romantically entangled."

Val laid her head on the back of the couch and groaned. "Why did I have to be right? I just told you, you have brains, but you're not using them. This is going to be a disaster."

"Let's see." Vanessa ticked off points on her hand. "Jeff learned a lesson about integrity. I sold a dog. I'm even earning money on training." She wiggled those three fingers in the air. "If that isn't enough, look at the more important issues: Nathan is now playing ball with the church team, and he's renewed his friendship with Kip. Jeff is going to the tide pools with the primary department—and Nathan is taking him!"

All five fingers stuck up in the air. She then tightened them together to form a scoop, turned her hand palm up, and lifted it toward heaven. "It's really not in my hands at all, Val. It's in God's."

Chapter 13

Once or twice a week, Nathan managed to find a time slot that Vanessa had free. They met at the park across from her shop and worked with Lick's training. Sometimes Jeff stayed at home with Consuelo. Other times, he was at a birthday party or at a friend's house. About half the time, he came along and enjoyed learning, too.

Nathan liked how Van paid attention to Jeff and never acted like he was a tagalong. The two of them often traded silly jokes and romped, yet she still earned and held his respect.

If they did puppy training in his backyard, she made a habit of bringing a snack of some variety and insisting that they all wedge into the fort to share it. Having deduced that he was all thumbs in the kitchen, she frequently managed to bring something she'd baked—cream puffs, cookies shaped like dog biscuits, apple tarts, or cupcakes with cherries made of gumdrops decorating the top.

Two adults, one wiggly boy, and two puppies in the fort's tight space always turned out to be the highlight of the day—and not because of the food. After lifting the dogs into the fort, Nathan could sit close to Vanessa, relish her sunny laugh, try to determine what odd combination of fragrances she'd put together, and swipe a nibble from her fingertips.

Whenever he and Vanessa met without Jeff, Nathan tried to find ways to prolong their time together. They'd eaten at several fast-food places that featured outdoor picnic tables so the dogs wouldn't have to be left in the car—something neither he nor Vanessa would consider. It didn't exactly qualify as the most romantic way to edge into a relationship, but he didn't care. Just being with Vanessa made his day.

One hitch bothered him. When they ate, she prayed. He knew the Lord was an integral part of her life. She'd mention things about a program at church or occasionally quote something he knew came from Psalms or Proverbs. If anything, he sensed she made a concerted effort not to swamp him with religious stuff.

He appreciated her restraint. It made him uncomfortable when folks got all churchy around him. Nathan knew it was guilt. He flatly refused to explore that emotion. God took Evie away. How could God ask for a man's soul when He robbed him of his heart?

Over time, he'd begun to feel less awkward when Vanessa would say a simple, quick grace. He'd turned down a few invitations to church by a couple of the guys on the team until Vanessa had grabbed the bull by the horns. After practice one evening, she'd faced the whole team and announced, "Nathan knows he has a standing invitation to church. I promised him I wouldn't wheedle or plot so he'd get roped into attending. When he's ready, he'll come. Until then, let's leave it be." Integrity. She had it in spades.

What kind of man was he, to want to court a woman who walked so closely with the Lord? He knew all about being in step with the Lord. He'd been that way once upon a time, and he'd willingly worn the mantle of the spiritual head of his home with an awareness of its responsibilities and blessings. His marriage with Evie blossomed under God's grace and leading—until Evie died, when simple faith suddenly wasn't enough. Vanessa deserved a man of faith. *But I can't let her go. What kind of man does that make me?*

✝

"Dad, that was so much fun! Can we go again? Please?"

Nathan looked down at Jeff's sun-kissed cheeks and silently agreed. They'd had a terrific day down at the tide pools. The group got there just as the tide went out, and the pocked rock formations held countless wonders. Children darted from one pool to the next, shrieking with joy. They'd squat next to a little hollowed-out retreat and point at darting, tiny fish or touch limpets. *Yeah, I could go for a day like that again. It was relaxing, fun. . . .*

"Please, Dad. I wanna go back there."

"I had a great time, too. Maybe we could do it again. What would you think about taking Vanessa and Amber with us?"

"That'd be super-duper! Let's go tomorrow."

"Sorry, sport." He lifted the blankets, and Jeff tumbled into bed. Covering his son, Nathan said, "Tomorrow's Sunday. Van works in the afternoon after she goes to church. The animals have to be fed and watered."

"But we could go in the morning!"

Nathan shook his head. "Van goes to church."

"Dad? Why don't we go to church? I gots lots of friends who go to Van's church. We're all good buddies."

"Church isn't just supposed to be about who you go to see."

"Then what is it about? I know!" Jeff popped up and gave Nathan an earnest look. "It's 'bout God and Jesus and stuff—like in the songs the kids were singing today, huh?"

"Yeah." Nathan tucked him back in, ruffled his hair, and kissed his forehead. "Enough talk. Go to sleep." Before Jeff could pursue the conversation, he left the room.

✝

"I'm going for the fives." Dad set aside two of the dice and dropped the other three back in the cup. They made a hollow, rattling sound before he dumped them out again. They tumbled across the flower-patterned vinyl tablecloth and came to rest a few inches past a small crease that acted as a speed bump.

Vanessa leaned back in the molded plastic patio chair and relished the night breeze off the sea. It rustled through the mulberry tree in the corner of the back-yard. She laughed. "Remember that year Val and I did the silk project?"

"Fourth grade," her mother recalled. "Those silkworms you raised were disgusting."

"Now I thought they were interesting, Mom." Dad set aside another five and plunked the last two dice into his cup. "The teacher said our Van was the only kid she ever had who actually kept them alive and spinning."

"Because we had the mulberry leaves. It wasn't hard at all—I just picked a few leaves and dumped them in each morning. We got a good grade on the project because of Val. She wrote a great paper to go along with it."

"And your illustrations were amazing," Mom added.

Dad sent the dice across the table and bellowed gleefully, "Yahtzee!"

"Can you believe that? The last roll of the game, and Dad gets a Yahtzee!"

As they put away the game, Mom asked, "What made you think of the silkworms?"

"The mulberry tree."

Dad took another sip of his tea. "It's a good source of shade, but the berries sure make a mess. Every year, I say something about taking it out and putting in something that won't be such a hassle, but Mom won't let me."

"Why not?"

"She's sentimental. You used to hold your animal hospitals under it."

Vanessa grinned at the memory. "It's amazing you didn't go broke, buying me gauze and tape for all of those bandages I made."

"What's amazing is, all of those animals just sat there and let you mummy wrap them!" Mom laughed. "Dad's just as sentimental as I am. He sticks nails into the ground by the hydrangea so the flower petals will turn pretty colors. Remember how you and Val used to play 'Wedding' and use those poufy flower balls as your bridal bouquets?"

"And the yellow chenille pipe cleaner rings!" Vanessa looked over at the hydrangea, then back at her parents. "We had a storybook childhood."

Dad cleared his throat. "Speaking of weddings. . ."

"Is someone getting married?"

"We're talking about you, sweetheart." Mom scooted her chair closer. "You're spending an awful lot of time with that Adams man."

"Did Val put you up to this?"

"Nope." Dad leaned on the table and shook his head. "Honey, we reared you to do the right thing, to live by the Bible. You know you're not to set your heart on a man who isn't walking with the Lord. My understanding is Nathan Adams lost his wife, and he's bitter toward God."

"He is."

"Then why are you dating him?" Mom frowned.

Vanessa sighed. "Once and for all, we are not dating. I get paid each time we meet, and you certainly didn't rear me to be that kind of woman!"

Her mom's eyes widened, and she chided, "Vanessa!"

"Okay, Mom. Sorry. I got a bit carried away, but all of this concern feels like such an overreaction." When her parents didn't respond, she hastened on. "I'm giving him puppy obedience lessons. Most of the time, we have Amber, his black Lab, and his son with us. We've never eaten out unless you count an ice cream cone or fast food. He's a friend."

"Friends can become more than friends"—Mom looked her in the eye— "especially when the woman is as compassionate and sympathetic as you are. Your whole childhood, you gravitated toward people and animals who needed special attention. You've grown into an empathetic woman who cares freely and deeply. I'm worried that you're getting absorbed into Nathan Adams's world. He's a wounded man, and you can't fix him."

Vanessa rubbed her face with both hands and looked away for a moment, then looked back at her mother. Quietly, she admitted, "I know I can't. I'm just trying to come alongside him as a Christian sister."

Mom dipped her head ever so slightly and looked at Vanessa with her I-mean-business glare. "Sister? Friend? Those are nice labels, but my radar is sending off boyfriend alarms."

"Mom, I'm not dating him. I'm so busy with the shop and the private lessons and the baseball team and the puppy training club, there isn't time. My life is full, and my heart isn't empty. I figure God will put the right man in my life when He wills it."

"Nathan is on that team, isn't he?" Dad asked pointedly.

"Yes, he is." Vanessa grinned. "And he just took his son to the tide pools with the primary department today. I have faith that the Good Shepherd will bring back His straying lamb. It's a matter of letting God be God."

"Don't get involved romantically with a man and expect him to change." Dad stood. "It's wrong, honey."

"I agree, Dad. I need to get going. I'll see you at church tomorrow."

✝

Nathan lay in bed and stared at the stained-glass window. A streetlight shone through it just enough to make the pattern apparent. Evie had surprised him with the window the year she was carrying Jeff. It was a Christmas present, and she'd managed to save up the money for it by squirreling away her change. He'd been so surprised. *Little things add up. Just think—we're going to have the best little thing of all.* She'd wear that dreamy look and rub her tummy.

Then, too, once he set the window into their bedroom wall, she'd lie next to him and imagine all the different things the window could mean. *Three flowers. . . you, me, and the baby. Or is it the Trinity? Father, Son, and Holy Spirit. . .the ribbon holding them is love. I'm sure of that. Nothing is stronger than love.*

Now, he lay there, and her words echoed in his mind. So did Jeff's. *Dad? Why don't we go to church?*

He rolled over and smacked his pillow.

God, You know why I don't go to church. I refuse to be a hypocrite. I'm not going to go and pretend I understand. I don't. I don't have the kind of faith that makes everything okay and lets me dump everything into Your hands. I'm mad. No, I'm livid. Bad enough, You took my wife, but how could You rob Jeff of his mother? I wouldn't want someone who held a grudge against me in my home. Why should I go to Yours?

Sleep wouldn't come. Hearing a light, puppy whimper, Nathan shoved aside his blankets and got up. He took Lick out to the backyard and grumbled, "Okay. Do your business."

How many times had he heard Vanessa give Amber that same command? He'd chuckled the first time he overheard it. That was back when he didn't know the special commands she used in training. Now it all made sense and came as second nature.

Lick complied, then ran to the other side of the yard. "Come." Nathan waited, but the puppy ignored him.

He squatted down and reached out. "Come, Lick."

The puppy continued to wander on his own path.

"Lick, come on, boy."

Lick perked up his head, his tail wagged, and he bounded across the yard, straight to Nathan.

Nathan felt a spurt of irritation, then squelched it. He couldn't punish this silly little, wiggly ball of fluff. Lick had obeyed the call and came. If he got punished, he'd be less likely to come in the future. Instead, Nathan cradled the puppy in his arms and took him inside. As he stuck Lick back in his bed in the corner of Jeff's room, Jeff stirred.

"Dad?"

"What?"

"You never answered my question. Can we go to church?"

Nathan stayed motionless and stared across the dim room at his innocent little boy. *I don't have to make a big deal of this. We'll go just once. That'll satisfy him.* Even that agreement felt like a huge concession.

"I wanna go."

Each word strained his vocal cords as Nathan said, "We'll go tomorrow."

Chapter 14

His shoes pinched. His dress socks had a hole in one toe, courtesy of Licorice. One of the buttons on his suit dangled by a thread, and he'd forgotten he'd tossed his favorite tie in the drawer the last time he wore it, so he had to settle for another one that had a small mustard stain. For being a successful businessman, he looked like a bum.

Man looks at the outward appearance, but the Lord looks at the heart. The verse ran through his mind, and as Nathan pulled into a parking space, he muttered, "I'm striking out on both accounts."

Giggling, Jeff bounced along the sidewalk as they headed toward the sanctuary. "Hey—there's Andy! He's in my class at school."

It didn't take much time to settle Jeff into a Sunday school class, then Nathan stared at the sanctuary. Each step took resolve. *I could just leave and come back to pick up Jeff, but I said we'd go to church. If I don't stay, I would be lying.*

He hadn't attended Seaside Chapel before and was surprised to discover how that very fact actually made it easier to go inside the sanctuary. Instead of having to endure the inevitable flood of memories from Mercy Springs, there was simple curiosity on his part. A greeter shook his hand, and an usher handed him the bulletin—familiar rituals that should have given comfort, but just left him feeling hollow. He could endure one day of this.

He saw Valene sitting near the aisle. Amber was lying curled up, "being small," just to the side of the pew. A couple sat beside Val—her parents, he presumed. Nathan slipped into the pew directly behind her, set down the bulletin, and leaned forward. Tapping her on the shoulder, he murmured, "Don't look now—the roof might cave in. I came to church."

"You'd better look," she whispered back. "I'm Val."

"I know." He flashed a quick smile at her. "Van couldn't sit as still as you do or stay quiet. She'd be chattering up a storm with half the congregation and make a last-minute mad dash for a seat." He glanced around, hoping to see Vanessa. With Amber right here, she had to be close—a fact that made him feel a little less anxious. Until now, he hadn't realized how much he was counting on her being there to be his lifeline. "Where is your sister?"

"Van's singing in the choir today. Amber's supposed to stay here, but I'm keeping an eye on her."

"She looks a lot more comfortable than I feel." He couldn't believe he'd blurted that out.

She gave him a timid smile. "I'm glad you came. Have you met our parents, Ellen and Bill?"

"No." He stood and shook Ellen's and Bill's hands. "You have wonderful daughters."

"Thank you. We hear you have a terrific little boy," Ellen said.

"And a powerhouse swing," Bill added. "The team's finally winning a few games this year."

"Why don't you come up and sit with us?" Ellen invited.

Just then, another family entered from the side and filed right in next to the Zobels. Nathan grinned. "Thanks, but I'm fine." He took a seat and pretended to study the bulletin.

Nathan figured it served him right that he assumed Vanessa would be waiting to sit next to him. She probably served on a few committees and substitute taught a Sunday school class, too. He'd never met anyone with her vitality. If something needed doing, she'd be in the middle of it.

Valene and her parents were gracious, but it just wasn't the same. He knew Van and Val were identical, but the odd thing was, he really never gave Val a second thought. Vanessa kindled something inside of him, and beside her, all other women paled to insignificance.

Shy Valene sat in front of him and dipped her head as she meditated before the service began. He'd noticed Vanessa tended to turn her face toward heaven when she prayed. She acted just as open with the Father as she did with people.

How can she trust the Lord and rely on Him so completely? Innocence? Is it just that she hasn't been burned by life yet? God let loose a nuclear bomb in my life. Nothing's left of my soul but a charred shell. I believe in Him, but how can I ever trust Him again?

He didn't have much time for reflection. The worship leader got up to the microphone and welcomed everyone. He directed them all to stand and greet someone. A couple of the guys from the baseball team came over and shook his hand.

Part of Nathan liked already knowing some of the folks—it made it seem a little less foreign. On the other hand, he felt trapped. Just because he came this once, he didn't want them all to start bugging him to show up again.

While his attention was diverted, the choir filed in. Nathan looked up and spotted Vanessa at once. She perked up and smiled at him. *Best welcome I got. . . .* Close on the warmth of that feeling, his common sense kicked in. *But this is just a one-time deal.*

The pianist played a couple of chords, and the choir started in. Soon, the music director had the whole congregation singing.

Funny thing, hymns. They're classics. Never paid attention, but they can be welcoming and comforting—probably the familiarity of them. Odd, after five years, I remember almost all of the words. Two of the worship songs were new—he didn't know the tunes, but that forced him to attend to the lyrics more closely. All in all, the music time didn't feel too awkward.

Nathan followed the music minister's directions to stand and sit when everyone else did. He took his seat again as an elderly couple tottered from the front row of the choir to the microphone and started to sing, "It Is Well with My Soul." Clearly, their hearts were in the right place, but their vocal cords weren't. Nathan never pretended to have a whole lot of talent in the music department, but even he knew they were each singing in completely different keys. To make matters worse, one of them wore a hearing aid that managed to buzz off and on. The microphone picked up the high-pitched tone and turned it into a shrill siren.

Amber stood up, right there in the center of the main aisle and started to "sing" along in howl.

"Hush!" Valene tried to silence Amber, but Amber wagged her head from side to side almost as if she were saying no. She tilted her head back and continued to howl.

Nathan glanced up at the choir and saw Vanessa's incredulous expression. Valene glowed bright red in embarrassment as she continued to whisper very softly, "Hush, Amber."

Having spent a lot of time with them, Nathan remembered the command Vanessa used on the rare occasions when Amber needed correction. He leaned forward and used her tactic. In a firm voice, pitched low enough to mean business, yet not so loud as to travel through the entire sanctuary, he said, "That's enough."

Immediately, Amber went quiet.

"Down," Nathan commanded.

Amber backed up a few steps, sat down, and rested her chin on the edge of his pew. Nathan glanced up at the choir, and Vanessa mouthed, "Thank you."

Fortunately the man in charge of the sound system managed to adjust the microphone so the duet finished without any further technical or canine embellishment. Nathan knew he'd never forget that hymn.

After the benediction, Bill Zobel turned around. "I have a hankering for Chinese. Why don't you collect your son and meet us all at the Paper Lantern?"

"Only if he'll promise to order something with some zing," Vanessa declared as she walked up. "My parents and Val all have sissy mouths. I'm tired of sharing bland stuff."

"The hotter, the better." Nathan grinned. "But Jeff is going to be a traitor. He always wants something sweet like orange chicken."

"My favorite!" Ellen smiled.

"See?" Vanessa groaned.

"I'll order hot-and-spicy Hunan beef if you get firecracker shrimp or kung pao chicken." He got a kick out of seeing how Vanessa perked up. The woman was so bright, she could masquerade as a thousand-watt lightbulb.

Val wrinkled her nose. "I'll order beds for both of you at Community General after you burn holes in your stomachs with that stuff."

Nathan shrugged. "If my cooking hasn't sent me to the hospital, nothing will."

⚜

"Dad, what is the duck peeking at?"

"Peking used to be a place in China, but they changed what it's called to Beijing," Van explained as Nathan gave his son a baffled look. "The people at that table across from us want to try a dish that is named after the city."

"Oh. So those people wanna eat funny stuff." Jeff leaned closer to Vanessa. "Did you hear them? They're getting mushy pork."

"Mu shu pork sounds good to me." Vanessa's dad closed the menu. He grinned at Jeff. "It's sort of like skinny pancakes they fill with pork. They're good. I'll get that, and we can try it together."

"My dog eats pancakes. My dog and Valene's dog are brothers. I wish I had a brother."

The muscle in Nathan's cheek twitched. His eyes narrowed for a split second. He took a long, deep breath, and his features smoothed. Poking his forefinger into Jeff's ribs, he rumbled, "Oh, no. You're enough for me. Between you and Lick, I've got my hands full."

Jeff giggled and squirmed. "Lick got one of Dad's socks today. He ran all over the house with it in his mouth."

Nathan looked into Vanessa's eyes. She felt her pulse speed up a bit. "See what kind of trainer you are? You swiped my socks, so now the dog's doing it, too."

"His socks?" her mother echoed. "You swiped his socks?"

Shaking his head, Jeff blabbed, "She wore Dad's socks. Dad and Van both had one with stripes and one that didn't have stripes. They matched each other."

Mom about spilled the tea she was pouring into Dad's cup as she croaked, "How did you end up wearing his socks?"

"Vanessa talks in her sleep." Jeff wiggled with delight. "She told me—"

Uh-oh. This is unbelievable. Damage-control time here. "Nathan had an emergency. At work. I went over—to his house, not to his work. He called me." She knew she was babbling, but she couldn't help herself. "Early in the morning—"

"Vanessa bailed me out of a tight spot. About a week ago, I had to dash off to a construction site, so she baby-sat Jeff for me." Nathan finished the explanation smoothly. It didn't escape her notice that he made it abundantly clear he hadn't stayed in the house with her there.

Whew.

"You ready to order?" The waitress held her pen poised over an abused pad of paper.

"Mom?" Dad prompted.

"I heard Jeff likes orange chicken, so I'd better order something different so we'll have an assortment. I'll go for some sweet-and-sour ribs."

"I'd like the mushroom chicken, please." Val snapped the menu shut.

"Mu shu pork," Dad added.

Jeff got up on his knees and leaned across the table. "Are those our pancakes?"

"You better believe it!"

"Goody!"

Jeff managed to give them all a rundown of his Sunday school lesson. The whole time he spoke, Nathan kept his arm around his son's shoulders, but with his free hand, he pensively turned his teacup in slow, exacting clockwise clicks.

What is he thinking?

When the food came, Jeff changed topics. "Looky, Dad! Looky! That thing in the middle of the table is a merry-go-round!"

"It's called a lazy Susan. We'll all put our food on there and spin it around so anyone who wants to can have a taste. Pretty nifty, huh, sport?"

"Can you put one in our table? It's cool!" He turned to Vanessa. "My dad can do anything. He can make anything!"

She thought of the beautiful, old oak pedestal table she'd seen at Nathan's house. "Your table is round like this one, but I think it would look kind of strange with a lazy Susan. It's just right the way it is."

"On rainy days, Consuelo puts a big blanket over it and lets me pretend it's a tent."

"Jeff, you need to quiet down," Nathan said matter-of-factly. "It's time to use your mouth to eat, not to talk."

As she dished rice onto her plate, Val piped up. "Yeah, well, Amber wasn't very quiet today, either. I wanted to crawl under the pew when she started in!"

Van muffled a laugh. "Nathan took care of it. And get this, Nathan: Eulla Mae and Harold came up to me in the narthex and thought it was hilarious that Amber wanted to make it a trio with them. They weren't upset in the least."

"Eulla Mae is gifted with grace," Mom said.

Nathan snorted. "I'm certainly not."

His words stunned Vanessa for a moment until she followed his rueful gaze.

He'd managed to drop a shrimp, and it had slithered away from the serving spoon, leaving a thin, messy, pinkish streak across the table.

"You can't escape me!" Vanessa nabbed it with her fork. "Ta da! Gotcha, you little rascal."

"Catching a shrimp isn't a big deal. I wish you woulda gotten a whale." Jeff's lower lip poked out in a classic pout. "I didn't get to see no whale on our trip."

"No, we didn't get to see any whales, but we did see lots of cool sea creatures yesterday at the tide pools," Nathan reminded him. "You saw anemones and urchins and hermit crabs. . . ."

"Van? Dad said we can go back to the tide pools again. Wanna come with us?"

"I'd love to!"

After the meal was over, Nathan swiped the check and paid the bill. They all walked out to the parking lot, and after he left, Dad and Mom bracketed Vanessa.

"Honey, he's a good man," Mom said.

"But he's not walking with the Lord," Dad said. "He's fallen away. I hate to see you get more deeply involved. It's a big mistake."

"Involved? It's friendship. And for the record, I have a deal with Nathan. He knows he has a standing invitation to come to church, but I don't bug him. Today was the first time in five years he's attended church, and I'm thankful for that answer to prayer."

"We're glad he came. We hope he continues, but Van, don't start wading into 'missionary dating.' You know it's wrong."

"Yeah. I understand. Just notice that it was Jeff who asked me to go to the tide pools—not Nathan."

Inside, she felt a niggling about that fact. She really wished Nathan had asked. . . . Then again, she was glad he hadn't—not because of her family's misgivings, but because she didn't want to have to start examining her feelings about him too closely. Deep down, she knew full well if he was an on-fire believer—*No. I'm not going there. This is about God and His relationship with Nathan. I'm not in the picture. I'm not. Well, okay, so I am—but just a little bit.*

Chapter 15

"Y" ou want me to what?" Vanessa stopped dead in her tracks on the aisle between the birdseed and kitty litter. Her hand wrapped around the cordless phone receiver more tightly. Amber stood patiently at her side, oblivious to the ridiculous suggestion Nathan had just made.

"Jeff mentioned it the other day at lunch—the tide pools. Why are you sounding so surprised?"

"I'm not exactly surprised you asked, but—"

"You're off on Monday, and I'm at a point in my projects that I can take a day off, too. Jeff's school booked a student-free day for the teachers, so he won't miss any class."

"So far, I'm fine with that—"

"You also said Amber is allowed there," he tempted without taking a breath, "so that's not a hitch."

Vanessa marveled at his delivery. He'd reasoned out all of the contingencies and her possible objections and delivered his sales pitch as smoothly as he banged a nail into place with a hammer. She grimaced. He'd failed to take one major point into account.

"C'mon, Van. Whadda ya say?"

Vanessa stuffed an outdated tablet of rebate coupons in the trash can under the counter. "You were doing fine until you started discussing high and low tides."

"You have to get there right as the tide is going out so you can see the best assortment of all of the sea life. Those first hours are awesome!"

"I have to be awake so I can see." She wiped off the counter and headed toward the kittens' cage. She'd sold all but two of them, and they looked like they could both use some attention. "I couldn't pry my eyes open at 6:43 a.m. if you dropped a python on me."

Nathan chuckled.

"I don't really even think," she mused as she dangled a feather teaser toy at one of the fluff balls, "the world is alive yet at that hour."

"It is. I assure you, it is."

"I'll take your word for it." She laughed at his impatient snort as well as at the kittens' antics. "I'm not about to actually discover that for myself."

77

"You already have. When you bailed me out that night, Jeff had you up by six thirty."

"Boy, oh, boy. I do a guy a favor, and he tosses it right back in my face."

"It's a good cause. Think about how disappointed Jeff was when we didn't spot any whales when we went whale watching. A trip to the tide pools will help make up for it."

"Nathan, you already took him."

"But you weren't there."

"Yeah, well, it's a safe bet that I'm going to be a no-show for anything that requires me to crawl out of bed before sunrise. My alarm clock and I have an iron-clad agreement: It doesn't wake me up before 7:23 a.m., and I keep it plugged in."

"7:23?"

"And not a second sooner. I have a routine all worked out so I can stay in bed until the very last minute." She tossed a jingly bell in for the kittens and fastened the cage's catch. "I told you I'm a night owl."

"You're not exaggerating at all?"

"Okay, I confess—Val dragged me out of bed and poured coffee into me so I'd make seven thirty classes in high school and college."

"So you can get up and function."

"Not really. She and I are polar opposites—she's a lark, and I'm an owl. It's probably one of the reasons she got As and I didn't in all of those crack-of-dawn classes. I was just sleepwalking with a commuter mug in my hand."

"Ah-ha!" His baritone laughter rippled over the phone line. "I've discovered your weakness. Jeff and I will bring a giant mug of coffee for you."

"Not good enough."

"No? Jeff will be so disappointed, Van. He really wanted you and Amber to go with us."

"Life is made up of all sorts of little disappointments." If anything, Nathan sounded rather downhearted himself. She couldn't tamp down her smile, even though he couldn't see her. "Chocolate has caffeine, you know."

"You'd eat chocolate at six in the morning?"

"As far as I'm concerned, if I'm breathing, it's a good time to eat chocolate. I'm a firm believer in eating my vegetables, and cocoa is a bean."

Nathan spluttered for a moment, then recovered wryly, "I suppose that is an example of the kind of stuff you, ah, 'learned' in one of those early morning science classes."

"The benefits of a good education." She laughed. "I probably ought to set a good example for Jeff, though. I'll settle for hot cocoa."

"Great! We'll pick you up at six on Monday."

"Six fifteen." After she hung up, Vanessa put the phone back on the base and folded her arms akimbo. "That man missed his calling in life. He should have gone into retail sales where he'd get a hefty commission. He'd be rolling in the dough in less than a month."

Amber looked up at her as if she understood and agreed with every last word.

"Come on, girl. We have work to do." Amber stood and followed along as Vanessa went along the aisle with all of her fish tanks. She sprinkled food along the surface of the water and watched as the fish tumbled about in the water like colorful sprinkles in a kaleidoscope.

When she and Val had worked here when they were in college, she'd hated cleaning out the fish tanks. It was a slimy, messy, smelly job. Her boss really liked fish, though. Pete would stand and admire the nearly translucent fins, the iridescent colors, and the grace with which the fish cruised through the tanks. He'd actually had a second aisle of exotics. She'd gotten accustomed to caring for them.

All along, she'd thought to go into veterinary medicine—well, until she'd gotten into anatomy and physiology. She'd sat in the corner of the lab and tried to force herself to participate, but she couldn't dissect the cat. It looked just like Elvira, the sleek black cat she and Val had for several years. As a compromise, she'd done her "dissection" on a computer instead. When she went to turn in all of the necessary pages, Dr. Bainbridge was visiting her professor.

Her professor made a disparaging comment, but Dr. Bainbridge came to her defense. He'd been the family vet for Elvira; the poodle, Fluffy; and later her first guide puppy, Thane. He'd gently suggested she was excellent at caring for healthy animals—perhaps she ought to think about running a pet store or kennel instead of going into veterinary medicine. He'd even put in a good word with Pete at the pet store, who promptly hired both Van and Val.

Val had enjoyed running the register, pricing things, and keeping the books. Van, on the other hand, had gone wild over the animals. She'd groomed them, played with them, kept the pens and cages spotless, and found tremendous satisfaction in helping customers find the perfect pet.

Pete had often remarked that his business had taken off once the twins worked there. He chalked it up to their beauty. Van teased it was because Val finally straightened out his books so he could keep track of his funds. Val declared it was due to Vanessa's knack for selling not only the pet, but all of the necessary start-up gear, as well. Whatever the truth, the job had paid for the rest of their schooling, and Pete had happily set their work schedules around the hours they needed off for classes.

Pete had waited until Van was almost ready to graduate before he told her he was thinking of selling his pet shop. Just the year before, Grandma had passed on and left a sizable legacy to her and Val. Val had just used her share to buy the condo. Van had prayed and felt the Lord was opening doors. . .but not fish tanks.

She'd bought the store, renamed it, and promptly sold off half the stock of fish. Now, she had five shiny tanks full of freshwater fish. Adding more puppies, dog chow, and gear made the store far more profitable—and she didn't have to clean as many tanks.

Nonetheless, the goldfish tank qualified as essential equipment. She often donated coupons to schools and the church to give to children for a free goldfish. Frequently those children came back to get another fish, or their parents bought inexpensive little aquarium accessories. When that family felt ready to get a different pet, they frequently came back to Whiskers, Wings, and Wags because they were familiar with it. Vanessa smiled to herself. Nathan and Jeff were the record holders for the shortest turnaround time.

Van polished a few fingerprints off the front of the last glass-fronted tank and watched the fish dart around. No doubt Jeff would want to know why she didn't stock sea urchins, sea stars, and hermit crabs. Under her breath, she murmured, "Nathan, your kid is as cute as you are."

☧

Sunday morning, Nathan set out cereal and grabbed a banana for Jeff. It was the last one—good thing, too. It had reached the eat-now-or-toss-it stage. They needed to do some grocery shopping. Nathan would rather haggle with a city inspector over a building variance than walk the aisles of the grocery store. Jeff always wanted to buy all the junk food he'd seen advertised. Invariably, Nathan would skip a row or two just to get out of the place faster, only to stand at the register and remember something he needed and hadn't seen.

There were times when he thought about asking Consuelo if she'd take on the grocery shopping and cook suppers, but that went against one of the lessons he wanted to teach Jeff. A man could get some help with a few things—even delegate—but overall it was important to be capable of coping with issues. Someday his son would have to face life on his own. Nathan knew he needed to equip Jeff with skills like shopping and, well, basic stuff like opening cans and nuking frozen junk in a microwave.

He took a swig from his mug and made a wry face. The aroma barely qualified as coffee, and the taste didn't. He'd used the last few grounds from the bottom of the can to make this pot. He scribbled "coffee" on the shopping list and underlined it.

"Sport, turn off those cartoons and come eat. We've got stuff to do today."

"We do?" Jeff had been lying on the floor next to Lick, watching TV. He stood and pushed the off button.

"Yeah. I'm gonna hop in the shower. I already poured milk on your cereal, so it'll get mushy if you don't eat it right away."

Nathan walked up the stairs and climbed into the shower. As he scrubbed, he made a mental list of other things he'd forgotten to put on the grocery list. He'd yanked up his jeans when Jeff traipsed in, covered from neck to toes with mud. "What happened to you?"

"Lick wanted out. You told me to be sure to let him out right away any time he wanted to go so he wouldn't have any accidents."

"I fenced off the dirt in the backyard, though." As he spoke, Nathan stripped Jeff out of his clothes and shoved him into the shower.

Jeff's scrawny little chest puffed out with pride. "Lick wanted to go out the front door."

"You didn't—"

"He was really good, Dad. He did his business, and when he started to run away, I called 'Come!' to him, just like Van told me to. He turned around and came right away."

"Let me guess: The living room is as muddy as you are."

"Nope." His grin took on a decidedly cocky flair. "I helped Lick wipe off his paws on the doormat."

"Judging from your clothes, he thought you were the doormat. Clean all of that off."

As his son showered, Nathan finished dressing and tossed the muddy clothes into his hamper. Consuelo did laundry—a chore for which he happily paid her extra. She'd definitely earn her money with that load. Nathan knew she wouldn't bat an eye at it. The clothes he wore to construction sites often came back equally gritty.

Thank God for Consuelo.

He stopped dead in his tracks. He couldn't remember the last time he'd actually been thankful to the Lord. In this case, he had to confess, it was a heartfelt emotion. Without her, he wouldn't have made it through the last five years.

"Dad?"

"What, sport?"

"It's Sunday, right?"

"Yep." He dabbed a glob of toothpaste on his brush, started to work on his molars, and froze. He caught sight of Jeff in the bathroom mirror. His son had pulled back the shower curtain and looked at him with hope shining in his big brown eyes.

"Can I go to Sunday school?"

Slowly Nathan pulled the toothbrush from his mouth. He spat in the sink, then turned around. "You already went to Sunday school last week."

"Unh-huh. It was fun."

"Why do the same thing again?" He hoped he sounded casual. This wasn't in his plan. He'd thought it would be a one-shot deal, then Jeff would latch onto some other activity. Normally, he grew distracted or bored and moved on to a new thing.

"We're going to the tide pools again. You told me we'd see different creatures. The Sunday school teacher told me they hear a new story every week, so it'll be different there, too."

Miscalculated on that score, Adams. Now what're you gonna do?

"Listen, sport—I thought maybe we'd go out for—"

"Lunch with Vanessa and her family again? Yippee!" Jeff disappeared behind the shower curtain.

Nathan turned back to the sink and ordered, "Wash behind your ears." He looked at his reflection. A thin line of toothpaste outlined the center of his lower lip. Deep, harsh grooves bracketed his mouth. *What have I gotten myself into?*

Chapter 16

Nathan sat in the sanctuary and thumbed the edge of the bulletin. Jeff was so excited about going to Sunday school, he'd gotten ready in record time, and they'd arrived a bit early. Nathan sat in the same pew he'd occupied last week. He hoped Van wouldn't be in the choir today. She could sit next to him and make it so he didn't feel quite so lonely or out of place.

Last week, the organ music had made the hair on the back of his neck prickle. Today, the softly played hymn flowed over his nerves. It fit his mood like his favorite hammer just kind of fit in his hand when he was working on a project around the house.

The bulletin featured the morning's hymns and scripture, then had another segment, LOOKING FORWARD. It listed all the upcoming activities and events. He smiled as he noticed the last ball game of the season was listed. A plea for tools and willing hands for building a church in Mexico piqued his interest a little. *What am I thinking? I didn't even want to go to church. Why would I get involved in a project like that?* He swiftly turned the bulletin over.

LOOKING AROUND mentioned a birth, a wedding, and the names of those who were or had been in the hospital. Fair enough. It was nice to see this place really functioned like a cohesive church family—really caring for its own.

There was one last little section, LOOKING BACK. It simply asked, "How was your walk this week?"

Nathan drew in a sharp breath. He set aside the bulletin and wished he hadn't read those words. *How was my walk? My walk? God, I'm the walking wounded.* He bowed his head in weariness. *This week.* The last two words of the question echoed in his mind. This week? This week had gone better than. . .well, than since he'd torn out of church five years ago. The realization stopped him cold. It really had been a better week. Less empty. Not the same struggle. But why? What had made the difference?

"Nice to see you here, Adams."

Nathan looked to the side and stood at once. He shook hands with Bill Zobel and glanced down at Amber. "What happened? You're missing all but one of your gals."

"Ellen volunteers in the nursery once a month. Val is working this weekend. Someone at work is sick, so she's been putting in a lot of extra days and overtime."

"That's a bummer." He tried to sound casual and fought the urge to look around. "What about Vanessa?"

"She'll be here in a minute. She made cupcakes for a bake sale, and I'd rather baby-sit Amber than carry a tray of food. I'd either accidentally dump it on someone or eat half of them before I reached the kitchen."

"You have more self-control than I do, because I've tasted her cupcakes. I'd have eaten all of them." The small talk wasn't exactly difficult, but Nathan knew he didn't measure up to Bill's dreams for his daughter's future husband. Granted, Bill behaved more than just cordially. Vanessa must have inherited her friendly, outgoing nature from him. Even so, there was a world of difference between accepting someone as a friend and welcoming him as the man who was dating your daughter.

Nathan wanted to sit at the edge of the pew so he could simply scoot over to allow Van to take that place and be close to Amber. With Bill standing there, he'd have to scoot in farther and have Bill sit between them. *It's probably exactly what he wants.*

"Your boy liked Chinese last Sunday. How do the two of you do with Italian?"

"I love it; Jeff wears it." Nathan grinned. "You saw him with the chow mein noodles last week. He's worse with spaghetti."

Bill chuckled. "How 'bout we all go out to Ruffino's for lunch?"

"Sounds good."

"I pick up the tab this time."

"Hi, guys!" Vanessa slipped up and gave her dad a hug.

It was a sweet sight. Vanessa was an affectionate woman, and her warmth never seemed out of place or forced. The way she acted around her family made Nathan think of how long it had been since he'd been on the receiving end of any such fondness. Sure, Jeff and he hugged and wrestled around—but the sentimentality a woman put into a hug—that was different. How would it feel to wrap his arms around Vanessa and have her put her arms back around him? To hold and be held—even for a fleeting moment? Five long years of not wanting any such contact ended abruptly, and the realization shook him. *Being in church really has me off balance.*

"Did I hear you say something about Ruffino's? I can already taste the veal scallopini."

"Songs and sermon before the scallopini." Bill pushed her closer to Nathan and glanced at his watch. "I forgot to sign up for the men's pancake prayer breakfast. I'm going to duck back and do that before the service starts. I'd be happy to have you as my guest, Nathan. It's Wednesday. What do you say?"

Nathan thought for a moment, then pulled a small Palm computer from his pocket to check on a date. "I have a site inspection Wednesday morning." He felt an unexpected twinge of regret and paused for a second before proposing, "Maybe another time?"

"I'll hold you to that."

☥

Vanessa hummed all afternoon at the pet shop. *He came to church today! Two weeks in a row, he's come and heard the Word. Lord, please do a mighty work in Nathan's heart. There used to be a bitterness about him, but now there's just a sadness. Leech away the grief and pour Your love out on him.*

The bell at the door chimed. Patsy Dinnit zipped into the shop with her pedigreed Border collie on a hot pink, rhinestone-studded leash. "Van! Jazzy's going to have a litter. Do you want to take the puppies on commission again?"

"Amber, stay." Vanessa left her and went around to the other side of the counter. Amber normally did well around other dogs, but Jazzy tended to act high-strung when she carried a litter.

Stooping to give Jazzy a couple of strokes, Van asked, "Did you use the same sire? The last litter was gorgeous."

"Sure did! Sire's owner would get pick of the litter, but you can have all of the rest. I'll do an even split on the proceeds with you again."

"Let me grab my calendar and see what I have booked. When is she due?"

"In about four weeks."

Vanessa went back to the register. "Good girl." She patted Amber and reached for her calendar. "That would make it about the twenty-eighth, give or take a few days." She then flipped two pages. "If I take them when they're about eight weeks, that'll be in August. I have dachshunds and Labs coming in about the same time. That'll be a nice variety."

A secretive smile lit Patsy's face. She looked this way and that, then whispered, "Jazzy's not the only one who's expecting."

"Patsy! Really? How wonderful!"

"You have no idea what a miracle it is. Hugo and I have been trying to have a baby for almost four years. I'm so excited, I can hardly stand it. I haven't said a word to anyone until today. We went and had an ultrasound Friday. Wanna see the picture?"

"I'd love to! When are you due?"

"January second. Hugo is already talking to the baby. Last night, he tapped my belly and told the kid to come early so we'd have a tax deduction!"

"Oh, no!" Vanessa giggled. "It's a good thing Hugo and Val didn't fall in love and get married. They're both so into business and accounting, they'd breed a whole tribe of bean counters."

Patsy gave an exaggerated wince. "They'd name them Lima and Chili."

"Those beans have some class. I was thinking more along the line of Jelly—can't you see it now?" Vanessa spread her hands in the air like she was holding up a banner. "Jelly Dinnit."

Patsy gave her a mock look of hurt and rubbed her still-flat tummy. "How could you say such a thing? I planned for something more affectionate. . .Sugar. Sugar Dinnit."

"I just finished lunch, but this is making me hungry!"

"I saw you go into Ruffino's with that gorgeous hunk. Who is he? He was at church last week, too. You work fast, girl!"

"He's just a friend. We met my family there. I sold him a dog, and he's taking obedience training."

"He is, or the dog?" Patsy gave her an impish wink.

Vanessa waggled her forefinger at Patsy. "Your husband is going to have his hands full if this baby is half as spunky as you are."

"You're calling me spunky? Ha! Now you—your kids are going to be balls of fire."

"Predictions like that are enough to make me stay a spinster."

"Not a chance. That guy—you and he are going to be an item. I can feel it in my bones. Mark my words: In a few months, you're going to be gliding down the aisle."

"Me? Glide? Only if I were on a skateboard. You're mixing me up with Val. She'll glide, for sure. If you see me going down the aisle, it'll be in a bridesmaid's gown."

"Nope. You're not going to dissuade me. It's my vision, and the groom was that fine-looking man you sat next to in church."

"You know. . ." Vanessa tapped her cheek and looked at the ceiling, as if lost in important thoughts. "I seem to recall prophets who are wrong are put to death. You're so wrong about any entanglement there, it's downright dangerous."

Patsy giggled and dug through her purse for the picture of the ultrasound. "Look at this. This is a miracle."

Vanessa turned it around and looked at the wedge-shaped picture. "Amazing. Just amazing. Look! I can make out his profile! Is it a him or a her?"

"We told them not to tell us. It's so delicious, just knowing we're having a baby. I like leaving that secret in God's hands until He puts this baby in ours."

"Oh, yes. Like Psalm 139 talks about Him creating us in our mother's womb. I'm so thrilled for you. What a blessing."

Patsy agreed and carefully tucked away the ultrasound picture. She smiled. "That is my blessing and good news. I'm standing by what I said earlier, though. Go ahead and call it dangerous thinking, but I'm sure you and that guy are going to be an item."

Patsy left, and Vanessa looked down at Amber. "Dangerous. Even thinking Nathan could ever change and find me attractive is so far from possible, I'd be a fool to waste my time considering it." She turned and saw her reflection in the shopwindow. *Am I looking at a fool?*

⚘

The alarm clock went off, and Nathan groaned. He'd been lying awake for the last twenty minutes, hoping the rain would stop. Instead, it kept falling. If anything at all, it seemed to be intensifying. There was no way they could go to the tide pools in this kind of weather. Reluctantly, he picked up the phone and dialed.

" 'Lo?"

"Hey, sleepyhead, it's raining."

"You woke me up to give a weather report?"

"We won't be able to go to the tide pools." He sat up and stacked several coins on his bedside table. Jeff would come in and swipe them. He loved to plink the dimes, nickels, and pennies into the enormous, multicolored plastic dinosaur-egg bank in the corner of his bedroom.

"Nathan Adams," Vanessa moaned over the phone, "you are rotten to the core. Cruel. Mean. There probably isn't a person on the face of the earth more vile than you." Her bed squeaked, and her blankets made a loud ruffling noise, tattling that she'd rolled over.

He smiled at how zany, impulsive Van could be so predictable about this one particular aspect of life. She'd been more than honest when she confessed she wasn't a morning person. "Need another minute to wake up?"

"Wake up? Why?" She yawned. "I'm going right back to sleep as soon as I tell you how barbaric you are to dare calling me at this ridiculous hour."

"Come on, Van. You can't be mad."

She yawned again—a long, luxurious, stretched sound that let him know she could easily shut her eyes and coast right back off.

"You were going to wake up now, anyway," he wheedled shamelessly.

"Not really. I had it all planned out. I'd get dressed, sleep in your car, and sleepwalk on the beach. Amber would rescue me if I accidentally walked into the surf."

"Don't forget that plan. We'll put it into play some other day." Nathan swept the quarters into the jar beside his bed for the once-a-month pilgrimage he and Jeff took to an arcade. The arcade! His heart galloped in anticipation. He'd come up with a great substitute for them. "I have an alternative plan for the day."

"It better start with, 'Van, sleep in 'til noon.' "

"Eight."

"Eleven." Her voice still sounded husky with sleep.

"Nine, and you still get hot chocolate."

Vanessa muttered something unintelligible and hung up the phone.

"Dad?" Jeff stood in the doorway, curling his toes on the cold, hardwood floor. "You promised we'd go to the tide pools again to see the sea creatures today."

Nathan opened his arms, and Jeff scampered across the room and launched into a hug. Nathan held his son, rubbed his bristly cheek in Jeff's sleep-mussed hair, and growled like a bear.

Jeff giggled and wrapped his arms as far around Nathan's chest as they'd reach. He paused a second, then asked in a sad tone, "Papa Bear, what're we gonna do? Vanessa and Amber wanted to go to the beach with us."

"I know you're disappointed, but I have a plan. . . ."

Chapter 17

I t's raining, it's pouring, the old man is snoring."

Vanessa stared at Nathan and Jeff as they stood on her doorstep. She yanked them through her door. "Are the two of you crazy? Standing in the rain, singing. . ."

She paused, then huffed, "Without me? Seriously. I'm hurt."

Nathan closed his huge black-and-gray-striped golf umbrella with a loud snap. Jeff continued to sing as water dripped off his bright yellow slicker. He fiddled with one of the fasteners. " 'Nessa, d'you know that song?"

"Yep. Val and I used to sing it when we were little. I forgot all about it." She looked at Nathan and frowned. A water-splattered plastic grocery bag hung from the crook of his elbow. "What is that?"

"Your hot chocolate, madame." He opened the bag and pulled out a carton of chocolate milk with a flourish.

"Nathan, I hate to break it to you, but that isn't hot."

He gave her a supercilious look. "Not yet, it isn't. My faithful sidekick, Master Jeffrey, will assist me in the delicate operation of preparing it for you." He helped Jeff peel out of his slicker and cleared his throat. "Come along, young man. We have serious work to do."

"Oh, boy. This I've gotta see." Vanessa tagged along behind them as they headed into her kitchen.

"Pop fly!" Nathan picked up his son and sat him on the kitchen counter.

"Pop fly?" Vanessa echoed. "How'd you come up with that saying?"

"It's from baseball, silly," Jeff said.

"And I'm his pop, and I made him fly." Nathan opened a cupboard, shook his head, and shut it.

Vanessa didn't say a word. She backed against the counter on the far side of the kitchen so she'd be out of the way and still have a bird's-eye view of the goings-on. Nathan opened the next cupboard and shot her a quick look over his shoulder. "Wow, this is impressive. Even if we hadn't tasted some of your goodies already, all of this junk in here tells me you make more than just cupcakes on a pretty regular basis."

She shrugged. "I like to bake."

"I like to eat!" Jeff gave her a greedy smile.

Nathan's smile matched it perfectly. "Me, too! Especially your stuff. We're willing to sacrifice our taste buds and stomachs to the cause anytime."

"I'll keep that in mind."

The third cupboard held the coffee mugs Nathan wanted. He pulled out the first one with a wave worthy of a game-show host. "Ta da!"

"You didn't have to search. I could have just told you where they were."

"Oh, but this is an adventure, and Master Jeffrey and I are sleuths."

"I hate to break the news, but sleuths are for mysteries, not adventures."

Vanessa watched Nathan get out more mugs and unbutton the sleeves of his tan-and-green plaid flannel shirt. He methodically rolled up those sleeves, revealing muscular forearms. He then did the same thing to the sleeves on Jeff's little blue denim shirt. He made quite a production of it, as if they were about to make a seven-course gourmet meal instead of heat up chocolate milk. Vanessa couldn't decide whether the show was for her or for Jeff. Either way, she enjoyed every last second.

Nathan scrounged up a saucepan, set it on the range, then ordered, "Son, find a spoon. I'll need to stir this."

Jeff turned onto his belly on the counter, reached over the edge, and jerked open the drawer. The silverware in it jangled. "Dad, do you want a big spoon or a little spoon?"

"A little one," Nathan said as he wrestled with the milk carton. It didn't open neatly. Instead, the waxed cardboard wouldn't separate, so he scowled at the carton as if his dark look would make it cooperate.

Vanessa watched the whole process with nothing short of delight. *I would have gotten up at six for this show. This is a riot.*

Nathan gave up on the first side of the milk carton and attacked the other side. It yielded.

Probably out of fear.

He poured the chocolate milk into the saucepan and dumped the mangled carton into the trash with more emphasis than the poor thing deserved. When Nathan turned back around, he gave Jeff a blank stare. "What is that?"

"A little spoon."

Vanessa bit the inside of her lip to keep from laughing as Jeff held out the quarter teaspoon from a set of measuring spoons that had gotten separated.

"When we look in my toolbox, you know how I have the great big mallet, and I have the regular hammers, then I have that skinny, little finishing hammer?"

"Dad, you're not going to stir the hot chocolate with a hammer, are you?"

Vanessa started laughing.

Nathan shot her a disgruntled look, then suddenly perked up. "Yes, sport, I am. See?" He took two strides, came close enough to Vanessa for her to inhale his expensive, spicy aftershave, and reached around her. He snagged her meat-tenderizing mallet and nodded. Holding it high, he declared, "Always be sure to use the right tool for the job, Jeff."

Humor mingled with disbelief as Vanessa watched Nathan hold on to the business end of the mallet, dunk the handle into the saucepan, and proceed to stir. She had to give him credit. He'd managed to recover pretty smoothly.

"Dad, what am I s'posed to do with this little spoon?"

"Yeah, Nathan," she chimed in. "What's that bitsy spoon for?"

"That is. . ." He paused for a split second. "The tasting spoon. Yes, the tasting spoon. Whoever holds the tasting spoon has the important job of deciding when the hot chocolate is ready."

Vanessa dug out three mismatched party napkins from the pantry and put them on the table. Soon Nathan set the cups of steaming cocoa on the table. He dumped a telephone book onto a chair to act as a booster seat for Jeff, and they were ready. The rich scent of hot chocolate filled the air, and Vanessa curled her fingers around the mug. She stopped short when Jeff drummed his fingers on the table.

"Aren't we gonna say a prayer?"

✝

Nathan froze. He hadn't seen that coming, but he should have. Vanessa always took a moment to pray. For the past two Sundays, her father had prayed over the lunches. A man should be the spiritual head of the home. . .the adage went through his mind. *It's not my home,* he tried to reason, but that excuse sounded pathetic. There had once been a time when speaking to the Lord came so naturally, so freely. Now here he sat, mute.

"When I was a little girl," Vanessa said to Jeff, "I learned some prayers. Maybe you'd like to learn one of them. You can say the words after me."

"That's a good idea." Nathan breathed a silent sigh of relief. Listening to Jeff's pure voice repeat each phrase after Vanessa did something odd to Nathan. *Evie would have wanted this. She wanted our son to grow up in the Lord. She wanted me to fall in love again and live a full life. How many times did she tell me that? I didn't believe her. I refused to listen because I couldn't bear to think of going on without her—but I have. I've had to, mostly for Jeff. But now I want to for me. Thank you, Evie, for being so sweet to give me your blessing to move on. Had you known Vanessa, you would have been good friends.*

In those moments, Nathan sensed a momentous shift. He had a past, but he wanted a future. For five long years, he'd not looked ahead. Now he saw a bridge in the guise of a simple child's prayer.

Am I using God and religion as a way of making it acceptable to court and love Vanessa? I've done nothing but shake my fist in God's face for five years. Now, suddenly,

I'm going to do this turnabout? How convenient is that? Is this a matter of my heart or of my soul?

"Da—ad. You're not listening."

"What?" Nathan snapped out of his contemplation.

"I asked you when you were going to tell Van about where we're going."

"If Van is willing to watch you, I'm going to Mexico."

"What about the arcade, Dad? I wanna play games!"

Nathan looked at Vanessa. "We'll play at the arcade today, but if that hammer in Vanessa's kitchen is anything like the ones going to Mexico, that team needs a lot of help to build that church."

"Why can't I go with you?"

"It's a school week." Nathan took a gulp of hot cocoa. He needed to get away to think. Vanessa needed time to be with Jeff to see if they could get along well for more than just a day at a time.

A short while later, while Jeff smacked buttons on a blaring machine at the arcade and Amber sat patiently at Vanessa's side, Nathan apologized. "I should have asked you privately about watching Jeff instead of blurting it out like that. If you'd rather not, I'll understand."

She shrugged a shoulder and laughed self-consciously. "Oh—I'm happy to watch him. He's a lot of fun. I was trying to find a way of suggesting it might be easier if I stayed at your place with him than bringing Lick to mine."

"You wouldn't mind?"

"Why should I?"

"It's closer to the school, but it'll be farther for you to get to and from work."

She hitched the strap of her purse up onto her shoulder. "I'm glad you're going to go. The team needs guys like you who know what they're doing. You have a lot of talent. It's generous of you to want to use it for G—" She caught herself. "For others."

Nathan slid his hand over hers and laced their fingers. Her eyes widened as Nathan said, "I need a chance to do some soul-searching and thinking."

"I got hundreds of points and this many tickets on that game!" Jeff half shouted the words and intruded on the moment. He stood before them and held up a long trail of pale blue raffle-like tickets the arcade machine spit out. "I wanna get so many, I can get something really cool."

"Oh, is that so?" Vanessa broke away and rose. "I'm lethal on Uranium Thief."

"Can I play you? Can I?"

"You'd better. I'd be horribly disappointed to come all of the way here with you and not get a chance to razzle-dazzle you with my ability."

"Oh, brother," Nathan scoffed. "Jeff, can you believe her? She really thinks she knows what she's doing, but she doesn't know who she's playing against."

Vanessa's chin went up at a stubborn tilt. "I challenge you here and now—and if I get to the third level before you, you have to eat a fried pickle."

"A fried pickle?" Nathan and Jeff said together.

Vanessa dusted her hands together. "A fried pickle. Now prepare for doom. You're about to wish you'd never brought me along today."

"Even if I have to eat a fried pickle, I won't feel doomed." Nathan looked at her intently. "I'd never be glad that you hadn't come along."

Chapter 18

Twenty-eight dollars?" Vanessa twisted in the seat and gave Nathan an appalled look. "We wasted twenty-eight dollars at the arcade?"

"It wasn't a waste, Vanessa. We had a good time, didn't we?"

"And look at all of the good stuff I earned!" Jeff sat in the middle of the backseat like Midas in the center of his golden treasures. He'd spent half of forever choosing bouncy balls, slink chains, squirt guns, a magnifying glass, crazy sunglasses, candy, and half a dozen other assorted "prizes" with the tickets he'd earned from the arcade machines. Had they gone to a five-and-dime, he could have bought all of it for five bucks, max. Nevertheless, they'd had fun, and his pride made it all worthwhile.

"Sport, here's that big, big bridge."

"Are we going on it? Really?"

"No kidding."

Jeff sat a little straighter and craned to look out over the very edge of the bridge.

The railing came up so high that Vanessa could barely see over it part of the time. The Coronado Bridge in San Diego swept in a huge, graceful, sideways arc. It boasted such height, military vessels passed under it with ease. This kind of height gave her a sense of freedom. She tried to concentrate on looking as far out at whatever horizon she could spot through the drizzle. Due to the weather, there wasn't the usual abundance of sailboats out.

Charming, little old houses covered the island. Well-manicured lawns and nicely sculpted shrubs reflected the orderly community of military officers and understated wealthy citizens. Vanessa watched a cat streak across a lawn and shoot up a tree.

"Oh! I was so busy gawking, I didn't notice we passed the restaurant. I'm sorry, Nathan. It was on the left back there."

He gave her a startled look. "You're serious."

"Of course I am. I blew it."

"No problem—that can happen to anyone. I meant, you're serious about that restaurant—that it has fried pickles!"

She bobbed her head. "And you two are going to eat them. I got to level three first."

Nathan pulled into a parking lot. Vanessa wrinkled her nose. "What are we doing here?"

"Getting antacids. If I have to eat a fried pickle, I want something to rescue my stomach afterward."

"Hey! Don't knock it until you've tried it!"

"Ever hear of 'an ounce of prevention'? Well, I'm subscribing to that theory." Nathan opened his door. "I'll be back in a sec."

Ten minutes later, he emerged from the drugstore. He carried a big paper sack and stuck it between the two front seats. Vanessa peeped inside and let out a disbelieving laugh.

At least a full-dozen bottles of pink liquid jumbled in the bag.

"If you don't want to eat the fried pickles, just say so. You didn't have to buy out the store."

He snapped his seat belt and hitched his shoulder. "I figured we'd need it for the Mexico trip. Two for one."

"You're a bargain shopper? Who woulda thunk it?"

"Bargain? Me? You've got to be kidding. I'm not talking about a sale. I'm saying I'm killing two birds with one stone—the pickles and the trip."

Ten minutes later, seated in the Red Oak Steakhouse, Jeff repeated the prayer after Vanessa said each line. Just before she said, "Amen," he blurted out, "And God, please don't let Daddy kill those birds. Amen."

"What birds, son?"

Jeff gave his father a sad look. "The ones on your trip that you wanna throw rocks at."

"It's just a saying, sport. It means taking care of two things at the same time."

"Oh."

Vanessa gave Jeff's hand a reassuring squeeze. "But you were right. You can pray about anything that bothers you. I do, and it makes me feel better."

Vanessa saw emotion flare in Nathan's eyes, but she couldn't interpret it.

"Your mom did that, too," he said quietly to Jeff. "She talked to God about all sorts of things."

The food came, and Jeff practically dove across the table. "I wanna try the pickle!"

Vanessa arranged the napkin in her lap and avoided looking at Nathan. Had she gone too far? Spoken when she should have held her tongue? Opened the door to his grief again? Being torn between living for Christ and being sensitive to Nathan's limits was like being stuck between third base and home—she was in a pickle, all right.

✝

Nathan didn't want the day to end. More to the point, he didn't want his time with Vanessa to be over. After lunch, he decided they ought to take in a movie. They'd just missed the beginning, so to burn up time until the next showing, he drove to the huge, red-roofed Hotel del Coronado. "Why don't we wander and gawk? This old place is fascinating."

"I need to stop at the desk and make sure they're okay with Amber on the premises."

"I'll drive up to the front, then." He pulled up to the entrance of the white main building, and a bellhop immediately opened Vanessa's door.

"I'll only be a minute." She hopped out, and Amber started to follow. "Amber, stay."

When Vanessa slipped inside, Nathan reached down and petted the dog. "She'll be right back."

Indeed Vanessa came right back out. A gust of wind blew her hair into wild disarray, but Nathan could see her laugh in delight rather than become upset. She found so much joy in simple things. He loved that about her. She ducked her head into the car. "They're fine with Amber as long as I have the training jacket and gentle leader on her. How about if Jeff and Amber stay with me while you park? That way we won't have wet fur and a soggy boy?"

Nathan looked beyond the portico at the gloomy drizzle and shook his head. As he scooted out of the car, he said, "I'll just have them valet park. That way, we'll all stay dry, and we'll be able to get back to the theater on time."

They entered the lobby, and Vanessa started to giggle. Nathan gave her a questioning look. "What's come over you?"

"The valet is going to see all of those bottles you bought at the drugstore and think I'm the world's worst cook!"

"You're a good cook, Van," Jeff piped up. "I like the stuff you make, and you know how to make lotsa different junk. Dad's a pretty good cook, too. He makes terrific hot chocolate!"

"Sport, you need to use your indoor voice." Nathan looked around. "So where do you want to go first?"

Vanessa looked around. "We can go downstairs and wander through a few shops. If it's not raining, we can peek at the swimming pool."

Nathan nodded toward one of the antique elevators. Its metal grillwork carried the grace of a bygone era. "They sure don't make beauties like that anymore. Should we give Amber a chance to ride?"

"Amber?" Jeff looked crestfallen. "What about me?"

Vanessa leaned down. "You get to be the tail guard. You come along and make sure her tail doesn't get caught in the door. That's an important job."

They spent a leisurely hour-and-a-half wandering around. Jeff kept twisting around to check on Amber's tail. "You're a responsible little guy," Vanessa praised.

When they got into the theater, Nathan used a small penlight he'd brought in from his glove compartment to illuminate the floor. They found a spot that didn't have any spilled soda or popcorn, and Amber curled up. Vanessa took her seat, and to Nathan's dismay, Jeff hopped into the seat right next to her. He thought about picking the boy up and plopping him down in the next seat over. That way, Nathan could slip his hand over and hold Vanessa's hand during the movie. . .or he could put his arm around her shoulders.

"No, that's not a good idea."

Nathan turned his head sharply. One of the men from the ball team held a flimsy cardboard tray laden with popcorn and drinks. He was trying to get four kids settled in and keep them from grabbing a drink all at the same time.

Nathan extended his arm and shored up the bottom of the tray. "You're about to lose the battle."

Doug groaned. "Thanks. Janey's mom and sister are in town. I volunteered to take all of the kids for the day—but that was when we had a clear weather report." He spied Vanessa and gave Nathan a keen look.

Nathan ignored it. "Hope you enjoy the movie." He sat down. Had he needed to give a review of the movie, he'd be sunk. The whole time it played, Nathan tried to sort out his thoughts. He liked her. . .as more than just a friend. Somewhere along the way, she'd burrowed into his heart and made him start to face life again. He wanted her to be an integral part of that life. As the movie flickered on the screen, Nathan didn't even follow the plot. He came to the rock-solid conclusion that he wanted to make their relationship a public thing. . .and hopefully a very private thing, too.

But wanting wasn't enough. Vanessa deserved someone who shared the joy and innocence of her beliefs, and Nathan didn't know if he could ever again be the man of faith he'd once been. Amber had howled during that hymn "It Is Well with My Soul," but Nathan had to admit, *It still isn't well with my soul.*

🕆

Two weeks later, Kip came into the pet shop. "Valene said you're going to watch Jeff so Nathan can go with the Mexico work-and-witness team. Knowing how clear he's been about not wanting to be involved with the church, I thought she got things mixed up. I couldn't imagine him hanging out with a bunch of us, building a sanctuary, of all things, but I just stopped by Seaside and got the paperwork. I'm sharing a tent with Nathan."

Vanessa stayed on her knees on the hard linoleum floor. She'd started cleaning the birdcages, and when she put the latest sheet of newspaper in the tray to line this one, she'd spotted the comic strips and had taken a moment to enjoy them.

Kip squatted down next to her. "Van, this isn't funny. I'm worried about you."

"You don't think I can handle Jeff and Lick for a week?"

"Stop it right there. You can play games and tease other people into changing a subject, but I know you too well to get sidetracked. You're losing your heart to Nathan." He held up a hand to keep Van from responding. "Don't bother to deny it or make excuses. It's a fact. The question is: What are you going to do about it?"

"Pray."

"That's a good first step. What about exercising some wisdom?"

Vanessa stared at Kip. He was known for being brutally honest at times. She had the sinking sensation she was about to get an earful. "I'm not going to pretend I'm at peace with everything, Kip. I'm being honest with God."

"But are you able to be honest with Him when you're not being honest with yourself?" He smacked his thigh in impatience. "I'm partially to blame. I told you to pursue the relationship because I hoped you might be the Lord's emissary to bring Nathan back into relationship with Him."

"You're not to blame, Kip. It's not that kind of situation at all. Since we're shooting straight from the hip, here's the truth: I really care for Nathan—as a friend and as a man. Until he can get over his grief and reestablish his relationship with the Lord, I know I can't let the relationship go any further."

"This whole thing bothers me a lot. Don't tell me you don't feel any hesitance, because you have to. Deep in your heart, you have to know God would want you to put a brake on this before it rolls into dangerous territory."

Vanessa slid the tray back into the birdcage. "I was reading Philippians 4 today." She sat on the floor and quoted, " 'Let your gentle spirit be known to all men. The Lord is near. Be anxious for nothing, but in everything by prayer and supplication with thanksgiving let your requests be made known to God. And the peace of God, which surpasses all comprehension, will guard your hearts and your minds in Christ Jesus.' " She let out a prolonged sigh. "I have to trust the Lord with this. I need to be patient about His timing and believe that He'll guard my heart."

"Don't stop there. What about verses eight and nine?" He locked eyes with her and quoted, " 'Finally, brethren, whatever is true, whatever is honorable, whatever is right, whatever is pure, whatever is lovely, whatever is of good repute, if there is any excellence and if anything worthy of praise, dwell on these things. The things you have learned and received and heard and seen in me, practice these things, and the God of peace will be with you.' "

She waited. Tension sang between them.

"It's not right, and you know it isn't," Kip finally insisted. "Nathan hasn't renounced the Lord, but he's miles away from a strong walk. You're not feeling peace, and I think you need to reflect on it, because the Holy Spirit may be telling you to back off."

They both stood. Kip shook his head sadly. He reached over and cupped her cheek. "There was a time when I thought maybe you and I might make a go of things. I've always loved your sparkle and wit. I've accepted I won't ever be the man for you. You and Nathan have a special chemistry folks talk about that I've never really seen in action. I often struggle to tell you and Val apart when you're together; blindfolded, even as short a time as he's known you, he could figure out which one you are. I hoped maybe it was just infatuation and your family would step in and make you see the truth. I've probably put my foot in my mouth here, and you'll likely chalk all of this up to a wild, jealous rant. It's not, though. Van, as a brother in Christ—and I know that's all I'll ever be—I felt compelled to speak the truth."

He patted her cheek, then pressed a chaste kiss on her forehead and walked out of the shop. The bell chimed over the door, and for once, its cheery noise seemed dreadfully out of place.

Chapter 19

Nathan stomped a few times and methodically dusted off his shirt front, sleeves, and the seat of his jeans before ducking into the tent. He was sore, dirty, and tired. He hadn't felt half as good in years.

"The place is really coming together," Kip said as he lounged on his sleeping bag. "We ought to be able to get the roof up tomorrow."

Nathan nodded. He rummaged through one of the athletic bags he'd brought, then pulled out a pair of granola bars. He tossed one at Kip. "I'm too hungry to wait for supper."

"I could eat the hind legs off a running buck." Kip chuckled as he peeled back the wrapper. "Who am I kidding? I'm getting so stiff, I couldn't catch a centipede."

"No more than anyone else."

Kip shook his head. "I was hoping playing ball would help get me back in shape. After all of that waiting at the hospital or sitting in a desk chair, I was pathetic."

"What were you at the hospital for?"

Kip set aside the Bible he'd been reading. "That was dumb of me. 'Course you wouldn't know. My sister had leukemia. She had a bone marrow transplant last year." He grinned. "She's doing great now."

"Wow. Bet your family feels pretty lucky."

"Blessed is a better word for it." He stretched and winced.

Nathan didn't say anything. For the past four nights, he'd stayed in the area after dinner for Bible study or fellowship. Around the fire they built in a big pit, they shared and spoke of life's disappointments and joys, of how God gave them strength in the hard times.

He'd learned Harriet, who was cooking all of their meals, normally took care of her mother with advanced Alzheimer's. Pete and Lily had a daughter who was away at cystic fibrosis camp. Hugo left Patsy at home, rejoicing in her pregnancy after they'd struggled in silence through several years of infertility. Ben's teenaged son was addicted to drugs.

Heartaches. Everyone had them. A little voice whispered, *"But they turn to Me."*

Kip grabbed a cell phone and toggled it in the air. "I'm due to check in with the folks back home."

"I just called home myself. Everything is fine."

"That's always good news. See you at chow." Kip left the tent.

Nathan looked at the Bible Kip had left behind. He'd brought his own. He hadn't read it in years. At first, it sat on the coffee table, but he'd moved it to the dresser, then finally tucked it in a drawer. Out of sight, out of mind. While packing for this trip, he'd tucked it in with his gear. He hadn't had the courage to open it. Steeling himself, he pulled it out of his bag.

The unusually thick latigo cover still felt supple in his hands. Sturdy. Enduring. *Unlike my faith.* He opened it up and braced himself for the pain. It didn't come. Instead, he traced the lettering inside with a wash of gentle feelings.

With all the love God has given me for you, Evie.

She'd given it to him the Christmas they were engaged. She'd fretted because the lettering went uphill slightly. He'd found it endearing. He'd told her it represented how they'd always look up.

But I didn't. To the end, Evie clung to her faith. Me? I railed at God, then hid away from Him.

He thumbed through the gilt-edged pages. . .many marked with sermon notes or comments. The faded purple ribbon placemarker lay with an odd twisted quirk at the center of Psalm 139.

"Where can I go from Your Spirit? Or where can I flee from Your presence? If I ascend to heaven, You are there. If I make my bed in Sheol, behold, You are there. If I take the wings of the dawn, if I dwell in the remotest part of the sea, even there Your hand will lead me, and Your right hand will lay hold of me. If I say, 'Surely the darkness will overwhelm me, and the light around me will be night,' even the darkness is not dark to You, and the night is as bright as the day. Darkness and light are alike to You."

Nathan felt like he'd been punched in the gut. *I've been trying to hide, but it's impossible. In the darkness of my grief and anger, I was overwhelmed—but that was because I didn't look to the Light and hold fast to Him. People told me that, but I didn't listen.*

The memory of Lick's disobedience came back to him in a whole new light. He'd called, and Lick had ignored him; he'd commanded, and finally, when Lick did come, he'd petted and praised him—hoping it would make it easier for Lick to come back the next time. *And I've ignored God's voice. He's beckoned me, wooed me, called to me. . .yet He will still have a place for me like the father did for his prodigal son.*

"Nathan?" He hadn't heard Kip come back in the tent. Kip hunkered down beside him. "Do you need time alone, or do you need a brother right now?"

"I've been so bitter at God instead of holding fast to Him." His voice cracked. "I've been such a fool."

Kip sat down and gently pulled the Bible from him. He glanced down at the page, then looked up somberly. "David was a champion repenter. He messed up so many times. He went against God's will, but he knew the Lord's forgiveness was his if he confessed his sins and truly sought to restore his relationship. Is that how you're feeling?"

Tears burned Nathan's eyes. He barely choked out, "Yes."

Kip ran his stubby finger along the last verses of that chapter as he read aloud, "Search me, O God, and know my heart; try me and know my anxious thoughts; and see if there be any hurtful way in me, and lead me in the everlasting way."

"That makes it all sound so simple."

"It is. You're complicating it. God knows you. He was waiting for you to turn to Him. His arms are wide open."

Someone slapped the side of the tent. "Supper's on!"

"Be there in a minute," Kip called.

Nathan grasped his hand. "Pray with me first."

☦

"Who was on the phone?" Vanessa came out of the bathroom with a towel wrapped around her head.

"Dad called." Jeff lay on his belly on the floor, his brow furrowed with concentration as he arranged several plastic figurines in specific places. "He said he'll call again tomorrow. I told him I'm fine."

"Good. I'm going to go start supper." Vanessa stood in the hallway for a second and sagged against the wall. *They're fine, but I'm not.*

Staying in Nathan's home was a huge mistake. She'd been sleeping in the guest bedroom next to Jeff's, but even it carried Evie's stamp. No matter where she turned, Vanessa felt the lingering ghost of Nathan's wife—in the silk pansy arrangement on the bedside table, the Battenburg lace comforter and curtains, the kitchen's pink-flowered dishes, floor, and wallpaper. Nathan couldn't bear to change Jeff's room, even though it looked woefully infantile. The first thing Vanessa did was to shut the door to Nathan's bedroom. A pair of portraits hung in there—one of Evie in her wedding gown, and another of her and Nathan.

Father, I went into this with the right intentions. Where did I go wrong?

She rewrapped her turban and dragged herself downstairs. Consuelo normally came in to do the housekeeping and laundry, but she had the flu. Vanessa tried to keep the house picked up as she went along, but between Jeff and Licorice, it wasn't a successful operation. She tucked his book bag against the couch, out of the way of traffic, and made a mental note that he still had to take a ruler to class tomorrow.

With Consuelo sick, Jeff didn't have anyone to go pick him up after school or watch him until Vanessa got off work. She juggled her schedule so Jamie was at the shop for the twenty minutes each afternoon that it took for her to zip over to the school and back. Jeff would do his homework in the back room, show it to Vanessa, then help her out with filling water bowls or playing with the animals. The makeshift arrangement actually worked out fairly smoothly.

Vanessa headed into the kitchen. Somewhere along the line, she'd gathered that Nathan's culinary skills encompassed the vital ability to open cans and microwave frozen foods. All week long, Jeff sat wide-eyed at the table as she put home-cooked meals in front of him. Tonight, she didn't have the energy. She opened a can of chili.

As it heated on the stove, the phone rang.

"I've got it!" Jeff shouted from the stairs. He rocketed across the living room and snagged the receiver. In a breathless voice, he said, "Hellowhoisthis?"

Vanessa bit her lip. Maybe they should talk about phone manners tonight at dinner. She'd arranged to have her phone calls forwarded here while she was staying with Jeff, so that provided a good excuse to teach him how to answer a call.

"Van, it's for you."

She took the phone. "Hello?"

"Vanessa, this is Dave."

Dave. Dave from Guide Dogs... She mentally placed him and said, "Yes?"

"I've got a tough one for you. They're starting a new training session up at the facility on Monday. One of the dogs they were going to use just got held back. He got into a tussle with an unleashed boxer."

"He didn't get injured, did he?"

For all of their work, the hardest thing the puppy raisers had to deal with was unleashed dogs. They disrupted all but the most polished, obedient, mature puppies, and even then, it could be dicey.

"No, but we think he needs another couple of months of citizen training before we put him through the program. You've done a marvelous job with Amber, and I'd like to go ahead and slip her ahead into that position."

Vanessa drew in a quick breath.

"I know we had her slated to go in six weeks, Van." He spoke quietly, his words measured with understanding of the sacrifice he asked. Vanessa knew he'd raised a puppy and relinquished it—he knew firsthand how much it hurt. "It's hard to let them go, even with a target date."

She let out a long, choppy breath. "Is there any other candidate you could have go?"

"That last trip we all made to Disneyland is what made me think of you. Amber performed like a pro. She got on and off the Haunted Mansion and Pirates of the Caribbean like she'd been on them a million times. When that little girl came up and yanked on her tail, she showed exceptional tolerance, too."

Vanessa remembered that trip. The puppy training club went on monthly outings to socialize and to expose the dogs to challenging situations. She'd posed Amber with characters for photos, sat on Main Street and watched the parade, and had been proud that Amber didn't bat an eye at the huge draft horses pulling a trolley.

In a small voice, she said, "So Amber passed the final, and I didn't even know it was an exam."

"It wasn't meant to be, Van."

"I know. You've always been right up front with me. It's heartache talking. You know me." She laughed sadly. "Always talking before I think."

"I'll make the flight arrangements and get back to you. You've done a fine job, and someone is going to be lucky to have Amber as their guide dog."

"Thanks, Dave." She tearfully whispered, "Bye," and quickly hung up the phone.

"Van?" Jeff tugged on the hem of her sleeve. "What's wrong?"

"Everything."

✝

Nathan scowled at his cell phone. He'd accidentally left it on, and the charge was almost shot. He dialed home. "Van? Listen, my battery's almost gone. I won't be able to call tomorrow. How are things going?"

"Jeff's over at the Wilsons' for Caleb's pizza party."

"I forgot about that! I didn't get a present."

"I called Caleb's mom to get approval. He's now the proud owner of a second hamster."

"I owe you big time. How about you?" Just then, his cell phone let out a pitiful beep. "Van? Van?"

He kicked a small stone, sending it flying into a metal trash can. The *ping* wasn't loud enough to tattle on his frustration, but Nathan hated having to wait to tell Vanessa his good news. *Then again,* he smiled to himself, *it's the kind of news best given in person.*

The next day, hundreds of tools rattled in the back of the truck. At one of the preplanning meetings, he'd assessed what folks were taking and deduced their team was grossly undersupplied. His construction company had donated materials, and he'd packed a generator and all sorts of power and hand tools in his truck. He hit a pothole, and everything made another loud *clunk*. Nathan didn't care. Normally, he took pains to treat his tools well, but it didn't matter this time. He was going home, and he wanted to get there as soon as possible.

Kip understood. He'd helped Nathan pitch the tools in and shoved him toward the cab. "I'll take down the tent. You go on ahead and get home. You have someone waiting for you. . .and I don't mean Jeff."

Nathan had paused for an instant and given Kip a searching look.

"Vanessa is yours, Buddy." Kip lifted his blistered hands in a gesture of surrender. "I gave it a try, but I know when to quit. You're the right man for her. Now that you squared things away with God, there's nothing standing in the way. Go home. Make her a happy woman."

Nathan remembered Kip's words as he pulled onto his housing tract. Everything had fallen into place. Life had a sense of rightness. A neighbor was mowing his lawn, and a few kids were tossing a Frisbee. His son and the woman he loved were just a few houses away.

Instead of the welcome he expected, his reception was anything but delirious. Vanessa sat on the steps with her arm around Amber. Jeff sat on the other side of the retriever. All three of them looked glum. Lick wasn't with them.

Nathan had barely jammed his truck into PARK when he bolted over to them. Lick's barking from the backyard relieved and confused him. "What's wrong?"

Jeff popped up and gave him a hug. "Van has to give Amber back."

Vanessa's pretty blue eyes were red-rimmed and puffy. If ever she needed comfort, now was the time. Nathan plopped down beside her and slid his arm around her shoulders. "When?"

"Tomorrow."

Even choking out that one word stretched her. Nathan could scarcely stand seeing her hurt. He tilted her head onto his shoulder and whispered into her soft, golden hair, "You can keep her if you really want to, can't you?"

Vanessa shook her head. "I gave my word. From the day I got her, I knew I'd have to let go."

"She's being honor'ble, Dad."

"Yes, sport, she is." He wondered aloud, "How are you going to do it?"

She lifted her head and looked at him. Tears glistened in her eyes. "God loved His Son supremely—but when it came time for mankind to stop walking in darkness, to shed spiritual blindness, God sent His beloved Son to lead us to eternal freedom. It was an unspeakable sacrifice—but I'm eternally grateful for it."

He let her talk, not knowing where she was going, but willing to let her talk if it gave her any comfort.

"Each time I've given up a guide puppy I've trained, I've remembered God's sacrifice for my soul. I've had to trust Him to give me consolation. He's been faithful, and that's why I've always taken on another puppy. By giving up Amber, someone who lives in darkness can find liberty. It's nowhere near the scope of the Lord's sacrifice, but drawing that parallel helps me let go because God proved that by giving, we're set free. I'm just following His example."

Tears ran down her pale cheeks. Nathan wrapped her in his arms and held her as she cried. He'd spent the last months thinking she was so innocent in her faith, yet she'd been far wiser than he'd been. She'd let God come alongside her in her times of loss. Oh, to be sure, the loss of a guide puppy didn't in any way equate with his losing Evie, but the God who cared about the lilies of the field and counted every hair on a man's head certainly covered every concern with His love.

Vanessa sniffled and pushed away.

"Van, we need to talk." He wanted to tell her his good news, to maybe shed some light in the midst of her sadness.

"No." She dipped her head. "I need time alone with Amber. I really need to go."

"Can't you stay just a little while? Maybe I could take a quick shower, and we could go out for supper."

"No."

"I'll drive you home. You shouldn't be driving right now."

"I need to drive. It'll help me clear my head." She flipped a swath of hair behind her shoulder and stood. Pasting on a smile that was anything but genuine, she said, "Jeff is a terrific kid. You can be proud of him."

"I'll help you put your stuff in the car."

She pulled her key ring from the pocket of her jeans. "Jeff already helped me. I need to go. G'bye."

He fought the urge to snatch her back, to hold her and let her pour out every last tear. She wanted to spend this last night alone with Amber, and she deserved that. Nathan stood on the porch and watched her drive off. If he had his way, she wouldn't be doing that again.

☩

Amber sensed something was wrong. She gently nosed Vanessa. That action opened the floodgates. Vanessa sat on the floor by her bed, wrapped her arms around her puppy, buried her face in her fur, and wept. Everything in her life felt like it was falling apart. She had no one to blame but herself.

She'd chosen to take on this puppy. All along, she'd known the time would come to give her up. What kind of fool was she to keep setting herself up for this kind of parting?

And then there was Nathan. The tears flowed even faster, wetting Amber's soft coat. Mom and Dad and Val and even Kip had warned her. They'd each come to her and discussed their concerns. *Oh, but did I listen? No.*

In the week that she'd cared for Jeff, she'd come to realize how much she adored him. The feeling was obviously mutual. He was a great kid. Cute. Smart. Tenderhearted, grubby-faced, and ultimately lovable.

The first few nights, she'd looked forward to Nathan's calls. Then she'd grown to dread them. As she stayed in his home, the truth became undeniable. What started out as an innocent business arrangement had ensnared her, and she couldn't let the relationship continue.

Vanessa had to face the heartrending fact that she'd unwisely let her heart get ahead of her spiritual welfare. A huge ball formed in her throat.

God, I've been so foolish, so arrogant. All along, I thought I was in control of my feelings. Ever since I accepted You, I knew I was meant to fall in love with a man who wanted to serve You as much as I did. In my dreams, we were going to have a marriage based on You as our foundation.

I didn't listen. Mom and Dad came to me. Val tried to talk sense into me, and Kip even confronted me. Instead of listening to wise counsel, I charged ahead. I really thought I was doing the right thing. I wore my faith as a shield and thought it would serve as a barrier against any heartbreak. How wrong I've been!

I love him, God. I do. I hate to admit it to myself and to confess it to You. How did I come to this point? In the past, I'd been so positive about setting my affections on a man who was on fire for Your kingdom. Nathan is burned out, yet I want him.

I know I have to make a choice. Nothing can come between me and You. Abraham faced having to choose, and he was willing to sacrifice Isaac. You gave Your Son. Nathan professes to still be Your child, but he isn't walking with You. What kind of home would we have if the foundation isn't built on Your will and holy Word? If my husband isn't following You, how can he lead me? What about any children we'd have? I know it's wrong. Father, I know it's so very wrong.

But in my heart, I long for Nathan to be restored to You. His bitterness has faded into. . .emotionless acceptance. It's progress, but it isn't enough. I have faith You can reclaim him. Until he comes to that point, I see how I cannot let the love I feel flourish. I don't know how to stop it. I've never understood how Abraham could put his son on the altar. Can't you work a miracle for me, just as you did for him?

Give me strength to cling to You and let go of Nathan. Help me make the right choices. Give me the courage to let go.

No grand or glorious thing happened. She didn't feel a blanket of peace descend. If anything, her prayer only served to sharpen her awareness of just where she stood. Tears burned behind her eyelids, and a deep ache radiated behind her breastbone.

She'd hoped for a fleeting moment that Nathan would say something when she spoke about giving Amber away, but he'd been silent.

Even if he did reestablish a firm relationship with the Lord, Nathan still loved Evie. His heart belonged to the woman who had borne his child. So did his home—their home, the charming little saltbox Evie rescued on their honeymoon and Nathan lovingly reconstructed for her. Every single room still looked as she'd decorated it. Her pictures hung on walls and sat in frames on tables. All of the patience in the world wouldn't erase his memories, and Vanessa came to the conclusion she simply couldn't shadowbox the rest of her life with a memory.

Amber. Strike one. Nathan's soul. Strike two. Nathan's heart. Strike three.

Vanessa tipped her head back and stared at the ceiling. The light fixture wavered and formed a halo through her tears. "God, I've struck out. I can't do this on my own. What more do You want from me?"

Chapter 20

Vanessa, let me drive you and Amber to the airport."

"Thanks, Nathan. It's nice of you to offer, but I have to do this myself."

"Honey—"

"I need to go. Bye." She hung up. Putting the bright green jacket on Amber was hard. It was yet another "last time" thing she was doing today. "You're a big girl now. You'll go to doggy college and wear a blue jacket."

Secretly, there was that selfish wish that Amber would go and "flunk out." Then, she could come back forever. . . . Vanessa clenched her eyes shut to keep from crying. *God, I really don't want to be that kind of person. Make me bigger than my selfish desires.*

Amber usually traveled in passenger compartments. She'd been on a plane twice and on a boat, busses, trains, even a hay wagon. Today was different. At the airport, Vanessa stayed with her until the very last moment, gave her a hug and kiss, and put her in a dog crate. She wept as they took Amber off to the plane, cried all of the way home, and flung herself across her bed. She lay at the very edge, her fingertips brushing the edge of Amber's bed. It was as empty as her aching heart.

⁜

Nathan had tried to contact Vanessa a half-dozen times in the last twenty-four hours, and she'd given him every version of a polite brush-off he'd ever seen. He wasn't going to put up with it any longer.

Nathan chuckled under his breath. Vanessa, impulsive in so many ways, managed to model patience. Today, he was the impulsive one, and he had no patience left. He strode to her door with resolve, gave it three solid raps, and jangled the keys in his pocket as he waited for her to answer. She didn't come, so he banged on the door a few more times. Still no response.

Unwilling to give up, he hiked around the corner of her place and drummed his fingers on her bedroom window. When he'd helped move Val out, he'd had a conniption that they were on a ground floor with no security. He'd come back and put in a security window. Now, he wished he hadn't.

One side of the curtain inched back. "Whaddo you want?"

"Doing that well, huh?"

109

The curtains opened wider, revealing a very sleepy woman bundled in a robe the color of shamrocks. Nathan thought she looked as if someone had tackled her and wrapped her up in Astroturf. She'd never looked better to him. She scrubbed her face with her palm, then swept her wild hair back behind her left ear. "Do you have any idea what time it is?"

"Time to talk. Get dressed."

"Nathan, go home."

"No can do. Hurry up."

She turned to the side and wheeled back around. Her eyes were huge. "It's five fifteen. Are you crazy? Who's watching Jeff?"

"Val is. I know what time it is, and we'll be late if you don't get a move on."

"The only place I'm going is back to bed." The curtains swished shut.

Nathan chuckled. He didn't doubt for a minute she'd be headed right back to bed, but he wasn't about to let her do it. He drummed his fingers on the window.

"Go away!" came the muffled shout.

A set of sprinklers started on the far side of the lawn. *I'm going to get soaked. May as well be a fool for love. . . .* He cleared his throat and began to sing. "It's raining, it's pouring, the old man is—"

The curtains didn't open. Vanessa popped up from beneath them like a crazed jack-in-the-box and flipped the safety latch on the window. Her cheeks glowed scarlet. As she opened the double-thick, shatterproof pane, she hissed hotly, "If you had any sense at all, you'd just leave." She drew in a breath and added, "Can't you see the sprinklers are coming on?"

"Why do you think I'm singing this song?"

"I have no idea. I didn't recognize it as music. The first time you sang it with Jeff was cute, but this is irri—"

"Jeans and a sweatshirt, Van. Put 'em on and meet me at the front door." He glanced down at his wristwatch. "You have ten minutes."

"You have ten seconds to go away before I call the police. You're disturbing my peace!"

"Nine minutes."

She huffed and shut the window. He heard her mattress squeak.

Four minutes later, he used his cell phone and called her. "Five minutes, and I have chocolate."

✞

He'd given her five minutes. . .like he had any right to make any dictates to her. Still, he had her so tied in knots, she wasn't going to get back to sleep, anyway. Vanessa clambered out of bed and headed toward her closet. He'd specified jeans and a sweatshirt, but she wasn't going anywhere. Not at this hour. Not with him.

She yanked on jeans, but her sweatshirts were in the bottom drawer over where Amber's empty bed lay. She couldn't go over there right now. Not a chance. She'd start crying all over again. Instead, Vanessa rummaged through her closet and pulled out a T-shirt that was as blue as she felt.

In her haste, she broke her shoelace. "Ohh!" She flung that shoe across the room and listened to the satisfying *thump* it made as it hit the floor right next to her shoe rack. Even in her frustration, at least she managed to keep her aim true. She scowled at her feet and hobbled over to that shoe rack. "Oh, forget it." She stopped looking and twist-stepped into big, rainbow-striped, fuzzy slippers.

Nathan Adams was about to get a piece of her mind. "Let's go." As soon as she said the command for Amber, she realized for the millionth time that Amber was gone. All of those things she said and did as a puppy trainer were empty gestures and phrases now—and painful reminders of the loss she'd sustained. A fresh wave of grief washed over her.

Nathan knocked at the front door.

Vanessa marched over, jerked open the front door, and gave him a belligerent look. How dare he show up at this ridiculous hour at all, let alone looking like that? Freshly shaven, lounging against her door frame, he could have just stepped from a magazine ad.

"Good morning, sweetheart."

"Give me the chocolates, and you might not get hurt."

"They're in the car." He grabbed hold of her wrist and yanked.

Vanessa struggled to free herself. "What in the world are you doing?"

"Kidnapping you."

"You're nuts. I don't want to go anywhere or do anything. Just leave me alone."

He tilted his head to the side, and his dark brown eyes shone with compassion. "Hiding out won't take away the pain, honey."

"Neither will running all over the place."

"True, but I have special plans. You'll have to trust me." He glanced down and shook his head. "I've got an extra sweatshirt in the car, but those slippers won't do."

"Just what is wrong with my slippers?" She folded her arms across her chest and tapped her toe.

"They'll get wet when you walk across the lawn."

"I'm not walking across the lawn!"

Nathan gave her a don't-be-difficult look. All of a sudden, he ducked, rammed his shoulder into her middle, and wrapped his arm around the backs of her legs. When he straightened up, she dangled over his shoulder like a rag doll. She turned her head to the side, saw him snatch her key ring from the hall table, then dizzily watched as he pulled the door shut and locked it.

She tried to stay calm. "What are you doing?"

"We've already discussed that. I'm kidnapping you and your goofy slippers. I'm even making sure they don't get wet."

A considerate kidnapper. She'd chalk this all up as another one of her wild nightmares, but blood rushed to her head. It pulsed and made her ears ring, proving she really was awake and Nathan truly had gone 'round the bend. "Let me get this straight. Valene is with Jeff and knows you're doing this?"

"Yup. So do your parents."

"Now I've heard everything."

"Almost. I've arranged for Jamie and your mom to mind the shop today."

"Great." She tried to catch her breath. It wasn't exactly an easy thing to do in this position. "I'm getting abducted by approval."

Nathan's shoulder shook as he chortled, and the action made her bounce. *It would serve him right if I threw up all over his legs. He's having far too much fun, and I don't want to play this game.*

"Really, Nathan, take me back. I'm lousy company right now."

"I'll take you however you come." He stopped, opened the car door, and lowered her inside with surprising care instead of dumping her like a sack of cement. He slammed her door shut, zipped around the car, and slid into the driver's seat.

Just then, Vanessa caught sight of herself in the visor's mirror and let out a breathless shriek. "Okay, the joke's over. I'm going back inside."

He started the car and put it into motion before she could open her door. "Buckle up, and the chocolate is in the glove compartment."

"I haven't brushed my hair. I don't have any makeup on, and I'm wearing slippers!"

"Yeah, so?" He shifted and pulled a black comb from his pocket. "Borrow this. Eat the chocolate."

She made a rude huff as she accepted the comb. The man needed to get his head examined if he thought this was going to mollify her.

"You're a natural beauty, sweetheart. You don't need a bunch of stuff all over your pretty face, and as for your slippers. . ." He let go of the steering wheel momentarily and lifted his palms in an "oh, well" gesture.

Vanessa pulled the comb through her tangles and gave him a disgruntled look. Leave it to him to give her a compliment on a morning like this. Clueless. The man was utterly clueless. Good thing, too. It meant she could stay mad at him about this escapade and use it as an excuse to distance herself and cool the relationship.

"So ask me about what I found in Mexico."

"Obviously you lost your wits."

"This is important, Van."

"Sure it is," she said flippantly. She tossed his comb onto the dashboard and rooted around in the glove compartment for the chocolate. Nothing. She unbuckled her seat belt and twisted around.

"You're not listening to me."

Desperation had her rummaging through the stuff he had stored in the backseat. She didn't want to face him right now. "You promised me chocolate."

Nathan's baritone filled the car:

"'When peace like a river attendeth my way,
When sorrows like sea billows roll,
Whatever my lot, Thou hast taught me to say,
It is well, it is well, with my soul.'"

Vanessa twisted around and stared at him. She clamped her hand around his arm and squeezed. "What?"

He gave her a soul-stirring smile. "I found my way back. My relationship with Christ is on track again."

"Oh, praise God!"

"The hurt and anger are gone, Van. I realized what a fool I was for blaming God for robbing me of my wife. Evie was His child, and He called her home. For a time, I was blessed to have her to love. I've mourned for her, and I'll always miss her, but now I can be at peace, knowing she's whole and healthy in heaven."

Vanessa took a deep breath. She didn't want to hear about Evie. Even the mere mention of her name was like a dagger through her heart, but how selfish was that? Nathan was freed of his shackles, and that was what was important. He'd begun to heal spiritually.

"Wow. Answered prayer."

"I know you were faithful to pray for me, Van." He gave her a piercing look, then trained his gaze back on the road. "I managed to push away everyone else, but you were different. You didn't push back or walk away. You've stuck around and let God work in His own way."

"So tell me about how God finally got through to you!"

"It's been so subtle—gradual, you know? At first, I couldn't stand anything having to do with worshiping Him. All of the essentials for a strong walk stopped cold. But God's used you to patiently reintroduce them to me: associating with believers, prayer, attending church." He hitched his shoulder. "The final step was down in Mexico. Kip got me to start reading God's Word again."

"Kip's a great friend, Nathan."

"Yeah, he is—to me. What about you?"

Father, how do I respond to this? The biggest hurdle is behind us—Nathan is Yours. With time, can he let go of Evie and learn to love me? Do I play it safe and tell him Kip is just a friend, or do I focus on the relationship that may or may not ever blossom between me and this man?

Vanessa took a deep breath and looked Nathan in the eye. "I hope I'm a great friend to you, too."

His rich, deep laughter filled the cab. Vanessa had the feeling she'd mistakenly answered Nathan's question the wrong way, but nothing mattered this morning.

"I finally realized the truth—I'd been longing for what was right in front of me all of those years. I was like a blind man, wandering around in darkness. I let anger and grief come between me and God instead of letting Him be my strength and solace at the darkest time in my life. Now I've come back to the Light. God's restored my spirit—just as He did for David in the Psalms."

"I'm so happy for you, Nathan."

"It's the craziest thing. I kept thinking the emptiness and loneliness were because I was a widower. I'm still a widower, but I can see that when grief should have started to wane, I stayed so empty because I'd shut down spiritually. You have no idea how free I feel."

His news started to fully sink in. He hadn't just made a decision with his mind—his heart and soul were behind it. The joy flowing from him touched her deeply.

"You once said God was bigger than my anger," Nathan continued. "I had plenty of people tell me I was a sinner for that; you were patient with me and let God chip away at my hardened heart. He is bigger than anything that I am or feel or do. But the other thing is, He doesn't expect me to pretend—He already knows how I feel, so I can live honestly before Him."

Vanessa nodded.

"I'm not trapped in the past anymore, Vanessa."

"The chains are broken. I'm glad for you."

He'd zipped down the freeway and turned onto a winding dirt road. Now he made a sharp hairpin turn and another wild jog to one side. A hot-air balloon came into sight.

"Oh, look!"

Nathan parked the truck and turned to her. "I wanted to celebrate with you in a special way. Let's go."

Still stunned by everything he'd said, Vanessa got out of the car when he opened her door. She watched him yank a paint-splattered, maroon sweatshirt from the back of his truck and gladly accepted it. Once she pulled it over her head, he slipped his strong hand along the back of her neck and freed her hair.

The sudden warmth felt good in the nippy morning air, but she wasn't sure whether it was from the sweatshirt, his good news, or his touch.

"Come on." He took her hand and led her all of one step, then stopped. He looked down at her slippers and shook his head. "Upsy-daisy."

Vanessa let out a surprised squeal as he scooped her into his arms.

Nathan carried her toward the balloon and stopped briefly to speak with one of the men who seemed to be directing the busy ground crew. Seemingly satisfied, Nathan gave her a squeeze and carried her to the basket.

"Ready to go?" the operator inside the basket shouted above the din.

Nathan raised a brow as he looked at her. She nodded enthusiastically, so he lifted her into the basket, then climbed in beside her. He stood close in the tight quarters and bumped a picnic basket with his knee. He pointed down, then put his mouth by her ear and half-shouted, "Once we get underway, you can have some coffee. I ordered breakfast for us."

"Breakfast in thin air? How fun!"

The basket shifted a bit beneath their feet. Vanessa grabbed one of the lines. Nathan grabbed her. She didn't mind one bit.

Filled with hot air, the balloon barely started to rise. "Away we go!" someone said from behind her. The noise from the burners ripped through the air and made any conversation virtually impossible. The ground seemed to fall away as their balloon continued to rise. The movement felt smooth, but the height change seemed almost dizzying. Soon Nathan's car resembled one of Jeff's toys. A stand of trees looked like frilled toothpicks. As they reached cruising altitude, the noise from the burners diminished.

"Isn't this outta sight?" Nathan's arm around her waist tightened.

"Amazing! I've always wanted to ride in one of these!" She let go of one of the lines and reached out. "I almost feel like I can touch the clouds from here."

Nathan turned her and held her close. His warmth and strength felt marvelous. Slowly, one of his hands slid up her back to her nape. He spread his fingers out and speared them through her hair, forcing her to face him.

Vanessa didn't want to look at him. If she did, he'd be able to read her like a book and know exactly how she felt about him. She tried to turn her head to the side. "Look at the horizon. We're going right toward the sunrise!"

"I don't need to look out there to see today or tomorrow." He exerted gentle pressure and had her staring up at him.

Vanessa could scarcely catch her breath.

"I'm already walking on clouds, Van, and when I look at you, I see all of the bright days ahead."

He caught her gasp with a toe-curling kiss. When he lifted his head, he smiled. "I've been wanting to do that for a while."

"Oh, my."

"I've already gone to your dad and mom. We have their blessing."

"Their blessing," she echoed, hoping she understood his meaning but afraid she was letting her wishes run wild.

"I know this is our first date, but I'm going to court you for a lifetime. I can't wait, though." Nathan's arm cinched tighter around her waist. He dipped his head and nuzzled her ear. "Marry me, Vanessa."

"Was that a request or a command?"

"It's a requirement." He pulled away a little and pressed his forehead to hers. "Live with me and love with me and laugh with me. God fills my soul, but you fill my heart."

There under a zigzag rainbow fabric canopy, soaring toward a sunny day, Vanessa didn't have to give more than a second's consideration to his proposal. "Yes, Nathan. I'd love to be your wife."

"Seal it with a kiss," he said in a husky tone.

After a kiss that promised happily-ever-afters, he cuddled closer. "Happy?"

She nodded, stood on the tiptoes of her slippers, and wrapped her arms around his neck. "I never want to touch down. I've been going crazy, loving a man who was so blind."

He looked deeply into her eyes. "Sweetheart, I can see forever from here."

Epilogue

Vanessa sat in the bride's room, brushed on a touch of mascara, and winked at Della. "I have a feeling you like these clothes better than our baseball uniforms."

Della fluffed her hair. "Don't you just know it? You taught me how to bat and how to snag a ball. Think you can teach me how to catch a husband?"

"We'll have to see if Nathan invited any good prospects. I'll have him introduce you and Valene to them at the reception."

Valene groaned.

Vanessa gave her twin a saucy smile in the mirror. "Guess what I just figured out?"

"What?" Valene adjusted the skirt of her smoky blue maid-of-honor dress until it hung with sheer grace.

Her twin had been fussing all morning, and Vanessa suspected it was because she hated to be on stage at all. Even being a maid of honor was more spotlight than she'd prefer to handle, but she filled the role because sisterly love trumped shyness. Vanessa decided to tease her to help lighten her anxiety.

"When we walk down the aisle, it's the last time in my life I'm going to be the last one. Alphabetically, I've always been dead last."

Della snorted. "What did you expect? With a last name like Zobel, you were sunk."

"No kidding," Val agreed.

"Yeah, but you still came before me," Vanessa said to her sister. "Val, then Van. My married name will be Adams." She stood and twirled about in her rustling satin slips. "And the last shall come first. . . ."

Mom made a worried sound and started to take the bridal gown off of the hanger. "If you don't get into this gown, you're not going to be first or last. You'll be an old maid."

"Are you kidding? Nathan would marry me if I walked out there in my ugly orange baseball uniform. He proposed to me in my rainbow slippers."

Della gave her a silly look. "Let me get this straight. He was wearing your slippers?"

"And you all think I'm daffy? Of course he wasn't. Have you seen the size of his feet? I was wearing them when he kidnapped me. It was so romantic."

Val held part of the bridal gown, and Della took hold of another section. "Come on. Let's get this woman into her gown before she gets so besotted with those stupid slippers, she wants to get married in them." They lifted the gown so Vanessa could slip into it.

As Val started to do up the zipper of the dreams-come-true satin-and-lace bridal gown, Vanessa worried aloud, "You all have everything you need, right? Jeff will stay with Val for the next few days, then he'll go stay with Mom and Dad. Mom, you and Dad will stop by Nathan's and get Lick tonight? He and Hero will tear up Val's condo. He needs your big backyard to romp in."

"Stop worrying," Val chided. "You're chewing off your lipstick."

"Girlfriend, you need to get your head examined." Della shook her finger at Van. "You're going off on a romantic honeymoon to Ireland and Scotland, and you're fretting about a dumb dog?"

"That dog and a silly goldfish are what brought them together," Valene said loyally.

"Yes." Vanessa dipped down so her mother could help her pin on an airy veil. She left the blusher veil back out of the way for the present. "And so did the grace and mercy of God."

Someone tapped on the door. Della opened it.

Dad stuck his head into the room. "We're ready."

Jeff nudged past him and stared up at Vanessa. His little mouth dropped open. He blinked, then said in an awed tone, "You look like a fairy princess."

"Yes, kitten, you do." Her father's voice sounded choked.

Jeff walked all the way around her and asked, "Do I get to call you 'Mom' now?"

"That would make me so happy!"

"Okay, Mom. Daddy said he wanted you to hurry up. He said he's waited long enough for his sweetheart. Did you know that's what he called you?"

"Yes." She smiled at the way Jeff wrinkled his nose. At the rehearsal the day before, Nathan had been eager to sweep her into a theatrical dip and give her a heart-stopping kiss. Jeff ended it all with a loud, "Eww, yuck!" Nathan later borrowed her strawberry lip gloss and let Jeff take a whiff. After that, Jeff decided his dad hadn't gone crazy, after all. His favorite bubble gum smelled like that. Nathan then had extracted a pledge from his "honor'ble" son that he wouldn't make any noises during the real wedding ceremony.

They all went to the narthex. Mom gave Vanessa one last kiss and allowed Kip to seat her before he took his place as best man. The music started, and Jeff carried a satin pillow with the rings tied to it. He stopped partway down the aisle to scratch his knee, then continued on with all the decorum of an English butler.

Della stepped off, and Val turned to Vanessa. She didn't say a word. She didn't need to. They'd always been able to communicate at moments like this with just a look. She nodded, smiled, and headed down the aisle.

"Kitten, he's a good man, a godly man. I had some real doubts awhile back, but I know he's the man I prayed for God to bring to you."

"Thank you, Daddy." She gave him a kiss, accepted his fumbling help to pull down her blusher veil, and took his arm.

Vanessa walked down the aisle with every assurance that waiting for this moment was worth every prayer she'd ever whispered. When she could see Nathan at the front of the church, she knew she'd never known a more handsome man. Love and happiness shone in his eyes. Daddy gave her away, and she stood beside Nathan, then knelt at the altar.

They'd consulted and counseled with Pastor MacIntosh, and now he began to read the scripture they'd requested for their wedding. It was from 1 Corinthians:

"Love is patient. . . ."

Love Is Kind

by Joyce Livingston

Dedication

I would like to dedicate this book to my irreplaceable black Lab and best friend, Lancelot. We lost Lancelot three years ago after having had him with us for seventeen years. Although he was an outdoor dog, he and I spent many happy hours together, swimming in the lake, planting flowers, chasing one another, and just sitting enjoying each other's company. I love you, Lancelot, and miss you terribly. You were a good doggie.

Chapter 1

Valene Zobel blinked back tears as she lovingly fingered the smoky blue, satin dress hanging in her closet. How she was going to miss her twin.

"Why're you crying, Aunt Val? Weddings are supposed to make you happy. That's what my daddy said."

She pulled her new nephew close and ran her fingers through his hair. "I am happy, Jeff. Sometimes grownups cry when they're happy. It's just that I'm going to miss Vanessa. Now that she and your daddy are married, we won't be together as much."

The boy seemed satisfied with her answer and turned his attention toward Hero, the black Labrador Vanessa had given Valene several months ago. "Come on, boy. Wanna watch me ride my new bike?"

Hero seemed happy with the idea, and the two of them raced off to retrieve the little bike from the living room of Valene's first-floor condo.

"Jeff!" she called out after him, remembering the rules Nathan had laid down before he and her sister had taken off on their honeymoon. "You can only ride your bike on the sidewalk! Not in the parking lot! And wear your helmet! Do you hear me?"

Jeff nodded over his shoulder as he mounted his prized possession, the shiny red bicycle his new stepmom had given him.

Valene had looked forward to being Jeff's baby-sitter while they were gone. She grinned as he slipped the helmet on his head and took off down the sidewalk, with Hero nipping at his heels.

"Be careful, Jeff!" she yelled out loudly, cupping her hands to her mouth. "I don't want you getting any skinned knees while your dad is away!"

She stood in the open doorway, watching, wondering what it would be like to find that perfect man, like Vanessa had when Nathan appeared in her life. She smiled as she recalled the funny way he and her sister had met, laughing aloud as she remembered the expression on Nathan's face when he'd first seen the two of them together. He'd done a double take, then blurted out, "You're twins!"

Valene had wanted to say, "Duh! You're kidding!" but had refrained. She'd never say anything that might offend or embarrass someone. How was she ever going to get along without her twin now that Vanessa was married? Just thinking about it made her sad.

"Watch, Aunt Valene! Watch me! I can ride really fast!"

"Remember what I said about—" Realizing what was about to happen, she screamed out, "Jeff! Watch out!" She ran toward him, picking up her pace with each stride, frantically waving her arms, trying to get his attention.

It was too late.

Instead of stopping where the sidewalk ended, the bicycle whizzed onto the crowded parking lot at full speed, right into the path of an approaching pickup truck.

A small boy's scream, the screeching of brakes, and a sudden *thud* all seemed to happen in slow motion as Valene raced into the lot, weaving her way among the parked cars, her heart pounding furiously, her mind whirring with thoughts of what-ifs.

"I didn't see him coming! Honest I didn't!" the driver yelled as he leaped from the oversized pickup and raced around to the front. "I tried to stop—"

"Jeff!"

"I'm sorry, Aunt Valene."

She blinked hard, breathing a prayer of thanks, her palm flattening against her chest as she heard the boy's voice. There was Jeff, on the other side of the truck, still straddling his bike. He was okay.

But the man was bending over someone.

Who?

After wrapping her arms about Jeff and making sure he hadn't sustained any injuries, Val cautioned him to stay put before hurrying to see if she should call for an ambulance.

But the man wasn't leaning over a person.

He was leaning over Hero, and the dog wasn't moving. He was lying frighteningly still in a small pool of blood.

"I didn't mean to hit him! I didn't see him! Oh, why did this have to happen? I never meant to do it! I hit the brakes when I saw the boy, but—"

Weeping, Valene dropped onto her knees and tried to comfort Hero, stroking his head frantically and praying he'd be all right.

"We need to get him to a vet!" the man said, stooping beside her and carefully scooping up the dog in his long arms, his face filled with sheer panic. "I can't leave him here to die. He needs attention immediately!"

"But—"

"Hurry!" the man ordered, moving quickly to his spotlessly clean truck and carefully lowering the injured dog onto the leather backseat. "Let's hope we're not too late."

"But, Jeff—" Valene said, almost incoherently. "What—"

"Hurry," the man said again.

Almost robotically, she rushed back to her apartment and grabbed her purse before closing and locking the door.

"You ride in the backseat with your dog. Your son can ride up front with me. Now hurry!" the man told her in a take-charge manner, although he was shaking as badly as she.

He placed the shiny red bike in the truck's bed while Valene and Jeff climbed inside. "You'll have to help me. Where's the closest vet or animal hospital?"

"Ah, let me think." For a moment, Val's mind went blank. "Two blocks down and. . .and turn to the left—no, right."

The man's concerned gaze caught hers in the rearview mirror, and she could see tears in his eyes. "Which is it? Left or right?"

"Right. It's right. About three blocks." *I've got to settle down,* she told herself, taking a deep breath before continuing. "It. . .It's across from the shopping center. A red brick building, I think. It's an animal clinic. I—I took Hero there when he got a thorn in his foot."

For the first time, she became fully aware of the turmoil the man must be experiencing. He'd nearly hit a boy on a bicycle. He could've killed Jeff. She couldn't even begin to imagine how she would feel if the same thing had happened to her, and suddenly, instead of anger, she felt sorry for him. All this time she'd been so concerned about Jeff, then Hero, she hadn't even considered how he must be feeling. "Ar—are you all right?" she mumbled through chattering teeth. "I mean, you. . ."

He nodded but kept watch on the road. "I—I'll be okay. Just a little shook up. Don't worry about me. You take care of that dog. He's the important one here. I'll have us there in a flash. What's your name?"

"I'm Valene Zobel. Jeff is my nephew, not my son. He's staying with me this week." A shudder passed through her body as she slipped her free hand over the seat and squeezed Jeff's slim shoulders. How close she'd come to losing him. *Thank You, Lord. If that truck had been just one second—*

"My mom got really sick and died a long time ago," Jeff said sadly. "Vanessa is my new mama. She's nice."

"I'm Jordan Young." The driver gave them a quick sideways glance, then turned his attention back to the oncoming traffic.

Within minutes, the truck pulled into the vet's parking lot. The driver leaped out, jerked open the back door, scooped up Hero, and dashed toward the clinic. Valene grabbed Jeff's hand, and the two ran in behind the man named Jordan.

The receptionist took one look at Hero and quickly called out for the doctor on duty as she guided the truck's driver toward an examination room.

"I'll need some information," she told him, motioning toward a desk in the lobby. "Your wife can stay here with the dog while we fill out a few papers."

Clutching Jeff's hand tightly, her fingers entwined with his, Valene inserted, "I'm not—"

But the man who'd introduced himself as Jordan Young took hold of her arm and stopped her. "It's okay. Stay with your dog." For the first time since the accident, his chiseled features softened a bit and he smiled. "Hero. Isn't that what you called him?"

She nodded, finding it hard to speak without crying.

"I'll take care of everything. After all, I'm the one who. . ." He paused, and she could see his Adam's apple rise and fall as he swallowed hard. "Who caused his injuries."

"But you didn't. I—"

He wagged a cautioning finger to silence her. "We'll worry about where the blame goes later. Right now, you need to be with Hero."

After spending several minutes checking Hero, Dr. Kinney momentarily diverted his attention from the limp, banged-up body on the table to Valene. "This dog's injuries seem pretty serious. It might help if you'd talk to him a bit. He might not hear you, but then again, he might. Right now, I think he could use a few words of encouragement."

Valene gathered her shoulder-length hair in one hand and pulled it to the side as she leaned over Hero and whispered in his ear. "I love you, Hero." She gulped hard, barely able to continue as the tears rolled down her cheeks. "I need you, Hero. Please don't die. Please—"

She felt a slight tug on her sleeve, and pulling herself away from her beloved Hero, she looked into the worried, tear-stained face of the six-year-old. "Is he gonna die?"

"Oh, no, sweetie." Valene gulped hard and forced a smile as she pulled her nephew close and held him tight. "I'm sure the doctor is going to fix him up just fine."

"You'd better go now," the veterinarian told them as he motioned them toward the door. "We're going to do the best we can for Hero. You can wait in the lobby, but it may be awhile before we can tell you anything for certain, after I've done a more thorough examination and we've X-rayed him. If his injuries are as extensive as I fear they might be, he's going to require some long-term care."

"But you will be able to save him, won't you, Doc?" a trembling male voice asked.

Valene turned and found the man whose truck had hit Hero standing beside her, apparently finished with filling out the necessary papers.

Jordan Young's hand cupped the doctor's shoulder. "You gotta save him, Doc. He can't die!"

The doctor stood upright and hung his stethoscope about his thick neck. "What happens to Hero from here on out somewhat depends on you folks."

Valene's gaze went to the doctor as she found herself finally able to speak. "What do you mean, depends on us?" She dabbed at her eyes, feeling slightly offended by his words. "Of course, I want him to be all right. He's my dog, and I love him. I'll do anything to keep him alive."

Jordan pulled a handkerchief from his back pocket and wiped at the beads of perspiration forming on his forehead. "Me, too, Doc. That dog has got to live."

"Does that mean he's gonna die, Aunt Val?" Jeff asked with big eyes, as he stared at the still figure on the table.

Before she could answer, with a reassuring smile, Jordan slipped an arm about Jeff's shoulders. "Hey, don't you worry. I'll betcha the doc'll be able to fix him up just fine."

The doctor seemed to be assessing their words carefully before speaking. "I have to be brutally frank with you. The possible surgery and long-term care we're talking about can get pretty expensive. Many folks decide to put their animals to sleep rather than go to such an expense."

Valene gasped. "Put Hero to sleep? I'd never do that!"

"Do whatever is necessary to get that dog well, Doc. I'm footing the bill on this. I don't care what it costs. I'm the one who hit him, and I aim to do the right thing."

With a raise of his brows, the veterinarian shrugged. "Well, like I said, the decision is up to you and your wife. I'll do whatever you tell me. I never like putting a dog down, especially when I can see how much he's loved."

Valene clung tightly to Jeff's hand. She started to speak, to correct the doctor's misapprehension but felt a reassuring arm slip about her shoulders. A feeling of gratitude warmed her heart and kept her silent. They could straighten the doctor out later. Hero's welfare was the important thing right now.

"Do it, Doc." Jordan Young's tone was firm and unwavering. "I've already given my credit card to your receptionist. It's as good as paid for."

Dr. Kinney looked from one to the other. "Just wanted to make sure you and your wife know what you're getting into. Like I said, some folks—"

"I don't care what some other folks do, Doc," Jordan Young answered quickly, breaking into the man's sentence. "Do everything you can for Hero. No matter what it costs."

Valene was so relieved, she wanted to throw her arms about Jordan's neck. Although her thoughts had been focused on Hero and his injuries, she had to admit she had been concerned about the cost. Not that she'd ever let the doctor put Hero down, as he'd so delicately put it. She wouldn't. She'd find the money somewhere, even if she had to refinance her nearly paid-off car. But his words had set her mind at ease.

"Hero? That's his name?" the kindly doctor asked with a slight grin as he placed a gentle hand on the big dog's back.

Valene nodded, still blinking back tears.

"He's Lick's brother," Jeff inserted, his eyes rounded with fear. "Lick's real name is Licorice."

"Hero and Lick came from the same litter. Lick is Jeff's dog," Valene explained in a shaky voice.

The doctor bent and clamped a firm, reassuring hand on Jeff's shoulder. "Well, don't you worry, young man. We're going to take good care of Hero." He motioned Valene and Jordan toward the door. "You two take your son and go on into the waiting room. Once I've taken some X-rays, I'll be able to tell you more about his injuries."

"But. . ." Valene sent a quick glance at the man standing beside her.

"I think we'd better do as the doc says." Jordan gestured toward the door.

She paused a second then, realizing how unimportant it was that the doctor know they weren't husband and wife, moved toward him, tugging on Jeff's hand.

"I'll come out for you as soon as I've finished," the doctor called out just before he closed the door behind them.

The three seated themselves in a corner, with Valene and Jeff on one side of a little square table, and Jordan on the other. She slipped an arm about Jeff, then bowed her head and prayed silently, asking God to be with Hero. When she opened her eyes, she found Jordan Young staring at her.

"I'm–I'm sorry about hitting your dog. If only I'd—"

"It wasn't your fault," Valene said, turning to face him. His cheeks were flushed, and although it was cool in the room, he was still perspiring.

"It was my fault," Jeff said, his rounded eyes filling with tears. "Aunt Val told me to stay on the sidewalk, and I didn't do it."

"I guess we were all at fault," Valene said in a raspy voice as she wrapped an arm about her nephew and drew him close. "Letting you ride your bicycle on that narrow sidewalk wasn't the smartest thing I've ever done. I knew it dead-ended at the parking lot. I just didn't think to tell you."

Jordan pulled out his handkerchief and dabbed at his forehead again. "I'm sorry I hit Hero, but I'm glad it wasn't the boy. I could never have lived with myself if—"

"But you didn't hit him," she reminded Jordan, trying to control her voice and the turmoil still going on inside her. "Neither Jeff nor Hero should have been in that parking lot."

She stared at him, trying to comprehend the pain and fear he must've felt when he thought he'd hit Jeff. No wonder the man was shook up. How would she feel if the same thing had happened to her? "Normally, I never let Hero outside unless I have him on a leash." She watched as a slight smile curled at the corners of his strong mouth.

"I know. I've seen you walking him." His grin turned into a full smile. "Or should I say, him walking you?"

She smiled back. "He does tend to get a bit rambunctious sometimes."

Jeff frowned and yanked on her sleeve. "What's a ram-but-yus, Aunt Val?"

She placed a loving hand on his shoulder and gave it a gentle pat. "It means sometimes he wants to run and check everything out when I want him to walk."

Jeff nodded and seemed satisfied with her answer.

"Hero, huh? That's quite a name for a dog." Jordan's eyes twinkled, and he seemed to be a bit more relaxed than when they'd first sat down. "How'd you come up with it?"

Valene let out a slight chuckle. "You'll probably laugh at me."

He grinned. "I'll try not to."

"My twin sister, Vanessa, gave him to me when I moved into my condo. We both love animals. In fact, she owns a pet store—Whiskers, Wings, and Wags. She thought I needed a dog for protection. At first she named him *Nero*, but I soon changed it to *Hero*. This is the first time I've ever lived alone, so it's nice to have a *Hero* around."

"Vanessa is my new mother," Jeff inserted.

"Vanessa and Jeff's dad were married a couple of days ago."

Jordan's jaw dropped. "Really?"

"I was the ring bearer!" Jeff lifted his head proudly.

Valene smiled back when Jordan sent her an amused grin. She pulled a children's magazine from the stack on the table and handed it to Jeff. He opened it and immediately began perusing the words.

"Hero is a good dog, and I feel much safer having him around. Especially at night."

"A woman can't be too careful. His name sounds like it suits him."

They sat in an awkward silence for a few minutes, the ticking of the clock on the wall and the sound of Jeff turning the pages the only sounds in the room. For the first time since entering the clinic, Valene became aware of the faint, clean smell of antiseptic. She glanced across the room at a man sitting opposite them, grimly holding onto a small cat. She couldn't help but wonder why the man had brought the cat in. Maybe it was there to be spayed.

"Doesn't Jeff go to school?" Jordan asked, his gaze going to the boy.

Her attention was quickly drawn away from the cat. "Yes, but they're having a state teachers' meeting next Thursday and Friday. School will be out anyway, so my new brother-in-law figured it wouldn't hurt Jeff to miss a couple of days and come to Spring Valley and spend the week with me. He's a bright kid and can make up the missed work easily."

The receptionist appeared. "Mr. and Mrs. Young, Dr. Kinney is ready to see you now."

The three filed quickly back into the little room where Hero still lay on the table.

"How is he, Doc?" Jordan asked, stepping quickly to the dog's side.

Chapter 2

Dr. Kinney pulled off his glasses and rubbed at his eyes. "Well, I'm afraid I have some bad news."

Valene let out a gasp as she stared at the still figure on the table. "Is he—"

"No, he's alive," Dr. Kinney assured her quickly. "I've given him something to make him rest."

"You can't let him die," Jordan said quickly, leaning over the still body on the table. "Please, Doc."

The doctor held up a palm toward them. "He's not going to die, but he is going to require a lot of care. Maybe more than you two are willing to give him."

"What's wrong with him?" Jordan asked, wringing his hands, his face void of color.

Valene found herself full of questions but knew if she tried to verbalize one word she'd begin to cry. *Hero! Oh, Hero! Why did I ever let you out without your leash?*

"Other than the obvious skin abrasions your dog has sustained, I'd thought perhaps his leg was broken." The man paused. "A broken leg would have been simple. I could've put a pin in it, and in a few days he'd be running around, almost as if the accident had never happened. But. . ."

"But what?" Jordan and Valene asked in unison.

"I'm sorry to say, his injuries weren't that simple. I hate to have to tell you this. He has a fractured pelvis."

Valene's tears gushed forth unashamedly. During her time at the pet store, she'd heard horror stories about dogs who'd fractured their pelvis and how long it had taken them to recover. Not Hero! Not her precious Hero!

Jordan raked his hands through his hair. "Exactly what does that mean? Surgery? Will he recover?"

"Oh, yes. He'll recover, in time. As to surgery? There's really nothing I can do. Dogs are different than people. That pelvis will heal by itself. Eventually. But in the meantime, you'll have to do everything for him." He paused as a deep frown creased his forehead. "And I mean everything. Twenty-four/seven. He'll be helpless and totally dependent on you."

"For how long?" Valene asked, finally able to string three words together without crying.

"A good six to eight weeks."

"Then?"

"Then, other than quite a bit of stiffness in his hind end, he should be fine. God, in His infinite wisdom, made us so these old bodies will heal. Dogs, too." The doctor gestured toward Hero. "I know he looks pretty sad right now with all those abrasions, but they'll heal and his fur will grow back. It's the inside I'm concerned about. I'd like to keep him here for a few days, then you can take him home."

Valene prayed in her heart, thanking God. Hero was going to live, and in time, he'd be his old self.

"That is, if you're sure you want to take on the responsibility of caring for him," the doctor cautioned. "It's not going to be easy. He won't be able to use his back legs at all for awhile."

She drew in a sharp breath and held it.

"He'll try to get up and walk. It's a dog's nature to want to move around, even when he's in pain. He'll try to drag himself by using his front legs, and there won't be much you can do to stop him. Because of those natural tendencies, you may want limit his space by keeping him in a box of some sort, when you're not helping him exercise. And let me tell you, it's gonna get messy! He's gonna be worse than a newborn baby. Only he won't be wearing diapers, if you get what I mean."

Valene nodded as she tried to imagine managing a dog Hero's size and his bodily functions.

"What about pain, Doc?" Jordan asked, seeming to grasp the doctor's implications as to the problems Hero's injuries would cause. "He's got to be in terrible pain."

The doctor nodded. "You're right. His pain is probably almost unbearable. I'll be giving him about one hundred milligrams of Rimadyl twice a day. That should keep him fairly comfortable. And for those abrasions, he'll be getting an amoxicillin tablet twice a day to make sure no infection sets in and that those injuries heal up properly."

"Will we need to keep some kind of salve on them?" Valene asked, trying to take in everything the doctor was saying.

"No. No salve. Wouldn't stay on. He'd lick it off. The tablets work much better, but the wounds will have to be kept clean at all times." He crossed his arms and leaned against the table, his eyes scrutinizing both Valene and Jordan. "Are you sure you want to go through with this? It's not the expense I'm thinking about; it's the inconvenience and time. I want you two to know up front what you're getting into. Taking care of a big dog like this when he's helpless is not going to be an easy task."

He paused, as if giving them time to comment. When neither did, he continued. "It's not too late to change your minds. If you're not up to doing this, it'd be better for Hero if you put him down now. He can't make it without you. It's going to be hard on him, too."

Valene's jaw dropped. "I don't care how much care he takes. I'll do it gladly!"

Jordan stepped up beside her, and she felt his arm slide about her shoulders. "I live nearby. I'm going to help her."

Dr. Kinney adjusted his glasses and gave them a funny stare. "You—you two are separated?"

"No," Jordan inserted awkwardly. "We're neighbors."

Dr. Kinney reared back with a laugh. "Oh, excuse me! I thought you two were married! I'm sorry. Oh, my. You were both so concerned, I assumed. . . ." He tugged at his lab coat with a grin. "Guess it's never safe to assume, eh?"

"I should've told you up front," Jordan said, sticking out his hand, "but all I could think about was Hero. I'm Jordan Young."

"I'm Valene Zobel, and this is my nephew, Jeff."

"So, Ms. Zobel, Hero is your dog?"

She nodded. "Yes."

The doctor turned to Jordan. "You were driving the pickup that hit the dog?"

"I'm afraid so."

"Well," Dr. Kinney said slowly, rubbing at his forehead, "that does indeed present a problem. I had thought, with you two being married, you could perhaps split the time that's going to be necessary to take care of this dog properly, but with only one person living with—"

"I can take care of him on weekends and some evenings," Jordan volunteered, "and I'll hire someone to help Valene during the week."

The doctor smiled at both of them. "I have a feeling Hero is going to get all the attention he needs. Now," he said, ushering them toward the door, "why don't you all go home and let me tend to your dog?"

Valene stepped aside. "Can I tell him good-bye first?"

When the doctor nodded, she slipped back into the room and bent over the sleeping dog. "I love you, Hero," she whispered. "Don't worry. We're going to do everything we can to get you back on your feet. Just rest, okay?" She stroked his thick, black fur lovingly. "I'll be praying for you."

She looked up to see Jordan standing beside her, his face showing deep concern. He could've yelled at her for letting her dog run loose. There were signs posted all over the condo complex, saying dogs must be kept on a leash at all times. But he hadn't yelled at her. He'd taken the entire blame and not once had he even hinted that she should bear any part of it. Not many men would've been so understanding, and he'd taken on the responsibility of paying all of Hero's bills. "I–I don't know how to thank you," she said, getting teary-eyed again. "You've been so kind and—"

"Thank me? I hit your dog! I'm surprised you don't hate me!"

"It was my fault. I let him out without his leash."

"That doesn't excuse me. I should've been more observant. What if I'd hit Jeff? I could have, you know."

"I'm so thankful you didn't. I wasn't thinking when I let him ride his bike on that sidewalk."

Jordan shoved his hands into his pants' pockets, rattling his change. "Why don't we quit playing the blame game? It's getting late, and I don't know about you, but I'm hungry. According to the doctor, there's nothing more we can do here."

She glanced at her watch and was surprised to find it was already eight o'clock. "Oh, it is late. Thank you for bringing us, but I have my cell phone. I'll call a cab." She reached out her right hand. "Thank you, Mr. Young. You've been very kind, and I appreciate it."

He ignored her hand and shook his head. "You're not going to call a cab. I brought you, and I'll take you home."

She pulled her phone from her purse. "No, I'll call a cab. You've done quite enough for us."

"Put that thing away. I'm taking you home."

Although tempted, she knew she shouldn't accept his offer. He was a stranger. From childhood, she'd been cautioned to never accept rides from strangers.

"You'll be safe with me," he said with a teasing smile that set her somewhat at ease. "You rode here with me."

She had, and she hadn't even thought to refuse his offer when he'd grabbed up Hero and told her to get into the backseat with the dog. This situation was different, though. Yet wouldn't he think her foolish if she refused, after all they'd been through together? They were going to the same destination. Surely, he wouldn't try anything weird with Jeff around.

"Well, are you coming?"

She hesitated while sending up a quick prayer for discernment. "I–I guess."

He led the way, and soon they were back in his pickup, headed for their condos.

"I'm starving, and I bet you are, too," Jordan said as he flipped on the left turn signal and entered the busy street, easily maneuvering into the oncoming traffic. "How about stopping for a burger and fries at Wilbur's Diner? My treat!"

"Oh, no. Thank you anyway. But we couldn't."

He turned his attention away from the street long enough to give her a questioning glance. "Why? You gotta eat, too."

"I have things at home to fix. We'll eat there."

"I'll bet Jeff would rather have a burger and fries. Right, sport?" he asked the boy, catching his attention in the rearview mirror. "Loaded with catsup!"

"Could we, Aunt Val?" Jeff asked, obviously pleased by the man's invitation. "I love fries and catsup."

"No, Jeff. Mr. Young has done quite enough for us. We'll eat at home."

"But, Aunt Val, I—"

"Enough, Jeff," she warned with a frown over her shoulder, wishing the boy would just settle down and be quiet.

They rode to the condo in silence. As soon as the pickup came to a stop, Jordan rushed around to Valene's door, but she already had it opened and was halfway out. He gave her a quick smile and moved to the back, lowered the tailgate, and pulled out the shiny red bike. "Offer still stands."

She took the bike from his hands and motioned to Jeff to push it toward her condo, then turned back to Jordan. "Thank you. You've been more than kind. But no."

"I'm going to the clinic to see Hero in the morning. I want to make sure he's doing all right. Want to come with me?"

She shook her head. "No, thank you. I don't want to impose."

"Impose? I'd consider it an honor. Not often I get a chance to take a. . ." He paused. Then with a smile that brought out his dimples, he added, "A nice young boy to see a dog."

She couldn't help but laugh. "Really, Mr. Young, we—"

"Jordan," he insisted. "Mr. Young is my father," he added with a snicker.

"Jordan." She liked the sound of his name, and it suited him. It was strong, yet friendly. Not pretentious, but authoritative. "I have a few errands to run tomorrow, so I need to take my car, but thank you for the invitation."

He gave her a shrug. "Well, I'm in 10A. If you change your mind, send Jeff over to tell me, or meet me in the parking lot about eight."

"Thank you, but as I said, I'll be driving. Good night."

He didn't answer but began walking alongside her toward her condo.

"Didn't you say you lived in 10A?"

He nodded. "Yep."

"Isn't it over that way?" she asked, pointing to the next section.

He grinned. "Yep. I'm walking you to your door."

"It really isn't necessary. I think I can make it on my own." She hoped her words didn't sound rude. She didn't mean to be rude; she just didn't know what else to say. Her dealings with handsome men had been quite limited.

"I know. I'm sure you're quite capable. But gentlemen always walk ladies to their door, and. . ." He gave her the grin that brought out his dimples again. "And I like to think of myself as a gentleman."

"Oh," was all Valene could think to say. When they reached her door, she fished her key from her purse and reached toward the keyhole. She wasn't used to having someone watch her do such a mundane task, and his presence unnerved her. What if—when she opened the door—he pushed her inside? He looked like a nice enough guy, but what did she really know about him?

"Are you having trouble with the lock?" he asked, as he leaned in for a better look.

"Aunt Val, open the door!" Jeff said impatiently, his bike leaning against him as he held onto the handlebars.

"Okay." She turned the key and pushed the door open, stood back, and motioned Jeff and the bike inside.

"Good night, Ms. Zobel," Jordan said as he backed away from the door. "I'm sorry about Hero."

"I know you are, and I appreciate your concern. Good night." She closed the door and quickly secured the latch.

"Boy, Aunt Val, that was dumb," Jeff said, as he leaned his bike against the wall. "Now you gotta fix supper."

☧

Jordan sat in the booth at Wilbur's Diner and locked his hands together on the worn Formica-covered tabletop. He'd said he was hungry, but now as he sat in the booth, watching others around him enjoy their food, he wasn't at all sure he wanted to eat. He'd hit a dog. Someone's family pet. He could just as easily have hit a six-year-old boy. A sudden shudder gave him a chill. Things happened so quickly in life. Things for which you couldn't prepare yourself. He well knew.

"What can I get you, sweetie?"

He pulled his thoughts together and glanced up at the waitress. Although she'd served him dozens of times, he couldn't for the life of him remember her name. "Oh—ah—sorry. I guess my mind was wandering."

"The special is chicken-fried steak with steamed veggies," she told him matter-of-factly. "It's pretty good."

He shook his head. Even the burger and fries, normally his favorite, didn't sound good tonight, not after what he'd been through. "Just a bowl of vegetable soup and a good strong cup of coffee, please."

"Sure you don't want the steak and veggies, honey?"

He pushed the menu toward her with another shake of his head. Once he was alone again, he replayed the accident in his mind, wondering if he'd been careless. Had his mind been on something else? He barely remembered seeing Jeff cut out in front of him, and he'd never seen Hero.

"Here's your coffee, sweetie. Black as night, and strong enough to waddle across the table by itself."

He gave her a feeble smile. "Thanks."

"You feelin' okay? You look a bit pale."

While he appreciated her concern, he didn't feel like explaining. "Long day, that's all."

"You ought to try standing on your feet for ten hours, serving cranky people, then going home to a house full of screaming kids and a useless hubby. Now that's a long day."

He watched as the woman moved to the booth next to him, and for the first time, he noted her slight limp. Funny how you never think about the people around you and what troubles they may be going through. He'd never had a hard day in his life. Not really. Basically he'd had everything he'd ever needed, or wanted, handed to him. Not everyone was that fortunate. He gazed at the busy woman with a new appreciation, deciding to leave her a bigger tip than usual.

The soup arrived, and he spooned up each bite without really tasting it. His mind was still focused on Hero, the little boy, and the woman who'd entered his life so quickly and completely unannounced. What was her story? She'd mentioned she lived alone. Had she been married? A divorcée like a number of the women he'd met since he'd moved into the complex? Was there a significant other in her life? Was that the reason she'd turned down his offer of supper and had nearly turned down a ride home?

He thought about her big, round, blue eyes, eyes that seemed to widen with innocence as she talked. He hadn't noticed those beautiful eyes until they'd reached her condo. Before that, his mind had been centered on the accident.

"More coffee?"

"Ah, no."

"Finished with your soup?"

"Yes. I'd like my bill, please."

"How about a piece of fresh strawberry pie?"

He gave the woman a smile. "No, thanks. Maybe next time."

When she brought the bill, he glanced at it, noted the total, which came to four dollars and thirty-seven cents, pulled out a twenty-dollar bill, and placed it on top.

"Keep the change," he said with a wink as he scooted out of the little booth.

"But this is a twenty!" she said, her voice filled with surprise.

He gave her a grin. "I know."

⸸

Valene lay on her back, thinking about Vanessa's wedding day. The day she and her twin sister had looked forward to since they were old enough to play dress-up. She smiled into the darkness as she remembered the many times they'd played "Wedding" and how they'd conned their neighbor boy into playing the part of the groom. Their mother had given them an old, white satin party dress that had yellowed with age, a long piece of white nylon netting to cover their heads as a veil, and a handful of hydrangeas from the yard to use as a bridal bouquet. Whichever girl wasn't being the bride on a given day took the role of the preacher.

What fun they'd had, and what hilarious vows they'd thought up. *Do you take this man to be your husband? Will you keep his clothes washed and ironed, the kitchen clean, and give him pills when he is sick?* They couldn't have been more than five or six at the time, and their groom was at least two years younger and had no idea what he was doing. They just draped him in one of their father's old black jackets and made him stand in front of the make-believe altar—a cardboard box covered with a bath towel.

She and Vanessa would fashion a cross from two small branches they'd break off from the mulberry tree in their backyard. Then they'd stick it into a glob of putty to make it stand. Next to it, they'd place a Bible opened to John 3:16, the first verse they'd ever learned. Since the homemade wedding rings they'd fashioned from yellow chenille pipe cleaners were usually misplaced between the mock weddings, their mother had suggested they use the tabs from soda cans, which were a little lopsided in shape but always readily available.

Valene flipped onto her side and scrunched up the pillow beneath her head. Now Vanessa was married. Her twin, her buddy. She couldn't imagine what life was going to be like without her. A ray of moonlight wiggled its way past the edge of the drawn shade and fell across her pillow. She traced its path with her fingertip, wondering where her sister was at that very moment. *Will I ever find that perfect man? The one God has prepared for me?* She frowned as another thought pushed its way into her mind. *What if I never find him? What if God has designed that I remain single?*

A bright light flashed across her room as a car pulled into the parking lot, causing her to blink. *Surely not! Not when He knows all I've ever wanted to be is a wife and a mother.* She thought about Jeff, who was sleeping soundly on her sofa, and how precious he was to Nathan and Vanessa. *Oh, God. Thank You for protecting him.*

Her thoughts went to the man they'd met that day. Was he, too, lying in bed, trying to sleep? She trembled as she tried to imagine how she would've felt if she'd nearly hit a boy on a bicycle, then hit someone's dog, causing serious injuries. Only now that it was over could she recall the look of panic and guilt she'd seen on Jordan Young's face when she'd rushed into that parking lot. The poor man! Her heart went out to him.

Eventually, sleep overtook her.

✝

Valene jumped when the phone rang at seven. It was Diane, her next-door neighbor. She'd heard about the parking lot accident from another neighbor who'd witnessed it.

"Yes, it was a pretty close call," Valene told her as she filled her in on the details. "But praise God, the truck didn't hit Jeff. Never even grazed him."

"How's Hero?"

Valene swallowed hard. "Not so good." She went on to explain Hero's injuries, then added, "I'm going to the animal clinic as soon as Jeff and I have breakfast."

"Look, I'm sure that clinic is no place for a boy of Jeff's age. Why don't you let him stay here with me? He and my son always have a good time playing together when Jeff comes to visit you. They can play video games this morning, I'll feed them an early lunch, then we can go to that new community park near the mall. I hear they have all kinds of new playground equipment there. They can burn off some of that boundless energy. I'll have him home by three, and you can spend the day with Hero. I'm sure the boys'll have a good time together."

"The playground, huh? I know Jeff would like that."

"Can I, Aunt Val? Please?"

Valene turned to see a sleepy-faced boy standing behind her, rubbing his eyes. She covered the phone with her hand. "You sure you want to go? I'll be gone most of the day."

He nodded.

She gave him a grin and removed her hand from the receiver. "He says he wants to go. If the offer still stands, and you're sure you want to spend the day with two energetic young boys—"

"Of course I do. It'll be fun."

Val thanked Diane and made arrangements to take Jeff to her condo as soon as he'd had his breakfast. She really wanted to spend some time with Hero, and Diane was right. It would be a depressing experience for Jeff. She grasped the boy by both shoulders and lowered her face to his. "Jeff, you have to promise me to stay with Diane every second. No wandering off, do you hear? And no talking to strangers."

The boy gazed back at her with big, rounded eyes. "I promise, Aunt Val."

The two enjoyed a quick breakfast of hot oatmeal topped with milk and brown sugar, then Valene took Jeff's hand, and they headed for Diane's condo. After handing Diane a piece of paper with the numbers of both her cell phone and the clinic and issuing a few last-minute instructions to Jeff, she started across the lot to her assigned parking space. She'd nearly reached her car when she heard footsteps behind her.

Chapter 3

Turning quickly, Val found Jordan Young smiling at her in an easy, friendly manner. He was dressed in a pair of jeans and a short-sleeved, pale blue polo shirt that brought out the blue in his eyes.

"Good morning," he chimed out as he approached her. "I hope you slept well. Where's Jeff?"

"He's staying with a neighbor. I kinda hated to take him to the clinic with me."

"Yeah, probably better if he doesn't go. Seeing Hero like that is depressing enough for an adult."

"Well," Valene said, as she pulled her keys from her purse, "I'd better be going."

He stepped between her and her car. "Are you going to the clinic now?"

She nodded.

"My offer still stands. I'd be happy to drive you."

"It'll probably be best if I take my car," she said quickly. "I may want to stay longer than you do."

He shrugged. "I'm not in any hurry. I've got all day."

"I–I need to stop at the store."

"Fine with me. I'm nearly out of coffee."

Valene stood gaping at the man, fresh out of excuses.

"I won't bite."

"I–I know," she mumbled, not sure what to say or do next.

"Aw, come on. Let me drive you there. We're both going to see Hero. Kinda silly to take two vehicles, isn't it? My truck's right there. A mere two spots from yours."

She quickly assessed the situation. Hadn't he taken them right home last night as he'd said he would? Surely, a man who was facing up to his responsibilities as he was could be trusted. "O–okay."

He led her to his Avalanche, opened the door for her, and soon they were headed toward the clinic.

Dr. Kinney was standing in the lobby when they arrived. "Good morning."

"Can we see Hero?" Valene asked without returning his greeting.

The veterinarian gave her a warm smile. "I'm sure he'll be glad to see you.

I'll be giving him his Rimadyl soon. Don't be alarmed if he seems to be in pain. The effects of last night's pill have worn off, but he'll be fine as soon as this one kicks in. We're keeping him as comfortable as possible."

"Ca–can I stay with him for awhile?"

"We'd both like to stay," Jordan added, stepping up beside her.

The doctor smiled and motioned for them to follow him.

Valene couldn't hold back her gasp when she walked into the little cubicle and found her beloved Hero lying on his side, strapped to a table, completely immobilized. He whined when he saw her and tried to get up, then let out a yelp.

Tears began to roll down her cheeks. "Does he have to be strapped down like that?"

"At this stage, the less he moves around, the better," the doctor explained as he stroked the dog's head. "Why don't you talk to him? Maybe pat his back. I'm sure your presence will have a calming effect on him."

Valene pulled her hair aside and leaned over the whimpering dog. "Shh, Hero. It's okay. I'm here."

Immediately, he calmed down, and his tense body relaxed.

"Looks like you two are good pals." Jordan moved close to her side and carefully wrapped his fingers around one of Hero's front paws. "Hi, fella."

Hero's pitiful whines tore at Valene's heart, and she had to force herself to keep from sobbing openly.

"I'll come back in a little while and give him his medication," Dr. Kinney said. "Meantime, try to keep him calm. We don't want him struggling to get up yet."

"We will," Jordan said, his thumb stroking Hero's paw.

"I know he's in terrible pain," Valene said, wiping her eyes with her sleeve as the door closed behind the kindly doctor. As she lifted her face to Jordan's, she was surprised to find tears in his eyes, too.

"He wouldn't even be here, if it weren't for me," he said sadly.

Without thinking, she patted the man's arm reassuringly, knowing the pain he must be experiencing in seeing Hero strapped to the table. "You mustn't feel that way. It was just one of those things that happened. I don't blame you."

Jordan brushed away his tears with the pad of his forefinger. "You probably think I'm a real wimp, but honest, I'd never hurt anyone intentionally."

"I know that." She wanted to slip her arm about his shoulder and comfort him. He seemed so forlorn. "Di–did you ever have a dog?"

"No. My mom wouldn't allow it. She thought dogs were smelly and dirty. But I always wanted one. Is Hero the first dog you've ever had?"

His mother wouldn't allow it? His words surprised her. What mother would deny a boy the joy of having a dog? Gathering her thoughts, Val answered, "No, Vanessa and I had one of those cute little white poodles when we were growing up. We called her Fluffy. But I'd always wanted a black Labrador. Hero is special in his own right, but he's extra special since he was a gift from my twin sister. We had a cat, too. Elvira."

He grinned. "Elvira?"

She laughed. "Yes. She was sleek with black hair and beautiful squinty eyes. Sorta flirty-like. It seemed the perfect name for her!"

"Yeah, the name *Elvira* does conjure up that image."

"What kind of dog would you have wanted if you could've had one?"

He tilted his head and pursed his lips thoughtfully. "What kind of dog would I have wanted? Well, to be honest, I don't know. What I really wanted to do was go to the Humane Society and pick out the scroungiest mutt they had. One that looked like he needed a home. Dumb, huh?"

"No, I don't think that's dumb. I think it's sweet. So many animals need homes and someone to love them. I actually thought about going to the Humane Society myself, although I doubt I'd have found a black Lab like Hero. I'd told Vanessa I wanted to get a dog, and being the kind, thoughtful sister she is, she gave me Hero as a gift. He's the best present I could ever have." She lowered herself onto the chair with a grateful smile.

"Well, I think Hero is the perfect name for this magnificent animal. His name fits him well. Like I told you, I've seen you walking him. He has a regal air about him. He looks like a hero."

Valene smiled at her dog. "He is my hero."

"Look how calm he's gotten since you've been here. He's barely moving now, and he's quit whining."

She brightened. "He has calmed down, hasn't he?"

"I'd say you have a magic touch."

╬

Jordan watched Valene as she wrapped an arm about her dog and whispered encouragement in his ear. She was pretty, no doubt about it, with her petite, shapely body, her honey-colored hair, and those gorgeous, big blue eyes. But her outward beauty wasn't what impressed him most. He'd been around attractive women all his life. It was her inner beauty. There was a sweet genuineness about her he hadn't seen in most of the women he'd dated, and he found it refreshing. He'd like to know more about Valene Zobel.

"Jordan, would you please get me a tissue from that box on the counter?" she asked, breaking into his thoughts.

"Tissue? Sure." He handed it to her, then watched as she carefully removed a bit of matter from one of Hero's eyes. Her touch was a gentle as a whisper.

142

"There," she said, tossing the tissue into a big metal wastebasket. "You're a good doggie."

With a slight yelp, Hero shifted his front legs, but Valene was quick to place a hand on him. "Stay still, Hero."

"He's a lucky dog."

She turned toward Jordan. "Lucky?"

"To have someone who cares for him like you do."

She grinned. "You're here, too. You must care."

"I do care. It's killing me to see him looking so forlorn, knowing I'm the one who caused his injuries."

"Jordan, you're a wonderful man. I want you to know how much I appreciate you and your interest in Hero. You didn't have to come here. I'm sure you have more pleasant things to do than spend your morning at an animal hospital."

"I'm wonderful? I nearly ran over your nephew, and I hit your dog! I don't call that wonderful."

"Enough of that."

He felt her hand on his arm. "Okay. You win. I'm wonderful."

Valene laughed. "Yes, you are. Learn to live with it."

He chuckled. "If I'm so wonderful, how about letting me take you to lunch after the doc gives Hero his medicine? I know this great little Italian restaurant down on Clifton Boulevard. Their specialty is *pollo alla cacciatora*. And you'll love their garlic bread. Only problem is, you can't breathe on anyone for a week after you eat it without them passing out!"

He watched as she laughed and seemed to be considering his invitation, hoping she'd accept. "Aw, come on, say yes. You've already told me Jeff won't be home until three."

Before she could answer, Dr. Kinney came in, carrying Hero's pill on a small plastic tray.

"Well, looks like having you here is better than medicine. I'm amazed Hero is this calm, considering his Rimadyl has worn off."

They watched as Dr. Kinney skillfully maneuvered the tablet down the dog's throat. Although Hero fought him a bit and tried to struggle, the doctor held him fast, and soon the dog swallowed the pill with very little difficulty.

"It won't take too long before he'll be getting sleepy," the doctor said with a gentle tap to Hero's nose. "He'll probably be out for several hours. If he gets along okay, you should be able to take him home in three or four days."

"Can I stay until he goes to sleep?" Valene asked quickly.

"You can stay as long as you like," Dr. Kinney answered. "It's obvious Hero likes having you here."

As soon as the doctor shut the door behind him, Valene turned to Jordan.

"You don't have to stay. I can take a taxi home."

"Valene, you have to eat. We'll both stay until Hero goes to sleep; then I want to take you to lunch. Please. Buying you a meal is the least I can do."

"Well, I'm not sure, I—"

"Please?"

"Umm, I guess, but I'll pay for my own lunch."

He smiled. She'd said yes. "We'll argue about that later."

Nearly twenty minutes passed before Hero fell into a deep sleep. Jordan's heart was touched as he watched Valene bend over the sleeping dog and whisper something in his ear. He knew she was hurting, and he wanted to take her in his arms and comfort her. There was something so sweet and innocent about her that tugged surprisingly at his heartstrings. But he also knew, since they were barely acquainted, his comfort could only come from words. "He'll be fine," he told her, reaching out his hand.

"I know. I'm being an old worrywart. But he's important to me. I can't imagine life without him. I'm also a fraidy-cat. There's no way I could sleep nights without Hero by my side." Although she ignored Jordan's hand, she gave him a smile.

"A beautiful woman can't be too careful these days." He pulled the door open, catching the delicate scent of her perfume as she moved past him.

"Look, it was nice of you to volunteer to help with Hero, but it's really not necessary. I'll manage somehow."

"Oh, but it is necessary. I would never forgive myself if I didn't help you. After all—"

She held up a silencing finger. "No blame game, remember?"

"Then you'll accept my help?" he asked as he pushed open the outer door.

"Maybe. We'll see."

The restaurant was crowded, but after a twenty-minute wait, they were escorted to a table in the far back corner. Jordan smiled at his luncheon guest over the menu. There was something about her that held him spellbound. Was it her smile? Her beautiful eyes? Or could it be her gentle ways? He couldn't be sure exactly what attracted him to her, but he found himself wanting to spend more time with Valene.

"What did you say was their specialty?"

"Ah, the pollo alla cacciatora? I think you'll like it."

She nodded. "Then that's what I'll have. If you say it's good, I'm sure it is."

When the waitress came to take their order, Jordan handed her their menus and ordered for both of them. "Thanks for coming with me," he told Valene once the waitress had moved on. "I hate eating alone."

She let out a slight sigh. "Me, too. Before I moved here and Nathan and Vanessa started dating, she and I always had lunch together. Now I have to eat alone."

"You love your sister very much, don't you?"

She nodded. "Yes, I do. But she's Nathan's now."

"You make her sound like a possession."

She frowned. "I do, don't I? She's anything but a possession. My sister is her own person. She's the strong one, the leader. I've always been the follower."

"Funny, you don't impress me as a follower," he said, meaning it. "From what I've observed in our short time together, I'd say you're very strong in your own right."

"Really? You think so?"

"Really."

"Everyone loves Vanessa," she went on. "She has what you call a sparkling personality. She's terrific."

"So are you." He almost wished he hadn't made that comment when she turned to him with a frown, but he couldn't help himself. She was terrific, and not at all like most of the women he knew. They were much more interested in themselves than in others. Valene impressed him as one who always put other's interests ahead of her own.

"You're only saying that because you haven't met my sister."

"I'm saying it because I've met you."

The waitress brought their drinks, a basket of hot onion-garlic rolls, and a plate of butter squares.

"These rolls are best when you slather them with butter." He offered the basket to her.

"Don't tempt me, Jordan," she said, hesitating before taking a roll from the basket. "I love butter, but I'm trying to keep my fat grams down to a reasonable number."

"You don't know what you're missing. Better try it."

"I will, in a second."

He watched as Valene bowed her head. He knew she was praying, but he couldn't help staring at her. It was obvious praying was a natural part of her life.

When she lifted her head, she spread a pat of butter onto her roll. "Umm, you're right. These are delicious and well worth the extra grams of fat."

"Told you so."

The two of them sat smiling at each other as they consumed their rolls. When their lunch arrived, Jordan grinned with satisfaction as Valene took her first bite of the pollo alla cacciatora.

"Umm, it's fabulous."

"Are you glad you came?" He hoped this would be the first of many times they'd dine together.

She ducked her head shyly and gave him a demure smile. "Yes, but I do feel a bit guilty having such a wonderful lunch when poor Hero is barely able to eat."

"Valene, Hero is in good hands," he reminded her. "He's probably sleeping right now and doesn't even realize you're gone."

She nodded. "I know, but. . ."

"If anyone should feel guilty, it's me. I'm the one—"

She lifted her palms to him. "I'm sorry, Jordan. I know I'm being foolish, but Hero is much more than a pet. He's my companion. My roommate."

He reached out his hand, palm up. "Let's make a pact. No more sad talk while we're enjoying our lunch. Okay?"

She placed her hand in his. "Okay, no more sad talk."

He knew he should let go, but he didn't want to and held on to her hand longer than he should. When Valene finally pulled it away, he smiled awkwardly. "It's nice to have company. Thanks for coming."

"Thanks for inviting me."

"You were a tough sell. I wasn't sure I was going to be able to convince you to come with me."

"I–I nearly didn't."

"I'm glad you did."

"Me, too."

"Well, if it isn't Jordan Young!"

At the sound of a woman's voice, both Jordan and Valene looked up into the gorgeous face of a tall, willowy blond.

Chapter 4

Jordan rose quickly. "Charmaine. Hello!"

"Where've you been keeping yourself, Jordie? It's been weeks since I've heard from you." The woman's words fairly dripped with honey.

"I—I've been busy." He gestured toward Valene. "Charmaine King, this is Valene Zobel."

The woman gave her a cool, indifferent stare.

"Hello, Ms. King. It's nice to meet you."

As quickly as she'd looked in Valene's direction, the blond turned away. "Jordie, dear, I'm giving a dinner party next Saturday night at the country club. I do hope you can come. I've missed you. All our friends will be there."

"Sorry, Charmaine. I'm going to be busy all weekend. But thanks for the invitation."

The look on the woman's face said she didn't like being turned down. "All weekend?"

"Long story." He shot a glance at Valene. "Some other time, perhaps."

Charmaine started to say something but stopped. She sent an icy stare Valene's way.

"I'll call you sometime," Jordan told the attractive woman, none too enthusiastically.

Charmaine gave him a coquettish smile as she ran a well-manicured fingernail down his arm. "I think that's what you said the last time we talked, but I never heard from you. You do have my phone number, don't you?"

"Like I said, Charmaine, I've been busy, and yes, I'm sure I have your number somewhere."

"Maybe we can play a game of tennis or take in a movie."

Jordan nodded. "Maybe."

Charmaine seemed a bit perturbed by his nonchalance. "Well, I'll leave you two to your lunch. Nice to have met you, Virginia."

"Valene," Jordan said, correcting her.

She shot an uninterested glance Valene's way. "Oh, yes. Valene." Then she smiled at him and, adding more honey to her words, added, "I'll be waiting for your call, Jordie."

"Good-bye, Charmaine." Jordan sat back down and grinned sheepishly at

Valene. "Sorry about that."

"You needn't be sorry. It's always nice to see old friends." She grinned back. "I got the feeling she was quite happy to see you."

"More coffee?" he asked, changing the subject, which was fine with her. However, she couldn't get the woman off her mind. Her gorgeous tanned figure, her beautifully coifed hair, her expensive clothing, all spelled wealth. Was this Charmaine person one of Jordan's girlfriends?

What business was it of hers? She wouldn't even be with the man if he hadn't hit her dog. That was his only interest in her. There was no way a handsome man like Jordan Young would choose her as his luncheon guest unless the two of them had been thrown together under such unusual circumstances.

"How about dessert?" Jordan asked as the waitress cleared away their dishes. "Spumoni ice cream!"

Valene shook her head as she placed a hand on her abdomen. "I'm too full to even think about it. Besides, I want to get back to Hero, and I'm sure you have plans."

"My only plan is to take you back to the vet's, spend time with Hero, and get you home before Jeff gets back."

"But—"

"Sorry, Valene. You're stuck with me."

After spending another hour with Hero, Valene and Jordan drove back to her condo.

"Want a ride in the morning?" he asked, as he stopped the truck in front of her place. "I heard the doc tell you it'd be okay to visit Hero."

She shook her head. "Thanks for the offer, but I'll be at church in the morning. I'll probably head over to see Hero after I have lunch with my parents."

His brows lifted as he leaped from the truck and rushed around to open her door. "Oh? Your parents live around here?"

"Yes, in Granite Cliffs, if you can call about fifteen miles away, 'around here.' I still go to Seaside Chapel, our home church in Granite Cliffs, even though I live here in Spring Valley." She slipped out of the seat and waited while he closed the door. "Do you go to church?"

"Me? Yeah, I usually make the early service, unless I need to be at the base."

"Then you're a Christian?"

He nodded and stuck his hands in his pockets, rattling his change. "When I was about ten, I went to my friend's church for some special meeting. They had this missionary speak, and he was pretty good. I went to the front of the church at the end of the service and accepted God into my life."

Valene brightened. *Jordan is a Christian?*

"I really meant it at the time," he went on, "but when I got home and told my dad, he said Christianity was nothing but a bunch of do-good, confused people." He grinned and wiggled his eyebrows. "I confess it made me question my decision. But when I was about fifteen and went to a youth meeting, I learned more about the Bible, and I knew I'd made the right decision despite my dad's ridicule. How about you?"

"I asked Jesus to come into my life when I was about that age."

"Like I said, I meant it at the time, but I was too young to really understand, and there was never anyone around to explain things to me. But I'm sure God heard that little ten-year-old boy's prayers."

"I'm sure He did."

Jordan looked off into space, as if avoiding her eyes. "I'm not as close to God as I should be. Maybe sometime we'll talk about it."

She wondered at his words but decided this might not be the best time to ask for an explanation. "You should visit my church sometime. The music is fabulous."

"Are you inviting me?"

Valene felt her heart skip a beat. "Yes, you're invited! I'd love to have you go with me any Sunday you can make it. We even have an orchestra. I love the music."

"Personally, I like country music."

"Oh, I've got some great southern gospel CDs you'd like," she told him with enthusiasm.

"I'd like that." Although he smiled, she detected a note of sadness in his voice.

"I'll loan you some, if you promise to listen to them." She pulled her keys from her purse and handed them to him. He took them with a grin, and the two walked to her door.

He unlocked her door, pushed it open, and handed her keys back to her. "Maybe by Monday, Dr. Kinney can tell us when you can bring Hero home, and we can work out a schedule."

She gave him a blank stare. "A schedule?"

"Sure. The doc said Hero's going to need constant care, twenty-four/seven. You can't do that alone. I told you I'd help."

"I know you did, but I really didn't expect you to go through with it."

He leaned his lanky body against the door jamb and smiled. "Hey, I don't say things I don't mean. Like I told the doc, I aim to do my part."

She ducked past him and stood in the open doorway, feeling as tongue-tied as a schoolgirl on her first date. "We'll see."

"I'll call you tomorrow night."

"Okay." She pushed the door almost shut, then stood watching him through the crack. Jordan Young was the kind of man most women only dreamed about. He'd barely stepped away from the door when his cell phone rang. Valene knew she shouldn't eavesdrop, but she listened anyway, assuming it was one of his many girlfriends. Maybe even that obnoxious Charmaine person.

Jordan quickly pulled the cell phone from his belt. "Hello," he said. "Yes, I can make it by five. No problem. I don't mind a bit."

She watched as he hurried to his truck and pulled into his parking place. Who was he meeting at five o'clock? *It's none of your business, dummy.*

Jeff arrived home right at three and chattered a mile a minute about the park Diane had taken them to. Val loved the way his face beamed with enthusiasm as he talked. When Vanessa and Nathan had first asked her to baby-sit Jeff while they were on their honeymoon, she'd been a bit apprehensive, although Jeff was a pretty good kid. Jeff had been to visit her with Vanessa before but had never actually spent the night. She found she enjoyed having him around. The two got along quite well.

"I hope you thanked Diane for taking you," she finally said when she could get a word in.

"I did, Aunt Val, and she said she'd take me again sometime."

She smiled at her nephew. "I told Hero why you didn't come and visit him today. He was a bit sleepy while I was there, but he's doing fine. Mr. Young was there, too."

"I like him. He's nice."

"Yes, he is nice."

Jeff hurried off to watch one of his afternoon cartoon shows while Valene put a load in the washer. She added the soap to the dispenser and had just hit the ON button, when the doorbell rang. She hurried into the little foyer and, after peeking through the peephole, flung open the door.

There, standing on her porch, was Jordan Young, and he was wearing a naval flight suit.

"You left your scarf in my truck. I thought you might need it." He reached the colorful scarf toward her.

She took it but stood gaping at him. "You're in the navy?"

He grinned. "No, I'm on my way to a Halloween party."

She suddenly realized how stupid she sounded. Of course, he was in the navy. Why else would he be wearing a naval flight suit?

He pounded his forehead with his palm. "That wasn't a very nice thing for me to say. You'll have to excuse me. Sometimes I speak before I think." His smile was quite congenial. "I'm stationed at San Diego. I'm a navy pilot. I fly the F-18 Hornet. You know, one of those planes that lands on aircraft carriers. I was supposed to be off all weekend, but a buddy called and asked me to file some reports for him. His wife has gone into premature labor."

"I–I'm sorry. I didn't mean to stare. It's just—well, we've never talked about our occupations. I—"

"Guess we didn't, did we? I don't even know what you do."

She shrugged. "I work in Medical Records at Community Hospital. Flying sounds like a lot more fun."

He laughed, and she once again felt at ease.

"I never had that problem. I've planned on being a navy pilot from the time I was old enough to know what one was. My dad served in the navy, too. My plan was to see the world before I settled down, just like he did. I've already seen a great deal of it. There's so much out there to see and do. Being a navy pilot gives me a chance to do just that, and I'm going to take advantage of every opportunity I can."

"You're lucky. I graduated college with a degree in business, which means I'm qualified for everything and nothing. I'm surprised you have a condo here. Couldn't you live on the base?"

"Yep, but when we're in port and not out on a mission, I prefer to have a place off-base, too. That way, I can stay here when I have free time and on weekends. I prefer my privacy and an abundance of entertainment and sports activities, not to mention a variety of good restaurants. Sure beats the base's elbow-to-elbow camaraderie, mainly military-centered activities, and base chow."

She snickered. "Isn't it scary to land on one of those ships? I've seen them do it on the news. I can't imagine being in a plane caught by its tail hook on a cable."

"I gotta admit, I've done it hundreds of times in my ten years with the navy, but the old adrenaline starts pumpin' each time I do it. I wouldn't give it up for anything." He sent her a grin as he backed away. "Well, I'd better scoot. I want to be at the base by five."

"Ah. . .sure. Thanks for returning the scarf."

"You're welcome. Say a little prayer for me when you go to church."

"I–I will."

Again, she closed the door all but a crack and watched as the handsome, uniformed man climbed into his truck and sped off. "Wow," she said aloud as she closed the door. "Does he ever look great in that uniform."

ℱ

Val's mother was waiting on the church steps when she and Jeff arrived the next morning. After making sure Jeff made it to the right Sunday school classroom, the two of them sat down on one of the sofas in the welcome center.

"I couldn't believe it when you called and told me about Jeff and that bicycle. I'd told your sister he should leave it at our house, but he insisted on taking it with him, and you know how she wants to please him." Her face filled with concern. "How's Hero?"

"Oh, Mom, you should've seen him. He was lying so still. I was sure he was dead, but Jordan rushed him to the vet's, and—"

"Jordan? Is that the man who hit him?"

"Yes, he's been wonderful. I don't think I could've gotten through this whole ordeal without him."

"He should be wonderful to you! Racing that truck of his through a parking lot—"

"No! It wasn't like that. He wasn't driving fast at all. I'd told Jeff to stay on the sidewalk. He disobeyed me. If Jordan hadn't hit the brake pedal when he did. . ."

Her mother grabbed her wrist. "Oh, Valene, don't even say it!"

Valene turned her face away and blinked back tears. "I should never have let Hero out without his leash. Now he's lying in the clinic with a fractured pelvis."

"Do—do you think perhaps it would've been better for him, if you'd—"

"Put him to sleep? No! I would never do that!"

"But, dear, do you have any idea how much his veterinarian and hospital bills will be? And how much care he's going to require? Can you handle all of that?"

"Jordan is paying all his bills, and he's volunteered to help me take care of him."

"He is?"

"Yes, Mother, he is. He's the most honorable, responsible man I've ever met."

"Oh, Valene, I worry about you. You're not strong like your sister. Please don't take on more than you can handle."

Jordan's words rang in Valene's mind. *Funny, you don't impress me as a follower. From what I've observed in our short time together, I'd say you're very strong in your own right.* "Perhaps I'm stronger than you think."

"Just be careful. You don't really know this man."

"He's a Christian, Mom. He accepted Christ when he was a small boy. I'm not sure how close he is to God now, but I'll find out more as I get to know him better. He goes to his own church, but I've invited him to go to church with me sometime."

"Good. Knowing that makes me feel better. You know how important it is that you two share the same faith. Are you sure you don't want Jeff to spend the week with us?"

"No, I've taken off the entire week. He'll be fine. I told Vanessa I'd take care of him. I'll be bringing Hero home probably Tuesday or Wednesday, and he can help me with him during the day. I think Jordan will be helping at night."

"Promise me you'll be careful."

"I will."

⁜

"Time to go," Valene called out to Jeff after a pleasant lunch and a leisurely visit with her parents. "I know you're having a great time playing with Lick, but we want to spend some time with Hero."

Jeff wrapped his arms about his dog and gave him a big squeeze. "Sorry, Lick, but I gotta go see your brother. He can't run and play like you can, and I think he's lonely."

"We'll take good care of him," Valene's mother assured the boy, patting him on the shoulder. "You'll be back with him next week, but right now I think your Aunt Valene needs you."

Jeff gave his dog one more squeeze, then bounded toward the door with Lick at his heels. "Okay."

⁜

When Valene and her new nephew arrived back at the condo after spending some time with Hero, they played a game of Clue, then put on one of her favorite CDs, while Jeff showed her how he could do somersaults across the living-room floor. They enjoyed hot dogs at a nearby drive-in, then stopped by the video store and rented a movie.

She fixed them tall glasses of fresh lemonade, popped the videotape in the VCR, and the two settled themselves on the sofa to watch the movie. She had to smile as she straightened the cover on the armrest, remembering how she and Vanessa and their friends had struggled, getting that sofa from their old apartment to her new condo. She'd bought it secondhand, but it still looked good. The pale blue upholstery was as lovely as when she'd seen it that first time.

Occasionally, Valene would glance at the phone. When it finally rang, she grabbed the receiver on the first ring and carried it into the hall, where she could talk without disturbing Jeff, who was engrossed in the movie. As she'd hoped, it was Jordan.

"Hi," she said, trying not to sound too eager. "How'd your day go?"

"Fine. It was just routine. How about yours?"

She smiled into the phone. "It was good. Jeff and I went to church, had lunch with my folks, visited Hero for an hour or so, then came home. Jeff's watching a movie now."

"That's it?"

"Well, we did play an exciting game of Clue."

He let out a chuckle. "Who did it? Colonel Mustard in the library, using a candlestick?"

She laughed. "How'd you guess?"

153

"I've played that game hundreds of times. Why do kids like that thing?"

"I don't know. My sister and I played it, too. I used to think it was exciting when I was little, but I had a hard time gathering up any enthusiasm to play it with Jeff. He enjoyed it, though, and that made it bearable."

"Did you pray for me?"

His question took her aback. "Ye—yes, I did."

"Hey, thanks. I wondered why things went so well today."

She laughed. "Then I'll pray for you again tomorrow."

"I have an early morning meeting, so I'm going to stay on the base tonight, but I should be back to Spring Valley by four. What time are you going to go see Hero?"

"I thought I'd go in the morning. Jeff's going with me."

"Oh."

She detected a tinge of disappointment in his voice. "Diane said she'd keep him if I wanted to go back later."

"About four?"

"Probably." Her heart raced.

"Want a ride?"

"Yes, that would be very nice. I hate driving in late-afternoon traffic."

"I'll try to make it by four. Don't leave without me."

"I won't."

"Valene."

"Yes?"

There was a pause. "Nothing. See you at four."

She cradled the phone in her hand long after the connection had been sev-ered. What had he started to say?

*

"Hey, Young! Wanna get a beer with us?" two of Jordan's squad members asked as the three of them walked along.

He shifted his briefcase to his other hand. "No, thanks. I have a four o'clock appointment, and I have to drive to my condo."

"A blond appointment?" one of them asked with a wink.

Jordan felt himself blushing. "Actually, I'm going to visit a dog in the animal hospital."

One of the men elbowed him as they walked along. "Aw, you don't expect us to believe that, do you? Come on, you can tell us. Who is she?"

"Honest, fellas, I'm going to visit a dog!"

"Give her a kiss for us, will you?"

He waved good-bye, then strode off in the direction of the parking lot. *Give her a kiss for you? I'd like to give her a kiss for me!*

154

It was exactly 3:55 when Jordan arrived at Valene's condo. She was waiting for him on the little bench on her porch. "You're early," she called out as he exited his pickup.

"I knew you were waiting for me. Ready?"

"You bet." She climbed into the truck as he held the door open for her.

He hurried around to the driver's side and slid under the steering wheel. "How was Hero this morning?"

"Pathetic."

The smile left his face. "He's not doing well?"

"I didn't say that. I said he was pathetic. All those places where he skidded on the pavement have turned crusty, and he's beginning to try to move around a bit more. It breaks my heart to see him like that."

"I know," he said softly as he guided the Avalanche out of the lot and onto the street. "He's been on my mind constantly. I wish I could trade places with him."

"Somehow," she said, her frown turning to a smile, "I can't imagine you barking and eating dog biscuits."

"Aw, you know what I mean."

"I know. I wish I could trade places with him, too."

"Did the vet say when you could take him home?"

"Wednesday."

His face brightened. "Really? Good. I know I can get someone to cover for me Wednesday. That way, I'll be able to help you with him."

Valene felt a sense of relief. She'd had no idea how she was going to manage bringing the dog home by herself. "I'd really appreciate the help, if you're sure it won't inconvenience you."

"No trouble at all. I'm one of the few single guys in my unit. A lot of the married men owe me time for covering for them."

As they entered the clinic, Valene felt Jordan's hand on the small of her back, and his touch sent chills up her spine.

"Ah, I'm glad to see you both," Dr. Kinney told them as they entered the waiting room. "That dog of yours is determined to get up. I think it's time we let him."

The doctor led them to the place where Hero was being housed during his stay.

"Ms. Zobel," the doctor said, reaching out a long piece of terry cloth, "since you won't have an apparatus with which to move your dog around when you get home, I'm going to show you a way to handle him so you won't hurt him or add to his pain. When Mr. Young lifts Hero, you and I are going to slip this cloth beneath him, directly in front of your dog's hind legs, okay?"

Valene nodded.

"Okay, Mr. Young. Wrap your arms around Hero's midsection and lift him on the count of three. And be prepared. This is going to hurt him, but it has to be done if he's going to get his strength back." He gestured toward Valene. "Ready, Ms. Zobel? One. Two. Three. Lift!"

Each did their job, and with only one loud yelp, Hero's hind end was lifted and supported by the makeshift sling.

"Steady, boy," the vet said, tugging up on one end of the cloth. "He won't be able to stand on his own, but he'll be encouraged. It's his natural instinct to want to stand despite the pain he's experiencing."

Valene wanted to cover her ears. The pitiful sounds coming from Hero as he struggled to stand were almost more than she could bear. A quick glance at Jordan confirmed that Hero's obvious pain was getting to him, too.

Dr. Kinney gestured toward Hero. "It's time for his Rimadyl, but I wanted him totally alert the first time we tried this. We'll let him struggle for a few minutes, then we'll lay him back over on his side, and I'll give him his medication."

Neither Valene nor Jordan could think of anything to say. They just watched the helpless dog make his futile efforts. Eventually, the doctor motioned for them to lower him.

"Now I want to show you how to exercise him. Each of you grab onto one end again while I assist Hero. As he tries to drag himself forward, we're going to help him by tugging slowly on the cloth. He won't get far, but with you taking some of the strain off his hind end and his skeletal frame and muscles, it will relieve his pain somewhat. When you take him home, this is what you'll have to do to help him learn to maneuver again. Do you think you can handle it?"

They both nodded.

"Okay, pull."

Valene winced when Hero let out another painful-sounding moan.

"Like I told you, it's going to get messy. He won't be able to take care of his bodily functions like he would if he were outside. You'll have to clean up after him until that pelvis heals and he's able to walk around by himself."

"We'll do whatever is necessary," Jordan said without hesitation, and somehow Valene knew he meant it. She wouldn't have to face this alone.

They watched as Hero stood on his front legs and tried to pull his back legs to a standing position, but it was impossible, even with their help.

"It'll come, boy. Just be patient," Dr. Kinney said as he again patted Hero's head. "That old adage is true. No pain, no gain. It's true for dogs as well as humans."

"He—he's so helpless," Valene said, her voice cracking with emotion.

"Ah, but he has you!" Dr. Kinney gave her a compassionate smile. "Not all dogs have owners who are as patient and as willing to work with them and nurse them back to health. After seeing you two and the love you both seem to have for this dog, I have no doubt he's going to be up and running around in no time."

"We won't desert him, Doc," Jordan added, speaking for both of them.

They allowed Hero another three full minutes on his front feet before the doctor said he'd had enough for one day. Within thirty minutes of taking his medication, the dog was once again stretched out on the table, strapped down, and fast asleep. Valene bent and kissed the tip of his ear before whispering, "Good night."

When she stood, she found Jordan staring at her. The look in his eyes told her he was as concerned about Hero as she was, and she was thankful. If Hero had to be hit by a truck, she was grateful he was hit by someone who cared and who faced up to his responsibility. That's exactly what Jordan Young was doing.

"Are you ready to go?" he asked softly, as if he didn't want to disturb the sleeping dog.

She smiled up into his kind face. "Yes. I'm ready."

As they moved out toward the parking lot, she felt Jordan's hand once again go to the small of her back. The same chill ran up her spine.

"How are we going to work this out?" he asked once they had turned toward home.

"You mean our schedule?"

He nodded as he sent a quick glance her way. "I'll try to be available any time you need me, but I figured the nights might be best. That way, you could get a good night's sleep."

She paused as she thought things over. "I knew it was going to be tough, but I didn't know how tough until this afternoon. I'm not sure what would be best."

"Maybe you could call me each time Hero needs to be moved. And I don't mind cleaning him up," he inserted quickly. "I'll take the night shift, too."

She frowned. "How would that work? He's too heavy to move back and forth from my condo to yours. We don't want to cause him any more pain than necessary."

He let out a long, low sigh. "I hadn't thought of that."

"I know!" she said excitedly. "I can take next week off, too! I've been working a lot of overtime the past few months—there has been so much sickness in our department. Instead of my usual ten-hour-a-day, four-day workweek, some weeks I've been working as many as six days. I know I have at least five or six days of comp time coming. Maybe more. This would be the perfect time to use them."

"That'd sure help," he said, "but what about the night thing? You can't take care of him all day and all night, too."

Her enthusiasm waned. "I guess we have plenty of time to work something out. He won't be coming home until Wednesday." *But what? I can't have a near-stranger spending the nights in my condo. Maybe he can take the day shift, and I'll take* nights. But that wouldn't work. It wouldn't be proper for him to spend his days taking care of Hero while I'm sleeping in the other room. Then there's Jeff to consider. He'll be with me until Saturday, when he goes over to Mom and Dad's to stay until Vanessa and Nathan get back from their honeymoon. And I have to go back to work after next week. What'll I do with Hero while I'm at work and Jordan is at the base?

"Yeah," he said, scratching his head as if he, too, were deliberating their dilemma. "We probably need to give it some more thought."

"Yes, I guess we do."

"I'm sure we'll find an answer that's workable for both of us," he said confidently.

They rode along in silence for awhile. Valene's mind was a blank. The situation seemed impossible, yet they had to come up with a workable solution.

"I don't know about you, but I think better with food in my stomach. Why don't we call and have pizza delivered to your condo? I'm sure Jeff would like it, and I hate—"

"To eat alone," she said, finishing his sentence.

"Exactly."

"But, Jordan, you've done so much already."

He glanced at her, taking his eyes off the road for only a second. "Not nearly as much as I'd like to."

She meditated over his comment before answering, wondering exactly what he meant. "Okay, but if you do this, you have to allow me to fix supper tomorrow night. Nothing fancy, but that way we can devote our full attention to Hero. Providing you're still willing to help me bring him home."

"Of course, I am!" He pulled his cell phone off his belt and handed it to her with a grin. "Hit six on the speed dial. That's the pizza phone number. I call it often. Order whatever you and Jeff would like. Me? I like it all."

"How about a large, half supreme, half pepperoni?"

"Sounds great."

When they arrived at the condo, Valene opened things up while Jordan went to Diane's to retrieve Jeff. By the time they'd returned, she had poured soda for them and set paper plates and napkins on the coffee table. "I thought we'd eat our pizza in here."

"Pizza? Kewl!" Jeff said in exaggerated tones. "I love pizza. Me and my dad eat it all the time."

"Pepperoni okay, sport?" Jordan asked as he sat down on the sofa and stretched his arms wide across its back.

"My favorite," Jeff said, sitting down beside him.

Jordan looked around the room. "Nice condo, Valene. I like the way you have it fixed. It looks like you."

She gave him a shy grin. "Is that a compliment? Other than the second-hand sofa, it's mostly garage-sale stuff."

"Are you renting your condo, or did you buy?"

"I bought it. I hated to pay rent and have nothing to show for it at the end of the year. My grandparents left my sister and me some money. She wisely bought the pet shop where we'd worked, and renamed it Whiskers, Wings, and Wags. Cute name, huh? Vanessa has always been the creative one."

"And you bought your condo?"

She nodded. "I figured any property in the San Diego area was a good investment. I hope I was right."

"I hope you were, too. That's the main reason I bought my condo. I like this complex."

Jordan leaped from the sofa when the doorbell rang, paid for the pizza, and gave the delivery boy a generous tip.

When he placed the pizza box on the table, Jeff called out, "I wanna pray," surprising Valene.

She gave him a smile. "Sure, Jeff. Go ahead."

"Dear Lord. Thanks for the pizza and Aunt Valene and Mr. Young and Hero. And thanks for the doctor who is going to make him well. Be with my daddy and my new mama and with Lick, too. Amen."

"Hey, that's pretty good," Jordan told him with a laugh. "Better'n I do."

Jeff gave him a quizzical look. "I talk to God all the time. Don't you ever talk to Him?"

Jordan frowned. "Sure I do, Jeff. Couldn't get through life without it." Jordan tousled the boy's hair. "Let's dig into this pizza before it gets cold."

Valene and Jordan consumed the supreme half of the pizza, while Jeff worked on the pepperoni half.

"I'm stuffed." Jordan leaned back into the sofa and rubbed his stomach. "How about you, sport?"

Jeff grinned. "Me, too."

Valene rose and began gathering plates, napkins, and glasses and placing them on her tray. "While you two boys relax, I'll take this stuff into the kitchen and take care of the leftovers."

Jordan stood quickly and grabbed onto the tray. "No, I'll do it. You relax."

They stood staring at one another, each wearing a challenging smile.

Valene let go of the tray and motioned him toward the kitchen. "We'll both do it."

She led the way and he followed.

"This has been nice," he said as he placed the tray on the counter. "Thanks for letting me stay."

"Thank you for the pizza."

"Maybe we can do it again after we bring Hero home."

She smiled over her shoulder as she placed their glasses and silverware in the dishwasher. "Maybe."

"I guess I'd better be going. I've got another early morning meeting scheduled with my work crew, but I'll be home about four. I could drive you to see Hero again. Maybe Jeff'll want to come along this time."

"I'd like that. Are you sure it won't inconvenience you?"

"Not at all. I want to drive you. I like being with you."

She felt herself blushing. She liked being with him, too, but she'd never tell him.

He leaned down and planted a quick kiss on her cheek. "See you about four tomorrow."

His sudden kiss rendered her speechless. "I. . .ah. . .yes, four. See you then."

She watched as he strode down her sidewalk and turned toward his condo. *Oh, dear Lord. I think I'm falling in love. Jordan is everything I could ever want in a man. But why would he ever want me?*

She and Jeff watched a skateboard special on TV, then worked a few puzzles in the workbook she'd bought him when they'd gone shopping. "Off to bed with you," she told him, as she closed the book and placed it on the coffee table.

"Do I have to go to bed now, Aunt Valene?"

She nodded. "Your dad gave me strict instructions for you to be in bed by nine. Don't forget to brush your teeth."

Valene smiled as she watched the boy pad off toward the bathroom. Someday she'd like to have children.

She pulled the toss pillows off the sofa and began making up Jeff's bed. She was just putting the quilt in place when she heard a soft rapping sound. After a quick look through the peephole, she opened the door.

Chapter 5

"I've got it!" Jordan called out excitedly as his hands grasped her shoulders.

"You've got what?"

"The way we can take care of Hero when he comes home! I was getting ready for bed when it hit me!"

She couldn't help but smile. He must've been serious about getting ready for bed when he was struck by inspiration. He had on a simple white T-shirt and a pair of khaki shorts and was barefoot. "So, what's this plan of yours?"

"You can stay at my condo!"

"Stay at your condo? I don't understand. Why would I want to do that?"

"Look, I've got it all planned out. It'd be much too difficult to move Hero from place to place, right?"

She nodded.

"So, until you go back to work, you stay with him days while I'm at work. I'll be home about four, and I'll come over and help you exercise him. Then, when it's your bedtime, you can go over to my condo and spend the night. That way, you'll get a good night's sleep, and I can take care of Hero!"

She gave him a frown. "But when are you going to sleep?"

"With the lights out, he'll probably sleep most of the night. But when he needs help or needs to be cleaned up, I'll be there to take care of him. I'll wake you up when it's time for me to leave in the morning."

His enthusiasm overwhelmed her. "But, Jordan, don't you see? You're getting the worst end of that plan. I couldn't let you do such an unselfish thing."

"Nothing unselfish about it. I owe it to you and that terrific dog of yours. Besides, it'll give me an excuse to spend the evenings with you. Maybe we can even have supper together again."

She didn't know what to say and just stared at him.

"Think about it. It's a good plan." He bent and kissed her on the forehead. "Now, you'd better get some sleep. Good night, sweet lady."

"Ah. . .good night."

Valene stood holding onto the knob even after she'd closed the door. Jordan had kissed her. Twice! Her fingers rose to touch her forehead. *Be still, my heart. It was only a friendly gesture. He meant nothing by it. If it weren't for Hero, he wouldn't take a second look at me. Vanessa, maybe. But not me!*

By four o'clock the next day, Val was a basket case. All she'd been able to think about was Jordan Young. Even Jeff had noticed her spaced-out look and had asked her about it. She'd awkwardly explained she was merely concerned about Hero, which she was.

She raced to open the door when Jordan arrived.

"Ready?" he asked.

She nodded and gave him a warm smile. "Come on, Jeff," she called. "It's time to go see Hero."

"Shut the door and make sure it locks," Jordan told Jeff over his shoulder as he led Valene to his pickup. Once they reached it, Jordan took Valene's hand in his. "Let me help you. I don't think they designed these Avalanches for women wearing skirts."

She let out a giggle. "I guess not." The warmth of his hand on hers made her heart sing. *Down, girl. He only took your hand to assist you. Nothing more. Don't read things that aren't there. You'll only set yourself up for disappointment.*

"So, how was Hero when you visited him this morning?" he asked as she settled into the smooth leather seat.

"The doctor said he's doing as well as could be expected, but I don't know. Hero's trying to move around even more, and it's so obvious he's in pain. It hurts me to see him that way."

"I know, and tomorrow it'll be up to us to help him move around. Think you can handle it?"

"I have to handle it. I don't have a choice, if I want to see him get well."

He closed her door, checked to make sure Jeff was secure in his seat belt and that the door was shut tight, then hurried around to the other side.

"It's very kind of you to drive us to the vet's," Val told him, wanting him to know how much she appreciated it.

"Yeah, I like to ride in your Avalanche!" Jeff chimed in from the backseat. "It's cool. Wish my dad had one."

"Avalanche? That's what you call this truck?" Valene asked, searching the dash for a brand name.

"Aunt Valene! Don't you know what an Avalanche is?" Jeff asked mockingly. "They show them on TV all the time."

"I'm afraid I don't keep up on things like that," she confessed, with a sideways glance toward Jordan.

He let out a chuckle as he caught Jeff's face in the rearview mirror. "Women don't care as much about that sorta stuff as us guys, Jeff."

"I know it's the nicest truck I've ever been in," Valene admitted. "I love the leathery smell. It must be quite new."

"As a matter of fact, I've only had it for two months now, so I guess you could say it's pretty new."

"I want an Avalanche when I grow up," Jeff said.

Jordan let loose a little laugh. "Jeff, by the time you get ready to buy a truck, they'll probably have wings!"

"Really?"

"He's teasing you, Jeff," Valene said, smiling over the seat at her nephew.

"Hey, Valene," Jordan inserted. "Did you give any more thought to my plan? About caring for Hero when he comes home tomorrow?"

"Yes, but I still think it's asking too much of you."

"It's not. Honest. I think it's the best thing we could come up with. I say, let's do it!"

⁜

Hero was wide awake and struggling against the straps that restrained him when they entered the cubicle. His fur was damp.

"Don't be alarmed," Dr. Kinney said as he began to unfasten Hero's straps. "He had his water therapy session, and you know how Labs love water."

Jordan moved to the dog's side and placed a hand on his damp fur. "Does that kind of therapy really help him?"

"Oh, yes. You'll want to continue his water therapy when you get him home," Dr. Kinney explained. "Simply fill the tub about half full and lower him into it. It'll not only make him feel better, but the water will give some buoyancy to his hind end and make it easier for him to start to stand again. Just make sure you have an abundance of old towels. He splashes quite a bit."

Jordan flashed a quick look toward Valene. "I don't think you'll want to try this without me."

She nodded. "You're right. I could never handle him by myself."

"There's something else I need to mention." The doctor handed one end of the towel to Valene. "Hero will be standing by himself in a couple of weeks, he'll be able to walk very soon after that, and then run, but he'll always appear a bit stiff when he walks. Those hips are never going to be quite right, and he may develop arthritis in them sooner than normal. I just want you to be aware of it, so you'll recognize it when it comes."

"I've heard arthritis is fairly common in older Labradors, Doc. Is that true?"

"Yes, it's common in many older dogs, but Hero is young, and he should have many good years ahead of him." He ruffled up the dog's damp fur. "As you can see, his abrasions are healing nicely, and his fur is beginning to grow back, but you'll still have to keep those places quite clean and continue to give him his amoxicillin for awhile. I've already taken the stitches out of those cuts he had." He pointed to several places on Hero's shoulders. "I'll have all the instructions

163

written out for you when you come for him tomorrow. He'll also need to continue with the Rimadyl twice a day. In some ways, this is going to require more effort on your part than taking a new baby home from the hospital—only thing is, you won't have to burp him."

Jordan laughed. "Gonna be a few years before that happens!"

His comment only reinforced Valene's resolve to keep their relationship from going beyond friendship, though she'd like to see it go much farther.

"He still looks sorta funny," Jeff said, wrinkling up his nose.

"He'll look fine, once that fur grows back," the doctor assured him. "Just be patient."

They worked with Hero, helping him drag his body by using the towel, until he seemed exhausted.

"I think he's had enough for one day." Dr. Kinney pulled the towel from beneath the dog. "I'll give him his dose of Rimadyl, and he'll soon be fast asleep."

"He looks so pitiful," Valene whispered to Jordan as the doctor left them alone. "Will he ever be himself again?"

Jordan took her hand in his and stroked her knuckles with the pad of his thumb. "Of course, he'll be all right. He has the two of us to help him."

"I'm so thankful for you," she declared as they stood by the dog's side. "I couldn't have faced this without you."

"If I hadn't been around, Hero wouldn't even be here now," he said with a sorrowful expression.

She shrugged. "But what happened, happened, and you've been with me right from the start. I really do appreciate all the things you've done for both Hero and me."

"Enough! I don't deserve this kind of praise."

They stayed until Hero was resting comfortably. Valene bent over Hero and whispered her love and good wishes for his returning health, adding that she was praying for him and his recovery, before she kissed the tip of his ear and said good-bye. Then Jordan ushered her and Jeff out the door and to his truck.

"How about spaghetti and meatballs for supper, Jeff?" Jordan asked as he turned the key in the ignition. "I know a great place right on the way back to the condo."

"Um, I like spaghetti," Jeff answered quickly, leaning forward excitedly.

"You shouldn't, Jordan," Valene said, shaking her head. "You really don't have to feed us every night. And remember, I was going to cook tonight."

"Have to? Did anyone here twist my arm?" he asked with a grin, keeping his eyes trained on the road. "Besides, I like taking you out to eat."

"I can fix us something when we get home," she volunteered, afraid they were taking advantage of his generosity.

"I really want to take you and Jeff out for dinner. Please say yes."

What could she say? He wanted to take them, and Jeff wanted to go. "Okay, but this has got to end. Tomorrow night, I definitely will cook."

"Does that mean you're inviting me to supper?"

She laughed. "Of course you're invited, but don't expect anything fancy. I'm not much of a cook, but I'm learning."

Before they arrived at the condo, Jordan's cell phone rang. From what Valene could hear of the one-sided conversation, it was one of his navy buddies. His car wouldn't start, and he wanted Jordan to bring over his jumper cables.

He looked disappointed as he explained and placed the phone on his belt. "I'll have to give you a rain check on the spaghetti, and you two are going to have to play Clue without me."

"We were going to play Clue?" Jeff asked from the backseat. "Yippee!"

Valene swatted at Jordan's arm playfully. "Looks like you got out of that one easily enough. But now I'm going to have to play, thanks to you."

"I'll make it up to you," he said, grinning at her. "Since someone is covering for me tomorrow, I can go with you to pick up Hero anytime you're ready," he told her as she stood on the sidewalk with Jeff at her side.

"Why don't we plan on going about ten? That okay?"

"Ten, it is."

She watched as the truck pulled out of the parking lot and onto the street.

"You ought to marry him, Aunt Val. He's nice."

She gave her nephew a sad look. "He's not the marrying kind, Jeff. He has plans to see the world before he settles down. That could be years from now."

"Maybe you could see the world with him."

Oh, if only it were that simple. "I don't think the navy would let a wife tag along."

"So, pray about it!"

Out of the mouths of babes. "You're one smart kid," Valene told her nephew as she put an arm about him and they headed for their front door. "I will pray about it."

✝

Jordan pulled into his buddy's driveway and stopped opposite his car.

"Hope I didn't take you away from something important," his friend said as Jordan opened the cargo bay and pulled out the jumper cables.

"Naw, I was just in the company of a beautiful woman, that's all."

"What'd you do with her? I don't see her in the truck."

"I told her duty called and dropped her off at her place."

"Sounds like I spoiled your evening. Why didn't you tell me? Maybe I could've gotten hold of someone else."

Jordan grinned as he snapped the jumper cable clamps over the battery's terminals. "Yeah, I had a terrific evening planned. I was gonna play Clue with her six-year-old nephew. Look what you made me miss."

"I hate that game! My daughter wants me to play it with her all the time. If I ever meet Colonel Mustard, I'm gonna strangle him myself! The guy who invented that game must not have had kids!" His buddy shook his head. "No man in his right mind would put himself through that kind of torture unless he was bonkers about the woman. When's the wedding?"

Jordan offered a feeble laugh. Somehow the single life didn't seem as satisfying as it used to, but he'd never admit it to his buddies. "No wedding! I'm gonna see the world before I get saddled with a wife, remember?"

The man gave him a friendly slap on his back. "You sure about that? Seems to me you've met a woman who might just change your mind."

"Nope. Just a friend."

Jordan checked the connections one more time, then motioned for the man to turn on the ignition. The car's engine roared into action. He disconnected the cables and began rolling them up.

"Hey, thanks, Jordan. I really appreciate your help. Guess I'd better buy that new battery tomorrow."

"No problem. That's what friends are for. You'd have done the same thing for me."

The man smiled. "I'm not so sure I'd have left a beautiful woman to come to your aid. If you hurry, you might get back in time to play that game of Clue."

Jordan climbed into his pickup, rolled down the window, and gave the man a wave. "I'll give your regards to Colonel Mustard!"

The light was on in Valene's condo when he drove by, and he was tempted to stop. But tomorrow was a big day for her. Hero was coming home.

⌖

"Jeff's fine. He didn't even get a scratch," Valene told her twin as they talked on the telephone. "He didn't mean to disobey, honest. I'd told him to stay on the sidewalk, but you know how the sidewalks all end at the parking lot here in our complex. Jeff got to the end and couldn't stop. Jordan was driving fairly slow and slammed on his brakes in time to avoid hitting him. Hero wasn't that fortunate."

"I just feel awful about this," Vanessa said on the other end. "I praise God Jeff is all right, but I know how much you love that dog. Jordan—is that the man's name who hit Hero?"

"Yes, he's been wonderful to us. And Hero's going to be all right. It'll take time, but with Jordan's help. . ."

"He's going to help you with Hero?"

"Oh, Vanessa, I can't wait for you to meet him. He's the most amazing man. He's paying all of the vet bills, and he's going to help me with Hero's exercises and water therapy. He's been driving me to the vet's every—"

"Whoa, sis! Who is this man? He sounds like a saint! Why do I get the feeling you're interested in him? Do I detect a bit of infatuation here?"

"No!"

"You could've fooled me. How old is this guy anyway?"

Valene twisted the phone cord about her finger nervously. "I'm not really sure. Several years older than us, I guess. Maybe even thirty. We've never talked about age."

"He lives near you?"

"Yes, he has a condo a few doors down, but he's a navy pilot. Sometimes he stays on the San Diego base."

"I can hardly wait to meet him. But Val, if he's a Christian and you two have feelings for each other, you need to keep your options open. I've never heard you talk about a man with such enthusiasm. I'll be praying for both of you."

"Yes, praise God, he *is* a Christian. I wouldn't have dated him if he weren't. He's not as strong in the Lord as Nathan, but I'm praying someday he will be. But, Vanessa, he's made it perfectly clear he's going to see the world before he settles down. That could be years from now. Please do pray for us. I really want God's best for our lives—with or without each other."

"You wouldn't be the first woman to change a man's mind."

"Since he's a Christian, I might be tempted to try, but there's no way he'd be interested in me."

"Why? You're gorgeous!"

Val chuckled. "You're only saying that because we look exactly alike!"

"Val, you always cut yourself down," Vanessa protested. "I can't imagine any man not being attracted to you."

"So, how's the honeymoon going?" Valene asked, needing to change the subject before she confessed how fond she was growing of Jordan. She'd never been able to keep a secret from her sister for very long. "Is Nathan as wonderful as you thought, now that you're with him twenty-four/seven?"

"He's even more wonderful. Oh, Val, Ireland is beautiful. Better than anything I could imagine! We're having a terrific time, but I know Nathan is anxious to get back to Jeff. Are Mom and Dad still coming after Jeff on Saturday?"

"That's the plan. But I've thoroughly enjoyed having Jeff here. I'm afraid it's been pretty boring for him though, with all the trips to the vet's. He's stayed with Diane a couple of times. He and her son always have a great time together."

"I know they do. Jeff's told me, and I like Diane. Well, I'd better let you go before my dear husband pulls the phone from my hand and hangs it up. I know he'll feel better about Jeff's near-accident now that I've talked to you. I hope all this hasn't been too trying for you."

"I'll survive. Just enjoy your honeymoon."

ꝸ

Jeff chattered about everything from Clue to his new Rollerblades, to bicycling, to frogs, as the three rode along on their way to the animal clinic the next morning.

"I'm nervous," Valene finally got in edgewise between Jeff's words about a cartoon he'd seen.

Jordan gave her a frown. "Why? The doc said he'd be ready to come home today."

"It's so hard to see him in pain. I'm afraid I'll hurt him."

Without looking away from the road, he reached over, took her hand, and gave it a squeeze. "You're not going to hurt him. Besides, I'll be there to help you. You'll do fine. That dog loves you. He knows you wouldn't hurt him intentionally."

"Oh, Jordan, what would I do without you?"

He gave her a grin. "Funny you should ask. I was wondering what I was going to do without you when this is all over. You kinda grow on a guy."

"Like fungus?"

"No, silly. You know what I mean."

"What's fungus?" a small voice asked from the backseat.

Valene let out a giggle. "It's a weird-looking kind of stuff that grows on trees."

"All fuzzy and green and nasty," Jordan added, screwing up his face.

Valene turned her head away. "Yuck! Did you have to say that?"

"You're the one who brought up fungus. Not me!"

"I guess I did."

"Hey, my words were only meant in the kindest way," Jordan explained with a grin as his fingers tightened over hers. "A compliment. Not my fault if you made light of them."

Valene sat still, not knowing if she should squeeze his hand back or just ignore it. "In that case, I thank you."

"You and Jeff go on back and see Hero," Jordan told them as they entered the clinic. "I need to take care of the bill."

Valene shook her head. "I can't let you pay for all of it, Jordan. That's asking too much. He is my dog."

He tapped the little bell on the counter to signal the receptionist they were there. "Look, I said I was going to pay Hero's bill, and I meant it. It's important to me that I do."

The woman appeared with the dog's long, itemized bill and handed it to Jordan. Valene gasped when she saw the total. It was far more than she'd anticipated, but he barely seemed to notice as he signed the charge slip.

She grabbed onto his arm. "Oh, Jordan. I had no idea it would be so much!"

"Don't worry about it."

"But I do worry about it."

He bent and kissed her cheek. "Best money I ever spent."

✝

Hero was lying on his side, fresh from a bath and his water therapy. The doctor's assistant was drying him off with a hair dryer.

"Well, don't you look handsome," Valene told the dog as she rushed to his side. "And you smell good, too!"

Hero lifted his head a bit, the whites of his eyes showing as he gave a slight whimper.

"We've come to take you home, Hero," Valene said sweetly as she stroked her friend. She scooted to one side and made room for Jeff.

"Hi, boy," Jeff said, patting the dog's damp back. "Sorry you got hurt chasing me."

"I've lowered Hero's dosage of Rimadyl." Dr. Kinney came in carrying two bottles of pills and a sheet filled with instructions. He conferred with the two of them, covering each point in great detail. "Any questions?" he asked finally.

Jordan shook his head. "None that come to mind right now. How about you, Valene?"

She took her attention away from Hero. "I noticed you have him lying on what looks like shredded newspaper. Should we do that too?"

The doctor gave a slight laugh. "It'd sure make it easier to clean up after him until he can get on his feet and go outside. If you're planning on keeping him in the house, I'd recommend using a large piece of cardboard or a crate of some kind for his bed, then cover it with a piece of plastic and a thick layer of the shredded paper."

"I've already got a big bag of shredded paper in my computer room, and I can get as much as we'll need from the base," Jordan told her. "And I always keep a large piece of cardboard on the bed of my truck. I'll bring it in for him."

"Well, you've taken care of his bill. It looks like he's ready to go home." Dr. Kinney turned toward Jordan after handing the bag containing Hero's medication to Valene. "I'd like to shake your hand, young man. In all my years as a veterinarian, I've never seen anyone face up to his responsibilities any more than you have."

Valene smiled. "He's been a rock through this whole ordeal."

"Okay, you two. Enough. I've only done what's right. Now," Jordan said moving toward Hero, "let's take this guy home." He carefully slipped his arms beneath the dog and gently lifted his rigid body, bracing him securely against his chest.

When they reached the pickup, Jordan held Hero while Valene unlocked the cab, removed an old army blanket from the truck's cargo area, and spread it across the backseat.

"Valene, why don't you ride back there with Hero, and Jeff can ride up front with me again? I think Hero would be much calmer with you sitting next to him."

She couldn't help smiling to herself as she climbed in beside her dog. Every inch of Jordan's Avalanche was spotlessly clean and highly polished. Not one speck of dust anywhere, not even in the cargo area. But here he was, insisting Hero ride on the leather seat instead of in the truck bed. What a man!

Once everyone was in their place and Hero seemed settled, Jordan turned the key in the ignition. "Hang on, Hero. We're taking you home."

⁂

Jeff held his nose and backed away quickly. "Aunt Valene, come quick. Hero smells!"

"It's okay, Jeff. He can't help himself." She rushed to the makeshift bed on the floor of her living room and dropped to her knees. "Wet one of these big rags, then get me one of those large paper grocery sacks from under the sink."

"Let me clean him up." Jordan dropped to his knees beside her and tried to push her away, but she held her ground.

"Absolutely not. You've already done too much."

"Valene, you shouldn't be lifting him. He's too heavy, and you'll have to put clean paper under him. Let me at least lift him for you."

She sent him a grateful smile. "Thanks. That would help."

Although Hero let out a yelp when Jordan lifted him, he quickly settled down. It took less than five minutes to get him cleaned up and back into a comfortable position on a fresh layer of shredded paper.

"Poor thing. I know he's in pain," Valene said, leaning over Hero and stroking his back.

"Hopefully that Rimadyl the doc gave him this morning is at least taking the edge off."

"Can't you give him an aspirin?" Jeff asked.

"Rimadyl is sorta like an aspirin, sweetie, only for dogs," Valene explained. "I know you're bored. Why don't you go into my bedroom and watch that new adventure videotape I got for you?"

"Okay!"

"Good idea," Jordan said. "There for a minute I was afraid you were going to suggest we all play Clue." He patted the sofa cushion beside him. "Come and sit with me. You don't have to stay by Hero every minute."

She gave one last pat to the dog's back, then moved to sit by Jordan. "I hadn't realized how heavy Hero'd gotten. I never could've gotten him home without you."

"Sure you could. All it would've taken was one call to one of your old boyfriends, and I'll bet he'd come running."

She wished that were so. But unfortunately, her old boyfriends were few and far between. Before she could explain, Jordan's cell phone rang.

"Hi." He turned to Valene and mouthed the word *"Mom."* "No, I can't. Not this weekend. But I'll come and see you and Dad soon. I promise."

Valene picked up a magazine from the table and leafed through it, feeling very awkward listening to his side of the conversation.

"I'll call when I know, Mom. Tell Dad hello for me." He grinned as he placed the phone back onto his belt. "She still tries to run my life. Your mom do that to you?"

"Some. She doesn't like the idea of me living here in Spring Valley. I have to keep reminding her I'm only fifteen miles away, and I do see them at church every Sunday. How did your parents feel about you joining the navy?"

"Oh, that was no problem. My dad graduated from the Naval Academy in Annapolis and served out his time before he joined my grandfather in our family business. Dad loved seeing the world before he settled down and got married. And he loved the navy. From the time I was a little boy, my life has been planned out for me. I studied hard, made good grades, and like my dad, got an appointment to Annapolis. Only instead of serving on a ship as part of the onboard crew like my father did, I opted for flying an F-18 and landing on one. Most guys know that sweet little number as the Hornet. It's the perfect plane for taking off and landing on an aircraft carrier."

"It sounds scary. Aren't you ever afraid you'll miss?"

"Naw, you get used to it. Like anything else you do in the navy, you train for it. It's second nature now." He gave her a mischievous smile. "I could almost take off and land with my eyes closed."

She winced. "Please promise me you won't even try."

He became serious. "I'm only kidding. When I'm flying that F-18, I'm all business. Every split second counts and could mean life or death."

"Life is very fragile. I'm glad to hear you're being careful." *And I'm thankful God is your copilot.*

"I've just about completed my obligatory time as a navy pilot, but I plan to stay in another four years or so, then join my father in the business."

"I guess you love flying."

"It gets into your blood. I like the navy, too, and I've seen quite a bit of the world, but not as much as I'd like."

"Do you ever worry about having to fly into dangerous areas? There always seems to be so much turmoil."

He paused thoughtfully. "Sometimes, but it's my duty to go where I'm needed. I not only love flying, I enjoy visiting other countries and learning about their cultures, but there's no place like the good old USA. I'm willing to do whatever it takes to protect her."

"Have you ever been in danger?"

His face sobered. "A number of times. Danger goes with the territory. I've been lucky. Some of my friends haven't. But I'd rather not talk about it."

"I'm sorry. I didn't mean to pry."

He slipped an arm about her shoulders and drew her close to him. "You're not prying. It's just that I'd prefer to forget those episodes. I made it through. That's what counts."

"When you were in danger. . ." She stopped mid-sentence, not exactly sure how she should finish.

"Yes?"

"Did you. . .pray?"

He stared off into space a bit. "Yeah, I prayed. Might not have made it out alive otherwise. I've always wondered what would've happened to me if I hadn't prayed. Guess I'll never know."

"I don't know how people get through life without praying."

"Like when you prayed for Hero? Boy, I thought for sure he was a goner. He was so still when I picked him up off that parking lot."

She sent a loving glance toward the sleeping dog. "I knew if he was to survive, God would have to perform a miracle."

"Well, if your prayers were what kept him alive, I'm grateful you prayed and God answered your prayer. I couldn't have lived with myself if Hero'd died, knowing how much he means to you."

Valene placed her hand on his sleeve. "We can't understand why things like this happen, but I know God wants only the best for me."

"Are you saying Hero's long, difficult recovery is best for you? For the next few weeks, your whole life is going to revolve around caring for that dog. Where is the good in that?"

She gave him a shy grin. "I–I met you."

He frowned. "That's the good? Meeting me? How can you say that?"

"You asked me about my old boyfriends." She paused and forced back the tears she was afraid would rise to the surface. "I've never told this to anyone, except my mom. I'm not even sure I should tell you."

"You can tell me anything, Valene. I'm here for you." His tone was kind, and for some unknown reason, she knew he'd never betray her confidence.

She took a deep breath and began. "My last year in college, one of the stars on the swim team asked me out to dinner. He was extremely popular, and I was flattered. I didn't even tell Vanessa about his invitation. She'd gone to some seminar that weekend about training guide dogs. I borrowed one of my sister's dresses from her closet and even fixed my hair like hers, hoping I'd appear more attractive than my plain old, dull self."

"I haven't seen your sister, but I can't imagine anyone being more attractive than you."

She gave him an appreciative smile. "We had a wonderful dinner at a quaint little restaurant out in the country. I laughed and tried to be witty and charming, like I'd seen Vanessa do. We talked and talked, and I was actually beginning to think he liked me." She gulped hard at the lump rising in her throat, just remembering that evening.

"When he turned off the highway and into an industrial area, I questioned him about it. He explained he was taking a shortcut back to town. Gullible me, I believed him."

Jordan winced. "I think I know where this story is going."

"Yes, it's the same old story we've heard time and again, but I was foolish enough to believe it couldn't happen to me."

"A wrestling match, huh?"

She lowered her eyes and bit at her lip. "Yes."

His grip tightened about her shoulders, and he pulled her close. "I'm so sorry. Guys like that give us all a bad name."

"I panicked. I didn't know what to do. In desperation, I grabbed the door handle and jumped out of his car when he stopped at a stop sign."

"Did—did he follow you?"

"No, he didn't. Although I was terrified, I knew I wasn't alone. I felt God's presence. The man made a terrible, obscene remark I won't repeat and drove off, leaving me there. When I finally found a phone, I called my mom to come and pick me up. I've never been so scared."

"Whew! I was so afraid he'd—"

"But he didn't, Jordan. Since then, I've pretty much avoided all men. Up to that time, I'd heard nothing but good things about that guy. Just shows how you never really know someone."

"I'm not that way, Valene. I hope you know that."

She smiled up at him. "I do know that, Jordan. You've restored my faith in men. That's what I meant when I said something good came out of all of this."

"Hey, don't let your guard down because of me. I couldn't stand the idea of anything happening to you. I'm in the navy, remember? I hear how some guys talk, and it makes me sick."

"I can imagine. I do believe God sent you to me though. To show me there are fine men in this world. If only—"

"If only what?"

"Never mind."

"No, I want to know what you were going to say. If only what?"

"If—if only I could find a good man. . .like you." There, she'd said it.

He grimaced, then smiled. "I do try to be a good man. I don't cheat on my income taxes. I help old ladies across the street."

The look on Jordan's face confused her. It was as though he were a million miles away, remembering a painful time in his life. She wanted to ask him about it. Hadn't she just shared her innermost secret with him? But somehow, she couldn't. She just couldn't.

"There are some things even God can't forgive," he said slowly, enunciating every word.

She planted a hand on her hip. "That's not true, Jordan. God is able to forgive anything and everything, but we have to ask Him. The only thing He can't forgive is if we turn our back on Him and reject Him."

"I wish I could believe that."

"You can." *God, give me the right words, please.* "I can show you in God's Word where He talks about forgiveness. You're such a kind man, Jordan. It's hard to imagine you ever doing anything bad enough to make you feel God couldn't forgive you for it."

He stood quickly, brushing his hands together. "Let's talk about more pleasant things. What do you want for supper?"

After a hastily prepared supper, Jordan helped Valene clear the table and put the dishes in the dishwasher. He'd done the same thing hundreds of times in his own condo and had always thought of it as work. But tonight, doing it with Valene, it was fun. He actually found himself enjoying the task.

"You look cute in that apron," she told him with a giggle as she pressed the dishwasher's ON button. "I wish I had new batteries in my digital camera. I'd take your picture."

"So you could blackmail me? No, thanks." He untied the apron and placed it back on the hook. "I put clean sheets on my bed, and I made up a bed on my sofa for Jeff. You ought to try to get to bed early. You've had a pretty busy day. Hero will be fine with me. He's had his Rimadyl and should sleep pretty well for the next few hours."

"I'm not going to run you out of your bed. You've had a busy day, too."

He pulled his keys from his pocket and handed them to her. "Valene, I hate to be tough about this, but we've already discussed this once. I'm going to spend the nights on your sofa so I can take care of Hero. You and Jeff go on over to my condo. Everything is ready for you, and I refuse to take no for an answer."

Jeff grabbed his aunt's hand. "We're gonna sleep in Jordan's condo? Cool!"

"No, Jeff. We—"

"Valene, I mean it. I am going to stay here nights and take care of Hero. Once he begins to get on his feet, we'll reevaluate the sleeping arrangements. But until then, I'm staying here. Don't even think about arguing with me."

"But—"

He held up his palm between them. "No buts. Now get whatever you'll need and go."

Jeff tugged on her hand. "Come on, Aunt Valene. It'll be fun."

"Well, if you're sure. . ."

"I am sure. Now go. I'll be over in the morning about six. I need to be on the base by seven."

"I need to change the sheets first, and—"

"Go!" he said firmly. "I'm not afraid of your germs. Besides, I can sleep on the couch."

"If you're going to sleep on the couch, then I'm not going," she said, resolutely crossing her arms.

He held up both palms in surrender. "Okay. I'll sleep in the bed."

Once the door had closed behind Valene and Jeff, Jordan wandered into the kitchen and had a cup of the coffee she'd put on to brew before she left. He checked Hero, then settled himself onto the sofa and clicked the TV remote. He flipped from channel to channel, finding nothing that interested him, and was ready to forget it and hit the OFF button when he heard music. He paused, turned up the volume, and began to listen, snapping his fingers to the beat. The singer was extolling God's grace and His forgiveness. He started to turn it off or switch to another channel but felt compelled to listen. When the song ended, he turned the TV off.

He picked up the little case he'd brought with him and moved into Valene's bathroom to prepare for bed. There, taped to the mirror, was a verse that he knew had to be from the Bible. She'd told him she regularly memorized scripture. Maybe this was how she did it. He leaned toward it and read aloud, "If we confess our sins, He is faithful and righteous to forgive us our sins and to cleanse us from all unrighteousness. If we say that we have not sinned, we make Him a liar and His word is not in us." The words went right to his heart. *Oh, Valene, you have no idea how I've sinned.*

Had she taped that on her mirror, knowing he'd see it? Of course not! Hadn't she tried to talk him out of staying in her condo for the night? He showered, slipped into his T-shirt and boxers, gathered up his things, and after checking on Hero, headed for Valene's bed. He set his alarm clock, pulled back the covers, and crawled in, taking note of the sweet-smelling scent on the pillow. The bed felt good.

Before he reached for the light switch on the bedside lamp, he glanced at his new surroundings. The room looked like Valene, with soft, feminine ruffles and frills everywhere in the room. A huge white teddy bear sat in a white wicker rocker opposite the bed, smiling at him. He smiled back. A pile of Christian romance novels stood in a neat stack on the nightstand, flanked by an assortment of hand and body creams. He lifted the lid on the one marked honeysuckle and took in a deep whiff. He'd noticed the fragrance on Valene that very day.

Visions of the lovely woman, no doubt sleeping in his bed by now, filled his mind. He'd never met anyone like her. If he could've laid out a recipe for the type of woman he'd like to marry eventually, it would describe Valene. Shy, unassuming, loving Valene. Her story about the college jock really disturbed him. Guys like that belonged in jail. Unfortunately, innocent women like Valene were entirely too trusting for their own good.

He glanced at the lace curtains covering the windows, the small ceramic birds on a wicker shelf hanging on the wall, and the silver comb-and-brush set on her dresser. He'd never spent a night in a woman's bedroom before. This was a whole new experience, one he was enjoying. With one last stretch, he turned out the light, slipped down between the sheets, and pulled the comfy quilt up over him. Being with Valene these past few days, hearing her laughter, watching her cry, seeing her loving ways with both Jeff and Hero had made him question his determination to see the world before he settled down.

Forget it, fella, he told himself as he lay there in the darkness surrounded by things that reminded him of her. *Think about your buddies who said the same thing you did. They wanted to see the world, too, but when some pretty young thing came along and swept them off their feet, they traded their freedom and independence for a wedding ring and a baby carriage. Not me. I've got a plan for my life, and nothing, not even a woman as beautiful and caring as Valene Zobel, is going to change that plan.*

A whimper, then a moan followed by a yelp brought him quickly to his feet. Hero!

He flipped on the hall light and hurried into the living room. "What's wrong, boy? Can't you sleep?" Jordan bent over the dog. "Oh, Hero! You smell! Not again!"

⊤

Valene glanced at the clock on Jordan's nightstand. Two o'clock. Why was she having so much trouble falling asleep? She'd read her Bible and prayed, and that usually made her relax. Could it be the fact that she was sleeping in Jordan's bed? The scent of his aftershave wafting around her? Or was she worried about Hero?

That's dumb! she told herself as she flipped over onto her back. *Hero is in better hands with Jordan caring for him than if I was there.* In the shaft of moonlight arching its way across the room, she could see some sort of certificates hanging on the wall. Curiosity getting the better of her, she crawled out of bed, turned on the light, and padded her way across the room. They were awards of some kind. She gasped as she read the various inscriptions. Every one of them was an award for bravery. Jordan was a hero? Were these for the incidents he'd mentioned but was unwilling to talk about when she'd asked him if he'd ever been in danger? She'd like to know more, but considering how adamant he'd been about not discussing it, she decided to keep her questions to herself. For now, at least.

She turned out the light and moved to the window. From his bedroom, she could barely see one of her windows through the bushes and trees that surrounded the complex. Was Jordan getting any sleep, or was Hero keeping him awake? She should've stayed with Hero herself. Jordan needed his sleep, too. Especially since he seemed to have so many obligations at the base. Why had she ever let him talk her into such a ridiculous arrangement?

Finally, she crawled back into bed. As she lay on his pillow and stared at the ceiling, she couldn't help but wonder what it would be like to be married to Jordan Young. Eventually, she drifted off to sleep with visions of the handsome pilot filling her dreams.

The ringing of the doorbell brought her out of a sound sleep, and for a moment, she couldn't even think where she was. She grabbed her bathrobe, rushed to the door, peered out the peephole, and, seeing Jordan standing there, pulled open the door a crack. "What are you doing here? Is something wrong with Hero?"

Chapter 6

It's six a.m. I'm ready to leave for the base. I was supposed to wake you up, remember?"

She rubbed at her eyes, suddenly realizing she was standing in the doorway in her bathrobe and pajamas. "I'll be right back."

She closed the door, leaving him standing outside his own condo. After rushing into the bedroom and pulling on jeans and a T-shirt, she hurried back to open the door. "Sorry."

He gave her a teasing grin. "I understand."

"Did you get any sleep at all?"

A smiled crooked at his lips. "Hero and I were up a few times during the night, but he settled down about four. After that, I slept so soundly I couldn't even think where I was when my alarm went off."

She dipped her head slightly. "Th–that's the way I felt when you rang the doorbell. Did Hero give you much trouble?"

"Umm, not exactly a lot of trouble, but you'll find some pretty smelly rags in your trash. You might want to dump them right away. I kinda think his medication might be the cause of some of his, um, accidents."

"You may be right. I should've been there," she said, feeling guilty as she crossed her arms to get warmer in the cool, morning air.

"Oh? And you could have lifted him all by yourself?"

"Maybe, but I might've hurt Hero in the process."

"Don't try to lift him while I'm gone. Let Jeff help you. Understand?"

She gave him a mock salute. "Yes, sir. Give me five minutes to gather my things and wake Jeff up."

He put a hand on her wrist. "No. Leave your things here. You'll be spending the night again."

"Jordan, I can't let you—"

He gave her a playful frown. "Let me? It's my decision. Now scoot! I have to get to the base."

By the time she'd brushed her teeth and raked a comb through her hair, Jordan had awakened Jeff, and the two of them were waiting for her on the porch. Jordan handed Jeff her keys and told him to go open the door. "I'll be back by four," he said to Valene. "And don't try to give Hero his water therapy until

I'm here to help you. Do you hear me?"

"Jordan, I can—"

He slipped an arm about her and pulled her close. "I know you can take care of Hero without me, but I want to help. I like being around both of you." He slipped a finger beneath her chin and lifted her face to meet his.

Her heart pounded. It was exactly like her dream.

"You're a very special woman, Valene," he said softly as his lips met hers. "See you at four."

She stood frozen to the spot as she watched him stride across the parking lot to his truck. Jordan Young had kissed her—not on the cheek as he'd done before, but fully on her lips. Could that be why she had goose bumps on her arms? *Oh, God, help me! I already love this man.*

꘏

Friday was nearly the same as Thursday, but Hero seemed a bit stronger and even more determined to stand. By Saturday morning, both Valene and Jordan had fallen into an unquestioned routine of spending their nights at the other's condo, and it was working out well.

"Jeff, pack up your things," Valene told her nephew. "Grandma and Grandpa and Lick will be here soon."

Jeff pulled himself away from the Saturday morning cartoons with a frown. "Aw, Aunt Val, do I have to go? I miss Lick and I wanna see him, but I wanna stay here with you and Hero, too."

Her brows lifted in surprise. "You do? I figured you'd been bored staying here. Hero has taken so much of my time, we really haven't been able to do any of the things I'd planned."

"You guys are the only ones who'll play Clue with me," the boy said, his lower lip hanging down. "My dad hates that game, and I like being here with Hero. He's a nice dog."

Valene shot a quick glance at Jordan, who only shrugged. "We haven't really played Clue with you that much," she confessed, wishing they'd played it more often.

Jeff hung his head dejectedly. "I know, but you had Hero to take care of, and I'm the one who got him hurt."

Jordan reached out and pulled the boy onto his lap. "You aren't responsible for what happened, Jeff. Yes, you disobeyed your aunt by riding into the parking lot, but the way that sidewalk ended so abruptly, there was nothing you could do to get stopped in time. I'm just thankful I didn't hit you."

"But I made you hit Hero."

"I should've had him on a leash," Valene inserted.

"No one made me hit Hero. It just happened, and he's going to get well.

Now, you just forget about all of this, mind your aunt, and gather up your things."

"You have a way with kids," Valene told him after Jeff disappeared into the bedroom. "You're going to make a great dad someday."

"I'm not so sure. By the time I finish serving my stint with the navy and find me a wife, I may be too old to be the kind of dad I'd like to be."

His words weren't exactly what she wanted to hear, but she knew anything else would have been wishful thinking on her part. "You won't be that old."

He seemed to be giving her comment some serious thought. "I hope not. My folks had me late in life. My dad never played games with me or attended any of my school functions. He never even made it to my game when I played in the state basketball finals. I want something better for my children."

She gulped. "Children? As in more than one?"

"Sure. I'd like to have at least four or five."

Jeff came dragging his suitcase into the room, hugging a basketball with his free arm. "Mr. Young, could you shoot some baskets with me while I'm waiting for Grandpa?"

Jordan grinned. "Sure, sport, if Valene says it's okay."

She nodded, wishing she could leave Hero long enough to go watch them. Maybe even shoot a few baskets herself, although she wasn't very good at it. She left the front door standing open, tidied up the room, put on a fresh pot of coffee, then squatted down beside Hero. Although his hips were stiff and he still couldn't move around much, his tail wagged rapidly. "You're a good boy," she told him as she stroked his ragged fur. "Even with all those funny-looking patches where your fur was worn off, you're still my beautiful dog."

"Yoo-hoo! Valene!"

"Come on in, Mom," she answered, pressing one hand against Hero to hold him down.

"Oh, sweetheart, I can only imagine how hard this has been on you. I know how much you love that dog."

Valene looked past her mother. "Where's Dad?"

"Shooting baskets with his grandson and that gorgeous man out there. Who is that guy?"

"That's Jordan. The man I've been telling you about."

Her mother pulled the footstool up next to Hero's bed and sat down. "You never told me he was that good-looking."

"Oh, Mom, I've never met a man like him. And best of all, he loves the Lord."

"Since your father and I have always stressed the importance of only dating those who shared your faith, I couldn't imagine any of my children ever allowing themselves to become infatuated with someone who wasn't a Christian."

Valene felt as if she was blushing as she patted Hero's back. "I—I think I'm in love with Jordan."

"Where's my girl?" a man's voice boomed from behind her.

Valene waved a hand in her father's direction. "Here, Daddy, on the floor next to Hero."

He dropped onto her sofa, pulled his handkerchief from his pocket, and began wiping his brow. "I'm not as young as I used to be. These guys nearly killed me." He gestured to Jeff and Jordan and Lick, who were following close behind.

Valene grinned. "Mom, I'd like you to meet Jordan Young. Jordan, this is my mother, Ellen Zobel."

"Nice to meet you, Mrs. Zobel," Jordan said, wiping his sweaty hand on his knit shirt before extending it. "You have a wonderful daughter."

Her mother flashed a quick look toward Valene as she grabbed onto Lick's collar to settle him down. "I think so, but thanks. I love hearing it from someone else."

Valene felt herself blushing. "Jordan's been a great help with Hero. I don't know what I would've done without him."

Hero let out a yelp as he tried to maneuver himself onto his stomach. As quick as a flash, Jordan rushed to his side, lifting him and holding him so his feet barely touched the floor. "It helps if we change his position pretty often," he explained with a glance toward Valene's parents.

"We've been trying to hold off on giving him his Rimadyl until after he's had his water therapy," Valene added, rising.

"He still looks pretty banged up to me," Mr. Zobel said, bending forward to touch one of Hero's scraped-up areas with his finger. "Will his fur grow back?"

Jordan nodded. "It's already beginning to. He'll never be quite like he was before the accident. The vet says he'll be able to get around, but his hips'll stay pretty stiff. At least he's alive. That's what matters."

Mr. Zobel put a hand on Jordan's shoulder. "Valene tells us you paid his veterinary bills. That must've set you back a pretty penny."

"I'm the one who hit him, sir. Paying his bills is the easy part. Nursing him back to health is what's going to take time, but Valene and I are both committed to see it through."

"Which reminds me, Valene. Have you had your phone number changed?" her mother asked.

"No. Why?"

"I tried to phone you a little before six this morning. I knew it was early, but I wanted to ask you about Jeff before Vanessa phoned me. I was sure I dialed the right number, but a man answered. I just hung up and didn't try again."

"Oh, was that you?" Jordan asked quickly.

Mrs. Zobel shot a glance at Valene, then back to Jordan. "You were in her condo at six this morning?"

"Yes, ma'am, but I had reason to be here."

"I wasn't here, Mom, because I was asleep over at Jordan's." Valene realized how stupid that sounded after she said it. "So was Jeff."

Her mother frowned and grew quite serious. "I think this calls for an explanation, Valene."

"Look, Mother, Hero needs constant attention. Until he's strong enough to stand. . ." She paused, trying to put Hero's bodily functions into acceptable words. "He has no choice but to, um, mess himself. I can't lift him by myself, so Jordan kindly offered to take the night shift and sleep here."

"While Valene is sleeping over in my condo," Jordan inserted hastily. "Then Valene takes the day shift."

Her father clapped his hands together. "I'd say that's a good, workable plan, wouldn't you, Mother?"

Her mother seemed relieved after things had been explained. "Yes, I guess so. It's very kind of you, Jordan, to help Valene with Hero."

"I stayed at Mr. Young's house, too," Jeff said proudly, as if staying there was a real accomplishment. "He plays Clue with me."

"Jeff, did you bring that awful game with you?" his new grandmother asked with a slight, teasing frown.

Jeff turned quickly to Jordan. "You like it, don't you, Mr. Young?"

Jordan nodded at the boy. "When I have someone I like to play it with, I do."

"Anything we can do to help you, honey?" Valene's dad asked her.

"Nothing I can think of."

"How about groceries? You need anything?"

She shook her head. "No, Jordan has taken care of that too. I think he nearly bought out the store."

"Well, then, I guess we'll be going." Her father turned to Jeff. "Tell your aunt thanks for taking care of you. Then go put your things in the car, Jeff, and take Lick with you."

Valene slipped an arm about her nephew. "He was a joy to have around. I only wish we could've done more fun things while he was here."

"I had fun!" Jeff said, smiling up at her and hanging onto his dog. "Just being here with you and Hero and Mr. Young was fun."

"I'm glad. Maybe you can come and stay with me another time."

"I'll put your bike in your grandfather's trunk," Jordan told Jeff as the two headed for the door with Lick following. "Just promise me you'll be careful where you ride it, okay?"

Both her father and mother lingered as Jeff and Jordan moved out onto the parking lot.

"You kinda sweet on him?" her father asked, gesturing toward the open door. "I sure hope he's a Christian."

"He is, Dad."

"Valene has always known getting involved with a man who isn't could mean trouble later on," her mother inserted quickly.

"I wasn't exactly Billy Graham when we were dating, Mama." He gave his wife a playful pinch on her arm. "As I recall, your folks weren't too happy about you marrying me. I wasn't a Christian then, or have you forgotten?"

Valene's eyes widened. "You weren't? I always thought you were."

"No, I was about as far from the Lord as a man could get. Oh, I don't mean I was a criminal or anything like that, but I didn't want anything to do with that God stuff. It was only your mother's and her parents' prayers and their godly lives that made me see myself for what I really was. Lost!"

"Daddy, I had no idea! When did you become a Christian?"

Her mother's eyes began to glisten with tears. "Your father accepted Christ when you and your sister were born."

"Really? I always thought Daddy was saved when he was young!"

"I was young. Barely twenty-three. I nearly lost all three of you, Valene." Her father slipped an arm about her waist. "I know you and Vanessa have heard parts of this story before, but having two babies at once is not the same as having one. Your mother had a hard time of it. She spent the last three months of her pregnancy in bed. The night she went into labor, which was about three weeks before her due date, I stood beside her hospital bed feeling totally helpless. Every minute of watching her struggle with you girls' delivery was torture."

He gulped hard before going on. "Finally the doctor turned to me and told me he doubted he'd be able to save all three of you. I—I'll never forget the look in his eyes when he warned me to be prepared for whatever might happen. His final words were, 'Bill, if you know how to pray, pray hard, and pray for a miracle.' I didn't know how I'd ever face life without your mother or be able to raise one or both of you girls by myself. If she died, I wanted to die, too."

Valene had never seen her father cry like this, and she, too, fought back tears as he dabbed at his eyes with his sleeve.

"So many times your mother had explained the plan of salvation to me, but I wouldn't listen. That night her words came back to me, and I could hear them as plain as if she'd just said them. I got down on my knees right there in that delivery room and finally admitted to God I was a sinner. I asked Him to forgive me and accepted Him as my Savior. Then, I promised Him, if He would spare your mother's life and let you girls be born, I'd serve Him until I died. And I meant it. I know now I should never have tried to bargain with God, but I had very little knowledge of the scriptures then. I'm sure God knew my heart was right, but that's the last time I've tried to bargain with Him."

Valene threw her arms about his neck. "Oh, Daddy. I didn't know. You never told us that part."

"But, Valene, that doesn't mean a young woman should ever become involved with a man who doesn't love God the way she does," her mother said, wiping at her own tears. "Sometimes things don't work out for the best."

"Your mother's right," her father said, touching his daughter's arm affectionately. "I'm just sorry it took something that serious to make me see my need for God in my life."

"You have no idea what life was like between your father and me before he accepted the Lord. We were like two corks bobbing in the sea. He went his way. I went mine. I've prayed my children would never have to go through rough times like that. That's why your father and I have always stressed that you girls only date people who share your faith."

"The bike is in your trunk, and Jeff and Lick are waiting in the car," Jordan said, as he walked through the open door.

"Then we'd better be going," her mother said, with a meaningful glance toward Valene.

"Good-bye, my little sweetie," her father told her as she slipped an arm about his waist and walked him to the door. Then, with a wink, he whispered, "I like your young man. I'll be praying for you. Just don't try to rush things. Wait on the Lord. If He wants you two to get together, He'll make it happen."

Valene and Jordan stood on the porch and waved as her parents' car exited the parking lot.

"Did I come in at a bad time?" Jordan asked once the car was out of sight. "I kinda got the impression your mother wasn't too enthused about me being here with you."

"She only does what all mothers do—worry about their children."

They gave Hero his water therapy, then Valene dried him with her hair dryer as Jordan held him so the dog's feet barely touched the floor.

"Do you realize it's been a week since the accident?" he asked as Hero struggled to stand. "I'd say he's making good progress."

"Thanks to you." She smiled up at him.

While Jordan held Hero on his lap, Valene bagged up the soiled shredded paper and replaced it with a fresh batch. Once Hero was settled, Jordan gave him his Rimadyl, followed by his dose of amoxicillin. "I think his skinned-up places look pretty good, don't you?"

Valene leaned over the dog and checked each abrasion carefully. "Doesn't look like any of them have become infected. I think he's well on his way to recovery. As soon as that fur fills in, he'll look as handsome as ever."

She sat down by Jordan, gently stroking Hero's back until he fell asleep.

"I'm not sure your mother likes me," Jordan said.

"Of course she does. What's not to like? You're a fine man. I know my dad likes you. He told me so."

Jordan brightened. "He did?"

She nodded. "Yes, he did. Right before he left."

"I like him, too. You should've seen him shooting baskets. He was pretty good. Probably made at least one out of every four shots. Wish my dad would have shot baskets with me like that."

"I think Mom worries about me because of Vanessa."

"Your sister? What's she got to do with it?"

"Vanessa always knew where she was going and how she was going to get there. I didn't." She gave a feeble laugh. "I still don't."

"I don't understand."

"Vanessa's the feisty one. I used to spend most of my time trying to keep her out of trouble. Not that she was a bad kid—she wasn't. But she wanted to enjoy life to the fullest. From the time we were kids and had that little dog, she knew she wanted to work with animals, and she set out a plan to do it. Much like you did with the navy. She got her degree as a veterinary assistant, just like she'd planned. Now she's not only using that degree, she's doing something worthwhile, training service dogs. What am I doing? Working as a medical records assistant at a hospital. Though I spent four years in college to earn a business degree, I now find I'm much more interested in marketing."

"I think you're selling yourself short, Valene. You're a beautiful, intelligent woman. You shouldn't be comparing yourself to your sister."

She smiled and patted his hand. "Thanks. Your affirmation helps."

"Only telling the truth." He stood and lowered Hero into his bed. "Think you can handle him for a few hours? I need to work on my computer for a while, then, after I call my parents, I thought I'd grab a quick nap."

"Sure. Go ahead. If I need you, I'll call. I've got a book I want to read."

He grinned. "One of those romance novels I saw on your nightstand? Those looked pretty interesting."

She gave him a coy smile. "Maybe."

She watched as he moved out the door and closed it behind him. There was no use denying it. She was in love with Jordan.

If only he were in love with her.

Although the book was interesting and the characters enthralling, she couldn't keep her mind on the story. She was tired of living vicariously through those characters. It was time she experienced real love firsthand.

She started up her computer and sent off a few e-mails, checked some items on the Internet, then browsed a couple of Christian Web sites. After that, she changed the shredded paper in Hero's bed and stroked his fur, telling him how much she loved him. By three, she was checking the clock every five minutes. All she could think about was the handsome pilot.

At four, a knock sounded on her door.

"Guess what! I ran into Diane on the way over here, and she volunteered to stay with Hero in the morning so you can go to church!"

Val gave Jordan a puzzled look. Hadn't he told her he'd be available all weekend to help her with Hero? "Are you flying tomorrow?"

"No, I thought I'd drive you."

She felt like pinching herself to see if she had fallen asleep and hadn't realized it. "To church?"

"Of course, to church. You do want to go, don't you? I'll go to my own church if you don't want me to go with you."

"I'd love for you to go with me. I just assumed you'd rather go to your church."

"What time should we leave? I have to tell Diane."

"I usually go to the middle service. It starts at nine-thirty. We should leave no later than nine, I guess."

"Good, I'll tell Diane."

She stood in the doorway, feeling numb. *Are you answering my prayers, God? Or am I reading something into this I shouldn't be?*

He came back, carrying a grocery sack. "I told her."

She nodded. "Good. Are you sure she wants to do this?"

"Yep," he said, pushing past her. "Her boy is coming with her. He can help her if Hero has to be lifted. I told her if he made any real messes to just put a heavy layer of fresh paper on it, and I'd clean it up when we got back. And that's not all. She's agreed to come over and stay with Hero during the day when you go back to work next week. Her boy'll be back in school, and she'll be alone all day."

"How much are you paying her, Jordan?"

His grin told her he wasn't about to tell her. "Enough to make it worth her while."

He headed toward the kitchen but stopped long enough to call back over his shoulder, "Steak sound good for supper? I brought over three nice big ribeyes. One for you, one for me, and one for Hero. I'm gonna stick some baking potatoes in the oven, and after I get the grill fired up, I'll put the steaks on to cook."

Valene's jaw dropped. How could one man be so nice? "I'll fix a salad."

✞

Once again, Val spent the night in Jordan's condo, and he in hers. Things were working out quite well. They exchanged condos at eight that morning, in order to give each other time to get ready for church.

Although her mother and father were surprised to see them come in, they welcomed Jordan cordially. Jeff insisted on sitting with them during the service. Valene could feel the eyes of those sitting around her, and she knew they were wondering what a good-looking man like Jordan was doing with her. He sang along with the congregation and was quite attentive during the sermon.

Everyone greeted him in a friendly manner at the close of the service, and he shook hands with all the men, as if he were glad to meet them. He even told the pastor, as he shook his hand on the way out of church, that he'd be back again.

They stopped at a drive-in on the way home and ordered carryout fried chicken dinners, since Valene thought it was only fair they get back and relieve Diane as soon as possible.

Once they were seated around her kitchen table, and she'd prayed over their meal, Jordan dropped a bombshell.

Chapter 7

My parents are having a dinner party next weekend. I want you to come with me."

Valene stared at him. *He wants me to meet his parents?* "I—I thought they lived in La Jolla."

"They do. I thought we'd go for the weekend."

"Oh, Jordan, I don't know. Are you sure you want me to go along? I can probably handle Hero by myself by then. Why don't you go on without me?"

He reached across the table and cupped her hand in his. "I want you to go with me. Please, say yes. It'll be fun. Mom's always telling me to bring a friend with me."

"I—I don't know. I'm not very good at meeting people."

He gave her hand a reassuring squeeze. "You'll do fine. Hey, it's only a dinner party. No big deal. Besides, I want you to see where I grew up. Meet a few of my friends. And we'll take Hero with us. Come on. For me?"

She sucked in a deep breath. "Well, okay. If you insist. But are you sure your parents won't mind if we bring Hero?"

"Why should they mind? It's not like he's going to be up running around through the house."

"But you said they never allowed you to have a dog."

He laughed. "We're not moving Hero in with them. He's only going for a visit! Are you looking for excuses so you won't have to go with me?"

"No! I'm flattered that you've invited me. I just don't want to be the cause of any trouble."

"Take it from me. There won't be any trouble." He took the carton of slaw from her hand and placed a big spoonful of it on his plate. "We'll plan to leave early Saturday morning. Okay?"

"O—okay, I guess." *What am I doing?*

✦

The week went even better than either of them had hoped. Diane got along fine with Hero during the day, and during evenings, both Valene and Jordan cared for him. Nights, Jordan took over while Valene slept in his condo. Each day the dog showed improvement, and by Friday evening, he was beginning to stand, bearing his own weight with the help of the towel.

"I'm not so sure we should be taking Hero to your parents' house tomorrow," Valene said as she spread out a fresh layer of paper in the dog's bed. "They may not appreciate his messes."

"Don't be silly. We'll both be there to take care of him. I'll toss a couple of big bags of paper, a big sheet of plastic for him to lay on, and a spray can of air freshener in the Avalanche. He'll be fine."

She stood, then fastened the twist tie around the top of the big bag. "You look cute sitting there on the sofa with Hero on your lap."

He gave her a silly grin. "I know this sounds stupid, but I enjoy holding him like this. I can feel his heart beating against my arm. Remember how he struggled those first few times when I tried to lift him? He doesn't do that anymore. I get the feeling he trusts me, and I like that feeling."

She placed the bag in the trash can, fastened the lid, and sat down beside him. "Of course he trusts you. You've been there for him ever since the accident." She gave his side a jab with her elbow. "He knows you like him. He's watched you clean up his messes!"

He gave her a melancholy look. "Being with Hero these past couple of weeks has made me realize how much I missed by not having a dog when I was a kid. Believe me, when I have kids, they're gonna have a dog like Hero."

She felt herself on the verge of tears. "Oh, Jordan, you've never had the opportunity to be around the real Hero. You've only seen him like this. Totally helpless. I wish you could've seen him when he. . ." Her voice cracked with emotion. "When he. . ." She couldn't say the words.

Jordan freed one hand and pulled her head onto his shoulder. "I know. You don't have to say it. We both know he'll never be able to run and jump like he did before, but the doc said he'd be able to get around fine. We should be thankful for that much. It—it could have been worse. We could've lost him."

She relaxed against his shoulder. It felt good to be able to share her feelings with someone and be understood. "Thanks, Jordan, for being here."

"I'm right where I want to be, and I promise you, I'll be here until Hero is as well as he's going to get."

Valene's heart clenched. *As well as he's going to get? What about after that? Does that mean you're going to leave us then? Go back to your life and forget about us?*

Jordan gathered Hero up in his arms and stood, leaving Valene on the sofa alone, plagued by unanswered questions.

"Well, I think it's about time this old boy takes his pill and goes to bed. I'd like to head for La Jolla by nine."

"It's not too late, Jordan. You can still change your mind and go by yourself. I won't mind. Really."

"And not take you with me? Forget it. If you don't go, I don't go. Your call."

"But they're expecting you."

"They sure are! So what is it? Go, or stay?"

"You're putting me on the spot, you know."

"I know. But I want you with me. You and Hero."

"All right, but remember, I'm not a sparkling conversationalist like my sister."

"All I ask is that you be yourself, and everyone will love you."

⁜

Valene nearly choked as they turned onto a magnificent, flower-lined, circular drive in front of a lovely, Spanish-style mansion. "Te–tell me this isn't your parents' home!"

"You don't like it?"

"Of course I like it. I've never been to such a grand place. Oh, Jordan, why didn't you tell me?"

He stopped the pickup in front of the ornate, iron-railed porch and gave her a blank stare. "Tell you what?"

"That you were raised in such elegant surroundings! You should never have brought me here."

"Why?"

Before she could answer him, the door opened and a uniformed butler stepped out.

"Hi, Henry," Jordan sang out as he shook hands with the man. "Good to see you." He turned to Valene. "This is my friend, Valene Zobel."

Henry bowed low as Valene scooted out of the Avalanche. "It's very nice to meet you, Ms. Zobel." Then turning to Jordan, he asked, "May I get your bags, sir?"

Jordan shook his head. "Later. Where are my parents?"

"In the solarium, sir, reading the morning paper."

Jordan opened the truck's back door and carefully lifted Hero out, motioned for Valene to follow, and headed toward the door.

She went along, but her heart wasn't in it. *Why didn't he tell me?*

The foyer took her breath away as they entered. Everything was black marble except for one wall completely covered by mirror. She wanted to turn around and run away as fast as she could. She would have, except that she couldn't leave Hero behind, and she couldn't break her promise to Jordan.

They crossed through a large room, what she assumed to be the living room. Unlike the foyer, everything in it was white. White damask sofas, white pillows, white ceiling-to-floor drapery, white carpets. The only color in the room came from a lighted painting of a conquistador and several potted palms.

"Coming?" Jordan called over his shoulder.

"Yes, right behind you." She followed him down a long hall swathed in a

190

deep scarlet flocked wallpaper, then entered a wonderful, sunlit room filled with plants of every sort. In the center of the room on heavily-upholstered, high-backed, white wicker chairs sat two glamorous-looking people who had to be Jordan's parents: a man, who looked much like Jordan despite his well-trimmed gray hair, and a woman dressed in a multicolored, floral caftan, who looked as if she'd just stepped out of the city's most elegant salon.

"Jordan, good. You made it. We've been waiting for you," his father said, leaping to his feet.

His mother moved a bit more slowly, seeming to size up the situation before rising. She looked from Hero to Valene, and back to Hero. "What is that?" she asked, pointing to the dog, without so much as a "hello" to her son.

"This is Hero," Jordan said, smiling as proudly as if he owned the dog.

The woman made a face and turned her head away, as if just the sight of the injured dog was repulsive.

"And you are?" she asked, turning to Valene with an expression not much different than she'd given Hero.

"Valene," Valene said timidly, feeling very awkward.

Jordan moved quickly to her side. "Mom, Dad. This is my new friend, Valene Zobel. Valene, these are my parents, Margaret and Colin Young."

"What are you doing with that mongrel?" Mrs. Young asked, turning her attention back to Hero, barely acknowledging Valene's existence.

"Long story. I'll tell you all about it later." He moved toward a brightly colored chintz sofa. "I brought a piece of plastic to lay him on. He'll only be here until I can fix up a bed for him. Valene can sit with him. He won't fall off."

"I'm not worried about him falling off! I don't want him there! He'll get it dirty!"

Jordan frowned, as if he couldn't fathom what she was saying. "He's not dirty. The poor dog's been having water therapy every day. I doubt if there's a speck of dirt on him."

"I can't believe you'd bring a dog into our home, Jordan," his mother said haughtily, pointing her finger in his face. "You know how your father and I—"

"Don't bring me in on this," Colin Young interjected quickly. "You're the one who would never allow pets."

"Get him out of here immediately, Jordan. I do not want him in this house." Margaret Young's face was red with anger.

Jordan scooped Hero up in his arms. "Either Hero stays or we leave. Which is it, Mother?"

"Come on, Margaret. It's only for the weekend," Colin said, slipping an arm about his wife. "Surely it won't hurt to have that dog around for two days. You don't want Jordan to leave, do you?"

All eyes turned to Margaret.

"Well, if he must stay, I guess it will be all right, but I do not want that dog on my furniture!"

Jordan's scowl relaxed a bit. "Fine. I'll keep him off your precious furniture, if that'll make you happy."

"I take it you plan for your little friend to stay for the weekend?" Margaret asked, turning to glare at Valene.

"I thought you told her I was coming with you," Valene whispered, feeling very unwelcome.

"I did," he whispered back.

"When you said you were bringing a friend, Jordan, I assumed it was a male friend," his mother said coolly.

"Male. Female. What difference does it make? You're always telling me to come and bring a friend. You have plenty of guest rooms."

"The problem is, Jordan, since I thought you were bringing one of your single, male friends, I've invited Melany Carlson to join us. You and Melany made such a cute couple. I think she thought the two of you would get married someday. She's bringing a friend along for your guest, or at least the guest I'd thought you were bringing. I certainly don't want to have to call and tell them not to come at this late hour."

Jordan shook his head and frowned. "Mother, why'd you invite Melany? You know we were never that serious. You should have asked me first."

"And you should've told me your weekend guest was that woman!" his mother shot back, her hands on her hips.

"Valene is more than 'that woman.' I'd appreciate it if you'd call her by her name!"

"Maybe I'd better leave." Valene's insides were shaking, and she was suddenly sick to her stomach. She'd never been in a situation like this before, and she felt sorry for Jordan.

"No, Valene. If you go, I go!"

His mother's expression softened a bit. "No, Valerie, stay. You're Jordan's guest. It's too late to do anything about it now."

Jordan bristled visibly. "Her name is Valene, not Valerie, Mother."

"Look," Colin said in a calming voice, raising his palms toward all of them. "Let's not make a big deal out of this. We have a nice dinner party planned for tonight." He turned to Valene. "We're glad to have you here, Valene, despite the way it looks. I think my wife was just unnerved by having Jordan bring your dog in here. She's never liked animals of any kind. I do hope you'll forgive her."

Valene nodded, not sure what to say.

His father gave both her and his son a warm smile. "Jordan, why don't you and Valene go fix up a place for the dog, either in your room or Valene's? She can use the guest room next to yours. I'll have Henry get your bags."

Jordan shot an icy glance toward his mother. "You okay with this?"

She tilted her chin haughtily. "Yes, I suppose so. It seems you give me no choice."

"No 'suppose so,' Mother. I'd appreciate either a direct yes or no."

"Yes, it's fine with me. Both of you may stay."

Jordan gave his father a wink, then turned to Valene with a smile that told her everything was going to be okay. "Come on, Valene. Let's get Hero settled."

Jordan asked Henry to serve a light lunch on the patio, next to the pool, after learning his mother was playing bridge that afternoon and his father was scheduled for a business meeting with one of his cronies.

After Jordan placed Hero on the ground beside them, the two watched as the dog stretched his body out full-length, obviously enjoying the sun's warmth on his stiffened hips.

"This is so beautiful," Valene said dreamily as she looked around the spacious grounds. "What fun you must've had growing up here, climbing these magnificent old trees. I'll bet you had a tire swing in that one over there."

"Are you kidding? My mother let me have a tire swing? It would've cluttered up her yard. She'd never allow it. As far as climbing the trees, ha! Not a chance! I might've damaged one of the limbs, and it would have thrown off the symmetry of the garden. You wouldn't believe what my parents pay their Japanese gardener to keep it looking like this."

After they'd thanked the Lord for their food, Valene nibbled on her crab salad, thinking of all the fun she and Vanessa had experienced during their growing-up years. They'd spent much of their childhood climbing trees, building crude tree houses, and digging in the backyard. Apparently Jordan hadn't been allowed to enjoy those same delightful pleasures.

"I'm sorry bringing me here has caused so much trouble," Valene said, remembering the look of displeasure on his mother's face when she'd seen her standing at Jordan's side.

"Don't worry about it. My mother thrives on trouble. She's never been a very happy woman."

"Why? She seems to have everything she could ever want."

"Got me! No matter how much they have, it's never enough. She always wants more, and fortunately with my father's income, she can have it. Maybe if he didn't pamper her like he does, she'd appreciate things more." He shrugged. "Don't get me wrong. I love my mother. But to be honest, sometimes I don't like her. She can be very rude and demanding, but you've learned that by experience, haven't you?"

She nodded as she let out a big sigh. "Yes, I have."

"Well, you'll only have to put up with her until tomorrow. Actually, I think she's a little frightened of you."

Her palm went to her chest. "Me? Why would she be frightened of me?"

"Because I've never brought a woman home before. I'm sure we have her wondering about our relationship. Remember? I told you my life has been planned out since I was a child. Getting serious with a woman before I leave the navy has never been a part of that plan."

"But we don't have a relationship."

He grinned as he forked up a bite of salad. "Sure we do. Haven't we been great friends since the day we took Hero to the vet's?"

"Yes, we have," she said, knowing that, on her part at least, they were more than just friends.

"But she doesn't know that. I'm sure she thinks there's something serious going on between us. I kinda like the idea of keeping her guessing."

"Oh, I see." Disappointment rippled through her body.

They finished their lunch then strolled through the majestic gardens. They sat in the frilly wrought-iron gazebo for more than an hour, each reminiscing to the other about their childhood.

Finally, Valene glanced at her watch. "It's nearly five. Didn't you say dinner was at six?"

"Actually, cocktails are at six. Dinner is at seven."

Valene winced at his words. "Cocktails? I don't drink!"

"Don't worry about it. I'm sure they'll have some soft drinks, too. I guess we'd better get back to the house. You'll want some time to get ready," Jordan said.

"I hope the dress I brought will be appropriate."

He smiled. "I'm sure whatever you brought will be just fine. It's only dinner."

"I wouldn't want to embarrass you."

"You could never embarrass me." Jordan turned to her with a grin. "Did you see that?"

She looked around but didn't see anything unusual.

"Don't look up, but my mother is standing on the balcony off their bedroom, watching us."

"She is?" Valene did her best to keep her eyes from wandering upward, but it was hard.

"Try not to look surprised. I'm going to kiss you. She needs to know how much I care for you."

Jordan pulled Valene into his arms and kissed her with a long, lingering kiss, the kind you see in the movies, then looked into her eyes and kissed her again. "Wow," he said, finally pulling away from her, "that was great!"

Valene's heart was fluttering so rapidly she could barely catch her breath. Jordan carefully picked up Hero, and they continued on into the house.

ᚦ

Valene showered in the amazing glassed-in shower. She'd never seen such a big shower, and she was intrigued by the brass serpent-head faucets. She dried her hair with the room's dryer instead of the one she'd brought, trying to fashion it into a style she thought might be more appropriate for the dreaded evening with the Youngs.

Somehow, the dress she'd liked so well in the store looked frumpy to her now, and she wished she'd had Vanessa there to pick one out for her. Unlike her, her sister always seemed to know the right thing to wear.

She applied her makeup meticulously, tugged on her pantyhose, and slipped into her dress before standing in front of the mirrored closet doors for one final check. *I should've gone for that sleeveless, plain black dress and borrowed Mom's pearls. I hate this ridiculous thing! I look like I'm going to a 4-H banquet! Whatever was I thinking of when I bought this childish-looking getup? Well, it's too late now. Other than the clean pair of jeans and the T-shirt I brought to wear tomorrow, there's no other choice.*

She slipped into her shoes and sat down on the rose satin love seat, nervously wringing her hands until a knock sounded on her door right at six.

"Hey, you look fantastic!" Jordan stepped back, giving her a full appraisal. "Ready?"

She nodded. "As ready as I'll ever be. It's not too late, Jordan. I don't mind staying in my room. You can go on down there by yourself and have dinner with your friends. I won't be the least bit offended, and I know it'd make your mother happy." She gestured toward the sleeping dog. "Besides, I really don't think we should leave him up here alone."

He held out his hand. "Don't worry about Hero. Remember that Japanese gardener I told you about? He's agreed to stay up here with Hero until we get back. He should be here any minute." He let out a chuckle. "Maybe he'll even teach Hero to bark in Japanese."

"You're one in a million, Jordan Young." She slipped her hand in his. The guy thought of everything.

Before he had time to come up with another clever remark, the gardener appeared. Jordan gave him a few instructions, then, holding Valene's arm, ushered her down the stairs and into the solarium, where the cocktails were being served. His father lifted his glass and gestured to them when they came into the room. His mother only offered a quick, disgusted glance, without so much as acknowledging she'd seen them. She was too caught up visiting with an attractive couple who looked as though they could have been movie stars attending an award function. Margaret Young almost looked like a movie star herself in her lime green pants suit with a huge red lily emblazoned on one side in bright red and green sequins. A quick glance around the room and Valene knew she was underdressed by far. Every other woman in the room either sparkled, glittered, or glowed.

"Let's go say hello to Mother," Jordan said, gently tugging Valene in her direction.

Do we have to? she mouthed silently so Jordan wouldn't hear her. If she had her way, she'd never have to meet Margaret Young face-to-face again, but that, too, was wishful thinking.

Jordan's mother turned away from her guests when he and Valene approached. Valene felt criticism in the woman's eyes as they scanned her from the top of her head to the tips of her shoes. It was obvious Margaret Young was not pleased by her appearance.

Valene clung tightly to Jordan's arm.

"Whatever did you do with that dreadful dog?" his mother asked, ignoring Valene.

Jordan took in a deep breath. "You needn't worry about him. He's being cared for by someone quite competent."

Margaret curled her finger, and instantly, a young woman dressed in a black uniform topped by a white apron appeared with a drink tray. "What would you like, Valerie?"

Jordan gave his mother a frosty look. "Her name is Valene, Mother. Is that so hard to remember?"

"I'll just have ginger ale, thank you."

Mrs. Young stepped back and, with a raised brow of amusement, gave her a ridiculing smile. "If you say so." Turning to her son she asked, "Wherever did you find this woman, Jordan? In a convent?"

"No, Mother. I didn't." He turned to the server. "Oh, and make that two ginger ales."

"That's an interesting little frock you're wearing." Margaret reached out and touched Valene's sleeve. "Polyester, isn't it?"

Valene's first thought was to respond with, "No, it's burlap," but she'd never want to embarrass Jordan, and the rude woman was his mother. Instead she smiled sweetly and said, "Yes, I like polyester. It takes very little care."

"Well, it's—it's charming," Margaret said, drawling out her words. "Polyester is quite durable, I've heard."

"Did someone get your drink orders?" Colin Young asked as he joined them.

"Oh, yes," Margaret said, her face frozen in the familiar smirk. "They've both ordered ginger ale."

Colin smiled as he lifted his glass and gave them all a wink. "Good idea. That's what I'm having."

Margaret latched onto Jordan's arm and pulled him toward a group of ladies standing by a brilliant display of red geraniums and white chrysanthemums. "Look who's here, Jordan," she said, nearly pushing him into the petite blond squeezed into a dress at least a size too small for her.

The woman spun around and gave Jordan a coquettish smile. "Jordan, how nice to see you again. You must come over and play tennis with me while you're home. Maybe tomorrow morning?"

Jordan turned and reached a hand toward Valene. "Melany Carlson, meet Valene Zobel. Valene is my guest for the weekend."

The woman's eyes widened. "But I thought—"

"I'm sorry if there was a misunderstanding, Melany. Apparently Mother thought the guest I was bringing was another man." He gave her a friendly smile. "Now if you'll excuse us, we have a dog to check on before dinner."

Melany gave him a puzzled look. "A dog?"

Jordan grinned as he pulled Valene toward the door. "A very special dog."

"Nice to have met you, Miss Carlson," Valene said quickly as Jordan led her away.

"You really didn't want that ginger ale, did you?" he asked as he pulled her through the door of the solarium and headed toward her room where the gardener was staying with Hero.

She shook her head with a laugh, glad to be leaving the cocktail party sooner than expected. "No, I'd much rather check on Hero."

A few minutes before seven, the two of them rejoined the others in the massive dining room. The table was splendidly set with sparkling china and crystal. Small vases of fresh flowers marked each place setting.

Still clinging to Valene's hand, Jordan quickly made a circle around the table, checking the name on each place card. When he found his mother had arranged for him to sit across the table from Valene and next to Melany, he quickly switched the cards. "Shh, no one will ever know."

"Your mother will," she whispered back.

Once everyone was seated, and not wanting to give Jordan's mother something else for which to criticize her, Valene discreetly bowed her head to pray.

"Aren't you feeling well, Valerie?" Margaret asked. "Perhaps you'd like to go to your room and lie down."

"Valene is praying, Mother," Jordan explained, sounding almost proud. "It's what some of us do before we eat."

Valene quickly finished her prayer and smiled up at him.

"Oh," his mother said with a tilt of her head. "I didn't realize Valerie—"

"Valene!" Jordan said in an exaggerated tone. "How many times do I have to tell you? Her name is Valene!"

"What I was saying was. . ." Margaret glared at her son. "I didn't realize Valene was one of those."

"And just what do you mean by 'one of those'?"

"You know perfectly well what I mean."

"Although I haven't always been as close to the Lord as He wants me to be, I'm a Christian, too, Mother. You know that, although you've always chosen to ignore it."

The room was suddenly filled with silence as every guest looked toward Margaret and Jordan.

"I propose a toast!" Colin rose quickly and loudly rattled his spoon against his glass. "To family, good friends, business associates, and neighbors. May each of us prosper!"

Everyone lifted their glasses and added a "Hear, hear!" Even Jordan and Valene lifted their glasses—their water glasses.

"Enjoy your dinner!" Colin said with a bow toward his guests.

Valene paused before eating her salad, waiting to see which fork everyone else used before picking up her own. The vegetables were nice and crisp, just the way she liked them, although some of them she didn't recognize.

When the butler came around with the basket of rolls, she reached in and took one.

"We have servants to do that for you, Valerie," Margaret said, chastising her and pointing to the ornate silver tongs in the man's hand.

Jordan reached past her and took a roll from the basket with a grin, as his mother grimaced.

Valene had never been so uncomfortable. Every bite she took was sheer agony. What if she dropped something on the pristine tablecloth?

"Relax," Jordan whispered, as he leaned toward her. "Don't let her get to you."

She smiled back and reached for her water glass, hoping the cool liquid would dissolve the lump in her throat. But her nervousness caused her aim to miss, and instead of picking up the water glass, she knocked it over. A river of water and ice flowed across the table, a portion of it dropping onto Melany's short dress. Others seated in its path jumped quickly to their feet, throwing their napkins onto the table to stop the flow.

"I'm—I'm so sorry. I never meant to—"

Jordan tossed his own napkin onto the puddle and wrapped a consoling arm about her. "It's okay. Don't feel bad. The servants will have it cleaned up in a second. Accidents happen."

"I think I'd better go to my room." Valene tried to stand but Jordan's hold on her tightened.

"No, you're staying right here with me," he whispered as he held her tight.

She sat rigid, feeling more foolish than ever before in her life. *Why, oh why, did I let Jordan talk me into coming? Or is it God's will that I be here? Maybe He's trying to make me see I'd never fit into Jordan's world!*

The rest of the dinner went without mishap. Afraid of making another mistake, Valene merely toyed with her food.

By the time dessert came, she had calmed down and was able to almost enjoy the rich chocolate cheesecake garnished with whipped cream and fresh strawberries.

"You have a bit of whipped cream on your chin, Valerie," Mrs. Young said, pointing her long finger.

Valene grabbed at her napkin. "Ah, thank you."

Jordan squinted as he bent close to her. "I didn't see any whipped cream."

There probably wasn't any, Valene thought, giving the woman a quick glance. *Just another one of her ploys to embarrass me.*

Jordan stood and pulled Valene up with him. "It was nice to see all of you again, but I'm afraid Valene and I are going to have to excuse ourselves. We have an ailing dog upstairs, and we want to go check on him. Enjoy your evening."

Mrs. Young grabbed his arm as he passed. "But Jordan, Vladimir is going to entertain us in the parlor. I know how you love hearing him play the piano. Perhaps Valerie could stay with that dog."

"Val–lene," Jordan said, emphasizing her name. "We both need to check on Hero. We'll see you in the morning."

With one final wave to his parents and their guests, he led Valene out of the dining room. "Sorry I put you through that."

"She hates me, Jordan. I know she does. I don't belong here. This world is completely foreign to me. But I do appreciate your father. He's been very kind."

"Nights like this, I don't know how he can live with her. I suppose they do have their good moments. Sometimes I think Mother is Father's trophy. She's normally a wonderful hostess to his business associates, and she gives great parties, which can be a real asset to his business."

"She's quite a bit younger than he is, isn't she?"

"Oh, yes, about fifteen years younger. I imagine her age and her good looks are what attracted him."

When they reached Valene's room, the gardener reported on how the evening had gone. "Hero did fine," he said. "He's a nice dog."

Jordan pulled out his wallet and gave the man a few bills, thanked him, and shut the door behind him. "Looks like he got along okay without us."

Valene stooped down beside Hero and patted his head. "Oh, oh."

Jordan shoved his wallet into his pocket and bent down beside her. "Oh, Hero, why didn't you do that when that guy was here to clean you up?"

"I'll do it," Valene said, slipping out of her shoes.

"No, it's my turn. You did it last time." He pulled off his jacket and began rolling up his sleeves.

"We'll both do it."

They'd no more than started the clean-up job when someone rapped on the door.

Chapter 8

D oor's open," Jordan called out as he lifted Hero from his bed of paper. "I've come to apologize—" Colin's eyes flitted from Jordan holding the dog, to Valene holding a huge bag filled with shredded paper. He reared back with a laugh. "Now, that is a sight!"

"You needn't apologize for Mother," Jordan said with a half-smile, awkwardly holding the offensive dog away from his shirt. "She needs to apologize for herself."

"You know your mother well enough, son, to know that will never happen." He stared at Hero. "What happened to him anyway?"

"He's this way because of me, Dad. I was driving across the parking lot at my condo and accidentally hit him with my truck. He has a fractured pelvis. As you can see, he's pretty helpless. Right now, he requires care around the clock."

The man patted Hero on the head. "Oh, Jordan, how awful! I can see why you're so concerned about him. Will he ever be able to walk again?"

Jordan nodded. "Yes, he's getting better every day, but his hips will always be stiff. We've been giving him water baths as therapy. The doc said he should be able to stand by himself before long. Meantime, he'll have to drag his hind end around. We try to help him by putting him on a towel and assisting him. He's a good dog."

"I had no idea. No wonder you wanted to bring him along."

"That's not the half of it. I nearly hit the six-year-old boy Hero was chasing. If I hadn't hit the brakes in time, I might have injured or killed a child. Instead, I hit Hero."

"I'm proud of you, son, for facing up to your responsibilities. And I'm glad you brought Valene along."

"She's become a good friend through all of this. We enjoy each other's company."

Valene, still holding the bag of paper, stepped forward with a smile. "Thank you, Mr. Young. Your words mean a lot to me. You've raised a fine son."

Mr. Young's smile left. "I'm afraid I can't take much credit for Jordan's upbringing, and neither can my wife. We left much of his care to our housekeeper. We were both too busy with things that really didn't matter. But I'm quite proud of Jordan and the man he has become."

"You should be proud. He's one of the nicest and finest men I've ever met."

"Hey, you two. Don't talk about me like I'm not here!"

Colin's smile returned. "I'll let you get back to that dog. Hero? Is that what you said his name was?"

Valene nodded. "Yes, I know it's a silly name for a dog, but it suits him."

"I like the name. This world would be a better place if we had more heroes. See you both at breakfast?"

"Yes, sir. We'll be there," Jordan told him. "I'd shake hands with you, but—"

The two men laughed.

"Carry on with your cleaning project. I'd better get back to your mother before she comes looking for me."

"I like him," Valene said as the door closed behind Jordan's father.

"Good. I can tell he likes you, too."

🌴

Colin and Margaret were already seated at the table in the breakfast room when Jordan and Valene came down the next morning.

"Well, how did Hero sleep?" Mr. Young asked as Jordan and Valene took their chairs at the table.

"He went to sleep right after Jordan gave him his Rimadyl and slept the rest of the night without making a sound.

"Good! You must keep me posted on his recovery."

"I do hope you're keeping that dog off the furniture, Jordan. I've heard an animal's smell is almost impossible to get out of upholstery." His mother raised a well-arched brow. "Carpeting, too."

"There is plastic sheeting on the floor under a double layer of cardboard. I doubt your carpet will smell," Jordan said, seeming almost amused. "I even brought a can of room freshener. I'll be sure to give the guest room a good spritzing before we leave. And Hero has not been on your furniture."

The maid brought in their breakfast. Valene opted for juice, coffee, and a bagel with cream cheese, while Jordan went for the whole works—eggs, bacon, biscuits, and gravy.

"Too bad you had to leave to take care of that dreadful dog last night, Jordan. We had a wonderful time visiting with our guests," his mother said, "and Vladimir's playing was astounding, as usual. Did you know Melany is going to Paris next month?"

Jordan dabbed at his mouth with his napkin. "No, I didn't know that."

"I think this will be her third trip abroad this year." Margaret took a sip of juice, then turned her attention toward Valene. "Have you been to Paris lately?"

"No. I've never been to Paris."

"Oh, what a pity. There are so many amazing things to do in Paris. Have you been to Rome? I love Rome. The Italian fashions are to die for."

"No, I've never been to Rome. In fact, I've barely been out of California," Valene confessed reluctantly.

"That's too bad. Traveling is such a stimulating way to broaden one's horizons."

"I'm sure it is."

Margaret reached over, her fingers cupping Valene's wrist. "I don't recall you mentioning your parents' business."

"They don't have a business. My dad will retire from the phone company in a few years. My mother has never worked outside our home, except for occasionally baby-sitting and helping at a friend's bridal shop."

Mrs. Young's eyes widened. "Really? The phone company? Well, I suppose someone has to do those things, or we wouldn't be able to have phones."

"Her parents are great people. I've met them. Valene has a twin sister, but she's been on her honeymoon, so I haven't met her yet."

"A twin? That must be interesting," his father said.

Valene smiled with pride. "It is! She and I have always been close. I'm afraid I'm going to have trouble adjusting to the fact that she's married now."

"Jordan, do you remember the Gallagers?" his mother asked, interrupting. "Mr. Gallager sold his investment company recently, and they've bought the old Kilmer place. They have a lovely daughter about your age. She's anxious to meet you. I think the two of you will have a lot in common."

Jordan speared a hunk of biscuit and gravy with his fork and twirled it in the air. "Sorry, Mother. Not interested."

"Jordan, mind your manners," his mother said sharply.

"Hey, Dad, how's the golf game going? Won any tournaments lately?"

Colin took his last sip of coffee and placed his cup in the saucer. "I'm not any better at golf now than I was ten years ago, but I have to say, I've made some pretty good deals on the course. Seems men are more relaxed when they're playing golf. Just last week, one of my golf partners signed a good contract with our firm, right there on the ninth hole. The caddy had to loan him a pen."

"Sounds to me like you'd better keep on playing golf!" Jordan said with a wink as he spread jam on a fresh biscuit.

"You need to spend more time at the office with me, Jordan," his father said, his expression turning serious. "It won't be too many more years before you'll be taking over the business. You need to keep abreast of what's going on."

"I've got a few years yet, Dad. Don't rush me."

"Jordan tells me you were a navy man, too," Valene said, feeling the need to participate in the conversation.

"I was. Graduated from Annapolis like Jordan did, but he graduated with honors. I didn't."

"He's being modest," Jordan said, beaming at his father. "I barely beat him out. You ought to see his awards."

"You're being quiet, my dear," Colin commented to Margaret.

"I'm a bit weary. I didn't sleep well last night. I may take an aspirin and go back to bed."

Jordan placed his napkin on the table. "Well, you needn't worry about entertaining us. Valene and I are heading home as soon as we get things loaded into the Avalanche."

"Why do you drive that hideous vehicle?" his mother asked, pushing away her dishes. "It's ghastly."

"Hey, don't talk about my truck that way. That's what all us jocks drive these days."

"I wish you wouldn't call yourself a jock. The word has such a vulgar connotation to it."

"I like that truck. It serves my purpose well, and if I ever get stuck in a snowstorm—"

"In California? You rarely go up in the mountains, and that's the only place you might need it around here."

"Ah, but having it gives me the option, in case I ever decide I want to."

Valene had to smile to herself as she listened to them bantering back and forth. How much his mother and father had missed by not spending time with him when he was a boy.

"Well, good-bye, you two. Been good to see you both. We'd better be hitting the road," Jordan said finally.

Colin held out his hand. "Good-bye, son. Drive carefully."

Margaret lifted a cheek toward Jordan and held it there until he finally kissed it. "Good-bye, Jordan."

⌘

Although Jordan apologized profusely for his mother's insolent behavior, Valene found it hard to forgive her. She'd never been around someone like Margaret Young, and she wasn't sure she ever wanted to see the woman again. Yet Valene knew that if she ever wanted to be near Jordan, she must recognize that Margaret came with the package. The woman would always be his mother.

"How come you're so quiet?" Jordan asked, reaching over to take her hand.

"Been thinking."

"About what? Your wonderful, entertaining weekend at the Young house?"

"Something like that."

They rode along quietly the rest of the way with Jordan occasionally trying to get a conversation started, but to no avail. Valene didn't feel like talking.

When they reached her condo, he gathered Hero up in his arms and carried him inside before going back for Valene's suitcase and the dog's bed.

Once Hero was settled, Jordan bent and kissed Valene on the cheek. "Thanks for going with me. I had no idea things would be that bad. I know my mother embarrassed you, and I'm sorry. You were a good sport, but I should never have put you in that position. I guess by being away from her as much as I have since I went off to Annapolis, I'd forgotten how vindictive she can be."

Valene dropped down on the sofa with a deep sigh. "This has got to end, Jordan."

He sat down beside her and slipped an arm about her shoulders. "What has to end?"

"Us. Our relationship."

"Why? I thought we were getting along so well."

"I know we're only friends, but can't you see? Other than Hero, we have nothing in common. Your world is wealth, prestige, and excitement. I'm a nobody."

"I don't see what any of that has to do with us being friends, and besides, you're wrong. You're selling yourself short, as usual."

She motioned toward the door. "I think you'd better go. Hero's getting along fine now. You've done more than your part in helping him get well. Between Diane and me, we should be able to take care of him until he's able to stand on his own. Go back to your world. Forget about us."

"What if I don't want to forget about you?"

"It's for your own good, Jordan. You've put off way too many things these past couple of weeks to spend time with us. I don't want you to sacrifice any longer."

"Who said I was sacrificing? Have you heard me complain?"

She pulled away and crossed her arms defiantly. "I really don't want to see you anymore. I have my life to live, too."

"You really want me to leave? You're sure?"

"Quite sure."

"You realize if I walk out that door, I may never come back?"

She wanted to throw herself into his arms and beg him to stay with her forever, but she couldn't. "Yes, I know."

"Have I done something to offend you? Are you mad at me?"

"No, of course not."

"Can't you see I care for you? You're much more to me than a friend."

How much more, Jordan? Am I just another one of your groupies? Like Melany? Will you cast me aside someday like you probably did to her?

"Valene? Did you hear me?"

"I heard you, Jordan. Please go."

"Okay! If that's the way you want it. We'll do it your way. If you need any help with Hero, give me a call. Otherwise you won't be hearing from me. But remember, Valene, this was your idea. Not mine."

Jordan grabbed his jacket from the chair, bent and patted Hero one last time, and stormed out, slamming the door behind him.

Valene rose and walked slowly to the door, pressing her cheek against it as her tears flowed. "I love you, Jordan, but you've never said you love me. You're out of my league. I've known that from the start. I can't set myself up for a broken heart."

Lord, I need Your help. Fill my heart with the peace that only You can give.

Just then the phone rang, and Valene rushed to answer it, hoping it was Jordan.

"Hi, sis," a cheery voice said on the other end of the line. "Nathan and I are back from our honeymoon. I'm coming over. I want to meet that hunk Mom said is helping you take care of Hero. You've got to tell me all about him."

"No, don't—"

"Hey, I know you're busy, but I'm coming. Nathan is going to stay here with Mom and Dad. I'll be there in half an hour."

Before Valene could explain why she couldn't introduce her sister to Jordan, Vanessa hung up.

☩

"You what?" Vanessa gaped at Valene. They'd been sitting on the sofa for a full hour. The first half hour, Vanessa spent telling Valene all about the honeymoon. The second half hour, Valene told Vanessa about the accident and everything leading up to the minute she'd told Jordan to get out of her life.

"I told him to leave. Don't you see, Van, even if he felt the same way about me as I feel about him, there are too many obstacles in the way. Right now, the navy is his life, and he has no intention of leaving it for probably another four years. There's no place for a wife in his plans. I'd never fit into his world. His mother hates me."

Vanessa leaned back into the sofa and clasped her hands behind her head. "You, dear sister, have a problem."

"But Vanessa, I never knew losing Jordan was going to hurt this much. He's only been gone a few hours, and I'm miserable."

"I know, kiddo. I know, and I'll be praying for the two of you. I hate to leave you, but I promised Nathan I'd be back in two hours. You gonna be all right here by yourself?"

Valene gestured toward Hero, who was trying to pull himself off the bed Jordan had made for him. "I've got Hero. He'll keep me company."

"Call if you need me, and I'll be here in a flash."

"I know that. You've always been there for me. Thanks for coming over. Tell Nathan 'hi' for me, and give Jeff a kiss. I love that boy. Oh, by the way, Jeff left one of his books in my car. It's unlocked. You'd better take it to him."

She watched as the door closed behind her sister before breaking down and crying until she could cry no more. Jordan was out of her life.

⚓

Jordan walked slowly toward his pickup. He wasn't exactly hungry; he just couldn't stand the idea of sitting in that condo one more minute, knowing Valene was just a few doors away. He'd nearly reached it when he noticed her leaning into her car as if trying to retrieve something.

He rushed over, grabbed her by the wrist, and pulled her into his arms. "Are you sure you won't change your mind?"

"You must be Jordan!"

Chapter 9

Jordan pushed away from her a bit and stared into her face. "Of course I'm Jordan. Who else would I be?"

"I'm Vanessa! Valene's twin sister," Vanessa told him with a giggle.

He couldn't believe it. The likeness was uncanny. "Whoops, sorry! I didn't know you were back in town. Have you talked to Valene yet?"

"Yes, I just spent the last hour with her. She told me all about you."

"Did she tell you she told me to get lost?"

Vanessa's smile disappeared. "Yes, she did, but she had her reasons. I'm sure she explained them to you."

"She did, but I just don't get it. I thought we were getting along fine. Then, *pow!* I take her to visit my parents for the weekend, and she turns on me."

Vanessa pulled Jeff's book from the car and closed the door. "I know what she's going through, Jordan. She felt like a misfit at your parents' house. We didn't have all the advantages you had growing up, but we had parents who loved us and did all they could for us. Val felt like the proverbial fish out of water in La Jolla."

He had to make her understand. "But I'm not like my parents. At least, not like my mother. I know she gave Valene a hard time, and I'm sorry. If I'd had any idea Mother would treat her the way she did, I would never have taken her there."

"There were other reasons, too. Valene's always wanted to meet Mr. Right, get married, and have children, but she—"

"I want that, too, just not now."

"Not for a number of years, from what Valene tells me."

Jordan clasped his hands together and stood staring at her. "Look, I'm a navy pilot. Right now, I couldn't offer anything permanent to any woman. Not even a woman as wonderful as Valene. When I'm out of the country on a mission, I may be gone for months at a time. What kind of a life would that be for her? I'd never want to be married and have a wife and kids to leave behind. No, ma'am. As long as I'm in the navy, it's better for everyone if I remain unattached. But I do want to keep up a relationship with Valene." He grinned. "You could put in a good word for me!"

Vanessa gave him a slap on the back. "Sorry, pal. You're on your own on this one. A woman can't wait forever. Especially a woman like my sister."

"I don't want our relationship to end this way. She's been too good a friend for that."

Vanessa tilted her head as she gazed at him. "I have one question I want to leave with you, and I suggest you give it some serious thought."

"Oh, what?"

"Do you love her?"

With that, she turned and walked to her car, and he was left standing alone in the parking lot.

֏

Although Hero slept fairly well, Valene had a miserable night. She couldn't get her mind off Jordan. Even praying didn't seem to help. Where was that peace God promised to those who love Him?

She routinely took care of Hero's needs, then dressed quickly for work. By the time Diane arrived, Val was ready to head out the door.

At five, when she walked back into her condo, Diane handed her a vase containing a dozen red roses. Their sweet fragrance filled the room. Valene held them close, their velvety petals caressing her cheek. The attached card bore only a few words: *I'm waiting for your call.*

Each of the next five days, flowers arrived with the same words on the card. Valene would hold them close and cry. She wanted to call Jordan and thank him and tell him Hero had stood completely on his own for the first time, but she didn't. The ache in her heart hadn't lessened one bit.

By Saturday, she was exhausted and nearly to the point of calling Jordan. Living without him in her life had become unbearable.

Late Sunday afternoon, after she'd given Hero his water therapy and his Rimadyl, she decided enough was enough. She had to see Jordan. She dabbed on a bit of lipstick, ran a comb through her hair, and hurried across the sidewalk to his condo, but no one was home. Disappointed, she started back to her place, when Diane's door opened.

"I heard you knocking. Jordan isn't home. He hasn't been for a couple of days now. I don't know where he is. He asked me to take in his newspaper and his mail until he gets back."

Valene's heart plummeted. Where could he be? Maybe he was staying at the base to avoid seeing her. She thanked Diane and rushed back to Hero.

The next two days dragged by. On Tuesday evening, by the time Valene had given Hero his water therapy, cleaned up the kitchen, and folded two loads of laundry, she was dead tired. She fell down onto her sofa and turned on the eleven o'clock news to check the weather report. But when the lead story came on, she sat up straight and quickly turned up the volume. "An F-18 Hornet from the San Diego Naval Base has gone down in the Philippines, killing the pilot," the newscaster was saying. "At this time, details are limited. The name of the deceased pilot is being withheld until the next of kin can be notified."

Valene went ballistic. That pilot could be Jordan! Why else would he be gone from his condo for five days straight, unless he was on a mission?

Frantically, she dialed Jordan's base apartment. His answering machine picked up, and she listened to the recording of his voice explain he was unable to take calls and to please leave a message.

She hung up quickly and phoned the base switchboard, asking if Jordan Young was on the downed plane.

"Sorry, ma'am, unless you are a close relative and can verify your identity, we cannot give out that information."

Terrified, Valene began to pace about the room. She had to know if Jordan was dead or alive.

Suddenly, a thought occurred to her. Next of kin! His parents, they'd know! But what if they hadn't been notified yet? She couldn't just call them and ask if the navy had contacted them. They'd be sick with worry. Maybe Jordan was safe somewhere. Maybe sitting in an arena watching a basketball game or playing tennis or. . .

She had to find out. Maybe she could casually ask his parents if they'd talked to him lately. What if his mother answered the phone? Margaret probably wouldn't tell her anything, even if they'd been notified. She had to take a chance and hope his father was the one to answer, or at least the butler.

With fingers almost too nervous to dial, Valene called the house in La Jolla. "Hello."

"Mrs. Young, this is Valene Zobel. I haven't seen Jordan around his condo for several days, and I've been concerned about him. I thought perhaps he was sick, or—"

"You have no right calling my son. Why don't you leave him alone? I know all about women like you. You find some unsuspecting man you think has money, and you chase after him shamelessly. Stay away from him, do you hear?"

Shocked by the harsh accusations, Valene hung up the phone without responding. Although she was hurt by the woman's words, she was also encouraged. Surely if Mrs. Young had received bad news about Jordan, she wouldn't be answering the phone. She'd be grieving.

In near hysterics, Val stayed up all night, scanning the television channels, hoping for more news about the crash, but most of the comments the newscasters gave were only repeats.

When Diane came over the next morning, Valene told her what she'd heard on the news and that she had decided to take the day off in case the pilot's name was released.

That night when the phone rang, she let the machine pick up, afraid to miss even one second of the local newscast. But when she heard Jordan's voice on the answering machine, she leaped to answer it before he could hang up.

"Oh, Jordan, it's you!" she said, tears blinding her. "I've been so worried. I was afraid it was your plane that crashed." She was sobbing so hard she was afraid he wouldn't be able to make out her words.

"I'm fine. I've been on a short-term training mission all week. I didn't even know about the crash until this evening when we got into port."

"Oh, Jordan, I was so afraid I'd lost you! I love you so much. If anything ever happened to you, I'd—" She stopped midsentence, realizing what she'd said.

"You mean it? You love me?"

"Yes," she said between sobs, "I know you don't love me, but I can't help myself. Outside of God, you're the most important person in my life."

"Oh, but I do love you. That's the main reason I called. The day I talked with Vanessa, she asked me, point-blank, if I loved you. I've never been in love before, Valene. I didn't have a clue as to how it felt or what it was. But when I thought I'd lost you, I realized what I was feeling was indeed love. Nothing means more to me than you. Not flying, not the navy, not my parents, not my future at my family's company. I'd give it all away rather than lose you."

Those were the sweetest words Valene had ever heard, and she was filled with such emotion, all she could do was cry.

"Oh, Valene, you're all I've thought about since we've been apart. I wish I wasn't so far away. I want to hold you in my arms and look into those beautiful blue eyes."

"I–I want that, too."

"Look, I won't be home from this mission until Friday. I'd like for us to spend as much time together as possible. Just you and me. . ." He snickered. "And Hero?"

She cupped the phone in her hands, feeling it was her lifeline to him. "Oh, yes, I. . .we'd like that."

"How is he, Valene? I've been worried sick about both of you. I should never have let you take care of him by yourself. I'll bet you're exhausted, but I'm going to pamper you when I get home. I promise I'll take care of Hero the whole weekend."

She let out a giggle. "He'll be glad to see you. He's not too crazy about the way I handle him. I've been putting him on the towel and dragging him to the tub."

"I almost didn't call. I was afraid you'd hang up on me. But I had to hear your voice."

She brushed away a tear and swallowed a sob. "I'm glad you did. I can't begin to tell you how much I've missed you."

"See you Friday night, sweetheart."

"I'll be waiting, and Jordan—please be careful flying."

"I love you, Valene. I think I've always loved you."

"I love you, too, Jordan. I can't wait to see you."

Valene cradled the phone long after he'd hung up. Jordan was safe, and he loved her! She bowed her head to thank God for answered prayer and for bringing Jordan back to her.

🌴

Jordan smiled as he hung up the phone. He could hardly wait to hold Valene in his arms.

He looked up a number in the directory and dialed the phone. The person he was calling picked up on the second ring.

"Chaplain Abbot."

"This is Jordan Young. I need to talk to you again."

"I'm free now."

"I'll be right there."

🌴

The next few weeks were the happiest ones Valene had ever known, as she and Jordan spent every possible moment together talking on the phone, listening to CDs, holding hands while walking in the park, cuddling in front of the TV, attending the Sunday morning services at her church, and falling deeper in love.

Despite his parents' insistence that he come to La Jolla for Thanksgiving, Jordan opted to spend the holiday with Valene and her family instead, at Nathan and Vanessa's picturesque 1865 saltbox-styled home, the one Nathan had lovingly restored.

After a sumptuous Thanksgiving dinner with all the trimmings, Valene and Jordan broke away from the rest of the family and wandered into the backyard.

"Wow," Jordan said, as they walked through the lush stand of green grass toward a lacy white gazebo surrounded by dozens of colorful chrysanthemums. "This is beautiful!"

"Yes, it is beautiful, but nothing like your parents' yard. Mmm, don't you love the smell of freshly mown grass?"

They pushed aside one of the vines twining its way around the lovely gazebo and sat down on one of the ornate benches.

"Nathan did all this work himself? My parents have a team of gardeners who take care of their lawn, and it doesn't look much better than this." He leaned back on the bench and crossed his ankles. "It must give him a great deal of satisfaction to know he's restored an 1865 house like he has and to have built this magnificent gazebo. I envy him, being able to work with his hands."

Valene laughed. "He probably envies you being able to fly like you do."

Jordan grinned. "It's a guy thing."

He pulled her into his arms and held her close, their foreheads touching as they gazed into each other's eyes.

"I love you, Valene. Will you marry me?"

She pulled back and stared at him. *Marry me? Is that what he said? After all his comments about staying single?*

"I can't promise you an easy life, not yet anyway. Not until I get out of the navy, which might be another four years. But other guys in my squad are married. If they can do it, surely we can if you love me as much as I love you."

She wanted to shout "Yes!" But despite their deep feelings for one another, so many obstacles still stood in their way. "I don't know, Jordan. You know I love you, and I want so much to say yes." She reached up and gently stroked his cheek. "Marrying you would be a dream come true. But your parents would be furious with you. Especially your mother. She'd never allow you to marry outside of your social circle. You know that. She'd much prefer you marry someone like Melany or Charmaine. Someone with breeding and class. Someone with social graces."

"It's my life, Valene. I can't live it for my parents. I don't want any of those women for my wife. I want you. I love you. Please say you'll marry me!"

"I want to marry you, Jordan. You know I do! I've told you how much I love you. I nearly went crazy when we broke up. I was miserable without you. But—"

"Look. Let's plan on announcing our engagement at Christmas. That'll give us a month to work out all the kinks. I won't let you go again. We can't let anyone, or anything, stand in our way. We have to be together!"

"You sure about this?" Valene asked. "Marriage is a lifetime commitment. When I marry, it's going to be one of those 'till death do us part' things. No escape! No changing your mind later!"

He kissed the tip of her nose. "That's the way I want it, too. Since God brought us together, I know our love will last a lifetime. Come on, say yes!"

She allowed her slow smile to turn into a broad grin. "Okay. I'll marry you! We'll tell everyone at Christmas! Like you said, that'll give us time to work out the kinks."

"If I can keep it quiet for that long," he said, his smile radiating his joy. "I'd like to plaster the news on a billboard! Tell everyone I know you're going to be my wife!"

She threw her arms about his neck, laughing hysterically. "I love you! I love you! I love you!"

When they walked arm-in-arm back into the house from their walk, Vanessa asked, "What's with you two? You look like you've just won the lottery, but I know that can't be so, because neither of you ever buys a ticket."

Jordan grinned. "We've sorta come to an understanding."

✝

The next month passed quickly, as fall turned rapidly to winter, on the calendar, at least. The San Diego area's weather was much the same year round. Bright and sunny.

Valene and Jordan spent a traditional Christmas Eve with her family at her parents' home in Granite Cliffs. After the Christmas story had been read from the Bible and all the gifts had been opened, Jordan clapped his hands loudly.

"Since I consider all of you to be my family now, Valene and I would like you to be a part of something special." He dropped to one knee in front of her, taking her hand in his and caressing it as he gazed up at her.

"Valene Zobel, I love you with all my heart, and you've said you love me. I want us to spend the rest of our lives together." He pulled a beautiful diamond solitaire ring from his pocket and placed it on her finger. "Will you marry me?"

Valene's heart leaped with happiness as she circled her arms about Jordan's neck. The day she had hoped for, yes, even prayed for, had come. "Yes, dear Jordan! I'll marry you! I love you with all my heart. My life wouldn't be complete without you."

There wasn't a dry eye in the room, as their loved ones shared in their joy.

Jordan pulled her to her feet and wrapped his arms about her. "I love you, Valene. I'll always love you." Then he kissed her. To Valene, it seemed the world began to swirl around them as her love for him overflowed her heart. Soon she would be his, to have and hold forever.

✝

"Remember, Valene," Jordan told her as they stood outside his parents' home the next morning. "You're marrying me, not my parents. Maybe when they see we're determined, they'll be happy for us."

She leaned her head against his shoulder with a sigh. "I'm so afraid your mother will go through the roof when she finds out we're engaged. I don't want to be the cause of any trouble between you and your parents."

"Hopefully, there won't be any trouble. I made it perfectly clear when I phoned them to say we were going to spend Christmas Day with them that I would not come unless both you and Hero were welcome." His reassuring smile warmed her heart and gave her courage. "Ready?"

She lifted her chin and pasted on a smile. "Ready."

Instead of the butler, Colin himself opened the door. "Merry Christmas, you two!" He threw his arms open wide. "It's so good to have you here." He shook Jordan's free hand and kissed Valene's cheek. "You, too, Hero," he added, patting the dog's head.

Jordan raised a brow. "Mother wasn't too thrilled when I insisted he come with us."

Colin gave him a wink. "Don't worry about your mother. I'll take care of her."

"Merry Christmas!" Margaret rushed into the foyer, dressed in a flowing red caftan that rustled when she walked, totally ignoring Valene's presence. "I'm so glad you made it, Jordan." She stopped short when she saw Hero.

"Merry Christmas, Mrs. Young," Valene said brightly, trying to ease the tension she'd already begun to feel.

Margaret barely cast a glance over her shoulder before adding a slightly cool, "Merry Christmas."

Colin put an arm about his wife. "I was just telling Jordan and Valene how glad we are to have them here."

Hero let out a slight yelp as Jordan tugged on his leash.

"Surely you don't expect that dog to have free rein of this house!" Margaret's nose wrinkled up as she turned her head away. "Can't you put that dreadful animal outside somewhere, Jordan? Maybe in one of the garages? But don't turn him loose. I don't want him digging in the lawn."

Jordan shook his head and narrowed his eyes. "Look, Mother, I explained all of this to you on the phone. I told you the woman who usually watches over him when we have to be away is spending Christmas with her parents in Oregon. You knew I was bringing Hero. Father has gone out of his way to make us feel welcome. Now either you quit being Miss Hoity-Toity, or we're leaving. Am I making myself clear?"

"You needn't speak to me in that tone of voice," Margaret said, looking hurt. "I am your mother."

"Then act like a mother!" Jordan's words were sharp, but considering the fiascoes during their last visit, Valene knew it was necessary that some ground rules be established if they were to get through the day without a major confrontation.

"Do we understand one another, Mother?" Jordan asked, tapping his toe impatiently.

"Oh, Jordan, don't be silly." His mother gave them both a warm smile that was about as genuine as a ten-dollar Rolex watch for sale on the streets of Times Square. "It's Christmas. Of course, we're glad you brought your little friend along, and if you feel you have to have that dog with you, as well, I guess I'll have to put up with it."

"Good, then we understand each other." Jordan gave Hero a quick pat on the head, then smiled at his mother. "Why don't you two show Valene the Christmas tree while I get some things from my pickup?"

Although she looked none too happy about his request, Margaret motioned for Valene to follow and led her into the living room, with Colin following. Valene caught her breath as she stood before the perfectly shaped Christmas tree. What looked to be a thousand tiny gold lights wound their way through its branches. And from its tip to nearly the floor, the tree was covered with hundreds of gold-colored ornaments and countless bands of shiny gold garland. It was magnificent, as were all the other decorations in the room.

"It's lovely," Valene said, stepping back for a better look. "I've never seen anything like it."

"I use the same designer every year. He's very much in demand, but I'm at the top of his list."

Valene's eyes widened. "You don't decorate your own tree?" She'd always thought decorating the tree was one of the highlights of the season. She loved decorating her family's tree.

"Of course not! Why would anyone want to decorate their own tree? It's so time-consuming, and I'm sure those branches are quite prickly."

"There you are!"

Valene turned at the sound of Jordan's voice and found him pulling Hero in a big cargo-type wagon.

"Look at Hero," he said pointing proudly to the dog. "I've been taking him for a ride. This was my old wagon. If we'd gotten him something like this when we brought him home from the vet's, Valene, then I wouldn't have had to sleep in your bed."

Margaret looked as though she was going to faint. "You—you slept in her bed?"

Jordan grinned. "Sure did. For two weeks."

His mother's hand went to her forehead as she let out a sigh of exasperation. "You needn't brag about it. Gentlemen usually keep their conquests to themselves."

He threw his head back with a robust laugh. "Mother, Hero couldn't be moved. And since he was too heavy for Valene to lift when he needed to be helped or cleaned up, we switched condos at night. She stayed in mine. I stayed in hers. It was all perfectly respectable. Apparently you don't know me or Valene, or you wouldn't have jumped to such a conclusion. We both have values."

Both his parents seemed relieved by his explanation, but neither commented on it, and the rest of the morning was spent on simple chitchat.

After an exorbitantly festive Christmas dinner, the four, along with Hero, moved into the solarium to open their gifts. Although the decorations in the living room had been breathtakingly beautiful, Valene found the solarium decorations more to her liking. The tree, though not as tall, looked more traditional and was filled with multicolored lights and ornaments. Most of the ornaments were the collector type, and no doubt quite expensive, but nonetheless, they were intriguing. Any child would have loved that tree.

Fresh greenery, wrapped with garlands of red and green and silver and entwined with tiny twinkling lights, was draped in half circles around the entire glass ceiling of the huge room. It was like a fairyland. Valene felt herself gawking and wondered what Mrs. Young would think of her naiveté. She'd never been around such blatant extravagance.

Once they were all settled and Hero was confined to the throw rug the maid had provided for him, they began to exchange presents. Valene handed Margaret her gift with trepidation—a large family-tree sampler she'd cross-stitched, with the names and birth dates of the past five generations of the Young family. Valene had loved stitching it. Evenings, Jordan would sit in the chair, watching her, smiling his approval. He'd even insisted that she stitch her name and the date in the lower right-hand corner. When she'd said his mother might not approve of that, he'd insisted, saying she was going to be part of the family, and her name should be there. It'd been a wonderful experience for both of them. They'd taken it to a store and had it matted and mounted in a lovely gold-edged frame.

She held her breath as she watched Margaret examine the package. Valene had been especially careful with the wrapping, using a lovely paper she'd found at a neighborhood store and some gold ribbon she'd been saving for a special occasion.

After reading the card, Margaret sent a mere flash of a look toward Valene, then proceeded to open her gift. Valene nudged Jordan, and he turned to watch.

Margaret pulled off the wrapping, opened the box, pushed aside the tissue paper, and frowned. Then with only an obligatory smile, she said, "How quaint," and put it aside.

Valene's heart sank. She'd spend every free minute since Thanksgiving working on that sampler, and Margaret had barely looked at it.

"Valene made that for you herself, Mother!" Jordan reached over and picked up the frame, holding it up for his mother to see. "It's our family tree!"

"So it is. How nice." Margaret quickly turned her attention to her next gift.

Valene put her hand on Jordan's arm and said in a mere whisper, "It's okay. Let it rest. Don't say anything, please."

Although his face was filled with frustration, he gave her a half smile and leaned back in his chair.

"Oh, Jordan, these are great!" his father said, smiling as he took a pair of golf gloves from their box. "I've been intending to get a new pair. Thank you."

Several presents under the tree were for Valene, all of them from Jordan. She loved each thing he'd selected for her. His parents gave him an abundance of gifts, mostly things she doubted he'd ever use. His tastes were not nearly as grandiose as theirs.

When the last package had been opened, Jordan turned to her, a frown etching its way onto his face. "What did my parents give you, Valene?"

She tried to avoid his eyes, knowing her answer would upset him, and whispered, "It's okay, Jordan. There really isn't anything I need."

His expression quickly turned to one of anger as he rose and pointed a finger at his mother. "You've known for over two weeks I was bringing Valene with me, and you didn't even get her a gift? You give gifts to your hairdresser and your mailman! You even give them to the UPS man! Why not Valene?"

His mother met his angry face with one of her own. "Because I'd hoped you'd come to your senses before Christmas Day and break up with that little fortune hunter, that's why! Can't you see, Jordan? She's way beneath you!"

Jordan closed his eyes and drew in several deep breaths. Valene knew he was struggling to control his temper.

He grabbed her by the arm and pulled her up beside him. "Give me your ring, Valene!"

She reached into the neck of her sweater and caught hold of the fine gold chain Jordan had bought for her to hold her ring until they could tell his parents they were engaged. He'd planned to do a grand presentation when he told them, dropping to one knee, much like he had at her parents' house. He'd wanted his parents to share in their joy. But as Valene had feared, it hadn't happened. Nothing that day had gone like they'd hoped.

She pulled back the lobster-claw clasp, slid the ring from the chain, and handed it to him.

Jordan laid it in his palm and extended his hand. "See!" he said, his voice still tinged with anger. "This is our engagement ring. I've asked Valene to marry me, and she's said yes. She's going to be Mrs. Jordan Young as soon as I can talk her into setting a date!"

His mother gasped and began to fan herself. His father simply stared at them.

"What about the navy? Our plans for your future?" Colin asked.

"We've worked those things out, Dad."

Margaret stood to her feet, her face nearly as red as her caftan as she glared at her son. "I forbid it, Jordan! I absolutely forbid it! You will not marry that girl!"

Jordan took Valene's left hand in his and slipped the diamond solitaire onto her third finger. "I am going to marry Valene, and there's nothing you can do to stop me. You're a hateful woman, Mother. You're your own worst enemy. I can't see how Father has put up with you all these years."

Colin stepped between them, his face now reddening. "You have no right to talk to your mother than way, Jordan! Apologize right now."

Jordan shook his head vehemently. "Apologize? For what? All I've said is the truth!"

"I'm so disappointed in you, Jordan," his mother said, moving to stand by her husband. "Don't you realize how important it is for a man of your position to have a wife with a fine background and the necessary social graces? Someday you're going to take over your father's business. The woman who will become Mrs. Jordan Young needs to be—"

"Someone like you? Someone whose rung on the social ladder is more important than having values?"

"Take it from me, son, those things do count," his father interjected. "Your mother has won over many a business client with her social graces and her business acumen."

"Well then," Jordan said, his voice still sounding sharp. "I guess maybe the family plans will have to change. Perhaps you'd better find someone else to run the Young corporation, because I'm marrying Valene—whether you like it or not!"

Valene couldn't believe what he was saying. "But—"

Jordan took her arm with one hand and grabbed onto Hero's leash with the other, then strode toward the door. "Get used to it, folks. Valene Zobel is going to become Mrs. Jordan Young, my wife, and there's nothing you can do to stop us."

He rushed through the house and out to his Avalanche, which was still parked in the circular drive, dragging Valene and Hero behind him.

"Jordan, you can't leave like this!" his father bellowed, panting for breath as he caught up with them.

"You marry that tramp, and you're no son of mine!" His mother looked as if she was about to burst with anger as she hurried toward them.

"What about our things?" Valene asked as Jordan opened the passenger door and nearly shoved her inside.

He carefully lifted Hero and placed him on the backseat. "Forget about them," he answered as he slammed the door and stalked around to the driver's side. "We're getting out of here."

Valene took a quick backward glance as they turned onto the road. Standing in the middle of the circular drive, both Mr. and Mrs. Young stood screaming at them. Especially Jordan's mother. Valene's heart ached. Although Jordan seemed willing to give everything up for her, she wasn't sure she should let him do it.

They were about half way back to Spring Valley when his cell phone rang, but he ignored it.

"You'd better answer it. It might be the base calling you."

"Or my parents with more advice?"

"Answer it, Jordan. Please."

He pulled the phone from his belt and punched one of the little buttons.

From the serious look on his face after he'd said, "Hello," she knew the call wasn't from the base.

Chapter 10

Dad's had a heart attack," Jordan announced as soon as he finished the call. "The ambulance is on its way."

Jordan waited for a clearing in the traffic, then spun the pickup around and headed back toward La Jolla.

Valene began to sob. "It's all my fault. If you hadn't taken me with you, this would never have happened. Oh, Jordan, what if he doesn't make it?"

"He's got to make it." His fingers tightened on the steering wheel. "I should've known something like this was going to happen. He had a mild heart attack last year. The doctor insisted he slow down some and alter his diet, but other than that, he's been fine."

"We did it to him. If we hadn't upset him with our news, this would never have happened." Valene's guilt was almost too much to bear. "Your poor mother must be terrified."

He gave her a puzzled look. "After all she's done to you, you're still concerned about her? Her rage didn't help my father any. She's as much to blame as we are."

"But she loves your father. She must be frantic! I wish there was something we could do."

He turned toward her quickly. "You want to do something? Then pray, Valene. Ask God to keep my father alive!"

She nodded, grateful for his suggestion. "Lord," she said, bowing her head, "we don't know much about Colin's condition—just that he's had a heart attack. But You know. If it be in Your will, we ask not only that You would spare his life, but that You would give him many more years. You are the Giver of life, the Great Physician. Be with him now. Restore him to health, and I ask You to be with Jordan's mother, too. Comfort her, Lord. Give her a sense of peace. I ask all these things in Your name, amen."

"Thanks, Valene." Jordan's softened features and his smile told her he appreciated her prayer.

Without taking his eyes from the road, he reached for her hand and squinted his eyes in reverence. "Lord God, please spare my dad. He doesn't know you and it frightens me. I haven't been as faithful in witnessing to him or to my mother as I should have been. Give me a second chance, please. I want my parents to come to a saving knowledge of You. I want them to know they're going to heaven as surely as Valene and I know we are. Forgive any words I may have said and anything I may have done that would keep them from You. Be with my dad. Bring him out of this. I beg You for that second chance."

Valene ached for Jordan. She knew how hard this had to be for him. "God is able, Jordan. He delights in answering the prayers of His children. We have to have faith."

When they reached the hospital, they were led to the cardiac care unit, where they were told Colin was alive. Margaret, who was crying hysterically, rushed to her son and buried her head in his chest.

Jordan wrapped his arms about her and pulled her close, patting her back much like he would a child who'd been hurt. "He's going to be all right, Mother," he told her confidently. "He's in good hands now. I'm sure they're doing everything they can."

She lifted a mascara-stained face to his. "H–he was so upset when you left, and he accused me of running you off. H–he went into the den and slammed the door behind him. I heard a crash, and when I rushed in to see if he was all right, I found him lying on the floor next to his desk." She burst into tears again, her chest heaving uncontrollably.

Valene wanted to rush to the woman and throw her arms about her, even though she knew that would only upset Margaret even more. Jordan put out a hand and motioned her to come to him. She shook her head, but he motioned again. She crept over silently, hoping his mother wouldn't notice.

Margaret lifted her face from his chest and stared at Valene coldly, without saying a word. Valene could see the woman's attitude toward her had not changed one bit.

"Mom, let's pray for Dad." Jordan bowed his head and closed his eyes. "Lord, my father needs Your healing touch. You are the Great Physician and You are in control of his life. Through all of this, may he realize his need of You. We come to You, gracious Father, asking that You will touch his body and even heal him, if it be in Your will. He's a good man. I need him. My mother needs him. She'd be lost without him. And Valene needs him, too. Please, God, give him back to us."

Valene said a soft, "Amen."

"You can go in now, but only for a few minutes," a nurse told Mrs. Young. Jordan and Valene stood holding hands, watching until the heavy double doors closed behind her.

It seemed an eternity before Margaret came back, although they knew it had to be no more than five minutes.

"How is he?" Jordan asked quickly.

Margaret blinked hard. "He's so still. I'm worried about him. I—I don't know what I'll do if he doesn't make it."

The three huddled together in the waiting room all night, with Jordan asking Valene to pray several more times, and he and his mother alternating the once-an-hour visits. At dawn, the doctor announced Colin had regained consciousness, and things were looking somewhat better. Although Colin was quite weak, the doctor encouraged them to continue their visits, just not to tire him by letting him try to talk.

Jordan took Valene by the hand and begged her, with pleading eyes, to go in and see his father. "Lay your hands on him, Valene, and pray for him. Please. He needs your prayers."

"But won't it upset him to see me there?" The last thing she wanted to do was get the man agitated by her presence.

"No. When I told him I was going to ask you to come in and pray for him, he blinked at me. I think he wants you there."

"I'm not so sure that's wise," Margaret said, grabbing Jordan's arm. "She's right. It may upset him."

"I know Father wants her there." He gently freed himself from his mother's hold and led Valene to the double doors. "Go on, sweetheart, please."

Valene ventured into the little cubicle with apprehension, but when she thought she detected the faintest smile on Mr. Young's face, she knew God would help her. She tiptoed to his bed and touched the helpless man's arm. His face was nearly as white as the sheets. "Hi," she said softly. "Jordan asked me to come in and pray for you."

With an almost undetectable nod, he blinked. Taking that as a sign he was agreeable, she patted his arm and began to pray, asking God to heal him and restore him to health. When she finished, she was sure his faint smile had broadened. She told him she'd continue to pray for him and excused herself. Praying for the man, like Jordan had asked, had been much easier than she'd imagined.

⁜

A couple of days later, as Valene and Jordan sat beside his father's recliner in the hospital room, Colin begged Jordan to resign from the navy and take over as CEO of Perfection Plastics in his place. With difficulty, he explained the doctor had told him his recovery was going to be slow and hard, and even if he was able to get most of his strength back, he was going to have to rid his life of much of its stress.

Valene, feeling the conversation should be between the two men, excused herself and headed toward the little chapel on the main floor, where she intended to pray that God would lead Jordan to make the right decision, the one God would have him make.

She was about to go into the chapel when one of the hospital custodians, a tall, gaunt-looking man who was cleaning up a spill from the floor, approached her.

"Hey," the man said, sticking his mop back into the bucket. "Ain't you related to that snooty Margaret woman? The one married to that guy who had the heart attack?"

"Do you mean Margaret Young?" She was surprised by his question.

"Yeah, I guess that's her name. I've been cleanin' her husband's room."

"No, I'm not related, but I am engaged to her son. Do you know her?" The chance of this man knowing Margaret Young seemed quite unlikely, but he had aroused her curiosity.

"Sure do. Her and me used to date when we was in high school in Nevada— long time before she married that guy upstairs. But she wasn't the high-and-mighty Margaret then. She was Maggie. We was both raised in the poor section of town. She lived in an old, broken-down trailer park, just like me. Her daddy was the town drunk."

He let loose a snicker, his grin lacking two front teeth. "That man spent more time in jail than he did at home. Don't think he worked a day in his life. Even less than my pa did."

Valene shook her head. Was this really happening? Surely the man had made a mistake. The woman he was describing couldn't be Margaret Young. "Didn't she have a mother?"

"She was workin' at the bar down on the corner some of the time. Home gettin' drunk with her hubby the rest of the time, I guess. Never saw much of her, but that Maggie was sumpthin'. Dated nearly every boy in town. She had a terrible reputation, if you know what I mean."

His snide laugh made Valene shudder.

"Yep, she was one tough cookie. Nuthin' but trailer trash. Last time I saw her, she was broke, pregnant, and unmarried, leavin' town in her old wreck of a car. Sure makes you wonder how she snagged that rich old geezer layin' up there in that bed. He seems like a right nice old fella."

Valene stood gaping, stunned by his words. *Broke, pregnant, and unmarried? He has to be talking about another Margaret.* "Are—are you sure you don't have the wrong person? Margaret is a fairly common name."

"It's her all right. I'd know her anywhere, despite them fine clothes and that fancy hair. You ask her! Ask her if her maiden name used to be Clark, and if she was from Dingo, Nevada. Then you'll know I'm tellin' you the truth."

Val stared open-mouthed as the man and his bucket moved on down the corridor. She knew she must keep his story to herself. If it was true, she had no right to tell it. If it wasn't true, telling it would serve no purpose.

By the time she'd prayed and returned to Colin's room, the two men had reached a decision. Jordan would resign from the navy in three months when his obligation was over and take over as CEO at Perfection Plastics. Considering the state of Colin Young's health, she knew they'd made the right decision.

"I don't know about you, Valene," Jordan said as the two sat quietly in her condo that night, "but I'd like to have a February wedding at Seaside Chapel. Maybe on Valentine's Day. I need you by my side as my wife when I take over Father's position."

"I'd like that, too. I know your mother doesn't approve of me, but I'm still hoping, once she realizes she can't stop our plans to get married, she'll give in and accept the idea."

"I don't remember Mother ever giving in on anything. Wait'll she hears we're having our wedding in Granite Cliffs. That'll set her off!"

⚓

"Absolutely not!" Margaret said, stomping her foot against the floor when they went to visit Jordan's father the next weekend. "Jordan, you are our only child, and you are going to have a proper society wedding, even though you aren't marrying one of your own kind!"

Valene bit her lip, trying to maintain her silence, deciding to let Jordan handle his mother's objections rather than blunder in and say something she'd later regret.

"I'll pretend I didn't hear that remark. I only hope Valene can forgive you. But you have to be reasonable, Mother! Father has just come through a heart attack. I'm going to have to wrap things up at the navy and take over a position I'm not prepared for, and I want to marry Valene as soon as possible. I need her to help me face the coming days. She's going to be your daughter-in-law. I'd think you'd want to start getting along with her. Even if we wanted it, which we don't, there isn't time to plan the kind of wedding you're talking about."

"Jordan, think! That girl is nothing but a tramp. A nobody. Can't you see she's not good for you?"

"Write February 14 on your calendar, Mother," Jordan told the irate woman as he stormed toward the door, his fists clenched at his side. "If you want to come, fine. If not, it's your loss. We are going through with this wedding." He turned to Valene. "I'm going for a walk to clear my head. I'll be back in a little while."

"You're the cause of this!" Margaret said, turning her wrath on Valene and shaking her finger in her face. "You're not worthy of being a Young!"

"Oh? But you are, Maggie Clark?" Valene blurted out before she could stop herself. From the look on Margaret's face, she knew the custodian had been telling her the truth. Maggie Clark and Margaret Young were one and the same person.

Margaret's face turned a sickly yellow as she let out a gasp. Her hands dropped to her sides.

"You are Maggie Clark from Dingo, Nevada, aren't you?" Valene asked, trying not to sound vindictive.

Margaret grabbed the armrest and lowered herself into a chair as she stared at Valene. "Who told you about me?"

Valene sat down opposite the distraught woman, her insides a jumble of nerves. "Th–that's not important."

Margaret's hands trembled. "Ha–have you told Jordan?"

The look on Margaret's face melted some of the hurt Valene had suffered at the woman's hands. "I've told no one."

Margaret fell on her knees at Valene's feet, tears running down her cheeks, a penitent look on her face. "Please, Valene, I beg you! Don't tell anyone. It would ruin me! I'll be disgraced, and so will Colin and Jordan. You wouldn't want to do that to the Young family, would you?"

"Have you forgotten? You were willing to push me aside. You said awful things about me to Jordan. Why should I be concerned about you?" In her heart, Valene knew she'd never betray the woman's secret, but she had to admit it felt good to see Margaret on her knees, contrite.

"I'll make a deal with you," Margaret said, cupping Valene's knees with her well-manicured hands. "Keep my secret, and I'll stop interfering between you and my son."

The woman's words shocked Valene. *Make a deal?*

"Please! I mean it. I'll do anything you ask, only don't let anyone find out about my past. All these years I've lived with the fear that someone would come along and expose me. I never thought it would be you."

"I–I must know about the baby you were carrying when you left Dingo. Was it Jordan?" The question had preyed on Val's mind since she'd first heard about Margaret's pregnancy.

The woman shook her head sadly. "No, it wasn't Jordan. I–I had an abortion. I've never forgiven myself for that. I nearly lost Jordan when he was born, and I've always thought it was God's way of punishing me for what I'd done." She placed her head in Valene's lap and wept until it seemed she could weep no more. "I'm so, so sorry."

Despite the way Margaret had talked about her, Valene's heart went out to the woman. All these years she'd held onto her precious financial and social standing, knowing her house of cards could come tumbling down any minute. But how could Val possibly keep something like this from Jordan? Something that would influence all of their lives if it ever came out? Wouldn't she be living the same sort of lie as Margaret? Fearing someday he'd find out she'd kept something this important from him, and he'd be furious with her?

But then again, she had no right to tell him. It was his mother's secret, not hers. "I don't know if I can promise something like that. I'll—I'll have to pray about it before I can give you an answer."

For the next few days, Valene agonized in prayer. Finally God gave her the answer she was seeking. One she could never have thought of on her own.

The following weekend, when they went to visit Jordan's father again, Valene faced Margaret confidently.

"Whatever you ask, I'll do," Margaret said with pleading eyes as she held onto Valene's arm. "Just tell me."

"First, I want you to start treating me with respect. No more of this she's-not-your-kind talk. I want to be treated as your equal."

Margaret hesitated. "I'll do it. I promise."

"Second," Valene said as she counted her requests off on her fingers, "you have to accept me as your future daughter-in-law and stop trying to break Jordan and me apart."

"I promise, if you promise not to betray me."

"Third. I want you to be nice to my dog. He's very important to me, and he's important to Jordan."

"Yes, if I have to, I will."

"Fourth. . .this one you may find quite difficult, but I consider it to be of the utmost importance."

"Anything."

"I want you to start attending church at—"

For the first time, Margaret smiled. "Oh, that won't be hard. I always go to church on Christmas and Easter, at that big new church downtown. Many of our friends and business associates attend there. They have such wonderful bazaars."

Valene lifted her hand. "You didn't let me finish. I want you to start attending church every Sunday, and I want to approve of the church you attend. It must be a Bible-believing, Bible-preaching church. Sickness will be your only excuse for not attending."

Margaret's eyes widened. "Every Sunday? And you're going to pick out the church? Isn't that a bit extreme?"

Valene shrugged. "Not if you want me to keep your secret. It's up to you, but I have one more condition."

"I'll pay you whatever you want!" the woman said quickly.

"I don't want money. I want a signed and dated document, written in your own hand, saying that if the truth ever comes out, you'll tell Jordan I only agreed to keeping this secret because I didn't want to hurt him or Colin. Will you do that?"

"Yes, of course, if I have no other choice. But how do I know the person who told you won't talk?"

"You don't, and neither do I, though I doubt he will. He could've said something weeks ago, and he didn't. I guess it's a chance you'll have to take."

Margaret seemed to think Valene's words over carefully before pulling a piece of paper from the desk and beginning to write. Valene read it through when the older woman finished. Everything she'd asked was included. "I guess this means we've come to an agreement."

Margaret gave her a grateful smile. "Yes, Valene, we have an agreement." To Valene's surprise, the woman threw her arms about her neck and gave her a hug.

"Thank you, Valene. Anyone else would've called the newspapers with my story. You didn't. I now realize you truly love my son and have the best interests of the Young family at heart. I'll never speak badly of you again."

That night, as Valene lay in her bed, she thanked God for showing her how to deal with what she'd learned about Margaret. Through it, He had touched her and made her realize she was as important to Him as anyone. That money and power couldn't buy true happiness. True happiness could only come from a close relationship with Him.

✝

No one was allowed to be married in Seaside Chapel without participating in premarital counseling with Pastor MacIntosh. Although Jordan seemed apprehensive about it when Valene had first told him about the requirement, he agreed, and they attended their first session. After covering the basics, the pastor turned to Jordan and asked, "Do you have a personal relationship with God?"

"Yes, sir, I do," he answered. "I accepted Christ as my Savior when I was ten, but because of Valene and her influence on my life, I'm closer to Him now than I ever have been. I love the Lord with all my heart and want my life to be in the center of His will. But to be honest, I still find it hard to believe He could forgive me for the things I've done in my life, even though I've confessed them to Him."

Valene stared at him. *What things? He's never told me about anything he's done that would make him feel so unworthy. Do I really know Jordan? From all I've heard from his parents, he was an exemplary child and a perfect son. I've seen dozens of awards he's received from the navy. He's never been in any scrapes with the law or caused anyone any trouble that I've ever heard of. What could he have done that's so terrible?*

She watched Jordan's reaction as he and Pastor MacIntosh talked, but she couldn't read any meaning in it.

When she mentioned the issue to Jordan that evening, he broke down and started crying. She sat down beside him and began stroking his back. It pained her to see him so upset. Something was troubling him, but what?

"I have a confession to make," he told her, lifting watery eyes. "One that will shock you and could ruin my family's reputation."

Valene's thoughts instantly went to the secret she was already keeping to avoid ruining the Young family's reputation. Did Jordan know about his mother after all?"

"I've done something, Valene," he said, clenching and unclenching his fists. "Something I'm terribly ashamed of. No one knows but me. That's why I haven't been able to accept God's full forgiveness. I'm afraid if I do, He'll expect me to make my sins public. I wouldn't mind it so much for me, but I have Mother and Father to consider, and now I have you. You may not want to marry me when you hear what I'm about to tell you."

Chapter 11

Nothing you could tell me would make me love you any less. Whatever it is, we'll face it together." Valene spoke with calm assuredness.

"The weekend before I left for Annapolis," Jordan explained, "some of my friends and I were carousing around in the new red convertible my parents bought for me. We'd each had about six or seven beers, and since I rarely drank, they went right to my head and made me dizzy. Then I got sick to my stomach. I remember letting my friends off at their houses and heading toward home, but I was light-headed and nauseous. From there on, I don't remember anything else about that evening. I don't even remember driving into our driveway and going to bed. But the next morning, when I went out to my car, there was a big dent in the fender, and one of the headlights had been busted out. I didn't have the faintest idea how it'd happened and thought maybe some kids had done it as a prank."

"Maybe they did," she said, hanging on his every word.

"No, that wasn't what happened! When I went back into the house to tell my father about the car, he and my mother were talking about something he'd read in the morning paper. Someone had hit a pedestrian walking along Beacon Road, the same road I always took home. Apparently he'd been hit by a red car, and its driver hadn't even stopped. A patrolman had found the injured man and taken him to the hospital, but he was in serious condition. I'm sure I was the one who'd hit him. I've been afraid to tell anyone. I knew I'd be put in jail for hit-and-run, and I'd never have the navy career I'd planned."

Valene held her breath, willing him to continue.

"I took my car to a body and fender shop in a town about a hundred miles away and had it fixed before anyone noticed, then drove back and finished packing up my things for Annapolis. All these years I've carried the guilt of what I'd done, never able to put it out of my mind. Then when I almost hit Jeff and ended up hitting Hero, it all came rushing back to me. That's why I freaked out that day. I knew I could never run away from my responsibilities again. I think I was hoping that paying Hero's bills and helping you take care of him would somewhat absolve me for what I didn't do all those years ago."

"D–did the man d–die?" she asked, almost fearing to hear the answer.

"No, he didn't die. According to the report on the news, the man was alive but badly hurt. His wounds weren't fatal."

Valene wrapped her arms around him. "Jordan, dearest, dearest, Jordan, don't you know there isn't anything God can't forgive? You don't need to carry this burden of guilt. Let Him carry it for you."

"I have to do something, Valene," Jordan said, rising and squaring his shoulders. "I have to make things right with that man. The one I hit with my car. I have to ask his forgiveness and try to make restitution. Regardless of the circumstances."

The next day, they went to the La Jolla newspaper's morgue, looked up the story on the accident, and wrote down the man's name and address.

"I hope he still lives here," Jordan said as he knocked on the door later that day.

The door opened, and the man they were looking for invited them in, but as Jordan began his story and told him what a coward he'd been, the man seemed confused.

"It wasn't a red car that hit me; it was a black truck. As usual, the newspapers got their story all wrong. They arrested the guy for drunk driving several months later, and he confessed he'd hit me and left me there. It wasn't you!"

Valene shrieked with joy as Jordan grabbed her up in his arms and danced about the room. The man stared at them, still looking bewildered.

"All these years I've carried the guilt of nearly killing a man and abandoning him, and I didn't even do it! It must've been kids vandalizing my car after all! Praise God, Valene! Praise God! I'm finally free!"

⁂

Valene leaped for the telephone when it rang in her old bedroom in her parents' house.

"Hi," a male voice said softly on the other end. "Know what day this is?"

"Umm, Valentine's Day?" she asked dreamily, loving the sound of that voice.

"Yes, it's Valentine's Day. But what else is it?"

"Umm, Saturday?"

"Yes, it's Saturday, but it's also your wedding day, unless you've changed your mind."

She cupped the phone tightly. "I'd never change my mind about marrying you, Jordan Young. You're gonna be stuck with me for life."

"Is that a promise?"

"That's a promise."

"See you at the church."

"Wait," she said, "someone wants to talk to you." She held the receiver out toward Hero. "Speak!"

The dog barked loudly.

"He said he loves you, too."

Jordan laughed. "Tell him I love him, and don't forget to bring him to the church. I have a boutonniere for him to wear. After all, he's the one who brought us together."

"I love you, Jordan."

"I love you, Valene."

⸸

"You look beautiful, sis." Vanessa stared at her twin sister. "That gown is gorgeous. I've never seen anything like it."

Valene tilted her head as she looked in the mirror. "I would never have picked out a wedding gown quite this ostentatious, but it was the one concession my future mother-in-law asked, that she get to provide my wedding dress. I couldn't refuse her offer. I have to admit, I do like it! It makes me feel like a princess. You know, I've almost gotten to like that woman, now that she's come down from her throne!" she added with a laugh.

"I just want you to be happy. Jordan's a wonderful man. You did good, Sis!"

"May I have a few minutes alone with Valene?" Margaret Young asked, pushing the dressing room door open a crack.

"Sure." Vanessa picked up her bouquet and moved into the hall. "I'll be right outside if you need me."

Margaret stared at Valene with misty eyes. "You—you are so beautiful, dear. The loveliest bride I've ever seen."

Valene wrapped her arm around her future mother-in-law and gave her a hug. "Thank you. I love the dress."

"I'm glad. I wanted you to like it. I–I just wanted to thank you one more time for keeping my secret. Even after I treated you so badly, you've treated me with nothing but love and kindness. Thanks to you, Colin and I have been attending that church you recommended, and I've heard things I've never heard before about the Bible and what it means to be a Christian. Although I'm not ready to be one yet, I am considering it."

Valene's heart leaped for joy. *Thank You, God!*

"Last Sunday, the preacher talked about God's love, His forgiveness, and His kindness. I've thought about his words a great deal this week, and I've come to a decision." Margaret paused, blinking a few times before going on.

"I've asked way too much of you, Valene, expecting you to keep my secret from Jordan and Colin. I can't go on like this anymore, wondering if someone will show up at our door and tell them. As soon as you two get back from your honeymoon, I'm going to tell both my son and my husband. It'd be better coming from me than someone else. I only hope they can forgive me for keeping this from them all these years. Then I think I'll ask for God's forgiveness."

"I love you, Mother Young," Valene said as she kissed Margaret's cheek.

"Y—you called me Mother! I—I like that."

A gentle knock sounded on the door, and it opened a crack. "Ready, sis?" Vanessa asked. "The organist is playing your song."

✝

"That's quite an unusual groomsman you have there," Pastor MacIntosh said, smiling at Jordan as they stood at the front of the church, waiting for the double doors to open.

Jordan grinned as he bent and patted the head of the black dog wearing a white carnation boutonniere on his new, gold-colored collar. "Hero has to be part of the wedding party. He's the one who brought Valene and me together and kept us together until we got this thing worked out."

Nathan, his best man and newest friend, let out a chuckle. "You mean she doesn't know?"

Jordan shook his head. "Nope, I wanted it to be a surprise. Actually, it was Jeff's idea."

Jeff's broad smile nearly covered his freckled face. "Jordan let me pin that flower thing on Hero's neck."

"Just don't drop the ring, Mr. Ring Bearer," Nathan told his son with a proud grin and a shake of his finger.

Jeff gave him a look of exasperation. "Dad, I've done this before—at your wedding!"

"You may have to hold me up," Jordan told his best man as the organist began to play. "I'm more nervous now than I was when I took my first solo flight."

Nathan gave his arm a quick pinch. "No more solo flights for you, buddy. From now on, you're flying double!"

"Nope, you're wrong about that. I'll be flying triple. Valene, me, and the Lord!"

As the music swelled, all eyes focused on the back of the sanctuary.

Vanessa looked radiant in her long, pink matron-of-honor dress, but Jordan barely noticed. He was waiting for Valene. When she finally appeared, all dressed in white, her face and shoulders covered by a delicate, nearly transparent veil, he thought she looked like an angel. As she seemed to float down the aisle toward him, he smiled to himself, remembering the look on his bride-to-be's face when his mother had said she wanted to provide the wedding gown.

Only Valene, with her sweet, understanding ways, would have allowed such an unconventional request in light of the way his mother had treated her. She was the perfect woman for him. How thankful he was that they'd each saved themselves for one another. She was his bride, the love of his life, and hopefully the woman who would one day bear his children. *Thank You, God.*

✝

Although the sanctuary of Seaside Chapel was filled with family and friends, Valene's gaze immediately went to Jordan as she held onto her father's arm and they started down the aisle. *It's actually happening! I'm going to be Mrs. Jordan Young. Oh, God, thank You. Only You could have worked out this miracle.*

A slight movement sent her gaze to the floor next to Jordan. Her heart did a flip as she caught sight of her beloved dog whose injuries had brought her and Jordan together. *Hero! Oh, Jordan, how thoughtful!*

When she reached the front, she bent and gave Hero a loving pat. "Good dog." Then she mouthed *"Thank you"* to Jordan.

He mouthed back, *"I love you."*

Everything went exactly as it had at the wedding rehearsal. She and Jordan remembered the vows they'd written and memorized, and Jeff didn't drop the ring.

The pastor smiled at the two of them. "Jordan. Valene. Nearly twenty years ago, my wife and I stood where you're standing, right at this very altar, and repeated our vows before our pastor." He gave them a tender smile. "That was before I went off to Bible school and became your pastor. I'll never forget that godly man's final words to us. They've served us well, and I'd like to pass them on to you. I think they're the secret to a happy and fruitful marriage."

Valene felt Jordan's hand tighten around hers as she turned and gazed into his eyes with adoration.

"Love God. Love one another. And at all times, treat each other with kindness."

In unison, although it had not been planned, both she and Jordan said, "We will."

Pastor MacIntosh continued, "By the power vested in me by the State of California, I now pronounce you, husband and wife. Go forth in peace."

As if on cue, Hero barked his approval.

Love Worth Finding

by Cathy Marie Hake

Chapter 1

Brandon Stevens spied his target and broke out in a cold sweat. He'd completed over a hundred missions, but none had ever affected him like this one. As a Navy SEAL, he'd done demolition work, rescues, reconnaissance. . .but of all the places he'd been, none ever seemed this foreign. The map in his pocket had proven to be accurate, so he hoped this would be one of those in-and-out operations that went off without a hitch.

A detailed sweep of the area showed little activity. Good. He slid out of the jeep, strode determinedly toward the entrance, and spotted his target behind the glass door. The minute he stepped inside, a motion detector went off.

It played "Here Comes the Bride."

For an instant, Brandon almost yielded to the temptation to bolt. Instead, he resolutely stepped forward to stop the stupid thing from pealing that song. His athletic shoes sank into deep plush carpeting the color of a Bazooka—the bubble gum, not the weapon. Silvery mirrors reflected billows of satin, lace, and fluff. Sensing a presence, he wheeled to the side.

"Welcome to Della's." A shapely woman rose from behind a mannequin and smoothed the shoulder of the tuxedo it wore. "May I help you?"

"Yeah. Gloves. I need gloves."

"This way, please." Her dark brown hair flowed in a cascade of curls clear down to her waist as she pivoted toward a gleaming display case.

"Military, marriage, magician, or mime?" She looked at him expectantly. A man could get lost in her deep chocolate eyes.

"Milit—oh, no. They're not for me." He crammed his hand into the rear pocket of his jeans and yanked out a piece of paper. Smoothing out the crinkles, he read, "Size six, elbow-length, white satin gloves."

She beamed at him. "It's always so nice when a man knows what his bride wants."

"No, no. That's not it. They're for my niece."

Laughter bubbled out of the woman. "Someone's going to owe you a big favor for running this errand."

"No kidding!" He grinned back at her. "The school play opens tonight. My niece is Cinderella, and my sister-in-law can only find one of the gloves."

"Mindy Stevens!"

"How did you know?" He held up a hand. "No, don't tell me. She probably got that fancy blue gown from over there." He cast a glance at the far wall of the shop where racks held a veritable rainbow of gowns.

"Yes. Here. Size six." Drawing a pair of shimmering gloves from a box, the gal laid them across the case. "They're washable satin, so Mindy'll be able to use them later for the prom."

"If they can find them," Brandon said in a wry tone.

A frown creased her face.

"That didn't come out right." Brandon prized loyalty, and he'd just made a flippant remark which could be misconstrued. "Annette's doing a great job with Mindy. It's not easy for her, everything considered."

The sales gal shook her head. "The stitching on the hem of these is flawed."

"Not a problem. The audience won't see that." He reached for the gloves. So did the woman. Stubborn little thing wouldn't let go.

"I sell only the best." She tugged.

"I'm in a hurry." He pulled. For all the missions he'd been on, the battles he'd fought, this one rated as the strangest—a ridiculous tug o' war over a slippery woman's glove! "Listen, lady, just sell it to me."

"Absolutely not." She grabbed hold of the glove with her other hand, too. "I refuse to take advantage of you."

"You're cheating." He tapped her left hand.

"Two gloves, two hands." Merriment danced in her eyes as she tried to tow the gloves closer to herself. The satin didn't allow her much of a grip.

Tightening his hold on the fabric fingers and twisting for better grip and traction, Brandon could feel her losing the battle.

"You're fighting for something you don't even value."

"Wrong. I value family. Mindy needs these."

"These are smudged and wrinkled." She let go.

Brandon scowled—first at her then at the limp, crumpled white fabric.

"I have more in the back room. Please give me a minute."

Brandon watched her walk away and set the ruined gloves on the display case. She'd better have another pair. The small town of Granite Cliffs didn't have anywhere else that would carry fripperies like this. His sister-in-law had been in a full-on, tears-in-her-eyes dither when she begged him to go out and buy gloves for Mindy. A silver anniversary cruise resulted in Annette's unexpected pregnancy, and Brandon would rather be caught in enemy territory without a weapon than upset a forty-five-year-old woman with morning sickness. Come to think of it, he *was* in hostile territory without a weapon. . . .

"Excuse me." The clerk peeped at him from behind a curtain leading to the back room. "How tall are you?"

The only time in his life that his height had been an issue was when he wanted to join the SEALs. They didn't have an official height requirement, but a more compact build was definitely the norm. "Six foot. Why?"

"I wouldn't normally ask, but you're in a hurry. I could go next door to the pet shop and borrow a ladder—"

"Say no more." He strode to the storeroom. "Point the way."

She motioned toward the top of a well-organized series of shelves. "Top tier, second row from the left, third box."

"Third box up, or third box down?" He headed back toward the goal.

"Both, actually, if you don't mind. I'd like a backup in case there's another flawed glove."

"Good thinking." His shoulder pulled as he reached upward. Brandon gritted his teeth against the pain. Stupid rotator cuff. The surgeon stated it would never be the same—and that cost him his place with the SEALs. "Here."

"Wonderful. Thank you so much!"

As she walked ahead of him to the register out front, Brandon resisted the urge to sweep his hand through her hair. She'd backed into something and had tiny bits of shimmering stuff winking at him from those luscious curls.

꙳

"Thank you for shopping at Della's." Though that was her customary line when handing a patron the purchase, Della couldn't resist adding, "I'd normally say, 'Come back again,' but I have a funny feeling you'd rather be shot."

A deep laugh rumbled out of the hunk as he accepted the gloves. "I've been shot more than once. This was less painful."

"I'll take that as a compliment."

"You do that, ma'am." His *ringless* hand dwarfed the pale pink and silver bag, and his head tilted back. He sniffed. "Besides, this place smells a whale of a lot better than a hospital." A rakish grin crossed his rugged features, transforming somber, gunmetal gray eyes into pools of silver. He winked. "And you can take that as a compliment, too."

The wedding chime to the door sounded as he left. Della leaned against the counter and sighed. "Now why can't I order one of those for me? Tall, dark, handsome. . .deep voice, rough hands, great sense of humor, loves his family."

She straightened the business cards in the sterling holder and looked around. Five years after opening her bridal shop, she still loved her job—but every once in a while, she suffered a few pangs. This was one of those days. A friend had just come in, thrilled to tell her all about last night's romantic supper and marriage proposal. Della loved hearing all the details. Once again, Della received the honor of being invited to serve as a bridesmaid. Selling the bridal gown, bridesmaids' gowns, and arranging for all the announcements, etc., would bring in a tidy sum for the shop, too. All told, it was fabulous news.

Except for the fact that all of the Mr. Rights are getting snapped up, and I'm not interested in Mr. Leftover.

The door chimed again. Vanessa Adams from Whiskers, Wings, and Wags next door tugged on the hem of her bright red T-shirt. "I'm running over to Pudgy's for a sandwich. Did you want me to bring anything back for you?"

A low-calorie fruit salad in the refrigerator awaited her. Feeling the need to be self-indulgent, Della cast caution to the wind. "Want to share a mile-high pastrami?"

Vanessa laughed. "Sure."

"Oh! While you're there, will you please grab their catering brochure?"

"I didn't know they had one."

"They do. I'm putting together a wedding reception for someone who wants to do it like a giant picnic." She didn't mention the catering company the bride chose just went belly-up, so Della volunteered to make all-new, last minute arrangements. Navigating through disasters while making everything seem effortless was just part of the business.

"A picnic? Really?"

Della smiled. "No one makes better potato salad than Pudgy's."

"*Mmm.* I'll pick up a pint of it now, and we can. . .uh. . .taste test it. Yeah." Vanessa gave her a sassy grin. "That's it. Taste test it. Just to be sure they haven't changed the recipe, you know."

"Oh, the things I suffer for the sake of my patrons!" Della giggled. "In fact, a new company contacted me this morning—a confectioner. They have all sorts of decadent things like mint truffles, candied almonds—"

"As your friend and retail neighbor, it's my duty to help you taste test them, right?"

Della tapped a finger on her chin. "I'll have to think about it. As I recall, the only samples you get are pet food. I'm afraid you'll reciprocate!"

Vanessa groaned. "You heard about that?"

"About what?"

"My son thought the doggie chews were beef jerky. I caught him with a half-eaten piece yesterday."

"Oh, no!"

"Yeah, and my husband was no help at all. Nathan hooted about it then asked Jeff how it tasted. I told him if he took a bite, I wouldn't kiss him for a week."

"As if you'd ever carry out that threat." Della shook her head. Van and Nathan were married just a year and a half ago. They were head-over-heels in love, and Della often saw them together on the baseball team. They called themselves a match made in heaven, and Della had to agree—they were one of the happiest couples she knew, and Vanessa adored Nathan's little son.

Della had been a bridesmaid in that wedding, too.

"Nathan's minding the store for me now. You'll notice I didn't suggest roast beef sandwiches."

"That's so gross!"

"You're being prissy again." Vanessa laughed. "Have you ever actually gotten dirty?"

"I've gotten hungry. Are you going to stand there, talking all day, or are you going to get the pastrami?"

Vanessa left, and Della spritzed cleaner on a case and polished the glass. She didn't mind Vanessa teasing her. Vanessa loved her for being just who she was. Their friendship started back in high school when Vanessa played the zany mascot and Della received the homecoming crown.

Growing up in a home like hers, Della didn't have a chance to be anything other than prissy. When she was less than a year old, her mother died. Her dad and two older brothers made a pact not to fall into the trap of turning her into a tomboy. As a result, she'd been their little princess—with enough frills, lace, and pink to smother a multitude of girls.

Daddy and the boys would go fishing and send her off to Miss Mannerly's Etiquette weekend. She took flute and piano lessons while her brothers tore up the lawn playing tackle football and practicing golf swings. The one "girly" thing she welcomed was dating—but they'd made utter pests of themselves and scared off most of the men after the first date.

Thanks to her overprotective brothers, the closest she would ever come to a groom was right now—when she fixed the mannequin's cuff links.

Chapter 2

"M*mm*. She's a beaut." Brandon whistled. "Do you know how old she is?"

"Not sure." Nathan Adams pulled to a stop. "She's pretty tacky. What do you think?"

Brandon continued to stare at the ornate building. "I want her." Hopping out of the truck, he started thinking aloud. "We'll need a safety inspection first—she's made it through several earthquakes, so the foundation may have shifted. Assuming the foundation's safe, all the wood will have to be sprayed for termites as soon as we pull off anything that's not salvageable." Even in his enthusiasm, Brandon meticulously noted each hazard and knew precisely where Nathan moved. "We'll need to contact Jim Martinez about supplying us with reproduction gingerbread and hardware."

"I already commissioned the foundation survey—I wouldn't pursue the project if there were problems with it."

"Great. Let's take a look inside."

"We have clearance, but there's no key."

"As if that matters." Brandon hustled up the stairs and quickly jimmied the lock. When his boss crooked a brow, Brandon chuckled. "Your tax dollars paid for that training."

Floor by floor, they walked through the old, rambling building. "Looks like it started out as a hotel then turned into a boarding house." Nathan stared out from a gabled window on the third floor. "I was thinking it would make a great bed-and-breakfast sort of place."

Brandon nodded. "The downstairs is cramped. Knock down a few walls, and you'll have big spaces that'd be great for meeting or reception rooms. It'll be a good investment. Rent the place out for weddings and business seminars."

"My plate's already full with the high school expansion." Nathan turned. "Do you want this project?"

"Yep."

"One condition." Nathan locked eyes with him. "You're to be the brains, not the brawn. You have carte blanche to make decisions regarding architectural alterations, landscape, and decorating—but I'll fire you on the spot if you lift anything heavier than a hammer."

Brandon snapped off a salute. "Sir, yes, sir."

"Now that's the kind of training my tax dollars can go for."

Brandon knocked the edge of his fist against a doorframe. "Someone did a slapdash job on repairs. I'm going to want to yank out the garbage and do it right."

His boss studied the window frame. "Replacing the woodwork with Victorian moldings won't be cheap."

"Nope. But you can have it done right, or you can have it done right now." Brandon wanted this job so badly, he could taste it—but only if he could do a quality retrofit. He stared at his boss. "I do things right."

Nathan nodded. "That's why I offered you the job." He headed back down the stairs. "By the way—I already signed the papers for the property. You can start assembling a team."

"Hoo-ah!" Brandon passed Nathan on the stairs and shot him a look over his shoulder. "That's military, too."

"Why do I have the feeling you're going to import a bunch of your SEAL buddies to do the grunt work?"

"Don't I wish. They do it right. First time. Every time." He shook his head. "Can't, though. Training schedule's a bear. I could probably round up some Seabees who just got out. They're great."

"Can't argue with that. I've got another reason I'm okay with it, too."

Brandon shot him a quick look. Nathan's tone warned he'd be delivering unwelcome news.

"The high school expansion is on a tight schedule. You'll be working with a skeleton crew, and I plan to pull them from your site on a few key dates."

"Good planning can make up for that—especially on a site this small."

Nathan paused on the last step. "I do everything aboveboard. Nothing under the table."

Most of the construction businesses in the area employed "day labor," which consisted of undocumented workers from across the border who were paid cheap wages that didn't show on the records. Doing so kept down the costs on a project, but it was illegal. Brandon hadn't risked his life serving his country for the past six years only to turn a blind eye to its laws. "Every man on the site is on the book. Wouldn't have it any other way."

"Good. Since that's out of the way, I have something important to discuss."

"Important, huh?"

"Think that shoulder of yours would let you play baseball?"

After the surgery, the doctor told Brandon it would be six months before he'd recover. Within three months, Brandon exceeded every goal the physical therapist set. Even then, they still gave him a medical discharge. He could have fought it, but it boiled down to whether his pride was more important than his team members' safety. Brandon made the only possible decision. He'd been lucky to fall into a job that he enjoyed with a decent boss.

He resisted the urge to rub away a twinge along his incision. "I do what I want. I don't consult my shoulder."

"No use overtaxing it, though."

Brandon walked around a rotting area on the floor. "Back to talking about taxes? No way. So what's this about baseball?"

"Church league. We're down a few players, and—"

"Forget it. I'm not the church type."

"You don't have to be a member of the church to play. We have a couple other players who don't attend services. No pressure—it's just for fun and fellowship."

"Fun, yes—but the fellowship part sounds touchy-feely."

"Nope. It's more like a prayer at the outset then grilled hot dogs before a game or ice cream afterward. Real low-key. Why don't you come tomorrow evening and give it a try? If you don't like it, or if your shoulder bothers you, you can walk away with no commitment, no questions asked."

"One time. No strings."

☩

"Supper's on!" Della thumped the biggest pot in the house onto the table and glanced over her shoulder.

Footsteps sounded on the porch; then the screen door banged shut. "I'm coming. Whatever it is, give me doubles. I'm starving." Daddy sniffled loudly. "It smells like lasagna."

"Spaghetti."

"Triples."

"Me, too." Justin plopped into a chair. "And no skimping on the meatballs!"

Shoving a pitcher of iced tea into Gabe's hands, Della scoffed, "Since when have you guys gone hungry?"

Daddy brushed a kiss on her cheek. "We're still making up for all the years when you didn't know how to cook." He grabbed the basket of garlic bread and headed for the table.

Della looked at her family and felt an odd twang. Her brothers had moved into an apartment four years ago, but they still came home for supper Monday through Thursday. Weekends, they dated or fended for themselves. She'd love to have a place of her own, too—but Daddy would be so lonesome by himself in the house. She'd taken a big loan to start her business, so it made sense for her to stay at home.

I'm tired of being sensible.

"You'd better get over here, sis." Sauce-laden noodles slithered across the tabletop as Gabe served himself. "Justin's going to eat the rest if you don't dive in."

"Go ahead, Justin." Della slipped into her chair. "Here. Have more garlic bread, too."

Justin stopped mid-bite and gave her a horrified look. "Oh, no. No. Not a chance."

"You don't want more garlic bread?" she asked oh-so-innocently.

"I'm wise to you. You can't pull that stunt on me twice. I said it once, and I'll say it 'til my dying day, no. Got that? I'm not going to put on one of those fancy monkey suits you rent out and get saddled into another show."

"Oh, Justin." Della gave him a disappointed look. "Why not? You look outstanding in a tux."

"Yeah, and three of the models gave you their telephone numbers," Gabe teased.

"That's just the problem." Justin made a disgusted sound. "Every last one of them thought that just because we met at a bridal show, the date was supposed to get them back into one of those gowns again—and I'm not talking about getting another job modeling. Ten minutes into a date, and every one of them started talking about marriage."

"What's wrong with marriage?" Thoroughly disgruntled, Della glowered at him.

"Nothing—as long as it's someone else's," Gabe said. He took a long gulp of his tea. "And count me in with Justin—I'm not gonna play model groom for you, either."

Her dad drummed his fingers on the table. "When's the show, princess?"

"Monday, the eighteenth. It's a luncheon in San Diego."

He nodded. "Power Electric is happy to supply you with men." He shot his sons a telling look. "Two of them."

Justin muttered, "Spare us the family-sticks-together speech, Dad. I should have known you'd pull rank on us."

"Talk about rank—" Gabe popped a whole meatball into his mouth and kept speaking. "Could you believe that skunk at the Java and Jelly? Whew!"

The conversation zipped all over the place, and Della didn't say much. She'd be interrogated to the *nth* degree if she confessed the scent she remembered from her day of work was left by a hunky young military man who bought gloves. He'd worn some kind of aftershave that lingered in the shop and left her inhaling deeply for the next hour.

"Earth to Della." Justin's voice registered.

"Oh—huh?" She shook herself.

"I said, since I'm going to have to strut around in that penguin suit for you, you have to help me with my billings tomorrow night. I'm behind."

Della shook her head. "I've got a game tomorrow night."

"When are you going to stop that and start dating?" Her father shook more Parmesan cheese on his plate. "I want my daughter walking down the aisle, not walking with crutches."

"If I get married"—she stabbed at an olive in her salad. It rolled away—"you won't have anyone here to cook for you."

"I can eat at a restaurant or hire a cook. I can't buy grandchildren."

"And I can't buy a groom." She finally speared the olive. "Besides, Justin and Gabe are older. Look to them for your first grandchildren."

Her father snorted. "Those boys gotta be roped into pretending to play married for your fashion shows. No way they're gonna tromp down the aisle for a long time yet. You—well, a woman's got to pay mind to her clock."

Just then, the grandfather clock in the living room chimed. Della laughed. "*That* is the only clock I'm minding."

Daddy could have given lessons to a pit bull. Once he got hold of something, he wouldn't let go. He knocked his knuckles on the table. "Boys, you need to help your sister."

"We are, Dad. You're making us do that show for her."

"Yeah, well, it's high time you dug up a nice young man to ask her out."

"Actually, we do know this one guy. . . ."

The way Gabe perked up made Della's blood run cold. "And you know me even better. If you dare try to pair me up with someone, I'll return the favor and double it."

Daddy slapped the table. "Good! You know someone for each of your brothers?"

Della pasted on the smile she knew gave her brothers the willies. "Oh, I know a couple of girls for each of them, Daddy. I'd want them to have a choice, you know." She turned to her father. "In fact, a bride came in the other day with her mother. Her mama's a widow, Daddy—just perfect for you. I—"

"You're at the table," he groused. "You should eat and not talk so much."

Chapter 3

O kay. You've got the stance right. Now choke up on the bat a little more."
Della wrestled with the bat as she listened to Vanessa's instructions.
Vanessa managed to drag her to church about three times a year, and
the second time Della attended, she'd seen the announcement in the bulletin that
they wanted more players on the softball team. "I'm on the team. You could join
up," Vanessa had urged.

"I'm not going to become a member of a church just to play ball."

"You don't have to. No strings attached."

Della confessed, "I'm miserable at sports. I've never hit a ball. They won't
want me."

Vanessa proved her wrong. For two years now, Della suited up in a hideous
orange and white baseball uniform and consistently played worse than anyone
else in the whole league. Still, everyone wanted her to come back for more. She
loved it.

But she'd only connected with the ball once. Kip called it the law of
averages—sooner or later, it had to happen by mistake. He pretended to do the
math and announced she ought to connect once every three seasons. From the
looks of it, he was probably right, too.

"Della." Vanessa giggled. "I said choke up on the bat—don't strangle the
poor thing! What did it ever do to you?"

She loosened her grip. "How's this?"

"Much better. Now keep your eye on the ball." Vanessa pitched, and the
ball came whizzing past. "That was in the strike zone. You were supposed to
swing."

"Give me another one."

Vanessa nodded, pulled another neon pink tennis ball from the pail, and
pitched.

"Aaand she swings and misses!" Jeff sang out from behind her. "Mom, can
we get them now?"

Della looked at Vanessa's eight-year-old stepson and waggled the end of
the bat at him and the sleek black Lab that pranced at his side. "You hang on a
second. I have three more to miss before you and Lick gather them."

"Okay, but hurry. He's been waiting a long time."

"It's a good obedience exercise," Vanessa called back. "Get ready, Della. One, two, three. . ."

She swung the bat.

"One more to go," Jeff told his dog.

"One more?"

Della turned as she heard Vanessa's husband's voice. "Nathan, are you making fun—" her voice died out. He wasn't alone. Walking alongside him was the gray-eyed hunk who bought the gloves at the shop yesterday.

"She still hasn't hit another one, Dad."

Della wanted to crawl in a hole and die of embarrassment.

Nathan rumpled Jeff's hair. "Someday, she will. Della, this is Brandon Stevens. Brandon, Della Valentine."

"Ma'am." Brandon nodded.

"She's not a ma'am; she's a miss." Jeff let out a boyish bark of laughter. "And she misses the ball every time!"

"Having trouble?" Mr. Make-Your-Heart-Go-Pit-a-Pat asked.

"Well. . ." Della knew she had to be as pink as could be.

"Here." He slipped behind her, wrapped his long, long arms around and molded his callused hands over hers. "What's your thumb doing up here?"

"That's how my brothers hold their golf clubs."

"Different sport, different grip." To his credit, he didn't laugh. Instead, he eased her thumb around the bat. "Here. Good. Now lift your left elbow."

She followed his instructions.

"You're gonna smack this one halfway across the park." Confidence rang in his voice. "Okay, Vanessa, let her rip."

Vanessa picked up the last ball. "Here goes nothing."

Thwop. The pink tennis ball arced through the air and sailed toward a vacant picnic table. Della stood frozen in place as she watched it.

"That was a beaut. Do it again."

"It was the last ball," Vanessa called. "Jeff, give Lick his command."

Jeff gleefully shouted, "Fetch!"

While they gathered up two-dozen balls, the guy behind Della didn't release her. "Practice your swing. Keep your grip. Yeah. That's it. Now the elbow. . ." He led her through a couple of swings, then let go and waved his arm in an arc. "Practice makes perfect."

She chewed on her lower lip, struck her stance, and copied the moves a few times.

"Good. Now make sure you follow through. When you stop the swing partway because you connect, you lose all the power."

Della laughed. "As if I'll actually connect again."

His face darkened. "With that attitude, you won't."

"Della, think like the Little Red Engine," Jeff said as he handed his mother the bucket of tennis balls. "I think I can; I think I can."

"Not good enough," Brandon said curtly. "I know I can. I know I can."

Vanessa smiled. "Brandon was a SEAL, Della. Watch out, or he'll have you doing push-ups, too."

"I'm good at those," she said.

The corner of Brandon's mouth twitched. "Girls' push-ups?"

"No, standard. I'm not half bad at chin-ups and pull-ups, either."

"So if you can do those things, you have the upper body strength to swing a bat. It's just a matter of hand-eye coordination and practice."

"Yeah, well, once you get her batting up to snuff, you can teach her how to run." Nathan chuckled.

"Oh, you don't, do you?" Brandon gave Della a pained look.

"Don't what?"

"Run like a girl."

"News flash. I am a girl!"

"A girly girl," Vanessa called out merrily. "Here you go, Della. Slug this one out of the park and show them you have it in you."

"Here goes nothing," Della muttered as she took her stance.

"And there went nothin'," Jeff said from behind her a few seconds later. "But your form was good. Tell you what: Tie a tennis ball on a length of twine in your garage. When you have a few minutes, bat at it. It'll take care of your hand-eye coordination. By next week, you'll connect."

"I wish the back room at the store were bigger. I spend most of my time there."

"In the back room?"

She laughed. "At the store. Maybe I could hang the ball from—no, I'd hit the wall with the bat."

"Hey you guys," someone hollered at them from the baseball diamond. "Are we gonna play ball, or are you planning to stand there and yak all night?"

Nathan picked up the bucket of tennis balls and wrapped his arm around Vanessa's waist. "We're coming."

Della watched their casual affection and smiled. Jeff and Lick dashed up to join them.

"Looks like a commercial for domestic bliss," Brandon said from beside her.

"If it's for sale, just tell me where and how much."

Brandon crooked a brow. "You don't know?" He took the bat from her and propped it over his shoulder. "You're ideally set up for reconnaissance and information gathering."

Della burst out laughing. "It's love, not warfare."

"Hey, all's fair in love and war, so the tools of the trade apply in both instances. Never waste an opportunity."

Della scooped her mitt from the grass. "It's too late by the time they reach me. The battle is fought, and they're ready to sign the peace treaty."

Brandon chuckled. "I wouldn't have guessed you'd think in those terms. You sound more like a warrior than a wedding planner."

She tossed the mitt into the air and caught it. "The secret lies in knowing when to put on the gloves and when to take them off."

꙰

"Hey." Brandon slid one leg over the bench and straddled it in the dugout. "Great strategy."

"Strategy?" Della wrinkled her cute little nose as a blush stole over her cheeks. "That wasn't strategy; it was shock."

She'd been up to bat when he was on second base. He'd seen her strike twice. The third time, she bunted—not intentionally, but because the ball was inside and didn't warrant a swing. Stunned, she stood there and watched it roll toward the pitcher as Brandon sped toward third.

"Aw, c'mon, Della. Stop being so modest. You bunted and sacrificed yourself so I'd be set up to make a run for home."

"If only that were true. I can't take credit. I just froze."

"You've got a lot to learn," Brandon agreed. *And I wouldn't mind coaching you.* The thought slipped into his mind, and it felt right. Brandon lived by his hunches. They'd saved his life on more than one occasion. "Why don't we meet and I'll—"

"Whip me into shape?"

He winked. "Your shape is just fine, ma'am. It's your talent that needs refining."

Easy laughter bubbled out of her. "I'll have to remember that line. My brothers would love it!"

"Just how many brothers do you have?"

"Two."

He squinted. "And you didn't learn how to bat?"

"Only her lashes." Vanessa yanked her ponytail through her cap. "Della's dad and brothers got caught in a time warp. They think a woman should be home, serving up food on a plate, not out running across home plate."

"They all love me," Della tacked on.

Her loyalty to her family counted for a lot in Brandon's book. He gave her an assessing look. "Love made them protect you."

She nodded.

"As if baseball is dangerous," Vanessa scoffed.

"My brother broke his leg sliding into home."

Twice, a member of his SEAL team broke a leg when they were out on a mission. Ugly, painful injuries. From the way her face paled, he figured she'd seen her brother suffer his injury. Brandon resisted the urge to smooth back a few of her errant curls. She'd been babied a lot. Judging by her presence here, she wanted to venture ahead. Anyone who had guts enough to try something deserved a chance in his book. "He's over it and running around now, right?"

Her face brightened. "Nothing slows him down."

Crack! Brandon automatically turned at the sound and whistled in appreciation as Kip hit a homer.

"Wow. I want to do that someday."

He smiled at Della. Never one to miss a golden opportunity, Brandon plowed right into the opening. "Fine. I'll take you to the batting cages. When are you free this week?"

Her pupils dilated—whether with pleasure or surprise, he couldn't say.

"Her shop is closed on Sundays and Mondays," Vanessa volunteered. She gave Della's leg a playful pat. "Go for it. Do it for the team."

Della looked up at him with her dark, shiny eyes and took his measure.

She's cautious. Smart, too. What's stronger—her loyalty to the team or her reticence?

A slow smile tilted her mouth. "For the team."

༘

Della locked the door, turned over the CLOSED sign, and dashed to the back room. Brandon would be here in ten minutes, and she couldn't very well go to the batting cage in a silk dress. Hastily changing into neatly pressed brown slacks and a cotton blouse the color of peach sorbet, she tried to decide what to do with her hair. *Tying it back would be smart, but I look like I'm twelve when I do that.*

She twisted her foot into an athletic shoe and was reaching for the other when someone rattled the back door with a single, solid thump of a knock. *It's him!* She snatched the left shoe then groaned at the sight of the knotted lace.

"Hey! You okay in there?"

"Yes." She giggled as she hobbled toward the steel door. Out of habit, she still looked through the peephole. Even distorted by the fisheye lens, Brandon looked too good to be true in a dark blue T-shirt and jeans.

As if he knew she was spying on him, he ducked down a little closer and gave an exaggerated wink. "The password's 'Team'," he said in a grave tone, but his smile could have melted the door.

"The team," she opened the door, "is suffering a delay due to—"

"—an equipment malfunction," he finished as he swiped the shoe from her hand. "I'll see to it. You go ahead and change."

She looked down at her outfit and confessed, "I already did."

"Don't you have real clothes? Jeans? Shorts?"

"My jeans were in the hamper."

He nodded somberly. "Gotcha. On your last outfit before you do laundry."

Della didn't disabuse him of his faulty assumption. Instead she turned. "I'll go grab a rubber band from the register so I can tie back my hair."

"Good thinking."

When she returned, he hunkered down, wrapped his callused hand around her ankle, and twisted the shoe onto her stockinged foot. "I gave up on trying to unknot it."

"Then what—" She looked down. "Oh." A small knot lay on the floor beside him. He'd cut it from the lace, connected the pieces, and now tugged on the ends as he finished tying it into a lopsided bow. "Thank you."

He plucked the knot from the floor and rose. "Nothing to it. Let's go."

She set the alarm and slipped out the back door. He shut it, then nodded. "Good setup. Secure."

Della hitched her purse onto her shoulder. "It ought to be. My dad and brothers put it in—they're electricians."

Brandon shot her a quick look. "What company?"

"Power."

"Power?" he echoed. "Gabe and Justin are your brothers?"

"You know them?" She caught herself. "Of course you do, if you know their names."

"I've worked with them a couple of times on a site." He scrutinized her features. "But your last name is Valentine. I didn't mentally place you with them."

"Oh, they're Valentines, too." She slipped her keys into the pocket of her purse. "Daddy said no one would trust 'Valentine Electric,' so he named the company 'Power.'"

He took a few long strides and opened the passenger door of a jeep. As she climbed in, he murmured, "You don't look anything like your brothers."

"They've each had a broken nose."

"Yeah," he drawled as he shut the door. As he walked around to the driver's side, he muttered, "They did it fighting back the men who wanted you."

Zing! Della shivered at the thrill of knowing the attraction wasn't one-sided. She pretended she hadn't overheard him and asked as he drove toward the edge of town, "So you work with Nathan's firm?"

He nodded.

She liked that curt, masculine mannerism. Growing up in a household of men, the abbreviated conversation, the brisk actions, and brusque ways didn't bother her. She found them oddly reassuring. If a woman wanted information from a man, she needed to prod each tidbit out of him. Della settled into her seat and started in.

"So you're a former SEAL?"

"Six years." He drummed his fingers on the steering wheel. "You didn't interrogate Vanessa about me?"

"Oh, I tried," she confessed merrily. "But she just got a whole shipment of puppies; Jeff's on summer break and 'helping' her at the shop; and I've spent hours on the phone trying to track down a certain pattern of Belgian lace for a client. The only time we actually connected on the phone, Van told me she's not a gossip and you're a good man."

"I knew I liked her."

"So the ball's in your court."

"You can't bat, but you use sports metaphors?"

"I'm all talk and no action." Once the words popped out of her mouth, Della groaned.

Deep, male laughter rippled in the air.

"See? You need to talk so I can keep my mouth shut."

"Crying for mercy, huh?"

She gave him a wry look. "You'd better believe it."

"Okay. Yeah, I was a SEAL for six years. Now I'm doing construction."

"Why did you leave the SEALs?"

His features tightened. "Got banged up." Just as quickly, he flashed her a cocky grin. "So for the sake of the team, I bugged out."

"Ah, yes, the all-important team," she nodded sagely. "What kind of injury, and how did you do it?"

"Shoulder. Training exercise."

Della dipped her head and studied a chip in her manicure.

Almost a mile later, the silence in the jeep nearly crackled. "Anything else?"

"It's not worth asking. I won't trust what you say."

"Why not?" He veered to the curb and gave her a disgruntled look.

"Because you just lied to me."

Chapter 4

What gave you that notion?" Features strained, she hitched her right shoulder. "I can tell. Listen, it's none of my business and—"

"Hang on a minute." She looked ready to open the door and bolt, so he curled his hand around her forearm. "Sorry. I'm used to dealing with people who know the rules."

"What rules? I thought you guys were all about honor and duty and integrity."

"We are. But that involves silence." He rubbed his thumb against the soft fabric of her sleeve. "No matter how or where a man's hurt, it's always a 'training exercise,' Della. The phrase is a shield for security purposes, and everyone accepts the need for that discretion."

Her brow puckered, but she didn't look up at him.

"I've been places and done things I can't discuss—not now, not ever. Flat out, that's just how it is."

"Like it or lump it?" She finally looked at him. Dozens of questions glittered in her eyes, ones he'd never address. National security relied on it, but even if he were allowed to say anything, he wouldn't. Not to her.

Just like the peachy-colored material beneath his fingers, this woman was soft. There was a fineness, a femininity, about her that brought out all of his protective instincts. Part of serving his country revolved around preserving the beauty and innocence of people like her who'd be destroyed by the ugly currents beneath the international scene. A warrior paid the price by keeping silent. He'd seen plenty of teammates' relationships tear apart under the stress that silence imposed. If Della couldn't innately trust him, he might as well find it out now.

"So," he looked at her and quietly asked, "you gonna like it, or do I turn around and take you back to your shop?"

"You don't believe in compromise?"

"There's plenty of give-and-take in relationships, but some things are non-negotiable. I don't compromise my values."

Finally, she smiled. "Vanessa was right. You're a good man, Brandon Stevens. Are you a good teacher?"

"Let's find out."

✝

Thwop.

"Run!"

Brandon's bellow set Della in motion. She sped toward first base. The first baseman laughed so hard, he dropped the ball as she approached.

"Tag the base!" Brandon hollered.

She stepped on it and turned to give him a triumphant smile.

He punched the air, let out a victory yell, then cupped his hands to his mouth. "You can let go of the bat now."

She looked down at the bat. Giggles of embarrassment shivered out of her. Even so, nothing took away the thrill of her achievement. He'd taken her to the batting cages three times now. She twirled the bat like a baton and called out, "It looks like the third time was the charm!"

He'd jogged out of the dugout. "There's no such thing as luck. Practice pays off."

"Be careful of your shoulder." She let him take the bat.

"Stop fussing and pay attention." The sparkle in his eyes took away the sting of his words. "We're behind. You need to earn us a run."

"Hey!" the pitcher yelled. "Is this a social or a softball game?"

Della propped a hand on her hip and called back, "Is there a third option?"

"You bet." Brandon gave her a stern look. "Winning. Never settle for anything but your goal."

The first baseman punched his fist into his glove and grinned. "That's my kinda thinking, and we're about to beat the socks off of you."

Brandon let out a derisive snort and walked to the batter's box. With a solid hit, Kip ended up on first and sent Della to second. She stood on second base and watched Brandon take his place at bat. Other guys would scuff their feet in the dirt, restlessly find a stance, change their grip on the bat and take practice swings, or look around the diamond. Brandon didn't. Exuding confidence, he stepped up, assumed his stance, and watched the first ball without moving an inch.

"Outside. Ball one."

A moment later, the ball went whizzing by. Della let out a whoop and headed for third.

"Run, Della!" Vanessa and her twin, Valene, shouted in unison. When she hit third, Vanessa waved.

Della waved back.

"Go home!" Vanessa screamed.

"I can't believe it," Kip said later as the whole team wolfed down barbequed hot dogs. "You didn't just hit the ball. You made it on base and got a run!"

She beamed up at Brandon. "I owe it all to my coach."

Brandon swiped the mustard from her. "Next, I'll teach you how to run."

"Told you she runs like a girl." Nathan tore open a bag of chips and passed them down the picnic table. "That's going to be a real challenge."

"Me being a girl, or me running like one?"

"No complaints about what you are, ma'am." The left corner of Brandon's mouth kicked up in a rascal's grin. "In fact, it might come in handy. Are you doing anything on Saturday, the fifth?"

She thought for a moment. "Yes."

"Change your plans, and go with me to my cousin Linda's wedding."

Della shook her head rapidly and blinked as if she couldn't quite process what he'd asked. "Only a man could blend running and a wedding in the same breath."

"Self-preservation." Kip slapped Brandon on the shoulder. "Makes perfect sense to me."

"Careful!" Della half rose. "Brandon—your shoulder! Is it—"

"I'm fine." He didn't look fine at all. Deep grooves bracketed the corners of his mouth.

Della's instinct was to fuss over him, but she quelled the urge. He had that macho, I-can-take-it look. Instead, she covered for him. "So that pained look is because you're thinking about having to wear a suit for the wedding?"

"Yup." Gratitude flashed in his eyes. "I'm going to swelter."

"Guess again." She took a long, lazy lick of her Chocolate Decadence ice cream and gave him a jaunty grin. "Now that you mentioned it's Linda's wedding, I remember all of the details. I planned the whole affair with her. It's an outdoor event, and they're doing a picnic-style reception. The invitations came with a map to Seaside Park and mentioned casual wear."

"Yes!" He made a fist and jerked it downward in a pumping action—the same one her brothers used whenever they were particularly pleased with something.

Come to think of it, Brandon managed to find joy in the simplest of things. It was a good quality. Admirable. Then again, she had yet to learn something about him that she didn't like. But it would have been far more thrilling if he'd been that excited about her going to the wedding with him.

"Were you already going?" Vanessa asked her.

"Most of Granite Cliffs is." Della smiled. "It's why they're holding it outside—so there'll be enough room."

"But you're going with me," Brandon asserted.

It sounded more like an order than a question to her, but Della smiled. She didn't mind a nice guy like Brandon getting a tiny bit possessive of her. She found it flattering.

That thought crossed her mind again later that evening. She'd never liked the guys around her acting domineering. In fact, she'd quickly parted company with more than one guy because he'd been too controlling. The fact that her brothers made pests of themselves actually came in handy on those occasions.

But Brandon didn't behave like a caveman who wanted to boss her around. He treated her as though she had a brain and was able to think for herself. Never once had he said she couldn't do something—he'd taken the time to teach her how to bat, promised he'd teach her to change the oil in her car, and yet never failed to be a gentleman by opening doors for her or showing small courtesies.

This guy is too good to be true.

So far, they'd met at her shop or in the park. Daddy, Justin, and Gabe didn't have a clue that she'd been seeing Brandon. The first two times Brandon picked her up at work, it had been simple expediency—the last time was because she still wanted a chance to decide if things stood well enough for her to endure the third-degree grilling from her family if her relationship with Brandon continued.

Pulling back her white eyelet duvet and sliding between pale pink sheets, Della wondered how "The Meeting" would go. When she'd seen the case of oil in Brandon's jeep, he'd offered to change her oil today, too. She'd gotten bold and told him she'd rather learn to do it herself. Tomorrow ought to be interesting.

Daddy wouldn't wait for Brandon to knock on the door—he'd stand on the porch so he could do what he termed, "Taking the man's measure." Over the years, Della learned that involved a complex combination of noticing not only what vehicle her date drove, but whether it was freshly washed, the engine sounded smooth, what any bumper stickers might say, how the man walked, dressed, and about two hundred other silly things.

For the first time, she had a feeling the man walking up to the porch would meet Daddy's requirements. Then again, Brandon had made such a stunning first impression on her, she wasn't exactly impartial. But her subsequent impressions were even more favorable.

Brandon Stevens just kept getting better and better.

Chapter 5

Brandon didn't bother to hide his grin. She said she wanted to learn how to do things for herself, and changing the oil in her car ought to have been a simple, straightforward exercise. Only with her, nothing ever was.

She'd insisted on learning the names of the components of the engine and singsonged them under her breath to recall their names. *Dainty little Della has a voice that would detonate grenades.*

She drew out the oil stick with more flourish than a swashbuckling pirate and tried to discuss the varying colors of clean-to-dirty oil with the intensity of an artist mixing a paint palette for a masterpiece. She thought maybe she ought to shake or stir the oil before adding it. Left to her own devices, the woman could destroy an entire motorcade in an hour.

"What?" Della shifted from one foot to the other and scrunched her nose.

"You're cute."

"I'm capable. That's more important. See? I knew if someone showed me, I could learn this."

He nodded gravely. "Just one more thing. . ."

"I thought you said that was all it took. Did I forget something?"

Brandon swiped a rag from the workbench and rubbed a streak of oil from her forehead. "Next time, don't rub your face when you've got goop on your hands."

"I've got oil on me?"

The glee in her voice made him laugh. "Yes." He dabbed at the bridge of her nose. "Hey. You've got freckles!"

She looked mortified at that discovery then quickly reached up and rubbed her finger across the spot he'd just bared, leaving another smudge. "I don't know what you're talking about."

Brandon propped a hip against the car and gave her an amused look. "Della, freckles are—"

"Don't say it!"

"What's wrong with looking—"

Her glower dared him to finish his sentence. He wasn't a man to back down from a dare. "Spicy."

Her eyes widened in shock.

"What?" he taunted. "You expected me to say something cliché like *cute*?"

"I should have known better. You're not like everyone else."

"Nope, I'm not." He leaned toward her. "And I'm not about to miss out on seeing all of the cinnamon and spice on your cheeks."

To his delight, she stood still as he wiped off the streak of oil she'd used to cover her freckles. He didn't stop at just that smudge, but flipped the cloth to a clean spot and continued to buff the makeup off her cheekbones. "Why do you wear all of this stuff?"

"Because I don't want to be cute. I want people to take me seriously."

"Sweetheart, you'll always be beautiful. It's not how you look that matters; it's how you act."

"Oh, great. I'm sunk." As soon as she spoke, she groaned. "See? I talk before I think. Daddy says I need to wear heels just so I can't run everywhere I go."

"I've seen you run. Heels wouldn't make any difference."

"What's wrong with how I run?"

"Everything," he said succinctly.

"Huh-unh! It gets me where I want to go!"

The memory of seeing her run around the bases caused him to let out a bark of laughter. "Della, your running does get you there, but the idea of running is to go directly to your destination."

"I just said I get there."

He strove to come up with a way to explain the problem. "Yes," he drawled, "You do get there, but you manage to go up and down and side-to-side as much as you go forward."

"Are you saying," she asked in an arctic tone, "I wiggle?" When he nodded, her chin raised a notch. "Impossible."

"Hey—you're the one who pointed out you're a woman."

"A lady. And ladies glide; they do not wiggle or bounce."

"Who fed you that line?"

"Miss M—" Her brows arched. "What does it matter?"

Everything about you matters. He didn't dare tell her that. Instead he slammed down the hood of her car and shook his head. "I can't figure you out."

"That makes two of us!"

"You can't figure yourself out, or you can't figure me out?"

"Both!"

"Babe, I'm easy. What you see is what you get."

"Well, it's the same for me."

"No, it's not. Underneath that makeup and behind whatever lessons Miss Someone-or-Other taught you, there's a real woman."

"For your information, I am a real woman, and I can cover my freckles if

I want to." She yanked at the hem of her strawberry-colored T-shirt, leaving oily streaks on it. "And you have no right to pass judgment on Miss Mannerly. She was a wonderful woman, and—" She huffed. "Oh, forget it. I don't have to explain myself to you."

As she turned to stalk off, Brandon grabbed her arm. "Hang on."

"Are you okay, princess?" her father called from the porch.

"Of course I am, Daddy. Just a little greasy."

Her father hustled down the steps with a roll of paper towels. "I saw that. Don't know why you're doing this. Your brothers and I can change the oil for you."

"A little oil never hurt anyone," Della placated as she accepted a paper towel and wiped off her hands. "You never fuss when it's olive oil."

"That's different," her father scoffed.

Brandon leaned against the car again. "How is it different?"

"It ruins everything."

"Like what?"

Her father seemed almost nonplussed by the simple question. He finally stammered, "The balance. Yes." He nodded as if he'd solved the complex question entirely. "It ruins the balance."

"What balance?" Della gave her father a quizzical look.

"Princess, you already do so much for the men in your life. You need to let us do things like this to make up for it."

"Since when," she asked her father in an exasperated tone, "did we keep accounts of who does what for whom?"

Brandon held up his hand. "Hang on. I didn't mean to cause a problem. It just occurs to me, Della needs some basic skills so if her car ever goes on the fritz, she isn't stranded."

"I gave her a membership in the Auto Club," her father shot back. "My daughter is demure, and it's insane for a girl to have to do these things." He looked at her. "Your brothers and I made a vow."

"Oh, not that again," she moaned.

"What kind of vow?" Brandon sensed he'd finally stumbled across something that would explain aspects of Della that puzzled him.

"She's a girl."

"This isn't important," Della cut in hurriedly. "Daddy, we need to clean up here. I—"

"Oh, we have a few minutes," Brandon drawled.

"Her brothers and I promised each other we weren't going to rear her to be a tomboy. She deserved to grow up to be a lady, and we've done everything we could to make sure she did."

"You've done a good job. Della's a fine young woman." Brandon lifted her hand and squeezed it, leaving a smudge. "But a little grit or grease won't ever change what's on the inside."

"Doesn't change the fact that we can do stuff for her."

"As much as Della loves you, I'd bet she'd rather have you do things with her instead of for her."

"You're changing the balance," her father muttered.

Brandon let out a chortle. They both looked as if he'd taken leave of his senses. "Fair's fair. Ever since I met Della, I've been off balance."

ᛜ

Brandon squinted through the dust and evaluated the effect of having knocked down the wall. "Looks good, guys. Let's do the other side, too."

Work boots crunched through fallen plaster as the men followed his instructions and demolished the second wall. Nathan hadn't been kidding when he said Brandon would be working with a skeleton crew. Then again, Brandon liked it that way. This project relied on detail, and his small crew took pride in the restoration.

As it turned out, the western exposure of the downstairs featured two walls that weren't shown in the original blueprints and bore no weight. Tearing down those walls was a no-brainer. Brandon watched the dust settle and knew a sense of satisfaction that this place would be functional, yet very true to the original design.

A little strip of old wallpaper appeared where it had been protected beneath one of the walls. Taking out his pocketknife, he painstakingly peeled a long swatch. With all of the choices available, he'd like to have the decorator find something that matched as closely as possible.

The hardwood floors upstairs were all in decent shape, but the downstairs ones were beyond redemption. Well—almost. He'd marked boards around the edges of the rooms that he deemed salvageable. Those were pried up, taken upstairs, and left in a room designated as a storage place for all hardware, boards, and trims they could reuse.

Brandon looked at the site with pride. It was coming along beautifully, and he loved coming to work each day to get more done. He grabbed a push broom and started cleaning up the mess as his team carted out the beams and plaster. A quick glance outside let him know the day was about over, and he wanted this place shipshape. Jim Martinez was coming over to show samples for restoration work. Better, though, when he'd mentioned it to Della, she'd invited herself along so she could see how the renovation was going.

Until now, he wouldn't allow anyone near the site who didn't have a job to do. It was just plain dangerous. With Della, it would have been downright insane. He'd found a daredevil streak in her that alternately pleased and appalled him. Visions of her twisting her ankle or falling kept him up part of the night, so he'd called this morning and told her she couldn't step foot on the place if that dainty little size five-and-a-half was in a heel.

Jim arrived with an armful of catalogs and went back out to his truck to bring in samples of hardware and moldings. Brandon gave the place a quick inspection then went out to offer to help carry things in. The minute he saw Della talking to Jim, jealousy flashed through him.

He and Della didn't have an agreement to date each other exclusively, but that didn't matter. No one else was getting a chance. Della managed to befriend everyone she met—the new checker at the grocery store, the county parking meter inspector—no one crossed her path without the woman cheerily making them feel as if they were the most important person in the universe. She had no idea how alluring that was to a man, and Brandon marveled she didn't have a ring on her finger and a slew of kids by now. One thing for certain: He wasn't going to step aside and let anyone else have a chance at her. She was his.

"I'll make a reservation," Jim said to her as Brandon jogged up.

"Perfect!"

He stopped dead in his tracks. She wanted to date Jim?

Chapter 6

B randon!" She turned her thousand-watt smile on him.

"You two know each other?" The question grated out of him.

"We sure do." Della stepped to Brandon's side and brushed plaster dust from his sleeve.

A glint flashed in Jim's eyes, and he shook his head. "Not that it means much. Granite Cliffs is so small, everyone knows everyone else."

Still not mollified, Brandon asked, "So what kind of reservations are you making?"

"Dinner." Jim hefted a case from his truck. "Della found out where Katie's dad proposed to her mom."

Realizing he'd reacted to a nonexistent threat, Brandon relaxed and tucked Della into his side and took the case of hardware samples away from Jim. "Obviously Granite Cliffs is bigger than you think, because I've never met anyone named Katie."

"She's been in Europe for the past six weeks." Jim pulled out another case, and they started toward the house. "Gawking at cathedrals and famous buildings."

Della slipped her arm around Brandon's waist and squeezed. "Katie's in college—an architecture major."

"And absence made Jim's heart grow fonder." Brandon steered her around a clump of azaleas he'd specifically guarded during the renovation.

Della entered the huge, old building and slipped from his hold. She slowly spun around, surveying the place. "Oh, this is magnificent!"

"Yeah," Brandon agreed, but her reaction pleased him to no end. "But it needs a bunch of work still."

She tugged on the case he held. "What are we waiting for? This place is perfect for wedding receptions!"

Jim chuckled. "There's no hurry, Della. Knowing Katie, she'll want a long enough engagement to plan everything down to the last detail."

Slowly rubbing his thumb back and forth while he continued to cup Della's shoulder, Brandon asked, "So if it were yours, sweetheart, what would you do?"

❧

"I must be out of my mind." Della crammed her hands into the pockets of her windbreaker. She'd been in such a great mood last evening, deciding on moldings and trims and a kitchen layout for the place Brandon was remodeling, he'd somehow managed to get her to agree to a morning jog. "I can't believe I'm up this early."

"Sissy." Brandon pulled her away from his jeep and toward the edge of the parking lot. "You said you didn't want anyone watching. This is perfect timing. Tide's going out. The sand at the tide line is hard packed, and we own the beach."

She didn't argue. He'd been good enough to honor her request for someplace that wasn't crowded. With anyone else, she'd feel vulnerable out here, all alone. Brandon could protect her against anything.

He wore a ratty T-shirt with an almost-washed-to-death U.S. Navy emblem on the front and a pair of gym shorts he should have pitched into the ragbag years ago. Impervious to the tendrils of morning fog drifting in the chilly air, he plowed ahead.

"I must be crazy," she muttered under her breath. *Love makes you do foolish things.* The thought made her stumble in a small pile of sand that had drifted onto the asphalt.

Brandon caught her, held her steady. "You okay?"

I'm falling in love with you. Afraid he'd see the truth in her eyes, she ducked her head and rested against him, listening to the steady beat of his heart. "*Mmm.* You're warm."

He didn't seem in a hurry to let go of her. For a few minutes, he held her close then briskly chafed his hands up and down her arms. "There. Let's get busy." He started doing some stretches, and she copied him. "Warm up. No muscle pulls on my watch."

"Aye, aye, sir."

"Feeling sassy, are you?"

"No, I'm still too cold to waste my breath arguing."

"You'll be warm soon enough."

Once they finished warming up, they hiked through the sand to the water's edge. Brandon stopped, rested his hands on his hips, and instructed, "Now run."

"With you watching?"

"Ten yards. Do it."

Self-conscious as could be, she did as he bade. When she turned around, he'd squatted near her footprints. "What are you doing?"

"Come look." He waited until she joined him, then pointed at the imprint her athletic shoes left behind. "Your heel imprint is the deepest, the ball of your foot leaves a perfect impression, and then your toe digs in."

"What does that mean?"

264

"You land wrong and don't push off. You lose your impetus by bouncing up instead of pushing off. When you have that impetus, you'll lengthen your stride, too."

"Oh." What else could she say? It made sense, but she didn't know exactly how to correct the problem. "I always thought running is just fast walking."

He shook his head. "No wonder you run like a woman. Listen up: Impact on the very back of your heel will hurt you." One of his hands curled around her ankle as the other cupped the top of her foot. "Put your hand on my shoulder."

She took care to use his left shoulder. Warmth and strength radiated from him.

He jostled her ankle. "Let loose. Relax."

"Oh. Okay." She forced herself to pay attention.

"You want to basically hit almost flatfooted and use your ankle to push off." His hands guided her foot as he gave the instruction. He did it a few times.

"So it's sort of like walking in heels, but not."

He looked up at her, eyes full of mirth. "I wouldn't know."

She laughed. "I land the same, but I don't toe off. If I pushed off with my ankle in heels, I'd walk right out of them."

Brandon chuckled, rose, and dusted off his hands. "Hold my hand."

She clasped his right hand with her left. "Now what?"

He briskly rubbed her hand. "I'll bring gloves for you next time."

"I'm starting to warm up a little."

"Good. Now start running around me. Begin with your normal form, and when you've hit your stride, I'm going to pull you faster. That'll give you forward impetus so you can feel the difference when you push with your ankles instead of toes."

"Good thing I don't get dizzy easily." She started jogging, and he rotated about like a hub as she wheeled round him.

"Pick it up." His grip tightened, and he rotated a little faster, then faster still. "I'm going to let go. Keep your form and run along the same line you ran last time."

Once he released her, she dashed down the beach.

"Okay. Come back!"

When she turned around, his grin made getting up so early and having sand in her shoes worth it. "Well?"

"Take a look at your footprints."

She stood beside him and compared them. "My stride is longer!"

"Significantly longer. Less effort, more distance."

"The ball of my foot dug deeper, and my toes aren't digging holes."

"Yup. Now that you have the basic form, let's get a move on." He started to jog in the dry sand, and she scurried alongside him.

"Loose sand is harder. I'll move—

"Nope." He gave her an indulgent smile. "I'm used to ten-mile runs in this each morning. I don't want to get soft."

"Ten miles!"

"You're going to that lifeguard station and stopping." He gestured toward a spot about half a mile away. "Respect your limits and push a little more each day. In a few weeks, you'll be going five miles and will barely break a sweat."

"Ladies, do *not*—" she refuted then took another breath before she finished, "—sweat."

"No?"

"They glow."

When they reached the lifeguard station, Brandon swooped her up, swung her around, and chortled. "You're pretty when you glow."

"When I. . .catch my breath. . ."

"Don't." His head dipped, and he kissed her.

Della was sure she'd never catch her breath again.

Chapter 7

Delicate, lily white. Soft. Brandon couldn't get over the feel of Della's hand in his. He'd positioned them on the bride's side of the park where Della would be able to see the ceremony, yet he'd be on the very outside edge so his height wouldn't block folks' view from farther back.

When he'd arrived to pick up Della for the wedding today, Mr. Valentine stood on the porch like a general inspecting the troops. After he'd taken his time, he shut one eye and squinted through the other, then rumbled, "Haven't run you off yet?"

Sensing plenty lay beneath the wry humor, Brandon stared him in the eye. "I'm not going anywhere."

"You're big, but if you make my baby girl cry, I'll make every last inch of you hurt and hurt bad."

Yeah. Well, Brandon couldn't blame him. Della called forth a man's instincts to shield his woman. Even now, a quick glance at her dainty, pale green sundress and strappy sandals made Brandon shift position so he'd cast Della into his shadow. She'd twisted her hair into a froth of curls at the top of her head, leaving springy little wisps at her nape. His brows knit. Fair skinned and freckled, she'd burn if he didn't keep her in the shade.

As weddings went, it was a nice one. Getting hitched when a couple was this wild about one another rated as a smart move, and Brandon liked seeing how this bride and groom were head-over-heels in love. But Brandon wished the pastor would limit the affair to simple vows and a short prayer. Instead, he inserted comments about Jesus' first miracle being at a wedding feast and other Christian stuff. Especially with it being summer and all, he could have taken mercy on the guests, who stood in the hot sun, and just gotten down to business.

As soon as the newlyweds kissed, Brandon swept Della into the shade of a big, old sycamore. She didn't come alone; she dragged Annette with her. He would have enjoyed trying to get a kiss from Della, but having an audience squelched that notion.

"Brandon, could you bring a chair for Annette? A glass of water, too."

He looked at his wilting sister-in-law. She rested a hand on a just-beginning-to-bulge belly. "I'm going to pound my brother into the ground for leaving you alone in this condition."

Annette's laughter sounded a tad faint. "Don't beat him up. I need him."

"He's a good man." The curls atop Della's head danced as she nodded her head to punctuate her praise. "In fact, Dave did a great job on the music. He's never let on that he's so talented. He needs to get cards made up, and I'll recommend him to my clients."

"Really? How nice." Annette stroked her belly. "This little one is going to be expensive, and we just blew through our nest egg last year when we went on our twenty-fifth anniversary cruise."

Brandon hadn't seen a woman who could be as animated as Della, yet turn into such a gentle listener. She definitely was one-of-a-kind. He hiked off and came back with two bottles of iced water in his pockets and a pair of folding chairs. "Both of you rest and cool off."

"Oh, I thought I'd go help spread out the picnic blankets and—"

Brandon winked. "Annette needs some company. I'll go help."

"He's afraid I'll start crying again," Annette said in a stage whisper. "It's gotten to be a habit of mine lately."

"Soon, it'll be the baby crying, not you." Della twisted off the top of the water bottle and handed it to her.

Brandon opened the other and tucked it into her hand. It didn't take long to help spread out a variety of nifty plaid blankets. A caterer had the picnic theme down pretty well—barbecued ribs and hamburgers, corn on the cob, big pans of fried chicken, and vats of salads. Brandon mentally planned on plowing through and piling up plates for Della, Annette, and himself.

"Hey, Stevens."

He turned. "Gabe. Justin."

"What do you think you're doing with our sister?"

Brandon didn't sense any hostility. Appreciating how they kept watch over their sister, he pretended to study the pair and kept his tone light. "Della's a sweet little gal. How'd she ever end up with brothers like you?"

"That's not the issue." Gabe closed in. "You'd better treat her right."

"Not a problem." After having worked with the Valentine brothers, Brandon wasn't in the least bit surprised that they matched their father's bluster. Reliable, good workers, a bit high-spirited, but solid through and through. They loved Della every bit as much as she loved them—and because of that, Brandon determined to earn their respect and trust.

Justin smirked. "Dad told us to find someone to date her. I was going to nominate you, but don't tell her that."

Brandon chuckled. "I won't—unless she asks. The little lady already had me promise to always shoot straight. I'm not going back on my word." He shoved a pair of blankets into Gabe's arms. "So stop swaggering and make yourselves useful. Spread these out."

Gabe stared pointedly at Brandon's empty arms. "What are you going to do?"

"I'm going back to your sister." He turned and strode toward the sycamore tree.

Annette laughed as he approached. "I told Della to stop fretting about you talking with her brothers. If they irritate you, you'll handle them."

"Yup." He winked.

"But you're too smart to irk them," Della decided. "I'm the one who'll bug you first."

"You already do." Brandon took her hand and lifted it in a silent bid for her to rise. She followed his lead beautifully in a single, fluid move, and he fought the urge to yank her close as he growled, "You make me crazy."

He escorted them to the reception line, and Brandon couldn't help thinking Della would be beautiful in a bridal gown. *Standing next to me.*

While in the SEALs, he'd refused to be in a serious relationship because it was just too hard on the woman and unfair to kids. Now his life was stable. For the first time, the idea of marriage, a little house, and kids slammed into him. The impact didn't blow him away, though. Elation filled him. He'd always loved family. Maybe the time had come for it to be his turn.

And Della would make a fine wife.

⚜

"Dry? Is that you?"

Della watched in surprise as Jordan slapped Brandon on the back. Valene's husband shook his head. "I almost didn't recognize you. You clean up well."

"Dry?" Della accepted the plate someone handed her and looked at the men in puzzlement.

"We ran into each other, compliments of Uncle Sam."

Brandon's casual voice could have fooled an acquaintance, but Della detected a wealth of information and feeling under the surface.

"I never figured out," Jordan continued, "whether you got that handle because you never drank or because you were famous for snaking."

"Both."

"You ate snakes?" Annette turned a hideous shade of green.

"Nah. Snaking is just crawling through stuff you don't want to know about." As if his height didn't give him a good enough view of the huge spread of food, Brandon craned his neck and gawked ahead. "Now I wouldn't mind crawling through this stuff one bit."

Della took the hint that he didn't want to pursue the topic and rescued him. "I get dibs on the potato salad before you do. It's from Pudgy's."

Annette regained her coloring and grabbed a fork. "Okay, I give up. You two go pick up the whole bowl and bring it back to me. I'll be sitting in the shade."

As she waddled off, Della started laughing.

Brandon arched a brow and warned, "She was serious."

"I know! That's what's so funny. I'm glad she's finally over her morning sickness. I'll make a plate for her and add a big scoop."

"I'll hold all three plates." He followed her down the buffet line and back toward Annette. "I'll go back for drinks."

"But Jordan just said you don't drink."

"I don't." He regretted his curt tone. "My granddad drank himself into the grave. The whole family suffered from what booze did to him."

She nodded somberly. "My mom was killed by a drunk driver. I understand."

"Sorry." He studied her. "How old were you?"

"It was just before my first birthday."

He whistled under his breath.

Della didn't want to spoil their day with a recitation of what she'd missed. She did a little hop-step to match his stride and laughed. "Yeah, I was at my dad and brothers' mercy for a long time, but I paid them back for all of their mistakes while I learned to cook."

"So you can cook?"

"Daddy taught my brothers how to do wiring by having them install smoke detectors in every room of the house. Whenever I burned anything, the whole neighborhood knew. You can bet I learned quick!"

"Her lasagna is to die for," Annette said as she reached for her plate.

"Is that so?"

Della laughed. "You're welcome to come try it, but you'll have to fight Daddy and my brothers to get any."

He gave her a slow wink that made her toes curl. "Some things are worth fighting for."

*

"You pulled that off beautifully," Brandon said as he drove away from the reception. "No one knew it fell in your lap as a last-minute deal, and if I hadn't seen your plans back at the shop, I wouldn't have known you plotted the set up and made all of the arrangements."

"That's the way it's supposed to seem—effortless. The spotlight is on the bride and groom."

"Yeah, well, this wasn't exactly the standard wedding and reception. Take some credit, Della. You stepped in and saved the day by putting this together. Doing the picnic theme was a stroke of genius."

"Coping with glitches is part of my business. It wasn't what Linda originally wanted, but I'm glad the outcome pleased her. I just used some creativity to get the job done. I'm sure you handle predicaments all the time, too."

"Not that kind." He changed lanes and glanced at her. "Linda turned into a basket case when the caterer bugged out."

"She looked serene today." Della twisted as far as her seat belt allowed and faced him. "Everyone pitched in to make it come together."

"The preacher got too long-winded." Brandon flipped the jeep's sun visor to the side. "He could have just stuck to the usual prayer and vows. Hot as it is, we all fried in the sun while he talked about Jesus and that stuff."

"Plugging some kind of minisermon is his trademark with all of the weddings he conducts. Pastor MacIntosh is a nice guy, but according to him, I'm doomed to hell because I'm not a Christian."

Brandon snorted. "You're a good person. If God is love and forgives, then you'll go to heaven."

"Whew!" Della shoved back strands of hair blowing about her face. "We've never talked about religion. I don't know why we have to believe in a bunch of stories in the Bible. Living right and doing good should be all that counts."

"I'm all for America, family, and clean living."

"I knew from the day we met you were a patriot and dedicated to your family. I could tell you didn't smoke because you don't smell icky. Today I found out you don't drink."

"Keeping a score card?" There was a wealth of meaning behind his question. "That sounds calculating."

"Hey—we've never shied away from a subject yet. Why start now?" He'd begun to think in terms of a future together, and he needed some reassurance that she felt likewise. Just how serious was she about making this relationship work?

"Okay." She paused. "What do you want to know?"

Survival skills like reading body language, nuances of expressions, the slightest shift of posture or change in blink rate didn't evaporate just because he'd left the SEALs. She'd folded her hands in her lap.

"Why are you withdrawing?"

"I'm not withdrawing."

He pulled to the shoulder of the road and swept his hand through the air at her posture. "The way you're sitting screams 'Not a chance.'"

Her brown eyes grew huge as color washed her cheeks. Her lips parted, then closed, then parted once again as her chin lifted. "No, there isn't a chance."

The words hit him with the impact of a mortar shell.

Chapter 8

I just can't." She looked down then back at him. "I mean—well, I know it's nothing to lots of people. I don't feel that way, though. Call me old-fashioned, but I'm waiting."

Her words sank in, and Brandon finally started breathing again. "Waiting."

She nodded jerkily. "For marriage."

"That's not where this was headed."

Wariness still radiated from her darkened eyes, and the corners of her mouth tensed. If anything, she looked worse. Brandon quickly replayed what he'd just said and wanted to kick himself. *She thinks I just said our relationship isn't headed for marriage.*

He reached over and rubbed his thumb over her whitened knuckles. "Face it, Della. After several dates, we've barely kissed. I got the picture at the very start, and it's fine. Maybe not easy"—he gave her a lopsided smile—"but good stuff rarely comes easy."

Her guard still didn't drop. Her voice sounded hoarse as she said, "I'm not just playing hard-to-get, Brandon. It's not a game."

"I understood that." He frowned. "You misunderstood me. What I'm saying is, I respect you. The first time we met, I said I didn't compromise my values; I don't ask others to ditch theirs either."

As his words sank in, she slowly slumped back into the seat like a parachute losing wind. The sweetest smile he'd ever seen erased the anxiety lines bracketing her mouth.

"You got all intense, and I figured you were. . ."

"Putting the move on you?" he supplied when her voice died out.

She nodded.

"The chemistry's all there, but that's only part of the equation." He leaned back against the door of the jeep and felt the whole vehicle rock as a truck whizzed past. "I don't know where this relationship is going to end up, but I like where it's headed so far."

"Me, too." She tilted her head to the side. "So what were you trying to find out about me?"

"Let's see. . ." He drew the words out slowly to tease her. "I already know you don't smoke. You favor one particular perfume that drives me nuts. You don't drink. You're highly intuitive and sensitive, which is probably why your shop is so successful. And your dad and brothers are overprotective."

"How did you know that?"

"Because Gabe's stalking toward us, and from the sounds of it, Justin's coming up on my blind side."

"Oh, no," she groaned.

Brandon couldn't believe what he was seeing. Then again, he should have. Wherever they went or whatever they did, one of Della's brothers or her dad usually managed to make an appearance. He raised his voice. "Justin, I'm taking your sister to the grocery store."

"Doesn't look like it." The reply sounded as if Justin was jogging closer.

"I'm going to talk her into making me some lasagna."

"No way." The brothers converged on the jeep at the same time. A greedy gleam replaced the anger on Gabe's face.

"I told you they decimate the pan," she folded her arms.

"So I'll be sure we buy a second pan along with the fixings."

Justin leaned against the car. "Just be careful. If Della offers you garlic bread, she's trying to rope you into doing something."

"Garlic bread, huh?"

"Homemade," Gabe said succinctly.

"Didn't know it would take that much time." Brandon winked at her. "Guess I'll just take you out for supper instead, babe. Say good-bye to your brothers."

"Bye, Justin. Bye, Gabe." Barely restrained laughter bubbled under her words. Moments after Brandon put the jeep in gear, she cleared her throat. "They're going to make you pay for this."

He caught sight of her brothers in his rearview mirror and smiled. "Some things are worth fighting for."

☦

"Camping?" Della repeated the word as if it came from a foreign language.

"Yeah. Jim and Katie, Val and Jordan are all on board. We'll head out Saturday morning—just to the San Bernardino Mountains."

"My shop—" She looked around then huffed when his grin didn't fade one iota. "I can't just shut down for four days."

"You don't have to. You're already closed on Sundays and Mondays. Ellen Zobel can cover for you on Saturday, Tuesday, and Wednesday."

"You already spoke with Van and Val's mom?"

"Hold on." He raised his hands as if to ward her off.

"This had better be a good explanation, because I'm pretty ticked off right about now."

The rascal dared to wink at her. If she were a violent person, Della thought she might kick him in the shins just to watch that cocky smile fade. He had no call to go arrange things regarding her business.

"Nathan brought Ellen by my worksite. He said it was to let her see the house, but I think he did it so I wouldn't deck him for telling me he's shutting my site down for half a week so he can swipe my men. Ellen volunteered."

She folded her arms and arched a brow. "Before or after you asked?"

"How would I have known she's filled in for you in the past? Come on, Della. We'll have fun."

"Fun."

His head dipped and rose once in a display of pure, arrogant assurance. "I'll teach you everything you need to know."

"I'll embarrass you," she warned. Secretly, she longed to go on the trip, but she felt obliged to confess something. "I've never been camping."

"Starlight. Campfire. Fresh air. . ."

"Dirt, spiders, and wild animals. . ."

He leaned so close, his breath teased across her face as he whispered, "Hot cocoa and s'mores."

"Oh, that's not fair." She laughed. "You know I can't turn down chocolate."

"I know." He kissed her, then straightened up. "I'll bet you have a few dozen things to tend to before we leave. Don't worry about gear. Just stuff a few shirts and a pair of jeans into a pillowcase."

"I have a sleeping bag."

"Fine. We're on."

⚐

"We're off!" she called to her father as she bounced down the stairs.

Brandon met her with a look of utter disbelief. "What is that?"

"My sleeping bag."

He snatched it from her, snorted in derision, and planted it on the floor in the corner.

"What's wrong with it?"

"Everything."

Della sat down on the steps and gave him a disgruntled look. "You said the same thing about how I ran."

"We fixed that. We'll fix this, too." He plucked her up and headed toward the door then stopped at the sight of a bulging suitcase.

"You are *not* 'fixing' that. I've cut it down to the absolute bare essentials."

"I've lived for a month out of a pack with less stuff than that, and my gear included a tent and sleeping bag."

"Men don't use curling irons or makeup."

"I carried camo face paint." He let out a world-weary sigh. "And you can ditch the curling iron because we're not going to have electricity."

"Nope. It's butane." She grabbed the handle and started to tow the suitcase over the threshold. "I thought of everything."

He shut the door and muttered, "You're taking everything."

After a quick stop at a surplus place where Brandon gave her a crash course on thermal ratings on sleeping bags, showed her how to judge quality of hip pads, and extolled the virtues of a few other doodads, they headed for the campground.

"Jim's flight was overbooked. He's getting in on a noon flight, so he and Katie will be here by supper. As soon as Val finishes her shift at the hospital, she and Jordan will come. We're going to select and establish a site."

Once they reached the mountains, Della couldn't sit still. "Look! Oh, it's beautiful here!"

"Yeah, but there's no water source."

She gave him a horrified look. "You're taking me someplace without plumbing?"

"Rustic accommodations."

After digesting that unwelcome and euphemistic explanation, Della decided to be a good sport. She pointed out other possible campsites.

"Not protected from the wind. Tents will blow over. . . . Too close to the creek, and the water's barely moving. Bugs would eat us alive after sunset."

Just about when she despaired of ever finding a place he'd find satisfactory, Della called out, "Wait! There." She pointed out the open window to her right.

Brandon steered the jeep into a clearing, scanned the area, and nodded. "See? All you needed was to know what to look for. Great choice."

He made the chores fun. A natural-born teacher, he'd show her how to do things and explain why it had to be done in that particular way. Everything from pounding tent stakes in at an angle to where to build a fire turned into an opportunity to learn and work side-by-side. Brandon didn't treat her like a fancy china doll that had to be cosseted—he treated her like a capable, thinking woman. No one had ever accepted her just as she was instead of trying to squeeze her into a mold and make her play a role. With Brandon, she felt free to be herself. He made it safe and fun to try new things.

By the time everyone else arrived, all three tents were pitched and a hearty stew bubbled on the camp stove. Jordan sat down at the picnic table and announced, "I'd like to bless the meal."

"Sure." Brandon thumped down his cup.

Della glanced around the table. She and Brandon were the only non-Christians. Katie and Jim didn't go to church much, but they'd immediately bowed their heads and chimed in on the *Amen*. Later, around the campfire, Katie taught them some songs she'd learned at high school church camp.

Curling up beside Brandon at the campfire rated as a highlight in Della's life. Feeling warm, cherished, and comfortable, she laughed as he torched another marshmallow into a charred mess. "How can you eat that? It's charcoal!"

"Think you could do any better?" He stabbed another marshmallow on a stick and handed it to her. "Have at it."

"I'm great at this," she boasted. "Just ask Val. We used to have beachside picnics in high school. I'm not utterly helpless, you know."

"No one," Brandon said as he speared another ill-fated marshmallow, "with a brain like yours is helpless."

Valene cheered.

"What got into you?" Jordan gave Valene a baffled look.

"In high school, Van and I hung out with Della. We were known as Zany, Brainy, and Prissy. Someone finally realized Della's smart!"

"Acting like that, we'll all think you're zany." Jordan's voice held affection.

"Well, I'm sleepy." Katie yawned and rose.

Brandon sandwiched his marshmallow between two broken bits of graham cracker and gobbled it down. "Della's still not done with that marshmallow. When it's done, we'll extinguish the fire."

She didn't regret the last five minutes alone as the others turned in. Brandon brushed his temple against hers and murmured, "I was an idiot to eat marshmallows. I can't kiss you without leaving sticky junk on your face."

She turned and whispered, "I haven't eaten any yet. Hold still." She brushed a kiss along his jaw line then pulled away. "I guess we'd better put out the fire."

"Yeah." His gravelly undertone gave a completely different twist to her words.

Della hopped up, but Brandon captured her hand. "Some fires you put out. Others, you bank the embers so you can bring them to life again at a later time." He paused. "Go on and join Katie in your tent before I douse this, so you have some light." He prepared to dump what was left from the coffeepot onto the dying flames.

Della scampered into her tent and zipped it shut. She didn't mention she had a tiny flashlight in her pocket.

Chapter 9

Della." Brandon stood outside her tent and hissed her name again. This time, he heard some rustling.

"Huh?"

"Come on out here." A few moments later, the tent zipper buzzed. He snickered when she held the flaps closed and barely peeked out with one eye. "We're on breakfast detail."

"It's still dark." Her whispered words carried more than a hint of accusation.

"Not for long."

She sighed. "Give me fifteen minutes."

"Three."

The zipper sounded, and the flap sealed completely again. Ten minutes later, she emerged. She'd pulled on neatly pressed tan slacks. He bet whatever shirt she had on beneath her jacket was just as impractical. The tip of her ponytail bounced along at her waist, and she'd somehow managed to slap on some makeup.

"You need to learn to tell time," he said as he tugged her along. He had to keep moving before he kissed her silly. Months ago, he'd thought his life was over. He'd left the "family" of SEALs. Suddenly, things had changed. He saw a future with Della, of them having their very own family—trips to the beach and camping. Rowdy little kids who jumped on their beds. . . . Seeing the woman he loved first thing in the morning jolted him. He'd found sheer contentment in a very disturbing package.

Their first stop was his jeep. Cracking open the first-aid kit, he searched for an alcohol swab. "No perfume up here unless you want to get eaten alive."

"Oh." She hastily swabbed off her wrists and behind each ear. She'd put in earrings. Dangly ones. Brandon grinned and wondered what she'd do if he told her—*oh, why not?* "Those earrings—"

"Aren't they pretty? I got them on sale."

"At Joe's Bait and Tackle?"

Her eyes grew huge. "What?!"

He reached over, unhooked it from her ear, and dangled it between them. "Looks like a great fishing lure to me."

She snagged it from him and popped it back into her earlobe. "You haven't had coffee yet. I forgive you." Leaning into the jeep to put the alcohol swab into his litterbag, she asked, "So what are we cooking?"

"Whatever we catch." He grabbed a pole from the jeep and shoved it into her hand.

"Fish for breakfast?"

Brandon chuckled softly. The glee in her voice made the whole trip worthwhile.

An hour later, Brandon sat on the shore and cast his line again. Della didn't have the patience it took to sit still and wait for a nibble. Soon after they'd started fishing, she'd stuck her pole into the dirt, tried unsuccessfully to dust off her seat, and wandered up and down the stream. She stayed in sight, and Brandon enjoyed watching her exploring the area with such intensity. Finally, she'd grabbed his net. "Careful," he called.

"It's only water." She nimbly made her way across several stones. "You said fish like cool, deep water. This looks like a good spot."

"You do know how to swim, don't you?"

"Only if I'm wearing arm floaties." Her laughter drifted to him.

Brandon smiled at her sass and spirit. She'd stolen his heart. Never one to hesitate when he'd decided on a course of action, he grimaced at the realization that Della would probably want a long engagement so she could plan the perfect wedding.

She skipped back to him. "Look what I got!"

He ignored the fish in her net and swept her in a circle then hugged her tight. "Nope. Look what I got."

⨸

Brandon couldn't get the camping trip out of his mind. Watching Della had been a real kick—the woman embraced life with such zest, he'd loved opening her eyes to all the little things around them. She'd actually gotten grubby, and he'd never seen a woman look more appealing than she did, sitting on a rock beside him, trying to copy how he held a blade of grass between his thumbs to make a whistle.

Coming back to work—well, at least he liked his job. If he didn't, he would have been sorely tempted to stay right up in the mountains with her. She'd invited him to come over for supper tonight—Power Electric worked on the site today, and her father volunteered that she'd stuffed the biggest roast he'd ever seen in the crock pot. The old adage about the way to a man's heart being through the stomach didn't hold true—she'd already captured him before he ate a bite of her cooking. . .but Della's great cooking sure sweetened the deal.

"Hey, Brandon! Did Della—" Gabe began.

"—rope you into the show, too?" Justin finished in a morose tone.

Brandon shoved his cell phone back into its holder and asked, "What show?"

"For her shop. She bullies us into tuxes, and we have to pretend to be besotted grooms." Justin measured a length of electrical wire from a spool and cut it.

"At least she's trying to line up safe 'brides' this time," Gabe said as he pulled more wire. "Van and Val are both married. Katie already has Jim."

"It's just a show. What's the problem?"

The wiring in Gabe's hands snarled just as badly as his voice. "The models are piranhas in white satin. They're total man-eaters. Get close, and your days are numbered."

Brandon chuckled. "Thanks for the warning. Della didn't ask, though, so I'm safe."

Just then, his cell phone rang again. "Hello? Della!"

Della's brothers started laughing like loons.

⁜

"Dreams can come true. . . ." Della lost her line for a moment as she watched Brandon step on stage in his tux. *There ought to be a law against men that good-looking being let out alone. And I'll volunteer to escort this one. . . .*

The microphone let out a small squawk, jarring her out of her own fantasy and back to the bridal extravaganza. "The styles this season are classic and more tailored, accentuating the groom's masculinity, and they photograph especially well. . . ."

Just about every waking minute for the past week had revolved around the details for this show. Two hundred fifty brides and their mamas or sisters filled the room. Caterers, photographers, florists, stationers, jewelers, two lingerie stores, and two other bridal shops put on this extravaganza twice a year. Almost a quarter of her year's sales would be generated from the contacts here, and she took every opportunity to promote her shop.

One look at Brandon striding down the walkway in that tuxedo ought to make every woman in the room swoon. The rascal hit his mark at the end of the runway, half turned, and winked—at her!

"Where's the bride?" someone called out.

Della only then realized the model who was supposed to be with him hadn't materialized. She quickly extemporized, "This is the best man." *The best man I've ever seen. . .* "Next, we'll see the bride with the man of her heart. Yes, ladies, here comes the bride. . . ."

Times like this, family and friends really helped. Vanessa and Nathan, Valene and Jordan, Katie and Jim—they all radiated the contentment of couples in love. As for her brothers—for all the fuss they kicked up about getting roped into helping, they'd actually gone the extra mile and rigged up special lights and a fantastic backdrop. Two of the three models she hired as brides/bridesmaids walked the runway with flair—but one seemed to be having difficulty.

Katie tugged on the back of Della's dress and whispered from behind the curtain, "Angela's sick."

Della waited until another couple posed on the runway and hissed, "Your mom's here, isn't she?"

"Yes. Pink dress, second row."

"I hope she'll forgive me. . . ." Della smiled at the audience and looked at them. "I'd like to do something a little different today. It occurs to me that my brides are all younger women. I'd like to have a mature woman come back and show us all that love is ageless."

The idea electrified the audience. "When love comes again, the son often has the honor of escorting his mother down the aisle. Let's have Brandon come out here to escort the 'bride' from our audience."

Brandon appeared and plucked a rose from the trellis and turned to Della.

He'd shocked her on the phone when he volunteered to help with the show before she even told him about it. Clearly, he didn't mind pitching in, and the extemporaneous action showed style.

Della stood on the toes of her already high heels. "How about if we match that rose to the dress of a woman in the audience?"

Brandon hopped off the runway with a lithe move and soon stopped in front of a pair of young, giggling girls. His voice cut through the air. "A lady in the second row since this is the second time around." He extended the rose to Katie's mother with a gallant flourish. "Milady?"

Tessa Garrett accepted the rose and stood. "I never had a son, but I'm more than willing to adopt you!"

"There you have it!" Della said into the microphone. "An adoption and a wedding in the same afternoon."

Valene and Jordan walked the runway as Della cheerfully praised the features of their formalwear. Katie and Jim came next; then Della glanced over and caught sight of Brandon. He stood behind the curtain, out of sight from the audience. The minute their eyes met, he held up four fingers. He didn't look apologetic or worried in the least about asking for more time. His confidence in her sent her spirits soaring.

Having done this event for the past three years, Della knew just how to organize everything backstage so the models could scurry back, change, and return. She also planned something to fill in a time lag, just in case. Taking advantage of a momentary pause, she lifted a basket. "I'm going to send this around. Slip in your cards, and at the close of the show, we'll have a drawing. Della's Bridal, Forget-Me-Not Flowers, and Genesis Photography have created a gift package valued at over one thousand dollars. . . ."

Minutes later, Brandon gave her a thumbs-up.

"Take a breath now, ladies, because once you see this next couple, you'll be breathless! Brandon is escorting Tessa to the altar." Brandon appeared with Tessa on his arm, and the audience burst into applause.

"Love is ageless, and so are the beautiful lines of Tessa's gown. . . ."

It barely seemed possible that she'd spent weeks planning the show and it was over in an hour and fifteen minutes. Della mingled with prospective customers then went behind the curtains, took one look at Brandon, and burst out laughing.

Chapter 10

We must've done well—you're happy." Brandon grinned at her as he slowly unknotted his tie and drew it off.

"Get some orders, sis?" Gabe asked.

"Five of the gowns are on reserve. I need to tag them." She took the tie from him. "Your feet hurt, too, Brandon?"

"I'll tag them," Vanessa offered.

"No one's toe-tagging me," Brandon protested. "I'm definitely alive and kicking."

"The gowns, not your feet."

"No kidding," Van teased. "I've seen his feet, and I'm not that brave! Just tell me which gowns."

While Della specified which ones, Brandon tugged her over to a chair and promptly yanked off her drive-a-red-blooded-man-crazy high heels. "Why did you wear these?"

"They match my dress," she said with insane, feminine logic. "Oh, my word! Brandon, what happened to your feet?" She popped out of the chair and tried to shove him from his kneeling position.

He didn't budge.

"Brandon!" Her voice took on a decided edge as she knelt beside him.

"It's nothing."

"Nothing?!" She stared at his blisters in horror.

He tilted her face up to his. "You must think I'm a real wuss if you think a couple of blisters are gonna bother me."

"Are you gonna kiss my sister?" Justin's words held unmistakable challenge.

"Your sister," Della declared as she threaded her fingers through Brandon's hair and dipped closer, "is going to kiss him."

"Over my dead body," Justin blustered.

"That can be arranged, can't it?" Della asked Brandon right before her lips touched his.

Brandon hadn't ever laughed through a kiss, but he couldn't help it. Their lips barely brushed, and their noses bumped, then Della pulled away.

"My life is safe if that's your definition of a kiss." Justin sauntered off.

Brandon pulled Della closer and murmured, "The only reason I put up with him is because I'm nuts about you."

"Brandon?"

"Yeah?"

"What happened to your feet?"

"Have I ever remarked on how stubborn you are?"

Jordan snorted as he hung up the tuxedo he'd been wearing. "Look who's talking."

Brandon stood and pulled Della to her feet. "It's impossible to carry on a conversation around here."

Jim curled his arms around Katie. "Get used to it. Once you have a woman in your life, you'll never get a word in edgewise."

"Hey!" Katie gave him a look of mock outrage.

"You all clear out. I'll help Della load up the racks," Brandon said.

"Gabe, please pull the truck to the south exit." Della turned to zip a gown into a huge vinyl casing. "We won't take long."

Everyone sauntered away. Brandon held a hanger aloft as Della zipped the next gown into the protective casing. "You have this down to a fine art, and you handled that glitch like a pro."

"Thanks. I was lucky Katie's mom happened to be here and was a good sport."

"I was proud of you—you're a great emcee and came up with extemporaneous comments to make things work. You ran with it."

"Speaking of running. . ."

"Tomorrow morning. I'll pick you up at five fifteen."

"Not a chance." She looked at his feet again. "Not with those blisters. The shoes did it, didn't they?"

He'd already put her off, but the woman could teach obstinacy to a mule. At the moment, Brandon rued his promise to always be totally honest with her. "The box says size thirteen, but they're elevens."

"And you wore them? And walked around like nothing was wrong?"

"No big deal. I've had blisters that deserved birth certificates. Let's bag up that last gown."

He thought he'd distracted her until they finished packing all of the gowns and tuxedoes into the truck with Gabe's help. Della spoke to her brother, gave him a hug, and waved him off. Brandon didn't think anything of hopping into her car to go back to the shop—until she turned the wrong way.

"Don't you give me that look," she snapped.

"What are you up to?"

"I'm making sure you don't die of blood poisoning."

He decided not to argue with her. . .even though the crazy woman stopped at three different places. Later, up to his ankles in a pan of Epsom salts, he ate a plate of her lasagna as she put everything back in place at the shop.

"There." She tucked away the last cummerbund and turned to him. "How are you doing?"

"Never been better. This lasagna is outrageous."

She knelt and carefully dried his feet. Brandon couldn't believe it. He didn't like anyone fussing over him; but here Della was, her classy silk dress pooling on the floor around her in wild disarray, showing him a tenderness that stole deep into his heart. He'd already mentally claimed her as his own, but the way she tended him tattled about how profoundly she cared for him, cared about him. In her own way, she was making him hers.

He wanted to grab her, hug her, and confess his love, but it was all wrong. Backward. He should be kneeling at her feet when he made that declaration. Tugging the towel from her hands, he said, "That's enough. I'm too ornery for this to bother me."

"I bought salve."

He shook his head. "Air is best. Trust me on this."

Not even hesitating for a second, she nodded. The phone rang. "Excuse me, Brandon."

As she hurried to the phone, he bent to pick up a bag she'd set on the floor. He peered inside. Bandages, witch hazel, peroxide, Merthiolate, salve, a tube of antibiotic ointment, cotton balls—the silly woman had practically bought out the drug store. But that wasn't why he smiled. She'd listened to his opinion and ignored all of her grandiose first-aid plans because she trusted him. A man couldn't ask for more—except for her heart.

⳨

"Babe," Brandon said as Della clicked her seat belt, "I've never eaten better lasagna. In fact, I've never eaten better chow, period."

She took the plate from him. "If you take me home, you can have seconds." Laughter bubbled out of her as he slammed the door and scrambled straight across the hood.

"Hey—I'm not wasting any time. I've seen how your brothers eat!" A few seconds later, Brandon shot her an exasperated look. "Stinkin' road work."

"You just complained a week ago about the potholes through here."

"That was before lasagna and your brothers were on the other end of the road!" A pained look crossed his face. "They've probably decimated the garlic bread, too."

"You already had three big slices!"

"I'd go for more, but you need a slice"—he waggled his brows—"to eat it in self-defense. Otherwise, you might not put up with me."

"I'll put up with you—anytime, anywhere."

The jeep coasted to a stop at a light. "Good thing, because you're not getting rid of me."

The certainty in his voice gave her an assurance she'd never had. Bless his heart, Brandon hadn't let her brothers or dad irritate him away. He'd accepted her as she was and taught her how to be more self-sufficient. He lived the SEAL's theme—"The only easy day was yesterday!"—and challenged her to test her own limits. Because of him, she'd discovered new strengths in herself, new abilities, new feelings.

"Truth is—" Brandon gripped the steering wheel tightly.

A loud honk made them both jump.

"All right, all right," he groused as he stepped on the accelerator.

Della wiggled to sit sort of sideways so she could see him better. "What's the truth?"

"When I set my mind on something, I go for it."

"Yes, you're stubborn. I noticed that right away. I've never had a customer hang on to damaged merchandise and insist they still want to buy it."

"Give me a challenge, I'll rise to it."

"You'll soar past it." Della adjusted the visor to block the late afternoon sun. "You don't settle for okay—you always want stupendous."

"Like you."

"I never thought of it that way, but yes. Like me. I don't want to settle for mediocre. Funny—we're almost opposite in most ways, but in others, we're so much alike."

He shook his head. "Della, I wasn't trying to point out our similarities."

"Oh." She tugged at the shoulder belt to hide her disappointment. "Well, I sort of figured that you like me."

"I don't like you," he half-roared, "I love you!"

"He looooooooves youuuuu!" a teenaged boy in the car next to them repeated back in loud, saccharine sarcasm, then cackled and zoomed off.

"And now the whole world knows," Brandon said as he made a turn onto her street and parked in the driveway beside Justin's car. He looked her in the eyes. "I'm not sorry it does. . .but I'd planned on telling you that someplace a little more private or romantic."

Happiness flooded her. "Brandon—"

"Hey, sis!" Gabe shouted from the porch.

She groaned.

"Later," Brandon muttered under his breath.

She nodded as Gabe continued to holler, "We're out of soda! Why don't you two go get more?"

"I have some in the trunk of my car," she called back.

A few minutes later, she and Brandon joined her dad and brothers at the table. They'd already scraped the first pan of lasagna clean. Della grabbed a spatula and rapped Justin's knuckles when he lifted his plate for more.

"Brandon?"

He grinned and slid both his plate and hers right next to the pan. "Ready when you are."

"No one's ever going to be ready for Della," Justin grumbled.

Della cut a huge chunk of lasagna and held it over Brandon's plate. There, in front of her family, she looked at Brandon and said, "Brandon? About what you said earlier—I love you, too."

❦

"How are the blisters?"

Brandon shoved Nathan's arm. "What's it to you?"

"Hey—I wondered if you needed a couple days' medical leave." A teasing smile lit his boss's face. "I heard they were bad."

"I wouldn't have thought Jim would blab."

"He didn't. Vanessa did."

"I should have guessed. Forget it. If anything, I thought maybe you'd back out on tonight." *Actually I hoped you would. I can think of a few million other places I'd rather be.*

"No way."

"Is your wife going to be okay?" Brandon took a seat in the stadium and gave Nathan a worried look. "I spotted Vanessa yesterday when I took Della to the shop. Don't take this the wrong way, but I don't like how your wife looks. I thought maybe you'd stay home with her or something."

Nathan grinned. "Nothing's wrong with Van that another eight months won't cure."

"No kidding? Congrats!"

"Thanks." Nathan beamed. "We're totally stoked. What a blessing, you know?"

"Yeah." Brandon nodded. He couldn't help thinking of Della, picturing her all rounded with child—his child.

Things were good between them, and since they'd finally broken down and admitted their love for one another, he'd been marching around with a fool's grin plastered on his face. He'd even dared to make a few veiled references about the future. Funny, how he was usually so straightforward, but with Della, he hadn't charged ahead. Some things deserved time. The old-fashioned word *courting* came to mind.

He wanted Della to feel cherished and certain. Marriage was a forever thing. One trip down the aisle, one mate for life. As their relationship deepened, Brandon had come to the point of knowing he wanted her by his side for the rest of their lives. From their first meeting, he'd been enchanted by her, intrigued and amused. . .and each time, things got better. Never before had he used the word *love*. With Della, there was no choice—she embodied all he could ever hope for in a wife-to-be. He'd do everything possible to make her happy. And though a jog down the aisle tomorrow would suit him just fine, Brandon resolved to let this whole romance unfold in such a way that her every dream came true.

If anyone knew I was this besotted, they'd never let me live it down. He cleared his throat to cover the chuckle that bubbled up.

"So what do you think?"

Nathan's question pulled him from his musings. Brandon looked around. "Pretty hard to believe a bunch of men fill a stadium, and it's not for sports."

Nathan merely chuckled.

"This better be good," Brandon continued. He shot his boss a sideways glance. "You know I'm not into all this Holy Roller stuff."

"It's a three-night thing, and you're off the hook tomorrow and the next night if you don't want to come. No pressure."

Brandon nodded curtly. He fully expected to cash in on that provision. He'd come because Nathan wasn't just a boss—he was a friend. Since leaving the SEALs, Brandon missed the camaraderie he'd shared with his team. For six years they'd trained together, worked together, practically lived in each others' pockets. Nathan hadn't just given him work to do—he'd given him a dream job and offered his friendship. Brandon took his measure that first day and knew full well that Nathan Adams was a man he could count on.

Their working relationship and friendship took on a new significance when Nathan asked him to play baseball. That little invitation gave Brandon the opportunity to bump into Della again. . . .

Yeah. One night of hellfire and brimstone. I can take it.

Brandon scanned the stadium. A platform with several microphones sat dead center of the field. A set of drums promised music of some sort. *I'd rather listen to Jesus-Loves-You music than a long-winded preacher.*

A weasely looking guy got up and welcomed everyone. Brandon winced. There stood a man who personified his idea of a Christian man—wimpy, indecisive, needing the crutch of religion.

"I praise God for my weakness," the man said in an unsteady tone, "because in my weakness, His strength is made perfect. . . ."

Nathan murmured, "Bill was once a world-class weight lifter. He's got cancer."

Like a grenade, the words blew all of Brandon's preconceived notions to bits.

The music that followed wasn't half-bad. . .until a strapping man with military bearing strode across the platform. *The guy squares his corners. Either he's still in, or he just got out.*

He got in front of the mike. Even from the distance, Brandon could see how he grinned. "I'm sure a bunch of you men are going to pick up on this real quick. If you ever served Uncle Sam, you got a different version of the words." He paused while chuckles rumbled through the crowd. "So join in with me. . . ."

Yeah, join in. Not a chance. I haven't known a single one of these songs.

The song leader stepped back from the mike and belted out, "I don't know, but I've been told. . . ."

How many miles had Brandon marched, jogged, run with a full pack to those words? Out of sheer habit, he sang back, "I don't know, but I've been told. . . ."

"The devil's trying to keep my soul."

Well, it was a song. Brandon didn't believe the devil had much to do with his soul, but he sang along.

"Did some things, and I'm not proud. . . . Some alone, some with the crowd. . . ."

Ouch. Those words struck a cord. Brandon tried to live a good life, but he had some stuff he wished he hadn't done.

"Count 'em," the resonant cadence went on.

"One, two. . ." Brandon sang along.

"Count 'em."

"Three, four. One, two, three, four." Only they weren't just words. Each number stood for something he'd done wrong. His chest went tight. A million thoughts and memories speared through his mind.

"Jesus died for all my sins. . . . I only have to ask Him in. . . . All my past is washed away. . . . All I have to do is pray. . . ."

Brandon didn't hear a word of the message. The cadence kept drumming through his mind.

Chapter 11

At the end of the evening, he walked out of the stadium and over to Nathan's truck.

Nathan slammed the door and turned to him. "What did you think?"

"Not bad. I guess I can take another night of it."

"Bet you felt right at home with Jonesy singing cadence. You belted out the words like you'd been a SEAL or something," Nathan teased.

"Yeah, or something." Brandon strove to hide behind a wry response. He had too much to think about, too much to process. They drove in silence until they passed the place he was renovating.

"Wanna show me what you've been up to here?"

Brandon grinned. "Sure."

They walked around the old building. Brandon summed up the overall accomplishments. "All the rot's gone. Had to strip it down to the bones in places and completely redo it. The lines are still the same, but she's stronger, better—more functional.

Nathan nodded. "Looking great. You've proven yourself worthy of my confidence. How are we on budget?"

"It didn't come cheap. I still have work to do."

"Life's like that—the things that matter most are often the most costly."

Brandon leaned into a doorframe. "You're not talking about the project, are you?"

"If it's all you want to discuss, I am. If you feel like talking about something else, I'm available."

Brandon stayed silent. *I don't know. But I'm not a coward. I have to face this. May as well do it now as later.* "Sure your wife doesn't need you?"

"Van and Val are having a girls' night." Nathan's face scrunched into a look just short of agony. "If I go home before midnight, I'll be forced to watch old Doris Day movies."

"Fate worse than death, huh?"

"You got it. I married a great woman, but her taste in movies stinks. So believe me, you're not keeping me from anything."

Okay, Stevens. Time's up. Handle it. He cleared his throat. "Nothing's black-and-white. At least, I never thought it was."

"But you're reconsidering that premise?"

Brandon nodded curtly. "Even in war, you don't just have combatants. There are neutral parties. I always figured that was me. God and the devil were welcome to duke it out, and I'd just stay clear of it all."

Nathan plopped down on a stepladder. "And now?"

"I never thought about the whole thing being polarized. A world war. You're on one side or the other. In the call-and-response, that guy singing cadence hit a nerve."

Nathan nodded.

"I've done good stuff, but I've also done things I regret. I sorta figured there's going to be a giant balance at the end of life, and as long as the good outweighs the bad, I'll get a pass into heaven. Only it's not that way, is it?"

"No, it's not. You can't be on both sides."

Brandon shook his head. "I'm not sure how to process it."

"In the end, you have to chose whom you serve."

"At what cost?" Brandon cut to the heart of the matter. "Why?"

"Because you're like this place was." Nathan swept his hand in an arc. "Parts of you are solid, but parts are rotten. If you're really going to be all you can be, you have to be willing to let God strip out the bad and rebuild you in His image. Sometimes, the process is a joy; other times, it's painful. In the end, I can promise you'll be glad of the results."

Brandon digested that analogy then said, "You didn't mention the cost."

"The cost was Christ. He paid the price. We don't have anything God wants except our hearts."

"So according to the cadence, we pray, and Jesus washes away our sins. Then what?"

"We obey." Nathan let out a long, gusty sigh. "It's not always easy. I blow it sometimes. It's not about me being perfect, though. It's about me being willing to do my best and seeking forgiveness when I blow it. I can't say what the cost is ever going to be—not for me, not for anyone else. What I do know is, God loves me and wants only what's best in the long run. Faith in His wisdom is why I obey."

Kicking the opposite side of the doorframe with the toe of his boot, Brandon said, "Like following a superior's order, hoping he's got intel that you don't?"

"Yep." A slow smile lit Nathan's face. "Only God is the ultimate in wisdom. You can always count on the intel when it comes down from Him."

"Slick."

"If you mean it's trite, I'm not going to try to convince you otherwise. The simplicity of salvation is undeniable."

"Black-and-white," Brandon said. "And I was satisfied living in the gray zone."

"Was?" Nathan studied him.

Brandon stayed quiet for a long count. When faced with truth, though, a man had to take a stand. His moment of truth had come.

"I've always viewed myself as one of the good guys. I guess it's time I joined the right side, huh? Think God would take me?"

"I know He will."

⁜

"Three nights in a row?" Della clamped the phone between her jaw and shoulder while arranging a new headpiece in the case. Tiaras and pearl-studded bands winked and glittered like promises of happily-ever-afters.

"We'll go out tomorrow night," Brandon said. "What would you like to do?"

"How about dinner and a movie?"

"Sounds great." Hammers pounded in the background. "Hang on a sec, babe. It's too noisy in here. . . . Better now?"

"Yes. What are you doing today?"

"Jim Martinez hooked me up with a bunch of vintage molding and ceiling panels. We're installing all of it in the big rooms along the beach side of the building."

"Oh, tell me you're going to paint them all white."

"Why white?"

"Because it'll look fresh and clean and airy. . . ."

"And?" he prodded as if he knew she'd left out something. He'd gotten good at reading between the lines.

"And because I plan to book rehearsal dinners and wedding receptions there. If you chose something dreary or dark, it'll spoil everything."

He chuckled. "We couldn't have that, could we?"

"Absolutely not."

His voice went muffled for a moment, "Yeah. No. Then take it all down and redo it. It's got to be level." He cleared his throat. "Okay, babe. Sorry. Ran into a minor disaster."

"It sounds as if you have it under control."

"Give it ten minutes. Another is bound to come up. It's been one of those days." He let out a pained chortle. "You ought to be glad we're not going out tonight. If my luck held, we'd have a flat tire, and we'd contract food poisoning."

"Hold it right there! You just keep your distance then." She laughed. "Hey. Speaking of food. . .how did that pantry idea work out?"

"Great. Even got Vanessa's approval. If you have any other brainstorms, let me know."

"See? Listen to me, and even your boss's wife is happy. Would I steer you wrong?"

Brandon's deep laughter rumbled over the line, making her shiver with pleasure. "I certainly hope not."

"Consider it payback for teaching me how to bat." She sighed dramatically. "You'll probably have to teach me all over again once we start up the team after the break."

"Count on it. Those games were a great excuse to see you."

"I've missed you so much, honey." She switched the phone to her other ear and clamped it in place so she could thread a new roll of paper into the cash register.

"How much?"

Laughter bubbled out of her. "Oh, no you don't. Last time we played that game, you talked me into going on a second camping trip."

"And we had a great time. You're becoming quite the outdoorswoman."

"Well, we can't go camping this weekend anyway. My summer sale just started, and Jim and Katie are moving."

"Moving?"

"Um-hmm. He proposed at that special restaurant and everything is falling right into place for them. The apartment they wanted came vacant, so he snapped it up."

"They're going to live together?"

Della swung the little side door on the register shut, and it gave a satisfying click. She advanced the tape with several *chings* and said, "Yes. Katie's okay with it. After all, they are engaged now."

"Humpf."

"And you used to think I was so old-fashioned!" Della smiled. Brandon let her know he found her more than appealing, but he never crossed the lines she set. It made her feel cherished and respected.

"You are." He paused. "And I see a lot of wisdom in those old-fashioned values."

"If nothing else, it kept us both alive. Daddy or my brothers would do something rash if we tried living together."

"Well, we have nothing to fear." The sound of his boots thumping up wooden stairs accompanied his words. "When our time comes, we're going to do everything right. Listen, babe, I need to go. See you tomorrow."

"Okay. I love you, Brandon."

"Love you, too. Bye."

After she put down the phone, Della couldn't resist spinning in a jubilant whirl. He hadn't said *if* their time came. . .he'd said *when*. In the past few weeks, he'd been dropping bombs like that, and every one of them shook her world.

Brandon didn't make false promises. He didn't just blithely make comments and off-the-cuff remarks. When he said something, he meant it. He loved her. He wanted to be with her—not just for right now, but also far, far into the future. And now, he'd given her another hint that he wanted to make her his forever.

What more could a woman want?

She opened a file on the computer and looked at the newest styles. As if the computer knew all about her phone conversation with Brandon, the very first thing she saw took her breath away. There it was—the perfect wedding gown. The one she would have designed for herself. Clear down to the details on the hem, it matched everything she'd ever dreamed of. Delighted, she gazed at it and followed her impulse. She e-mailed off an order for it—custom-made to her own measurements.

⚶

Brandon slid his arm around her shoulders and nestled Della close. "Nippy breeze tonight."

She wrapped her arm about his waist. "But you're always nice and warm."

They walked along the sidewalk, toward the park on Balboa Island. The movie they'd decided to watch was only showing at the small theater on the island, and it had been a mad dash to get there on time. He'd managed a hasty shower and changed out of his work jeans into chinos, but Della still wore one of her dress-for-feminine-success silky outfits.

Navy brass lived on and around the island. In fact, naval personnel tended to frequent the theater and restaurants here because of the quaint, intimate atmosphere. That being the case, men Brandon knew by sight, but not by name, passed by. Their gaze would go from him to Della, slow smiles would sketch across their faces, and they'd look back at him and give a nod of silent approval.

Yes, Brandon felt proud of his woman. Della was a looker—but even more, inside, she held a beauty that mattered most. Let the other guys eat their hearts out. Della belonged to him.

"Hungry now?"

She laughed. "Are you kidding?"

"I promised you supper."

"After that huge vat of popcorn?"

"That little snack?"

"If that tub were any bigger, they'd have to put it on the oceanographic charts as a newly discovered gulf of something-or-other."

"Sounds interesting. We could be the first to explore it. Have you ever gone sailing?"

"No, but I'd go anywhere with you."

His hold tightened slightly. *Thank You, God. I prayed for a chance, and this looks like a good one.* "Really? Then how about coming to church with me this Sunday?"

"You're going to church? You just went to that thing at the stadium three nights this week."

"Yeah, I did." He stopped. "I'm glad I did, too."

"Okay." She didn't bat an eye. "If it makes you happy, I'm okay with it. I can't go to church, though. I already promised Katie I'd help her unpack and hang pictures. I have to keep my word."

"Some other time. Soon." He looked at Della steadily.

"Yeah. I do go every once in a while with Van. If I'd go with her, then you know I'd go with you."

"Thanks, Della." He kissed her softly. "That means a lot to me."

She stood on one leg and used the top of her other foot to rub the back of her calf.

"I wanted to talk with you about something important."

Chapter 12

She reached up and rubbed the back of her neck. "Yes?"

Brandon brushed her hand away. "Mosquitoes eating you?"

"I don't know. I don't think so." She shuddered. "All of the sudden, I itch all over."

He tugged her under a light post. One look, and he whistled under his breath. "Babe, you've got a primo crop of hives starting. What are you allergic to?"

"Nothing."

"You'd better be, or you've got some kind of kid disease."

"I can't." She chafed her arm. "I had all my vaccinations."

He yanked out his cell phone and dialed. "Doc. Dry. My girl's got hives."

"I don't need a doctor!"

Brandon's eyes narrowed to deny her assertion as Doc started pelting him with questions. "Yeah. Breathing's fine. No, she says she's not allergic to anything. Okay. Gotcha. What kind of antihistamine?" His cell phone bugged out.

"*Aargh!*" Brandon dialed again, but he got no response. "Come on." He grabbed her hand and started striding toward the corner.

"Brandon!"

"Yeah?"

"You may be Daddy Longlegs, but I can't go that fast—especially in heels." He swept her into his arms and kept walking.

"Your shoulder!"

"Is fine. Stop fussing."

She wound her arm around his neck. "What are you doing?"

"Taking you to the drug store. We're getting you an antihistamine, pronto."

"Now who's fussing?"

"I'm responding, not fussing." Traffic was light, so he didn't pause or go to the corner.

Once he stepped out into the street, Della squawked, "You're jaywalking!"

"Nope," he said as he sped up. "I'm jay-jogging."

She held on tight. "You're going to get us killed."

He stepped up on the curb and shouldered past a few pedestrians and into the drug store. "Babe, as long as you're in my arms, I'll die happy."

Someone clapped him on the back. "Hey, Dry. I think that counts as PDA."

Brandon glanced over his shoulder. "I won't deny the affection, but this isn't a public display. It's an emergency."

"Man, if emergencies look like that, I'm gonna have to become a doctor like my mama wanted me to."

Della laughed self-consciously. "Hi. I'm Della."

"She has hives," Brandon tacked on as he headed down an aisle.

"Grant Luvelle." Grant followed in their wake. "Get calamine lotion. My sister always used it. She's allergic to blueberries."

Brandon stood in the middle of the aisle with Della in his arms. "Two bottles."

"You can put me down, Brandon. I can walk."

His eyes narrowed. "How are you breathing?"

"Just fine. My only problem is, I itch."

He put her on her feet, grabbed the calamine lotion, and ordered Grant, "Go get a basket and the pharmacist."

"Aye-aye!"

"Water," he muttered to himself. He raised his voice. "Lurch—toss me a bottle of water!"

Della yelped as a bottle shot through the air in a perfect spiral that would have done any quarterback proud.

"You need this to wash down the pills." He cranked off the lid in one savage wrench.

"Pills? Just how much stuff do you have in mind?"

"Whatever it takes." He scanned the shelves and started filling his arms with products that looked promising. "Hey, Lurch—what's taking so long? Where's that pharmacist?"

"*Shhh*, Brandon. I'm okay. Really." Della tried to take a box of pills from him and shove it back on the shelf.

He picked up that box again and the one next to it for good measure. "Behave yourself."

"Lurch?"

Figuring it would be a good idea to keep her distracted, Brandon nodded. "Scratching Luvelle's handle. The man can get anyone, anytime, on the radio."

Clenching her hands together to keep from scratching, Della bobbed her head. "Oh, I get it—after the guy on the *Addams Family*." She dropped her voice and intoned, "You rang?"

"Oh, man, she really must be sick if that's the best impersonation she can manage." Lurch marched up with a white-jacketed man. "Help's arrived."

"Ahhh." The pharmacist squinted at Della and nodded. "Diphenhydramine."

"*Gesundheit*," Della said.

Lurch cackled. Brandon glowered at him then focused back on the pharmacist. "Do I have it?"

"No, no. It's not a disease. It's a medication."

Della got the giggles.

"I mean, do I have the dye-pen-hydrant stuff here?" He jerked his chin toward the gear he'd grabbed.

"You must. You're holding half the store," Lurch said.

Della laughed harder.

"At least you're breathing well, young lady," the pharmacist said. "That's good. Do you have any allergies?"

"Of course she does," Brandon snapped in exasperation. "Why do you think she looks like that? Let's get the show on the road here."

The pharmacist exhibited calm that would have impressed Brandon under other circumstances. Now, his demeanor only served to irritate him because the man simply wasn't sufficiently impressed with the gravity of Della's condition. "Did anything sting or bite you?" the pharmacist asked Della.

"No."

"Did you just eat anything unusual? Change to a new soap?"

Della and Brandon exchanged a look. "The—"

"—hot dog," he groaned. "Babe, I'm so sorry." Thinking the yellow stuff in the big pump-top container next to the catsup was mustard, he'd covered their hot dogs with it. Her eyes almost popped out of her head when she took her first bite. He'd teased her about having a sissy mouth, so she took a second bite before he robbed her of it, ate it, and got popcorn.

"I had some double jalapeno nacho cheese sauce," Della told the pharmacist. "Only a little."

"It doesn't take much if you're allergic." The pharmacist ignored everything Brandon gathered. He stooped, took a small box from the lowest shelf then grabbed another type of stuff from above it. "I have it in the regular and non-drowsy variety."

"We'll take both."

Della reached over and helped herself to the box that proclaimed *Non-drowsy* in screaming red letters. "I'll take one of these."

"Nope. Take the regular ones," Brandon insisted. "You need to sleep through this ordeal. You can take the non-drowsy ones tomorrow."

"I'm not going to need them tomorrow!"

"Just in case." Brandon popped one out of the package and had her take it. He grabbed the basket from Lurch, filled it with everything he'd collected, and asked the pharmacist, "What else does she need?"

"I'm telling you, you have half the store there already." Lurch waved toward the basket. "As long as you have calamine lotion, you're set. Oh—and cotton balls. To dab it on."

"It's unnecessary." Della patted Brandon's arm. "Really, I'll be fine."

"You'll be fine," the pharmacist agreed. "But keep her hydrated."

"I have water right here." Della lifted the bottle. "He takes good care of me."

"The diphenhydramine will work shortly. Drink plenty of water and get some rest. You'll be fine, come morning."

Brandon's cell phone rang. "Yeah?" He frowned at the pharmacist. "My man said she needed to take Benadryl. Where is it?"

"She took the generic." The pharmacist scowled. "You navy guys. If you're going to call your medic, why do you bother to ask my opinion?"

"We never go in without backup," Brandon rapped out. "Thanks for the help."

"Yes, thank you," Della chimed in. "I think I feel a little better already."

Brandon snorted. "You look worse."

Lurch followed them toward the register. "Keep it up, Dry. A few more sensitive comments like that, and I'll be here to catch her when she boots you out."

"I don't wear boots," Della declared promptly. "He's stuck with me."

"You don't happen to have a sister, do you?"

"No such luck," Brandon said tersely. "Two big, ugly brothers who are almost as big a pain as you." He chucked a box of Popsicles into the basket then added Della's favorite candy bar.

Della gave up protesting. She let out a long-suffering sigh and scratched her elbow. Brandon opened the Popsicles and stuck one in her hand. "Eat that instead of scratching. It's good for you."

By the time he walked her up to her door, she'd started yawning. "Is your bedroom air-conditioned?"

She shook her head.

"You need a fan. Do you have a fan?"

"Ceiling fan. I'm fine, Brandon."

"You go on up and take a cool shower." He'd already planned out the rest of the night. She'd take a shower and put on her swimsuit. He'd cover her with a whole bottle of the calamine then pour more fluids into her. After that, if her breathing was still okay, he'd let her go to sleep. On the couch. With him sitting across from her, keeping watch.

Smart. Safe.

Besides, he was scared out of his wits. Really, hives were a minor annoyance, but with Della—well, even the little things mattered a lot. *Hey, God? I'm not very good at this prayer stuff, but could You please make Della better?*

"Brandon, are you going to turn the key or not?" Della's baffled tone broke into his prayer. He nodded, and she asked, "What were you thinking?"

"I was praying."

She yawned again. "Any port in a storm."

The time wasn't right for him to tell her. He'd wanted to take time tonight to share his newfound relationship with Christ—to let her know how incredible salvation was. To invite her to discover it for herself. Then everything would be perfect.

Chapter 13

So Daddy threw him out at one o'clock and threatened to melt the fuse box at his place if I ever get hives on a date again." Della thrust one last book onto the shelf.

Katie laughed. "Your dad would do it, too! Here. These go on the next shelf."

"I don't know." Della accepted the next stack of books and started putting them in place. "Daddy's finally getting the idea that Brandon's going to stick around."

"I'm not looking forward to what my dad's going to say when he finds out Jim and I are living together."

Sliding a Bible onto the bookshelf, Della said nothing.

"But it's really none of his business. It's just between Jim and me," Katie said. "And we're engaged. Besides, he and Mom aren't together, so it's not like they're exactly experts on successful relationships."

Uncomfortable with the topic, Della shrugged. "That's it for the books. I thought you wanted me to help get the kitchen set up."

"I already lined the cabinets, so we can dive right in. With all my school loans and stuff, money's tight, but I found this little dollar store that had the neatest organizers. Come on!"

Nesting. . .setting up a home of her own. Della felt a surge of excitement. Brandon had mentioned Nathan's construction firm's next major project would be a housing tract. The high school retrofit and expansion had only two weeks' work to go. How long would it take to get the houses built?

"You know that plastic tub we used for a sink when we went camping? Valene got me five more from the hospital." Katie knelt by the sink. "I thought they'd be great to hold my cleaning supplies."

"Valene gets them for Vanessa to use at the pet shop, too." Della opened a small, heavy box and peered inside. "Hand me the spare ones to hold the packing peanuts around your china."

"Isn't my china beautiful? I talked Jim into buying some. We only bought four place settings because it's so expensive."

"You can list it on your wedding registry." Della carefully put the china in the cabinet Katie indicated.

"Jim suggested we register for camping stuff. I'm not keen on the idea—I'd rather get things for our home. Who wants a tent when they don't have a bed-spread? Jim surprised me. He's usually easy-going, but he dug in his heels. You know how guys are—they don't like to borrow someone else's gear."

"Brandon took me to a surplus place to get my sleeping bag. Jim can talk to him—he'd make sound recommendations on the sturdiest stuff."

Katie sat back and grinned. "You light up when you talk about him. Sounds serious to me."

"It is."

"The real thing?" Katie perked up.

"I love him with all my heart."

⚜

Brandon sat down in the gazebo in Nathan's backyard and stretched out his legs. "So when I called this morning, her dad said she was fine."

"Good." Nathan threw a battered tennis ball across the lawn for Licorice to fetch. "Jeff got hives once when we ran out of milk and I tried that powdered stuff. Didn't last long but gave me a real scare."

Licorice raced back and dropped the ball at Nathan's feet. Nathan threw it again. "He sure misses Jeff. I do, too."

Brandon chuckled. "You just put him on the bus after church."

"But it's so quiet without him. I'm not sure he's really ready to go away to camp for a whole week."

"I'm sure you'll find stuff to fill the time. You could take Van out for a fancy supper—maybe ask Jim where he took Katie to propose. Della said it was the most romantic place around."

"Not a bad idea. As long as Vanessa's having a good day. Her morning sickness comes and goes with no rhyme or reason."

Thunk. The tennis ball landed between Brandon's feet. He leaned over, picked it up, and tossed it. "I've decided to surprise Della. I'll take her to the beach at sunrise. She'll think it's just for an early morning run. Later that evening, I'll do the candlelight dinner thing, but—"

"Wait." Nathan's smile faded. "Surprise her?"

"Yep." Brandon felt downright smug. "Ring's a beaut. Little though. Size five."

"I didn't realize you two were that serious."

"Crazy serious." Brandon chuckled. "Man, I'm not even embarrassed to admit I'm wildly in love."

Nathan groaned as he rubbed his forehead. "Have you talked with Della about Jesus?"

"I wanted to, but the hives ruined the evening." He watched as Nathan's face went grim. "What's wrong?"

"We need to pray for Della's salvation."

"I already have."

Nathan sat in silence. Brandon could see how he struggled to frame his words. "Whatever you have to say, spit it out."

"You asked the cost of salvation."

"Yeah. And you told me Jesus paid it."

Nathan nodded. "It's only by grace that we're saved. But we also discussed obedience."

Instead of continuing to play fetch with Lick, Brandon stroked the Lab. "I'm the first to admit I don't always like the rules, but I play by them. So what does this have to do with Della?"

"It means for the two of you to seek God's blessing on your marriage, you both need to be believers."

"Hold on." Brandon bolted to his feet. "My love for her isn't conditional."

"Your love isn't, but biblically, your marriage is." Nathan rose.

"You show it to me. Prove it. I don't believe it."

Nathan got his Bible and leafed toward the back. He scanned a page then passed over the thick leather Bible. "Second Corinthians, chapter six."

Brandon took the Bible and started reading, *"And working together with Him, we also urge you not to receive the grace of God in vain—for He says, 'AT THE ACCEPTABLE TIME I LISTENED TO YOU, AND ON THE DAY OF SALVATION I HELPED YOU.' Behold, now is 'THE ACCEPTABLE TIME,' behold, now is 'THE DAY OF SALVATION.'"* He looked up triumphantly. "See? Now is the time. Not just for me. For Della, too."

"Man, I pray you're right—that she hears the good news and asks Christ into her heart. But you need to read the rest of the chapter—especially the last part."

Brandon scowled. He skimmed through the next verses, then hit fourteen and fifteen. *Do not be bound together with unbelievers; for what partnership have righteousness and lawlessness, or what fellowship has light with darkness? Or what harmony has Christ with Belial, or what has a believer in common with an unbeliever?* "What's Belial?" he asked hoarsely.

"Satan."

"So if you're not with God, then you're with the devil," Brandon said heavily. He didn't need any further explanation. There it stared back at him in black and white—it wasn't just Nathan's opinion.

"Being married means blending yourself—not just physically and emotionally, but spiritually, too. You haven't proposed yet. My advice is to pray for Della's salvation. In the meantime, asking her to marry you would be wrong."

"God wouldn't have given me Della only to take her away."

Nathan's eyes shone with pity. "I said the same thing about Evie. She was my first wife. Died of kidney failure."

"Hey, man, I'm really sorry. But if your point is that God gave you Vanessa and you're happy, that's fine—it's your story." Brandon's throat ached with the strain of trying not to shout. "I'm not going to be happy with anyone else. I don't want anyone else. I love *her*."

✝

"I've missed you so much!" Della dove off the porch and into Brandon's arms. His arms closed tightly around her, and his head dipped, but he didn't kiss her. Della understood. Affection belonged between them, not as a show for others.

"Get her out of here, will you?" Daddy groused. "She's been moping ever since her hives spoiled that date."

Brandon set her down.

"I'm sorry. Did I hurt your shoulder?" She reached up to rub the place where a wicked scar sliced from beneath the edge of his tank top.

Brandon grabbed her hand and twined their fingers. "I'm fine."

Della didn't say anything more about it. He refused to admit it ever bothered him and hated to be reminded of his injury. "So where are we going?"

"To The Spindles."

She did a hop-skip beside him. "Is it official? Nathan approved?"

"Yes. Vanessa says it's a perfect name, too. I'm even having a sign painted."

Della beamed. "When you started putting all of that fancy gingerbread trim back on, the name just came to me. It sounds elegant. Old-fashioned."

"It's been a challenge to match some of that woodwork." Brandon talked about the renovation and a few little things he planned to do in order to complete the project. "Just the finishing touches," he said. "Then we're going to have an open house. We're already getting calls about booking meetings and conferences."

"You need to have a 'No Red Punch' policy. Red punch stains carpeting and floors."

"Good idea." He flashed a smile at her. "Anything else?"

"Not that I can think of offhand." They rounded a corner, and she caught her breath. "Oh, Brandon! The landscaping is done!"

"Like it?"

"I love it! That little arbor off to the side looks inviting, and the fountain! Oh, look at it!"

He chortled. "If I never see another fountain again, it'll be too soon. I must have looked at five hundred of them to find the one that looked okay."

"Well, you found just the right one." She hopped out of the jeep and stuck her hand into the cool water. "Take a picture of this view and have postcards made."

"I already took a picture for the website. Come look inside." He chafed her wet hand to dry it off. "I wanted to put in cobblestones, but they're too dangerous. Someone would twist an ankle and sue."

He opened the door.

"*Oooh*, Brandon!" Della crossed the threshold and stepped into the center of the entryway. Slowly turning to take in the whole view, she didn't even want to blink. "It's incredible!"

"Vanessa and her mom met with an interior decorator. I gave them a basic list of essentials. What do you think of the furniture?"

"Ellen always has impeccable taste. It's elegant, but inviting. Some of the styles from that period were stuffy, but this—it just oozes 'Welcome!'"

They went from room to room and finally ended up back at the entry. Brandon led her over to a window seat. During the tour, Della kept sensing something was up. She didn't want to rush him. By the time she sat down, she could hardly stay put. Suddenly, his behavior made sense. She couldn't have asked for a more romantic place to receive a proposal.

Smiling up at him, she patted the cushion beside herself.

Brandon sat then stood back up again. Della didn't want to spoil the moment by laughing at him. It had to be nerve-racking for a man to summon the courage to ask a woman to marry him.

Not that he had any reason to worry that she'd refuse.

"Babe, I brought you here because I came to the most important decision of my life in this room. I hope you will, too."

His eyes went the color of buffed pewter, and he gently cupped her hand in his.

Her heart filled to overflowing.

Chapter 14

"Give my heart to Jesus?" she echoed his words in disbelief.

Brandon nodded. "Yes. I used to think being good was enough. It's not. I can't do it on my own merits. Christ died for me. Accepting that fact is the only way I'll ever make it to heaven."

Della snatched her hand from his.

Brandon's heart twisted. He could see the confusion in her eyes. "Let me explain." He crouched on the floor in front of her. "God loves you."

"Well, since He does, then He won't damn me to hell."

"No, babe. It doesn't work that way."

She drew back from him. "Brandon, if you're happy with doing the whole church-and-Jesus thing, that's fine by me. You've never asked me to compromise on things that matter most to me. I won't ask that of you, either."

Lord, this isn't going how I wanted it to.

"I'll even go to church with you sometimes. You already know that."

"It's not just a behavior. It's a change inside," he tried to explain.

"I'll love you, no matter how you change." Hurt shone in her eyes. "Why do I have to change just to suit you?"

"It's not just to suit me. I love you, no matter what."

Her chin lifted. "Then I don't see what the fuss is about."

"I love you with my heart. I love God with my soul."

Her brows puckered. "It's not some kind of competition."

He shook his head sadly. "No, it's not. Listen, I'm not trying to be pushy. I wanted to share something precious with you because I love you."

"Well, you shared it. I'm happy for you." Her smile looked forced. "So what else did you want to do today?"

He'd hoped she'd see the truth and respond, but how many times had he heard the salvation message and not taken action? Being forceful would only push her away. She'd closed the subject, and he'd play along for now. There would be plenty of chances for him to witness to her. Brandon twirled a lock of her hair around his finger. "What would you like to do?"

She thought for a moment. "Why don't we go to Balboa Park and wander around the museums?"

"Only if you promise we won't get lost in the Aerospace Museum." He tugged on that tress. "Last time, I never got to the Timken."

Della laughed. "How was I to know you liked fine art more than a bunch of military artifacts? I was trying to make sure you enjoyed yourself."

"Babe, I could lead you through that place blindfolded. I spent almost every weekend of my early teens there. The day we went there, I was far more interested in the woman by my side than anything on display."

"And when we get into the Timken, will you still feel that way?" She batted her lashes.

"Hmmm," Brandon teased. "I don't know. That place is small, but the pieces they have on display are incredible. You, on the other hand. . ."

"Brandon!"

He grinned. "Gotcha!" He winked. "In my eyes, you are God's greatest work of art."

✝

Signing her name with a flourish, Della accepted the shipment. From the label, she knew exactly what it contained: her dress! Of all times for it to arrive, why now? She had a nitpicky mother of the flower girl who didn't like the dress the bride had chosen for the little girl to wear. It took every shred of Della's diplomacy to deal with the woman and her whiny daughter even before the interruption of the shipment's delivery. Now, all she really wanted to do was shoo them out, flip over the OUT FOR LUNCH sign, and relish the sight of her very own wedding gown.

But that wasn't professional. She tamped down her wishes, bumped the box toward the back of the shop, and returned to her customers.

"Let's have Audrey try on the dress," she said brightly. "It's one of those styles that always looks so much cuter on."

"But it's pink," her mother repeated for the third time as she smoothed her hand down her daughter's copper-red hair.

"Yes, and it's very feminine." Della tried to turn what had been intended as a flaw into a selling point.

"I want my daughter to wear white."

"You mentioned that on the phone," Della said in her most diplomatic tone. "But the bride insists on all of the party wearing pink."

"I like pink, Mommy," Audrey whined.

"Well, then, this is just right!" Snagging the dress from the hook, Della slipped between mother and child and nudged her into a dressing room. "You're a big girl, Audrey. Why don't you put this on, and we'll have Mommy keep her eyes closed when you come out. I'll zip you up and stand you on that platform over by the big mirror, just like the brides do when they model their gowns."

"Yeah!" Audrey couldn't shut the door fast enough.

Looking thoroughly disgruntled, her mother muttered, "Pink," and headed for the rack of children's-sized formalwear.

Usually, brides came in and were part of this event. In this case, the bride intentionally skipped being present for the fitting. She'd confessed to Della that the little girl was sweet as could be, but nothing ever pleased the mother.

No novice to such circumstance, Della knew how best to handle things. She had suggested the bride give the mother some nominal choices regarding the accessories. "Anything," the bride had begged, "just get Audrey into the dress!"

Della approached the mother. "It'll take Audrey a little time."

"She's only seven. I don't know why you think she can get into that dress by herself."

"I'm sure it'll be difficult." Della nodded agreement and cast a glance over her shoulder then lowered her voice conspiratorially. "That's why I have her try here. It'll make her glad to have your help on the Big Day."

"Oh. Yes. Good."

A little soprano called out, "I can't do up the zipper thing. Mommy, don't look!"

Della winked at the mother, who suddenly became an ally.

"I'll wait over here, honey."

"Actually," Della paused then pointed toward a display case—the one where she and Brandon had met. "The bride left it to your discretion whether Audrey wears gloves. I have both lace and cotton ones, if you think she should wear them. Why don't you take a quick peek?"

Della zipped up Audrey's dress, led her to the platform, and smiled as the little girl squealed in delight at her reflection. "Let's make sure everything is just right before—"

"Oh, Audrey!"

"Aren't I pretty, Mommy?"

Della held her breath.

"Honey, you are beautiful. Just look at you!" Her mother drew closer.

By the time they left, Audrey's mother couldn't stop gushing. "I love pink. People always told me redheads couldn't wear it, so I didn't buy any for Audrey. I can't believe how silly I was. The truth was right in front of me, and I never saw it!"

As soon as she shut and locked the door, Della flipped over the sign and dashed toward the box. She'd no more than picked it up when someone started banging on the door. Letting out a resigned sigh, she set down the box and turned around.

"Della!" Vanessa stood there, rapping on the glass like a demented woodpecker.

"I'm coming."

"No!" Vanessa shouted through the glass. "Hurry! Go shut off the electrical main!"

Since their shops adjoined, they shared the same box. It took a lot to rattle Vanessa, so Della reacted at once. She ran through the shop, out the back, and over to the fuse box. Once she shut down the power, she dashed back to Vanessa.

"What—"

"Oh, you'll never believe it," Vanessa used her fingers to squeeze water out of her hair.

"It's you. Of course I'd believe it."

"I'd just finished grooming Mrs. Rosetti's terrier. She's such a dear. So is her dog. Anyway, I went into the back to rinse out the tub, and the faucet broke."

"So. . . ," Della ventured slowly, "you want me to call a plumber?"

"No, I'll have Nathan come fix it. I need you to call your dad. When the faucet broke, I had it on full blast. The shower massage thing turned into a bull-whip. It jerked out of my hands."

"You're okay? You didn't slip?"

"I'm fine."

Envisioning the five-foot-long fiberglass hose still wreaking havoc, Della headed back through the shop. "I'll turn off the water main, too. What about Mrs. Rosetti's dog?"

"She took him home before it happened," Vanessa called. "Hey, you don't have any towels in your back room, do you?"

All the years of listening to her brothers and father didn't help. They'd never let her come close when they were working. Brandon, on the other hand, had commented on the shared utilities one night when they'd left the shop. Because of him, Della knew where the shut-offs were.

She snagged a cordless phone and a linen tablecloth as she headed back to Vanessa. Once she'd wrapped Van in the tablecloth, Della froze. "I didn't think—are you sure you're okay? Van, with all of the wiring you have for the radiant heaters, you could have electrocuted yourself!"

"I'm fine. Really. Your dad insisted on the rubber floor mats. They probably saved my life. I jumped out of there and came running for help." She let out a weak laugh. "I don't think I've ever prayed so hard, so fast!"

Della knew Nathan and her dad were both supposed to be at The Spindles today. She called Brandon. She'd no more than started to explain what had happened when he boomed, "Are you okay?"

"Yes. It was at Van's—"

"Is Van all right?"

"Yes—"

A tussle sounded, and Nathan's voice came over the phone. "Van—is—"

"She's right here." Della handed her the phone. Three minutes later, while Vanessa was still talking to her husband, Brandon's jeep screeched to the curb.

He and Nathan bolted from it as Daddy's truck rounded the corner and skidded to a halt. The fact that two police cars pulled up behind with lights and sirens only added to the effect.

Brandon grabbed Della and held her tight. Her dad stood behind her, yanking her back toward him. In the midst of their tug o' war, Della watched as Nathan scooped up Vanessa—tablecloth, phone, and all, and plowed toward a cruiser.

"Sir—"

"My wife just about got electrocuted. Get us to the hospital." The one squad car left.

Della remained sandwiched between Brandon and her father as the other officer approached. "You men were speeding."

Brandon yanked Della closer still. "I was going faster."

ᚶ

"I don't understand how anything so right can be wrong." Brandon could barely get the words past the tightness in his throat.

Nathan squeezed his shoulder—the bad one. The pain didn't even begin to compare with the anguish Brandon felt.

They stood at the head of the stairs, looking down as the caterer carried the last bag of trash away.

Della, radiant in a russet-colored dress, thanked the worker as Vanessa closed the door. The women shared an exuberant hug. "Oh, it's been a splendid affair!"

"Everyone loves it," Vanessa agreed. "I'll bet Nathan has this place booked solid for the next six months!"

The two women chattered as they headed for the kitchen.

Brandon gripped the banister until his nails dug grooves in the highly polished oak. "I love her."

"I know you do," Nathan said in an equally muted tone.

"We're opposites on just about any level. She's a princess; I'm a jock. She's—well." He groaned. "It works for us. We're a perfect fit. Why can't we be different about God?"

Nathan jerked his head toward one of the upstairs business suites. They went in, shut the door, and sat across from one another in the made-for-big-men upholstered chairs. The silence between them ached.

Finally, Nathan asked, "Have you prayed about it?"

"I have. I can't. I do." Brandon banged his fist on the arm of his chair. "God must be sick of hearing me. I've been begging Him for three weeks solid."

"God isn't sick of hearing you. He'd love to have Della as His daughter. Ultimately, she has to make the decision, though."

"What's so wrong about me marrying her? I'd get her to come to church. She'd hear the gospel. I can't see anything wrong with that."

"It's tough." Nathan winced. "But you're assuming a lot—that she'll eventually make a decision to follow Christ."

"She has to."

"There aren't any guarantees. We live by what we value. Since you've been saved, you're using your time differently. Can you honestly say that Della wouldn't be jealous of the time you spend alone in the Word and in prayer? You said she's uncomfortable when you pray at meals now."

"She could get used to it." Brandon resented the question. He resented the need for the question. Why couldn't Della just see the light?

"You don't marry with the expectation of changing your mate. You have to say your vows with the understanding that you fully accept Della as she is. It'll make for an unhappy marriage if she feels like she doesn't measure up to your expectations or hopes."

Nathan's words held a lot of wisdom.

Brandon didn't want to think about it though. Given enough time, surely, Della would have to. . .but his thoughts came to a grinding halt. Wishing for something didn't make it happen.

"And what about your children? You'll want to dedicate them to the Lord and train them up to know Him." Nathan's words hit hard. "A mother's example is vital."

Brandon raked his fingers through his hair. "I can't make this decision. Not yet."

"Hey, you guys!" Vanessa's voice cut into the conversation. "Stop hiding away and gloating alone. You promised to take us out for a celebration dinner!"

Nathan popped to his feet and headed toward the door. He cast a quick glance back at Brandon. "Take a minute." He left and shut the door.

Brandon could hear Della's heels clicking up the wooden stairs. Every beat sounded just like a nail being driven into a coffin.

⁜

"Guess which fork," Della teased as dessert arrived. They'd gone out to supper with Vanessa and Nathan—an elegant dinner at a fabulous restaurant. Nathan and Brandon both complained about the "arsenal" of silverware on the table, but neither had a bad thing to say about the wonderful food and service.

Brandon didn't pause for a moment. He reached over and swiped hers. "This one."

Laughter bubbled out of her. Brandon's playfulness cropped up at the most unexpected times, but whenever it did, it never ceased to delight her. She held out her hand.

His brow hiked in unspoken challenge.

"That's cheating." She wiggled her fingers in a beckoning motion. "I know you always play by the rules."

"You can share," Vanessa suggested.

"Are you kidding?" Nathan gave his wife a disbelieving look. "Della ordered chocolate cream pie. No man in his right mind deprives a woman of chocolate."

Brandon laid the fork back in Della's hand. The silver felt warm from his touch. "Truer words were never spoken. Get this: Della keeps a stash of chocolate behind the cash register."

"With all of those expensive gowns?" Nathan gave Van an astonished look. "Did you know that?"

"Of course she did." Della gave the men a you-have-to-be-kidding-me look. "Girlfriends don't hold out on one another."

"In fact, Della invited me over to taste test the chocolates." Vanessa grinned. "We decided on the best ones."

Brandon gave Nathan an I-told-you-so look. "Women and their chocolate."

"Since when did you care about chocolate?" Della tapped the back of his hand with her fork. "When we went hiking, you took away my chocolate and made me carry beef jerky!"

"Chocolate melts. The sugar attracts insects. It's a refined carbohydrate, so you don't get long-term energy from it."

"See?" Della cast a knowing look at Vanessa. "He not only plays by the rules, he can quote them." The waiter served the desserts. Della cut a bite of her chocolate cream pie and held it up to Brandon's mouth. "I'm going to tempt you. Forget the rules and live a little."

His eyes darkened, and for a moment, Della had the strange feeling she'd said something wrong. Embarrassment swept over her. Had they mistaken her words to mean something racy?

"Oh, eat that." Vanessa picked up her own fork and dug into her mud pie. "Della, just don't blink, or Brandon will inhale his pie and yours."

Everyone chuckled, but the tension didn't dissipate. Della couldn't shake the odd sensation that she was missing something important, but she didn't want to ruin the supper by asking. This was Brandon's big day. He'd proven his skills by completing a detailed, difficult renovation. Nothing was going to dampen the joy.

҂

"Something's wrong," Della said as they sat in the cool sand the next morning. Tendrils of early morning fog swirled around them, but they'd finished their run and were warm.

But Brandon's blood ran cold. "What do you mean?"

She shrugged. "I don't know. I can't figure it out. Everything used to be so easy between us. Suddenly, it's strained. I don't get it."

The time's come. Brandon whispered a prayer for a miracle. . .and if that miracle didn't happen, for the strength to do what he had to. He reached over and folded her hand in his.

Chapter 15

I 've changed, Della. I'm a new man." The confused look in her eyes made him continue, "When you accept Christ, you're a new person."

"Don't be ridiculous. You're the same man."

"No, babe, I'm not. I've come to know the Lord, and that makes me different—different from who I used to be, and"—he paused and added quietly—"different from you."

A wariness crossed her features. "I told you that doesn't matter to me. I'll do the church thing with you sometimes."

"That's a good start, and I appreciate that you're willing to meet me halfway."

"But?" Her voice nearly broke on that one syllable.

"But it's not enough. Some things in life can't be halfway."

"What are you saying, Brandon? That if I don't get religious, I'm not good enough for you?"

"I'm not religious, babe. What I am is forgiven."

"You're a good person. So am I. We had this talk and agreed that was enough. Suddenly, you're changing the rules, and I have to change or I don't measure up? Give me a break, Brandon. Those rules don't matter. Christians don't even keep their own rules. Look at Katie and Jim—they're Christians, and they're living together."

"We both know they shouldn't." He didn't know how to respond to her comment. For people to call themselves Christians and live against God's precepts didn't just affect their own lives. It also ruined their witness. The pastor had a term for that—being a stumbling block. How could non-Christians understand what it meant to be different—to be set apart, when Christians acted just like non-Christians?

He let out a big sigh. "The wrong things others who call themselves Christians do make me sad, and I can't condone their actions."

"So if they do something wrong and God still loves them, then He can still love us. We're not even doing anything."

"There are going to be times when I blow it. I'm not saying I'm perfect. But when I do mess up, I'll go to the Lord and ask forgiveness and try to follow Him more closely. I'm responsible for my own behavior."

"But you're not responsible for my decisions. Just because I don't wear a cross and sing hymns, it's not your fault."

"Being a Christian isn't just something you do; it's what you are on the inside."

"Well Katie and Jim say they're Christians. I don't see any difference. Why are they any better than I am? I'm not sleeping with you. I haven't done anything wrong." Tears filled her big brown eyes. "You want me to buy into this whole God-and-religion thing, and I don't. All of a sudden, who I am isn't good enough for you. I can't lie, Brandon. So we have this—this"—she slashed her hand up and down—"this *wall* between us. I didn't put it there. You did. Isn't my love for you enough?"

Pain washed over him, lapped and pulled at him like the outgoing tide. He cupped her cheek. "Babe, you're the only woman I've ever loved. You're the only woman I will ever love—but I can't lead you on."

"You're not leading me on. I know what the score is. We're different in lots of ways, but we get along just fine."

"This is the one thing that's not negotiable. I'll wait for you. I'll pray for you. But I can't keep dating you or ask you to marry me until you've given your heart to Jesus."

She sat there in stunned silence. Slowly, her eyes filled and huge tears began to roll down her cheeks. "You don't mean that."

God, help me. He rasped, "I do."

She fell apart on him. Brandon held her as she soaked his T-shirt with her tears. Some of his joined hers. He'd made the decision because it was the only honorable and righteous thing to do—but the anguish was unbearable. The depth of Della's emotions only plunged the dagger more deeply into him. He'd done this—and he couldn't do a thing to change it.

╬

"I can't believe it," Della told Katie two days later. "Van and Val were my best friends in high school. We were all still so tight—and then *poof!* They just side with Brandon."

"That's rough," Katie sympathized.

"I still can't believe it. We were so right together. Everything went like a fairy tale; then he just dumped me."

The ice clinked in their glasses as Della wiped away her tears. "Van spouted off something about him being a Christian so we'd be 'unequally yoked,' as if we're stupid oxen."

"Oh, yeah." Katie nodded. "Now I get it." She hastily held up her hands. "Don't get me wrong. I think it stinks. You and Brandon make a great pair."

"So then what's the problem? He can go to church. I already promised him that. What more does he want?"

Trailing the tip of her fingernail in a water drop on the tabletop, Katie sighed. "From what Jim's said, Brandon's a play-things-by-the-book sort of guy. Christians make rules. They think there's only right and wrong—nothing in between. That leaves you here." She made a wet dot on one side of the water streak on the table, "and him here." She made another dot on the opposite side then looked up.

"You and Jim aren't like that. You accept me just the way I am. Why can't God? Why can't Brandon?"

"God will accept you—but there's a hook. You have to accept Him as your personal Lord and follow Him. That's what Brandon wants out of you, too."

"Why can't you Christians get your story straight? You're a Christian. You aren't forcing me to agree with you or be damned to hell."

Katie shrugged. "I'm not hard-core Christian. I was once—back in high school. But life happens, you know? My parents split up, and God didn't make it better. I still believe in Jesus, but I don't feel like I have to walk around quoting the Bible and show up in church every time they open the doors."

"Then I don't see the difference." Della couldn't hold back the tears. "I figure God is there somewhere, too. Why should I have to conform to their rules just so I'm good enough to love?"

Squirming in her seat, Katie shrugged. "I don't know."

✝

"Stevens."

Brandon glanced up from the blueprints and knew he was in for a rough time. Della's dad and brothers looked ready to electrocute him. "Yeah."

"I told you back at the start, if you made my baby girl cry, I'd—"

Brandon nodded once, curtly. He didn't need to hear the threat. If having the Valentine men beat him to oblivion would solve the problem, take away Della's pain, or mute his own, Brandon would willingly stand still and let them take him down.

"You hurt her." Gabe's accusation hung in the air.

"I know." He didn't bother to hide the ache in his voice.

"You love her," Justin ground out. "We all know you do."

Brandon looked him in the eye. "I can't deny that. But it's not enough."

"Not enough?" Della's father bellowed in outrage.

"Sir, I respect your daughter. I can't ask her to change."

"My daughter is perfect. She doesn't need to change."

"I've accepted Christ as my personal Savior. Because of that, I'm not the same man I used to be."

"You're no man at all to hurt my sister," Justin sneered.

"I'd hurt her every day by wishing she were something she isn't. I can't do that to her." Brandon rested his palms on the table. "I told her I'd pray for her. That I'll wait. I'll have faith that someday—"

"Forget it." Gabe slashed the air. "Just forget it. Della doesn't need you and your religion. It's you who's not good enough for her."

Nathan sauntered up. "Gentlemen?"

Della's father shook his finger at Brandon. "As long as he works for you, I don't. Power Electric is canceling our contract bid on the housing development."

"I'm sorry you feel that way. I value Brandon."

"You made your choice." Della's family stalked off.

Brandon stared down at the blueprint. It was the one he'd chosen as the home he'd buy for his future with Della. No matter where he turned, reminders of his loss swamped him. He rasped, "I thought God was supposed to give me peace about this."

"This is a different kind of war. Peace doesn't mean an absence of struggle. It means you're certain that, no matter what happens, God wins in the end."

"Ultimately, God wins the war, but I never wanted to put Della in the line of fire. What kind of man am I to let the woman I love become a battle casualty?"

"You're a man of faith," Nathan stated firmly. "God can bind every wound and heal the brokenhearted. Put your trust in Him."

Brandon thumped a weight down on a fluttering end of the blueprint. "I used to think only weak men turned to God. I'm coming to discover it takes more strength to believe than to deny Him."

🌴

"I'm sure he's a nice guy, but—"

"Oh, come on." Katie yanked on the cord to close the blinds in her apartment then nudged one of Jim's shoes toward the corner, next to the backpack overflowing with her new textbooks. "You have to quit moping, Della. I already told Harvey all about you. We'll double-date. You can choose where you want to go. Saturday night—"

"I'm already busy Saturday night." Della jumped on the opportunity to avoid another of Katie's matchmaking attempts. "I know you're trying to help me, but I need some time."

"I can't help it if I know dozens of guys. I'm surrounded by them in school. Brainy, hunky engineering and architectural majors. You could do a lot worse."

Della didn't respond. Katie had a habit of asserting herself, and most of the time it was okay, but this wasn't one of those times. After Manny just "happened" to run into them at a movie, Della didn't say anything. It felt like a set-up, but she didn't want to make unfounded accusations. Lunch with Ashley seemed like a nice break—until Ashley turned out to be "a true Southern gentleman" with an obsessive need to cut his sandwich into precise, one-inch squares.

"It'll be fun," Katie singsonged.

"I told you, I already have plans."

"You're serious!" Landing on the sofa with a pounce, Katie squealed. "Tell me all about it."

"I'm going on a weekend hike."

"You? Hike?" Hysterical laughter poured out of her. "I've been camping with you. You could barely make it with"—she caught herself—"all of our help."

"I'm an independent woman. Whatever I don't have in ability, I make up for in effort."

Looking thoroughly unconvinced, Katie squirmed for a minute then brightened. "Oh, I get it. You know with skiing how they have the little bunny hills and the advanced runs? You're just going to do one of the little ones, right?"

"No. It's a real hike. Five days."

"Five days!" Katie gawked at her as if she'd lost her mind.

Della nodded with far more confidence than she felt. "It's real camping. Pup tents. Boots and backpacks and marshmallows." Memories of toasting marshmallows and snuggling by Brandon at the campfire threatened to swamp Della. She straightened her shoulders and suppressed the memories. "My boots are broken in, and I'm great at toasting marshmallows. I'll do just fine."

"You're going to break your neck." Katie shook her head. "I've never heard a more ridiculous idea in my life."

"Hey—where's the support? Friends are supposed to cheer you on, not knock you down."

"Friends," Katie said in a doomsday voice, "are supposed to stop you when you're doing something dumb." She pulled a throw pillow onto her lap and hugged it. After a pause, she asked quietly, "Does anyone else know you're doing this?"

Della knew she meant Brandon, but she purposefully ignored the thinly veiled question. Pasting on a cheerful smile, she proclaimed, "Ellen Zobel is watching the shop for me. She always does such a great job. I don't know if she's told Van or Val. That whole clan sits together in church, so they'll find out soon enough."

"I don't think this is such a bright idea."

"I'll be fine. I'm going with a group—Rugged Adventure."

"Never heard of them. Did you check them out?"

Della leaned back into the sofa. Finally, a question that didn't feel like the Spanish Inquisition! "I looked all over. You know me and the Internet. I narrowed it down to three different companies, and this one is close-by and had an opening for dates that Ellen could cover the shop for me. It worked out perfectly. You should see their brochure on the Internet."

Katie waggled her brows. "Are the guides hunks?"

"You're impossible." Della swallowed one last sip of coffee then stood. "I need to get going. I have a lot to do." After giving Katie a hug, she ran a few errands before heading home.

Sitting at the curb was Brandon's jeep.

Chapter 16

Brandon knew the minute she drove up. Her brothers and dad had been in the garage when he arrived. They came out to "greet" him. Their idea of hospitality left a lot to be desired. He put up with it though. Della was more important than their anger.

Brandon ignored Gabe's latest snarl and looked right over the fuming man's shoulder to see Della slide from her car. Dainty heels. Swirly lavender dress. Big, hurt eyes.

His heart wrenched.

She turned to go into the house.

Brandon took a step forward.

The Valentine men formed a wall.

Brandon didn't want to fight them. It would be ugly. All three would be in a bloody heap in a few seconds.

"Della, I need a minute with you."

"Nobody here cares what you want," Mr. Valentine roared. "Della needs you to get out of here."

Slowly, Della turned. She refused to look Brandon in the eyes. "Say what you came to say."

It didn't escape his notice that she kept several feet between them. Her vulnerability tore at him. Brandon wanted nothing more than to shove her family apart and gather her into his arms, but he didn't have the right. He cleared his throat.

"The hike you're going on—it's not safe." In revealing that, he knew she'd realize someone had talked with him about her. She didn't need to know who. Fact was, Ellen told Van and Val, who both told their husbands. Jordan and Nathan discussed it, and Nathan came to him. He hadn't known the details, though, until Katie called him. Della didn't have a clue that so many people truly cared about her.

Since they'd broken up, she'd withdrawn from almost everyone. Van and Val both said once Della knew they supported his decision on a biblical basis, she'd avoided them.

She held her purse like a shield. "I'm going."

"It's not safe, Della." He strove to reason with her, but from the way she hung back and stared off at nothing warned him she wasn't receptive to what he came to say. Still, he had to try. "I checked into it. Rugged Adventure is a two-bit, seat-of-the-pants—"

"Rugged Adventure is a business. They know what they're doing."

He changed tactics. "Then I'll go along. Just as a friend. Just to be sure—"

"No." She finally looked him in the eyes. "You're not my friend. I could never be just friends with you. Leave me alone, Brandon." She pivoted and headed toward the porch.

Brandon watched as her shoulders began to shake. She'd started weeping, and he was powerless.

Thump.

Air whooshed out of him from being sucker-punched. Brandon didn't defend himself.

Justin glowered and kept his fists raised. "You made her cry."

"I'm more sorry than you'll ever know." Brandon got into the jeep and left. He went to the beach and ran several miles. The steady beat of feet pounding the sand didn't bring oblivion. All it did was punctuate the unending waves of grief at having hurt the only woman he'd ever love.

Finally, he walked to cool down and sat in the icy solitude of the star-blanketed beach. *God, don't let her hurt like this. Do whatever it takes. If she's never going to come to You, then let her fall in love with someone who will make her happy. I'll take the pain. I'll handle the loneliness. Just please, God—don't make Della pay for my decision to follow You.*

⸸

"We'll make camp here tonight."

Della watched in disbelief as Chet unbuckled his backpack and let it drop to the ground. The guide chose a lousy location. They were close to water—too close, because the water wasn't moving much at all. It smelled brackish. The clearing was large enough to handle their group, but the ground sloped. The wind cut through at a nasty angle, too.

Ten other hikers struggled out of their gear. Della decided not to give her opinion. Resigned to slapping on extra bug repellant, she decided to position herself between other tents so they'd serve as nominal windbreaks.

Chet sauntered up. "Della, you'll be with Misty and Madeline."

"I thought you said they're two-man tents," she said.

He studied her from head to foot and shrugged. "Man. You're all woman, and—"

"Hold it right there." She glowered at him.

"Hey, I'm not trying to come onto you or anything." He waved his hand as if to erase the words. "I meant to say, you're all women. The other two are small. Three of you'll fit fine."

She didn't say another word. He'd gotten the message that she wasn't about to put up with any flirting. Still, just about the last thing she wanted was to share a tent with the two bickering teens. The sisters didn't want to be here, and they'd made no secret of that fact. If tonight went badly, Della decided she'd have cause to ask for a reassignment. For now, she wanted to put up the tent and eat.

Rugged Adventure outfitted its hikers—but for a small fortune. Della had borrowed Gabe's backpack and brought her own sleeping bag and hip mat. A trip to the surplus place filled in the rest of the essential gear. Seeing the poor quality of the others' sleeping bags made her glad she'd seen to her own equipment.

"Tents!" the other worker shouted as he dropped bundles every few feet. The fact that one of the employees carried the tents had seemed like a great idea. Della didn't feel capable of toting the additional weight. Now that she saw the flimsy nylon structures, she consoled herself with the fact that California Septembers weren't especially cold. They'd brought five, two-man tents. With ten campers, two workers. . . The math simply didn't add up.

"I guess we'd better pitch this thing," Della said to Misty.

"The only thing Misty is pitching is a fit," Madeline said as she kicked the small bundle.

"All I care about is having a warm, dry place to sleep." Della methodically opened the bundle and started fitting together the fiberglass framing poles. The girls disappeared, so she ended up doing the work by herself. Once she had the tent up, Della started driving in stakes.

Chet came over. "Here. I'll do the rest." He took a stake, shoved it straight down into the ground, and banged on it with a hammer.

It's wrong. It should go in at an angle, just like Brandon showed me. Especially with the wind, we'll need it secured. "I can do this. Really. Why don't you help someone else?"

"Not a problem. It'll only take a minute." He flashed her a smile. "Besides, it gives me an excuse not to cook."

"What's for supper?"

"Shish kabobs. Packed 'em frozen, and they'll be thawed and ready to stick on the fire."

"Sounds good. I'm hungry." She smiled, even though he pounded in another stake the wrong way.

Supper tasted great. The day's activity and cool air sharpened her appetite. Della decided the trip was working out well enough. There were bound to be a few glitches here and there, but for the most part, the group seemed happy. A few songs at the campfire, rich hot chocolate, and they turned in for the night. Misty and Maddy both argued about the limited space. They complained about the hard ground.

Della wished she'd brought earplugs. She burrowed into her sleeping bag and tried to ignore them. Then she decided she'd wished they hadn't fallen asleep. At least their arguing served as a diversion. Now she couldn't stop the flood of memories from the times Brandon took her camping.

The wind howled. Someone snored. The corner of the tent lifted and started flapping. Della fought the crazy urge to laugh because she couldn't decide whether it was the wind or the snore that blew it loose. In her heart, though, she knew if Brandon had tacked down that stake, it wouldn't have given way.

They hiked farther into the San Bernardino Mountains the next day and made good time. At one point, they passed through a vacant campground. Della drank at a fountain then refilled her canteen. She wondered why they didn't set up for the night here, but Chet clapped his hands. "Gather up. We still have plenty of light. No sissy camping. We're stouthearted adventurers. Open trail for another hour or so before we stop."

"Well, there's truth in advertising," someone said in a wry tone. "This is definitely a 'rugged adventure.'"

Folks laughed and fell into step. They chattered along the path, but Della couldn't help remembering how Brandon was as he hiked—he'd point out types of trees, plants, rocks. Interesting little facts. According to what Brandon taught her, Chet led them out of the chaparral, past the yellow pine forest, and crossed through montane meadows. From what she could judge, they'd come to the lodgepole forest. But Chet didn't talk about the different geological regions or point out the tracks in the earth from deer or raccoons. He just plowed on ahead. Compared to her hikes with Brandon, this so-called adventure was nothing more than a harsh march.

Chet consulted the GPS then adjusted their course when a rockslide obliterated part of the trail. It added some excitement to the trek, and by the time they reached their destination, everyone needed to use a flashlight to find footing.

"You folks go ahead and pitch your tents along here." Chet swung his arm in a line.

Della's brow puckered. "Why not over by the rocks? Wouldn't it be warmer there?"

"That's where we're having campfire."

"Oh." The minute Della dragged the tent to a spot, Misty and Madeline disappeared. The sisters didn't care to do much of anything. Their parents heaved sighs and raised their hands as if to say, "Oh, well," but Della noticed they didn't offer to help her pitch the tent. Once she had it up, she stored her gear inside.

Chet mentioned he had a permit for them to use deadwood and to have open fires. He and the other man scraped back a clear area, made a nominal ring of stones, and started the fire. They'd worked hard to gather the wood and chop it to size while folks pitched the tents, so Della dismissed the thought that the ring was too small. *They do this for a living. It's okay.*

Only it wasn't okay. Logs slid from the pyre, and one fell outside the perimeter stones. A few dried twigs and some grass caught fire, but folks stamped it out.

That wasn't the only problem. Chet arranged for everyone to sit against the rock wall and had the fire farther out, away from them. *Brandon taught me to build a fire close to the wall so the heat would radiate back and give double the heat. . . .*

A warm, hearty stew made from dehydrated stores bubbled on the fire and restored Della's faith in Rugged Adventures. They'd had no mishaps, and Chet showed fair navigation skills when they'd run into the need for a detour. *There's not just one way to do things. Brandon knew one way, but things are working all right this other way.*

Della snuggled into her sleeping bag and listened to the sisters complain about the hard ground and how cold they were. When she'd taken a closer look at their hip pads, she knew they had cause to grumble. *Brandon told me those were cheap. If it froze, they'd turn into sleds, and they didn't keep any cushion factor.* Only she couldn't share her pad—by design, they were only shoulder-to-hip pieces. Even turning it sideways wouldn't help. The quality of the sleeping bags equaled the one he'd sneered at and left behind on their first camping trip.

By the next morning, Della drank the rest of her canteen and went to the creek to refill it. The other worker chuckled as she added water purification tablets.

"See how the water's running over all those rocks? That's nature's purifier. You don't need to use those pills."

"I thought the water had to rush over the stones and be white to be safe." *At least that's what Brandon said.*

"It's close enough."

Della hitched a shoulder. "Oh, well. Better safe than sorry." As soon as the words came out of her mouth, she bit her lip to keep from crying. Better safe than sorry. . . Brandon always said that when he took her camping.

Chapter 17

I've got a bad feeling about Della's trip," Brandon said as he rolled up an electrical extension cord.

"Nothing you can do about it." Nathan looked out at the stakes in the bulldozed plot of earth that would soon become a housing development. "Put her in God's hands."

"I do. I have." Brandon dumped the bright orange, coiled cord onto a piece of plywood. "The problem is, I keep snatching her back. It's like I have her on a yo-yo string. She's God's. . .she's mine. . .she's God's. . . ."

"You don't know what she's learning. Could be, God's plan is going to unfold because of the things she finds out about herself on this trek. From what Jordan and Val tell me, when you went camping, you babied her."

"I most certainly did not. I showed her how to do things the right way."

Nathan shot him a telling look. "You made the decisions. Her dad and brothers do the same thing to her. Maybe on this trip, when she has to do things for herself, she'll iron out some issues."

"Who says Della has issues?"

"Everyone has issues. You're having an issue right now—trying to make her out to be a saint when we both know she's a sinner. Just because you love someone and are loyal doesn't mean you view them as perfect."

"You could drive a man to violence," Brandon muttered.

"I'm trying to guide you to reason." Nathan unrolled the layout for the tract and weighted it down on the table. "I can't say Vanessa's helping, though. She insists that we need to have faith. We prayed last night, and we've decided to put a fleece before the Lord on your behalf."

"What's this fleece thing?"

"In the Old Testament. There was a mighty warrior, Gideon. He wanted to be sure of God's will, so he set a fleece on a threshing floor one night. If it was wet and the rest of the floor was dry, then he'd take it as God's will for him to go to battle."

"Well? Was the fleece wet?"

"Soaking. He squeezed out a whole bowlful of water."

Brandon nodded. "So he went to war."

"Nope. He decided to ask God for confirmation. The next night, the fleece was to be dry, and the rest of the floor was to become wet."

Brandon lifted a brow.

"Fleece was dry as a bone—the floor was wet."

"So Gideon sorta bugged God, too." For some reason, that thought pleased Brandon. He didn't feel quite so bad for having a hard time following the Lord's direction. "I'm gonna have to read more about that guy. Where is his story?"

"In the book of Judges."

"Okay. So what does that have to do with me?"

"Vanessa and I prayed over the tract. We walked it last night and felt led to a particular plot. If you select that plot, we're going to set it aside as a home for you and Della. We'll take it as His direction for your life. If you don't select it, I'm going to pray with you to let go of her completely."

Brandon stared at the horizon. "I already did that. The other night at the beach. I told God if she's not going to be His daughter, I wanted her to find someone else to love."

Nathan stayed quiet for a long while. Finally, he said, "That was part of it, but not all of it. You asked God to have her let go of you. I don't hear you asking God to have you let go of her."

"I don't want to play this game."

"It's not a game. You decide. Van and I felt called, but we can't force you to do anything you don't want to. The offer's there. You decide."

Brandon wouldn't look down at the layout. He refused to.

Nathan quoted a line the SEALs used during training. "Sweat today or bleed tomorrow."

Ouch. That hit home like nothing else would. Brandon stared down at the paper. A decision like this ought to be made with a lot of forethought. Corner lots had bigger yards. Inside streets were quieter. In the past, when things were still good between him and Della, he'd secretly decided on just which place would be theirs. Fist tight, he passed it over the layout and fully intended to rap his knuckles on that segment, only his hand wouldn't go there. Instead, it veered to one side, and before he could figure out what he was doing, he'd decisively tapped a completely different lot.

"Number seventy-four." Nathan's voice sounded strained.

Brandon lifted his hand. "Don't say it."

"I have to. That's the one. It's the one Van and I consecrated last night to the Lord's will."

"Don't mess with my mind," Brandon rasped.

"I'm not. Here. Open this." Nathan took a small slip of paper from his pocket. "Van wrote a number on it."

Brandon's fingers shook as he unfolded it. There, in black and white was the number 74. "I'm not doing a second fleece. This is it." Brandon whooped. "She's mine!"

※

Things fell apart fast. After the second night, half of the hikers decided they'd had enough adventure. Cold and weary, sore-muscled and blister-footed, they couldn't imagine continuing into the rougher territory. The other guide led them back as Chet continued on with the rest of the group. Refusing to give up, Della stuck with those who would continue on.

"Babies," Chet muttered as they set out. "Soft. Why sign up for this if you want all the comforts of home? It's supposed to be something different."

"It's certainly been a challenge," Della said.

"Yeah. It's supposed to be." Chet looked pleased.

Della wasn't sure how he'd taken that as a compliment, but it didn't much matter. It wouldn't hurt for him to hear something nice after all of the complaints and criticism he'd heard over breakfast.

By late afternoon, Della's confidence in Chet's ability hit an all-time low. She felt sure she'd seen this stretch of the trail already today. They'd gone in a complete circle over the last hour. "How about if we look at the map?"

"Don't need to."

One of the other men stepped up beside her. "Don't growl at the girl. Seems to me, it was a reasonable request."

Della flashed him a smile of thanks.

"You can just GPS us," another hiker suggested.

"Battery went dead," Chet muttered.

A quick survey had them all on edge—only two of them had cellular phones, and neither was able to connect. Their batteries were incompatible with Chet's GPS.

They all crowded around the map. Brandon hadn't shown her how to read a map, but he'd taught her to gauge distance and direction. What the others decided made no sense to Della, but she held her tongue. Amongst them, they probably knew far more than she did about navigating.

"Okay. We'll need to set a good pace to reach the next site," Chet announced. "It'll probably be dark when we get there, but we managed just fine last night in the dark."

"We can do it," Della declared.

Two hours later, her confidence sank along with the sun. She'd refilled her canteen and followed Brandon's survival tips, but her feet and calves ached, and her back protested the weight of the backpack. Clouds started to roll in. Dusk turned to near dark, and still, they didn't stop.

"It's up here just a short ways. I know exactly where we are." Chet's declaration didn't inspire her as it did the others. Della stopped for a moment to rest then tagged along at the back of the line. One minute, her footing was solid. The next minute, her boot landed in empty space. The weight of her pack sent her careening over the edge and into darkness.

Chapter 18

Della groaned. Her leg hurt—not a little ache, but full-on, horrible pain. She couldn't even see it. About five feet away, a small circle of light let her know where her flashlight landed. She needed that light.

Gritting her teeth against the pain, she tried to stand. Impossible. Whimpers poured out of her as she worked her way to the flashlight. She stopped moving and caught her breath then yelled, "Hey! Somebody!"

No one answered.

Della figured they'd be back soon. In the meantime, she needed the flashlight. Once her hand curled around the plastic, she trained it on her knee to assess the damage.

Air shivered out of her lungs. Her jeans were shredded, and what she could see of her leg scared her. She laid back and talked to herself. "Stay calm. They'll come back. At least no bones are poking out. That's good."

Good? That opinion didn't last long. Within minutes, Della was cold. She shed her backpack and looked around. She couldn't have been unconscious for very long. Her party would be back for her in a few minutes, once they realized she was missing.

In the meantime, she needed to take care of herself. She had nothing to wrap her knee except her bandana. It would suffice for now. Surely, Chet carried an Ace bandage. Gritting her teeth, she poured water over the scraped mess and bound her knee as best she could. "Hey guys! I'm stuck over here. I could use some help."

Her voice shook with cold and pain. Tugging on her backpack, she shifted it so she could pull out a hooded sweat shirt.

One thing at a time. Think ahead. Plan. Brandon's words kept streaming through her mind. They kept her from panicking. Della couldn't find the whistle she'd brought along. Brandon made everyone in their party wear a lanyard with a whistle in case they got lost. *Just pucker up your lips and give me a whistle. I'll come running, babe.*

"Oh, Brandon. Why can't you come get me now?" She raised her voice, "I'm hurt, guys. C'mon and find me, will you?"

Only she heard no one.

The place she'd landed had plenty of sticks and branches—but that was about as stupid of a place as possible for her to stay. She wouldn't be spotted, and the danger of snakes. . .she cut off that line of thought. Della searched her surroundings and decided on where to go.

Hug a tree. You get lost; you hug a tree. People wander all over and can't be found because they don't stay put.

A tree about eight feet away looked like a good spot. She scrabbled toward it one painful inch at a time. About a yard from her goal, she felt something hit her hand. Then her face.

Rain.

Sobbing, Della pulled herself the last few feet and slumped against the tree. "Why, God? What did I do that's so bad? Why are You punishing me?"

🕆

Slowly, she opened her eyes. Daylight. Surely they'd come looking and find her. They couldn't be far away. Della groaned as she unwound the extra-large trash bag from around herself. It kept her warm and fairly dry last night—another one of Brandon's little helpful hints. She popped two aspirin and washed them down with a big gulp of water. *How did that commercial go? Take two aspirin and call me in the morning.*

"Me! Oh, me—eeee!" she shouted. "I took the aspirin. I did my part. Now come help me!"

No one answered.

After a few hours, Della's hopes began to flag. At first, she'd thought maybe Chet and the others had a little trouble. Then she thought they couldn't very well look for her during last night's rain. But they should have come back by now.

A galling fact glared at her: Chet couldn't punch his way out of a plastic garbage bag. *He has no right to run a business when he doesn't know anything. They've left me here. What am I going to do?*

As if she didn't know what she'd packed, Della emptied her backpack entirely. Taking stock of her supplies now took on a whole new significance. The big bag of Brandon's favorite beef jerky looked better than anything she'd ever eaten. A container of trail mix, two candy bars, a fruit leather, and a package of gum. Not a promising supply, but adequate for a day or two if she paced herself.

Water, though. A slosh let her know her canteen stood about half-full. She'd need more water—soon. By midday, thirst and the understanding that no one was searching for her forced Della to decide to find a water source. Using a stick as a cane, she jump-hopped her way around. Each move sent spears of agony through her.

She lost track of time. Lost track of where she was. Cried. Finally, Della found a creek. She sat down in the water and let the coolness surround her swollen knee. After drinking the last sip from her canteen, she refilled it. Then she wondered if she ought to skip using the purification tablets. One man said yes; the other said no. *Who do I trust?*

She added the tablets.

At first, getting wet felt good. Clean. Bracing and refreshing and helped lessen the pain. But then reality sank in. Her jeans wouldn't dry before sunset. She couldn't light a fire to signal for help or to use for heat. Though she had a lighter, she couldn't collect enough wood to do the job and still set up a safe fire ring. The last thing she wanted to do was start a forest fire and be its first fatality.

"Water. Warmth. Food." She kept chanting the priorities. Della wished she'd been carrying a tent now. Her sleeping bag and garbage bag would have to suffice. Gnawing on a piece of beef jerky, she studied her surroundings. She needed a big, solid, friendly-looking tree. Then she'd get there, change her clothes, and wait.

Someone would search for her. Brandon would.

Only she'd told him to leave her alone.

✝

"He left her alone up there?" Brandon's bellow nearly shook the construction trailer.

"Yes," Della's father answered in an anguished tone. He shoved his hands in his pockets. "Listen. I know we told you to leave her be, but I'm asking—"

"I'm going after her."

"Good."

Having been in the military set habits that he'd not yet broken. Brandon always kept a pack ready so he could roll out the minute he got a call. His pack sat at the ready in the bottom of his closet at home. As he went to claim it, he dialed Lurch. If the guys were on maneuvers, that was that—but if they were home, Brandon couldn't come up with a better team of men to help him find his woman.

Lurch's phone kept ringing. No help from that quarter.

Soon as he hung up, Nathan called. "I'm coming along. Jim Martinez, too."

"I'm heading out now."

"Pick me up at Jim's."

"No way. I'm not wasting a minute."

"We're on the way, Brandon."

"Be out front. If you're not, I won't stop."

Nathan and Jim stood on the curb. Katie and Van were there, too, with a crate and a duffel bag of junk. Brandon itched to gun the engine, and the women were gabbing about food and clothes and stupid inconsequentials.

"Later," he rumbled. "She's been out there alone for two nights already. We can't waste time."

"God go with you!" Van called.

Brandon pulled out into traffic and growled, "The guys are out on maneuvers. We're on short team."

Nathan grinned at him like a madman. "Did I ever tell you about a guy named Gideon?"

"Yeah. Him and the fleece."

"There's another story about him. He had a big army, but God only let him take the warriors who drank from their hands instead of burying their face in the water."

"Let me guess. His side still won."

"God always wins." Nathan smacked the dashboard. "You can count on that."

☩

"Let's see. . ." Della spoke aloud to herself all of the time now. She didn't care if it was odd. It gave her a little comfort. "What next?"

She'd calculated things as best she could. Chet would have spent time searching for her, but because of the rain, he wouldn't have much luck with tracks. Sad truth was, even if it hadn't rained, Della seriously doubted he would have been able to trace her footprints back to where she'd fallen, let alone to where she'd wandered from there to the creek. After a nominal effort, Chet would give up then head back with the others. Even at a full run, that meant they'd still have a day and a half to hike out; then help would take another day or two to come here. From that point, they'd have to look all over the forest to find her. Five days. Yes, five. That sounded about right.

But the pain in her knee said she couldn't wait for help that long.

Della counted out how many aspirin she had and rationed them to last five days. She did the same with her food. By dumping the trail mix into the pocket of her sweat shirt, she was able to use that pint-sized container to hold more water.

She'd hacked off her blue jeans and cut off the leg at thigh-level of the other pair before she pulled them on. Every move sent shards of pain through her.

Don't tense. Don't fight the pain. Let it be there. Brandon's words to her as he'd rubbed out a nasty charley horse she'd gotten during a morning beach run echoed in her mind. *Blow like you're blowing away the pain.*

She'd practically hyperventilated when she changed her clothes, but she got it done. Brandon was right—it worked. Sort of. Not that all the pain disappeared, but she'd coped.

He was right about the tent stakes and gauging distance and. . . She stopped cold. "What if he's right about God?"

"No. It's not like that," she answered herself. "I'm going to stay busy. I don't have to think about God and Jesus and all that religion stuff."

Lying on the hip pad with her head pillowed on a wadded-up sleeping bag nearly drove her crazy. Thoughts of Brandon swirled around in her head. "I'm thinking of him because I'm in the wilderness. It's just mental association. What I need to do is stay busy." She sat up and pulled over her backpack. With all the supplies she had stuffed in there, she could rig up some kind of a tent between the two shrubs with her garbage bag.

⁜

The others started to turn in for the night. They'd put in half of yesterday and all of today searching for Della, but to no avail. Chet couldn't be specific about where he'd led his party that last night, let alone where he'd lost Della. Thick vegetation made it impossible for helicopters to give much assistance. Thermal imaging should help, but to Brandon's frustration, it hadn't yielded anything useful. Search dogs hadn't picked up her scent either.

"Rest up. We'll start first thing in the morning," Nathan urged.

Brandon shook his head then dug through his gear and pulled out night vision goggles. "I'm heading out north by northwest."

"Alone?" Jim gawked at him. "We don't need another—"

Brandon's glower silenced him. He bent, snagged his pack, and shrugged into it. "Grab me more water, will you?"

Jim trotted off, and Nathan offered, "I'll come with you."

"No can do. My NVGs will keep me from breaking my neck. Thanks, but no thanks." He accepted the bottles Jim brought back, stuffed two into the pockets of his pack, and glugged down the third. He shoved the empty bottle back into Nathan's hand. "Wanna know something weird? I was just reading about the shepherd leaving the flock to search for that one lost lamb."

His boss grinned. "And we all know He succeeds. God go with you."

Brandon set off at a steady pace and yanked on the NVGs. The band pulled at his hair—something it never did when he sported a near buzz cut. The greenish glow from the lenses felt good. Familiar. He was on a mission, and this one—it had to be successful.

'Round about midnight, Brandon came upon a spot that showed excessive trampling. His pulse rose. The fire ring and divots in the ground showed a group had camped here overnight very recently. At least now the search field could be focused. According to his GPS, they were miles off course—a massive distance in this terrain.

"What would you do, Della?" he muttered as he unfolded a detailed satellite map of the area and flipped up the NVGs. The green tint on this map made it difficult to read. Training his flashlight on it, he looked for a water source. If she followed all of his teaching, she would have hugged a tree, but thirst would drive her toward water after a day.

There. A small stream. It meandered off toward the east. He would locate it then search the full length along both sides. After taking a fix on his location, he set out. It didn't take long before he heard the subtle trickling of water flow. Pine and fir trees blocked any distance vision.

Ten thousand feet altitude. The temperature dipped to the low 40s. Brandon hoped Della had brought the sleeping bag he'd selected for her instead of renting one of the cheap jobs Chet used. She had to be hungry. Hypothermia was all she needed. Poor woman had to be scared out of her mind.

God, lead me to her. Help me find her. Let her be okay.

Brandon tamped down his fears. That fleece thing—that meant he and Della had a future together. She'd make it through this. Once he got her out of here, though, he'd never let go of her.

Methodically using trees as points of reference, Brandon searched both sides of the creek. No human footprints joined those of raccoons, mule deer, and coyotes. No signs of human habitation—no footprints or drag-and-scrape lines showed anyone had been here. Brandon knew he might miss signs that would stand out in daylight—a scrap of cloth, a food wrapper. *I have to have faith. God will lead me.*

Coyotes howled. Crickets sang. Water bubbled. Wind soughed. He strained to detect anything out of the ordinary. By now, even if she'd rationed use of the flashlight, her batteries would be toast. Della, huddled alone in the dark—cold, hungry, and scared. The thought made him sick. He forged on.

Lord, I'm seeing a new side of Your love—of how You relentlessly pushed on and pursued me. Only I didn't even know I was lost, so I kept marching farther and farther away. This time, it's You and me together—looking for Della—both body and soul. I want it all, God. I want her in my arms. I want You in her heart. . . .

Then he saw it: a stack of rocks in the center of the narrow creek. They'd been carefully arranged from large to small to form a stack several inches high—something that wouldn't have happened in nature. She'd left him a signal! Plowing ahead, Brandon sloshed through the icy water and stared at that stack then scanned the banks. One bore deep grooves and left-sided footprints. *Della's hurt. But she's nearby!*

"Della!" he shouted as he headed up the bank and followed the marked earth. His goggles illuminated a lump. Della. Only she didn't move or make a sound.

Chapter 19

D ella!"
   She jarred awake to something crashing into her makeshift shelter.
Della screamed then shrieked even louder when she saw the monster.
Clutching her flashlight, she clobbered him.

"Hey! Della!"

She froze.

"Babe—"

"Brandon!" She dropped the flashlight and grabbed for him, trying to assure herself she hadn't gone crazy. He was here. Holding her. "You came. It's really you."

"You bet it is."

"What are you wearing?"

He yanked off the weird lenses and blinked. "Night vision goggles." He pressed her back down.

"You scared me half silly." She lay back and stared up at him as he pressed fingers to the side of her neck. "My pulse is about three hundred from that scare."

"I noticed." His tone held wry humor. He proceeded to take stock of her.

"If you dare touch my leg, I'm going to start banging you with the flashlight again."

"Which leg?"

"Right."

Brandon sat back on his heels and shed his pack. It made a loud thump on the earth, and Della wondered just how much gear he'd been toting. He'd done it for her. What did that mean, though?

"Shhh, babe. Don't cry. It'll be all right." He leaned over her and rubbed his whiskery jaw against her cheek.

Della hadn't realized she'd started to cry. The sandpapery feel of his jaw testified to his masculinity, to the fact that he was here—strong and capable. She didn't have to be strong anymore. Until now, she'd convinced herself to be courageous, but the strain of it finally took its toll. Once the tears started to fall, she couldn't stop them.

Cupping her hand over her mouth, she tried to tamp back the sobs. Brandon had come for her—but only as a friend. They'd never been closer, but they'd never been further apart.

Grim determination painted his features and colored his voice. "I'm going to take a look at your leg."

If he wanted to think pain prompted this reaction, Della decided that would be okay. At least it would help her save face later. Being offered nothing more than friendship by the man she loved caused her far more pain than her injured leg.

He rested his forehead against hers. His warm breath whispered across her face. "You lie still."

She wanted him to kiss her, to promise everything would be okay, but he didn't. He pulled away and passed his flashlight up and down over her until he figured out how she'd wrapped herself in the sleeping bag. The man was all business. Methodical. Careful. Swift.

The cold night air hit her, but he quickly tucked the sleeping bag back around all but her right leg. He blew on his hands, rubbed them together for a second to warm them, then began at her ankle.

She'd started to regain a little composure. Della wiped away her tears and rasped, "It's my knee."

"Okay." He ignored her and continued to examine her from ankle upward prodding at her with all the compassion of a Sherman tank. Then he started to unknot the bandana she'd tied around her knee.

"Aaghh—no—no—no!" She'd bolted into a sitting position without realizing it. Waves of pain caused her to hit his hands away.

"All right, babe. It's all right." He held her by the shoulders and eased her to lie back down again. Tugging the sleeping bag back up to warm her, he grated, "I'm sorry. It's real sore. I know."

"Don't—"

"I'm not going to touch your knee. I'm checking above it."

The next several minutes turned into a blur of agony. She heard his voice, but whatever he said didn't make any sense. All Della wanted was for him to stop. Finally, he scooted upward and cupped her cheeks.

"I've immobilized it. I can't tell whether you've just wrenched it, cracked the kneecap, or torn ligaments. It's too swollen to guess. The pulses are strong— that's a good thing, babe. Really good."

Through her tear-glazed vision, in the muted beam of the flashlight, his remorse came through. Della bit the inside of her cheek and nodded.

Nothing escaped him. His lips thinned. "I don't have anything to give you for pain."

"I'm okay if I stay warm and don't move."

"Come morning, I'll signal for help. I can carry you to a clearing not far from here, and we'll airlift you out." His eyes narrowed. "You're starting to shiver."

The man wouldn't give up. He ripped open a foil-like survival blanket and tore back her sleeping bag.

"Brandon!"

"You'll build up heat again in a sec." He spread the survival blanket over her, tucked the sleeping bag around her shoulders again, and then brushed strands of hair away from her face.

She gave him her bravest smile. "It's not so bad now."

A smile chased across his face, but he remained intense. "Hungry? Thirsty?"

"I was going to ask you the same thing. My canteen's about a third full, and I still have a piece of jerky left."

"You brought jerky?"

She nodded. No use reminding him of how he taught her to bring high protein, lightweight food. That was all over. . .in the past.

"How about some cocoa?"

"I don't have any."

His chuckle sounded rough. "I didn't expect you to have anything at all left to eat or drink. I've got rations in my pack—even cocoa."

"Oh, that sounds good."

A can of Sterno, and the man turned into a gourmet. The unmistakable aroma of cocoa filled the night air. He held up her head and shoulders and poured a cup of the rich, warm drink down her throat. "Better?"

"The best."

She watched as he looked around and tied up the fishing line he'd broken when he ripped down her shelter. She'd knotted fishing line to her towel and strung it between shrubs then tied the torn-open trash bag over it. Crumpled pages from a book and pine needles stuffed between the towel and bag acted as insulation to help keep her cooler during the day and warmer at night—a trick he'd told her about. Approval colored his voice. "You did a good job establishing a base camp."

"I had a great teacher." She looked at him. "When I got going on this trip and Chet did things differently, I thought there were probably other ways to do the chores; but everything went wrong. Some things, there's just one right way, isn't there?"

"Yeah." He studied her at length. "Are you just talking about camping?"

"No." She sighed. "I had a mother bring in the flower girl a few days ago. Because her daughter is a redhead, she didn't ever dress her in pink because she'd gotten the notion that it wouldn't look right. By the time she left, she said the truth was in front of her, but she'd refused to see it."

Brandon didn't say a thing.

Della closed her eyes. "What if I've been wrong? What if you're right? That there's only one right way to live? That I'm not good enough for God? I've been lying here for days now, and I can't get away from it. I figured it out. You couldn't compromise because we couldn't be a team with both of us going off in different directions. But I didn't want to change for you."

"It's not a decision you make based on someone else. You have to do it for yourself."

She nodded. "I figured that out, too."

He started making more cocoa. Deft, purposeful movements, and silence reigned. "Here."

"No, Brandon. You drink that one. In fact, you need to get in your sleeping bag, too. It's cold out tonight—colder than the other nights."

She tried to scoot closer to him, but the effort hurt.

"Hang on, babe." He opened his own sleeping bag and draped it around her. "Better?"

"I'm warm enough."

"Ahhh." Brandon sat cross-legged and reached under the sleeping bags to hold her hand. "So what have you been thinking?"

"All my life, I've tried to be good enough—to be what Daddy and my brothers wanted me to be. To please teachers and customers and, well, to be perfect. Not that I ever managed all of those things, but I tried. Then I met you, and you showed me I didn't have to do anything to make you like me—you just took me as I was. You gave me a chance to try stuff and encouraged me even when I was lousy at batting or running or camping. For you, I didn't have to be perfect. I was good enough—just me."

She couldn't stop the flow of words once she started. "Then, suddenly, you told me I wasn't perfect. I had to change. If I didn't change, I wasn't good enough for you anymore."

He looked like he wanted to say something, but Della was afraid if she let him, she'd lose her nerve.

"But I've been lying here thinking. God doesn't expect me to be perfect, does He? To Him, I'm already a disaster. All the things I've done wrong, all that stuff—He already knows it. The bottom line is, He'll still take me, right?"

"God loves you, Della. He knows everything about you, and it breaks His heart to have the distance sin created between you and Him. He gave His Son just so you could be forgiven."

"So what you're saying is, I blew it a thousand million billion times, and He still wants me."

"Yeah."

"But what do I have to give Him for that? Jesus died for my sins, and I can't do anything to repay my debt."

"The debt's been cancelled—but you have to accept that fact. The cost is that you have to be sold out to God. You get a new life—a different life. I still blow it, but He forgives me, and I try to do better."

"What about all the rules and stuff?"

"I always thought there were a lot of rules for Christians. Now that I am one, I'm discovering there really aren't many. I'm to live in obedience to the Bible and to the directions I feel God leads me. The Golden Rule and the Ten Commandments pretty much cover it all"—he paused—"except for what happened between us."

Tears slipped down her cheeks. "You were right though. If we'd gotten married, I wouldn't have stayed happy. In my heart of hearts, I'd sense you wanted more from me, that I disappointed you."

His shoulders slumped. "I'm glad you understand that. It nearly killed me, hurting you like that."

"It's torn me apart."

Chapter 20

Brandon didn't say a word. He didn't need to. Agony pulled his features taut.

Della winced as she reached to reassure him. "I never want to live through that kind of pain again. At first, I blamed you. I blamed God. Then I had to admit that I made a choice."

He sat so still, so somber. Della wasn't sure he understood what she was saying, but she strove to order her thoughts so they'd make sense.

"I decided, being stuck out here with nothing to do but think, that I'm like that little redhead's mom—the truth was right in front of me, but I hadn't accepted it. I just don't know what I'm supposed to do."

"Della, are you saying you want to commit your life to Christ?"

She nodded.

"It's not just so you and I—"

"No." She squeezed his hand. "I couldn't live a lie."

"Oh, babe, I prayed so hard for you to open your heart to Jesus."

"What do I do?"

"We pray. You confess to God that you've sinned and know Jesus is the price to rescue you from sin. You ask Him into your heart. It's that simple."

"I can't figure out why He wants me, but I'm glad He does."

"It's a special kind of love—a love worth finding. We have to search our souls and make the decision, but I promise you, Della, you won't be sorry."

"Well, here goes everything." She laid her head back, switched off the flashlight, and stared up at the stars. "I like the idea of looking up at the heavens to say my first prayer."

Brandon rubbed his thumb across her palm in agreement.

"Dear God, it's me. Della. Oh. You know that. You know everything. Then You know what I'm doing here. I've tried to live right, but I blow it. I can't do it on my own, and there's no way I can earn my way into heaven. I'm offering a trade here—my old life for a new one. You'll have to work on me with this new life, because I'm bound to mess up on things. But I'll do my best to follow what You ask of me. I'll even go to church and read the Bible and all that stuff because—well, not because it's a rule, but because I'm grateful and love You. Amen."

"I've never heard sweeter words in my whole life, babe."

※

She wasn't hypothermic or dehydrated, and though her knee hurt, the circulation to her lower leg was fine. Brandon knew he didn't need to transport her out tonight. If he did, he'd have to carry her several miles—something he wouldn't mind in the least. He had hold of her and wasn't about to ever let go. Though a new Christian, he knew the gift God had bestowed upon him tonight was a rare and precious thing. A man couldn't want more than the woman he loved to find the Lord. But trekking out would pose too much of a strain on Della. The terrain was too uneven, and though he'd take every precaution to plot out the smoothest course and carry her with every scrap of devotion he felt, she wouldn't be able to endure much jarring. If he waited until morning, he'd be able to carry her to a nearby clearing, signal, and airlift her smoothly.

The strength of the pulses in her foot and ankle gave much-needed reassurance, because from just above the knee down, she was a bruised, battered wreck. Trying to get the cocoa into her made sense—warm fluids, sugar—they'd help in case she was shocky. Only she wasn't. Despite her pain, she stayed uncannily calm. His woman had gumption.

Brandon flicked on the flashlight. "Babe, about getting you out of here. . ."

She shook her head and yawned. "I'm glad you said we'd wait 'til tomorrow. I don't want to be a sissy or anything, but my leg hurts a lot more at night when it's cold."

"No one in his right mind would call you a sissy. You're a gutsy woman. I'm proud of you."

She squeezed his hand. "You've got to be getting cold, and I'm roasting under two of these sleeping bags."

"Hang on a few minutes." He took the small pan of water he'd left over the Sterno and soaked it up with a pair of Handi Wipes. "Wash up. You'll relax and sleep better."

She started scrubbing at her face. "Do I look that bad?"

"You're the most beautiful woman in the world."

"I haven't," she asserted as she washed her jaw and throat, "shampooed my hair in a week. I'm filthy."

"To God, you're pure as snow. To me, you're lovely."

"You're nice to say those things. Really, you are. But I feel atrocious." She whisked the cloth over her forearms and hands, then grimaced at how dirty the wipe had become. Brandon silently took it and gave her the other one. Just like a fastidious kitten, she set about washing her face again. "I ran out of my sunblock lotion two days ago, and vain as it sounds, I really didn't want any more freckles."

"I'm wild about your freckles. They make me want to kiss you silly."

"So what are you waiting for?"

Brandon leaned forward then pulled back. "Sweetheart, I love you. Before I found Jesus, I knew you were the woman I wanted for my wife—and I gotta tell you, I've had a ring about burning a hole in my pocket. . .because I had to have faith that you'd find your way to the Lord. His love is worth finding, Della. I want my love for you to be worth it, too. Will you marry me?"

"Oh, yes. Please, yes! I love you so much, Brandon."

He leaned to one side and yanked his wallet from his back pocket. Inside nested the ring he'd chosen for her. "I'm putting this on your finger and allowing myself one last kiss." He smiled. "But then, no kisses until the wedding. Otherwise, I'm afraid you're going to dally for months planning an extravaganza, and I don't want to wait anymore. All I want is you and me, blessed by God, being husband and wife."

The ring fit just right. Their lips fit just right, too. A kiss never held so much promise and love. Brandon finally pulled away, crawled into his sleeping bag, and had her use his chest as a pillow. She settled in with a sigh.

"Brandon?"

"Yeah, babe?"

"I already know what tux I want you to wear."

"Good."

"And I already know my favorite music. Do you have any songs you like a lot?"

"I'm not picky. But I do want you to carry white flowers. Roses."

"Could we compromise? Valentine brides always carry red roses."

"By compromise, do you mean you'll carry pink ones, or a combination of red and white?" He chuckled. Of all the times he'd lain out under the stars, most had been consumed with the tension of a mission. He'd never imagined he'd spend time worrying about the color of flowers.

"Either."

"Red and white," he decided. "I'll talk Nathan into letting us have a reception at The Spindles. How does that sound?"

"I'd love that!"

"Great. So all the big decisions are made. We can get this done soon."

"My gown—"

He groaned. "Oh, no. Linda's mom said it took five months for her gown. You can't do that to me. I'll go insane."

"She wanted a special Belgian lace that was on back order."

"No Belgian lace." He tapped her shoulder to make sure she heard him.

"I love Belgian lace."

He sighed. Once upon a time, he'd decided to give her time to whip up the wedding of her dreams. Right about now, he'd gladly have her dad wheel her down the aisle in a wheelchair with her dressed in a coonskin cap and swimsuit.

Her cheek rubbed his shirtfront as she looked up at him. "Really, no Belgian lace?" She sounded so disappointed. But lace was so. . .impossibly trivial.

"Belgian is for waffles, not lace."

"Oh." She sighed. "I didn't know you felt that way. Next thing you're going to say is Brussels is out because of sprouts. French is out because of toast."

"And fries," he added. "What is this, anyway? Who goes around naming frilly stuff after European countries?"

"The people who've perfected the art of creating beautiful lace."

He groaned. "Just how long is this Belgian lace going to take?"

Her shoulders began to shake, and her voice filled with laughter. "The gown I love with Belgian lace is at my shop right now."

"Hot dog!"

"You're making me hungry."

"You're making me crazy. Go to sleep."

⚜

"Mornin', beautiful."

"Hi." She hitched up on both elbows. "You're up early."

"I got a signal out. You're due for a ride in about half an hour."

"Half an hour?" She sat up and groaned at how the action pulled her leg.

Brandon nodded then wondered as she rummaged in her backpack, "What're you looking for?"

"My brush. Ouch! Found it!" She looked at him pleadingly. "Can you take me to the creek and help me dunk my head? I have shampoo."

He frowned.

"It's biodegradable. It won't hurt the environment or ecosystem or anything."

"Honey, it's going to take me twenty minutes to get you to the extraction point."

"Then we don't have time to waste!"

"The water's cold."

"Refreshing," she shot back.

He heaved a sigh. "Vanity, thy name is woman."

Della gave him a sassy smile. "I'm a Christian now. Cleanliness is next to godliness."

It took a little fancy maneuvering, but Brandon humored her. After laying her on his trash bag, he used the small pan to help rinse out the shampoo then tackled one side of her hair with his comb as she used her brush on the other. While she braided it, he packed up their sleeping bags, took the gear out of her backpack and stowed it in his, then used the frame to rig a splint for her leg.

Della reached over and threaded her fingers through his hair as he used the cording to tie the last knot. "You're an incredible man. You know how to do so much."

"I'd better warn you; I can't cook."

"So what? I love to cook. You know that."

"Then we're definitely a match made in heaven, because I've eaten your food." He tugged on his pack. It looked impossibly heavy. Della marveled at his strength.

Then he scooped her up.

"Brandon!"

"Put your arm around my neck. I know it's hard on you—"

"Hard on me! Do you know how much I weigh—no, don't answer that."

"I've carried ugly old rafts that weigh more than you." He set off walking.

"If you get me a stick, I can hobble."

He snorted—a purely masculine sound that dismissed her offer without bothering to even entertain it for a moment. He acted as if this were his own backyard—picking his path with the absolute assurance of where he was going, twisting to the side to avoid banging her leg on trees and bushes.

"Brandon, how did you signal?"

"Mirror."

"No kidding? I thought you'd have some super-spy satellite thingamabob. You mean I could have just used my compact?"

"The mountains make signals bounce. Electronic gear's unreliable out here. As for the mirror—you were under a canopy of trees. Not enough room to refract back up. Besides, I'd guess you don't know Morse code."

"It's on the inside cover of my survival book, but the directions don't tell how to make a dot or a dash."

Her leg burned. Even though he did everything humanly possible to ease her way, Della hurt. He distracted her as best he could with tidbits of information and idle conversation. It was so unlike him just to chat about nothing—but he did it for her.

It made Della love him that much more.

They reached a clearing, and he laid her down in a small, grassy patch then consulted his watch. "We made good time."

"Even with washing my hair." She smiled at him. "Did I thank you for that?"

"Only a hundred times or so."

She looked down at herself. "Now I understand why the military uses those grays and khakis. They don't show the dirt. I'm covered in grunge."

"It's about to get worse." His voice rang with unrepentant glee.

"Why?"

"Chopper backwash."

Once the helicopter arrived, everything happened quickly. A basket came down, and Brandon lifted her into it, strapped, buckled, and stood.

Fear suddenly swamped her. She'd be hanging in this basket by a mere rope! *God, I know it's awful early for me to be asking things of You, but I'm so scared. Please help me.*

Brandon writhed in a few blurring motions then took a hook and clipped it to the rope. "Ready for the ride of your life?"

"With you?" Her heart stopped thundering. God answered her prayer more quickly and much better than she could have imagined.

"Yeah." He gave a signal, and they lifted off.

Once inside the helicopter, Brandon scooted off to one side. Medics converged around her, asking questions and yanking back the covers.

In one slim minute she had an IV and felt like she'd been caught in a spider web of electronic wires. Brandon leaned forward and barked, "Give her something. She hurts."

They radioed, took an order, and pulled a syringe out of a package. Brandon leaned close and hollered in her ear, "You're okay now, babe. You'll feel lots better in just a second."

She tried her hardest to smile at him, but the world started to tilt crazily then spin. Reaching toward him to grab his hand, she cried, "Bra—" but the world went dark.

Chapter 21

W e need permission to treat. Who's the next of kin?"

Brandon dumped Della's bag on the floor of the Emergency Department. "She has an emergency treatment consent card signed in her wallet. Do what you need to."

When they'd gone camping, she'd laughed at his attention to that seemingly ridiculous detail and proclaimed she trusted him to keep her safe. He'd insisted; now he was glad he had.

"I want to go back to be with her."

"Are you family?"

"We're engaged." Happy words, those.

"I guess it's okay. She's in bay three."

Brandon strode back and stood outside the curtains. "Permission to enter?"

Someone chuckled. "Permission granted."

"Thanks." He parted the curtains and stepped inside. Dressed in one of those ridiculous hospital gowns, Della lay on the gurney fast asleep. It did his heart good to see the deeply etched lines of pain gone from around her eyes and lips. "How is she?"

"Minimal exposure. She did a great job of staying hydrated and warm. We're taking her to X-ray her leg."

"Thanks." While they took her off, he ducked into the men's room, splashed off, and shaved. As he swiped off the last swatch of his day-old stubble, he had to laugh. "Who would have ever guessed that I'd become this domesticated?"

It hurt to raise his arms to peel off his shirt. Between sleeplessness, sleeping on the hard ground, and carrying two packs and Della at the same time, his shoulder took considerable strain. He'd pay for it, but the cost was negligible; the joy he'd gained from leading Della to the Lord and asking her to become his wife were priceless. Eternal. He yanked on a clean T-shirt, grinned at his reflection, and headed back to sit by Della in the treatment room.

Wheels and rubber-soled shoes squeaked on the linoleum floor, and Della's gurney rolled back into the bay. He squinted at the nurse's badge. "Mary Jo. What did the X-rays show?"

"Doc will talk with you." She pointed to a jumble of lightweight aluminum tubes on the floor. "That was an ingenious splint."

"If you have a bag, I'll haul it out of here."

"How long was she lost?"

A lifetime. "Five days.

"Hurt, scared, and alone. Poor girl."

"She'll recover. She'll be better than ever."

"That's the spirit." Mary Jo took another pasty-colored flannel blanket out of a steel cabinet. "These are warmed. Ought to feel good to her."

"Thanks." Brandon helped her spread it over Della and noted how the nurse took care to leave Della's knee exposed, yet tucked the blankets back around her foot so she'd be warm enough. The ER was drafty.

"If I didn't know better, I would have thought she took a spill off a cycle." Mary Jo tucked towels under Della's leg and started cleaning it with Betadine. "She's got quite a road rash down the side of this leg. It's amazing it's not infected."

"She told me she poured hand sanitizer on it."

"Oh, *ow*. That had to hurt. Those are alcohol based."

The doctor came back in and shoved three X-rays onto a light box. "She's got a hairline fracture at the head of the tibia. Patella's not cracked. We had an MRI cancellation, so I want to slip her in that slot and see if she tore any ligaments."

"Great!"

The doctor gave him a dark look.

Brandon shrugged. "I believe in miracles. God let that machine be available for my Della."

"I see," the doctor said, but Brandon could tell by his tone he didn't see at all. What a pity.

"Her ring—she can't have on any metal in the machine." Mary Jo tugged off Della's engagement ring. "How about if you hold this for her?"

"Yeah."

An hour and a half later, the doctor shook his head. "Someone's guardian angel was watching out for her. The preliminary reading by our radiologist says the ligaments are okay. The swelling's from the fracture and blood in the joint. She's too swollen to cast, but I can tape her knee."

"Do it," Brandon decided aloud as he slipped the ring back on her finger. He smiled at Mary Jo. "Let's not tell her that came off. She's sentimental."

✠

Della hobbled across her shop on the fiberglass walking cast. "Brandon!"

"What are you doing here?" He scowled. "You need to be taking it easy."

"I got my cast last night. See?"

He looked down and burst out laughing.

"I thought it looked spectacular."

346

"Who did that?"

She glanced past the hem of her pale blue-and-white floral sundress at the pale pink fiberglass affair that went from her toes to just above her knee. "Vanessa glued on the pearls and silver beads. Valene painted the designs and lettering."

Ellen Zobel straightened a gown on a nearby mannequin. "I wish I had my daughters' artistic talent. I can't get this right."

"Once you accessorize it with the necklace and bouquet, it'll look perfect." Without Ellen's help, Della would have had to close down the shop. She'd been, literally, a godsend.

Brandon ignored their exchange and stayed focused on Della's cast. He read aloud, "Here comes the bride," then tilted his head to study the hearts and curlicues. "It's great. Especially the top. Who did that?"

She didn't dare look down again and played coy. "Oh, that little thing?"

He nodded. "I like the blue ribbon on it."

"Well, you know the old saying, something old, something new, something borrowed, something blue, and"—she wiggled to give him a side view of her foot where they'd glued one last item—"a penny in her shoe."

He threw back his head and belted out a deep, wonderful laugh.

Della slipped her arms around his waist—as much for balance as affection, and he held her. "I'm one of a kind, Brandon."

"Babe, I'm so glad I found you!" He shifted her to the side, stooped, and swept her off her feet. Striding toward a padded bench over by the dressing rooms, he tacked on, "But I'm not happy at all about you zipping around. I want you to heal"—his voice dropped to a thrillingly deep, low level—"fast."

Della rested her head on his shoulder. "Doc said four weeks."

Brandon growled.

She laughed. "That's barely enough time to order, receive, and send out the invitations."

"You're on your own there. You've seen my handwriting." He seated her on the bench and tickled her newly painted toes.

"It would help if you gave me a guest list."

Ellen groaned aloud. "You don't know what you're asking for. When Val married Jordan, he invited hundreds of guys he'd known in the service."

"That's fine with me." Della beamed up at Brandon. "This is the happiest day of my life. Everyone's welcome to share it!"

"How many does the church hold?" Brandon gave her a calculating look.

"Five hundred." Demurely tugging down the hem of her dress, she added, "I did a layout of The Spindles and figured if we use the entire downstairs, we can seat four hundred and twenty-five for a meal."

He whistled. "That's gonna be steep."

"Nope." Della gave him a perky smile. "One of the benefits of my business—the caterer, musicians, photographer, and Forget-Me-Not Flowers all offered to do everything at cost."

"Great." Brandon clapped his hands together and rubbed them. "I've got a bunch of men who'll never go to church, but they'll come to my wedding—especially if I tell them you've invited single friends."

"Okay. I know a lot of single women. We can have Pastor MacIntosh do what he did at your cousin's wedding—give the salvation message."

"One other important thing." Brandon tilted her face upward. "No negotiating. I want you to promise me you won't wear heels."

"You, too? What is this?" Della let out a sigh. "Daddy, the doctor, my brothers, Van and Val—everyone is nagging me about that."

"Ellen? Did she listen to them?"

Ellen bustled over and showed him a pair of beaded satin ballet-type slippers. "I chose these for her. What do you think?"

He took one and shoved his thumbs inside then pulled on it. "It stretches. If it were a little bigger, it would fit over the cast. . . ."

"You're nuts!" Della cried.

"Yep. Certifiably crazy about you." He set the slipper onto the bench beside her and straightened up. "We're pouring the foundation of our house this afternoon. Wanna come watch?"

"Yes!" She hopped up from the bench and hobbled toward the cash register.

"What are you doing?"

"I want to put something in the cement."

"Like what?"

The small metal box made a racket as she set it on the counter. Brandon opened the lid. "A glove."

"From the first time we met."

He nodded. "Tennis ball—from batting practice."

She peered into the box. "Sand from our morning jogs on the beach."

"And a rock?"

She touched the water-washed stone reverently. "From the creek where you found me. Because Christ is the Solid Rock of our relationship, and no other foundation will do."

✝

Satin rustled, and Brandon couldn't wipe the grin from his face even if he wanted to. His bride was the most beautiful woman in the world. The answer to his prayers, gift-wrapped in satin and lace, let go of his hands after they'd exchanged vows and wedding bands. Brandon helped Della kneel at the altar. Her snowy gown flowed behind her, and the veil softened his view of her face.

He took his place beside her and slid his left arm around her tiny waist. It was all so right—this special closeness they felt as their pastor prepared to serve them Holy Communion.

They'd had premarital counseling, and he'd developed a whole new view of marriage. This would be the first time he and Della would break bread together as man and wife. Sharing the Lord's cup held deep significance—God was the center of their marriage. Through Him, the two of them became one.

Hands and heart joined, they finally rose and turned to one another. Lifting her veil gave him a rush of joy. Love lit her eyes, and the kiss they shared was the sweetest thing in his life.

"Ladies and gentlemen," Pastor MacIntosh said, "I'd like to introduce you to Mr. and Mrs. Brandon Stevens."

Vanessa was Della's matron of honor. She hastily gave the bouquet back to Della, and Brandon tucked Della's hand into the crook of his arm. He led her up the aisle, out of the church, and on to the bright future God had given them.

Love Worth Keeping

by Joyce Livingston

Dedication

I dedicate this book to my wonderful children, their sweet spouses,
and their families who stood with me through this very trying year
as we faced the eminent death of my dear husband—their father and grandfather.
I could never have made it through this time with you and your unselfish love:
Dawn Lee, Don Jr. and Helen, Mark and Cat, Dari and Wally,
Matthew and Sherry, Luke and Tammie.
I love you all more than words can say.
You are all a gift from God. Thank you, thank you, thank you.
And, as always, this book and any other book I may ever write
is dedicated to my precious husband and my greatest fan, Don Livingston.
Don, you may be gone but my love for you will never die.

Chapter 1

A Christmas wedding?" Tessa Garrett stared at her daughter in wide-eyed amazement then shook her head disapprovingly. "Impossible. Christmas is only two weeks away!"

"Mom, Jim and I have already decided we're not going to wait until spring when I graduate from college. We want to get married on Christmas Day, like you and Daddy did. I've already called about the church and. . ." Katie's eyes lit up as she chattered on, apparently oblivious to her mother's bewildered response.

Tessa held up her hands in defeat and heaved a sigh, knowing from experience that once Katie's mind was made up there was little use trying to argue with her. That child was just like her father—strong-willed and stubborn. This was not at all what she'd wanted for her precious daughter. She'd envisioned a spring wedding, maybe held in the arboretum, with bridesmaids in pastel gowns, winding matching ribbons around a maypole, and—

"Earth to Mother," Katie chimed in a playful manner as she waved her hands before Tessa's face. "Yoo-hoo!"

Tessa offered a weak smile and attempted to keep disappointment from tainting her voice. "Well, I suppose I should be grateful you've decided to get married, rather than continue to live together, like you two have done for the past few months. Given the two choices, I'd opt for a wedding any day."

Katie's eyes widened. "What? You're not going to try to convince me to wait?"

Tessa eyed her beautiful daughter, her heart filled with love for this child who had so quickly grown into a woman. "It sounds like an impossible task but. . ." She swallowed hard, trying to avoid the argument she knew was inevitable if she didn't agree to this sudden wedding. Knowing how impulsive Katie could be, her headstrong daughter might even elope, and she'd miss being a part of the most important day in her child's life. "I—ah—I guess Christmas Day is as good as any. If you're certain you want to go through with this—"

"Yes, I do want to!" Katie threw her arms about her mother's neck and kissed her cheek repeatedly, her face shining with joy. "Oh, Mom, I love you. I told Jim you'd see it our way. This is so exciting! I'm going to be married. In just two weeks!"

"Look," Tessa began as she glanced around the busy restaurant, her voice now soft and pleading, knowing full well her determined daughter was not one to be reckoned with under the best of circumstances. "I'm happy you've decided to tie the knot. You know I've never liked the idea of you and Jim living together. It's just something we Christians don't do."

Katie stole a quick glance at her fiancé of six months who was sitting silently beside her, their chairs pulled close together at the small, round table. "I guess that means you're okay with our Christmas wedding?"

Tessa leaned back in her chair as a slow smile crept across her face. "Of course I am. Are you sure you want Christmas Day, not Christmas Eve?"

"Jim wanted it to be Christmas Eve. I wanted Christmas Day, early evening."

"So, which is it?"

Jim, who'd uttered barely a word until now, slipped an arm about Katie's shoulders and pulled her close. "Christmas Day."

The three laughed.

Tessa's mood sobered. "What about premarital counseling? I know Pastor McIntosh requires it of all the couples he marries."

"We've already met with him, Mom. He really laid it on the line for both of us. I've decided it's time for me to get my life back together. I've been away from the Lord way too long."

"I've accepted Christ as my Savior. Katie and I are both really excited about our relationship with God. I have a lot to learn, and Katie said she does, too. We're going to start attending the Young Married Class at Seaside Community Church. Oh, and Katie forgot to mention that I've moved out of the condo temporarily. One of my single coworkers offered to let me stay with him until after our wedding."

Tessa wanted to shout hallelujah. She'd been praying for Katie for so long, and God had answered her prayer. She reached across the table and cupped her soon-to-be son-in-law's hand. "You have no idea how happy this makes me."

Katie leaned her head onto Jim's shoulder affectionately. "I knew you'd be happy about it, Mom. I probably should have told you after we met with Pastor McIntosh, but I wanted Jim to be here when I told you."

"So Christmas Day it is. But Christmas, Katie? Couldn't you have at least made it New Year's Day? Two weeks to plan and prepare for a wedding, even a small wedding, isn't nearly enough time." Tessa pulled a little calendar from the pocket in her checkbook and began to scan the dates in December.

"Enough time for what?" Katie's good-looking father asked as he removed his coat, kissed the younger woman on the forehead, and then dropped into a chair beside Tessa. "Sorry I'm late."

Tessa felt her smile disappear and her face blanch. She avoided the man's eyes and stared at her daughter. "What is *he* doing here?" she asked, wishing he weren't yet suddenly feeling self-conscious. The ambivalence she felt toward Mike was infuriating, and his presence always made her behave irrationally.

"I," the man announced proudly as he tossed his coat onto a nearby empty chair, "was invited here to have lunch with my lovely daughter." With a tender smile and a nod, he gestured toward Katie, who was seated directly across the table, then shook hands with Jim. "And although I'm not sure why she'd want the two of us to be in the same place at the same time, considering how you feel about me, I'm glad she did."

Tessa answered by crossing her arms and tilting her chin. "You'll find out soon enough."

He rubbed his hands together vigorously as if in anticipation and focused his attention on his daughter. "What's up, kiddo?"

Katie's eyes sparkled as she latched onto her father's hand and gave it a squeeze. "Jim and I are getting married!"

His face brightened. "No more of this cohabitation stuff?"

Katie blushed. "Nope, we're tying the knot, as Mom says."

He let out a long sigh of relief. "Glad to hear it. I never did like that arrangement."

"You sound like Mom! You should also be glad to hear that Jim is staying with a single coworker temporarily. Jim is a brand-new Christian, Daddy."

"You're right; I am happy to hear that—both parts. Congratulations, Jim. Glad to see you'll be starting out on the right foot to build a solid marriage."

Tessa waited until the waiter moved on before speaking her piece. "Yes, but I'm sure Jim won't follow Mike's example—"

Katie thumped her hand on the table. "Mom, please! Can't you two be in the same room for five minutes without sniping at one another?"

"I never said a word," her father interjected defensively. "Your mother started it, as usual."

Quickly shoving back her chair and rising to her feet, Katie wadded up her napkin and tossed it onto the table. "Either you two call a cease-fire, or I'm leaving, and Jim and I will elope."

Tessa grabbed at her daughter's wrist. "Katie, you're making a scene. Please sit down," she urged quietly.

"Say you're sorry, Mother, or we're outta here." Her daughter waited, her accusing gaze fixed on Tessa's face.

She swallowed hard. "Okay. I–I'm sorry."

Katie sank slowly into her chair. "Don't tell *me*," she said with a nod toward her father. "Tell him."

"Katie, I—"

Her daughter narrowed her eyes and cocked her head, her expression serious. "Now, please, or we're history."

Tessa sucked in her breath and held it. If there was anything she hated to do when it came to the husband she'd separated herself from, it was to admit she'd been in the wrong—about anything. But apparently, this time, she had no choice. "Oh, all right," she said, her gaze still pinned on Katie. "I'm sorry, Mike."

"At least you could look at me when you apologize, Tessie," Mike remarked with a taunting smile in his voice. "I can't remember the last time I heard you apologize. For anything."

Tessa watched as Katie's finger flew into her father's face. "And now you need to tell Mom *you're* sorry! That remark was uncalled-for, Daddy."

"See?" Tessa snapped, no longer caring about those seated around them hearing their conversation. "That's what I knew I'd get from that man. Nothing but snide remarks." *Even though what he said is true,* she reluctantly admitted to herself, trying to recall her last sincere apology to Mike.

Katie rose slightly, bent toward the quarrelsome pair, and stuck her chin out defiantly, her hands braced on the table, a look of disgust etched across her face. "I can't believe this. You two are worse than a couple of kindergartners. Why can't you be like other divorced or separated parents and bury the hatchet somewhere other than in each other's heads? You've been apart for eight years now. It's about time the two of you grew up!"

Mike leaned back in his chair, linking his fingers over his chest with a look of contrition. "Oh, pumpkin, I'm sorry. Your mom seems to bring out the worst in me."

"In you?" Tessa retorted, her anger rising again. "What about what you do to me?"

Katie's fist hit the table. "Stop it! Now! I refuse to tolerate this childishness one second more!"

The entire restaurant grew silent as waiters and customers stared in their direction. Jim, his face now a deep crimson, raised his water glass and took a long drink. Tessa slid down in her chair, wishing she'd kept her voice down to a whisper. "I'm sorry, Katie. I never meant to upset you."

Mike gave Tessa a pensive glance before turning his attention back to Katie. "I'm sorry, too, pumpkin."

"Good. Thank you," Katie said as she sat down. "Now that we've all settled down and will hopefully stay that way," she added softly, eyeing first one parent and then the other, "do you want to hear about our wedding plans?"

Each gave her a sheepish nod.

Donning a fresh smile, Katie took Jim's hand, her enthusiasm obviously rekindled. "Jim and I thought—"

"First," Tessa interrupted, still rankled at having to share this moment with her estranged husband, "I just want to say that this incident wouldn't have happened if you'd told me he was invited today. Although I wasn't expecting him, your father's late arrival was a vivid reminder—"

"Mother! Let it rest! It's not important now," Katie warned, looking highly annoyed again.

"I'm just trying to say I got upset because he was late for something so important to you. Nothing has changed."

Katie leaned forward, her elbows resting on the table and, gritting her teeth, said in an almost monotone, "Water under the bridge, Mom. That was years ago."

Her daughter was right, and Tessa was ashamed of allowing her own bitterness to spoil what should be a celebration. "For your sake, I'll try to leave it in the past." The deep hurts she'd tried to bury for the past eight years always tumbled to the surface whenever Mike was around, and Tessa already feared she wouldn't be able to keep her word.

Katie reached across Jim and gave her father's hand an affectionate squeeze. "You and Daddy may be separated and living apart, but he's still my dad and an important part of my life. You both are. You have to accept that, Mother."

"I know that, Katie." Long ago, Tessa had imagined her daughter's wedding as a happy time—that she and Mike would be a good example for their daughter and her future husband to follow. She knew now just how miserably they had failed.

Acting as though he'd been ignoring their exchange, Mike picked up the menu and began to peruse it. "I'm sure your mother is as interested in hearing about this wedding as I am. When is it going to be? After your graduation?"

Katie giggled as her face brightened. "Oh, Daddy, I knew you'd be happy for us. No, not after graduation. It's going to be Christmas Day, and we—"

Her father closed the menu and stared at his daughter, open-mouthed. "*This* Christmas Day? That's only two weeks off." A smile tilted at his lips. "Oh, I get it! You're going to elope, and you want your mother and me to go with you, right? That sounds like fun. Where are we going?"

Again, she giggled. "No, silly, we're not going to elope! And yes, it's *this* Christmas!"

Finally, after sitting quietly during the bantering and arguing, Jim spoke up, his arm circling his beloved. "Katie wants to be married on Christmas Day, just like you two were."

"We were going to wait until I graduated in the spring." Katie leaned into Jim and smiled lovingly into his face before going on. "But we suddenly realized that if we'd hurry, we'd have time to plan the wedding and most of our close friends could attend since they'll be in town for the holidays. Isn't that a great idea?"

"But—"

Katie went on, "We already have our condo. And with us married, it'll be much easier for me to concentrate on my studies this last semester instead of worrying about planning a wedding."

"But with going to school and your job and getting married, can you keep it all up?" Tessa asked, still not sure a Christmas wedding was a good idea.

Jim smiled confidently. "I want Katie to quit her job, Tessa. Since the construction company is doing so well, I'm making enough to support us both. This way she can spend all her time finishing up her schooling."

"And," Katie added, her excitement and enthusiasm bubbling over, "we've already talked to Pastor McIntosh and reserved the chapel at Seaside Community Church for Christmas Day. We'll have plenty of time to put up the decorations. The wedding is set for eight o'clock that evening."

"And," Jim said after giving his fiancée a quick peck on the cheek, "we have the chapel reserved for the rehearsal the evening of the twenty-third."

Katie grinned at her parents. "Pastor McIntosh said—"

Mike pursed his lips and shrugged. "Sounds to me like this wedding was going to happen whether your mother and I agreed to it or not. Looks like you two have things well in hand."

"But your wedding gown, Katie. . .what will you wear?" Tessa asked, still in shock over her daughter's announcement. She'd looked forward to her daughter's wedding day with eager anticipation for years, expecting they'd have months to plan and prepare for it. She'd wanted it to be the best wedding ever. Not the simple no-frills kind she and Mike had, but an all-out formal wedding.

Katie beamed. "Remember the gown I showed you in that bridal magazine when we were at your house for Thanksgiving? The one with the long train and the beaded organza bodice?"

Tessa nodded. She well remembered the dress. It was exactly the kind she would have picked for Katie. Expensive, yes, but this was her only daughter. That gown would be well worth the price.

"I called my friend Della at her bridal shop, and she said she could order it and it'd be here in three days! The very same dress! Isn't that just too cool?"

Tessa's jaw dropped. "Am I hearing you right? You're planning on having a *full formal* wedding? With all the trimmings? In only two weeks?"

Katie's smile broadened. "Uh-huh, just like we've always talked about."

"With only two weeks to pull it together?" Tessa nearly choked, just saying the words.

"There's plenty of time," Katie said confidently. She paused long enough to take a deep breath then offered her mother a loving smile. "*If* you'll help me."

Still struggling for words, Tessa gave her head a slight nod. "You—you know

I'll help you, dear, but—"

"Thanks. I knew I could count on you, Mom."

Mike unfolded his napkin and placed it on his lap. "Yeah, you can count on me, too, pumpkin. I'll help you in any way I can."

"You'll help? When would you ever find time?" Tessa asked, her voice laced with sarcasm she instantly regretted.

"Mother!"

"It's okay," Mike said, gesturing toward Tessa. "Old habits are hard for your mother to break."

"So, dear," Tessa said, forcing herself to ignore his comment and concentrate on the issue at hand, "who is going to be your maid of honor? And what about bridesmaids and a flower girl and a ring bearer? Invitations? There is so much to do. I'm not sure, even with my help, that you're going to be able to pull this off in fourteen days."

"We've already purchased our invitations. They should be ready by tomorrow." Katie reached into her purse, pulled out a list, and began to read. "Let's see. Valene Young will be my matron of honor, of course, since she's my best friend. I'm only having two bridesmaids—Valene's twin sister, Vanessa, since she's almost as close a friend as Val—and Della." She continued to check her list. "Do you think Carrie is old enough to be my flower girl?"

Tessa nodded. "That little cousin of yours is almost four now. I'm sure she'll be able to sprinkle rose petals with no trouble at all. Who else?"

"Ryan is nearly eight," Katie went on. "Do you think he'd act as ring bearer? I don't want to embarrass him."

Her father shrugged his broad shoulders. "Getting him to be the ring bearer might not be a problem, but getting him into a tux? I don't know about that."

Katie shot him a confident smile. "Well, you're his uncle. I'll bet you can convince him."

He returned her challenge with a consenting wink.

"Jim is asking Jordan Young, his best friend, to stand up with him. Nathan, Vanessa's husband, and Della's husband, Brandon, will be his groomsmen." She turned back to Mike. "You will give me away, won't you, Daddy?"

Mike blinked hard in a rare show of emotion. "Sure, honey. I'd be honored."

"Maybe not when you hear the rest of my request," Katie said as she glanced nervously from one parent to the other. "I want Mom to give me away, too."

"Is that proper?" Tessa asked, stunned by her daughter's strange request.

"Hey, it's their wedding. If she wants us both, I'm agreeable to it. What about you, Tessie?" Mike eyed his wife warily.

Tessa bit at her lip. Why did it always seem he was offering her a challenge? It was as if he enjoyed putting her on the spot every chance he got. Well, she'd show him! "I think it's a lovely idea. Of course, I'm agreeable. Now, what other plans do you have?"

Katie seemed surprised her mother didn't offer any flack but didn't mention it and went on checking her list. "Mother, I know you're busy helping at Grandpa's plumbing shop so I'm going to take care of almost everything. The florist, the caterer, the photographer, the organist, and I'll ask Jane Moray to sing, of course. I love her voice. I'm going to ask her husband Keene, too, if he'll be in town. Wouldn't it be fabulous to have a famous opera singer like Keene sing at our wedding?" Katie paused thoughtfully. "I've already arranged for Valene and Vanessa to go to Della's bridal shop and choose their dresses." She turned to Jim. "You'll have to set up the tux fittings for the men, and don't forget one for Ryan."

Jim nodded. "Gotcha."

Then turning to her father, she added, "Daddy, you need to go, too, and—"

Mike stared down at the table. "Whoa, I'm getting dizzy just thinking about all of this. Sounds to me like a lot still has to be done to pull off this wedding. Are you sure you two can handle it, honey? You'd better let me and your mother help with some of those things." He grinned. "Or wait until spring! You have enough to do just finishing up your last semester of college. You need to keep your nose to the grindstone if you want to be an architect and make the big bucks."

Tessa bit her lip, finding it almost impossible to not respond. *Oh, Mike. You offer to do something, then you disappear when it's time to do it. You've been that way as long as I can remember. I know you're going to disappoint her again.*

"Thanks, Daddy. If it weren't for you paying my tuition and other expenses, and the scholarships and grants I've qualified for, I wouldn't be able to be a full-time college student. Being an architect major is more work than I'd anticipated. But I'll make it. I have to, and someday I plan to pay you back." Katie tossed her father a confident smile as she patted his arm. "If I find I'm having trouble getting all of it done, I'll call and tell you. I just figured the holiday season was probably one of the busiest times of the year for you and—" She stopped abruptly when Mike's cell phone rang.

"You can forget about paying me back. I wouldn't take it anyway. Paying your way through college was the least I could do for my only daughter." He snatched the phone from his jacket pocket and put it to his ear. "Garrett here. Uh-huh. Uh-huh. Where? Call the coroner. I'm on my way."

Tessa shoved back from the table hard enough to make her chair squeak on the restaurant's highly polished hardwood floors. "Couldn't you have turned that thing off, Mike? This is an important time for your daughter! Surely the San Diego police force can get along without their star detective for at least one hour."

Obviously ignoring Tessa's remark, he rose from his chair and grabbed his coat. "Sorry, pumpkin, gotta go."

"I know. You don't have to explain, Daddy." Katie gave him an understanding smile.

"Sure, Mike, she's used to her father being gone at the important times of her life," Tessa snapped, silently chastising herself for breaking her word again.

Katie slapped at her mother's arm. "Daddy can't help it if someone needs him. It's important, or they wouldn't have called him!"

Mike's unresponsive silence irked Tessa.

Smiling, Mike stretched out his hand to his prospective son-in-law. "Congratulations, Jim. You're getting the very best."

Still ignoring Tessa, which he seemed to be doing all too often for her satisfaction, he bent and gave his daughter an affectionate peck on the cheek.

"I'll help anyway I can, and don't worry about the cost. Let's do this wedding up right."

Then, with an appeasing look Tessa couldn't understand—especially considering their earlier bickering—he told her with a sly grin and without raising his voice, "Nice to see you again, Tessie. You're lookin' good."

Caught off guard by his surprise compliment, which actually seemed sincere, Tessa stared at him, whispering only a timid, "Thank you."

"Too bad your dad had to leave early, honey," Jim said once Mike was gone, consoling Katie with a pat on her shoulder. "At least we got to tell him our good news."

Katie's fingers reached up and cupped his hand before turning to her mother, a deep frown furling her brow. "Did you have to make that remark about him being gone at the important times?"

Tessa felt very small. She'd known before she'd finished saying it that her comment had been snide and out of place. "For your sake, if for no other reason," she told Katie meekly, "I should've kept my mouth shut. I know that. But when I think about all the times—"

"Mother! Can't you drop that old subject? It's been hashed and rehashed hundreds of times. We're here to discuss my wedding, not beat up on Daddy."

✝

Mike arrived at his destination in less than five minutes. Although he'd tried to concentrate on the information he'd been given over the phone, his mind kept wandering back to the restaurant.

Tessie. That woman could whip him into a frenzy without even trying. They hadn't had a decent conversation in more than eight years.

He checked the rearview mirror and quickly pulled into a narrow alley, bringing his car to a stop near a battered blue Dumpster.

"Hated to call you," Hal Lester, the officer on duty, explained as he hurried toward him, clipboard and pen in hand. "I heard you were having lunch with your daughter, but—"

"Don't worry about it." Mike shrugged. "It's part of my job. My daughter's used to it, but your call sure bothered her mother."

The man frowned as if confused. "I thought you've been divorced for years."

"Not divorced. Separated." Mike shoved his keys into his pocket with a sigh. "Might as well have been divorced, but she doesn't believe in it." He grimaced. "Actually, neither do I."

"It's tough. My wife has always hated me being a cop. I'm waiting for the day she gives me the old ultimatum. Her way or the highway, as they say. I'd sure hate to have to choose."

"Goes with the territory, my friend. Now," Mike added as he pulled out his notebook, "let's get at it." He put his hand on the man's shoulder, eager for a change of subject. "Who found our Jane Doe?"

The officer checked the notes on his clipboard. "Some teenage kid who was skipping school and wandering around the neighborhood. Said he was looking in the Dumpster for aluminum cans. He was pretty shaken up." He gestured toward the black-and-white vehicle parked farther down the alley. "He's sitting in my car."

"Any ID on her?"

"Nope."

"Cuts or bruises?"

The man nodded as he pulled the woman's hair back from her face, exposing a mass of purple, green, and yellow bruises, some appearing to have been there for several days. "Oh, yeah. Big-time. Looks like she's been used as a punching bag."

"Just like the other Jane Does we've had in the past few months. We've got to catch this guy. The whole area is in a panic. I worry about my daughter crossing the campus at night. No woman is safe." Mike crouched down and stared at the woman. "I hate calls like this. Never get used to them, but someone has to do the job. Think what the world would be like if there weren't guys like us around. I look at this job as a calling. If I didn't, I'm not sure I could stay with it. Things like this make me sick to my stomach. Sometimes I wish I'd decided to be a plumber instead of a cop, like my wife wanted me to be."

Hal squatted down beside him. "I know. Me, too. I try to explain the importance of our job to my wife all the time, but all she can think about is the evenings I'm away from her and the kids, the weird hours we work, and the moods we're sometimes in because of what we've had to deal with during our shift. Not to mention the danger."

"I know exactly what you mean. Each time I left for work, Tessa was afraid

I wouldn't come back. It became an obsession with her. It was all she could think about. Every siren she heard, she thought was an ambulance coming after me because I'd been shot. When the phone rang, she expected to hear I had been killed in a gun battle. Her paranoia drove me crazy. I tried to explain to her I rarely even had to draw my gun, but she was too obsessed to listen. Eventually, her unfounded worries and my dedication to the job became the wedge that drove us apart, and our marriage ended." With a sad shake of his head, Mike stood, his gaze still pinned on the unknown woman who lay at his feet. "Enough of my sad tale. Guess we'd better get moving. Dealing with this Jane Doe situation ain't gonna get any easier."

Tessa sat at her desk at Calhoun's Plumbing, Heating, and Air-Conditioning, staring at the invoice in her hand, not really seeing it. Her mind was elsewhere. *A Christmas Day wedding?* she asked inwardly with a shake of her head. *That girl! I hope she realizes what she's getting herself into, planning a formal wedding in less than two weeks.*

"Good lunch with Katie?" Unannounced, Tessa's father strode into her office, dressed in his gray uniform with the Calhoun's Plumbing, Heating, and Air-Conditioning emblem sewn over the pocket. "How is that granddaughter of mine?"

Tessa turned to the man with a smile, still clutching the invoice in her hand. "She and Jim are getting married Christmas Day."

He perched himself on the corner of the desk and gave her a broad grin. "Eloping, huh? But when you elope aren't you supposed to keep it a secret from your parents?"

"They're not eloping, Dad. She's having a full formal wedding, complete with gown, bridesmaids, and men in tuxedos, at the church."

He took the invoice from her hand and placed it on a stack of papers, but she barely noticed. "You serious?"

"Ridiculously serious. She announced it at lunch."

"Guess that means you'll be taking some time off. Well, don't worry about it. The girls in the office can handle everything, and they can call you if they can't. I really appreciate you helping out like this while Caroline is on sick leave. It may be months before she's able to come back to work."

She nodded. "I hate to leave you high and dry, but thanks, Dad. I have a feeling Katie will be needing all the help I can give her."

"Mike know yet?"

She propped her elbows on the desk and rested her chin in her palms. "He was there, too. She'd invited him."

He stood, walked around the desk, and slipped an arm about her shoulders.

"I know that must have been difficult. But, Tessa, it's been eight years. You've got to get over your hard feelings toward Mike. That man has suffered, too, and he's going to be a part of your daughter's life as long as he's around."

She leaned into his side with a sigh. "I know. When Katie asked me to help her with her wedding and Mike volunteered to help, too, I behaved rather badly. Katie was pretty upset with me, and I don't blame her."

Her father took one of her hands and stroked it as he held it in his grasp. "Maybe it's time you divorced Mike and found someone else—"

"Someone else? Surely you don't mean that, Dad." She lifted her gaze to meet his. "I can't. The scriptures won't let me."

"Do you really think God expects you to spend the rest of your life alone?"

Tessa stared up into his eyes. Her father was a good man—one of the best. However, he had never felt the need to have God in his life. How well she remembered the last time she'd tried to share her faith with him. He'd made it perfectly clear he could get along just fine without God. He claimed he'd never done a single thing in his life he need be ashamed of, so he was convinced a God of love would never condemn him. He'd even asked Tessa to never bring up the subject again. She had resigned herself to trying to live the Christian life before him and let it be her witness. Why couldn't he understand the worst sin of all was to refuse God's love and sacrifice?

"You could always let Mike back into your life."

She pulled away from him. "Not after what he did!"

"Other than devoting his life to his job, exactly what did he do, Tessa, that would make you cast him aside like a old piece of jewelry you'd tired of? I know you worried about him all the time, but danger and the risk of injury go with his job. You knew that when you married him. Didn't you take vows at your wedding that said for better or for worse? Seems to me the *worse* part was Mike's job. I would think your God—"

"I'd rather not discuss it." How could she discuss it without admitting that, even though she had meant those vows at the time, she had been sure she could talk Mike into quitting the police force and take a simple nine-to-five job, one that wouldn't put him in danger?

He placed his hands on her shoulders and spun her around to face him. "Look, Katie's getting married. She's already moved out. You really don't want to spend the rest of your life rattling around in that big house all alone, do you?"

"I like that house." Though she hadn't given him a direct answer, she had given that very question more consideration than she cared to admit. Would she be happy living in that house alone? She'd never be comfortable living in an apartment or a condo. She loved that house. It was exactly what she and Mike had wanted—the house of their dreams.

Tessa drew in a deep breath and let it out slowly. The house on Forrest Street was no longer *his* home. It was stupid, she knew, but although the man had been out of her life for eight years now, she still thought of it as *their* home. Hers *and* Mike's. The nightstand on his side of the bed still contained every item it had held before he left, right down to the little dispenser of dental floss he used every night.

Why, she didn't know, but she could never get rid of those things. Even his suits and shirts still hung in the closets. He'd never asked for them, and she'd never been able to get rid of them. Occasionally, on long nights when Katie was sleeping soundly in her bed, Tessa would pull one of his suits from the rack and hold it close, savoring the faint lingering smell of his aftershave. Sometimes, she'd even wrap the sleeves about her shoulders and pretend he was holding her close.

"I know Gordon Banks has taken a liking to you," her father was saying. "Rod told me he invited you to have coffee with him after church Sunday evening. Maybe you ought to take him up on his offer. He's a good man, and he's been mighty lonely since he lost Sarah."

She pulled from his grasp and slowly made her way to the window, her eyes glazing over. "Even if I felt God would allow it, I could never love another man, Dad. Not the way I loved Mike."

Her father moved up behind her and gently began to knead her tense neck muscles then softly whispered into her ear. "Loved? Or still love?"

Chapter 2

D on't be ridiculous!" Tessa scoffed at her father, appalled by the idea. "Any love I had for Mike died long ago."

Mr. Calhoun raised a questioning brow. "Methinks the lady protests too much."

She gave him a flip of her hand. "Come on, Dad, don't you remember how Mike never had time for me or Katie? He was too busy playing detective. His job always came before his family."

He perched himself on the corner of her desk again and pulled a ballpoint pen from the mug where she kept them, eyeing it and twirling it between his fingers. "Did you say *playing*? I wouldn't exactly call putting your life in constant danger to protect the community *playing*. Seems like a ton of work to me. Dedicated work. Dangerous work."

"Exactly! Extremely dangerous work, but he loves it, Dad—thrives on it. Even though he knew I was always crazy with worry, I doubt he ever considered the danger involved. His dad was a cop. He's a cop. He claims it's in his blood."

"As I recall, you knew that even before the first date you two had. I distinctly remember you telling me the first day you met him he'd told you he was going to be a cop, or did you forget that little fact?" After placing the pen back in its place, he sat quietly, as if expecting the outburst that was about to erupt.

"You're right, but that was before we started dating! If he loved me and knew how I felt about it, I was hoping he would change his plans."

"Oh? You actually thought his plans were going to change? Just because he met you and you were squeamish about his chosen occupation?"

"My plans changed. I was going to be a nurse. I gave mine up for him!"

"Not the same thing."

She felt her anger rising. How dare he defend Mike! "Of course it's the same thing!"

"Nope. He couldn't have the babies."

"Have the babies? That gives him the right to take a job that allows him no time for his family and sets him up for possible death? Why was it my responsibility to be there twenty-four/seven? Where was he when Katie ran a fever, cut her teeth, or fell down and required stitches? Where was he when she was in the programs at school? Played team sports? Had teacher's conferences?" She rammed her finger into her chest. "I was the one who was there! The one who was both mother and father to her. The one who took her to church. Taught her right from wrong. Punished her when she needed it. Held her when she was afraid. Kissed her hurts away. Not Mike!"

He strode around the desk and slipped his arm about her shoulders. "Who made all those things possible?"

She pushed away and gazed up at him. "Who made all those things possible? What do you mean?"

"You were a stay-at-home mom, sweetie. Mike brought home the paycheck, paid the bills, and shielded you from the traumas of life. From what I've heard, he still is. Isn't he making the house payments and giving you a living allowance each month? And you're still covered by his insurance. I'm not sure you realize how lucky you have been. Many women would have given anything to stay at home like you did and be there for your child. Did you ever thank him for that?"

His words stunned her. "Thank him for letting me be a mother to his daughter?"

"He was the one who went off to work every day."

Now her dander was up. "I worked, too! Probably as hard as he did. Raising a daughter is not an easy task. Especially without your husband being around to help."

"And being a cop isn't hard?"

There he was, her own father, taking Mike's side again. "He didn't *have* to be a cop. He could have come to work with you. I know you offered him a partnership in the plumbing shop. That was a very generous offer. He should have taken it."

Her father let out a chuckle. "Yes, I offered him a partnership, but only because you wanted me to. I knew he'd never accept it. Can you imagine Mike Garrett as a plumber? I sure can't!"

"If he truly loved me, he would have accepted your offer."

"If *you* truly loved him, knowing his lifelong dream was to be on the police force, perhaps you would have accepted him for who and what he was."

A lump rose in Tessa's throat, making it hard to speak without tearing up. "I truly loved Mike, Dad, and you're right. I did know—even before we were engaged—that Mike had already chosen his profession to ultimately become a San Diego detective. But I had foolishly hoped once we were married he would change his mind. But he never did. He never even considered it—not once—though I begged him over and over. Our life was one big argument. Can't you see? He was married to the force, never to me. When push came to shove, he chose being a detective over being my husband."

Mr. Calhoun wrapped his long arms about his daughter, hugging her close.

"Ask yourself this question, daughter. Who did the pushing and shoving? Who gave Mike the ultimatum that forced him to make a choice?"

Though she would never voice it, in her heart she answered, *Me.*

He lovingly stroked her hair as she rested her head on his shoulder. "Whoever did that pushing and shoving was the one who ended your marriage," he whispered into her ear. "Perhaps that same person could put it back together again—if she wanted to."

It's too late, her heart said. *Much too late. Our marriage has ended.* "Mike was more interested in the partners he's had over the years than he was in me!"

"Wasn't that remark a little childish?"

"I don't think so. It's true," she shot back defensively.

"Partners have a common bond, Tessa. It's important that they work closely together. Their lives may depend on that trust and bonding."

"He never talked to me about the things *I* cared about, but he seemed to know everything that was going on in his partner's life."

"Perhaps some of that was your fault," he told her in a kindly manner. "Maybe it was your fault as much as Mike's that the two of you never had time for each other."

Tessa's heartbeat quickened. "What do you mean by that remark?"

He held up his fingers and began to enumerate. "You were a soccer mom, president of the Parent-Teacher Association, leader of the weekly women's Bible study class, and helped with the church bulletin. You attended jazz exercise classes three days a week, lunched with your friends, took painting classes, chauffeured Katie to her ballet lessons, kept score for her T-ball games, baked cookies for dozens of projects, worked on the voter registration, helped Katie with her homework—all kinds of things. Who knows what else? No wonder the two of you rarely communicated. You barely saw one another. From my perspective—let's face it—you were as inaccessible as he was."

Tessa gave her head a violent shake. "That's not true! I would have put those things aside if Mike would have taken a regular job."

"Like being a plumber?"

"Yes! Like being a plumber!"

Mr. Calhoun let loose a slight snicker. "Guess you don't remember all the calls I got when you were young and our family sat down to dinner. From customers whose sinks had stopped up and they were having company and needed me to come and fix their problems right away to toddlers flushing toys down the toilet. Or the hot water tank was leaking. Or it was ninety degrees outside and their air conditioner conked out on them. I wish your mother were here. You could ask her. I don't know how many meals she had to warm over for me because some customer had a problem—many times on holidays. But you know what?

She loved me, and she understood that my dad started Calhoun's Plumbing, Heating, and Air-Conditioning, and it was my legacy. Did she ever tell you what I really wanted was to be a pilot?"

Tessa stared at him. "A pilot? You?"

"Yes, I had loved flying since I was a young boy and took my first flight, and I wanted more than anything to be a pilot. But that would have meant leaving home and joining the Air Force, since that was the only way I could have afforded it. I'll never forget the day I told my dad I didn't want to be a plumber. It nearly broke his heart. It was only after I found out how much he had sacrificed to start the company he had wanted to pass on to his son—me—that I knew I could never do anything but follow in his footsteps. Though my desire to be a pilot never left me, I can honestly say I have never regretted giving it up. The love and sacrifice my father made for me was far more important than any old dream. That man worked round the clock, seven days a week, to get this company going. Like you resented the time Mike gave to his job, I resented the time my father gave to his. I remember one time, especially, when he didn't show up at the most important football game of my life. I was so mad when I saw my mom sitting in the stands by herself, I threw my helmet at the wall hard enough to crack it."

"Why wasn't he there?" Tessa asked, amazed at the emotion displayed on her father's face.

"His biggest client's toilet stopped up while he was entertaining some important people. He called my dad and demanded he come right then, or he was going to pull all his business from him. Dad had promised to buy me a new car for graduation and knew if he lost that account, he wouldn't be able to do it. So, not wanting to disappoint me, he fixed the stool and missed my game. Later, he told me it was the hardest decision of his life. Whatever he chose, one way or the other, I would be disappointed. I felt like a heel when I found out about it."

Tessa weighed his words thoughtfully. "That's so sad. The poor man."

"Mike didn't leave you or Katie to go play golf or take up a hobby. He left you for his job. A job he loved, despite the danger and long hours involved. I doubt you or I, or anyone who isn't a cop, have any idea of the dreadful things he faces every day. He meets the slime of the earth on their turf, not knowing when one of them is going to turn on him and perhaps put his life in jeopardy. Think what the world would be like without people like Mike. Not many are willing to put their own life on the line to protect the rest of us. Because of Mike and others like him, we live relatively safe lives, leaving them to deal with those who would cause us harm."

"You make him sound like a saint."

Ben Calhoun slowly made his way to the door, pausing and turning toward her as he reached for the knob. "I don't know much about saints, but I know a good man when I see one. Mike Garrett was, and is, a good man. The years are slipping away from both of you, Tessa. If you have any feelings left for Mike, I'd suggest you try to reconcile with him."

"Reconcile with Mike? How can you even say that?"

He sent her a tender smile. "Like I asked you before, don't you think that God of yours would expect you to work things out with your husband? Besides, nothing would make your daughter any happier than to see her parents together. Think about it."

Before she could give him all the other reasons reconciliation would not be possible, nor state that she was not interested in one, he stepped through the door, closing it securely behind him.

Tessa stared at the closed door, startling when the phone rang. "Calhoun's Plumbing, Heating, and Air-Conditioning. Tessa Garrett speaking. How may I help you?"

"I think we need to talk. How about having dinner with—"

"Mike? Is that you?"

"Yeah, it's me." The voice on the other end was unmistakable.

"I—I don't think that would be wise." Why was her stomach doing flip-flops?

"Even if I promise to behave myself and act like a gentleman?"

"What do we have to talk about that we haven't already said?"

"Come on, Tessie. Our daughter is getting married. Can't we put our differences aside for the next two weeks and be civil to one another? Is that asking too much, knowing how pleased Katie would be to see us getting along for a change?"

"Are you sure you could work it into your busy schedule?" The old sarcasm tinged her words and tasted bitter to her lips. "What I meant was," she said softly, "I wouldn't want to keep you from—"

"You name the time, and I'll be sure to be there."

There were a few things about the wedding they needed to discuss. Perhaps doing it face-to-face would be better than trying to do it over the phone. "About six thirty tonight?"

"Six thirty is fine."

"Where shall I meet you?"

"I could pick you up," he offered.

"I—I guess that would work, if you're sure it won't inconvenience you," she said, taking care to say it politely.

"No inconvenience at all. I'll see you at six thirty. Maybe we can have dinner at that Mexican restaurant in the mall."

She couldn't help smiling. That restaurant was one of her favorites. "That'd be nice. I'll be ready."

₮

Tessa changed her clothes four times before she decided on a simple navy blue pantsuit and silver jewelry then settled into the chair in the living room, her hands locked together in her lap, as nervous as she'd been waiting for Mike before their first date.

Six thirty arrived, and no Mike.

Six forty-five, and still no Mike.

I knew it! I knew he wouldn't make it. This is just another one of his hundreds of broken promises.

When the clock on the mantel chimed seven, she rose, kicked off her shoes, and headed to the kitchen to make a sandwich, glad that Katie wasn't there to see how angry she was.

At seven thirty, the phone rang.

"Sorry, Tessie. I was within two blocks of our house when a call came in about an armed robbery in progress at that convenience store down on the corner. I was the closest one, so I answered the call. I was sure glad I did. I was actually able to apprehend the guy when he came running out. He'd shot the young clerk behind the counter. I told the kid I'd go get his mother and bring her to the hospital. The poor woman took the news pretty hard, so I stayed with her until another family member could get to the hospital and take over."

Tessa squeezed her eyelids tightly together and clamped her lips shut. He'd done it again. Put total strangers' needs first.

"I know I should have called you, but the boy's mother was crying so hard, all I could think about was trying to comfort her," he went on without missing a beat. "The doctor said he's going to make it, but it was touch and go for a while. We can still make a late dinner."

She released a heavy sigh. "Forget it, Mike. I've made myself a sandwich."

"I'm sorry, Tessie. Really I am. I had no idea something like this was going to happen."

"You never do, Mike, but when duty calls, you always answer, no matter what."

"How about tomorrow night?"

She gave her head a sad shake. "No, not any night. Nothing's changed. Tomorrow night it'd just be somebody else who needs you while I sit and wait."

"Come on, Tessie. Give me a break. You didn't expect me to ignore the call for help, did you? Or to leave that wounded boy? Or not volunteer to get his mother and take her to the hospital?"

"Mike, I expect nothing out of you. I can't. I refuse to allow myself to be hurt again."

"But we need to talk."

"Let me put it this way: I'm going to do everything I can to help Katie with her wedding. When, and if, you have a few minutes to spare, you are welcome to assist me. Otherwise, I'll go on without you. I will not let you ruin our daughter's wedding because of some detail you may not have had time to take care of."

"I'll be there, Tessie. I promise. I want to do what I can to make her wedding the kind of wedding she deserves."

"You shouldn't make promises you can't keep, *Detective* Mike Garrett. I should think you'd know that by now. Now, if you don't mind, I'd like to finish my sandwich."

"Sure. Yeah, go ahead. I'll catch you later. You know you can call me anytime, don't you?"

"Good night, Mike."

"Night, Tessie."

Slowly, Tessa placed the phone back in its cradle, glanced at the half-eaten sandwich on the plate, and then picked it up and tossed it into the trash. *Reconciliation, Dad? No way!*

⸸

Mike closed the lid on his flip phone, cutting the connection.

"Hey, Mike. You still here? I thought you were having dinner with your ex-wife tonight."

He turned toward one of the EMTs who'd brought the boy into the hospital making his way toward him. "Yeah, I was, but it didn't work out."

The man put a hand on his shoulder. "Too bad. I kinda got the idea you were really looking forward to it."

Mike nodded. "I was."

"Wanna go home with me? My wife's got a platter of fried chicken waiting."

Mike gave him a smile then grew serious. "Thanks for the invitation, but no. You go on home, but let me give you a piece of advice. Don't let your job consume your life like I've done. Women don't understand our dedication. They need us there. Be there for your woman or, take it from me, she won't be there for you. I always thought I was doing the right thing—even defended it. Now I'm not so sure."

The man stuck out his hand. "Thanks for the advice, Mike. Me and my wife have been having conversations about the same thing lately. I love her, and I sure don't want to lose her. No job, no matter how important it is, is worth that."

Mike took the man's hand and gave it a vigorous shake. "Remember that and you'll get along fine. Life stinks without the people you love in it. It's taken me all these years to find that out. It's too late for me, but you're still young. Don't blow it like I did."

He watched as the handsome EMT headed for the ambulance. *Take my advice, kid. Cherish what you've got while you still have it with you, 'cause once you lose it, you may never get it back.*

Tessa turned out the kitchen light and made her way toward the stairs, deciding to go to bed early, too angry to even try to read the book on her nightstand—the one she'd picked up at the bookstore earlier that week and had been eager to read. When she reached the top of the landing, the phone rang again. Thinking it was Mike she raced back down the stairs to answer it, snatched it up, and shouted an impatient, "Hello."

"Tessa?"

She recognized the voice immediately.

"This is Jim. I have bad news. Katie and I are at the hospital. She tripped over a skateboard one of the neighbor kids left in the parking lot and broke her ankle."

"Oh, Jim, that's awful! Is she in much pain?"

"Yeah, quite a bit. I was sure glad I was with her. I carried her to the car. She wants you to come. We're in the emergency room at Community Hospital."

"I'll be right there, Jim. Thanks for calling."

"Could you call Mike and tell him? In my haste, I left my cell phone behind and had to use the pay phone in the hall. I really want to get back to Katie."

Call Mike? After the conversation we had tonight? Well, he did say to call him anytime. "Sure, I'll call him. You get back to Katie and tell her I'll be there right away."

Tessa ended their conversation then dialed Mike's cell phone number. "Jim just phoned and asked me to call you. Katie fell and broke her ankle. She's in the emergency room at Community Hospital. I'm heading there now."

"I'm on my way, too. Poor kid. I wonder what this will do to their wedding plans."

"I have to go. I need to get to Katie." Without even adding a good-bye, she hung up the phone then grabbed her car keys and purse from the table and rushed toward the door.

Katie was lying on a gurney in a crowded cubicle when Tessa entered, her cheeks stained with tears and dark rings under her eyes where her mascara had run from crying. "I'm sorry to be such a baby, Mom, but it hurt. I can't believe something so stupid as tripping on a skateboard could happen to me. I'd like to wring that kid's neck."

Tessa cradled her daughter's hand in hers, stroking her knuckles lovingly with her thumb. "I know, honey. I'm so sorry this happened. Is it a bad break?"

"They've taken X-rays. The doctor should be back soon with more information," Jim volunteered from the other side of the bed, his face contorted with concern.

"How's my girl?" Mike rushed into the tiny cubicle and bent to kiss his daughter's forehead.

A fresh tear ran down Katie's cheek. "I'm okay now, Daddy. This whole thing is a nightmare."

"She tripped over a skateboard someone had left in the parking lot," Tessa explained, suddenly remembering she hadn't taken time to fill him in on how it had happened.

"The name and address of the kid who left it there were written on the bottom of the skateboard," Jim said, crowding in and patting Katie's hand. "I'm going to have a talk with his parents."

"Want me to do it?" Mike asked, leaning to kiss Katie's forehead again. "I'll put a little fear into the kid. He won't leave that thing lying around again, I assure you."

"Sure, sir, if you want to."

"Show him your badge; that'll scare him," Tessa blurted out without thinking.

Mike turned and gave her a hard look. "You're great at those zingers, aren't you?"

Katie let out a moan. "Please, you two! Can't you stop? I'm hurting. I don't need this!"

"I'm sorry, baby." Tessa wished she could take back her remark. "It slipped out. I shouldn't have said it."

"I'm sorry, too, pumpkin. I had no business responding like that. I should have kept my mouth shut and not let her get to me."

"Well, I see your family has arrived." A middle-aged balding man in a white lab coat moved in between Mike and Jim. "I have some good news and some bad news. The good news is, it's a clean break and should heal nicely with time. The bad news is, you will need to stay off that leg until the swelling goes down and we can put a cast on it. Then, if all goes well, you'll be on a walking cast in a week or so. Maybe less. I hope you didn't have any plans to go skiing over the holidays."

"We're getting married on Christmas Day," Katie explained tearfully, wiping her cheeks with the back of her hand.

The doctor grimaced. "Oh? What bad timing for an accident. You'll probably want to put that wedding on hold for a while."

"No, I don't want to put it on hold," Katie said firmly, shaking her head. "I want to get married on Christmas Day, just like my parents did, and I'm not going to wait a full year."

"But, honey," Tessa began, "you can't get married wearing a cast."

"Why not?" Mike asked. "She's going to wear a long dress. No one is going to see it anyway."

"It's not the cast," Tessa shot back, wondering whatever possessed him to make such an outlandish statement. "Preparing for the kind of wedding Katie wants takes time and lots of planning, not to mention all the running around, making selections, and picking things up. She'll be confined to bed for several days and then have a cast on her ankle. There's no way she can do all those things!"

"Why not? She's got us! The two of us can do what she needs to do."

Filled with frustration, Tessa glared at him. "Us? You and me? You mean *me*, don't you? She'd never be able to count on you!"

"Mom!"

"I mean it, Katie. He was supposed to take me to dinner tonight to discuss your wedding. He promised he'd be there. Did he make it? No! More than an hour after he had arranged to be there, he phoned to say—once again—his job had kept him from making it."

"I couldn't help it. I was the closest one to an in-progress armed robbery. I had to take the call," Mike explained in his defense as he leaned over the bed.

"You aren't the only member of the San Diego Police Department, Mike. Someone else could have taken that call. Be honest. You wanted to take it. You're like an old fire horse that gets all excited when the fire alarm goes off. It's in your blood. Admit it!"

The doctor looked from one to the other, frowning, then cleared his throat. "We need to get Katie's ankle immobilized now. You folks can continue your discussion in the waiting room or outside."

Tessa started to protest but realized the doctor was right. All she and Mike were doing was upsetting their daughter. "I'm sorry. Let me know if Katie wants me," she told Jim as she kissed her daughter then exited the cubicle.

"I'll be in the waiting room, too," Mike said in an almost whisper. "Forgive me, Katie."

He followed Tessa to the waiting room. The only two seats available were side by side in a far corner. They seated themselves but remained silent.

"Aren't you Katie's parents?" a young woman holding a baby asked.

Tessa nodded.

"I saw Jim bring her in. Too bad about her ankle. I hope this doesn't interfere with their wedding plans. She told me all about it when I saw her at the grocery store this afternoon. I live in the same group of condos."

"We're not sure about the wedding yet," Tessa answered, glad Katie had such a concerned neighbor.

"She's lucky to have the two of you. My parents are divorced. They can't be in the same room without starting a big argument and hurling angry words at each other."

Tessa glanced at Mike and found him staring at her. "We both love her very much."

"Well, here comes my friend. She burned her hand on the stove, so I brought her in. Looks like she's ready to go home. It's been nice meeting you. Give Katie my love."

"We will. Nice to meet you, too." Tessa gave a little wave as the girl, her baby, and her friend departed.

"Why didn't you tell her *we* can't be in the same room either?" Mike asked, picking up a sports magazine from a side table.

"Because I'm embarrassed to admit it. It's your fault, you know. I thought we'd agreed to a truce."

"You sure didn't keep your part of the bargain. You tore into me like a wet hen when I phoned to tell you why I didn't show up tonight."

She huffed and turned her head away. "I had every right to tear into you. As usual, you broke your promise. I don't know why I ever expected you to show up. Not with your track record."

Mike idly flipped through the pages of the magazine, finally closing it and placing it back on the table. "I deserved that comment, but not because I intentionally broke my promise. Only because I didn't call sooner to let you know why I would be late. I fully intended to take you to dinner tonight." He pointed to his shirt. "I put on this stupid blue polo shirt because you used to tell me you liked me in blue." He offered a bashful grin. "I even bought you a bouquet of flowers. They're still out in my car."

Her eyes widened with surprise. "You bought me flowers?"

He nodded. "Yes. Red roses. Your favorite."

"That's because the first corsage you ever gave me was made of red roses and white carnations."

"You remember that?"

She tried to control the tiny smile that threatened to erupt but failed. "Of course I remember. You were so cute, standing in my parents' doorway, holding that corsage. You even pinned it on my dress."

He laughed. "I stuck you with the pin."

She laughed, too. "Yes, you did. I tried not to flinch, but I couldn't help it. I was afraid I'd bleed on my white dress."

"I felt all thumbs."

"I was nervous, too."

"You were so beautiful. You—you still are."

"And you were very handsome. I'd never seen you in a suit before."

"I spent every penny I made working at the grocery store that month to buy that suit and your flowers. I was so afraid you'd want to go out for a hamburger and fries after the party. All I had left were two one-dollar bills."

"We had such a good time that night, didn't we?"

He nodded. "The best. You were the prettiest girl there. I couldn't believe you were my date. All the guys envied me."

"All the girls envied me. You were dashingly handsome."

"What happened to us, Tessie? Where did we go wrong?"

His question kindled the old fire of resentment. "How dare you ask me that? You cut me out of your life, Mike. You cut our family out of your life. It was no longer you and me against the world. Everything was what *you* wanted. My wants and desires went by the wayside."

"What I wanted? Everything I did, I did for us, Tessie!"

"Oh? I wanted you to become a cop? Work weird hours? Be gone from me all hours of the day and night? Put your life in jeopardy?"

"Those weird hours on those weird shifts no one else wanted to work were what made it possible for you to stay home with Katie. I thought *that* was what you wanted!"

She bristled. "What I wanted—was you! I missed you, Mike. I—I loved you!"

"You loved me? If you loved me so much, why did you make my life miserable?"

"I made *your* life miserable? What did you have to be miserable about? You were working your dream job, having fun with your cohorts, flaunting your badge around the bad boys while I stayed home with a sick baby cutting teeth and crying into all hours of the day and night."

"Every cent I ever made went into our joint account. Did I ever complain about the way you spent my money?"

"Excuse me." They both looked toward a young woman who was sitting nearby, cradling her fussing baby. "My son is not feeling well, and I'm trying to get him back to sleep."

Tessa nodded and wished she could crawl into a hole. "I'm sorry. Our daughter broke her ankle tonight. I—I guess we're both a little unnerved."

"Yes, I'm sorry, too," Mike said.

The woman gave them a smile then turned her attention back to her son.

"Sorry, Tessie. When will I learn to keep my big mouth shut?"

She blinked back tears of regret. "My fault, too."

They sat silently, each pretending to read a magazine that held nothing of interest to either of them. Tessa had to smile when she realized the magazine in her hand was about wrestling and Mike's magazine was one about foods.

Finally, Jim appeared. "They're going to release her as soon as they have her prescription for pain meds and paperwork ready. Why don't you two go on home? There's nothing more you can do here."

Mike stood, his long arms dangling awkwardly by his sides. "Won't you need help getting her back to the condo?"

"No. Val and Jordan will be there by the time I get her home. Valene insists on staying with her tonight, and Vanessa will tomorrow night, if she needs someone there. We'll take good care of her."

"I could stay with her," Tessa volunteered. "They have husbands to care for."

Jim placed his hand on her arm. "It's already settled. She'll be fine. I'll have her call you in the morning."

Tessa felt Mike's arm slip about her shoulders—a familiar sensation she'd sorely missed but would never dare admit aloud.

"She'll be fine, Tessie. Don't worry. Jim and her friends will take good care of her."

She smiled up into Mike's reassuring face. "I know they will. That's very nice of them to help."

He took her hand in his and tugged her to her feet. "I'll walk you to your car."

"I'd like that." Her hand still tucked into her husband's, she gave Jim a smile and a wave. "Call if she needs me."

Though no words were exchanged as they crossed the parking lot, Tessa felt a warmth and safety she hadn't felt in a long time as Mike continued to hold her hand. When they reached her car, he took her keys and opened her door. Tessa crawled in then tossed her purse onto the passenger seat, feeling as awkward as a bowlegged ballerina. "Thanks, Mike."

He closed the door then rested his hands on the ledge when she rolled down the window, stooping to meet her gaze. "My pleasure."

"Do you really think she'll be all right?"

"I'm sure of it."

Tessa dipped her head shyly. "Remember when I broke my arm? You had to change Katie's diapers."

He chuckled. "I remember. Poor kid couldn't keep them on. I could never get those tapes stuck on right."

"You tried. That's all that mattered."

"That was before I made detective. After that, I barely made it home long enough to take a shower and catch a little shut-eye."

She nodded. "I had so hoped making detective would give you regular hours. Guess I was pretty naïve."

"Don't forget, making detective meant a big increase in pay. I doubt you would have been able to stay home with Katie and maintain our lifestyle without that extra pay."

"But it took you away from us."

"After a little while, it seemed you didn't care. Your life was full without me."

"I filled it with those things only because you didn't have time for me!"

Mike stood and rested his flattened palms on the roof of her car. "Our life sounds like a dog chasing its tail. The faster he chases it, the further it seems out of his reach, and he runs even faster. Our lives were like that, weren't they? You weren't there because I worked long hours, and I worked long hours because you didn't seem to care."

Tessa leaned her head toward the window, her gaze locking with his. "Do you have any idea how frightened I was? Knowing you were out there on the streets? Being the possible target of some criminal's bullet? Putting your life on the line when other fathers were home with their wives and children? No wonder the divorce statistics are so high among law enforcement officers. I often thought divorce might be the best thing for us. I couldn't live like that, Mike. Never knowing where you were or what was happening to you."

"I didn't think you believed in divorce."

"I don't, but perhaps it would have made things easier—for both of us."

He cupped his hand around her wrist and leaned toward her. "Tessie, I haven't been to church in years, but I want you to know I still believe in God. You and I may not be together, but that doesn't mean I'd have the right in God's sight to marry another woman. Nor have I ever wanted to. You're the only woman I've ever loved."

"I find that hard to believe. If you loved me as you say you did, why wouldn't you accept my father's offer? He's made a good living, and you know he wanted to pass his business on down to the two of us."

"Me—a plumber?"

"Being a plumber wouldn't have been so bad. It's an honorable profession."

Mike paused, staring at her with a look she almost considered disgust. "You've never forgiven me for saying no to your father and staying with the San Diego PD, have you?"

"I—I guess not. Rejecting that job was like you were rejecting me."

"Tessie, turning down your father's unselfish offer was never meant to be a rejection of you, but in all sincerity, I never could understand why you couldn't see my side of things. It hurt me that you wanted me to become something I never wanted to be, and give up the job I've dreamed of having ever since I was a kid."

She covered her face with her trembling hands, her heart pounding in her ears. "I'm sorry, Mike. I know you've always wanted to be a cop, but I never wanted to be a cop's wife!"

He backed away, stuffing his hands in his pockets and shaking his head sadly. "Then I guess we're still at a standstill. We've never seen eye-to-eye on this, and I guess we never will."

She nodded. "No, I guess we won't."

"Good night, Tessie."

"Good night, Mike."

Chapter 3

Despite the late hour, the phone was ringing when Tessa entered the house. It was her closest and dearest friend and fellow Christian, Ellen Zobel. The two women had been friends since high school, and now their daughters were close friends.

"I started trying to call you as soon as I heard about poor Katie's accident. How awful! Was the break very bad? Will she need to have surgery?"

Though weary and still trembling from her encounter with Mike, Tessa smiled faintly into the phone. She could always count on Ellen to be there when she needed her. How wonderful it was to have a friend like her. "Actually, it was a clean break and should heal fine. They're going to send her home, and Val's going to stay with her tonight."

"Yeah, Jim called Valene and Jordan from the hospital. He told them you and Mike were there."

Snapping the switch on the lamp on the end table, filling the room with light, Tessa sat down in the recliner that had been Mike's. "Things were a bit tense between Mike and me at first," she told her friend in a shaky voice, "but after a few words neither of us should have said, we settled down and actually had a fairly civil conversation."

"I'm glad to hear that. I know you hate for me to say it, sweetie, but both Bill and I still think you and Mike were made for each other."

Tessa closed her eyes and took a deep breath before answering. "You wouldn't have thought so if you'd heard the ugly words we said to each other after we left the hospital. I can't help it, Ellen, I still hurt. Even now, eight years later."

"I know, honey. Being that close to Mike again, especially in a tense situation like Katie's accident, must have been difficult for both of you," Ellen said with genuine concern in her voice. "Jim said you had agreed to help with the wedding, but I guess now that Katie has broken her ankle they'll put it off for a while."

"Not unless they've changed their minds since Mike and I left the hospital. That stubborn daughter of ours has her heart set on a Christmas Day wedding, and she refuses to budge, despite her accident."

"What's Jim think about that?"

Tessa huffed. "You know Jim. Whatever Katie wants is fine with him. I don't know how we're ever going to pull things together that quickly, but we're going to try. Dad says he can spare me at the office, so I'll be free to do whatever she can't do herself."

"Well, it looks like you've got a big job ahead of you. Let me know if there is anything I can do to help. Valene and I have been looking through bridal magazines for ideas for the bridesmaids' dresses. I guess you know Val is going to be Katie's matron of honor and Vanessa and Della will be her bridesmaids."

"Yes, she told me, and she also said Jim had asked Jordan to be best man and Nathan and Della's husband to be his groomsmen. I'm so pleased our children are such close friends." Tessa let loose a nervous giggle. "Oh, by the way, I'm not the only one who has offered to help. Her father volunteered his services, too."

"Mike?"

"Yep, Mike. The man who thinks the San Diego Police Department can't function without him. I don't know how he's going to find the time, with the crazy hours he works. When he's on a case, he doesn't stop until it's solved. He'll probably end up fizzling out on her like he has all her life but, knowing how that girl dotes on her father, she'll probably forgive him like she always has, and I'll end up doing everything without him."

"Well, like I said, I'm willing to do anything I can to help, and I'm sure Valene and Vanessa will, too, and you know I'll be praying for you, Katie, *and* Mike."

Tessa released a long pent-up sigh. "Thanks for calling, Ellen. I covet your prayers. These next two weeks are going to be trying, to say the least."

"You'll make it. You're the perfect organizer. With God on your side, how can you fail? Just don't let being around Mike get to you. Love you, sweetie. Get some rest. See you at church Sunday."

Tessa turned off the lamp then sat in the chair in the dark, thinking over the events of the day. Amazing! And with only two weeks to plan a wedding, the bride had broken her ankle. To top it all off, Mike had offered to help with the wedding plans. She lifted misty eyes heavenward, remembering the hurts of so long ago, hurts she had never been able to forgive. *God, please! I'll never get through this without Your help.*

ༀ

Mike pulled a wad of keys from his pocket and, after inserting the proper one into the keyhole, gave it a twist and pushed the door open. It'd been a long day, and he was tired. He tossed his jacket onto a chair then made his way through his cluttered apartment into the tiny kitchen. Searching the cabinet for a clean cup and finding none, with a shake of his head, he pulled a dirty one from the sink and rinsed it out before filling it to the brim with water.

"Gotta clean this place up sometime," he told Felix, the stray cat someone had placed in his car as a joke while he was interrogating a burglary suspect.

Felix sat in the middle of the kitchen floor, preening himself and ignoring his owner's comment.

"Don't care how dirty it gets, huh? Just so long as I make sure you have food and water, with an occasional cleaning of your litter box."

Still Felix ignored him.

"Want a cup of coffee? I hate drinking alone."

Without even a glance in his direction, Felix turned away and walked regally out of the room, his tail arched high over his back.

"I guess that means you don't want coffee." Mike placed the cup in the microwave then punched a few buttons. Once the water was hot, he pulled the jar of coffee granules from the cabinet, scooped in several spoonfuls, and gave it a stir. "Umm, that smells good. Nothing like a good strong cup of coffee at the end of a lousy day."

He grabbed a bag of stale doughnuts from the counter and carried them, along with the coffee, into the living room. After shoving a pile of old newspapers off the end table and onto the floor, he placed both the bag and the cup on its marred surface. "Tessie would have a fit if she could see this table. She always made sure I had a coaster under my cup."

He pulled a doughnut from the sack, broke it in half, and dunked the larger portion into his coffee before stuffing it into his mouth. "Stale doughnuts and instant coffee—what a meal. I wonder what Tessie had for supper. Probably left-over roast beef, or maybe a thick slice of ham between two slices of the famous garlic-onion bread she makes in that bread maker of hers. Maybe even a wedge of lemon meringue pie for dessert."

His mouth watered just thinking about it. The last time he'd had a piece of Tessie's homemade lemon meringue pie was eight years ago, just a few days before she had ordered him to move out. She'd baked one for his birthday—a tradition, since he'd rather have lemon meringue pie any day than a standard birthday cake. Now that he lived alone, each year on his birthday, he had to settle for either a store-bought pie or pick one up at the little diner a few blocks from his apartment, neither of which could even begin to compare with Tessie's pie.

Felix jumped up onto the sofa, curled up on one of its loose cushions, and lay staring at him.

"She was a good wife, Felix—the best. She made our home a haven. Took great care of our daughter, too. I loved that woman, but I guess I never told her. I just supposed she knew."

He dunked the other half. "She never understood me, you know. Always complaining about the time I was away from home. Griped about the times I missed supper—the weird hours I worked. I thought she'd be happy when I made detective, but she wasn't. I have to admit the hours I work as a detective are even worse than when I worked the streets, but detective work is different. The bad guys don't keep office hours. You gotta get them when you can. She never understood how I could pull an all-night surveillance, then go back to work the next day, sometimes without even taking time to come home for a shower."

Felix stretched out on the pillow and closed his eyes.

"That's okay. Don't listen. I'm used to being ignored." Mike took the final swig of coffee then twisted the top on the doughnut sack. "Did she care that I had a dozen commendations on my office wall? Did she care that the mayor awarded me a medal of honor for bravery? That I made sure I crossed every *T* and dotted every *I* when I worked a case, so the lawyers couldn't dispute the evidence?"

He shrugged his shoulders. "What am I saying? Of course she cared. She was the one who made sure those commendations were framed and hung on the wall. I guess she had a right to complain—sometimes. I did miss most of my kid's ball games, and I don't remember making one teacher conference with her. The thing that seemed to aggravate her the most was when I quit going to church with her. But my work was important. Why couldn't she see that?"

He pushed down the lever on the dilapidated recliner and allowed the footrest to lift his feet. "Tessie sure looked good today. How long has it been since I've seen her smile?" He pulled off his glasses and rubbed his eyelids.

Twisting to one side, he tugged his billfold from his hip pocket, pulled out a small snapshot, and stared at the image. "You were only about twenty-five when this picture was taken, Tessie—a real knockout. I was a fool to let you go."

Mike cradled the photograph to his chest and closed his eyes. Within minutes, he was asleep.

⁜

Tessa could stand it no longer. At eight thirty the next morning, she phoned Katie's apartment, determined to make sure her daughter was okay.

"Good morning, Valene. How's Katie today? Is she awake yet?"

"Morning, Tessa. She's doing great. I'm taking the phone to her so she can tell you herself. Here she is," Valene told her.

"I'm fine, Mom. My ankle barely hurts. The pain meds are really helping. Valene is taking good care of me," Katie told her. "Can you come over right away? I've already made a list of the things you can do for me. Like picking up the invitations, checking with the florist, and stopping by the caterer, and selecting the punch bowl for the reception. Val already has her hands full with just trying to help me get from room to room!" she added with a chuckle.

"I'd love to help out. Give me an hour to run a load of laundry through the washer and do up a few things around the house, then I'm yours for the rest of the day. Okay?"

"Thanks, Mom. You're the best. By the way, how did you and Daddy get along last night? Jim said he saw Dad walking you out to your car. I hope you two didn't get into another argument."

Remembering the more pleasant parts of their conversation, Tessa smiled. "We did all right."

"Well, come over as soon as you can. Della's shop is supposed to deliver my wedding gown sometime this morning. I can hardly wait. Can you believe in just two weeks I'll be a married woman?"

"Sure you don't want to postpone your wedding?"

Katie giggled into the phone. "Not a chance. This wedding is going to go off on schedule if I have to go down the aisle in a wheelchair."

"That's my impulsive Katie! See you in an hour or so. Love you."

"Love you, too, Mom. Bye."

Tessa loaded the washer, cleaned the kitchen, ran the sweeper in the family room, and then dressed for the day in a pair of jeans and her favorite T-shirt. After tossing the clothes into the dryer and pressing the button, she grabbed her keys and was heading for the door when the phone rang.

"Mom! Help!"

Tessa tightened her grip on the phone. "Katie? What's wrong? Are you okay? Is it your ankle?"

Chapter 4

M y ankle is fine. It's my dress!"

Tessa listened helplessly as Katie began to sob on the other end. "Your dress? What are you talking about?"

"My beautiful wedding gown! It arrived a few minutes ago. It's the wrong size!"

Tessa breathed a sigh of relief. "Oh, honey, don't worry. Maybe we can alter it."

"It's three sizes too small!" Katie blurted out between sobs. "Someone put the wrong tag on it! What'll I do? I phoned Della, and she said her supplier's orders are backlogged so she can't get another one. It was just a fluke that this one was available. I've called at least another six shops and no one else has it! I had my heart set on that dress."

Tessa racked her brain for a solution. "Maybe we could find a similar one."

"I can't go shopping! The doctor said I have to keep my leg elevated until the swelling goes down and I can get a walking cast on it!"

"Do you still have that picture of the dress? The one in the magazine?"

Katie sniffled loudly. "Yes."

"Maybe I could take it to Della's shop and try to find one something like it, in the right size."

"Would you?"

"Of course I will. I'll come and get that picture and start my search. I'll bet I can find one you'll like every bit as much. Maybe Della will let me bring several of them home for you to see."

Tessa picked up the list and photograph at Katie's then hurried to Della's shop.

"Mrs. Garrett, how nice to see you again," Della said.

"Della, we've been on a first-name basis for years."

"I know, but I prefer being more formal in my shop, even with close friends. It sets a more professional, respectful tone toward all of our customers. Anyway, Katie called and said you were on your way. I can't tell you how sorry I am about the mix-up. Someone at the factory must have put the wrong size tag on the dress when it was constructed. I called them, hoping to get a replacement, but they didn't have another one in stock in her size. With the wedding only two weeks off, there isn't time to get another one made and delivered. I told Katie she could have any dress we have in stock for half price to help make up for it. I do hope you can find something she'll like."

Tessa's eyes flitted around the shop at the dozens of bridal gowns adorning the racks and walls. "I hope so, too. Katie is pretty picky. I just wish she could have come here herself."

"I have a feeling you'll do just fine. Why don't you select six or eight gowns you think she will like, and we'll bag them up so you can take them to Katie for her to choose from."

A sigh of relief washed over Tessa. "You'd do that?"

Della nodded. "Of course. I'm so embarrassed that the supplier sent the wrong size gown." She led Tessa to the far wall. "All of these are Katie's size. If you'll excuse me, I'll be back in just a minute. I need to make a quick phone call."

Tessa nodded then stared at the voluminous mass of white satin and crepe. She wanted to cry. How could she possibly select a gown for her daughter? There were so many styles and shapes. She hadn't realized the selection would be this vast.

"How about that one?" a male voice asked from behind her.

Startled by the sound of Mike's voice, she whirled around, nearly knocking over a mannequin. "What are *you* doing here?"

He gave her a broad smile. "Katie sent me. She thought you could use some help."

"From you?"

The lines around his eyes crinkled as he gave her a second broad smile. "Sure! Why not? I've been to a couple of weddings in my time. How hard can it be to pick out a wedding dress?"

"You'd be surprised. Are you sure you can spare the time? How will the San Diego Police Department get along without you?"

The corners of his mouth turned up as he shrugged. "I guess they'll have to struggle along as best they can. I've told them not to call me unless it's an emergency."

"As if that would stop them." She gave him a look of irritation. "As I recall, everything that happens, even when you are supposed to be off duty, is an emergency."

He raised a brow. "Your fangs are showing, Tessie."

She ignored his remark and didn't respond, although a snappy comeback was on the tip of her tongue.

He pointed to the mannequin she'd nearly toppled. "How about that dress?"

Appalled by his suggestion, she gave him a blank stare. "That one would never do!"

"Why? It's white and has some of those bead things on it. I think she'd like it."

"Mike! That's a long-sleeved sheath. Katie wants a strapless one with a full, flowing skirt and a long train."

"Strapless? Won't that be uncomfortable? How'll she keep it up?"

Tessa rolled her eyes. "Strapless wedding dresses typically have plastic or metal staves in them that hold the bodice in place. They're quite comfortable."

He gestured toward the wall of dresses. "So let's find a good one." Selecting a hanger from the rod, he pulled out a strapless gown with a heavily pleated bodice and skirt. "I'll bet she'd like this one."

"I don't think so. Too much fabric around the bustline and through the hips."

"It's got a long skirt."

"But the skirt is pleated. Katie wants an A-line."

Mike gave her a puzzled look. "A line of what? Those bead things?"

"The term A-line refers to the shape of the skirt, Mr. Garrett," Della inserted as she returned.

He placed the hanger back on the rod. "Whatcha think of this one, Tessie?" She cringed as he pulled another dress from the rack, this one made with a heavy layer of tulle covering the skirt. "Too fussy. Katie would never go for it."

"Here's a nice one." Della pulled another gown from the selection and splayed the skirt out over a chair. "This is a beautiful dress, much prettier on than it looks on the hanger. The low-cut back is especially nice." She sized Tessa up. "Why don't you try it on, Mrs. Garrett? You and Katie are about the same size."

Tessa held her palm up between them. "No, I don't think so."

"Aw, come on, Tessie—try it on. Let's see what it looks like. You still got a good-lookin' figure."

"Yes, Mrs. Garrett, do try it on."

As Tessa took a closer look at the gown, she decided it was lovely, and more like what she thought Katie would want than any she'd seen so far. "I guess I could—"

Mike moved to one of the rose-colored slipper chairs and seated himself. "I'll wait right here 'til you come out."

She allowed Della to lead her to the fitting room and once she was alone slipped off her jeans and shirt and wiggled into the dress, letting out a little gasp as she peered at the image staring back at her in the mirror. The gown fit her perfectly, and Della was right. It did look much better on than it did on the hanger.

Della tapped gently on the door. "Could you come out, please? Mr. Garrett would like to see the dress on you."

Tessa stared into the mirror. Mike wanted to see her in the dress? The man who all too often wore navy socks with his black suit had suddenly turned into a fashion guru?

"It's much easier to see the dress in the large three-way mirrors in the show-room," Della added. "The back of that gown is so beautiful. You really need to see it in those big mirrors to get the full effect."

Tessa twisted from one side to the other, trying, without success, to see the back of the gown. It was impossible, with the small size of the dressing room, to see the entire back view. She pushed the door open a bit and said to Della, "I'd feel a little foolish strutting around out there in a wedding gown at my age."

"That's not a problem. Right now, you're the only customers in the store. No one, other than your husband and me, will see you. Besides, I'll bet you look beautiful in that gown. Times have changed. Although we recommend a pastel color, you'd be surprised how many older women come in and purchase a white gown for their second, or even third, wedding."

Tessa gathered up the train in her arms and moved warily through the door. "Times have changed. I always thought white was for your first marriage. Isn't it supposed to be a symbol of purity?"

Della grabbed onto the train and gestured toward the showroom. "I always thought so. But with so many couples living together before marriage, to most, it no longer matters."

"I know what you mean. Mike and I hated that Katie and Jim were living together. We've never approved."

"I was impressed when Katie told me Jim had moved out of their condo until after the wedding. Talk about living your values as a new Christian," Della said.

"I agree," Mike chimed in, rising as the two women approached him. "Our daughter and Jim are clearly devoted to one another and their Christian values. I expect those two will be together until death do they part."

Tessa bit her tongue, fearing he was going to elaborate and mention that a certain Christian couple, though they had married *before* living together and the bride had worn the traditional white, had not stayed together as they'd vowed to do. But he didn't. She wondered just how much Katie had told Della and her husband about the details of their breakup.

Della nodded as she lowered Tessa's train to the floor and stooped to arrange it around her feet. "I'm so glad to hear that, Mr. Garrett. It sounds like you approve of Jim for a husband."

"Jim? You bet I approve of him. He's a fine young man, and he loves my daughter. He's going to make a great husband." He nodded toward Tessa. "Even Tessie approves."

The woman rose. "Well, what do you think, Mr. Garrett? Will Katie like this one?"

Tessa felt herself blushing as Mike stood back, squinted, and sized her up from head to toe.

"She'd be nuts not to, if she looks anything like Tessie in that dress."

Della turned toward Tessa with a giggle. "What a sweet husband you have, Mrs. Garrett."

"Oh, he's a sweetie all right," Tessa answered, trying to keep any sarcasm from her voice. She turned her attention to another gown, this one with a heavily beaded lace bodice.

"Oh, you've chosen one of my favorites." Della moved aside the other dresses and pulled the gown from the rack. "This one is so feminine."

Mike smiled his approval. "Put it on, Tessie."

Tessa stepped back, appraising the dress with a frown. "You don't think it's a bit overdone? There are a lot of beads."

"The one Katie selected had a lot of beads," the stylishly dressed young woman reminded her.

"True, and it is beautiful. I like the self-piping at the top of the bodice." Nodding her approval to Della, she headed toward the fitting room.

A few minutes later, she appeared again before Mike. "I do like it. What do you think? This one is a lot like the one Katie had wanted."

His eyes widened. "I'd say it's a keeper. Let's take it to show Katie."

She bobbed her head, unable to mask her smile of approval. "It's my choice. I can visualize Katie in this dress, but we decided on taking six dresses. Let's find at least two or three more."

One hour and eight dresses later, they had selected five dresses to present to their daughter.

"Hey," Mike said as he leaped from the chair and headed toward a mannequin near the front of the store. "What about this one?"

Spinning around, Della gave him a smile. "Good choice, Mr. Garrett! That one came in yesterday. I'd forgotten all about it. Other than the one on the mannequin, we haven't even had a chance to check the others in yet and bring them to the sales floor. I'll go to the stockroom and see if we have it in Katie's size."

The two waited silently for her return.

"We have it," she announced victoriously when she reappeared. "You must try this one on, Mrs. Garrett. It's going to look fabulous on you."

Mike nodded with enthusiasm. "Yeah, Tessie, try it on. I wanna see you in it."

When she emerged from the fitting room, he rose to his feet with a whistle of approval. "Now that's a dress. Let's buy it!"

Her jaw dropping, Tessa blinked at him. "Without Katie seeing it?"

Smiling, his eyes locked with hers. He stood and moved toward her, the expression he wore looking more like that of the Mike she'd loved and married. A chill ran down her spine causing an involuntary tremble as he took her hand in his and gave it a squeeze. "Tessie, you're beautiful."

"Oh—I—you—" She found herself stammering like a fool.

"You are," he continued, his thumb gently rotating across her knuckles. "You're as pretty as you were on our wedding day."

Della nodded in agreement. "You do look lovely in that gown. It fits as though it were made for you."

Tessa felt a flush rise to her cheeks. "Thank you for the compliments, but the question is—how will it look on Katie? She's the bride. Not me."

"If Katie looks half as good as you in that dress, Jim will go berserk!"

"Mike!"

"I mean it. We guys like our women to look like women. All I can say is wow!"

"I guess we'll take this dress along with the others for Katie to see," Tessa told her, struggling to keep her voice under control. Mike's freely given, unsolicited compliments had unnerved her. He hadn't given her a compliment like that since long before they had separated.

"Six gowns are going to be hard to handle. Would you like us to deliver them to Katie's condo?"

"We'd really like to take them with us," Tessa told her, remembering the short time until the wedding. "I have a minivan. I can lower the seats, and we can lay the garment bags on the carpeted floor. I'd really like to get them to Katie as soon as possible. She's so anxious to get this thing settled."

Mike gave a snort. "Yeah, Della, that mistake with the gown size really sent her into a tizzy. You should have heard her yell. I thought she was going to bust a gasket."

"I feel awful about that. I'll do whatever I can to make things right for Katie. Of all the people it could have happened to, it *had* to be one of my best friends! Unbelievable. Anyway, I'll have these gowns bagged in no time, Mrs. Garrett, and loaded into your van."

Mike stuck out his hand. "Give me your keys, Tessie. I'll go on out and lower the seats."

She pulled them from her purse and handed them to him.

"Be back in a flash."

By the time she had taken off the final gown and handed it to Della, redressed, and run a brush through her hair, they were finished placing all but the last garment bag in her car. "Thanks," she told the helpful woman. "We'll get these back to you as soon as Katie makes a decision."

Della placed the final bag on top of the others and lowered the door. "If for any reason she doesn't like any of these, I'll be happy to help you select others."

Mike shook his head confidently. "I can tell you right now, she's gonna choose that last one."

"Thanks for your help, Mike," Tessa told him sincerely after Della said good-bye and disappeared through the shop's door. What she'd expected to be a real ordeal had actually been fairly pleasant. It was obvious Mike had been on his best behavior. "I'll let you know which one Katie selects."

He gave his head a vigorous shake. "Hey, no, you don't. I'm going with you!"

"Can you spare that much time?"

"I told you I'm taking some time off. People do that, you know."

She slid into the driver's seat and rolled down the window. "I suppose I should be impressed that you spent the last hour or so with me and no one from the SDPD called you."

"Impressed? No, but you might give me a little credit here. This is my daughter's wedding, too. I want to be there for her."

"Isn't it a little late to start being there for her?" Tessa shoved the key in the ignition and gave it a twist. "Where were you all those years when your daughter was growing up?"

"Is that a rhetorical question?"

She revved up the engine and yanked the gearshift into DRIVE. "Call it whatever you like. I'll see you at Katie's." With that, she drove off, leaving him standing in the shop's parking lot, staring at her rear bumper.

Mike arrived just seconds after Tessa's car pulled into the parking area in front of Katie and Jim's condo. By the time she reached the minivan's rear door, he was matching her stride for stride. Each gathered up three puffy garment bags and headed for the front door.

Jim pulled open the door before they could knock. "Katie's on the sofa waiting for you. I stopped by for an early lunch and to check on her."

"How's she feeling?" Tessa asked, pushing past him and into the comfortable, eclectically decorated room.

"She says fine, but I can tell she's hurting."

From her place on the sofa, Katie gave both her father and mother a teasing smile. "The two of you arriving together? That's a switch!"

"We've brought six beautiful gowns for you to try on," Tessa said, laying her garment bags on a chair and refusing to respond to her daughter's prodding question. "Della said we could bring more if you didn't find one in this group that you liked. She also said you could keep these until you felt like trying them on."

"But I know which one you're gonna pick," Mike told Katie as he placed his garment bags over a second chair.

Grinning, Katie splayed her flattened palm across her chest. "Daddy! You surprise me. I didn't think you'd be able to tell one gown from another."

"Hey, give me a little credit. I watch TV. I read the newspapers. Wait'll you see it. You'll look every bit as good in it as your mom did when she tried it on at the shop."

Katie's eyes sparkled. "You tried it on?"

"She tried on all six of them, and a couple of others, too."

Tessa felt the flush rise to her cheeks again. "It was Della's idea."

"We had to talk her into it," Mike confessed, grabbing Tessa's arm and giving it a squeeze.

"That's so sweet, Mom. I never expected you to try them on, but we are the same size. What a great idea. Will you model them for me?"

Before she could answer, Mike did. "Sure she will."

Though upset by the fact that he answered for her, with a mother's concern, Tessa placed a hand on her daughter's forehead. "You look great, but are you sure you're up to all of this?"

Katie lovingly tugged her hand away. "Mom, are you kidding me? Other than having a broken ankle and being a bit uncomfortable, I'm fine. I haven't even taken any pain pills since four this morning." She motioned toward their bedroom. "Please put the gowns on so I can see them. I really want to get a decision made."

She turned toward Jim. "Sorry, sweetie, but this would be a good time for you to go back to work. Grooms aren't supposed to see the bridal gown until the bride walks down the aisle."

"I really hate to leave, but I understand. I'll just pick up a sandwich for lunch on the way." Jim stood still, as if unable to move.

Mike sat down on the sofa beside Katie. "You might as well give up and go back to work, Jim. You know how women are about those things."

After picking up his cell phone and car keys from the table, Jim kissed Katie, shook hands with Mike, and kissed Tessa on the cheek. "Call me if you need me."

"Put my favorite on last," Mike instructed Tessa once Jim had closed the door behind him.

Tessa nodded then gathered up the garment bags and headed for the bedroom. Since she'd decided to put them on in the same order she'd done at the store, Mike's selection would have been last anyway, so she decided to let him have his way.

Katie leaned back against the sofa's cushion with an appreciative sigh as Tessa entered wearing the first gown, the one with the low-cut back. "Oh, Mother, I'd never considered that style, but it's beautiful."

Tessa took a slow turn in front of her daughter. "You don't think the back is too low?"

"Not too low for me," Mike said, eyeing Tessa carefully.

"I was asking Katie."

"I like it." Katie motioned for her mother to take another slow turn. "It looks fabulous on you, Mom."

"Wait'll you see mine. It's even better."

Tessa couldn't help laughing. Much to her surprise, Mike was really getting into this thing.

Katie let out a giggle. "Daddy! I've never seen you like this."

"No one has ever asked me to help select a wedding dress before!"

Tessa did another slow spin for Katie before retreating to the bedroom to don the next dress, the heavily beaded one with the piping along the bodice. *Her* personal choice.

"Umm, I don't know which one I like best," Katie said when her mother appeared in the doorway. "This one is pretty, too, and I love the unusual beading."

"This one is my favorite." Tessa ran her fingers over the beads, noticing their delicate design and sparkle. "I can just see you walking down the aisle in this one."

Mike shook his head. "It's pretty, but not as pretty as mine."

"I do like it, Mom."

He adjusted his position on the sofa's edge, giving his daughter a bit more room. "I like this one, too, but my selection is much better."

Katie tilted her head, first this way then that. "The one Mom has on now may be the wedding gown for me. She looks great in it. I may not even need to see the others. This one would be the perfect substitute for the one I'd picked out."

"She does look great, but wait until you see her in my dress."

Katie let out a giggle. "Your dress, Daddy?"

"He put a claim on it the minute he saw it on the mannequin," Tessa explained, ready to retreat to the bedroom for the next change. "You should have seen him going through those racks of dresses."

Tessa appeared three more times, with Katie oohing and aahing over each gown.

"You guys did a wonderful job selecting these dresses. I couldn't have done better myself. They look so different on Mom than they did hanging on those impersonal hangers. Now I don't know which one I like best. Any one of them would do, especially since I'm not able to have the one I really wanted. But I think the beaded bodice one is my favorite. The one Mom likes."

"She's not through yet," Mike reminded her. "There's one more. Mine." He nodded toward Tessa. "Go put it on, Tessie, and pull your hair up on top your head like I like it."

Tessa stared at her husband in disbelief. He remembered how he liked her hair? After all these years? He'd rarely mentioned her hairstyle to her. Even when she'd had it cut.

Mike gave her a gentle smile. "You look good with your hair up like that."

Tessa fingered the hair at the nape of her neck. "Uh—thank you, Mike. You—you never told me."

"If I didn't, I should have." His expression sobered. "I should have told you a lot of things, Tessie—complimented you more. I know that—now that it's too late."

She turned toward the bedroom, blinking back tears. The last thing she wanted was to let Mike see that his words had touched her so deeply. Despite the scoundrel she thought him to be, she still loved him. She always would, no matter how much she denied it to the rest of the world.

"Now for the very best one of all," Mike told his daughter, his face aglow when Tessa entered the room, her hair swept up on top of her head as he had requested. "I present my wife, one of the loveliest women I've ever met, wearing my dress."

Katie turned and let out a gasp. "Oh, Mama, Daddy was right! This is the best dress of all. And you are so beautiful in it!"

"She's right, babe." Mike rose and strode toward Tessa, taking her hand and enfolding it in his. "You *are* beautiful!"

Tessa struggled against the tears that filled her eyes to overflowing. For the first time in a long time, she actually felt beautiful. *Oh, God,* her heart cried out. *I love these two people more than life itself. Why, oh why, did our marriage have to fall apart? All I ever wanted out of life was to be a wife and mother and to serve You. Where did I go wrong?*

"That's it, Mother," Katie said in a mere whisper as she motioned her mother to come closer and reached out to touch the soft, satiny white crepe. "That's my wedding gown."

"See, I told you so!" Mike sat back down beside his daughter, smiling a victory smile. "I knew Katie would like this one best."

"It appears you were right," Tessa conceded, a little chafed and wishing Katie would have picked her choice, the one with the heavily beaded bodice, instead of Mike's. "Good thing you like it since, as the father of the bride, you'll be paying for it. Have you checked the price tag?"

He shrugged. "Nope. How much is it? Two hundred? Three hundred?"

Tessa fished the tag from inside the bodice, grimaced, and then bent close to Mike so he could see it, too.

"Twelve hundred dollars!" he shouted, his eyes bugging out as he peered at the tag. "What's that thing made of? Spun gold?"

"Don't blow a gasket, Daddy." Katie patted his arm. "Remember, Della said she's giving it to me for half price since the supplier goofed up my order. That's only six hundred dollars."

"*Only* six hundred dollars? I had no idea wedding dresses cost that much!" Katie's face fell. "Maybe we could find a cheaper one."

"Well, this is just dandy!" Her hands on her hips, Tessa glared at him. "Mike Garrett! This is your daughter's wedding gown we're talking about—for a once-in-a-lifetime event. I hope you're not going to do this with every thing for the wedding. Nothing is cheap, believe me. I've helped with dozens of weddings at the church. Sometimes people even have to take out a mortgage on their home to pay for their children's weddings."

Katie brushed a tear from her cheek and sniffled, obviously upset by her father's words. "It's okay, Mom. I don't want to throw Daddy into debt. I've got a little money set aside to buy a new car in the spring. I'll pay for my wedding gown."

Mike stood and began to fiddle with the change in his pocket. "No, you won't. Your mother is right. This wedding is important. I'm sorry for complaining. I shouldn't have said anything. It's just that I never expected it would cost so much. Go ahead with your plans, okay? I don't want to throw a wet blanket on things."

"I'm really surprised at you, Mike," Tessa flung out at him. "As long as you've worked for the San Diego PD, you should be making some pretty good money. I can't believe you're being such a cheapskate about this."

His fist came down on a nearby desk with a thud. "I'm not being a cheapskate! I'm only being practical. Where do you think all that *good* money you're talking about is going? I'll tell you where it's going. It's going to pay the mortgage for the house you live in. It pays your utility bills, the groceries in your cupboard, the insurance on your car, and the clothing on your back. How many men do you know whose wife kicked them out of the house would continue to pay the bills like I have? Not many, I can assure you. But I promised God the day I married you, Tessie Garrett, I would provide for you and take care of you, for better *and* for worse. These past eight years have been for the worse, but I've hung in there. I also have to pay to keep a roof over my own head. I live in a tiny one-bedroom apartment, drive a five-year-old car, and often fix myself a bowl of soup in the microwave and call it a meal, just to keep you in the lifestyle you deserve. Does that give you an idea where my *good* money goes?"

Katie covered her face with her hands and began to sob. "I'm sorry. I never m—meant to cause all this trouble. For—forget about the dress. Forget about the w—wedding. Jim and I will elope."

Mike reached his arm toward his daughter, but Tessa pushed her way in between him and Katie, wedging her body between the two of them. "Don't cry, sweetheart." She sent a meaningful glance toward Mike as she wrapped her arms about her precious daughter and pulled her close. "You'll have your wedding—just the way you wanted it. Your father was only letting off steam."

Mike began to pace about the room, nervously running his fingers through his hair. "I'm sorry, Katie, honest I am. I'd like to give you the moon, the stars, and anything else you want. I may not be able to do that, but I *can* give you a decent wedding. I promise I'll try to keep my mouth shut."

Katie lifted watery eyes, her face stained with tears. "I had hoped my wedding would bring you and Mom together, but I've just made things even worse!"

"No, you haven't, honey. Your father and I had a good time at Della's shop, didn't we, Mike?" Tessa shot Mike a warning look, hoping, for Katie's sake, he'd take the hint and agree with her.

"Uh—yeah—we sure did. We even had a few laughs. That hasn't happened in a long time."

"Neither of us wants to upset you, Katie, or have you cancel your wedding plans." Tessa placed a gentle kiss on Katie's cheek. "Now that you've chosen your wedding gown, the rest will be easy. Just tell us what else you want us to do, and your father and I will put our differences aside and get busy on it. Won't we, Mike?"

His face brightened, and he smiled at Tessa. "Yep, we sure will. Your mama and I love you, pumpkin. This is gonna be the best wedding Seaside Community Church has seen in a long time."

Katie winced as she shifted her leg on the ottoman. "You're sure about this? The two of you don't mind working together?"

"For you, my sweet girl, I'll do anything." Tessa sent a questioning glance toward Mike.

"Me, too, honey. Your mother and I used to be a great team. No reason we can't do it again."

Katie dabbed at her eyes with her shirttail. "So the wedding is on?"

Tessa brushed a lock of damp hair from her daughter's face. "The wedding is on."

⚓

Tessa sat in her favorite family room chair staring at the TV screen but not hearing a word of the six o'clock news. Her mind was on the events of the day. Who would have ever thought she and Mike would actually offer to work together and promise to get along until after the wedding?

When the doorbell rang a few minutes later, she debated about even answering the door, not in the mood to talk to anyone. Her minivan was in the garage. No one would even know she was there. But when it rang a second, third, and even fourth time, she leaped from the chair and rushed toward the door. Who could be that persistent? "Okay, okay! I'm coming!"

But when she looked out the door's peephole, no one was there. About ready to back away from the door and return to her chair, she decided to take a second look. Though she hadn't noticed it the first time, on the little wrought iron bench she kept on the front porch was a pizza box from the local pizzeria. Had they made a mistake and left the box at the wrong address? Without getting paid? That didn't make any sense—unless the caller paid by phone with their bank or credit card.

Thinking surely that was what had happened, she opened the door, planning to call and tell them they had left it at the wrong house. But when she bent to pick up the box, she heard a familiar voice from behind the hedge near the door.

"Hi." Mike stepped up onto the porch with a boyish smile that made her heart zing. "I hope you haven't eaten. Do you still like sausage and onion pizza?"

Though Mike was the last person she had expected to see at her door, she allowed the corners of her mouth to inch up into a smile. She had promised Katie she was going to get along with Mike. Perhaps now would be a good time to start.

⁜

To his surprise, she smiled and motioned him inside. "Sausage and onion *is* still my favorite. I'm surprised you remembered."

"I remember many things about you, Tessie. I think about them sometimes when I'm alone in my apartment or sitting by myself in my car while out on a stakeout." After giving her a sheepish grin, he moved in past her. "I'm sorry for what I said today. It was stupid and uncalled-for. As you know from experience, I'm not famous for keeping my mouth shut."

"You're not the only one. I say things, too—things I'm sorry for later." Tessa followed him into the family room and motioned toward the recliner, the one that had been his. "Sit down. I'll put the pizza on some plates and get us something to drink. Coffee okay? I just made a fresh pot, or would you prefer something cold?"

"Whatever you're having." He started to lower himself into the recliner but stopped midway, bracing himself against the chair's arm. "I could help."

She gestured toward the CD player. "You could put on some nice music."

Mike selected one of the many CDs by Christian artists filed neatly on the shelf then stood glancing about the room as the music began to play. Roses. There were roses everywhere. On the drapery, the pillows on the sofa, in vases on the tables and mantel, on the delicate figurines Tessa collected, everywhere. And there were mirrors, too—beveled mirrors, ornately trimmed mirrors, even mirror-trimmed sconces on the walls.

In no time, she was back.

"Whatcha call this type of decorating? With all the roses and stuff?" he asked after Tessa prayed and thanked the Lord for their food.

She pulled a string of cheese from her chin with a laugh. "Shabby chic."

"Oh, yeah, I remember that crazy decorating term. Wonder who thought that one up? I also remember the trips you and Ellen made to antique stores and flea markets to find all these pieces."

"It's a bit gaudy for some tastes, but I love it. It's warm and homey and inviting."

"I like it, too. Always did." Mike bit into his pizza with enthusiasm. "This is like old times."

She seemed to weigh her words carefully before speaking. "Yes, it is like old times, but you missed many of those old times—times Katie and I wished you were with us."

He stared off into space, and Tessa seemed suddenly uncomfortable.

"I didn't say that to upset you, Mike. I was simply stating a fact. We did wish you were there with us. You were a part of our family—the head of our family. Our family unit was incomplete without you."

Mike stared at her for a moment then asked, "Do you have any idea how difficult you made it for me, Tessie? I loved my family. Still do. I wanted you to be able to be home with Katie instead of going to work like so many other women were doing. All those extra hours I worked made that possible, yet instead of thanks, all I received from you was criticism."

She wore a look of frustration. "I would rather have gone to work part-time and had you home! Didn't you realize that?"

"But you preferred to be a stay-at-home mom, didn't you?"

"Not at the risk of losing you! I wanted to be with you! I needed to be with you!"

"Then why were you always so angry?"

"Me angry? You were the one who was always angry! Not me!"

"Only after you lit into me for being late or missing supper! You never seemed to realize I wasn't gone by choice. It was my job!"

Tessa visibly bristled. Jumping to her feet, she leaned over him, her face blanketed with hurt, her finger jabbing at her chest. "A job for you maybe, but I was the one waiting at home for you, praying to God that you were safe! And you call me angry?"

He grabbed her wrist and glared at her as she leaned over him, his face so close she could feel his hot breath on her cheeks. "I loved you, Mike. You were everything to me, and you rejected me."

His grip lessened some, but he continued to keep her imprisoned in his grasp. "Didn't you know I loved you, too?"

"I used to think you did, but then I began to wonder. You quit holding me, kissing me—paying any attention to me at all."

"I didn't think you wanted me to kiss you."

"I did. I wanted—"

Before she could finish her sentence, he tugged her to him and, taking her in his arms and pulling her onto his lap, he kissed her tenderly, passionately, like he'd kissed her the first year of their marriage.

Tessa wanted to pull away, but she couldn't. Her lips wouldn't allow it. It was as if she and Mike had suddenly been transported back twenty-some years, to a time when they couldn't keep their hands off each other. When each did everything they could to please the other. She tried to stop her hands when they moved to cradle the back of his neck, and her fingers as they twined themselves in the hair at his nape, but they wouldn't obey.

"This is where you belong, Tessie," he murmured against her willing lips. "Here in my arms."

Waves of pleasure swept over her as she leaned into him.

"You're my wife, Tessie," he whispered, nuzzling his chin in her hair. "This is where God intended you to be."

Tessa shifted in his arms as reality struck. Other than the two of them having a few good times as they'd worked on Katie's wedding, nothing had changed. Mike was still Mike the cop. Mike, the man who always put his work above all else in his life. The man who cared little about the time he spent away from his family or the danger he faced every day. Needing to free herself from his grasp, Tessa placed her hands on his chest and pushed away. "I may have belonged in your arms once, but not now. The only thing that has changed between us, Mike, is that we've grown older and probably each more set in our ways. While I don't like living alone, I've resigned myself to it, and I'm doing quite nicely. And yes, I'm sure God wanted us to be together, but apparently the only way you wanted us to be together was on your terms. Not His."

With a grunt of exasperation, Mike stood and gave his head a shake. "Maybe I'd better go."

Working hard at keeping her tears at bay, she turned her face away from him. "That's probably a very good idea."

Mike grabbed the remaining slice of pizza from his plate and, without looking back or saying another word, moved quickly through the house and out the front door. It slammed hard behind him, leaving Tessa brokenhearted and dreading her next meeting with him.

Chapter 5

T hat woman!" Mike shouted into the air as he slammed the car door and rammed the key into the ignition.

He shoved the pizza into his mouth, yanked the gearshift into reverse, and hit the accelerator, his tires squealing as the car backed into the street. "How can one woman claim to be a Christian and be so cantankerous?" he mumbled, his mouth still busy with the pizza. He pounded his fist on the steering wheel.

Why is it you never see her side of things? a still, small voice said from deep within his heart.

"Her side of things? What does she expect from me? I'm only a few years from retirement. Does she want me to quit my job? I'm too old to start over. If she's the wonderful Christian everyone thinks she is, why doesn't she understand my needs?"

Your needs? What are your needs, Mike? The biggest need in your life is Me. Think about it. You've quit attending church. You quit praying. You quit fellowshipping with Me. How long has it been since you've prayed? Come to Me with your problems, instead of either ignoring them or trying to handle them yourself.

"I had to work Sundays, God. You know that. I'm a San Diego police detective. Working Sundays was part of my job."

You volunteered to work most of those Sundays. Are you sure the demands of your job weren't simply convenient excuses to avoid attending church?

Mike let out a sigh. "Like I've always told Tessie, the bad guys don't take Sundays off. They work seven days a week."

Couldn't another detective, perhaps one who didn't claim My name and didn't have a family who needed him, work on Sunday?

Though Mike tried to come up with a viable answer, he couldn't. It *had* been his choice to work on Sundays. Oh, not at first. The first few times he'd done it, it had been because of the high-profile case he'd been working on. He'd been so close to solving it that every hour he'd spent on it had been necessary, even the hours he'd worked on Sunday. Because of his hard work and meticulous attention to detail, a hardened criminal who'd been frightening the entire city had been captured, prosecuted, and was serving time behind bars. Mike had fully intended to get back into his regular church-attending routine once that case was settled, but it hadn't happened. Another important case needed his attention, and the rest was history.

To his relief, a call coming through on the police scanner broke into his thoughts and caught his attention, taking away the feelings of guilt that constantly plagued him. Within seconds, he was off and running, adrenaline flowing through his veins like a healing salve, heading to assist Brad Turner, his partner, who'd just uncovered some new evidence in a case the two of them were working on.

Pushed into the recesses of his mind and forgotten, the still small voice again became silent.

✝

Sleep eluded Tessa most of the night, not because of what Mike had said, but because of her attitude and the words she had allowed to escape her own mouth.

By five thirty, she was up, dressed, and working out her frustrations in the flowerbeds.

By eight, she had cleaned out the refrigerator, mopped the kitchen floor, run a load of laundry, and vacuumed the family room, none of which needed to be done.

By eight thirty, she was sitting at her desk, staring at the phone, wondering if it was too early to call Katie. Deciding to risk waking her, she reached for the phone, only to have it ring as she touched it.

"Hi, Mom. I know you were concerned about the gowns being returned. I phoned the shop a few minutes ago, and Della said she'd send the truck to pick them up later today. Oh, by the way, other than hating to spend my days on this couch, I'm fine. Don't worry about me. My ankle barely hurts now."

Tessa smiled into the phone. "I was just about to call you. I'm glad you're feeling better and that the return of the gowns has been taken care of. Now—what do you want me to do next?"

"I kinda hate to ask."

"Ask away. I said I'd help in any way I could."

There was a pause on the other end. "Dad called a little while ago to see how I was. I told him I really needed him to go with Jim to select the tuxedos the guys will be renting."

Tessa let out a snicker. "And you want me to go along, to make sure they don't pick out something that will embarrass you, right?"

There was a giggle on the other end. "I knew you'd understand, Mom. Do you mind going? They're meeting Jordan, Nathan, and Brandon there at ten."

"Of course I don't mind, sweetie. Anything else?"

"I think I can trust Della, Valene, and Vanessa to pick out their dresses and one for little Carrie, so you don't need to bother with those, but you'll need to decide on your own dress as soon as you can."

"Sure, honey. Got any suggestions?"

"I was thinking of something in a very pale green for you, almost to the pastel shade, full-length, and maybe in a soft, flowing crepe. Whatcha think?"

"I think it sounds perfect, but with the wedding being only two weeks away, you'd better give me a backup color choice in case I can't find a green one."

"If you can't find green, how about ivory?"

"Whatever you say. I'll stop by Della's shop tomorrow. I'm sure she'll have the perfect dress. Now, I'd better hustle if I'm going to get to the formal wear place by ten. I'll call you later."

Tessa was already in the store, waiting, when Mike and the other men entered. They were so caught up in a conversation about a football quarterback who had just signed a multimillion-dollar contract that they didn't even notice her.

Mike spun around at the sound of her voice. "What are you doing here?"

Tessa closed the magazine she'd been idly scanning and rose to join them. "Katie mentioned you men were selecting your tuxedos this morning. I thought perhaps I could help."

He gave her a puzzled look. "Help with what? There's nothing to help with. A tuxedo is a tuxedo, isn't it? Black and boring."

The salesman, overhearing their conversation, stepped in. "Oh, no, sir. Not anymore it isn't. These days, tuxedos come in all colors and dozens of styles. You name it, we have it."

Jim gestured toward a mannequin. "How about something like that, Mike?"

Mike crinkled up his face. "Too fancy for me. I think we should stick with something plainer. That looks kinda sissy-like."

"The last wedding Valene and I attended," Jordan said, "the men all wore that off-white color. It looked pretty good."

Mike gave his head a shake. "Off-white? That'd get dirty too quick."

Nathan and Brandon chortled.

"You're only going to wear it once, Mike," Nathan said.

Jim nodded. "From what Katie said, I think she'd prefer we go with the off-white. She'd suggested off-white shirts, too."

"What color ties and cummerbunds?" Jordan asked, fingering a heavily pleated-front shirt on the display rack.

Jim frowned. "If Katie had a preference on that one, I don't remember."

Tessa was trying her best to keep out of the conversation, but Katie had specifically mentioned having the men go with a monochromatic theme. "Off-white. Katie told me she wanted everything off-white."

"Do you prefer the traditional length jackets, or perhaps the wonderful new longer length?" the clerk asked, sizing up the five men. "The longer length is complimentary to any man's build."

Grinning, Mike glanced at his companions then patted his stomach. "I guess he means me."

"I like the longer length," Jim said with a patronizing smile. "I think Katie would, too."

Tessa wanted to voice her approval but decided to stay out of it, rather than risk letting Mike think she was taking over in an area that should be left to him.

"This one is nice." The salesman pulled a hanger from the rack and proudly held out a longer-length, off-white tuxedo. "How about something like this?"

The five nodded their approval.

"Now that the color and style has been decided upon, let's select your shoes, and you can try them with the tuxedos, to get a better idea of the whole picture," the man suggested, gesturing to the wall of shoe boxes at the side of the salesroom.

Mike shook his head. "We don't need shoes. We'll wear our own."

The man stopped in his tracks, turned, and stared at Mike. "You are joking, sir, aren't you?"

Seeming mystified, Mike frowned. "No, I'm not joking. We each own perfectly good shoes, and wearing our own will be a lot more comfortable than breaking in a new pair. He turned to his companions. "You each have a pair of black shoes, don't you?"

Brandon burst out laughing. "Good one, Mike! You almost had me believing you were serious."

Jim gave him a warning frown. "I think Mike was serious, Brandon."

Tessa could stand it no longer. "Mike, you can't wear black shoes with off-white tuxedos!"

His gaze locked with hers. "Why not? No one is going to be looking at our feet. They'll all be looking at Katie."

Convinced this was the reason Katie had suggested she tag along, Tessa took charge but tried to keep her voice soft. "Mike, this is your daughter's wedding. She wants the men to wear off-white tuxedos with off-white shirts, ties, and cummerbunds, and shoes that will complement the look. I think you'd better go with whichever shoes the salesman suggests."

After much discussion and finally agreeing on the shoes to be worn, the group moved to the shirt area.

"The ruffled front shirts. Definitely, you'll want the ruffled front shirts." The salesman pointed to a display model. "This shirt is perfect with the tuxedos you've selected. They're a bit more expensive, but well worth it."

Screwing up his face and holding his hands up between his companions and himself, Mike backed away. "Me? Wear a ruffled shirt? Forget it!"

"I don't know about that, Mike. I think Katie would prefer the ruffled shirts," Jim countered meekly, sounding as though he was afraid to cross his future father-in-law. "I heard her talking about them."

Mike gave Jim a shrug and expression of surrender. "Okay! I give in. Whatever Katie wants is what I want, too."

Tessa busied herself in the waiting area while the men tried on their outfits, impatiently looking at more of the store's magazines until the five appeared, each looking more handsome than she could have imagined. She clapped her hands and smiled her approval. "Bravo! You guys look great! Katie will be so pleased."

Mike gave her a half smile as he smoothed at his lapels. "You really think so? We don't look dumb in these frilly shirts?"

She returned his smile. "You all look terribly handsome."

He turned to the clerk. "So, are we all through here? That's it?"

The man nodded. "Yes, sir, that's it."

Jim came out of the fitting room area with Jordan, Nathan, and Brandon following close behind. "Hey, Dad," he called out to Mike, "got everything taken care of?"

Mike turned long enough to wink at Tessa. That was the first time Jim had referred to him as "Dad." "Everything is under control."

✝

"How'd it go, Mom?" Katie asked Tessa when she stopped by her condo an hour later. "Did Daddy behave himself?"

Tessa smiled as the morning's events rushed through her mind. "They went okay. You should've seen how handsome your father and the others looked. I really think you're going to be pleased with the tuxedos and other things they chose."

Katie leaned forward and gave her arm a playful jab. "*They* chose, or you chose?"

"I guess you could say we all picked them out together."

"Has Daddy seen the bill yet?"

"Yes, he saw it."

"Did he come unglued or go into shock?"

Remembering Mike's request that she not tell Katie his initial reaction, Tessa chose her words carefully. "He was a little startled at first, but he did quite well once the initial shock wore off. You would have been proud of him."

Katie leaned back in the cushions surrounding her on the sofa and rubbed at her temples. "Jim and I hate it that Daddy is going to pay for our wedding. We know he can't afford it."

"It's traditional for the bride's parents to pay for the wedding. I'm sure your father wouldn't have it any other way."

"Mom, he's still paying on my college bill! I can't expect the man to do everything! Jim is making good money now. It just doesn't seem fair to put the entire cost on Dad."

"Just this morning, your father told me he wants you to have the best wedding ever. If he didn't mean it, I'm sure he never would have said it." Tessa smiled at Katie. "Now that we have the tuxedos taken care of, what's next?"

Katie tugged on her mother's sleeve. "*Your* dress, Mom. Valene called while you were helping Dad with the tuxedos. She and Vanessa went to Della's bridal salon this morning and selected their dresses and one for my flower girl." Katie paused with a laugh. "It took a little doing. Since Vanessa is about four months pregnant now, they wanted to find a dress that would disguise her slightly bulging tummy. I'm so excited for them. She and Nathan are wonderful parents. Maybe someday Jim and I will have a baby."

Tessa smiled at the thought. How she'd relished that idea.

"Just think, you and Daddy—grandparents. What would you think about that?"

Her heart swelling with love for this child who might one day become a mother herself, Tessa answered, "I'd love it. I know your father would, too."

Katie let out a wistful sigh. "Someday, Mom, someday. I have to establish myself as a full-fledged architect first. Now back to the wedding. Other than the tux for Ryan—he's going to be such a handsome ring bearer—which is being taken care of this morning, your dress is the only wedding garment left." Katie gave her a mischievous grin. "Want me to get Daddy to go along and help you decide on it?"

Tessa responded with a nervous laugh. "No, thanks. That's one chore I think I can handle all by myself."

"I've seen him giving you the eye lately. I'm sure he'd be more than willing to—"

"Katie! I said no!"

✝

Mike sat in his apartment at his makeshift desk, which was nothing more than a card table with a folding chair, scratching his head while going over his monthly bank statement. "My credit cards are nearly maxed out, and the wedding expenses aren't even added yet. I sure wish that daughter of mine and Jim would have put off their marriage until spring," he told Felix, who wasn't even interested enough to look in his direction. "Maybe by that time I could have had some of these bills paid off."

Letting loose a deep sigh, he leaned back in the chair and locked his hands behind his head, his legs extended beneath the table. "Pride is sure a vengeful thing, Felix. Mine's gotten me in hot water more times than I dare to count."

He closed his eyes and tried to imagine what the past years would have been like if he would have valued his family more and not spent his life being caught up in the pursuit of criminals. His thoughts went to his friend, Bill Zobel, his former accountability partner. How long had it been since the two of them had spent even five minutes together? Up until he'd become so busy with his job, he'd looked to Bill as his role model. Now he barely thought of the man.

At one time, Bill was everything Mike wanted to be. A fine, upstanding Christian, whom men looked up to and admired—a real friend when you needed him, who seemed to sense your need even before you realized it yourself, and a man of prayer. How many times had Bill placed a hand on Mike's shoulder and prayed for him, asking God to have His way in his life? When had the two men begun to part ways?

Searching his heart, Mike had to admit their close friendship had begun to deteriorate when he no longer had time to attend the men's fellowship group at their church. Bill Zobel had phoned him over and over, even come down to his office at the SDPD to try to talk to him, but Mike had become so involved with his excessive caseload he'd barely had time to say more than a pleasant hello. Looking back now, some of Bill's sage advice replayed in his mind.

"Your family needs you," he'd said. *"Are you sure you have to work this many hours? Mike, it's not good for you to miss church. You need to hear God's Word, and you need the fellowship and strength of other believers in your life. Your wife loves you and needs you in her life. Mike, you're playing with fire. You're not giving God first place like you used to. He's a jealous God. He wants you to love and worship Him."* And his final words the last time the two men were together—*"Mike, you're way off base. You need to get your life in order before it's too late."*

Mike grimaced as he remembered how he'd blown his stack and told the man to stay out of his life and mind his own business. Bill had responded by staring at him, openmouthed, and then walked away. Other than an occasional hello when they met on the street or at the hardware store, though he still greeted him warmly, his friend had done exactly what Mike had told him to do—stayed out of his life. Through his own actions, Mike had lost not only his wife, family, home, and best friend, he'd lost touch with God.

What'd I tell Jim this morning? Everything is under control? Everything is far from under control. And me and my selfish, uncaring attitudes are the reason!

✝

Tessa stared at the doorbell. Should she press it? She knew Mike was home. His car was parked at the curb. Maybe she could go on to the caterer by herself. After all, what did Mike know about planning a wedding reception? But he was being such a good sport about paying for everything; shouldn't he be included in any decisions made in regards to the wedding?

Maybe she should go on to the bridal shop and select her dress, but that was one chore that could be put off until later in the day. The most important task now was to make sure the caterer could do the reception on Christmas Day.

She reached toward the doorbell but before she could press it, the door opened and Mike appeared, looking haggard and weary.

"Tessie! I thought I heard a car drive up. What are you doing here?"

"I'm on my way to see the caterer, and I thought you might like to come along." She glanced past him into the dingy room. It was a mess. Worn clothing was draped over furniture. Dirty dishes cluttered the end tables. Empty food wrappers lay scattered on the floor. The place looked like a pigsty, and not at all like Mike had kept things when he had lived at home.

Seeming to note her concern, he stepped out into the hallway, pulling the door partially closed behind him. "I–I'd invite you in, but I've been so busy I haven't had time to tidy the place up, and I know how you hate a messy house."

She forced a slight grin. "I've learned there are other things more important than a meticulously kept house."

"I'd really like to go to the caterer with you. Can you give me a minute? I need to shut down the computer and get my jacket."

"I could meet you there."

He shook his head. "Why don't you let me drive you?"

"It's really not necessary."

"I know, but there's no sense in taking two cars."

Ride around with Mike? She wasn't sure that was a wise idea.

"I promise not to bite."

Not being able to think of a single excuse that wouldn't ignite another argument, she reluctantly agreed.

"Maybe you'll let me take you to dinner afterward." He grinned then moved back into his apartment, closing the door behind him before she could respond.

Tessa stood in the empty hall, waiting, feeling as awkward as she had the first day Mike offered to drive her home from school. In less than two minutes he was back, his hair combed, jacket on, and looking more like himself. She followed him out the building's front door to his car and waited until he opened the door for her, as he'd done so many times before. But one glance at the cluttered interior told her he wasn't any better at keeping his car clean than he was his apartment. Without comment, she pushed a bag of potato chips and an empty pop can onto the floor and climbed in.

"Sorry about the mess," he told her as he slid into the driver's seat.

She shrugged. "No problem."

The traffic was light, and they reached the caterer's shop in less than ten minutes, which left little time for conversation.

"We no can do Christmas Day wedding. No way!" the little man at the shop said in broken English, without even hearing them out.

Undaunted, Mike and Tessa made their way to the second caterer on Katie's list, receiving the same answer. "No!"

The man at the third catering shop took even less time to decline.

"Now what?" Tessa crossed her arms over her chest and stared glumly out the window of Mike's car, blinking back tears of sadness. Katie was depending on them to work things out, and they were failing her. "You can't have a wedding without a rehearsal dinner and a reception. Katie is going to be brokenhearted when we tell her the wedding is going to have to be canceled after all."

Mike circled his arms about the steering wheel, staring straight ahead. "We could always do it ourselves."

Tessa's jaw dropped. "Do the rehearsal dinner and the reception? Surely you're kidding!"

His eyes twinkled. "Think about it, Tessie. You could fix some big pans of your famous lasagna and maybe some of those caramel pies everyone likes. It'd be great! Or maybe we could have pizza delivered to the church."

The man was mad! She'd never be able to do such a ridiculous thing. Besides helping Katie with the wedding, she had Christmas shopping to do.

"We could get some cans of that tropical punch-type stuff to put in that fountain punch bowl for the reception, and we could buy several kinds of cookies from that deli down on the corner."

"And maybe we could use paper plates and napkins, and plastic forks," Tessa added facetiously.

"It'd sure save me a few bucks!"

Tessa couldn't believe her ears. "You're serious."

"Don't you think it'd be better than canceling the wedding?"

"Mike, there is no way we could do such a ridiculous thing! Do you have any idea how much work we're talking about? Not to mention the time it would take. Time we don't have. And it'd be totally inappropriate."

He screwed up his face. "You're probably right. It was a dumb idea, but we can't give up. Is there another caterer on that list?"

She checked the paper then sighed. "One more, but this one is way on the other side of town."

Mike started the engine and pulled out onto the street. "Can't hurt to try."

"You're not giving us much notice," the final caterer on the list said when they explained they wanted him to provide the rehearsal dinner on the evening of the twenty-third. "But we don't want to disappoint your daughter. Sounds like she's had enough trouble already. Since we'll be dealing with a fairly small group,

I think we can handle it. Now when is the wedding?"

Chafing from the refusals of the other three, Tessa sent a cautious glance toward Mike then back to the caterer. "Late afternoon—Christmas Day. Four o'clock."

"What? You want us to cater a wedding reception on Christmas Day? Impossible!" the caterer told them excitedly, waving his hands in the air. "I'd have a terrible time pulling a crew together. No one wants to work on Christmas Day!"

Tessa once again explained Katie's broken ankle was what kept her from coming to speak to him herself. "Her father and I"—Tessa gestured toward Mike—"were married on Christmas Day. Katie has her heart set on doing the same thing. We'd really hate to disappoint her."

He appeared a little calmer. "That's an admirable reason. Not many couples stay together as long as apparently you and Mr. Garrett have." Rubbing his chin, the man frowned thoughtfully. "I'd have to charge you more. My employees would expect overtime pay."

Mike tugged at his collar and cleared his throat. "Whatever it takes. I just want to make my daughter happy."

As if in deep thought, the man eyed them both then rose. "Give me a few minutes. Let me talk to my crew."

As soon as he disappeared into the back room, Tessa turned to Mike with concern. "You're already counting pennies. Can you afford to pay the caterer more?"

Mike fingered his chin. "Not really, but I'll manage. Just don't mention it to Katie, okay?"

The man came back before she could respond.

"Believe it or not, when I told them about your daughter's situation, several of my staff members offered to work on Christmas Day. Now tell me what you have in mind."

Both relieved and encouraged by this good news, Tessa pulled Katie's notes from her purse and handed them to him. "This is basically what she had in mind, but she's wide open to suggestion."

He read the notes slowly, nodding, and occasionally jotting details in the margin, smiling when he reached the end. "My hat's off to your daughter. She's done a good job. I would suggest adding a lovely, fresh green salad to the dinner, and maybe make one of the cakes chocolate instead of vanilla for the reception but, other than that, I like what she's done. Now let's select the tablecloths, punch bowl fountain, and the other things we'll need to make her wedding as spectacular as she'd like. It shouldn't be too difficult. Katie was very specific in her written instructions. She said there would be around twenty at the rehearsal dinner, but she never mentioned how many would be at the wedding." He poised his pen over an order pad.

Tessa gave him a confident smile. "I can answer that one. Since their wedding will be over a holiday, most of their college friends will be home and able to attend. Then, in addition to our neighbors and friends and church members, there'll be a number of family members. We figured between two hundred and two hundred fifty."

Mike turned to stare at her. "That many? I thought this was going to be a small wedding."

"Katie tried to keep the guest list small, Mike, but she simply has to invite certain people," Tessa explained, wishing they could have discussed this in private instead of in front of the caterer.

Looking over the half-glasses perched low on his nose, the man glanced up from his pad. "Two hundred and fifty *is* a small wedding, Mr. Garrett. You should see some of the weddings we cater."

Mike stuck his hands into his pockets, rattling his change. "So what's it gonna cost me?"

The man pulled a small calculator from a nearby shelf and began punching buttons.

Tessa jabbed an elbow into Mike's ribs when he tried to peer over the man's shoulder.

"Remember I said I would have to charge you more because I'd have to pay my employees overtime," the man said while jotting a few figures on the order pad.

Mike nodded. "Yeah, I remember."

The caterer leaned forward and pointed to the pad. "Here's the total, and of course you'll want to add a generous gratuity."

Tessa thought Mike was going to pass out. His face turned white, and he began to gasp for air.

After shooting a quick glance at Tessa, he sucked in a deep breath. "I—I never dreamed it would be that much! Is there any way we can cut the cost down?"

The man pursed his lips. "I guess we could eliminate the fresh green salad for the rehearsal dinner, but I wouldn't recommend it."

Tessa looped her arm through his. "The green salad would be a nice addition, Mike."

Mike stared at the figures again. "You really think so?"

She nodded. "We could ask Katie to trim the guest list."

"I'd hate to ask her to do that." Mike stared at the floor for a moment then, taking on a faint smile of surrender, told the caterer, "Let's leave the salad in and plan on two hundred fifty guests for the reception. My little girl is getting married. I want things to be right."

"We'll do our best," the man assured him.

"Well, we did it," Mike told Tessa with a shrug and a halfhearted smile as they left the shop. "We actually booked a caterer."

Tessa returned his smile, knowing he still hadn't recovered from the shock of receiving the caterer's bill. "We sure did, thanks to you. Let's go tell Katie."

Grabbing her hand, he tugged her toward the car. "Not until I take you to dinner. Do you realize we've been so concerned about finding a caterer we forgot all about lunch?"

She muffled a snicker. "We did, didn't we? Are you sure you can afford it?"

He grinned. "I still have a little bit of pocket change. How about that Chinese restaurant we used to go to on Friday nights? You always liked their food."

She pulled back her sleeve and checked the time. "I'd like to, Mike, but I really need to pick up my car and go home and check the answering machine. The pastor was supposed to call me once he confirmed our use of the fellowship hall for the rehearsal dinner."

"No problem. I'll run you by the house, you can check the machine, and then I'll take you to dinner. We'll get your car later."

Tessa hesitated. The time the two had spent together, so far, had been because Katie had requested it. What he was proposing was different. Dare she accept his invitation and risk an informal evening with him? Though she'd never been able to forgive him, she still loved him. But he was still a cop—still working those long, demanding hours that drove her crazy. Nothing in their relationship had changed. If anything, it was worse due to their long estrangement. "I don't know, Mike. I'm sure you have things to do, and I really need to get back—"

"You have to eat, Tessie. Come on. Pig out on Chinese food with me. Umm, crab Rangoon, doesn't that sound good? It's your favorite."

He remembered!

Mike gave her a tantalizing smile. "Sure beats eating leftovers alone."

✝

"You want to come in?" Tessa asked when they pulled into her driveway. "No sense waiting out here in the car."

Mike nodded and pushed his door open, surprised that she had invited him. He stepped inside the house and gave a quick glance around.

"Make yourself comfortable," she told him once they were inside. She moved to the answering machine and pressed the button. Katie's voice came on.

"Hi, Mom. It's me. How did the trip to the caterer go? Okay, I hope. Surely one of those caterers I listed came through for us."

Mike laughed at her comment. "Good thing she put several on the list!"

"Mom," Katie's voice continued, "I know this is hard for you, working with Daddy and being around him, but I want you to know I appreciate it."

The smile on his face faded.

"I hated it that Daddy wasn't around when I was little. My friends at church and the kids at school had daddies who were there for them. I didn't. I love you for always being there." Katie snickered. "Especially the night you took me to the father-daughter banquet at church. Remember how we sat there, me wearing my brand-new red dress and patent leather shoes, waiting for Daddy, hoping he'd remember his promise to be there on time to pick me up? Then, when he didn't show, rather than have me disappointed, *you* took me. Looking back, I'm sure you were as embarrassed as I was when you were the only female father in the fellowship hall. But you graciously explained to anyone who asked that something came up and Daddy couldn't get away."

Mike looked in Tessa's direction, but she was standing with her back to him, her head in her hands. He could tell Katie's words had touched her, too.

"Oh, Mom, I couldn't bear it if he didn't show up for my wedding. He's disappointed me so many times, I couldn't begin to count them. I know his job is demanding and important, but I never understood why he quit going to church with us. I think that hurt more than anything."

Mike felt as if a dagger was being jabbed into his heart and twisted, and his life's blood was spilling onto the floor. He'd had no idea his absences in her life had affected her this deeply.

Tessa reached for the answering machine.

"No! Let it play!" Mike nearly shouted at her.

Misty eyes met his. "But, Mike—"

"Let it play," he repeated, this time keeping his voice down to a reasonable level.

She nodded, and again turned away from him.

"But, Mom—I'm gonna say this now because I don't know if I'd get through it in person without you stopping me—we can't continue being angry with Daddy for things that happened so long ago. God wants us to put those things aside and forgive him. No matter how hard that might be. And I want Daddy to be as much a part of my life as you are, Mom. Especially now that Jim and I are to be married. I want our family to come together. Of course, I want you and Daddy to be reconciled, but if that can't happen, at least I want you two to be civil to each other. We need to be able to be in the same room without hateful words and accusations ricocheting off the walls. I want us to celebrate Christmases, holidays, and birthdays together." Katie's falsetto laugh echoed through the tension-filled room. "I sound like one of those Miss America contestants. Maybe I should add that I want world peace!"

Neither Mike nor Tessa joined in their daughter's laughter.

"Well, I'm not sure how much your answering machine will record. Maybe my long-winded message was cut off several minutes ago, and you won't even hear this part. But—if you do, Mom—I want you to know I love and respect both of you. I know I've hurt you at times, and I apologize. I realize I hurt both you and Daddy, and especially God, by moving in with Jim before we were married—that's one reason I want to marry him as soon as possible. That and I wanted to be married on Christmas Day, like you and Daddy. Be kind to Daddy. I so want him to come back to the Lord, and I know you do, too. Call me when you get home."

As the machine clicked, signaling the end of Katie's message, Tessa rushed from the room in tears, leaving Mike alone with his thoughts.

Chapter 6

Mike felt numb, thoroughly chastised, and very much alone. And he felt bad for Tessa.

He sat down in the recliner and stared through watery eyes at the room. The very recliner he sat in had been a gift from his wife. It was his chair. No one else was allowed to sit in it. On the table beside the chair was his Bible, also a gift from Tessa. She'd given it to him on their tenth anniversary. He'd loved that Bible. Flipping open its pages, he found numerous notations he'd made in the margins. Notations he'd made while listening to their pastor on Sunday mornings or doing his early morning scripture readings and meditations at home. He'd highlighted James 4:8 on the open page that lay in his hand: "Draw near to God and He will draw near to you."

Is that where I began to go wrong, Lord? When I quit communing with You and ceased reading Your Word? He carefully closed the Bible and placed it back on the table, making sure to put it in the exact same spot.

Next, his gaze went to the clock on the wall. The clock he had given Tessa the year they moved into their house. What a time he'd had hanging that clock. She'd wanted it mounted directly on the brick fireplace. When he'd told her it was impossible, she had put it in the hall closet where it had remained until one evening when Ellen and Bill had come for a visit. When she'd mentioned the clock to him and where she'd wanted it, Bill had asked her to bring him the drill and, within a few minutes, the clock was hanging on the fireplace in the very place she'd wanted it. Mike remembered how foolish he'd felt. He could have put that clock there himself, but instead of admitting he didn't know how to mount it there, he'd lied and told her the job was impossible.

The matching sofas caught his attention. He could never imagine why anyone would want matching sofas. Two sofas in one room seemed foolish to him, but that's what Tessa had wanted. Though he'd bought them for her, he'd never admitted how wonderful that pair of sofas had been in their home. They made the perfect conversation area, the way they faced one another in front of the fireplace. Why hadn't he told her how much he'd grown to like them? Tessa had gone out of her way to make their house a home, doing the decorating herself, scouting out bargains at garage sales and flea markets. Every nook and cranny of their home was warm and inviting, and he'd barely been there to enjoy it.

He glanced at the wall over the desk and was surprised to see how many of his framed commendations were still hanging there. She hadn't taken them down! Why not?

Across the room on an upper shelf in the bookcase sat two glass bluebirds, mementos of their honeymoon. Though he'd been short on cash when they'd taken their honeymoon to Thousand Oaks, he'd managed to buy those bluebirds for Tessa, and she'd kept them all these years, displayed in one of the most prominent places in the room.

Other items about the room caught his eye. Most were filled with memories, symbols of the happier times of their marriage. Others were simply decorative pieces, but all were treasures of the past.

Pulling himself out of his reverie, he stood, embarrassed and ready to depart without saying good-bye, but he remembered Tessa's car, which was still parked in his apartment's lot. He couldn't leave. She'd be stranded without transportation. And what would Katie think of him if Tessa told her he hadn't taken her back to get her car?

"Tessie," he whispered softly toward the hall.

When she didn't respond, he whispered her name a little louder.

Still no response.

Not sure what to do, he tiptoed down the hall toward the bedroom he'd shared with his wife. A room he hadn't seen for eight long years. There was Tessa, stretched across the bed on her stomach, her face buried in the pillow shams, and she was sobbing like her heart was broken.

Mike stood in the doorway, his arms dangling by his sides. "Tessa," he repeated softly. "Are you—okay?"

"I–I'm fine," she said between sobs.

"I was thinking of going."

"Th–that's probably a good idea."

"We have to get your car."

Sitting up slowly, she rubbed at her eyes and lifted her chin high. "D–don't worry about it. I'll get Ellen to t–take me to pick it up."

He cautiously took a few steps toward her. "I'm sorry, Tessie. I know Katie's message upset you. It upset me, too. Please don't tell her I heard it."

"I—I don't want to discuss it, Mike. Please l–leave. I'll take care of getting my car."

He moved toward the bed. "Can I get you anything? A glass of water? An aspirin?"

"No, th–thank you. Go on home. We have a b–busy day ahead of us tomorrow."

"You still want me to go to the—" His cell phone rang and, though he hated to answer it, he knew he had to. "Garrett."

He listened a moment, told the caller he'd be right there, and hung up.

"Duty calls?" Tessa asked, sniffing and lifting her tearstained face once more.

"Yeah, they wouldn't have called unless it was important. We've got another victim. They think it's the woman I've been looking for—the one who abandoned her physically abused four-month-old baby in a cardboard box at the bus station."

Tessa waved toward the door in a shooing motion. "Go on, Mike. Do what you have to do."

"I don't want to leave you this way."

She rubbed a hand across her face. "You were already leaving, Mike, before you got that call. Go."

"I'll have them get someone else to—" His phone rang again. "Garrett," he snapped impatiently. "Okay. Okay. Yes." He listened then shook his head sadly. "That's good. It should help us find her boyfriend. Thanks for letting me know. See you in a sec." He turned to Tessa, his face somber. "They found a picture in her pocket. Her, some guy, and the baby. I gotta go. If we don't hurry, the guy may get out of state. I'll call you in the morning about going to the florist." He hurried toward the door, turning only long enough to say again, "I'm really sorry."

"Yeah, me, too," he heard Tessa say as he headed down the hall toward the door.

⌖

"I would never have called you, Mike," the officer on duty told him as Mike bent over the Jane Doe, "especially since you're taking a few days off and asked that we not call, but I knew you'd be interested in this. Makes you wonder what would possess a woman to make her let a man do this to her. I'll bet that baby in this picture is the one we found at the bus station." He held the picture out toward Mike.

"Sure looks like the same baby." Mike examined the picture carefully then checked Jane Doe's face. Though she'd been badly beaten, and her face was swollen and marred with dried blood, he was sure she was the woman in the picture.

"Somebody really had it in for this woman," the coroner said, standing and pulling off his latex gloves. "I hope you get whoever did this."

"Notice anything that might help me get him?"

The man nodded. "He was wearing a big ring."

Mike rubbed at his chin thoughtfully. "Anything else?"

"Don't know where it came from, maybe from the guy, but someone had spit a wad of chewing tobacco on her chest."

"Maybe the lab tech can tell us what brand. That might help. Might even find a DNA match."

The coroner tossed his gloves into a bag and sealed it. "I'll bag the sample and get it to him right away."

Mike knelt and stared at the woman. "We humans do horrible things to one another, don't we?"

The duty officer huffed. "Tell me about it. I've seen more strange and cruel behavior in the five years I've been on the force than I expected I'd see in a lifetime. Wives stabbing husbands. Husbands strangling wives. Makes you wonder how these people ever got together in the first place. Don't couples usually get married because they love each other and want to be together? Kids are even killing their parents. What's this world coming to?"

"Good question."

"Well, every time one of these tragedies happens, I go home and thank the Lord for my wife and kids and our happy home. I'm way more blessed than any man deserves to be."

"You are a lucky man. I hope you know that." Mike gave the pitiful victim one final glance, then rose. "I'm heading to the station. I'll probably be there most of the night. Call me if anything else comes up."

On the way across town he drove past Tessa's house, still guilt-ridden for leaving her stranded without transportation. But there it was, her car, parked in her driveway. Maybe she'd called Ellen for a ride just as she said. All he knew was he'd let her down—again.

⁜

As promised, Mike phoned Tessa the next morning, fearful she might not answer when she noticed his number on her caller ID.

"You really don't have to go to the florist with me," she told him coolly. "I'm sure, what with the important case you're working on, you have things to do that can't wait."

"No, Tessie, I want to go with you. If anything further develops, the guys will call me."

After a bit of hesitation, she agreed to let him pick her up and drive her to the florist rather than take her own car.

Merry Sinclair, the owner of Forget-Me-Not Florist Shop and a member of their church, greeted them warmly as they came through the door.

"It's good to see you both," Merry said as the two women greeted one another with a hug. "I was really happy when Katie phoned and said she and Jim had decided to get married," the woman told her with an understanding smile. "But you certainly have your work cut out for you, putting together a formal Christmas Day wedding in such a short time."

"Then you'll be able to help us?"

"Of course, I'll help you. What are friends for? Besides, my son and his wife aren't going to be able to come for Christmas until the twenty-sixth, so I was going to spend Christmas Day by myself. Helping with Katie and Jim's wedding will be a lot more fun." She motioned toward a large refrigerated case along the far wall. "Katie mentioned red roses and white carnations. She was so adamant about it, I figured there must be some special symbolism involved."

Mike had to smile when Tessa ducked her head shyly. "We—Mike and I—had red roses and white carnations at our wedding."

"On Christmas Day," he added.

Merry sent him a smile. "Red roses and white carnations make a lovely setting for a Christmas wedding. I think Katie has made a wonderful choice. For major impact and to take advantage of the traditional red and green Christmas colors, for the sanctuary I would suggest a gigantic arrangement on each side of the altar, tall red candles in the candelabra with fresh green ivy intertwined, and red roses, white carnations, and more ivy anchored with huge red bows at the end of each pew."

Tessa nodded and from the look on her face Mike could see she agreed with each suggestion Merry was making. "Would you use the same colors and flowers for the wedding party's corsages and boutonnieres?"

"Definitely." Merry pulled a single long-stemmed red rose from the case and handed it to Tessa. "And I'll get together with Jim and make sure he uses the same combination for a lovely, vine-trailing bridal bouquet for Katie. How does that sound?"

"Expensive!" Mike rubbed at his chin. "Do we have to use so many flowers?"

Tessa gave him a look. *That* look.

He shrugged. "Sorry, Merry, but it seems this whole thing is mushrooming out of control. I don't want to look like a skinflint, but I'm not Mr. Moneybags. Cops don't make as much money as most folks think we do."

He was surprised when Merry gave him a pleasant smile instead of looking at him like he had two heads.

"I completely understand, Mike. So many times, I see folks spend way more than they should on a wedding for their children. I hate to see people go into debt." She placed her hand on his shoulder placatingly. "Don't you worry about it. We'll use silk flowers and ivy wherever we can. I doubt anyone will even notice. I'll go get a few pieces from the stockroom so you can see what I have in mind."

From the look on Tessa's face, Mike knew he was in for it once Merry was out of earshot.

"Do you have to sing your poor song to everyone we meet?"

Her words stung. "I'm not claiming poverty, Tessie. At least, I don't mean to. I'm just being truthful."

Her expression softened a bit. "Look, Mike. I know this wedding is going to cost way more than you expected, and I can understand your concern. But this constant complaining about the costs embarrasses me, and I'd think would embarrass you. I'm not used to discussing our finances with anyone, especially friends from church."

He took a step toward her, nearly knocking a huge Oriental vase filled with colorful silk flowers off a nearby display table, catching hold of it just in time. "Look, Tessie. I'm sorry. I mean it. The last thing I want to do is embarrass you *or* Katie."

"Here they are." Merry hurried toward them, a lovely bouquet cradled in her arms. "Aren't these pretty?"

Tessa reached out, gently touching several of the blossoms' petals. "They *are* silk! I would never have guessed it. They're beautiful."

"Yeah, those sure look real," Mike chimed in approvingly.

"Many brides actually prefer silk flowers to fresh ones. In addition to a savings in cost, with a little care the flowers literally last forever. Some brides have us rearrange all the flowers into bouquets after the wedding and use them as floral arrangements about their home. They make wonderful mementos of one of the happiest days of their lives."

Mike took a single red rose from Merry's hand and examined it carefully. "Tessie, you think Katie would go for these?"

"I think so. I couldn't say for sure."

"I'll box up a few of these so you can show them to Katie."

Mike grinned. "Good idea."

"They are beautiful, and they do look real," Tessa told him as Merry scurried off toward the back room again. "But there's no fragrance. Nothing can duplicate the exquisite aroma of the real thing."

"Yeah, you're right."

"Well, let's not worry about it now. We'll let Katie make that decision."

"Tessie?"

"Yes?"

"Don't mention my complaining or the difference in cost when we show these to Katie, okay?"

She frowned. "But I thought that was the reason we were considering silk."

"It was, but I want Katie to have whichever kind she chooses."

She tilted her head quizzically. "You're sure about that?"

"Absolutely."

"Then I won't mention it."

He gave her a grateful smile. "Thanks, Tessie."

She returned his smile. "You're welcome."

He sent her a sideways grin. "You know what?"

"What?"

"Seeing Merry holding those flowers in her arms like that reminded me of you on our wedding day. You sure were beautiful."

Her eyes widened. "Uh—thank you, Mike."

The shy smile and look on her face sent chills down his spine. As much as he hated to admit it, he still loved that woman.

"Here you are." Merry handed a long white box to Mike. "Tell Katie to call me if she has any questions. I hope she knows how lucky she is to have the two of you helping her. Where are you off to now?"

"The photographer," they answered in unison.

⚜

Tessa glanced at Mike as they sat waiting in the lobby of the Creative Images Photo Shop. "I've heard great things about this photographer. He photographed Valene and Jordan's wedding as well as Vanessa and Nathan's. He did Della and Brandon's wedding, too. Ellen said he was great to work with and highly recommended him."

"I still don't understand why Katie has to use a professional photographer. Jim said Bill Zobel has a brand-new digital camera. Why doesn't Katie let him take pictures? I've heard digital cameras do a great job. Didn't Nathan take video of Jordan and Valene's wedding? Maybe he'd shoot video of Katie and Jim's."

Tessa stared at him in the same quizzical way she'd stared at him at the caterer. "You've got to be kidding! For truly professional wedding photographs, you have to have top-quality cameras, special lighting, knowledge of settings and how to group people—all sorts of things."

"Hello." A handsome young man in a black turtleneck pull-over and black trousers greeted them with a smile. "I'm Eric. What can I do for you?"

"We need you to photograph our daughter's wedding," Mike said after a quick glance in his wife's direction. "Several of her friends recommended you."

"And when is this wedding to be?"

"Christmas Day."

"Well, we are planning things early, aren't we? A full year in advance? Most people only give us a few months' notice. Unfortunately, we never shoot a wedding on Christmas Day!"

"It's this Christmas Day," Tessa said quickly.

His mouth gaping, the man stared at them. "That's not even two weeks off!"

"Isn't there some way you could do it?" Mike asked, almost wishing the man would say no so he could ask Bill to do it with his digital camera.

"On Christmas Day? No! My mother and father would never forgive me if I didn't show up at their house on Christmas Day!"

Tessa looked as if she were about to cry. "Can you recommend another photographer who would be willing to do it on Christmas Day?"

The man thought for a moment. "Not a one. Sorry."

"Now what?" Tessa asked once they were both back in the car. "And don't say anything about having Bill and Nathan do it. They can take all the extra pictures you want them to, but we must have a professional photographer for Katie's wedding. She loved the other couples' pictures. That girl has her heart set on this Eric fellow doing it. What if we can't find another photographer? What then?"

Mike watched as Tessa blinked a few times; then he turned and climbed out of the car. "I'll be right back."

He entered the shop and found the man still standing at the counter. "Look, Eric, Katie is my only daughter. She's laid up at home with a broken ankle and has had to depend on her mother and me to do the footwork for this wedding. She's seen the work you've done for her friends and she wants you to be her photographer."

"Most brides begin planning their wedding months ahead of time. Why did she wait so long? Two weeks is not much notice at any time of year, but especially in December." Eric gave Mike a look of disgust, but he ignored it. He didn't want to alienate the man when he was about to try to bargain with him.

"Long story, which I won't go into now, but take it from me, Katie and Jim *are* going to be married on Christmas Day." Mike pulled his credit card from his wallet and held it out toward the man. "What's it going to take to get you to be the one to photograph it?"

Five minutes later, he climbed back into the car. "The guy's gonna do it after all."

"He is? On Christmas Day? How did you get him to change his mind?"

Momentarily putting aside the thought of the exorbitant amount of money he'd had to promise the man to get him to cancel his plans to be with his parents on Christmas Day in order to be Katie's official photographer, he gave her a victorious smile. "Just had a little man-to-man talk with him. That's all."

Tessa scooted toward him, her face beaming with delight. "Mike, I don't know how you talked him into it, but thank you. Katie will be so pleased." Bracing herself on the console between them, she pushed herself up and kissed him on the cheek. "I'm pleased, too. More than I can tell you."

For the first time in more than eight years, Mike felt like a king. Whatever this wedding was going to cost him, it would be worth it, just to be back in Tessa's good graces, if even for a moment. "Good. What's next on our agenda?"

"Actually, we're pretty well finished. All of the really important things have been taken care of. We still have to select and purchase the various gifts for the wedding party, but we can do that tomorrow. The most important thing left to do is address the rest of the wedding invitations. Katie has already mailed hers to their friends and associates, but she's asked us to do the rest. We need to get them in the mail by tomorrow at the latest. Even then, we'll be giving people extremely short notice."

"She isn't going over the two hundred and fifty mark we told the caterer, is she?"

Tessa laughed and slapped at his arm playfully. "No! I think she said her list consisted of about two hundred names. That means you and I will have to keep our list down to about fifty."

"That shouldn't be too hard," Mike said with confidence.

In no time they reached Tessa's house.

"Look, Mike," Tessa said, giving him a warm smile as he pulled the car into her driveway, "you've amazed me by the way you've put your detective work on hold this week. I know you have things that need to be done, and I have a few things to tend to, as well. Let's take the rest of the day off."

"What about the invitations?"

"I was about to suggest you come to the house for supper tonight. We could work on them then."

Her invitation was welcome—and something he certainly hadn't expected. "Yeah, that'd be nice," he said, savoring her words. "What time?"

"Six okay?"

"I'll be there!"

🌴

Tessa felt as nervous as a contestant in a cooking contest as she did one more final check through the house, making sure everything was in place. Why she invited Mike to dinner, she'd never understand. But she had, and now she'd have to go through with it.

When the doorbell rang at exactly six, she took a quick glance in the hall mirror, smoothed her hair with her fingertips, and then hurried to open the door.

"Hi." Mike stepped inside, a small bouquet of fresh red roses gripped tightly in his hands. "Got them at the gas station. They didn't have white carnations."

Her heart racing, she took them and lifted them to sniff their sweet fragrance. "Thank you, Mike. I love them."

"You're welcome." His smile turned to a frown. "I've been thinking. Maybe the silk flowers aren't such a good idea for Katie's wedding. I sure like the smell of the real ones."

"But think of the difference in price," she reminded him, clutching the flowers to her breast, still amazed that he would do something so thoughtful. "Silk won't be so bad."

He moved closer to her and sniffed the air. "Is that meat loaf I smell?"

"Sure is."

"I haven't had your meat loaf—"

"For over eight years," Tessa interrupted, finishing his sentence and putting a little distance between the two of them. "Since Katie moved out, I rarely fix it for myself. It'll be nice to have someone to share it with." She uttered a nervous laugh. "But don't expect lemon meringue pie. I didn't have time to bake one."

"Hey, I really don't care what we're having. Just you inviting me here is enough. I've—I've missed being in our home."

She noticed he nearly choked when she ducked her head and in a voice nearly inaudible said, "I've missed having you here." Had those words really come from her mouth? Gathering her wits about her, she pushed past him toward the kitchen. "Make yourself comfortable. I'll have things on the table in a minute."

Tessa leaned against the refrigerator and tried to catch her breath. She couldn't let herself be drawn into Mike's erratic lifestyle again, no matter how much she wanted to be there. It didn't work then—it wouldn't work now. Nothing had changed, except she had grown older, lonelier, and more vulnerable. No matter how much she claimed otherwise, she didn't like being alone.

"Want some help?" Mike appeared in the doorway a few minutes later, looking every bit as handsome—except for the paunch he'd acquired over the years—as he had eight years ago.

"You're just in time. Dinner is ready."

They laughed their way through their meal, reminiscing about the early years of their marriage, Katie's birth, and the good times they'd had together, each clearly going out of their way to avoid any mention of the bad times.

"I'm stuffed," Mike finally said, pushing back in his chair and rubbing his belly. "That meat loaf was fantastic! Everything was. My compliments to the cook."

Tessa felt herself blushing as she mouthed a demure, "Thank you."

Mike helped her with the dishes, something he'd never even considered doing before, as she recalled; then the two of them moved into the family room to get started on the invitations.

"Who would you like to invite, Mike?" Tessa picked up the pad she'd left on the coffee table and poised her pen over it.

He screwed up his face thoughtfully. "I dunno. Captain Ferrell and his wife, I guess. Four or five other detectives and their wives. That's about it. Oh, and the police chief and his wife. I nearly forgot him!"

Tessa wrote down all the names and information while Mike looked up the addresses in the phone book. "Now that you've completed your list, we can start on mine." She pulled her address book from the table, flipping through the pages slowly. "Our assistant pastor and his family. Ellen and Bill Zobel. Katie probably already added them to her list. Our neighbors on both sides... The Reeds across the street..."

She went on to add a second entire page to her list, most of them friends from church she knew weren't on Katie's or Jim's lists, while Mike looked on.

Finally, with a cautioning smile, he gave her a tap on the shoulder. "You do realize your list alone has way over fifty people on it?"

She scanned the names. "Oh, Mike, I'm sorry. I hadn't realized."

"I hate this, Tessa. Even if I could afford adding more names, I'm not sure the caterer would agree to serve more than two hundred and fifty on Christmas Day."

She started at the top of her list, crossing off a name here and there. "I'm sure I can eliminate a few names, but I don't want to offend anyone by not inviting them. And there are so many others I'd like to invite that I haven't even added to this list."

He let out a sigh. "Me, too. I've thought of at least ten others since I finished my list. Keeping this wedding down to a reasonable size is hopeless."

"I still have that piece of property up near Turner Falls my aunt left me. Maybe I could sell it and—"

"No, absolutely not," Mike answered firmly, his hand grasping her wrist tightly. "I know how much that piece of land means to you. Don't worry about it, Tessie. I'll come up with the money."

"But I—"

He pressed his finger to her lips. "Not another word. I'll call the caterer tomorrow and ask if we can add another twenty-five to our total."

"But Katie doesn't—"

"Not a word about this to Katie, understood?"

She gave him a nod. How nice it was to have Mike taking charge and being an active part of her life again. If only he'd done this years ago.

"I'll pick you up about nine tomorrow," he told her when they'd finished their lists.

"You really don't need to go with me, Mike. All I'm going to do is shop for gift items for the members of Katie's wedding party, the candles for the candelabra, the guest book for the reception, and a myriad of other last-minute things on Katie's list. I know how much you hate shopping. Let me take care of those things."

He shook his head. "No, I want to help. I wonder how Katie is getting along with her walking cast."

"She's doing fine. I talked to her first thing this morning. She says it's much better than having to hold her foot up and hobble around with the walker. Too bad it was her right foot so she can't drive, but at least she's able to get around the condo more easily. That really helps. She wanted to go shopping with me, but I encouraged her to stay home and concentrate on any final wedding details."

"Good idea. Are you sure you don't need any help? I'm still willing."

"No, I'll manage just fine. Oh, by the way, Katie and Jim want us to have dinner with them tomorrow night. She said Jim is cooking. Can you make it?"

"Dinner with you two nights in a row? Sure I can make it. What time?"

"About seven."

"Want me to come by for you?"

She shook her head. "No thanks. I want to stop by Ellen's on the way and return a book I borrowed. I'll meet you at Katie's."

⸸

Tessa greeted Mike at Katie's door when he arrived the next evening, looking bright and fresh and prettier than he'd seen her in a long time. "Wow, you look terrific!" was all he could think to say. She took his breath away.

"Hi, Daddy."

Katie thumped her way to the door then gave his cheek a kiss, ending it with a childlike smacking sound that made him laugh. He might not have been the best father when she was growing up, but he loved his precious Katie dearly and wanted to make things up to her. "Hi, pumpkin. Sure nice to see you up and around. How's the ankle?"

"Doin' good." Katie gave him a generous smile. "I'll be able to walk down the aisle with no trouble at all." She motioned toward the little dining area where the table was beautifully set with glowing candles and colorful place mats. "Jim's out on the patio turning the steaks. Dinner should be ready in no time. Would you like some iced tea or a cup of coffee?"

"Iced tea would be. . ." He stopped to answer his cell phone. "Garrett."

Mike listened a minute, excited to hear the news the chief of detectives was giving him on the other end, then said good-bye and hung up, disappointed he wouldn't be able to have dinner with his family after all. "I've got to go," he told Katie and Tessa as he headed for the door. "That was my boss. We finally got a big break in the case I've been working on. They need me at the station to interrogate a new witness. I'm really sorry. I'll try—"

Tessa's face grew red as her hands anchored on her hips. "Mike, you're doing it again! Jim and Katie have worked hard to prepare this dinner for us and you're leaving?"

"Mom!"

Mike shot her a troubled frown. "You think I want to leave? With you and Katie and Jim here and those fabulous steaks cooking on the grill?"

Tessa jutted out her chin. "But you *are* leaving, aren't you?"

"Daddy has to go, Mom! Why do you always make a big deal out it? It's his job!"

"Because it always was a big deal, Katie. Did you ever tell him how many times you cried yourself to sleep because he ran off to some crime scene when you needed him? When you had a ball game or a school play, or something else important to you?"

Katie blushed and glanced toward her father but remained silent.

"I was there," Tessa went on. "I knew what you were going through. I was going through it, too! We could never count on your father to be there when we needed him. His work was more important than we were. We always took second place."

Obviously upset at being placed in the middle, Katie glared at her mother. "That's not fair."

Trying to keep from saying words he'd regret later, Mike crossed the room and stopped in the doorway. "I'm sorry, Katie. I never meant for this to happen," he told her in a level tone, "but this case affects a lot of people in our community. I can't go into detail, but believe me, it's important, or I wouldn't be interrogating this witness myself. I'll call you later."

Just before closing the door, he glanced in Tessa's direction. "I'll call you in the morning."

✝

Infuriated by his sudden departure, Tessa clenched and unclenched her fists at her sides as she stared at the closed door. To her, it was history repeating itself all over again, and she didn't like it one bit better now than she had years ago.

"I'd hoped, when I arranged for you and Daddy to spend time together, the two of you would begin to get along, but I can see I was wrong. It was a waste of effort," Katie told her, leaning against the table as she lowered herself into a chair. "You're both as stubborn as you ever were."

Tessa turned to gape at her daughter. "What do you mean—arranged for your father and me to spend time together?"

"Mom, surely you didn't think I was as helpless as I appeared! Yes, I broke my ankle, but did it ever occur to you that I could have phoned the caterer and the florist and the photographer? Vanessa and Valene begged me to let them help, but I saw this whole thing as an opportunity to bring the two of you together! The two people I love most in the whole world, next to Jim, of course."

Tessa felt her heartbeat quicken as she stared openmouthed at her daughter. "You tricked us? Katie, how could you? You knew how I felt about your father!"

Katie met her intense stare with one of her own. "I should know how you felt. You've told me often enough." The expression on her face softened as she reached out and took her mother's hand in hers. "Mom, it's time to move on. From the time I was a little girl, you've tried to convince me God was in control of your life, but He hasn't been. He was only in control as long as He allowed you to call the shots."

Shocked and hurt, Tessa found it hard to speak but finally the words, though difficult, came out. "I can't believe you would say such a thing. I love the Lord with my whole heart. Surely you remember all the times I worked at the church, doing many jobs others refused to do, all the years I've taught Sunday school, the dinners I've cooked and taken to the sick, the many people from our congregation I've visited at the hospital."

"Granted, Mom, those are all wonderful things, but were all those things done for God? Or did you do them because you enjoyed them and they filled a void in your life?"

Tessa squared her shoulders and lifted her chin. "I did them for God, Katie! I can't imagine why you'd ask me such a thing! I'm a Christian!"

Katie turned loose of her mother's hand and leaned back in her chair. "I'm not saying these things to hurt you. Honest, I'm not. But, Mom, I accepted the Lord as my Savior when I was a child, and I meant it. I actually asked Him to forgive my sins and come into my heart, but with all the fighting and bickering going on in our home when I was a little girl, I began to wonder if God was real. If He was, why would my parents, who I thought loved each other and who both claimed to be Christians, behave in such an ugly way toward each other? I felt like we were playing church, like actors in a play—that what our family had was not the real thing at all, but the actions and speech expected of us because everyone thought we were good people, and good people were supposed to attend church."

Tessa searched her heart and came up short. Had she really done all those things, those works, simply to glorify and draw attention to herself? To solicit the praises of other people instead of performing them to please God? What had she done to her daughter? Were her actions and those of Mike, responsible for Katie pulling away from the God she had assumed her daughter loved? "Is—is that the reason you quit going to church? Because I let you down?"

Katie hung her head, avoiding her mother's eyes. "That was one of the reasons. I was disillusioned with the church, you, Daddy, my so-called Christian friends, all of it. But mainly it was because of some of the things I got into in high school—things I've never told you about. Things I knew displeased God."

Tessa's jaw dropped. "Katie Garrett! Whatever do you mean? I had no idea you'd ever been in trouble!"

"Only because I never told you! I was great at hiding things from you, and Daddy was never home, so I didn't have to worry about him finding out."

Unable to even comprehend that her sweet, innocent teenaged daughter could have been guilty of any wrongdoing, Tessa simply stared at her. "You must tell me, Katie. I have to know. What did you do when you were a teenager?"

Chapter 7

A number of things I'm not very proud of, but I guess the worst was during the Christmas break of my junior year."

Tessa's heart sank. "Oh, Katie—from the look on your face, I'm almost afraid to hear it."

"You remember when you thought I went skiing with the Clarkson family to Colorado? Well, I—"

"You *did* go to Colorado with them, didn't you? Oh, please say you did."

Katie fiddled with a fingernail and seemed to be avoiding Tessa's eyes. "Not exactly."

Her patience wearing thin, Tessa reached out and cupped her daughter's chin with her hand, lifting her face. "What do you mean—not exactly? Either you did or you didn't."

"I had planned to go with them," Katie confessed, still avoiding her mother's eyes, "but at the last minute, Mr. Clarkson had to cancel. He ended up having gallbladder surgery. Since his wife wanted to stay with him, he let us take his van, and we three girls went on alone."

Tessa gasped. "Without a chaperone? Clear to Colorado? Oh, Katie, if I'd known, I would never have let you go!"

Katie hung her head, a guilt-ridden look on her face. "That's the reason I didn't tell you. But there's more."

Tessa sucked in a deep breath. "What else, Katie? I need to hear all of it."

"We—we met some really cute twenty-year-old guys and drove all around the mountains with them in their SUV. I know it was dumb but—"

"Katie! You were sixteen! Please tell me nothing happened."

"Sorry, Mom, but it did. I tasted alcohol for the first time and after a few drinks, I found I liked it."

Tessa's mind reeled. "I don't like the direction this is going, Katie Garrett."

"I've wanted to get this off my chest for a long time. I hate to admit it, Mom, but I got drunk as a skunk. It was a dumb thing to do but, at the time, it really seemed cool. And yes, I know all the things that could have happened to me, but they didn't. I guess your prayers were protecting me. Even now, I shudder to think what might have happened." The guilty look on Katie's face twisted into a slight smile. "Actually, all three of us girls got so sick we vomited all over that new SUV. Those guys literally dumped us off at the hotel, and we never saw them again."

Aghast at her daughter's confession, Tessa imagined all kinds of scenarios, sending her mind spinning. "Is that the whole truth, Katie? You're not covering something up, are you?"

"Just one other tiny thing."

Tessa's hand went to her forehead. "Oh, no. What?"

"Those stupid jocks drove off with our purses. We didn't have money to pay the hotel bill or purchase gas for the drive home. So—"

Still in awe of what she was hearing, Tessa gave her head an accusing shake. "I guess I'd have to say you deserved it, taking up with strangers like that. So you called the Clarksons?"

Katie lifted wide eyes to meet hers. "No, I called Dad."

"You called your father? Why, Katie? You could have called me!"

Katie gave her head a vigorous shake. "No way, Mom. You would have had a coronary! It was bad enough having to call Dad. Believe me! Though he wired me the money, he read me the riot act. Big-time!"

"You turned to your father instead of me?" Tessa asked, both angered and hurt that Katie had contacted Mike. "Why, Katie? Why would you do such a thing? Haven't I always been the one who was there for you?"

After propping her foot up on the ottoman, Katie leaned her head against the back of the sofa and didn't answer for a moment. "Mom," she said finally, "yes, you've always been there for me, and I love you for it, but why can't you understand I love Daddy, too? He may not have been there the many times I wished he would have been, but he's worked hard all his life to provide the kind of lifestyle he's wanted for me. Because of Dad's willingness to provide for our needs, you were able to be a stay-at-home mom and never had to work like most of my friends' moms did."

Tessa swallowed hard. Every word Katie was saying was true.

"If he'd been an accountant, a lawyer, or even a plumber like you and Grandpa wanted him to be, maybe he would have worked regular hours. But he didn't, Mom, and he would have hated it. From the time Daddy was a little boy, he wanted to be a policeman. You told me yourself, you knew that long before you two were engaged. Did you expect him to forget his dream just because the two of you got married? I sure hope Jim never does that to me!"

"I—I hoped he'd forget about it once we were married. Especially after you were born," Tessa shot back defensively.

"Mom! That was an unrealistic expectation! What if Dad had decided he wanted *you* to become a waitress? Or maybe a flight attendant? Would you have accepted that?" Crossing her arms over her chest, Katie huffed. "I think not! Not you! You're much too independent. Thanks to Daddy, you've always done pretty much as you pleased."

Though the words stung, Tessa had no counterargument. For the most part, she had done whatever she'd wished all her life, with neither her parents nor Mike stepping in to even try to change her mind.

"Perhaps it'd be wise if we let this subject drop. I doubt you and I will ever see eye-to-eye when it comes to Daddy." Katie grabbed onto the arm of the sofa and struggled to her feet. "Make yourself comfortable, Mom. I'm going to check on the steaks."

Tessa's eyes filled with tears as she watched her lovely daughter hobble across the room and out the patio door. What had started out as a lovely evening had turned into a nightmare because she had lost control and exploded at Mike over that phone call. Why hadn't she kept her mouth shut? *We've been separated for over eight years. I have absolutely no right to question what he does and why, any more than he should tell me what to do.*

Slowly she crossed the room and gazed at the framed picture her daughter had placed prominently on the fireplace mantel—a picture of the three of them on Katie's tenth birthday. What a wonderful day that had been. They'd had so much fun celebrating. How handsome Mike had looked in his blue plaid shirt. As usual, his hair was badly in need of a cut. She smiled at the funny little way his mouth always turned up when he posed for a photograph. He hated having his picture taken.

Lifting the frame from the mantel, she pressed it to her heart. With a tear rolling down her cheek, she closed her eyes and whispered, "I'll always love you, Mike Garrett. Though I've tried to fight it and not admit it to myself, being with you these past few days has only made me realize how much I still love you. No one will ever be able to take your place in my heart."

✝

Tessa leaped to answer the phone when it rang at seven the next morning. It was Mike.

"Hi. I hope I'm not calling too early. I was at the station all night, and I'm bushed. I really need a couple hours of shut-eye. I heard you say you still had a few things to purchase. I—I wonder if it'd be okay if we put off the rest of our shopping for those last things on Katie's list until this afternoon?"

Remembering she had abandoned all rights to Mike's time when they'd separated, she answered quietly, "That would be fine or, like I said, I can finish myself. There's not that much to do."

"No." His answer was firm. "Katie asked me to help you, and that's what I intend to do. I'll be there by one o'clock." The phone clicked in her ear.

As promised, Mike appeared at her door at one, looking rested and ready to go, a pleasant smile on his face. "Look, I'm sorry about last night. Not that it's any excuse, but this case I'm working on has made me crazy. I had no right to snap at you that way."

Her heart doing a leap, she returned his smile as she led him into the room and seated herself beside him on the sofa. "I'm the one who should apologize. I had no right to criticize your actions."

To her surprise, Mike turned and placed a quick kiss on her forehead. "Let's pretend it never happened."

Though Tessa tried to hold it back, a broad smile broke forth. "I'd like that."

"What's on the agenda for today?"

"I finished most of the shopping yesterday, but we need to pick up the rolls of white satin ribbon for decorating the church, and I need to purchase a pair of ivory shoes, and—"

Mike reared back with a laugh. "Guess we'd better hurry if we're gonna get all that stuff done." Still smiling, he extended an open palm.

A wave of pleasure swept over her as she placed her hand in his and they headed for the door.

♰

Tessa awoke early the next morning after enjoying one of the best night's sleep she'd had in a long time. She actually let out a giggle as she remembered the good time she'd had with Mike as they'd gone from one store to another, crossing off the things on both hers and their daughter's list. Not one time had Mike's cell phone rung, for which she was grateful. She wondered if he'd threatened those at his office to only call in case of a dire emergency.

Though Mike hadn't mentioned he would call her, she leaped to answer the phone when it rang at nine o'clock, half expecting it to be him.

"Mom! It's happened again!" It was obvious by the screech in Katie's voice something was radically wrong. "Della's shop just delivered the wrong gown!"

"Are you sure?" she asked, nearly as panic-stricken as her daughter.

"Of course I'm sure! This one has stupid-looking ruffles from head to toe and is made of some weird fabric."

"Now, honey, let's not overreact. I'm sure it's nothing more than a simple mistake. Have you called Della?"

Katie sniffled. "I've tried a dozen times, but the line is busy. What am I going to do, Mom? It seems everything is going wrong, and here I am with this stupid cast on my leg! I can't even drive."

"Don't worry, sweetie. I'll hop in the car and hurry over to Della's shop. I'm sure they just delivered your dress to another customer by mistake, and you'll have the right one in no time."

"You don't mind?"

"Not one bit. I'll call you from the shop."

In less than five minutes Tessa was in her car, inserting the key in the ignition. But nothing happened.

No engine noise.

Nothing.

Now what? She lowered her head onto the steering wheel and closed her eyes. *Lord, please. I know You're displeased with me, but don't let this wedding fall apart.*

She turned the key again.

Still nothing.

She pulled out her cell phone and dialed Mike's number. He answered on the first ring.

After explaining about Katie's dress and the trouble with her car, she asked, "Can you come after me? I need to get over to the bridal shop as soon as possible. Katie is a basket case over this."

"I really want to, Tessie, but I can't," he explained, sounding genuinely sorry. "That guy I was interrogating just gave me some vital information that may solve the case. I have to check it out immediately. It could be the break I've been looking for."

She felt the old resentment rising. "Can't someone else do it?"

After a slight pause, Mike told her apologetically, "I'm afraid not. This is my case, and I don't want any slipups. I want to be there to personally make sure all the *t*'s are crossed and the *i*'s dotted. When I get the guy I'm looking for, I don't want some fancy high-paid lawyer getting him off on a technicality. This guy deserves to be locked up for the rest of his life, and I'm going to make sure that happens."

Tessa clutched the phone tightly. "I'd think, just once in your life, you could put your family first, but I guess that's never going to happen. Forget it. I'll call a cab!" With that, she cut off their connection.

An hour later, she arrived at Katie's condo, carrying the proper dress. "The delivery boy just delivered the two gowns to the wrong addresses. All it took was one quick phone call from Della, and the mystery was solved. She's sending him by later this afternoon to pick up the one he left for you."

Katie dabbed at her eyes with a tissue. "Thanks, Mom. I didn't mean to sound like such a baby on the phone, but so many things have gone wrong. I'd just had my fill."

Tessa sat down and slipped her arm about Katie's shoulders, giving her a much-needed hug. "It's okay, baby. Your dress is here, most of the things for your wedding are done, and you're marrying one of the nicest, most responsible men I've ever met. On your first wedding anniversary, you and Jim will laugh at all the trouble you've had."

Katie wiped away another tear. "Dad called."

Tessa gave a flip of her hand. "So? What did the busy man have to say?"

"He was concerned about you. He told me about your car trouble."

"Did he tell you he refused to come and take me to Della's shop? That he was too busy playing detective?"

Katie let out a long sigh. "He's not *playing* detective, Mom. I don't know why you keep saying that. Daddy's work is important."

"More important than his family? Surely he's not the only competent detective on the police force. This is not about how important his job is. I think this is more about your father feeling important by playing his role as a detective. And it's the only role in life he's chosen to play. He's abandoned that of husband and father."

"I hate to say this, Mom. I don't mean to upset you, but I don't understand how you can call yourself a Christian and talk about Daddy the way you do. What about all the forgiveness God speaks about in the Bible? Doesn't He say we should forgive our enemies? And Daddy wasn't your enemy; he was your husband. Does all that scripture about forgiveness pertain to everyone but you?"

Tessa's hackles rose defensively. "Don't be insolent, Katie. You can't begin to know how badly your father hurt me."

"But, Mom! You still need to forgive him. He didn't do it intentionally. He loves you, and I know you still love him, and—"

"Where did you get that idea?"

Katie's lips twisted into a slight smile. "It's obvious, Mom. I can tell."

Tessa lifted her chin defiantly. "You're speaking foolishness, Katie Garrett."

"Yeah, sure."

"If your father had any love for me, he would have quit that job of his."

"And if you'd had any love for him, you would have put up with his crazy hours!" Katie shot back.

Tessa crossed her arms over her chest and turned her head away. Though she couldn't see Katie's face, she knew Katie was about to add more to her outrageous comment.

"You—and Daddy—are incorrigible. And stubborn. And afraid to admit when you're wrong. I just hope Jim and I never get like the two of you! I want our marriage to last."

Deciding to put an end to this ridiculous conversation, Tessa pulled the cell phone from her purse to follow up on her car's problem. After a brief call to the mechanic, she took up her purse and headed for the door. "Carl towed my car to his garage. It was the solenoid, just as he'd suspected. He already has it fixed, and one of his staff is coming after me. I told him I'd be waiting out front."

Katie struggled to her feet then gently grabbed her mother's arm. "I'm sorry,

Mom. I didn't mean to be so smart-mouthed. I—I hope you'll forgive me."

Tessa cupped her daughter's hand and gave it a squeeze. "Forgive you for what? Being honest? Or for speaking from your heart?"

The two women smiled at one another. Tessa kissed Katie's cheek then headed for the door. "I'll be home if you need me. Love you."

✝

Mike glanced at his watch as he stood on Tessa's front porch. Seven thirty. He knew she was there. Katie had told him Carl had repaired her car, and it was parked in the driveway.

Maybe he should have called first instead of just turning up on her doorstep uninvited. No, he was already there. He'd just take his chances and hope she'd cooled off and wouldn't rail at him for not being available when she'd needed him.

He pushed the doorbell button and waited.

Tessa pulled open the door and eyed him suspiciously. "Well, look who's here."

Nope, she hasn't cooled off. She's still mad. He forced a smile. "Hi. Had supper yet?"

She merely gave him a vacant stare.

"I really am sorry about this morning, Tessie. Katie told me Carl got your car running and that you had taken care of the dress problem. I figured you'd had a pretty rotten day and the least I could do was take you out to supper."

She tilted her head to one side and stared at him. "I promised myself and Katie I wasn't going to get upset about this."

He ventured a grin. "Then you'll let me take you to supper?"

"If you'll do something for me."

"Anything within my power. Just name it."

Tessa presented him with a challenging smile. "Go to church with me in the morning."

Go to church with her? He certainly hadn't expected that to be her request. "I—I guess I could do that," he answered reluctantly, hoping to make peace between them. "I haven't been for a long time."

Tessa's smile broadened. "Good. I'll count on it. Give me a second to lock up and get my purse."

Both relieved and surprised by their docile conversation, since he had expected a tirade when he arrived, he nodded. "I'll wait in the car."

✝

"And that's what happened with the dress. Pure carelessness on the part of the delivery boy, and poor Katie went into a tailspin," she told him as they sat at the corner booth in their favorite little Mexican restaurant. "Let's hope nothing else happens to our daughter before this wedding is over. I'm not sure she or Jim could handle another problem."

"Yeah, I agree." Mike stared into his cup as he stirred his coffee. "I'm really glad to see those two are getting married. I've hated that they were living together."

"Me, too. I did my best to talk Katie out of it, but our stubborn daughter wouldn't listen to a word."

Mike felt her hand touch his. He wished she'd ask him about the two important cases he was working on, show some interest in his work, but she didn't. He needed to talk to her about it and its importance to the community, to share the highs and lows of police work, like he had done those first few years after they'd married.

"You will make it to the rehearsal dinner and the wedding, won't you?"

"Look, Tessie. As I've told you, these two cases are really important ones. Two of the most important I've ever worked." His free hand cupped hers, and he gave her a smile. "But I'll be there. I promise."

After lingering over a final cup of coffee, Mike drove Tessa home. He'd barely climbed back into his car when his cell phone rang. He listened, grinned, then hung up as he hit the car's accelerator and raced toward the lower east side. Finally, he had the lead he'd been hoping for.

Chapter 8

Deciding to retire early for a change, Tessa donned her nightgown, propped the pillows up against the headboard, grabbed the TV remote, and crawled into bed. The ten o'clock news was just beginning.

"A little less than an hour ago, little three-month-old Marilee Carter, who had been kidnapped from her crib as she lay sleeping in the room next to her parents, was found alive and well, thanks to the dogged pursuit and intense investigation of one of San Diego's longtime detectives. Detective Mike Garrett had promised Mr. and Mrs. Mark Carter he would not rest until he found their precious little girl. By working round the clock and following up on hundreds of leads, tonight Detective Garrett was able to apprehend the young woman who had kidnapped little Marilee and reunite the child with her joyful parents. When questioned, twenty-eight-year-old unemployed waitress, Margaret Peterson, admitted she had planned to pass Marilee Carter off as her own daughter and sell her to a desperate couple who had advertised in the newspaper for a baby."

Tessa sat glued to the spot, unable to believe what she was hearing. Mike— her Mike—had brought that family back together? That's why he'd gotten all those phone calls? Had to duck out on her all those times?

"When asked why this case was so important to him," the news anchor continued, "Detective Garrett said, 'I have a daughter myself. I can't imagine ever being separated from her. Nothing is more important than family. I determined I was going to follow up on every lead, regardless of how insignificant it was, until I located the Carters' baby.' And Detective Garrett and the San Diego Police Department did just that. I also asked Detective Garrett if he ever doubted they'd find the child alive. This was his response. Again, I quote. 'In a kidnapping case,' he said, 'time is of the essence. Fortunately, we were able to find and return little Marilee to her parents alive and well. Not all infant kidnappings turn out that way. Just seeing the joy on her parents' faces made all the hours of searching for Marilee worth the time and effort we put in.' Because of dedicated men like Detective Mike Garrett," the announcer said, smiling into the camera, "little Marilee Carter is sleeping in her own bed tonight, safe and sound."

"Mike! Why didn't you tell me?" Already knowing the answer, Tessa shuddered. "Because you thought I didn't want to hear, and you were right. I've been

436

too caught up in my own selfish little world to even think about what your life was like."

A tear trickled down her cheek as a short video clip ran of Mr. and Mrs. Carter weeping as they cuddled and kissed their adorable baby. "No wonder you get such satisfaction out of your job, and I didn't even care enough to ask you about it or understand why you would suddenly take off when you got a phone call. How callous you must think I am."

Her heart racing, she reached for the phone. "Mike, I was watching the news about little Marilee. I—I just wanted to congratulate you," she told him when he answered. "What a thrill it must have been to find that child."

"Thanks, Tessie. It was pretty exciting, all right." From the tone of his voice it was obvious he hadn't expected a call from her, especially a congratulatory one.

"I—I'm very proud of you."

"You are?"

She swallowed at her pride. "From what the newscaster said, without you, the Carters may never have found their baby."

"I got lucky. I had a hunch that baby was going to be sold, so I followed a few leads, called in a few markers and, praise God, found that little girl before something dreadful happened to her. Fortunately, her kidnapper took good care of her."

Did Mike say "praise God"? Perhaps he wasn't as far from God as he appeared. A chill ran down Tessa's spine when she considered what might have happened if Mike hadn't been so persistent in his pursuit of that child. "You're a hero, Mike."

He huffed. "All in a day's work, Tessie, all in a day's work."

"Well, I don't care what you say. You're a hero in my eyes."

"You have no idea what it means to me to hear you say that."

Gripping the phone tightly, she whispered softly, "I—I should have said it long ago."

There was a pause on the other end, as if her words had rendered him speechless. "I—I'll see you in the morning. About ten? I figured you'd want to go to the late service."

Tessa's heart leaped. Mike was still planning to go to church with her. "Ten is fine. Congratulations again. Good night."

" 'Night, Tessie, and thanks for calling.' "

She lay in bed, alone in the dark for a long time, ashamed to think she'd let her own petty needs take priority above that of an innocent child. But how could she have known? He never mentioned the missing child.

The reason hit her right between the eyes, jolting her into reality. He had failed to mention the missing child or any of his other cases because, other than their first couple of years together, she'd never shown one iota of interest in his work as a detective. Now she began to understand why he couldn't give it up.

As promised, Mike rang the doorbell at exactly ten the next morning. Though heads turned as the two of them entered the sanctuary of Granite Cliffs Seaside Community Church, neither she nor Mike took notice. Tessa led him to a front pew—the pew he and Tessa and Katie had claimed as their own the first day they'd visited that church.

Both Ellen and Bill, who were seated directly behind them, smiled and greeted them warmly, as did other members of the congregation. To Tessa's delight, Mike joined in the singing and even read along when Pastor McIntosh led in a responsive reading of the scripture. She loved hearing Mike's deep husky voice. How she'd missed it. A wave of joy swept over her as their shoulders touched and Mike smiled at her.

✝

Mike stole a glance at Tessa. How long had it been since they'd sat together in a church service? How long since they'd felt comfortable in each other's presence?

He'd forgotten how beautiful she was. Maybe the ugly words they'd had over the years had masked her beauty and made him forget how much he loved her.

He scooted a tad closer and gently, hesitantly, took her hand, afraid she might pull away from him. Instead she, ever so slightly, leaned into him. How lonely he'd been. How he'd missed the closeness they'd once shared. A pleasant, familiar fragrance jarred his senses. Was that the same perfume he'd bought her for Christmas those first few years they were married?

The offering taken and the choir's special number sung, Pastor McIntosh moved to the podium and after a lighthearted anecdote began his sermon. Mike tried to avoid listening as Pastor McIntosh told of the prodigal son who had wandered away from his father, cutting all ties, but he couldn't. The message seemed to be aimed directly at him, striking a too-long dormant chord in his heart.

"It makes no difference how far you've wandered from God, or how many times you've turned your back on Him." Pastor McIntosh paused, his gaze sweeping the audience of listeners. "He's there, waiting to forgive you. God longs to have fellowship with you, to walk with you when the storms of life beat you down. Forget your foolish pride. God knows the thoughts, the desires, and the intents of your heart. Surrender. Turn it all over to Him. Ask the forgiveness of the only One who can truly forgive. Oh, wandering soul—return to the God who loves you."

Deeply touched, Mike clamped his eyes shut and gulped hard. Wandering soul. Those two simple words described the life he'd lived for so many years he'd dared not count them.

Pastor McIntosh held his arms open wide as he moved down the carpeted steps from the podium. "Return to the God who loves you. Return to the God who cares. Only God can straighten out the mess we make of our lives. God can forgive you when you can't forgive yourself. Cast your burden upon Him. Give Him your life—your all."

It was all Mike could do to hold himself in the pew. He wanted to run to the front and kneel at the altar. *My life is a mess—a mess I created.* He fidgeted uncomfortably in his seat as the choir sang a hymn of invitation.

"We're going to sing one more verse. Don't let this opportunity to make things right with God pass you by." Pastor McIntosh bowed his head low and stood silently waiting.

Mike wanted to steal a look at Tessie. Was she looking at him? The pressure he felt to respond to the pastor's invitation was overwhelming. His hands fiercely gripped the top of the pew in front of him as a battle raged inside. Were those beads of sweat he felt on his forehead?

"If you've felt God's call today and you haven't made the decision to accept Him and His forgiveness, remember, you don't have to be in a church to commune with the heavenly Father. He's ready to listen to you anytime, anywhere, on your turf or His."

Mike's hold on the pew relaxed. The altar call was over. But try as he may to put it out of his mind, the almost overpowering urge to confess his sins and ask God's forgiveness remained long after the pastor had said the benediction and the congregation filed out.

"Good to see you here," Bill Zobel told him, shaking his hand vigorously when the two met in the parking lot as Mike was closing Tessa's door.

Though still shaken by the morning's message, Mike uttered a friendly, "Yeah, nice to be here. Good to see you, Bill."

Smiling, Bill placed his hand on Mike's shoulder. "You know, Mike, it's been way too long since you and I have had a good round of golf. I've missed our times together. As soon as Katie's wedding is over, let's hit the greens and lose a few balls. Whatcha say?"

Mike returned his smile. "I'd like that, Bill. Let's do it."

Tessa was fastening her seat belt and smiled over at him as Mike climbed into the car. "Great message, wasn't it?"

He nodded, Pastor McIntosh's words still ringing in his ears.

"I–I'm so glad you came with me, Mike."

He cast a quick glance in her direction. She was smiling at him like the old Tessa had smiled at him, and he found himself in awe of her beauty. "Thanks for inviting me," he said simply, not wanting her to know the turmoil that had been going on in his soul. "I've always liked Pastor McIntosh. He's a good guy."

Before she could respond or mention anything else about the morning's sermon, he headed the car across the lot and onto the street. "You are going to let me take you to lunch, aren't you?"

She let loose a giggle that sent his heart reeling. "I was hoping you'd ask."

✝

Tessa couldn't contain her grin as the hostess seated them at a cozy table for two in the beautifully decorated restaurant. She and Mike, together—attending church, having lunch, being civil to one another—something she'd doubted would ever happen again in their lifetime.

"What?" Mike asked, reaching across the table to cup her hand in his as they pushed away their dessert plates and the waitress poured each of them a final cup of coffee.

Her smile broadened. "What, what?"

"I just wondered what you were thinking about."

She felt his grip tighten and knew she must be blushing. "You. Me. Us together. That's all."

"Yeah. This is like old times. I kinda like it. How about you?"

Tessa gazed at this handsome, though somewhat older and a bit stockier man who, at one time, she had loved and pledged her life to. *Be still, my heart. Remember—nothing has changed except that the two of you have called a temporary truce until after Katie's wedding. Once it's over, he'll go back to being the same old Mike. Never there when you need him. Always at the beck and call of some murder scene, robbery, missing person, and on and on and on. You can't open up yourself for hurt again just because he's performed heroic deeds and taken up temporary residence in your life. It's too painful. You can't go through that again. You haven't even recovered from the first time.*

"Tessie? Did you hear me?"

His deep, husky voice jolted her back to her senses, sending up her shield of protection between them. "Yes, I heard you, Mike, and I agree it is somewhat like old times but—"

"Hello, you two. What a nice surprise!"

Both Tessa and Mike turned toward the voice. It was Gina Alexander, Mike's former partner and friend of many years who had retired from the police force and moved to Washington.

"I'm so glad to see the both of you together," the woman went on. "Some of our friends at the police station told me you had broken up."

With a slump of his normally broad square shoulders, Mike nodded. "We are still separated, Gina."

"We've been helping our daughter plan her wedding," Tessa added, smiling. She'd liked Gina and had been glad when she'd been assigned as Mike's partner.

"It's really good to see you again."

"Mike was the best partner I ever had," Gina said, her hand clamping his shoulder affectionately. "Partners develop a close relationship. Learn to trust each other. Sometimes our lives depend on that trust. That's the way it was with me and Mike. We were a great team." She smiled at Tessa. "He'll probably be furious with me for telling you, but Mike confided in me about some of the things that were causing trouble in your marriage. Believe me, all married cops have the same problem. You weren't unique. Spouses never understand our dedication to our jobs. Not even my dear husband, God rest his soul."

Tessa gasped. "You lost Kirk?"

Gina nodded, her eyes filling with tears. "Yes, just two months ago. Life will never be the same without him."

"Oh, Gina, I'm so sorry," Tessa told her, reaching out to cup Gina's wrist. "I didn't know."

"Me, either," Mike said, shaking his head sadly. "I liked Kirk. I know you miss him."

"I do," Gina said, her voice quivering. "Sometimes we don't know what we have until we lose it." Turning her full attention to Tessa, she added, "You're a lucky woman, Tessa Garrett, whether you realize it or not. Mike is a good man, and he loves you. I know you and Mike are Christians and you know the power of God's forgiveness. You can't continue to let something that happened many years ago keep you two apart. You belong together."

Tessa's mind was a whir. "But—"

"I know it's none of my business," Gina added, looking from one to the other, "but it grieves me to see two people who were meant for each other separate because of foolish pride. Life is short. Whatever is keeping you apart is not worth the effort." With a smile, she backed away and blew them each a kiss. "Take this lonely woman's advice. Kiss and make up. You'll be glad you did."

Before they could respond, she disappeared into the crowd of Sunday diners.

Mike sat at the table, his hands cradling his empty coffee cup. Tessa could tell Gina's words were niggling at his mind. They were niggling at hers, too. *How could I have been so blind? So selfish? Because of my arrogant refusal to compromise, I lost the most precious thing in my life. Mike. The husband I loved dearly.*

Clutching her purse to her chest, Tessa rose. "I—I'm sorry, Mike. I need to be alone." She hurried away from the table before he could rise and try to stop her. Swallowing her pride, she rushed toward the maître d' and instructed him to call her a taxi and ask them to come quickly, then hurried outside. Having to face Mike right now, after hearing Gina's words, was more than she could handle. *I've got to be alone, to pray and talk to my heavenly Father. Only He understands me and knows how I feel.*

✝

Mike was touched by Gina's words. He waited for what seemed an eternity then, concerned about Tessa and unable to stand being separated from her any longer, hurried toward the ladies' room where he was sure she had gone.

"There was no one in there but me," a kindly lady told him as she exited the restroom.

He thanked the woman, then leaned awkwardly against the wall, not sure what to do next. Where could Tessa be? In the lobby? Maybe out by his car? "I've got to find her."

✝

Tessa had barely arrived home from the restaurant and flung herself across the bed before Mike appeared on her porch, shouting her name and ringing the doorbell over and over until she thought she would scream. Didn't he realize she didn't want to talk to him now?

When he finally gave up and she heard his car back out of the driveway, she dropped to her knees by her bed and called out to her heavenly Father. Soon Mike's persistent phone calls began, and she found it difficult to even concentrate. Finally, she could stand it no longer. With her heart pounding in her ears, she lifted the phone, shut off the ringer, and clicked off the lamp. If there were a dire emergency, Katie would call Tessa's cell phone, which was still on and inside her purse atop the dresser.

After a fitful night of turning and tossing and praying, Tessa crawled out of bed, her makeup still on, her hair disheveled, and her mouth tasting like her teeth hadn't been brushed in days. It took only one look in the mirror, and all she wanted to do was crawl back in bed and pull the covers over her head. Where was the comfort God was supposed to give when you called out to Him? She was as miserable now as she'd been when she'd raced out of that restaurant.

Eventually, she forced herself out of bed, stumbled toward the window, and pulled the curtain aside, half expecting to find Mike's car in the driveway, but it wasn't there. *Oh, Mike, what have I done?*

Suddenly remembering the wedding rehearsal and dinner was today, she hurriedly dialed Katie's number.

"Hi, Mom. What's up?" Katie's cheery voice answered.

"I—I just wondered if there were any last-minute things you wanted me to do today," Tessa answered, trying to sound upbeat. The last thing she wanted was to upset her daughter. "Do you want me to call the caterer and make sure he has everything set up like you'd planned it?"

"I got up early and went over my list. I've already made a few calls. I'm going to call him as soon as I finish talking with you. I think everything is taken care of. You and Daddy have done a fabulous job of pinch-hitting for me. I can't thank you enough." Katie let out a slight giggle. "Do you realize in just two days I'll be a married woman? Mrs. James Martinez. I'm so glad we decided to go ahead with the wedding, but we couldn't have pulled it off without the two of you."

"I've loved helping you. How's the ankle doing?"

"The doc said I'm doing great. The break is healing well and even though I'll have to wear the strap-on cast, I'll be able to stand at my wedding with no trouble at all and, hopefully, the cast won't even be noticeable."

"That's wonderful news, Katie. I'm glad to hear you're doing so well."

"Oh, by the way, Mom, I tried to call you last night, but your line just rang, and the answering machine didn't pick up. Was something wrong with it?"

"No, I shut the ringer off and went to bed. The answering machine must be full of messages I should delete." Tessa didn't bother to mention they were all from Katie's father.

"It wasn't urgent. I was just calling to tell you that Jim had to fly to Kansas City yesterday to meet with the CEO of one of his major accounts, but he'll be back in plenty of time for the wedding rehearsal and dinner tonight."

Tessa sat down on the edge of the bed and leaned back against the pillows, the back of her hand resting across her forehead. "Oh, sweetie, did he have to go? Couldn't someone have gone in his place?"

Katie laughed. "Don't be such a worrier, Mom. Of course he had to go, but he's catching an early afternoon flight. That client always insists on Jim's personal attention. They're negotiating some big deal. He'll be back in San Diego by four o'clock."

"But tonight's such a special night for you. Couldn't they have put it off until after the first of the year?"

"Mom! Jim would never have gone if he didn't think it was necessary. You know that."

Tessa sighed. "I guess you're right."

"You are still planning to open the church for the caterer this afternoon, aren't you?"

"Yes, I plan to be there by three thirty."

"Thanks, Mom. Oh, I've been meaning to ask—how did it go with Daddy yesterday? We went to the early service with Valene and Jordan since Jim was taking a noon flight, so we missed seeing you. Did he go to church with you like he said he would?"

Tessa felt her pulse quicken. "Yes, he made it. We had lunch afterward; then I—I came on home."

"That's it?" Katie sounded disappointed. "I'd hoped the two of you would spend the afternoon together."

"No. I—I had things to do, and I'm sure he did, too."

"Well, I'd better let you go so I can call the caterer. I'll remind them you'll have the church open by three thirty. I love you, Mom."

"I love you, too, sweetie."

Tessa cleared Mike's phone messages as soon as she hung up. Although the phone rang a number of times during the day, she let the answering machine pick up. With the exception of two calls from Ellen and one from Pastor McIntosh, all of the calls were from Mike. "I really need to talk to you, Tessie," he'd say, a distinct air of concern in his voice. "Please pick up if you're there, or call me when you get home."

But she didn't. Her mind was in far too much turmoil.

She was just leaving the house at three when the phone rang again. Thinking perhaps it was another call from Ellen she paused in the doorway and listened. But it wasn't Ellen; it was Katie.

"Hi, Mom." Katie's voice sounded strange. "I'm afraid I have bad news. Jim's flight has been grounded. They're having an ice storm in Kansas City. There's no way he's going to make it in time for the rehearsal and dinner."

Leaving the door standing open, Tessa raced for the phone. "Katie, don't hang up! I'm here! What are you going to do?"

"Oh, Mom, there's not much I can do, but go ahead as planned. Jim is sick about missing the dinner. He suggested Daddy stand in for him at the rehearsal; then he can fill Jim in on the routine when he gets back. Jim phoned again a few minutes ago and said the storm is letting up some and the forecast for tomorrow is good. If his flight doesn't make it out tonight, at least he'll be out tomorrow morning."

Tessa dropped her purse onto the sofa then sank down beside it. "Oh, honey, I'm so sorry."

"Me, too, but there is nothing we can do but, as Jim says, go on without him. The important thing is that he gets back safely."

"I'll open the church then come after you."

"No, that's okay. Daddy stopped by on his way to the station. He's offered to pick me up."

Tessa huffed. "You'd better pray he makes it."

"Mom! Would you please try to go at least one day without bad-mouthing Daddy? For my sake?"

Hating herself for being so judgmental, Tessa bit her lip. "I'll try."

Tessa stayed at the church the rest of the afternoon, assisting the caterer and his team when needed. The remainder of the time she spent tying the satin bows that would be hung at the ends of the pews for Katie and Jim's Christmas Day wedding.

"Phone for you, Tessa," Mary Margaret Hughes, Pastor McIntosh's secretary, called to her from across the dining room thirty minutes before time for the dinner to begin. "It's Katie. She said it's important."

Tessa rushed to the woman's office and grabbed up the phone. "What's wrong?"

"Dad just called. He's going to be late. Can you come after me?"

Her anger rising, Tessa ground out, "I knew we couldn't depend on him. What is it? Another big case only he can handle?"

"He didn't say, Mom. Just that he was running late. Can you come, or should I call someone else?"

"I'll be there in a few minutes."

They arrived at the church just in time for the dinner to begin. Pastor McIntosh prayed for their meal, for Katie and Jim as they prepared for their marriage, and for Jim's safety and quick return. With Katie and Tessa leading them, the line of attendees moved through the magnificent buffet line the caterer had prepared, oohing and aahing at the vast array of attractively prepared food, filling their plates to overflowing.

Though miffed at Mike for letting Katie down, Tessa did her best to enjoy the food and appear cheerful. The caterer was already clearing the serving table when Mike appeared in the doorway, a bandage across his forehead.

Chapter 9

Katie rose from her place at the head table and hurried toward him, deep concern etched on her face. "Daddy! What happened to you?"

Mike put his arm around her and pulled her to him. "Don't worry about it, pumpkin. I'm okay. It's merely a surface wound."

Katie lifted worried eyes. "It doesn't look like it."

Tucking a finger under his daughter's chin, Mike lifted her gaze to meet his. "I had a little trouble with a suspect I was arresting. That's all. The doc said I could take the bandage off tomorrow. I'm really sorry I missed your rehearsal dinner."

"I'm just glad you're here now." Katie turned to Tessa. "Mom, would you get the plate I asked the caterer to save for Daddy?"

While avoiding Mike's gaze, Tessa forced a smile for Katie's sake. "Sure, honey. Be glad to." While everyone fussed over Mike, Tessa fetched his plate from the kitchen then set it down on the table in front of him without a word, though inwardly she was as concerned about his injury as everyone else was.

Mike grabbed her hand before she could get away, his gaze locking with hers. "Thanks, Tessie. I've been trying to call you."

Not wanting to appear rude in front of their friends, Tessa managed a slight smile. "I–I've been busy. Last-minute things to take care of, you know."

Pastor McIntosh took charge when the wedding party gathered in the sanctuary at seven o'clock for the rehearsal. "Since Jim has been detained in Kansas City due to an ice storm, he has asked Mike to stand in for him as the groom."

Before the attendants walked down the aisle, Mike hurried to the platform and took the place Jim should have taken—next to where Jordan, his best man, and Nathan and Brandon, his groomsmen, would soon be standing.

Moments later, with the attendants now flanking the bride and substitute groom, Jordan gave Mike a mischievous smile. "Hey, *Jim*, you've put on a bit of weight, haven't you?"

Mike responded with a wink. "You, Brandon, and Nathan better hope you're in as good of shape as I am when you're my age. Just ask that perp I arrested this evening. He's sitting in a jail cell right now, thanks to this old guy and his agility."

"We have another substitution," Pastor McIntosh said, grinning at Mike's comment. "Since Mike is tied up pretending he is the groom, Bill Zobel is going to stand in as the father of the bride and walk Katie down the aisle."

"Don't forget," Katie reminded him. "I want both Dad and Mom to give me away."

"I was just about to add that, Katie. I think it's a lovely idea." After a few more comments and instructions, Pastor McIntosh motioned to the organist and the strains of the wedding march filled the sanctuary. He nodded toward Bill Zobel and Katie and her attendants. "Slowly now, walk slowly. This is your time, Katie. Everyone wants a good look at the bride."

When they reached the altar, Pastor McIntosh asked, "Who gives this woman to be married to this man?"

Tessa rose and stood beside Bill. Gazing at her beautiful daughter, Tessa couldn't hold back her tears of joy.

With an oversized grin toward Mike, Bill answered, "Her mother and I do," as the entire wedding party muffled giggles and Bill led Tessa back to her seat.

When the laughter subsided, Pastor McIntosh instructed Mike and Katie to move close together and hold hands.

"Jane and Keene will sing their duet here," Pastor McIntosh said, nodding toward the Morays.

"I just want you to know, Katie," Keene said, smiling as he reached out and took her hand, "it's an honor to sing at your wedding. I just hope you and Jim can be every bit as happy as Jane and I are. Keep God first in your life and all will be well."

Jane nodded as she slipped her arm around her husband's waist. "He's right, Katie. God needs to be the center of your home."

"He's going to be the center of our home, Jane. Jim and I have already decided that."

Keene gave her a thumbs-up. "Then you two are on the right track."

"I'm really glad you weren't out on one of your concert tours, Keene," Mike added, "so you two could be a part of our Katie's wedding. She looks up to both of you."

"We wouldn't have missed it." Jane sent a smile Katie's way. "Katie and Jim are two very special people. We want only the best for them."

"I know Keene and Jane's duet will touch hearts. I've heard them rehearsing," Pastor McIntosh said. "You'll love the words. They're right out of the scriptures." He motioned toward Katie. "Katie, while Jane and Keene are singing, you and Mike hold hands and gaze into each other's eyes, like you and Jim will be doing during the actual ceremony."

The two moved into place.

"Now," the pastor said, "when their lovely duet ends, you both need to face me, and I want you to continue to hold hands. I will be reading some scripture here; then I will give the short sermon I always give before I perform the actual wedding ceremony. I'm going to do that tonight so you'll get a feel for what I have in mind, but I'll try to keep it fairly brief, since this is only the rehearsal. Remember, some in your group of friends, family, and coworkers attending your wedding may not know the Lord. We want to give them the opportunity to hear what God's Word says about accepting Him." He glanced toward Katie. "How you doing, Katie? You seem a little tired. Think you can stand awhile longer?"

Katie frowned and let out a sigh. "Actually, Pastor McIntosh, I really am tired. I've been on my feet most of the day taking care of last-minute details, and this cast is so uncomfortable. Maybe I should sit down for a while."

"That's probably a good idea," he told her, showing great concern. "But we'll need someone to stand in your place so everyone will know what to do and when to do it during the actual ceremony."

Katie turned to Tessa. "Would you stand in for me, Mom?"

"M–me?" Tessa stammered, totally caught off guard by Katie's surprising request.

"Please, Mom. I'd really appreciate it. I need to get off my feet."

After casting a quick glance toward Mike, then at the pastor, Tessa nodded and rose. "Sure. I guess I can, if you're sure you want me to, but maybe Vanessa or—"

"Please, Mom. I'd feel better if you did it." Katie, with Mike's assistance, moved down the steps from the platform. "I'll watch from your place, that way I can prop my foot up on the pew."

Feeling a flush rise to her cheeks, Tessa made sure Katie was seated then joined Mike at the altar.

Pastor McIntosh looked from one to the other. "Good. Now we're ready. Let's proceed."

Tessa moved next to Mike and flinched slightly when she felt his fingers entwine with hers. Just the touch of his hand sent shivers down her spine. Her mind flashed to another time—years ago—when she and Mike had stood before the altar holding hands. How young they were then, and so much in love. She gulped hard. Her grandmother's and grandfather's words, said many years ago, filled her mind and made her wish she'd taken their advice. If she had, perhaps things would have been different.

"Tessa," her grandmother had said, "you must be sure you're making the right decision and that God is leading you and Mike together. God doesn't look lightly on marriage, nor does He accept any excuse for a husband and wife to separate. When you marry Mike, it will be until death do the two of you part. If you have any doubts—"

"But I don't have doubts," she had told her grandmother. "I love Mike. I'll always love him. Nothing will ever be able to separate us."

Her grandfather had reminded her, "God must always be first in your home, and you must respect your husband, Tessa. You may not always agree with him, but you must respect him and his decisions. A good marriage takes work. Hard work. There will be times you'll want to throw in the towel, give up, but you must never do it. Mark my words, Tessa, true love is worth finding but—more importantly—true love is worth keeping. When you pledge your life to Mike, before God and your friends, that pledge is for a lifetime. There's no turning back."

But, Granddad, Tessa whispered within her heart, *I tried, Granddad. Honest, I did. It just didn't work. You know that. You saw how Mike pulled away from me, putting his work and everything else before me and Katie. I couldn't live that way. Living with Mike was impossible!*

Tessa ventured a glance toward the handsome man holding her hand and found him gazing at her. Though she tried with all her might to hold it back, a slight smile played at her lips. Who was she kidding? She'd never stopped loving Mike. She'd only tried to convince herself she had. Was she blushing? She hoped not. Turning away, she looked in Katie's direction and found her daughter's attention focused on the two of them. Had Katie planned this? Was this another of her sly little ways of trying to get them back together?

⸙

Mike tightened his grip on Tessa's hand and was surprised when she didn't pull away. *Oh, Tessie—if only we could turn back the clock, become the naïve young people we were when you and I said our I dos. Where did we go wrong, babe? Was my career as a police officer worth separating myself from my family like I did? I'll be retiring before too many more years. What will I have to show for the time I spent away from you and Katie? A gold watch? A decent retirement check? A lonely apartment?*

" 'Love is patient, love is kind and is not jealous; love does not brag and is not arrogant,' " Pastor McIntosh quoted. "Most folks search for true love all their lives—some find it but never realize what they have is exactly what they've been searching for. They refuse to compromise and seek a common ground acceptable to both parties. True love rarely runs smoothly, but—at the end of the day—when lovers come together, they have one another to count on, to encourage, to share their joys and sorrows. When you find that kind of love, hold on to it. Cherish it. Nourish it, because true love between a husband and wife is worth keeping."

Mike glanced Tessa's way and found her gazing at him. What was it he saw in her eyes? Not the hatred or ridicule he'd expected to find. Nor the I-don't-care look she gave him so often. No, this look was kind, gentle—maybe even—dare he think it? Loving? The way she used to look at him before the humdrum daily routine of life took over and they went their separate ways? *Oh, Tessie—dear, dear Tessie. You'll always be the girl I love. The girl I married. I thought our love was so strong nothing could ever tear us apart. If only you could forgive me—if only it wasn't too—*

"Love can be an elusive thing. You think it is within your grasp, never to escape from you, and then, *poof!* Something happens, and the love you thought you had for that other person, your better half, begins to dwindle. They're no longer the wonderful person you thought you married. Sometimes you even find yourself avoiding one another. Other people take over the role as confidant, encourager, and the one they turn to, and you're hurt. You feel deserted. Alone. Maybe you seek the companionship of others. You feel righteous indignation. How dare your partner treat you like that?" He paused, his look scanning the wedding party, and then resting on Mike and Tessa. "But was the other person totally responsible for the failure of that marriage? Or does the fault and blame lie with both parties? What is the missing ingredient in that marriage? The glue that holds it together?"

Every eye was fixed on Pastor McIntosh as he dramatically paused again, the silence deafening. The beat of Mike's heart pounded in his ears.

"God. He's the glue. The *super* glue that never fails. When two people begin to leave Him out of their relationship, their love for each other can begin to wane. God wants to be the foundation of every marriage. The glue that binds the couple together."

With a look of tenderness, Pastor McIntosh reached out and took Mike's and Tessa's hands in his. "At this point, if Katie and Jim were standing before me instead of Mike and Tessa, I would ask them to look each other in the eye and declare their love for one another by reciting the vows they've written. But, even though I have a copy of those vows, we'll omit them tonight. The vows they've written are very personal. They'd best be held until the service."

Mike blinked hard. His heart was deeply touched as Pastor McIntosh's words replayed in his thoughts. *"When you find that kind of love, hold on to it. Cherish it. Nourish it, because true love between a husband and wife is worth keeping." Why didn't I realize that? Why didn't I do everything in my power to be the husband and father I should have been? I was a fool, such a fool.* He lifted his eyes heavenward. *God, is it too late? Can even You put our family back together again?* He gave Tessa's hand a slight squeeze. How he needed her in his life. How he loved her.

Pastor McIntosh led them through the rest of the service, pausing and repeating instructions where necessary, then said, "This is where I will say, 'By the power invested in me by the State of California, I now pronounce you husband and wife.' And I'd say, 'You may kiss the bride.'"

On impulse, and feeling very nostalgic as he remembered his own wedding, Mike grabbed Tessa up in his arms and planted a kiss on her lips, a kiss much like he'd given her on their wedding day.

Hoots and hollers sounded from the wedding party.

"Hey, Mike—way to go!" Jordan teased as he led the audience in an impromptu applause. "Looks like the old guy has still got it!"

But Mike's attention wasn't on those who were cheering him on, or the pastor, or anyone else. His attention was centered on the lovely woman in his arms, and he never wanted to let her go.

Placing her hands on his chest, Tessa tried to push herself away, a look of shock blanketing her face.

"Hey, what's going on here?"

All eyes turned toward the door. It was Jim. He'd made it back from Kansas City, safe and sound. The wedding rehearsal was over.

Mike's heart sank as Tessa and the others rushed toward Jim, leaving him and the pastor alone at the altar. He hoped Tessa wasn't mad at him for his impulsive behavior, but even if she was, the kiss was worth it. He'd wanted to kiss her like that, really kiss her, since they'd first begun working together on Katie's wedding. The opportunity had presented itself, and he'd seized it.

"You really love Tessa, don't you, Mike?"

Startled, Mike looked up into Pastor McIntosh's kind eyes. "It's that obvious, huh?"

"You two vowed before God to love and cherish each other until death. God wants you together, Mike. You've not only left Tessa, you've left God. Isn't it about time you did what you could to make amends with both of them?"

Mike hung his head dejectedly. "I'm afraid it's too late."

"It's never too late. God is always ready to hear the prayers and confessions of His children. And Tessa? Though her heart has been deeply wounded, she still loves you, Mike. I know she does." He placed a hand on Mike's shoulder. "If I were you, I'd set things right with God, then I'd go after that sweet lady. Tell her how much you love her and want to put your marriage back together. If you love her like I think you do, it's worth a try, isn't it?"

Mike thought about his words then nodded. "I'll do it."

By the time he finished talking to Pastor McIntosh, Tessa's car was moving out of the parking lot. Mike waited until she pulled into the line of traffic then followed her, keeping a few cars between them. He turned in behind her when she pulled into her driveway, leaped out of his car, and rushed to open the car door for her. "I was hoping you'd invite me in for a cup of coffee," he told her, half expecting her to reach out and slap his face for his impulsive kiss at the rehearsal.

✝

Tessa stared at Mike, not sure how she should respond. Though he'd definitely stepped over the line when he'd kissed her, she had to admit she'd enjoyed it. "Sure. I guess. Come on in." She moved quickly toward the door, key ring in hand. "I think we could both use a cup of coffee."

Tessa motioned Mike toward his old recliner chair then moved quickly into the kitchen to start the coffee maker. When the coffee finished dripping, she filled two mugs with the hot, brown liquid and carried them into the family room, handing one to Mike before settling herself on the sofa.

"Thanks," Mike said simply, eyeing her as she placed her cup on the coffee table.

"You're welcome."

Mike set his cup on the end table then leaned forward, resting his elbows on his knees. "I'd say I'm sorry for kissing you in front of everyone like that, Tessie, but I'm not. I've wanted to kiss you since—"

"No harm done," Tessa said, shrugging her shoulders and doing her best to appear nonchalant. "You were just caught up in the moment."

Mike rose and joined her on the sofa. "No! That wasn't it at all, Tessie. I kissed you because I love you. Pastor McIntosh and I talked about it at the church. He encouraged me to try to set things right with you and with God."

He seemed sincere enough, but hadn't he seemed sincere hundreds of times before when he'd told her he loved her and was going to spend more time with her and with Katie? And hadn't he forgotten those words in a matter of days? Going back to his old routine of working round the clock? Letting anything and everything take him away from his family?

"Mike," she said softly, trying to keep her composure and not cry, "I appreciate what you're saying, and I do hope you get yourself straightened out with God, but so much has happened between us. Things I find hard to forget."

"You mean forgive, don't you? Why can't you forgive me, Tessie? Is it that you don't want to forgive me? Do you enjoy being the martyr?"

Though offended, his words caused her to examine her heart. "I want to forgive you, Mike. Really I do. These past two weeks have made me see you in a different light."

"I will put you first, Tessie. I'm a new man. Being with you these past two weeks has made me see what I've missed. I—"

His cell phone rang, and though he didn't answer it immediately, he finally snatched it from his belt. "Garrett," he barked into it impatiently.

Tessa watched with annoyance as he listened and scribbled a few notes on the pad he'd pulled from his pocket.

"You're sure? Absolutely sure? Because if this is a wild-goose chase, I don't—" He nodded. "Right. Gotcha. I'll be right there."

While Tessa watched, her dander rising, Mike shoved the phone back into its belt clip and reached for her hand.

"I'm sorry, babe. That call was really important. I've got to go. We've got the best lead we've had yet in the murder that happened at the Fairbanks Mall last week."

Rejecting his hand, Tessa rolled her eyes. "Go on, Mike. You have a job to do. You can't put me first, in spite of what you promised me not two minutes ago." She rose and snatched his cup from the table and headed toward the kitchen. "I certainly hope the SDPD can spare you long enough to attend your daughter's wedding."

"That's not fair, Tessie."

"Tell me about it. Life isn't fair, Mike. Haven't you learned that by now?" She shooed him toward the door, an angry edge to her voice. "Go on. Get out of here. You're needed elsewhere."

"I love you, Tessie. Can we talk about this later?"

Jamming her hands onto her hips, Tessa whirled around to face him. "I love you, too," she told him, letting the words slip out unbidden, "but sometimes—love just isn't enough. Now go."

Mike stared at her for a moment, started to say something but didn't, then headed for the door, slamming it behind him.

"I do love you, Mike Garrett!" Tessa shouted at the closed door. "I'll always love you, but I cannot take second place in your life."

Chapter 10

Christmas Day dawned bright, sunny, and beautiful, the perfect day for a Christmas wedding. Her little girl was getting married.

Tessa stared out her bedroom window, the bedroom she'd shared with Mike, wondering where he was, if he was safe, and if he'd make it to their daughter's wedding. She'd thought perhaps she'd see him when she'd spent Christmas Eve with Katie and Jim, but Katie said he'd called and told her he was working on that murder case and wouldn't be able to make it. *Just like him*, she thought as she turned away from the window. *Mike will never change*.

She stumbled through the day, pressing the lovely ivory lace dress she'd selected from Della's shop to wear as mother of the bride, gathering the things she'd need to take to the church for decorating the sanctuary, and doing a few mundane chores—but no matter how she tried, she couldn't get Mike off her mind.

About two o'clock, after loading everything in her car, Tessa headed for the church, determined not to let her lousy mood deter her from enjoying what should be one of the happiest days of her life.

After hanging her dress in the changing room, she went about her tasks placing the candles in the candelabra, attaching the big satin bows to the pews, unrolling the white plastic runner down the center aisle, placing the guest book in the foyer, and dozens of other things she'd told Katie she would do. Both the florist and caterer arrived at five. Tessa checked the final details with both then left them to their work while she tended to a few more unfinished chores. At last, everything was in readiness. Katie and the rest of the wedding party wouldn't begin to arrive for well over an hour.

Tessa stood back admiring the lovely, decorated sanctuary, the ivy-bedecked arch where Katie and Jim would repeat their vows, and the beauty of the flowers she and Mike had selected and the florist had so perfectly placed. Mike. What fun they'd had helping with Katie's wedding. She smiled to herself as she remembered how Mike had tried to save money by having the groomsmen wear their own shoes, and how he'd suggested they buy cookies at the deli and make punch from that tropical-type stuff for the reception. And how later he'd said he would do whatever was necessary to give his daughter the kind of wedding she deserved.

By working together, even the worst of situations had been handled and resolved, including the fiasco of the wrong wedding dress. *These are the kind of things we'll laugh about in years to come,* she told herself, smiling.

Then she sobered. "We?" she asked aloud. "Mike and me? There is no Mike and me!"

Tessa lowered herself onto one of the kneeling pads that graced the foot of the platform and, speaking aloud since she was alone in the church, called out to God. "God, am I being unreasonable? Is spending a few nights alone while Mike is off working worth giving up the time we have left to spend together? He'll be retiring in a few years and maybe then we would have time together, but what about now? I hate being alone. Why hasn't he been able to understand that? All I ever wanted was my husband by my side, not having to run off every time the telephone rang. Was that so wrong?"

She pulled a tissue from her purse and dabbed at her eyes. "God, how can You love me when I'm so unlovable? How could Mike love me?"

Tears of repentance rolled down her cheeks. "I'm so sorry! Sorry for not trying to work out a compromise with Mike. . . For all the times I've complained about him to our daughter. . . For being so quick to judge him. . . For turning away from You when You didn't make Mike bend to my will. . . I'm a mess, a pitiful mess. All the things Mike has done on his job have counted. Because of his bravery and dedication, lives have been saved and perhaps hundreds of criminals have been placed behind bars."

She lowered her head, sobbing from a broken heart. "The works I've done for You are as filthy rags in comparison to his, especially since I did them all to seek the praise and favor of people. God, I know I have no right to ask You, but I beg You, forgive my hardened heart. Give me a spirit of forgiveness. Help me accept the fact that Mike didn't leave me because he wanted to. He left me to protect and serve the people of San Diego. He's asked me over and over to forgive him, but my foolish pride wouldn't allow it. I need that spirit of forgiveness. Help me to put aside the things that separated us. I—I don't want to lose whatever chance we may have to get back together. I love Mike dearly. I'll always love him."

✞

Mike stood at the back of the sanctuary, the garment bag containing his tuxedo held tightly in his hands, his insides aching as he listened to Tessa pour her heart out to God. Tears of remorse he was unable to control flowed down his tough-guy face. *Oh, Tessie, I love you, too! I don't want to lose you either!* Not sure what to do or if she would be offended that he'd been listening to her private conversation with God, he quietly draped the bag over a pew and crept slowly forward.

Lifting tear-filled eyes, Tessa stared at the huge stained-glass window of Christ and the one lost sheep. "God—I'm like that little sheep. I've wandered so far away. I'm leaving this in Your hands. Melt me, God. Mold me into what You would have me to be. Only You can put back the miserable pieces of our lives."

Mike moved silently up beside her and knelt, slipping his arm about her. "Tessie—sweetheart," he whispered into her ear, "I spent most of yesterday with Pastor McIntosh. I've made my peace with God. I confessed my sins and asked Him to forgive me. Now I'm asking you to forgive me." His grip about her shoulders tightened. "No, I'm *begging* you to forgive me. We've let eight long years slip through our fingers, babe. Let's not waste what time we have left."

He waited, not sure if she was going to slap him, tell him to get lost, or if a miracle would happen and she'd forgive him.

✝

Tessa's quickened heartbeat thundered in her ears. What did Mike say? That he'd made his peace with God? Oh, if only that were true! It had torn her apart watching him ignore God, the God that at one time he'd loved dearly and had taken great pleasure in serving.

"I'm a different man, Tessie. My priorities have changed. If you'll forgive me and give me another chance, I promise I won't let you down."

Her heart overflowing with love, Tessa reached up and cupped his face between her palms. "You have no idea how much I want to believe that, Mike."

"With God's help, dearest, I'll always be there for you. I don't want to face life without you any longer."

Tessa stared into Mike's eyes and found love radiating there. True love. A love she could trust. Casting all her concerns aside, she slipped her arms about his strong neck, twisting the curls at the nape like she'd done so many times during their first years of marriage. "I can and will forgive you, Mike, but promise you'll forgive me, too. I've been a selfish, stupid fool."

Mike brushed a lock of hair from her forehead and kissed her cheek. "No, Tessie—I'm the one who has been a fool—a fool for putting our marriage in jeopardy by letting too many things come between us. I'm the one who needs to ask forgiveness."

Tessa leaned into him, pressing her cheek against his and nestling into the safety and security of his strong arms. "I love you so much, Mike."

"And I love you, babe. I can't begin to tell you how much."

Mike's cell phone rang, piercing the silence in the sanctuary. Instinctively, Tessa pulled away.

Mike pulled the phone from his belt. "Garrett."

He listened a moment then said, "No, not this time. I don't care how important it is, someone else will have to follow up on it. This is my day off. From now on, I'll be working only my regular hours. I'll be spending the rest of the time with my wife. Understood?"

Tessa couldn't believe what she was hearing. Mike actually refused to go when the SDPD called him? Amazing!

"I mean it, Tessie," he told her, holding her close and stroking her hair. "No more running every time the phone rings. I'll put in my shift and fill in if one of the guys is sick or his wife is in labor, but that's it. From now on you—if you'll let me share my life with you—you and the Lord are my number one priority. I want us to grow old together, enjoy our grandkids, and take care of one another in the sunset of our lives. I can't bear living without you, Tessie. Being with you these past two weeks, holding your hand, seeing your smile—well, I just know we belong together."

Tessa thought she would explode with happiness. Her dreams had come true. "I want that, too, Mike. I've never wanted anything but to be near you and be your wife in every way."

Chapter 11

Mike stole a glance at the friends and relatives who had gathered for his daughter's wedding. His and Tessa's best friends, Bill and Ellen Zobel; their twin daughters Valene and her husband Jordan, Vanessa and her husband Nathan and their son, Jeff; Katie's friend Della and her husband Brandon; and so many others who had meant so much to them over the years. What a day this was. A real milestone in his and Tessa's life. One they'd never forget. Their baby girl was getting married.

He turned and lovingly smiled at Tessa where she sat on the front row of the beautiful, candlelit sanctuary holding his hand. In his eyes, Tessa had never looked lovelier, nor had he ever loved her more than at this moment.

"Who gives this woman to be married to this man?" Pastor McIntosh asked, looking toward them.

Mike lifted his chin high as he pulled Tessa to her feet. After wrapping an arm about her and pulling her close, in unison, they answered, "We do."

Beaming, Katie gave them an approving thumbs-up as the pair sat down.

"She's so lovely," Tessa whispered in Mike's ear. "How could we be so lucky?"

Mike leaned and planted a kiss on her cheek. "She looks exactly like you, babe."

Blushing, she gave him a smile that made his heart sing.

They listened attentively to every word the pastor said as he preached the sermon he'd practiced at the rehearsal. Finally, Pastor McIntosh turned to Katie and Jim. "It's time to pledge your love and your lives to one another. You may repeat your vows."

Katie, instead of turning to face Jim, whirled around and looked directly at Mike and Tessa. Wondering what was going on, Tessa cast a quick glance toward Mike.

"Mom, Dad," Katie said, holding out her opened hand. "Would you please join Jim and me at the altar?"

Katie had called Mike to her dressing room just minutes before the wedding and told him she'd witnessed her parents' conversation in the sanctuary, and then filled him in on her idea. It was brilliant; he'd give her that. Mike couldn't keep a broad smile from traveling the full width of his face. Before Tessa could protest, he pulled her to her feet and up onto the platform.

"Mom, Daddy has something he wants to ask you," Katie said with a grin and a wink toward her father.

Mike dropped to one knee in front of Tessa then pulled a shiny gold band from his pocket and held it up for her to see. It was the very ring she had thrown at him the day she'd ordered him out of the house eight years ago—the ring he'd been carrying in his pocket for the last several days.

"Tessie, my precious, you're the only woman I've ever loved. Will you marry me? Again?"

A hush fell over the audience as Tessa stared into his face. Legally, she was still his wife. But Mike prayed, hoping she was as eager to renew their vows and let God help them start their marriage over as he was.

Suddenly she broke out into an adoring smile. "Mike," she said, touching his face with her fingertips, "of course I'll marry you, my love."

Mike had never been so happy. "How about now?" he asked, holding out the ring again.

Tessa glanced toward the bride. "Katie?"

Katie nodded. "Nothing would make me happier than to see my parents together again."

Turning back to Mike, Tessa nodded. "Now would be wonderful!"

The audience broke into loud applause as Mike and Tessa moved hand-in-hand to join Katie and Jim at the altar for another Christmas wedding.

Epilogue

Three months later

Mr. and Mrs. Mike Garrett sat propped up in bed, leisurely reading the Saturday morning paper.

"I could take early retirement," Mike said, peeping over the top of the page.

Tessa tilted her head to one side and frowned. "And do what? Play golf? Maybe sit around the house all day wishing you were still working at the SDPD? I don't think so. Besides, we're still paying on Katie's wedding."

He folded the paper then moved closer and slipped an arm about her. "I'd do it, if it'd make you happy. We'd manage somehow."

She kissed his cheek then gently thumped his nose with the tip of her finger. "Now that you've informed the chief of police you'll no longer work on Sundays so we can attend church together, I'm totally happy."

He chucked her chin and gave her a teasing smile. "You're sure about that? It'll be nearly four years before I can retire and draw my full benefits."

She nodded. "I think I can wait that long. Now that you're spending so much time with me, I don't even mind the occasional calls you get from the SDPD wanting you to work on your days off."

She'd barely gotten the words out of her mouth when his cell phone rang.

"Garrett." He frowned as he listened.

The serious expression on his face told Tessa the call was urgent.

"Sorry. Gotta go, babe. They found another Jane Doe. I could be gone all day, maybe into the night. We've got to catch this guy before he strikes again. He's terrorized the women of San Diego far too long."

Tessa scooted off the bed and pulled on her robe. "I'll fix you a hot thermos of coffee."

Unable to resist another opportunity for a kiss, Mike grabbed her wrist and pulled her to him. "Sure you don't mind?"

She shook her head. "Not one bit. Just promise me you'll be careful. I'll be waiting for you, no matter how late it is." Standing on tiptoes, she planted a kiss on his lips. "Go get 'em, big guy."

CATHY MARIE HAKE

Cathy is a Southern California native who loves her work as a nurse and Lamaze teacher. She and her husband have a daughter, a son, and three dogs, so life is never dull or quiet. Cathy considers herself a sentimental packrat, collecting antiques and Hummel figurines. In spare moments, she reads, bargain hunts, and makes a huge mess with her new hobby of scrapbooking.

JOYCE LIVINGSTON

Joyce has done many things in her life (in addition to being a wife, mother of six, and grandmother to oodles of grandkids, all of whom she loves dearly). From being a television broadcaster for eighteen years, to lecturing and teaching on quilting and sewing, to writing magazine articles on a variety of subjects. She's danced with Lawrence Welk, ice-skated with a Chimpanzee, had bottles broken over her head by stuntmen, interviewed hundreds of celebrities and controversial figures, and many other interesting and unusual things. But now, when she isn't off traveling to wonderful and exotic places as a part-time tour escort, her days are spent sitting in front of her computer, creating stories. She feels her writing is a ministry and a calling from God, and she hopes readers will be touched and uplifted by what she writes. Joyce loves to hear from her readers and invites you to visit her on the Internet at: www.joycelivingston.com

A Letter to Our Readers

Dear Readers:

In order that we might better contribute to your reading enjoyment, we would appreciate your taking a few minutes to respond to the following questions. When completed, please return to the following: Fiction Editor, Barbour Publishing, Inc., P.O. Box 719, Uhrichsville, OH 44683.

1. Did you enjoy reading *San Diego*?
   ❏ Very much—I would like to see more books like this.
   ❏ Moderately—I would have enjoyed it more if _____
   _____
   _____

2. What influenced your decision to purchase this book? (Check those that apply.)
   ❏ Cover   ❏ Back cover copy   ❏ Title   ❏ Price
   ❏ Friends   ❏ Publicity   ❏ Other

3. Which story was your favorite?
   ❏ *Love Is Patient*   ❏ *Love Worth Finding*
   ❏ *Love Is Kind*   ❏ *Love Worth Keeping*

4. Please check your age range:
   ❏ Under 18   ❏ 18–24   ❏ 25–34
   ❏ 35–45   ❏ 46–55   ❏ Over 55

5. How many hours per week do you read? _____

Name _____

Occupation _____

Address _____

City_____ State_____ Zip_____

E-mail_____